DRAGON'S GAME

BOOKS BY CAROL L. DENNIS

DRAGON'S PAWN

DRAGON'S KNIGHT

DRAGON'S QUEEN

GUARDIAN'S GAMBIT

DRAGON'S GAME

CAROL L. DENNIS

WILDSIDE PRESS

DRAGON'S GAME

Wildside Press, LLC
www.wildsidepress.com

For more information, contact **Wildside Press**.

HARDCOVER: 1-59224-211-1
PAPERBACK: 1-59224-213-8

To my dream believers
Charlotte Hardwick
Richard King
Michele Free

TABLE OF CONTENTS

DRAGON'S PAWN

PROLOGUE

The Keepers met in the vast Hall of the Gate. Twelve pairs of concerned eyes watched Andronan, their silver-haired leader, his long-fingered hands resting quietly on the table before him. The ancient mage said, "We must act now, before it is too late."

Nods of agreement came from the group.

The irrepressible Rory asked, "What is it you'd be havin' us do?" The leprechaun had never lost his thick Irish brogue although he had left Earth for the planet Realm centuries earlier.

"It is dangerous to use the gate," Librisald said, raising an admonitory finger, dust motes drifting to the stone floor from his gray robe.

The Keepers turned their heads, startled to hear dissent from this source.

The frail librarian peered from beneath his shaggy brows. He had spent so many hours poring over books in the university library that it was difficult for him to focus on anything more than a foot in front of his face.

"That is why I have called you together," Andronan said, drawing their attention by the tone of his voice. From a pocket in his deep blue robes he drew a black velvet box. It fit easily in the palm of his hand. Nevertheless, on seeing it the Keepers became more alert.

"You will open the box now?" Krom asked. The group had been summoned so hastily that he still wore his trader's trail garb instead of the Keeper's traditional robes. "The situation is that dangerous?"

"This box has remained closed for six hundred years. The time of peril to all Realm is now!" answered Andronan. The very curls on Andronan's head seemed charged with energy as he gently lifted the lid. Within, a circlet of metal in the shape of a dragon lay quiescent. "Wyrd," Andronan said gently.

As the Keepers gathered around to watch, one green eye opened lazily. The talisman had awakened.

"You have need of me?" The words echoed in the minds of the Keepers. "Ah, yesss," the sibilant thought touched each one. "You do."

"Rory," Andronan said, "you must be our messenger to Earth."

"Me," the leprechaun spluttered, "and why should I be goin'?"

"Because of your close—" Andronan's eyes twinkled as he continued soberly, "—ties with our alternate world."

The leprechaun had made clandestine trips to Earth to sample the whiskey of his native Ireland on several occasions. Rory's quick glance at the mage told him Andronan knew of his forbidden jaunts, and the leprechaun's protests subsided immediately.

"A fire wizard will send you easily. Wyrd will provide your destination." With these words, Andronan handed the dragon bracelet to Rory. As soon as the bracelet touched Rory's hand, he disappeared.

The ancient mage smiled at the astounded Keepers. "The search for a hero begins!"

CHAPTER ONE

The blaze in the stone fireplace glimmered, dimly lighting the main room of Jarl's comfortable cabin. A shower of sparks fell on the hearth with a loud pop. Minou, his yellow coon cat, bounded across the room away from the grate. "What ails you, cat?" he muttered. He stopped typing and rubbed the golden stubble of his beard. His bleary eyes scanned the room and he reached for his whisky glass automatically.

"You could be a wee bit more hospitable."

Jarl put down his drink. He focused, not without difficulty, on the place from which the voice came. The foot-high figure of a man dressed all in brown jumped on his word processor. The creature wore a white owl's feather in his cap. Jarl's huge hand dwarfed the small being as he lazily batted it to one side in an inebriated gesture of negation.

"Demon damnation, it's drunk you must be! Didn't you hear me speak, Jarl Koenig?" the angry voice shrieked the last words as the tiny man stood upright and shook his minuscule fist in impotent fury.

"Bu-but you're not here. You're only a—a figment of my imagination, so there's no need to pay any attention to you."

"Figment, indeed!" The little man drew himself up to his full height and puffed out his cheeks. "If it wasn't for the sheer waste, I'd upend that glass on your addled mortal noggin," he concluded with a screech as he slapped out a spark that left a scorched patch on his leathern britches. "Should have known better than to trust a thrice-bedamned fire wizard to send me anywhere on a quest." he grumbled.

Jarl raised his hand to cover the amused grin he couldn't repress.

"Well, are you going to stand there starin', man? Or will you be pourin' poor Rory a drink? Unless these old nostrils deceive me, I smell real Irish whiskey." He smacked his lips at the thought.

"Some people see pink elephants. I've dreamed up a nutso vision this time, one of the little people, no less. A brownie with a Gaelic accent." Jarl smiled ruefully at his folly.

"I'm a perfectly good luchorpan," the small figure corrected him irascibly.

"Ha! Now I know I'm drunk! Leprechauns dress in green."

"Me father was from over the water, and I dress like him. Make no mistake, even after being gone almost two thousand years, I'm still as Irish as Paddy's pig." The leprechaun rubbed his small hands together. "I'm glad to see you're not totally hopeless. Now pour me my whiskey," he demanded.

"What do you mean, not totally hopeless?" asked Jarl somewhat diligently, holding the bottle behind his back.

"You recognized the old word for leprechaun, so you're not as ignorant as I expected you to be."

"My grandmother was from County Cork, and during much of my misspent youth I heard the old tales. Ah, beautiful queens and heroic deeds," said Jarl. He paused to consider aloud. "I'm talking to a little man who can't be here. I must be crazy as well as drunk." Jarl focused on his hallucinatory visitor.

"It's crazy you'll be driving me with your foolish, misbelieving ways." As he spoke, the wee manling jumped down on the top of the oaken desk and beckoned the man closer. When Jarl bent his blond head, Rory reached out quickly and punched him in the nose.

"Ouch!" Jarl jerked, spilling whiskey from the bottle he still held behind his back.

"Now do you believe I'm real?" Rory asked with a merry chuckle as he tipped his cap. "You've spilled more whiskey than I could drink, so stop this foolishness and pour me a sip."

Jarl reached for his glass, intending to take a drink. "You surely seem to be here. I never heard of a tactile hallucination of one of the little people, so maybe you do exist." He gently touched his throbbing nose.

"Toadstools spare me from a thick-headed lackwit! What will it take to convince you?" The leprechaun hopped up and down, venting his frustration. He reminded Jarl of Rumpelstiltskin.

"Oh, tomorrow when I wake up, no leprechaun. Then I'll know I dreamed this whole conversation."

"You certainly don't look like very promisin' material to me. Give me a drink, man. Talkin' to mortals is thirsty business."

Jarl picked up the top of the whiskey bottle. He filled the cap to the brim and solemnly held it out between his thumb and forefinger. His guest took the proffered refreshment with alacrity, tipped the cap, and drained it. Then, without saying a word, he offered it to his host. Jarl refilled it a second, and then a third time.

"Ah, that was a potation to remember." The leprechaun exhaled happily and rubbed his red-bearded chin. "Now I'd best be gettin' to the real purpose of my visit."

"Real purpush?" Jarl had matched his visitor drink for drink.

"Boyo, there's a job you must be doin'."

"Job? I've got one already. This computer program is due in three weeks and I'm only two-thirds finished." Jarl pointed to the printout. Small, sooty footprints decorated the first sheet.

"Humankind is a bad way. If you won't accept the challenge, your world may well be doomed."

"Okay, I'll play. Tell me your story." The alcohol is Jarl's system made him expansively affable.

"To start at the beginnin' would take too long, but I'll give you some background so you can understand." Rory peered into Jarl's flushed face. "You are still capable of listenin' to me, aren't you?"

Jarl managed a careful and deliberate nod.

"Years ago the little people disappeared. Magical creatures went through a gate between two alternate universes, because there were more men and fewer of us each century. Men became increasingly logical. Logic! Fine thing! Tell logic to bring joy to the heart or a laugh to the lips. It was a poor exchange, if you ask me."

"I thought Christianity drove you away."

"Priestly propaganda said so, but the real reason we left was the development of science. Magic and technology don't mix. Mortal man made a poor choice when he decided to accept science."

"Well, the world is more technologically oriented now than when you left, so why are you here making footprints on my papers?"

"That's a good question. Don't think I asked for this job. When my name came up before the Council—but that's neither here nor there. Don't rush me. Impatience was always a mortal failin'." He eyed the whiskey bottle hopefully, but Jarl didn't seem to notice. "Through our magic we were able to transport ourselves to another place—I suppose your scientists would call it an alternate universe." He spoke with disdain. "Science! The very word dirties me mouth." He cocked his head to one side. "You wouldn't consider giving a poor thirsty fellow another wee drink, would you?"

Jarl slowly unscrewed the top of the bottle. The effort of coordinating his brain and hand was almost too difficult a task.

"Your mystics would probably call it another plane, but whatever you choose to name the place, Realm exists."

"Realm? What's that?"

"Has all the whiskey you've been sipping gone to your head? Realm, I said," Rory repeated in exasperation.

"If you've moved off Earth, what brings your return?"

"Because we lived here so long, there are affinities or bonds between us and you. And frankly, we're findin' it difficult to live with the evil creatures the human race keeps creatin'."

"We're creating evil creatures?" Jarl shook his head to clear it. He knew the next day he would have the father of all hangovers, but this really was some hallucination he'd dreamed up this time. "How?"

"By creatin' them in your thoughts."

"You mean we're manufacturing them in our minds?"

"Exactly! Now you're getting' the idea." Rory nodded his satisfaction.

"Mankind has always dreamed and created," Jarl said, rubbing his hand across his eyes in a tired gesture.

"Now too many of you read books and see movies with horrible monsters. If humans believe, even temporarily, in a blood-drenched wizard, he becomes real in our world. We normal magical folk don't like your monsters."

Jarl's laugh drew a frown from Rory. "Preposterous!" Jarl said.

"You may well laugh. Before you're through, mortal fool, you won't think what I've told you is so humorous."

Jarl recognized that the leprechaun was quite serious. "If we believe in fairies, they exist?" he murmured incredulously. "James Barrie used that idea in his story of Peter Pan, but adults don't believe it."

"You'd better start believin'," the unsmiling Rory told him in a grave little voice. He seated himself on a stack of books on the desk corner.

"You're actually serious? In your world the products of human minds are real?"

"Indeed, they are."

"I'm sorry to hear it, but why are you telling me about it? I don't write wild fantasy stories."

"When the time is right, you'll know. The talisman will take you when you're needed." Rory grinned. He flickered with the firelight and disappeared.

The confused and drunken man, seated alone in the room, blinked. Jarl shook his head in a vain effort to clear it. "Minou, you've got to remind me not to stare at the fire too long. What an imagination I've got. I'm wasted on nonfiction. Maybe I should try my hand at some of this fantasy stuff after all." At this point he noticed the cat curled up sound asleep. He ended his monologue and went unsteadily to bed.

The next morning Jarl stretched sleepily as the golden tracery of sunlight shot through the branches of the trees that surrounded his cabin. The cottony feeling in his mouth and the anvil chorus playing full tilt in his throbbing head signaled a class-one hangover.

Carefully holding his head so it wouldn't fall off and shatter, he plodded stolidly into the bathroom. He turned on the shower and tested the water with his hand.

Firmly clasped around his right wrist was a bracelet in the form of a dragon. "Lord, where was I last night? I can't remember buying this," he said sleepily. The multifaceted gold crystals that formed the eyes of the metallic creature drew his attention like a magnet.

"Now where the devil did I get this?" he pondered aloud. The bracelet refused to slip from his wrist; he could find no clasp to release.

Deciding he needed his shower, he took it, bracelet notwithstanding. The scales shed water. For a moment in the steamy stall he could have sworn the eyelids of the dragon drooped with languorous pleasure. He told himself the idea was ridiculous.

After dressing, he decided to forgo the doubtful delights of a breakfast his stomach might not be able to keep down. He noticed the whiskey bottle was almost empty. "No wonder I'm hung over this morning," he muttered. He tipped the scant remainder into his glass and tossed it back as if he were in need of the pick-me-up. Which he was.

His blurry eyes roamed the room. In mute testimony, small sooty footprints marched across the top sheet of paper on his desk.

CHAPTER TWO

Jarl slowly lowered himself into his chair, trying to orient the sight of the elfin footprints with a reality he could understand. The bracelet seemed warm, and tighter. It curled around his arm and he imagined he could feel a faint pulse from the metal body. The dragon's eyes were so green! He lifted the bracelet closer to his face so he could see the lifelike details. The whole thing was a work of art, especially the emerald chips that formed the eyes. As he watched, they seemed to grow larger and larger, holding his gaze in spite of his will.

He raised his shocked face to look at where he was. What had happened to his comfortable armchair? He felt the rough wood of a fallen tree under him. The bracelet was once again an inanimate piece of metal, but Jarl had the strangest notion. He could have sworn the transformation caught the left eyelid of the dragon in midwink. He had to be in his house. There was no logical way he could have moved outside into the woods around his home. Could he be hallucinating? The fallen tree he sat on seemed real enough. He reached out his hand to touch the green grass that grew before him. It felt like grass. It looked like grass. He pulled a piece, placing it in his mouth. It tasted like grass, too. A bird flew across the clearing before him. It ruffled its bright green feathers and sang a few notes. Jarl thought he recognized the opening bars of "The Wearing of the Green." He could have been dreaming except there was none of the wispy feeling of unreality a dream produced when you looked at it in detail.

The forest of oak and ash trees spread away in all directions. The small glade in which he sat seemed to be the only open space for miles. Far overhead, lacy white clouds decorated a teal-blue sky in which nothing moved. Under other circumstances he would have enjoyed the quiet isolation of his position.

In the center of the open space he saw a raised mound covered with bracken. He rose rather gingerly and rubbed his sore behind. Thank heaven, he thought, his hangover had disappeared. Almost like magic, he decided wryly. The rough bark felt permanently etched into his carcass. His corded brown work pants had provided him little protection.

When he approached the mound, he noticed that some small animal had been digging into its side. The sunlight reflected from a shiny object that sparkled in the loose dirt. His hand parted the vegetation cautiously.

"That's funny. It looks like a handle," he murmured to himself. Grasping it firmly, he tested his strength as he pulled it fully into the light. It was a sword.

Vaguely he got the impression of great age, even though the weapon shined brightly and seemed as sharp as new. He raised the sword and swung it in the air experimentally. The jeweled hilt fit his hand perfectly and grew more familiar with each swing. Every swish called a different note from the air. The sounds almost formed a musical pattern. "Like music," he said aloud.

"Stop, thief!" a nasty little voice shouted.

Jarl looked in the direction of the sound and saw a strange creature. Its yellow catlike eyes glittered evilly, and its pointed nose resembled the beak of a bird. Spindly legs held it partially erect. Between them he saw a scrawny tail projecting. Its clawed, four-fingered hand pulled distractedly at the patches of long, ragged fur that stood out over its head. Two tufts of fur looked as if they might cover pointed ears.

"I wasn't going anywhere," Jarl answered the weird apparition. His voice was calm despite his surprise and uneasiness at being transported to the glade so rapidly.

"Steal from a spriggan's treasure mound, will you!" The voice grew louder and more booming with every word as the creature inflated itself into gigantic proportions.

Jarl shaded his eyes with one hand as he looked sunward, for the head of the spriggan now towered over the surrounding trees. This had to be a dream!

"I wasn't stealing anything. If folklore is anything to trust, isn't it the spriggans who take things that don't belong to them?" Jarl refused to be intimidated by the huge form.

"That's a lie! It's a mortal lie! Only a thieving human would say a thing like that!" The spriggan's tremendous arm shook in the air as his finger emphasized every angry word.

At this point Jarl was more astounded than frightened, and his answer angered the creature further.

"Call me a thief, do you?" It tee-heed grotesquely. "So, I'll steal something of yours!"

Suddenly Jarl was looking up into his own face.

"This is a lovely body that I've got now."

To Jarl's horror, the words were coming from the mouth of the man-shape the spriggan was inhabiting. Jarl decided to sit down but came to an abrupt halt when he realized his tail made sitting awkward. His tail? The wicked sprite had stolen Jarl's body.

Busy flexing its new muscles and bending its new legs, the Jarl-creature laughed. Jarl in the spriggan's shape struggled to wield the shining sword.

"Dullard, are you?" Jarl-creature said in the man's voice. "Turn my own treasure on me, would you?" it questioned dourly. With a wave of Jarl's hand, it conjured a whirlwind. The whirlwind spun around Jarl's spriggan body and carried it away in a cloud of leaves and dusty sand.

Dusty sand? In a forest? Jarl thought as he opened the slitted eyes he had automatically closed to protect his sight. When he felt the wind abate, he dropped a foot into soft yellow sand. Blinking his eyes, he tried to adjust to the bright light. The trees had disappeared. Not even cactus grew in the arid region where Jarl found himself. He stood next to an outcrop of rocks that looked as if some giant had dropped his blocks and gone to play elsewhere. The hot, dry wind sucked the moisture from his body. The heat from the sand struck at him like a blow. Even the rocks denied him shade, for the sun was directly overhead.

"Shades of L. Frank Baum, I'm in a desert. All this crazy dream needs now is a yellow brick road."

"Spriggan, you are out of your place and time," a cool voice told Jarl.

"I'm no spriggan," he replied. Jarl looked for the source of the sounds he heard inside his head. He wanted to wake up. The body he inhabited was ill-kept and sandy. The hot sand burned his feet.

"Not?"

"No, not!" Jarl told the invisible speaker in angry tones. His new voice sounded petulant. "Where are you?" he demanded.

"Right here," the voice chuckled. A fennec, or desert fox, daintily stepped from behind a rock. At least it looked like the pictures of fennecs Jarl had seen once in a nature magazine. It had the typical large pricked ears and foxy brush.

"Small one, is there any way out of this desert?" Jarl addressed his companion politely. Courtesy never hurt anyone. If he wasn't dreaming this wild adventure, he just might need all the friends he could make, he reasoned silently to himself. After all, it wasn't in every dream that you met a talking fennec. In fact, he'd never actually seen one, not even in a zoo on his world. His world? Where was he? He knew with certainty he was not on Earth. If this wasn't a dream, what was happening to him?

Green eyes sparkled mischievously into his as the fennec replied, "Who's calling who 'small one'? You're just my size, you know."

"Sorry." Jarl made his spriggan's voice sound suitably repentant. It would be folly to lose contact with the only living being he could see in this Sheol of heat, sun, sand, and rock.

"What do you want me to call you?"

"Call me—" the fennec paused as if considering, "—Mirza."

Jarl's first instinct was to give his name. The fennec's pause reminded him of the old superstition that said knowing a person's name granted power over that person.

As if sensing his dilemma, Mirza said, "I already know your name. Jarl Koenig, I need your aid."

"How can I help you?" Since he was obviously out of his mind, he might as well play along, he decided.

"You wear the Dragon Wyrd, a powerful talisman. Use it to free me."

For the first time he noticed the silver chain that circled her neck. It was fastened to an oddly carved metal ring, which vanished into the stone of the entrance to the cave behind her. He looked down at his scrawny arm, noticing the bracelet curled tightly around it. "I'd do it if I could, but—"

The small dust devils that whirled over the sand in the distance coalesced into the form of a djinn. The djinn approached with malevolent rapidity, growing larger as it came. Jarl just stared.

"It figures. All the trappings of an Arabian Nights tale. My subconscious has a lot to answer for. The next time I decide to drink with a leprechaun, I'm sticking to lemonade," Jarl said ruefully, forgetting about the fennec at his side.

The djinn stood before them, his humanoid body clad in baggy harem pants. The six pointed horns on his head gleamed exactly like his mammoth yellow teeth, which were visible in his cavernous mouth. He laughed down at them.

He is Caschcasch, the fennec whispered inside Jarl's skull.

The djinn's voice boomed. "Ho, ho, little shape shifter. So you plan to escape me?"

Jarl wondered if all the evil in this adventure was going to come in giant economy size. How did this genie know the spriggan had swapped forms with him?

The gigantic hand of the genie reached out, first finger extended. Jarl just had time to wonder what a djinn did with such long, curved fingernails when a bolt of magic flashed at him. In his haste to duck, he threw up his spriggan arm on which the dragon bracelet glittered. It acted like a magnet, attracting the bolt to itself. The bolt reversed its direction, causing it to blast the djinn who sent it. An earsplitting crack reverberated from the surrounding rocks.

CHAPTER THREE

Neatly done, Jarl, the fennec commented.

"What was?" he asked.

Destroying the power of your oversized host and regaining your own form. You're a very handsome man.

Suddenly he was aware that the little beast was female. Her feminine remark had clinched the vague suspicions he harbored. Professional heroes got to rescue beautiful princesses, but he had saved a fox. Well, he supposed one had to start in the hero business somewhere. He could sense Mirza's amusement. She "spoke" directly into his mind. Did that mean she could read his thoughts?

It takes great power to break a changeling spell. The dragon channeled power into your change and returned the excess to the djinn, she explained kindly. *It will be centuries before he regains his full powers. In the meantime we can return to Realm.*

"Realm?" he questioned.

The small auburn-haired animal ignored his query. She stepped lightly over the sand and commanded, *Pick me up and hold me.*

As Jarl reached down to comply, he briefly considered the events of the last few minutes. Or was it hours? In this setting, time had no meaning. He suffered from concept overload. Nothing made much sense to him.

The Keepers approve, Dragon's Pawn. She touched noses with him gently. *Let us go.*

Shaken out of his reverie by her last remark and the cool moistness of her nose against his, he felt the clean warmth of her fur. Her nose reached out gently to nudge his chin. The gesture was strangely erotic. He received sensations like those of holding a beautiful woman in his arms, but he was becoming too shockproof to worry. He slipped his hand over the front of the fennec's chest to hold it more firmly, preparatory to walking out into the desert sands. He promptly received a bitten finger for his pains. Clearly there were definite rules for handing a fennec.

Visualize where you want to go, she instructed sharply, *back to the spriggan's mound.* Seeing his incomprehension, she added, *Look at the dragon, Jarl.*

The eyes of the mythological beast, which were golden at first, gradually turned to green. The color expanded until the whole universe shone emerald. Then there was a wrench and a moment of vertigo. Jarl and Mirza stood in the glade of the spriggan.

"Take the sword! Quickly!" Mirza told him. It lay where he dropped it when the wind whirled him away.

"It's not mine. The spriggan said it belonged to him."

Nonsense! He stole it from a hero's tomb centuries ago. As Dragon's Pawn, you'll have need of it. Take it and we'll go. Here the fennec nodded in a northern direction, where a faint path through the trees began.

"Who's stealing my sword?" a familiar voice questioned. At once Mirza leaped from Jarl's arms. "The Dragon's Pawn, you fool. Stand at your peril," she warned, teeth flashing.

The spriggan stopped in midhop. "My lady—a thousand pardons," it whined.

"No more tricks, or we'll turn another scale to gold by destroying you."

In an eye blink the spriggan disappeared into his hill, leaving a clear path for Jarl and his new friend. Jarl picked up the abandoned sword. "I thought scales weighed gold, Mirza," he said.

"Not that kind of scales. Dragon's scales," she told him patiently.

He glanced around the glade. "What dragon?"

"The one on your arm. You have only to look carefully to see the change." She sounded exasperated.

"If it's all the same to you, I'd just as soon skip looking at the bracelet. That's how I got myself into this m—" Prudence stopped him from completing his statement. "Realm," he corrected himself, remembering his conversation of the night before.

Mirza cast him a look over her shoulder, pink tongue lolling as if in a grin. Did she know what he had almost said?

The dragon wristband gleamed bronze, all except for its tail, which was now formed of two golden scales.

Follow me, Mirza commanded. She led the way along the narrow path that wound through the silent forest of giant trees.

The dim green light filtered through the thick, leafy branches overhead. The brightest object Jarl could see was the ruddy glow of the fennec's lustrous red pelt. Jarl remembered a girl he had once dated with hair of the same shade. He found himself thinking what a beautiful woman the fox would make if the spriggan used his shape-shifting magic on her. After an hour of following at the steady pace that Mirza set with little apparent effort, Jarl ventured to speak.

"Where are we going?"

North.

"Are you fennecs all so short-spoken?"

"Usually we prefer not to speak at all."

"Well, I'd like some answers and I'd like them now."

The fennec turned and sat in the middle of the path with her tail curled neatly around her paws. Her amusement was evident.

"Where are we?"

"On Realm, an alternate Earth. Realm is Earth as it might be had man followed magic instead of science."

"How was I brought here?"

"Curiosity is not a virtue here, Dragon's Pawn. Remember the cat in the adage and what curiosity did to it."

"But—" he began, and then glanced down at the bracelet on his wrist. A tingle passed along his arm. The eyes of the beast glittered with life, greenly beckoning. With a wrench Jarl recognized the vertigo, which was becoming all too familiar. When his stomach settled, he saw the dragon had transported him again.

He stood at a fork in the path. There was no sign of the fennec. Momentarily stunned by his rapid transition, he looked blankly at his two choices. The left branch seemed inviting, broader and well traveled. The right path led deeper into the forest. He felt a slight movement on his arm, but he carefully refrained from looking at the bracelet. Being jerked hither and yon as if he had no will of his own annoyed Jarl. He was deliberately being deprived of information. He turned his face to the left, preparatory to taking the first step down the path. The metal around his wrist constricted painfully.

"All right," he grumbled, taking the pointed hint. He clasped the hilt of the sword firmly as he set forth. The sword was an extension of his arm. He realized that sooner or later he would need a scabbard. Traveling around with an unsheathed sword in hand asked for trouble. He felt he had all the problems he needed without any additions.

As he stepped confidently on the right-hand trail, abandoning what looked like a road to civilization, the other path disappeared.

The afternoon had advanced to dusk when Jarl and the fennec arrived in the spriggan's glade. Now the shadows the trees threw across the trail grew longer, like the reaching fingers of the night they presaged. Already the warmth of the afternoon was sliding into the cool of evening.

Jarl forced his footsteps to a faster pace. All roads eventually arrived somewhere; accordingly, the sooner he got to the end of this one, the faster he would find shelter for the night.

The vacant sensation in his midsection predicted correctly the hunger he expected. The distance between his backbone and his navel seemed like a mile. First he had missed breakfast and now a nonexistent evening meal. He began to think of all the things he wished he had to eat.

An errant breeze frolicked across the air before him, carrying an odor redolent of spices.

"Apple pie!" Jarl's nostrils twitched at the scent, which overpowered the piney smell of this part of the forest. He was so hungry he thought he was imagining the scent of pie. Then he turned a sharp bend and saw a croft in a small glade beside the path.

The shutters on the small window to the left of the wood door were open. One the sill sat the pie Jarl had scented from the woods.

Flat stones were set in a complicated pattern to make a walk to the door. Multicolored flowers crowded together on each side of him as he approached. Little mists of steam rose from the still-hot vents in the nicely browned top of the pie. His wallet was on his dresser at home, and the few coins he had in his pants pocket probably wouldn't be any good here. He raised his hand to knock when the door opened from within.

"Come in," the wizened granny said, her alert black eyes snapping.

In spite of himself, Jarl smiled. She was exactly what one might expect to find in a small out-of-the-way cottage like this. The fire merrily crackling in the grate and the caldron bubbling over the flames heightened the storybook atmosphere. The contented tabby drowsing in the hearth completed the setting. The coziness of the room reached out and enfolded him. He felt immediately at home.

"Sit," his hostess commanded. She ladled fragrant stew from the pot over the fire. She set a full dish before him.

"You act as if you expected me," Jarl said after a brief thank-you. The stew was delicious.

"Eat first, then we shall talk." She put hunks of fresh bread and cheese on the table.

Then she retreated to the corner of the room and begin to spin. The soft whirr-whirr of the wheel made a quiet accompaniment to the hearty meal Jarl ate. Before the huge bowl was empty, the silent old woman added a generous wedge of the pie to the food before him. She pointed to the caldron, indicating that he might have more stew if he wished.

When Jarl finally finished, he pushed the bench back from the table. "Thank you," he said to the little old woman, who now rocked with the cat on her lap.

"You're welcome," she said quietly, eyes intent on what she was doing in the flickering light.

"Can you tell me where the road past your cottage goes?" Jarl broke the companionable silence.

"In the morning"—the old woman smiled warmly at him—"you'll be able to see the hill behind the house. When you get to the top of that hill, you'll see your destination in the next valley."

Her cryptic words mildly annoyed Jarl. Nobody in Realm answered his questions. When someone was ready to shed a little light on his situation, like Mirza, the crazy wrist shackle that he refused to look at zapped him off somewhere.

"Have you no other questions for me?" She cocked her head like an inquisitive sparrow.

"You weren't surprised when I arrived at your door," he said.

"That's right." She raised her eyebrows and waited for his next words.

"Why?"

A cheery peal of laughter was his answer. "My dear boy, why do you suppose a little old lady lives alone in the woods? Don't you remember the fairy tales from your youth—or don't they tell them on Earth anymore?"

For the present Jarl overlooked her knowing where he came from. "You mean you're a—a—" He floundered. He couldn't bring himself to say the word.

"Witch?" she concluded for him. "What a lovely compliment! You may consider me to be a wise woman instead of a witch if that makes you feel any more comfortable."

"How can I return to Earth?" If she knew where he came from, presumably she also knew how he could get home again.

"I'm not wise enough to answer that for you. A little way into the future I can see, but past that—"

She shook her head ruefully. "Too much depends on the choices you make."

"Spriggans, djinns, talking fennecs . . . I can't make any sense out of what's happening to me," he told her. He ran his hand over the flat of the exposed blade of the sword he held balanced across his knees.

The old woman took note of the sword for the first time. "I have a gift for you," she said.

"A gift?" Jarl repeated, showing his incomprehension.

"Open the box in the corner." She gestured. "The scabbard is yours."

Jarl took the scabbard from the box. "Thanks," he said, sheathing the sword for the first time since he had taken it from the spriggan's mound. The belt fit him perfectly, but he unbuckled it when he found wearing it made sitting difficult. He laid it on the bench beside him and waited for what his hostess had to tell him.

"Now, let's see," the old woman muttered softly to herself. "Have we all the ingredients? Hero, magic talisman, weapon, fair maiden, and villains in plenty . . . " Suddenly raising her voice, she said, "Ah, I know what's missing! You need to know the prophecy!"

"What prophecy?" Jarl burst out. "What about that fair-maiden bit—"

"Shush now. How does it go . . . " She rocked silently for a time.

"How can you know a prophecy about me?" he questioned, hoping to speed her mental processes. He impatiently waited for her to continue.

She began to recite:

> " . . . with evil's stain
> Lest dark wizard's powers reign.
> Every hap shall come aright
> When Dragon's Pawn is Keeper's Knight.
> Let in tiny sparks of day,
> Free those who are wizard's prey,
> Web of universe shine bright,
> Turn the Darkness into Light."

"But, but—" Jarl stammered, not helped at all by the rhyme.

"You're the Dragon's Pawn, Jarl," she told him seriously. "A riddle-prophecy does no one any good unless he solves it himself." Then taking pity on his bewilderment, she added, "I can only tell you this. The shortest way through is often the longest way around."

"I don't think I like being anyone's pawn," he began. "That's not exactly what I'd call a big help," he told her, forgetting for a moment that she was no ordinary woman.

"When you do the right thing, you'll know," she promised.

"How?"

"By watching the dragon." She pointed to his wristband.

"Every time I look at the darn thing, I get zapped from one place to another," he complained.

"The talisman will act on its own if you don't give it direction. Concentrate on what you need and see if the dragon can't provide it," she suggested.

"Can it take me home?"

"Not immediately. You have been summoned for a purpose."

"Will it tell me when I do the right things to get home?"

"You need only to look. You earn the dragon's scales through correct decisions and virtuous acts. There are three golden scales now. They mark three correct decisions on your part."

"What decisions?"

"Gaining the sword, rescuing Mirza by vanquishing the djinn, and choosing the way to my cottage. They were all correct choices. Each one changes a scale to gold."

"So I keep choosing, and bit by bit, if I'm lucky, the dragon turns to gold. Then what happens?" he asked. He had a curious feeling. It was almost as if he were a contestant in some kind of game show. Things didn't seem real. They couldn't be—could they?

"Then you'll be Dragon's Pawn no longer," she concluded on a note of satisfaction.

"And—"

"Then you'll not need me to tell you the answer to the riddle. You'll know yourself."

Later, as Jarl settled himself on the comfortable pallet in the loft above the cottage, he tried to make sense of what had happened to him. He still had more questions than answers, but tomorrow was time enough to find out about the powers of his bracelet. He gave his wrist an absentminded pat. A sense of warmth and approval came from what so short a time ago had seemed only a piece of inanimate metal.

CHAPTER FOUR

Jarl woke to the smell of frying bacon. "She must be a witch, all right," he muttered to himself. Running his hand over the golden stubble on his chin, he decided he could let his beard grow. Electricity was one of the scientific comforts that he had left behind him, along with his razor.

"The smell of bacon is one of the few things that can get me up in a hurry in the morning," he called down to his unseen hostess. He stretched luxuriously before throwing the quilt aside and springing to his feet. He picked up his cowboy boots, smiling to himself at the incongruity of a hero in a fairy-tale realm wearing a Texan's hallmark. This was the only place where things were bigger—and stranger—than the Lone Star State. As he started to walk to the ladder that led to the lower floor, the bracelet gave a warning twitch.

"What the—" Jarl said, wondering why the dragon was active for no reason he could understand. Well, perhaps that wasn't correct. What was the coiled talisman trying to tell him? He glanced down without thinking, as if the sight of the dragon could give him the answer to his question. Somehow it did. He returned to his pallet on the floor of the loft and neatly folded the guilt over the top of the crude mattress. He looked at the bracelet and said, "Okay now?"

He descended with no further movement from the dragon. Who ever heard of a tidy talisman? He had taken it for granted that the shape on his arm belonged to a masculine creature. If he was going to start doing things like making his bed neatly every morning in approved Boy Scout fashion, he might begin to believe his bracelet was female. At the conclusion of his thoughts, he jumped involuntarily as the tail of the dragon gave him a sharp slap on the wrist. It felt like the rubber bands he and his friends had snapped each other with when they were children.

He stood dumbfounded in the middle of the cottage floor downstairs. The dragon's movement hadn't bothered him. Perhaps he was finally getting used to this place. After all, last night's witch seemed to be a kindly old granny in the morning's light. Hearing the old lady chuckle, he looked at her with one eyebrow raised in inquiry.

"How else is the dragon to get into communication with you? Oh Jarl!" She laughed. "The problems you face! May you always surmount them as you have this morning," she added in a more serious vein. "Come eat," she urged.

He obeyed quickly, for the table had dishes that appealed both to his eyes and his nose. Eggs, bacon, crusty bread, fresh butter, and tall glasses of cider to wash it all down sat on the table. He alternated honey and pink jam on his bread slices, unable to decide which he preferred.

"Would you like to join me? I'm having a hot cup of tea," his hostess said.

"I usually drink coffee for breakfast, but I'll try a cup." The bracelet twitched uneasily. "Please," he finished.

The witch's amusement showed in her smile, which she made no attempt to hide. "Poor man, bitten by the fennec he befriended. Then chastised by his talisman," she said in a tone that told him she didn't really pity him at all.

"How the dev—" He corrected himself at once. "—dickens did you know about that?"

"Secrets of the trade, my boy. Secrets of the trade."

He looked into his cup and noticed that his tea was pink. "Pink tea?" he asked. He had never tasted anything like it before.

"Coralberry. You liked the jam I made from it," she told him with satisfaction.

"It was delicious."

"Many plants grow here that no longer survive on Earth." She rose from the table and bustled over to a small box on the mantel above the fireplace. "Here, keep this in your pocket." With these words she handed him a sprig of vivid green. It had a clean, fresh scent that he did not recognize.

"What's this?"

"Moley," she answered.

"Holy moley!" he said half jokingly.

"Yes, indeed. It wards off enchantments and sweetens the air."

"Thanks," he told her, peering at it closely. "The last fellow on Earth who used this was Odysseus," he mused.

"Right!" she told him delightedly as she cleared the table. "It is always scarce, and unicorns cannot resist it. Fortunately, it was so rare that men didn't discover it and use it to hunt the unicorns to extinction."

He gulped. "Are there unicorns here?"

"Naturally," she punned, seeing his lips curve at her little joke.

"Will I see any?" He stopped himself abruptly. He was asking questions like an ignorant teenager instead of a full-grown man. He didn't like feeling childish.

"Perhaps sooner than you think," she told him cryptically. Then, changing the subject, she said, "Now it's time for you to chop a little kindling for me. The logs are out behind the cottage. Split enough to fill the woodbox over there in the corner."

"I'll be glad to," Jarl answered, feeling it was the least he could do. He really liked his weird hostess. He wondered if her witchly powers told her things like that. He willingly chopped away at the mammoth pile of logs with the ax he found stuck in the chopping block. Women weren't so different here after all. No man would have let a good ax stand out in the weather. He split the wood neatly and piled it in the box inside the house. When he turned to put the last pile in the diminutive wheelbarrow, he saw a unicorn come out of the woods.

He stood gawking at the beautiful animal, afraid to move. One of the pieces of wood fell from the top of his sagging load and hit him sharply on the toe, breaking the spell.

"Ouch!" he said, carefully placing the wood down so he could wheel it in and add it to the pile. He was sure his movement would frighten the creature away. He remembered enough of his mythology to know how shy unicorns were. To his surprise, the unicorn approached until it was only a few feet away.

Moving slowly, he wiped his hands on his pants. He thought the unicorn scented the moley in his jacket pocket. Reaching out to stroke the glossy neck, he settled the long silvery mane all on one side. Then he saw a frayed rope around the beast's neck. He severed it with his pocket-knife, saying, "There you are, beautiful."

Thank you, the unicorn thought inside Jarl's head.

The thought reminded him of the telepathic conversations with Mirza. He missed the little devil. She had made a good companion. The unicorn nudged him gently. Her horn was quite short, nothing like the length he expected from old tapestry renditions and pictures of unicorns that survived on Earth.

I'm a female, she thought. *There is no necessity for me to have a long horn. Only males need to use them in the mock battles at mating time*, she told him, answering the question he hadn't voiced.

Jarl felt a little nervous. Did everybody here know his name—or were they all reading his mind? He didn't care much for that idea.

It's Wyrd, she sent gently.

"Yeah. It sure is weird," he told her, surprised when a feminine giggle tickled his mind. A giggling unicorn? This whole experience had to be real. In his wildest dreams he couldn't have envisioned a mirthful unicorn—but here she was.

Jarl, the name of your bracelet is Wyrd. Not weird—strange. Wyrd-fateful, she explained.

Light dawned. "Oh, I understand. W-Y-R-D," he spelled. He did not see anything incongruous in spelling a word to prove to a unicorn he knew what she meant.

You felt no desire to capture me?

"Unicorns need to be free, I'm sure," he answered.

The unicorn eyed his bracelet.

"Don't be afraid," he told her. "It would not hurt you." He tried to reassure her. If it was within his power, the dragon talisman would be her protector, not a feared thing.

He felt her soft laughter within his mind. *Silly man*, she nodded. *You have done well. Another scale has turned to gold.*

When Jarl looked at his bracelet, he saw it was true. He thought the female creatures of Realm were very attractive. The unicorn nudged him, inviting him to continue petting her, which he did. He continued thinking. The witch was a charming person, in spite of her age. Erotic visions flashed through his mind as he pondered what the young women of Realm might be like. A dainty unicorn hoof came down on his foot, and she pulled away from him with flared nostrils. The unicorn acted just like a jealous woman. It amused Jarl when he realized this; it was his turn to enjoy humor. Usually around here the laughter was at him. It was a welcome change.

"Jarl," the old woman called, "I have something for you. Are you finished?"

Her words broke the spell that bound Jarl and the unicorn together.

Good-bye, she thought. She trotted majestically back into the forest while he raised his hand in farewell.

The witch appeared around the corner just in time to see the creature enter the belt of forest that surrounded the clearing.

"That girl," the wise woman told him, "is getting to be a real little minx."

"You mean the unicorn?"

"Who else?"

"Does she come here often?"

"Often enough to be a real nuisance sometimes." The old woman's smile told him she was not seriously disturbed by the unicorn's visits.

Still bemused by his meeting, Jarl asked, "You know her well, then?"

"Known her family for years. She gets more like her father every day." She chuckled. "One of these times she's going to get her tail feathers singed, pushing her magic in here where it's not needed. She'll learn. She'll learn," she went on, almost as if she had forgotten Jarl's presence. Then with a jerk she brought herself back to the present. "Well, are you going to finish the job you started or not?"

"Yes," he said awkwardly. He tried to recapture his sense of normalcy. On Earth he hadn't believed in the fantastic beasts of fairyland, but seeing the unicorn had made a great impression on him. He wondered if he would see it again. Then he completed stacking the kindling. "I'm finished," he said.

"Well done," she told him shortly. "I've something you'll be needing before long." From behind her back she took a bridle. Jarl noted the fine workmanship. It weighed almost nothing in his hands.

"It's light, but it's strong," the witch told him.

"The gift is a nice idea, but I have no horse to put it on."

"The hero always rides a horse," she said. Then she took pity on his incomprehension. "You'll have one soon, or I'll turn in my crystal ball." She picked up a leathern pouch from the ground. "Here is your lunch—and dinner, if you should need it," she said, giving it to him. "Your time here is over. Now go." She gestured toward the path that ran along the clearing and vanished over the hill behind the house.

"Thank you for everything," he told her sincerely. Moved by an impulse he didn't understand, he bent over and kissed the old woman's cheek in good-bye.

Shocked by his impulse, he stood still. If his kiss offended the witch, she might make him hop through the rest of his life with a green skin.

CHAPTER FIVE

"Go along with you," the old woman said in a flustered voice.

He saw the kiss pleased her. As he walked along the path to the top of the hill, he thought, I've just kissed a self-confessed witch. This is one crazy adventure.

A chestnut mare stepped from behind a dense clump of bushes in front of him just as he reached the top of the hill. *It was very good policy to kiss the old dame good-bye.* The horse's thought reached Jarl's mind.

He stood and stared, the bridle handing limply in his hand.

Well, the voice echoed in his head, *are you going to stand there all day like a ninny, or are you going to put it on me?*

He bridled the mare and ran his hand down the chestnut neck. It reminded him of the unicorn's. He led her over to a convenient rock and, using it as a mounting block, got astride the mare's bare back. While he gathered the reins, she turned around to face the cottage far below them. The old wise woman was a tiny figure in the distance. They saw her remove her apron and wave it at them before she reentered her cottage. As soon as she disappeared inside, the mare turned and began moving.

Her walk became a trot, and her trot, a gallop. It was like riding the wind, and yet Jarl wished she could travel even faster. He felt a sense of urgency in the very air that rushed by them. A blackbird rose from the limb of a lightning-blasted tree on the edge of a swamp. He felt the muscles of his mount redouble their effort, increasing their pace. He gave up all thought of guiding the mare and concentrated on staying astride. He promised himself that he would never again be unappreciative of a saddle.

He missed the solid feel of stirrups under his boots. They left the woods and swamp far behind them. The mare seemed tireless. It was well past noon before her pace began to slacken. They traveled down a broad valley between a range of ever-taller mountains. She finally veered from the almost invisible trail she had followed to ascend an old, well-defined path.

Giant boulders strewed the side of the mountain, a reminder of some ancient catastrophe of monumental proportions. The mare slowed, and he could feel how the exertion had weakened her. For the first time since mounting, he applied pressure to the reins. She stopped obediently at his command. He dismounted and prepared to sit on a nearby rock while she rested.

Not here, the mare told him, speaking to him for the second time that day. *Up. There's water,* she added as an inducement, waiting for him to remount.

"Far?" he questioned.

Not too far; only a small distance.

Then I'll walk," he told her, removing the bridle from her head. She might want to nibble the sparse grass as they traveled at the much slower pace his walking caused.

This way, she urged as they rounded an especially large boulder.

A huge flat area held what remained of an old building. It had been fairly large, but not one stone was standing on another. Only in the exact center of the cleared space was there something remaining. A mosaic in the shape of a pentagram encircled a small well that had escaped the general destruction. Jarl followed the mare into the tiled space around the well. He felt the lessening of the constriction of his bracelet, which had gradually been growing tighter. The sun sank lower on the rim of the mountains.

We will rest here, the mare told him. *It is safe.*

"What do you mean safe?" Jarl asked, somewhat out of breath. In Realm even the animals understood more of the situation than he did. On Earth some of his best friends were four-footed. In fact, he preferred animals to people. He accepted them as companions with no urge to dominate the relationship. The fiercest watchdogs sensed his amity. No animal had ever bitten him—except that dratted fennec, he thought half-fondly. He wondered where the fennec was now.

You miss Mirza? the horse inquired.

"Do you know her?" he asked eagerly. Maybe the creatures had a bush telegraph in Realm. They all knew who he was. Perhaps they were all familiars of the witch.

The horse gave a very feminine chuckle. He stared at her in horror. She sounded just like the unicorn! Her acid comments were just like those of his foxy friend. His mind raced over his adventures, kaleidoscoping them into a whole picture instead of separate, unrelated fragments. Awareness in his eyes, he asked, "Are you a, a, uh—shape shifter?" he concluded delicately. He did not want to use the prefix 'were.' Werewolf, no. Were-fennec—maybe, he thought.

Approval emanated from his equine companion. *Intelligent as well as kind*, she commented. She neither admitted nor denied her ability to change form at will.

He narrowed his thoughts to the time with Mirza. When the djinn had appeared, what had he said? It was something like, "So, little shape shifter, you plan to escape." Jarl's features lit with his discovery. "He didn't mean me; he meant you! That silver chain around your neck bound you to the rock. Silver kept you from changing shape to free yourself. That was why you needed me to rescue you, wasn't it?"

Correct. The mare nodded.

As the sun finally disappeared entirely, Jarl could see the faint green glow that seeped from the rocks. The glow illuminated the pentagram upon which they stood. The air, which had been distinctly chilly, with a sharp nip to the wind, stilled. It became comfortably warm within the aura of the green light.

"Well, why don't you change back into a fox so you can get more comfortable?" he asked. He wanted to see how she managed the change. "There's not very much room inside the pentagram," he explained.

There will be enough. You will have to wait awhile before I satisfy your curiosity, the mare told him. The coquettish shake of her head was reminiscent of a young girl.

"Why?" he asked. He felt more at home now that he knew he could recognize her in more than one shape. How he had remained ignorant so long puzzled him.

Because within the pentagram I cannot change.

"Why not?"

Because it is a—She paused, obviously searching for an explanation he would understand.

He felt inexplicably stupid as he waited for her to speak.

—a magic field itself, she continued. *It protects us from any evil in the vicinity. It's the reason I ran so hard to get us here before night.*

"Well, I appreciate your efforts, but what kind of evil do you mean? I haven't been here long enough to make anyone angry with me."

The Dragon's Pawn has enemies because he is what he is, not because he has done anything to deserve them. When Good meets Evil, there is always total war, all-out confrontation, whether Good wishes it or not.

"I hope I'm one of the good guys," he said lightly, trying to dispel a sense of impending trouble. It wasn't coming from the bracelet this time. The hair on the back of his neck had risen like the hackles on a good watchdog as she spoke.

Tomorrow, if you wish, when we leave I will conjure you a white hat, she offered teasingly.

"No, I'm quite all right as I am." Conjure? he thought. She must be a witch herself. Perhaps she's the sister of the old wise woman. They surely know each other.

The mare nudged him playfully. *I'm not that old,* she said flirtatiously. She blew through her nostrils and nudged him again.

It was somewhat disconcerting. He wasn't expecting the second gesture. He almost fell outside of the pentagram. Only her quick warning caused him to twist himself and remain inside the greenish glow that spelled safety.

I'm sorry, she apologized. *Gone—or hurt—if you'd fallen outside,* she thought hesitantly.

"This is no time for horseplay, evidently," he said. He put his hand on her neck to show her he didn't mind.

It's no joking matter. Seeing the future isn't one of my talents, but I know there will be trouble in plenty before we reach Realmgate safely. She turned to the well. Jarl saw it had mysteriously filled while they talked. It now was so full his companion could drink from it easily.

"How will I feed you?" Jarl asked. His hunger had reminded him of the amount of food a horse could eat. No vegetation grew within the pentagram, and outside was unsafe.

Open the pouch and see what's inside, she sent confidently.

He untied the bag from his belt. He felt lopsided for a moment with the sword unbalanced by the weight of the witch's food sack. He opened it and reached inside. One apple followed another. He bit into one, holding the bag under his arm and offering the other apple to the horse. She ate it, core and all. She removed the core of his apple from his hand and ate it, too.

"There are some advantages to your shape I hadn't thought of," he teased her gently.

Try the bag again, she advised.

This time there were two sandwiches within.

No roast beef for me, she told him. *You eat them.*

"What will you eat? A horse can't make a meal on an apple and two cores."

Put down the bag with the top open, she commanded.

Jarl placed it on the ground. He watched, astounded, as she began to pull wisps of hay from the bag during the whole time he devoured the two sandwiches.

"There must be a whole bale of hay in that bag, but I don't believe it."

You should. My gr—she stopped abruptly. *The old wise woman isn't a witch for nothing. The bag has a very potent spell on it. It will feed us whatever is best for us at the time. Want to try for a little dessert?*

He reached within and found a large apple tart for himself and a measure of oats for the mare. "Darned if that isn't a handy gadget." Magic was beginning to seem normal to him. He didn't try to rationalize how such things as shape shifting and food materializations were done. He only knew that on Realm they worked. Somehow he began to think that life back home—where he naturally desired to return—would seem a little mundane. He did want to return, didn't he? He throttled his doubt instantly.

The bag obligingly fluffed up with hay like a pillow, so he curled up on the stones to rest. The mare stood sentinel over him, watching the blackness outside the circle grow deeper and deeper. The man slept on, unaware of what was happening a scant yard or so from his place of refuge.

The darkness grew until it blotted out the moon and the stars; still the mare kept vigil. A disembodied voice began to speak, but the mare gave no sign she heard.

"Give the Dragon's Pawn to us."

"Us—us—us," echoed small sibilant voices after their master's.

"You cannot win," the Unseen continued.

"Not win—not win—not win," the tiny voices mocked mindlessly.

Only the mare's flicking ears showed she heard, but she refused to answer.

The one-sided conversation continued. The voices promised the direst revenge for noncompliance and the sweetest rewards of which the evil presence could think. "Power, wealth, knowledge!" the Unseen ended its oration.

Still the horse said nothing in answer. The blackness was a pall close around the pentagram. The only light was the greenish glow emanating from the stones within the shape and from the well. The light streamed upward into the starlit sky that the mare knew existed far above the local gathering of evil power. She was tiring. The glow grew fainter. It took great effort to summon the power of the well. Every faculty she had concentrated on coaxing and controlling the power to protect Jarl and herself.

Jarl awoke with a start. As his eyes slowly adjusted to the pale green glow, which faded as he watched, he remembered the events that preceded their arrival in this place.

For a second the green phosphorescence paled to almost nothing, and the mare gasped, "Jarl! Concentrate on the Dragon's Wyrd! Summon its power or we die!"

CHAPTER SIX

He felt the pulsing evil waiting greedily without. He wondered why he
didn't feel more afraid. Perhaps it was the total unreality of the situation . . . No, unreality was not the word. The whole situation was different
from anything he had ever encountered. His mind told him that what was
happening couldn't be real, but some much more basic part of him fed him
information that he knew instinctively was true. He sensed that the unseen
creatures waited hungrily for the chance to attack and destroy them utterly.
He looked into the eyes of the dragon on his wrist. They glowed richly
amber. Slowly the green light that surrounded them turned to gold. The
golden light spread, wider, ever wider, farther and farther, driving back the
blackness until it finally faded, allowing stars to shine through dimly.

"You'll be sorry, my lady. There will be other meetings, other places. I
promise you shall be most sorry." The voice sank to the lowest of whispers
and the echoes whined, "Sorry—sorry—sorry."

Jarl felt a ripple of distaste flow through him. The sound of the whining
voice still grated on his nerves. "What in the name of all that's holy was
that?" he asked in an awed tone. He shook his shoulders to rid himself of
the unpleasant crawling sensation those small "sorrying" voices had
raised within him.

In the name of all that's unholy, the mare corrected. *That was a minor minion
of the dark wizard.*

"Who is this wizard? What's his name?"

*Even if I knew it, I would not say it. Do you not have a saying about speaking of
the devil?*

43

"Speak of the devil and there he is." Jarl repeated the old maxim.

Yes, that's what I mean. Names have power. Anytime you think of evil, its power grows. If you actually say the name of a wizard, you may summon his attention. The attention of the Dark Lord is something none of us needs just now.

"What do we do next?"

We need to get to Realmgate.

"How about if I just get on your back, look at Wyrd here, and have him zap us there?" In his enthusiasm, he was sure he could solve their problem easily. He remembered the surge of power he had called from the talisman he wore. It made him feel confident of success.

Even magic has its limits. We must save the dragon's might for really dangerous situations and as a backup for the magic which I can summon.

"Why didn't you ask for help sooner? If I hadn't awakened—"

Before this day is over we may well use the powers that you have in reserve. Don't worry. You'll get your chance to battle all too soon now that the Shadowlord has some idea where we are.

"Look at you! You're too exhausted to walk, much less trot or gallop, carrying me. I can't ride with you in such a shape," he protested. "Couldn't I change myself into something and carry you for a while?"

With me as big as a horse? she quipped. Her soft laughter had more than a touch of a whinny in it.

Her exhaustion showed, and she was more female than anything else, Jarl thought compassionately. *She got that way while I slept like a child through all that danger.*

Don't berate yourself, Jarl, she thought gently. *There is still magic here, of a kind. For me,* she added, seeing his curious look around him. *If you would help,* she requested.

"Surely. What shall I do?"

His hand went to his sword automatically, she noted. It was a good sign. Her chosen one was hero material, although he probably didn't realize it. *Gather some water in your hands and carry it over there behind those rocks.* She gestured with her head to show him the direction, which was easy to see because the sun was rising.

Behind the rocks were the remains of what had once been a good-sized pool. Rocks now filled most of it. A small corner showed blue water, the deep color indicating an almost bottomless depth.

Put more water in the pool, she commanded. *Hurry, before you spill it all. It is precious; do not waste it on bare ground,* she told him as his amazement slowed his reactions.

When the water left his hands, it flowed smoothly into the blue pool, which slowly changed to green before his eyes. The mare stepped into the water from a little shelf that Jarl had not noticed. When he peered into the emerald liquid, he faintly saw a series of wide, shallow steps leading down into the depths. His horse immersed herself completely.

"Hey! What are you doing?" he called, leaning over the pool anxiously.

I'm quite all right now, she told him happily. *The goddess has allowed the power of the water to refresh me. I'm as good as I ever was,* she told him. She scrambled out of the water and heaved herself onto the dry bank.

The water gradually returned to its original hue as he watched. "I could use a dip myself. Have we time?"

Yes, she answered. She stood in the sun, letting the breeze dry her mane and tail. *Go ahead,* she invited. *The water is quite ordinary now.*

Jarl stood, undecided. He didn't mind bathing in front of a horse. Nevertheless, he wasn't too sure just what shape Mirza really inhabited when she was normal. Skinny-dipping in mixed company wasn't his usual habit.

I'll wait over by the well on the other side of the rock, she told him. *The bag will still have hay in it, and I'll begin breakfast while I wait for you,* she transmitted understandingly.

He would have felt better if he had not caught the undertone of amusement her thoughts carried. The longer he conversed with her, the more meaning he got from her thoughts. At first, all he understood were the words themselves. Lately he found he read the tones of her thoughts as well as he could tell emotions from the faces of people who spoke aloud. He already knew her better than anyone else he had known for so short a time. He laid his clothes on the bank and slipped into the blue water.

"Yee-ow!" he gasped, finding the water icy cold. He felt, rather than heard, her chuckle. "Mirza, you little devil, you knew darn well this water is freezing!"

A little cold water never hurt anyone. You're wide-awake. That's an added benefit of bathing in the mountain pool.

He spluttered, rose to the surface, and climbed out. He toweled off with his shirt, knowing it would soon dry in the sun. He hated to put on his pants, which were full of horsehair from the previous day's travel. He beat at them and horsehair flew.

"Mirza, is there any way to get a saddle?"

So you don't like riding bareback?

"I don't mind feeling a little stiff, but the real problem is the dirt and hair I've ground into my pants. I beat them on a rock, so they're cleaner than they were. As soon as I ride a while, I'll have as much hair on my breeches as you have on your back. Wouldn't a saddle feel better to you, too?"

A saddle you want, a saddle we'll get. I know just the place, she assured him.

As they walked slowly down the trail from the refuge, Jarl began to think about the comfort of a saddle. He wasn't sure he really wanted one after all. There was a pleasant feeling of being one with Mirza as he sat on her broad back. Using a saddle would make her seem more of an animal and less of a companion.

"Er—ah, Mirza," he began.

It's too late to change your mind, Jarl. We're too close to the ogre's keep to back out now. If you want a saddle, you'll have to fight for it.

"Ogre's keep?" he repeated, hoping it was just a name for a local landmark.

Yes, she told him sweetly. *Ogre's keep, complete with resident ogre. His name's Mog. Defeat him in single combat, and the saddle is yours.*

"Hold it right there. I'm a peaceable person. I don't actually want a saddle anyway. I especially don't want one I have to win from an ogre. They're supposed to be pretty ugly customers," he told Mirza seriously.

"Ugly!" A gigantic voice roared out in almost unintelligible syllables. "Who dares call Mog, the handsomest ogre in all Realm, ugly?"

A huge brown shape that Jarl had mistaken for a small hillock reared up and turned. Jarl was face to knee with the owner of the saddle Mirza expected him to win. In armed combat, he reminded himself. He wondered if he could force her to turn tail and run away so rapidly the ogre couldn't catch them.

My hero, she thought.

Jarl noted he could tell when she was being sarcastic as she charged forward into battle of her own accord. Jarl had no choice. His sword sprang to his hand, and he whirled it through the air. He hoped the speed of his mount and the dexterity of his attack would work. Not very bright, ogres moved ponderously. His only chance lay in riding in, slashing, and escaping the downward blow of the tree-sized club Mog was raising.

To Jarl, even though Mirza was galloping rapidly, it felt as if things were happening in slow motion. On closer inspection, Jarl could understand why he had mistaken the ogre for a small hill. Size only partly caused his error. Moss and lichen grew in the folds of Mog's soiled brown tunic. The buckle of the belt that girdled the monster's titanic paunch was green with age. Jarl wondered how long creatures of this sort lived. The gigantic gnarled fist grasping the club and the moss-gray beard and hairy thatch upon the ogre's head, coupled with his fangs, indicated not only age, but great wickedness. As Mog roared, Jarl saw the stumps of his browned teeth were interspersed with gaps, which looked as if the ogre had been chewing megalithic boulders.

Mirza danced sideways as the club thudded harmlessly into the ground on the space she had occupied seconds before. The blow left an indentation as long as Jarl was tall. As she ran behind Mog, Jarl stood on her back. He reached up as high as possible and brought the sword across the back of the tremendous knee. Jarl felt a satisfying crunch as the sword bit deep into cartilage and ligaments. Mog shouted in mingled pain, rage, and surprise. Jarl nearly fell off Mirza's back when the ogre lurched. The ogre kept himself semi-erect with the help of his club, which he pulled back in agony. The club grazed Jarl's shoulder more by accident than design.

The puzzled look on Mog's face as he felt his knee with his hairy hand gave way to anger as his piglike eyes searched for his enemy. He stumbled to a nearby ledge of rock, upon which he leaned. Mirza quickly carried Jarl to an elevation where Jarl was in a position to reach Mog's neck.

Strike! she commanded, shocking him into action. Only the snick of the ancient sword's passing through the vertebrae apprised Jarl of his success. Great gouts of blood poured from the severed trunk of the ogre, which twitched grotesquely. The head lay face down in the dirt at the foot of the ledge. Jarl was glad. He didn't want to see the look on the dead face. He felt ill and relieved at the same time.

It is never pleasant to kill a living creature, no matter how wicked, Mirza consoled him mentally.

"I didn't need any saddle he had," he said. "We could have simply avoided passing this way."

Yes, that's true. Still, there were many others who fought Mog and lost. He preyed on everyone in his vicinity.

"So he stole an occasional cow or goat," he defended his former adversary.

He lived on human flesh. He deserved to die, Mirza said mercilessly. *Look at your bracelet for proof.*

Another scale gleamed gold. He didn't know what to say. No one told him, but the turning of the dragon's scales to gold on his bracelet must gain points of some kind. Maybe when he earned enough, he would be zapped back home. The area of golden scales was becoming slightly larger as the thin, gilded tide crept up the body of the dragon. Jarl hoped his antagonists weren't going to increase, too. Mog was about the biggest thing he'd ever seen—alive, that is.

CHAPTER SEVEN

His mount stepped daintily around the pool of blood that was gradually soaking into the earth. In the side of the hill was a cave. Mirza boldly stepped into it. The opening was so large Jarl didn't have to lower his head to pass through, although he remained on her back.

The remains of human bones strewn carelessly on the floor proved the truth of her words. A pile of objects Mog had stolen from his victims sat at the back of the cave.

Mirza snorted fastidiously. *Find a saddle and let's leave this place.*

He couldn't tell whether her horse's shape influenced her distaste or if she herself was revolted by the ogre's den. The area reeked of an unnamable odor that brought to mind fear, gluttony, and corruption. Jarl scanned the pile, seeing jewelry, sacks of coins, and bits and pieces of clothing that caught Mog's eye and must have seemed worth saving to him.

Jarl hesitated to rummage, but Mirza urged him on, so he finally dislodged a burlap-wrapped package. Behind it, wedged on the side of an overturned bronze jar of magnificent proportions, was a leathern saddle. There was something about the saddle he could not clearly see in the dim light cast by the two torches Mog had left burning along the rough natural walls of the cave. When he pulled it close, he saw an embossed design decorated the saddle.

He hoisted the saddle awkwardly to his shoulder and began to walk toward the entrance. Mirza advised, *Take a sack of those coins.* She nosed a second pile of clothing beside the treasure stack. *Take this, too,* she ordered, pawing the floor next to a heap of green cloth.

He picked up the bag of coins as commanded. When he went to look at the green cloth, he laughed. Holding it in front of him, he said, "What do you want with this? It's a dress."

Don't be foolish! Don't argue, either. Just take it with you and we can go.

Burdened as he was with saddle, dress, and sack of gold, he was making slow progress.

Mirza ordered, *Here. I'll help carry the saddle.*

After it was on her back, they left the cave. Both took deep breaths of the fresh air. The stench in the cavern had been sickening. Jarl awkwardly made a ball of the green material.

Mirza interrupted his efforts, *Don't do that! Hold it by the waist and double it over. You can carry it thrown over the pommel of the saddle.*

His horse sounded as if she intended to wear the dress. His chuckle did not go unremarked.

If you plan to ride, I suggest you mount directly. These hills are host to some other creatures of the Shadowlord. Death always calls scavengers.

"Creatures of the Shadowlord?" he asked, as she lost no time in trotting away from the ogre's cave.

"Yes," she answered tersely, keeping up the trot.

Her manner of speaking reminded him that she was really the fennec he had met earlier. He suspected that they were trotting to punish him for his laughter and inept handling of the dress. He remembered the pleasant feeling of contact with Mirza's living back and compared it to the sensations given by the dead leather. He wished he had not complained about a few horsehairs stuck to his pants.

"Mirza," he said, forcing a part of his mind to think about posting to save him the slap he got from the saddle every time he made a mistake.

Yes?

"This saddle is too heavy to bother keeping," he told her, longing for a resumption of her exhilarating gallop, which she had given up when he saddled her.

The saddle isn't nearly as heavy as you are. If you've discovered a conscience about riding, you can always walk, you know.

She made her unreasonable offer in such reasonable tones that Jarl was sure she was still annoyed with him. She seemed to be becoming more and more womanlike. Was that why some women were called vixens?

Her abrupt cessation of movement almost cast him over her head. *Are you serious about wanting to spare me the burden of carrying you?*

50

"Yes." There was no denying his irritation. He hoped his short answer made his emotion plain to her.

Look.

"Where?" They stood on a trail over looking a valley far below. He could see for miles, but he wasn't sure what she wanted him to focus his attention on.

Down there. Below us. It's a group of traders.

"Do we want to buy something?" he asked, not understanding her.

You have the sack of coins, don't you?

"Yes, but—"

You can easily afford some supplies and a packhorse, or riding horse, if you wish.

"Is it what you want?" he inquired, strangely reluctant to think of riding another animal.

Well, it's easier for me. You're a pretty hefty specimen, you know.

"Let's get moving. We've got to see a trader about a horse," he told her, half expecting her to bolt down the trail.

Mirza contrarily resumed a decorous trot that eventually brought them out of the hills and into the valley. They entered the camp of the trader at dusk.

Teamsters were setting up beside the road in an open spot that looked as if it had been used this way many times. The guards drew their weapons, not sure if the newcomer threatened their master. Although they saw Jarl dismount, they continued watching him. All but the largest of the men sheathed their swords.

"Do you claim shelter and fire rights for the night?" the guard asked.

"Yes, and I would buy, if this is a trader's caravan."

"This is the outfit of master trader Krom," the guard said, more hospitable now that he realized a prospective customer stood before him.

A heavyset man dressed in rich clothing joined the group around Jarl and Mirza. At his appearance the others faded away to attend to their allotted tasks. Krom radiated authority.

Jarl could see who commanded here easily. Without a word being spoken, the master trader created order from disorder.

"What can I do for you? It is not often I meet an honest man bent on business while traveling this stretch of road. It's too near the territory of Mog to appeal to any but hurried travelers."

Mirza pawed the ground restlessly.

"Ah," said Trader Krom, "would you like to sell the mare? She would bring a good price in Kingstown," he continued, walking around Mirza as he spoke.

"No, I'm afraid not," Jarl told him.

"Pity. I could give you an honest price and still turn a tidy penny on her at the court." The trader began to run his hand over Mirza, but suddenly stopped when she stepped on his foot. "Ah, that's the way it is," he said.

"I'd like to buy two horses from you. I have ridden my mount hard and would prefer that she rest for a few days," Jarl said.

His last words went unnoticed. The guards started a fire. The first bright flames illuminated the saddle, showing the embossing clearly.

"By the Bright Ones," the master trader breathed. "How came you by this?" He indicated the saddle.

"The ogre Mog is dead," Jarl said flatly. "This saddle was within his cave. Since I needed one, I helped myself."

The trader traced the designs with a gentle finger. "This is the saddle that Ordovan leather masters crafted for Prince Leon."

A number of guards had gathered around Mirza, Jarl, and the master trader since organizing the camp. Jarl could feel the hostility in the air around him."

These guards are hillmen, owing their allegiance to King Caeryl. Prince Leon, his son, has been missing for weeks, Mirza whispered in Jarl's mind.

"Shall we bind him, master?" asked the burly leader of the guards.

"For what reason?" inquired the trader with a slight smile.

"He has our prince's saddle. Mayhap he can tell us of the lad's where-abouts."

"Didn't the king's seer say that the little prince's disappearance was the result of black magic?"

A dumb nod was the guard's answer. He waited for further information from his leader.

"Although this man has the saddle of the prince, I do not think he is in the pay of the Shadowlord." The guards shuffled uneasily at the name, some glancing over their shoulders into the darkness. "His"—he paused with a twinkle in his eye—"horse is not ensorcelled by any dark power."

"But, master," the guard protested, reluctant to give up his desire to question Jarl under duress.

"Enough! You may well ask yourself how the saddle came into the possession of—" He looked at Jarl expectantly.

"Jarl."

"And—" the trader asked, indicating the horse with his head.

"Mirza, I call her."

"Very well. Ask how the saddle came into the possession of Jarl here."

"How did you get the saddle?" the guard asked Jarl.

"It was in Mog's cave in a pile of treasure the ogre stole from his victims."

"How did you happen to be there when the ogre died? He was under the protection of the Shadowlord, like most of the hellish creatures who have been appearing here in Realm."

"Aye," the other guards muttered, shifting uneasily. Mentioned for the second time that night was the dreaded name Shadowlord.

During this exchange, the master trader said no words, clearly wanting to know more details himself.

"Tell us," the guards demanded.

"Yes, now!" ordered a man whose slight build contrasted with the husky build of the other guards. "To meddle with the servants of evil often calls down woe."

Nods of agreement went around the circle.

"He attacked me and I—" Jarl took a slight breath before admitting, "—killed him."

"You?" the huge guard scoffed openly.

"Quiet, Snell," Trader Krom reprimanded. "He wears the ancient Sword of the Dragon."

A dozen pairs of eyes looked at Jarl's sword as the fire sprang up unexpectedly in a chill wind that eddied around the camp. For no reason Jarl could discern, a shiver passed over him, causing the hair on the back of his neck to stand on end. The bracelet on his wrist tightened, then released to a comfortable level as the temperature returned to normal.

"We offer you the hospitality of the camp," the trader said.

"Thank you. I accept."

Jarl unsaddled Mirza.

Ah, that feels better, she told him. *Don't worry, I'll be here in the morning*, she promised, rolling in the grass at the edge of the clearing where the camp ended.

"Very well," Jarl acknowledged.

When he returned to the fire, the guards had prepared a simple meal.

The trader ate the same fare as his men, Jarl noticed. That would help to account for the respect they showed him.

Jarl bargained for a rough, but clean, fur cloak-blanket in which he rolled up close by the fire. When morning arrived, he chose a likely-looking pair of hill ponies from the trader's string. Jarl paid for them with a gold piece from the ogre's hoard. Mirza came and waited for the saddle without being called. This impressed the guards who were preparing their own mounts, but it didn't seem to surprise the trader. Telling her to rest, Jarl readied the sturdier of the two ponies for their northward journey.

CHAPTER EIGHT

Jarl, astride the pony, rode beside Mirza at a steady gait. She set the pace at a rapid walk that did not quite break into a trot. Without words, he sensed they were traveling at a rate they could keep up all day if necessary. He wondered if there were further adventures awaiting him. She seemed familiar with the area. His talisman was quiet, so it was probably safe to enjoy the ride—if he could forget about returning home, that was.

His companion was silent, concentrating on the trail. He eyed the scenery, since directing his mount was not difficult. Squirrels inhabited the branches of the oak trees; birds occasionally flew across the trail; a deer bounded out of the forest, but scenting man, dashed back into the safety of the woods. Jarl decided he could have been at home, judging from what he saw as they rode.

Were you really so content there? Mirza questioned abruptly.

"Why, of course. It's my home."

Then Realm holds nothing for you?

"What could there possibly be here for me? I can't even do card tricks, and this whole place is magic. The sword actually conquered the ogre, you know. Without it, I'd be pretty much at the mercy of anyone who attacked me."

Mirza snorted and picked up the pace. For the remainder of that day she said nothing to him. She led the way until they came to a small island in the middle of a broad river. She entered the water with no word to her companion, giving him no option but to follow. Even drawing up his legs didn't keep his feet out of the water.

Exasperated with her, he said, "Why are we going off the path now? Shouldn't we be searching for a safe place to spend the night?"

There is none such near enough for us to reach. Tonight we shall have to depend on the properties of running water. Only a strong spell, aimed specifically at us, can do harm over the protection of the water.

"Why don't we keep moving until we come to a town or another of those star-wells?"

The pentagram at the well is what remains of the Old Magic and is much stronger than any we command now. The Old Ones used up their powers defeating those who would have opened the Realmgate and this universe to beings of unadulterated evil. The Shadowlord is not courting the same beings. There are few places in Realm that are so proof against Evil.

"Wyrd stays wrapped around my wrist all day. Hasn't he rested enough to take us to Realmgate?" Jarl touched the dragon's head fondly, receiving in exchange a sense of approval and acceptance.

You don't fully understand that danger we passed through at the star-well, she explained patiently. *The forces the dragon vanquished there were incredible.*

"You said our opponent was a minor minion!"

Even a minor minion of the Shadowlord can call forth evil of such potency that few in Realm could withstand in full force. I could not have battled alone to save us.

"Someone besides me was helping?"

It is best that we not discuss that until we reach Realmgate, far to the north. Fellkeep, gate of the Shadowlord, is to the south. The farther north we go, the stronger our magic becomes, the weaker his. That is why I have hurried so. I would not dare to stop here if we were not leagues distant from his seat of wickedness.

"The force of magic abates with distance?"

She nodded. *It would take tremendous power to reach us here. That is why we are safe. If the Shadowlord was certain of who you are, he would have attacked in force at the merchant's camp. Killing Mog is not definitive proof that you are Dragon's Pawn. At Realmgate you will learn to use your talisman to the fullest, and when you awaken its total abilities, the Shadowlord will find you easily. He must not discover you until you are ready to harness Wyrd to your purpose.*

This was the longest speech Mirza had given him. Jarl pondered the incredible ideas it contained as Mirza led him ever deeper into the island. It didn't seem fair to have a talisman and then be warned against using it until he reached their allies at Realmgate. Most of the heroes in the books he read had hopped right in swinging, like Beowulf, and hacked their way to victory. Impatiently, he wished he could do the same. Then a thought caused him to ask, "And after I fight the Shadowlord—what happens next?"

That depends on whether you win or lose, she told him dryly.

"Lose! I'm supposed to be the hero!"

Some heroes do lose, you know, she thought gently.

"But—"

Don't think of losing. Think of winning. When you have vanquished our enemy, you may return to Earth—if you wish.

"What's this 'if I wish' stuff? That's why I'm going north. To get to the gate so I can return home."

Is all so safe in your world that you would return so speedily?

He had the feeling that she knew more about Earth than she was admitting. When he considered the current tension on his planet, he knew she meant the remark ironically.

Exactly, she interrupted his thoughts. *It depends on what type of dangers you prefer to live with.*

They stood in a small cleared area almost dead center of the island. He unpacked the spare pony as Mirza, for once, condescended to tell him what lay ahead within the next day's travel. Out of the corner of his eye he saw her pick up the green dress. She disappeared into the densest underbrush that the island offered. Thankful for his camping experiences, he made a stone-encircled bed for a fire. Soon the blaze cast cheery light beams and welcome warmth into the somewhat chill air. He thought it was perceptibly colder than it had been at the spriggan's mound. As he considered what Mirza told him, he gained new respect for the powers of the witch who had been so hospitable. Perhaps her cottage was the outpost for the good guys.

Correct, Mirza's thought reached him. *She is a Keeper.*

"Keeper? Oh, I see. The good guys are keepers, right?"

Right, she thought.

Used to hearing her within his mind, he was startled when he actually heard her call from across the clearing.

"Jarl?"

The sound of her soft laughter brought him to his senses. He closed his mouth, realizing he was gawking like an idiot. Everything was happening too fast for him. He felt a flash of sympathy for the dull-witted ogre, with whom he had a bond at that moment. She was beautiful. In human form she yet retained portions of her former shapes. Her fennec-red hair flowed like the unicorn's mane. Her body was every bit as well-proportioned as it had been when she was a horse. Because she was human, she appealed to him even more strongly than she had ever done in the past. Her smile indicated she knew it.

"Is that your real body?" Jarl blurted like some callow youth at the mercy of his glands.

Her nod was a graceful gesture of agreement. He was dumbstruck. At last he understood how Romeo must have felt the night he first saw Juliet. He didn't know how long he stood there looking at her.

Then she said, "The fire's going out," in a conversational tone.

"I'd better get more wood," he muttered gruffly, sure he had made a fool of himself.

He was returning with the second load of faggots when Wyrd almost amputated his wrist. He heard Mirza scream. He plunged through the underbrush and burst into the clearing just as a vast black dragon arose from the ground with Mirza in its talons. As rapidly as he drew his blade, he was still too late to reach the dragon. Wyrd tightened on his arm, a signal that this creature was the Shadowlord's. Jarl knew he had to do something, but he realized his inability to attack an airborne dragon. The beast was magical, so what better weapon could he use than magic itself? He wasn't a trained shape shifter, and he didn't know if Wyrd could transform him, but he was ready to try anything. Jarl didn't know much about commanding magical powers, but he had to learn sometime. This was an emergency! Jarl held the talisman before his eyes, ready to command the aid of Wyrd's power to transform himself into an even larger, fiercer, swifter dragon, or to hurl a bolt of death. The green eyes stirred to life under Jarl's summons. Then a thought, faint as a whisper, reached him from Mirza.

Don't use the power of Wyrd. Go to Realmgate. Follow the trail north. The Shadowlord must not discover how close he came to you . . .

Her admonition faded into nothingness as a clap of thunder followed the total disappearance of dragon and woman. Jarl felt panic setting in. His first impulse was to saddle one of the ponies and start riding south. Further reflection told him Mirza and the dragon were already at their destination, moved by some magical transportation, snapped from here to there—wherever that might be. Wrapped in his cloak-blanket, Jarl spent a restless night drowsing and awakening, tossing and turning, waiting for the faint rays of morning sun to arrive over the horizon.

As is usual in such cases, Jarl dropped off to a sound sleep shortly before dawn and missed the sunrise. The scent of hot bread awakened him.

"About time," a familiar voice chided.

"Rory? Is that you?"

"Get the sleep out of your eyes and look, man. Of course it's me. Who did you expect, the witch herself?" He took a large bite out of the bread and honey he was holding in his hand.

"Where did you get that?" Jarl asked.

"Witch sent it." Rory chomped on, delivering his answer between bites. "Delicious." He swallowed. "Wash up and join me," he invited. "It's your breakfast I'm eatin'."

Jarl lost no time in washing. He hoped he would return fast enough to eat at least some of the witch's gift. For a little man, Rory had an amazing capacity for food. And whiskey, Jarl remembered belatedly.

Fortunately, there was still plenty for him to eat. The witch had sent a small jar of his favorite pink jelly. Jarl munched his way through a hunk of warm bread before asking, "What brings you here?"

"What else?" I'm a messenger boy sent hither and yon whenever you need information," Rory complained. "Why send a perfectly peaceful leprechaun into danger like this? At least the witch didn't materialize me half in the fire like that flame wizard who sent me the last time."

"Do you have a message for me, then? I suppose you know a black dragon snatched Mirza away last night."

"Yes, I know. You showed good sense for a mortal. You waited here for directions and didn't waste the power of your bracelet."

"Well, now I want to get started. How many days' journey south is Fellkeep?"

"You're not going to Fellkeep."

"Yes, I am!"

"Humans! You are a rattleskulled lot, as I've always said. You plan to rush south into the full power of the Shadowlord with no way to harness your major weapon, Wyrd? You shouldn't be called Dragon's Pawn. You should be named Dragon's Dimwit, lackbrain," Rory berated.

"What am I supposed to do if I can't rescue Mirza now?"

"Sensible. Most sensible. You need to do another major deed, removin' some evil, to repower your bracelet, and you also need to become the ally of a dragon."

"Doesn't Wyrd count?"

"If he did, would I tell you to befriend a dragon? Lackwit!" Rory stamped on the ground.

Jarl noted, and not for the first time, that the leprechaun had the temper to match his flaming hair and beard. "Great!" Jarl mocked. "If there are any dragons who aren't already recruited by the opposition." He paused. "Is my major deed already picked out for me, too?"

"We like to leave a hero a choice or two on his own. I was sent to deliver a message, and I did. Now it's time for me to go," Rory said, pocketing the empty jar the witch sent the coralberry jam in.

"Oh, no, you don't," Jarl yelped as he advanced to grab Rory.

"Look!" Rory shouted, pointing behind Jarl.

Naturally Jarl glanced over his shoulder. Rory's merry chuckle as he disappeared was the next sound Jarl heard. Nothing stood behind him at all. It was a typical leprechaun trick. The minute Jarl took his eyes from Rory the leprechaun was free. "Probably still has the first pot of gold he ever found," Jarl muttered into the empty glade.

Gloomily Jarl hefted his belongings. He had a nice collection of articles: sword and scabbard, fur coat, magic lunch pouch, a prince's saddle, two hill ponies, and a bag of ogre's gold. Jarl would have traded it all with no hesitation for Mirza's return.

Leaving the island, which hadn't proved a protected enough spot in spite of Mirza's faith in running water, he wet his feet for the second time. It didn't improve his mood any. The bright sunshine might just as well have been drizzle or pouring rain for all the notice he took of it. When he came to a spot where the road allowed him to look ahead, he saw a broad valley below him. The small-holdings were laid out in neat patterns. A rural village had grown at the place where another road crossed the one he traveled. He twitched the reins and started down.

When he reached town, a meeting was taking place in the wide spot in front of the local inn.

A hulking rustic grabbed his horse's bridle. "Here be one!" he growled in stentorian tones. His huge hands on the bridle pulled the pony into a clear space in the middle of a group of villagers. Jarl didn't particularly like someone's taking charge of his mount, but he was thirsty for something besides water. The magic bag only supplied food. The water in Realm was so clear that any stream was a good source. If the beverages matched the houses and the dress of the populace, Jarl expected to find ale at the inn. So he dismounted and started toward the inn door.

"Where d'ye think yer goin'?" the gorilloid type who still held Jarl's mount asked. He moved in front of Jarl, pulling the pony.

Since the bracelet gave no sign, Jarl figured he had no reason for concern. Jarl glanced up into his questioner's face before replying politely. "I'm going to have a drink, if you'll excuse me." He was glad his sword rested in his scabbard. He felt this fellow was looking for a fight. He had no intention of ending his long ride with any broken bones.

"Plenty to drink—after ye agree, hero," the man said.

"Now, Cruncher, that's no way to recruit a champion. He wears a sword and rides a saddle fit for a prince. When he understands our plight, he'll be happy to assist us," a jovial man said from the door of the inn. "The Oak Tree Inn welcomes you, hero. Enter, enter," he encouraged Jarl.

"Stable his horses, Cruncher."

"Yes, master. I'll take good care of them."

"Jack Cruncher is a good man, if a little clod-patted," the innkeeper said as he poured a thick mug full of brown ale.

Jarl took a long drink, finding it excellent. Others came and sat. A peach-cheeked maid began to serve them. The late afternoon sun slanted in the doorway, lighting the dim interior of the room. Jarl drank his second mug of ale more slowly, savoring the flavor.

He told the maid who served him, "I'll stay the night."

"My mother herself will prepare your chamber, sir. I hope it will be to your liking."

"Isn't this the best inn in town?" Jarl teased, knowing that a place as small as this could only support one hostelry.

"Oh, yes, sir, but it's the dragon—" she began to explain when her father came over to the table.

"Go on, girl. Have you no work to do in the kitchen?"

With a "Yes, father," and a bob to Jarl, she disappeared through the back door of the room.

"This dragon she spoke of—"

"He's the bane of the whole valley. Fafnir's his name. He lives in the crags to the east," the innkeeper said.

"Scarce a decent piece of livestock left in the whole valley," a grizzled old farmer put in, wiping his mouth on his sleeve.

"I lost two."

"And I four."

"All my flock but two," added another lugubriously.

"What do you expect? Your farm is nearest his cave."

Ready to deny any interest in the situation, Jarl stopped when he felt the tightening of his bracelet.

Shrieks and screams from outside drew the men to the door. A dark form came between the awed watchers and the setting sun; it was the dragon, flying low. Fafnir strafed the village like a Messerschmitt. Two thatched roofs blazed. It was late before the bucket brigade that Jarl joined doused both fires. Bone-weary, Jarl tumbled into his bed after dinner. Tomorrow was soon enough to play the hero. He directed his sleepy mental question to Wyrd: "How am I going to kill this dragon and yet make a dragon my ally?"

The bracelet gleamed, inert in the moonlight that streamed through a slit in the shuttered window. The teeth of Wyrd were exposed in a toothy smile.

CHAPTER NINE

Jarl wakened at dawn. He was not looking forward to this day. Fafnir. The very name sent shivers down his backbone. Well, the sword had killed an ogre. Perhaps it could kill a dragon, too.

Leaving his pony behind, he set off directly after breakfast, assured by his well-wishers from the village that the dragon rarely attacked before noon. Jarl didn't find the thought particularly comforting. Perhaps it would make more sense to keep going north once he was out of town. It wasn't his problem. Then he chided himself for his moment of cowardice. He wanted to rescue Mirza, not be quick-toasted by a dragon.

Anyone with any sense would be asleep this early. Maybe he could kill the dragon before it awakened. One snick, and the job finished. If this dragon had a treasure hoard, he could give it to the villagers for reparations. The hillside grew too steep for riding. He didn't want to continue. He considered how much faster a horse could run than a man. Further thought told him that neither a man nor a horse could outrun a flying dragon. The day seemed colder. Or did the chill originate inside him? He knew a hero never showed his fear. He wondered how brave he looked. Either he was no hero, or a hero felt fear like any other man. He took a deep breath to steady himself. Then he did one of the hardest things he had ever done. He dismounted, unbridled the pony, and left it to graze. It wouldn't go far with so much grass to eat. He put the saddle on a convenient boulder. If he didn't return, the pony was free; if he did, he could always resaddle.

He slogged higher and higher. The grass gave way to scree and rock. For each step he took forward, he slipped back a half step. Before he reached the mouth of the cave, he was quite out of breath. Perseverance won. Finally he stood peering into the large, black opening. He puffed a few times, catching his breath.

"Tsk, tsk, young man," a rumbly voice purred. "For a hero, you're badly out of shape."

Two green eyes appeared in the darkness. They were looking at him! So much for slaying a sleeping saurian, he thought, amazed at how being in Realm had changed him. He could contemplate slaying a dragon using alliteration. Perhaps the witch had put a spell on him. Actually, the eyes didn't unnerve him as much as their height from the cave's floor. Jarl looked up into them.

"Er." He paused. He swallowed, shoving his fear down deep inside. He would deal with it later. A tiny thought trickled through his fear. If you survive. "Er." How did one address a dragon? "Fafnir?"

"Brilliant deduction, dear boy. I shall be quite sorry to have to parbroil and eat you. Intelligent brains are so crunchy. You'll be a rare treat."

"Oh, but I'm not very smart. If I were, would I be here, where you can eat me? Definitely not. I'd be on my way out of this valley as fast as my horse could carry me if I had any sense?"

"Hmmm." The eyes blinked. "I still appreciate your coming up here. You'll save me a flying trip to shop for a nice sheep or cow for lunch. I hate to eat out," the dragon mused aloud.

"That's why I'm here. I'm kind of new to heroic doings. I had to kill Mog, the ogre, with my magic sword. Wyrd here zapped a genie for me earlier." Jarl tried to sound confident. The dragon couldn't know Jarl was wringing wet. Jarl took a deep breath while he awaited the dragon's reply.

"Just a moment. Come closer," Fafnir commanded.

"I'll admit I'm not brilliant, but I'm not a total clot, either. Why should I approach and give you a better chance to make things hot for me?" Jarl winced at his inadvertent pun. He decided he must be catching it from hearing the dragon.

"A joke! A joke!" The dragon smiled as he slithered into the light. His long neck snaked from the cave. He looked almost moth-eaten. His front claws fumbled among his scales and finally brought out a pair of spectacles that he perched on his nose. "Now, my boy, let me have a look at you." Fafnir lowered his head until one plate-sized eye was only inches away from Jarl.

The glasses slid down until they halted behind Fafnir's huge nostrils. Jarl looked at the imposing bulk of Fafnir and decided he was as good as dead anyway if the dragon decided to eat him. What had Jarl to lose? The matter was out of his hands. His sense of resignation to his fate ended the worst of his fear. Jarl reached up and gently pushed the dragon's glasses back into position.

"Thank you." The dragon's old eyes sighted the bracelet. "Oh, you're the Dragon's Pawn. That puts a different complexion on things. Are you agreeable to negotiation of our—er—difficulties?"

"You'll have to stop stealing livestock from the villagers. They'll all starve if you don't."

"I'll starve if I do," Fafnir said in an injured tone.

"There are plenty of woods around here. Why not eat the wild animals you can catch?"

"That's the trouble. I never thought I'd have to admit it, but I've grown so old I can't catch anything but those stupid, tasteless, tame animals. Every time I go into a power dive, my glasses slip down and I can't see. I bruised my nose just the other day when I tried. I hit a tree." A tear the size of a grapefruit plopped wetly on Jarl's head, drenching him. He patted the dragon in commiseration before moving to a drier distance.

"I'm sorry to hear that, but the village livestock is *verboten.*"

"*Sprechen Sie Deutsch*?" Fafnir quavered. "*Wunderbar!*"

"Only a few words. Not enough to hold a conversation with anyone," Jarl admitted.

"I haven't had anyone to speak German with for nine hundred years. I've been alone ever since my boy left," the dragon explained with a shrug, which unfurled his wings and caused such a draft that Jarl almost fell over.

Jarl sneezed.

"My dear boy, you mustn't stand about with a wet head. Whatever are you thinking of? You'll catch cold." Fafnir backed a few paces, snaked his head into his cave, and came out with a towel draped over his fangs. He offered it to Jarl. Hrumph," he said.

Jarl undraped the towel. "Thank you."

"Use it to dry yourself. Can't have the Dragon's Pawn with a cold, you know."

"Getting back to the livestock situation," Jarl said, "am I correct in assuming you aren't raiding for the fun of it, but to survive?"

"Well, sometimes I celebrate a little with a quick pass over the village—"

"If I solve your food problem, you'll have to give that up, too, although for holidays we might work something out. You might start bonfires for the village." The dragon was a crusty old fellow with no real harm in him, and if lighting a fire or two pleased him and salved his pride, the villagers ought to let him do it gladly. It shouldn't be too hard to arrange, since he would leave their animals alone in the future.

"How can you solve my problem? I don't eat much anymore, but I still like two square meals a day and a little snack before bedtime—something warm for my tummy, you know."

"Wait here for me. I've got just the thing, but I left it down with my saddle." Jarl found it easy to retrace his steps. He picked up the witch's bag and started the return journey. The trip upslope hadn't become any easier. He puffed his way to the cave ledge. "Fafnir," he called softly. He noticed the dragon's eyes were closed.

"I wasn't asleep. I just closed my eyes to rest them," the old saurian said in a crotchety manner.

"I never said you were. It's crouching here on this ledge in the sun. It looks like a good place to—close your eyes to rest them," Jarl told him.

"Well, what have you for me? I love surprises."

Jarl handed Fafnir the pouch. "It's magic. If you open it, you'll find your breakfast in it." Jarl crossed his fingers. It had to work for the dragon. He watched. Fafnir's claws fumbled with the bag.

"Kippers! My favorite! I haven't had a breakfast like this in centuries. When I used to visit my cousin, the Loathly Worm, he always had kippers for me." Here Fafnir tipped the pouch into his mouth. Jarl looked on in awe as a barrelful of fish slipped down the dragon's throat. "Would you care for a few?" Fafnir offered hospitably.

"No, thanks," Jarl hurriedly refused. "I've already had my breakfast."

The dragon put the bag on the ground. He patted it several times with a gentle claw. "Charming magic," he commented.

"Do we have a deal? You stop raids and you may keep the bag."

Fafnir picked a stray kipper from between his teeth.

"Oh, and you'd better give me a dozen pieces of gold to pay for the damages the farmers have suffered."

Fafnir's head shot straight up into the air. "Gold? What makes you believe I've got any gold? Money! That's all you humans think of. It isn't worthy of you, my dear Pawn, if you'll pardon the informality." Fafnir delicately placed one claw on the bag.

"Oh, that's all right." Jarl looked Fafnir in the eye. "You mean you're a poor dragon?"

"Of course not!" The dragon turned his head and emitted a short belch that withered a bush growing on the hillside. Then he raised his nose and blew seven perfect smoke rings into the air.

"That's a neat trick."

"Oh, when I was younger, I could blow a dozen or so and then loop the loop through each one as they dissipated into the air," the dragon said modestly.

Jarl felt Fafnir was trying to take his mind from the idea of reparation payments. He returned to the subject. "Now about the gold—"

"Well, if you insist, I might be able to find the odd piece or two—"

"Twelve," Jarl reminded the dragon.

"Six," Fafnir bargained.

"Ten."

"Nine," Fafnir said firmly.

"Agreed. Nine pieces of gold to repay the farmers." Jarl felt relieved. For a moment he thought he had not been outrageous enough in his first demand to allow room to bargain.

"You need to do me a small favor," the dragon added silkily.

"A favor?" Something in Fafnir's voice warned Jarl. What kind of a favor could a man do a dragon?

"A little something you can do for me," Fafnir repeated very casually.

Jarl took a deep breath. "Very well," he told Fafnir, hoping he wasn't going to regret making the promise. Befriend a dragon, indeed! "In return you faithfully pledge no more raiding in the valley."

"I do," the dragon said, solemnly blowing a cloud of white smoke upward.

"What's the favor?" Jarl asked.

"My worthless son, Fafnoddle, is a disgrace to dragonry. We Fafnirs descended from the original in Norse mythology—you are from Earth, are you not? I thought I recognized your accent—Noddle's betrayed his lineage. I want you to go to his cave in the Black Mountains and take him with you on your quest."

"What quest?"

"My dear Pawn, all heroes go on quests. It's the nature of the job, you know. They rescue fair damsels, break enchantments, and kill monsters. You are planning on being a hero, aren't you?" Fafnir got very heated about his subject, and he belched a flame that narrowly missed his listener. A scorched-hair odor permeated the air.

Jarl ran his hand over his head nervously. It had been a close call. "It looks like it."

"Well, then take Noddle with you. Perhaps if he becomes involved in the adventurous life, he can still be a credit to the family."

"But what if he, er—"

"Out with it, Pawn. Out with it. Don't dillydally."

"Perhaps he is otherwise engaged, I meant."

"Nonsense!" Fafnir unfurled his wings and brought them back against his body with a crack that reminded Jarl of a Spanish senorita's use of her fan. He was ready, half expecting another burst of fire, but the rush of wind generated by Fafnir's wings almost blew him off the ledge. The dragon grabbed him by the scabbard belt as he was going over the edge. He felt a sickening sense of vertigo, followed by the stomach-wrenching scent of charred kippers, as the dragon opened his mouth and set him gently back on the ledge.

"As I was saying before you so rudely flew away," Fafnir continued, burnishing one of his large claws on his scaly chest, "as a hero you should be able to fight him in battle and bend him to your will." What looked to Jarl like a crocodile tear shimmered in the dragon's dinner-plate eye.

"Don't worry. I won't hurt him."

"Oh, I'm not worried about that! All you'll have to do is threaten him, and he'll agree. That's Noddle's chief weakness. He's a pacifist."

"How can you say he's a pacifist when he kills all the animals he needs to survive?"

Fafnir turned his head and sighed. Jarl was glad of the courtesy. He had not enjoyed his flight off the ledge.

"He's a vegetarian," Fafnir hissed in some distress. Seeing the look on Jarl's face, he added, "He's the first lettuce licker we've ever had in the family. That carrot-crunching son of mine is so cowardly he'll never be able to attract a mate. He may well be the last of the line. I'm glad his mother didn't live to see the day. A more vicious temper I've never encountered. In her heyday she would have laid waste to this whole valley in hours," he concluded admiringly, allowing himself a gap-toothed grin at the thought.

"Well, I'll try to get Noddle to join me." Privately Jarl wondered what help a pacifistic vegetarian would be in a fight, but was wiser than to say so in front of the pacifist's father.

"You're a hero! You'd better succeed!" At this point Fafnir's tail reached out, snaked around Jarl, and removed him from harm's way. Fafnir emitted a gout of blue fire that melted a few of the pebbles where Jarl had been standing.

"Rather clever, don't you think?" Fafnir preened himself like a great bird, ignoring his captive's white face. "I can reason a priori and a posteriori," he commented, waving his tail, which still clutched Jarl, who wondered if heroes ever lost their breakfasts in situations such as his. "Sorry," his captor told him, releasing his hold at last.

"How shall I be able to find Noddle in the mountains?" Jarl said carefully, waiting as his stomach settled.

"Ask Wyrd. He'll tell you. It's not out of your way." With these words, Fafnir lowered his head on the magic bag and closed his eyes.

"Good-bye," Jarl said, but his only answer was a rumbling snore. Dragons seemed a rude and unpredictable lot. This one was too old to be his ally. Jarl carefully pocketed the gold coins Fafnir had stacked nearby with his tail as they talked. He would return to the village, get directions to the Black Mountains, and then fulfill his promise to the old saurian.

CHAPTER TEN

The citizens gathered at the inn watched silently as Jarl approached. A farmer spoke his mind bluntly.

"Horse must be faster than I thought," the old man said in a quavery voice.

"Probably didn't even go to the cave," another added, wiping his nose on his sleeve.

"Well, maybe the dragon was out," a third offered more charitably.

"Not a mark on him," growled Cruncher in a disappointed tone.

"Bet there's not a mark on the dragon, either," cackled the village wit.

"Fine hero he turned out to be."

Amis, the innkeeper's daughter, rushed out the inn door, hurried the last few steps to where Jarl was dismounting, and threw her arms around him. "You killed the dragon!" she gushed.

Jarl, not expecting such a buxom reception, almost disgraced himself by falling. At the last moment an instinct for self-preservation caused him to steady himself by putting his arms around her cozy figure. He did not bask in his hero's welcome long. Wyrd tightened on his arm immediately.

Shrieks from the villagers alerted Jarl to the source of the danger. Fafnir was lazily circling, preparing to make a dragon-point landing in the village square. His imposing bulk shadowed the open area, eclipsing the sun. He settled himself neatly, coiling his tail in a semicircle to take up the least space possible. His thoughtful gesture was neither necessary nor appreciated, because the fleeing populace cowered inside their homes as they frantically barred their doors.

Amis had such a stranglehold on Jarl that his major worry was enough oxygen to survive. "Hey, there. It's all right," Jarl told her, to no avail.

"Is this the way you keep your promise?" Fafnir roared, puffing agitated smoke rings in the air.

"I haven't broken mine," Jarl averred. "You're the one who's come without an invitation." His attempt at righteous annoyance was ineffective. Amis kept pushing him backward in her desire to get as far from the dragon as possible and still keep in the closest physical contact with Jarl.

"I'm not hurting a thing," Fafnir protested with an air of innocence that ill became his mammoth presence.

"You're scaring the villagers half to death. I thought we'd agreed that you would stay in the mountains," Jarl told him sternly. He pried Amis's hands from his neck and forced as much of her as he could behind him.

Cracks were appearing in doorways as people heard the conversation. Amis peeped wide-eyed from behind Jarl. Rumpf, her father, made the most of his opportunity and waddled from the inn, grabbed her, and hurried her inside his establishment.

"You've got to keep your side of the bargain!" Fafnir hissed.

Jarl shrugged resignedly. "All right. I'm going. Let me explain to innkeeper Rumph here, and then I'll be on my way."

Jarl's horse moved restively each time the dragon spoke. When Fafnir sidled closer, the hill pony bolted for the safety of the stable.

"Very well. No more dillydallying with local wenches!" Fafnir lowered his head until his huge eye was level with Jarl's. "Understood?" he hissed, then placed a taloned claw delicately over his mouth as a loud rumble and the stench of sulfurous, half-digested kippers followed.

"The sooner you leave, the sooner I'll be able to go," Jarl reminded him, trying not to breathe until the dragon was aloft.

With a final rip-roaring belch that Fafnir directed to the ground, he carefully raised his wings and floated upward like a huge balloon. Only a charred belch mark and the lingering scent of half-digested kippers proved Fafnir had paid the village a visit.

Jarl explained his bargain to the innkeeper, who kept a firm hold on his daughter. She seemed about to attack Jarl with further cries of "My hero!" Jarl hoped her father found a husband for her soon. Her unsolicited affection definitely unnerved him. Jarl gave the gold pieces to Rumpf, who promised to distribute them fairly. This earned him a cheer from the people who had crowded into the inn to hear what Jarl had to tell. When they realized that Fafnir promised not to set any more dwellings on fire, but instead would appear only when summoned to light bonfires for celebrations, the women and children gave a cheer.

Warmth around his wrist caused him to look at his bracelet. Another scale had turned to gold.

The grateful villagers gladly filled two saddlebags with provisions. Jarl thanked them before setting out for the Black Mountains. He was impatient to find Noddle, Fafnir's son. Rory had told him he needed to make an ally of a dragon. Against all logic, Jarl hoped he might be able to convince the vegetarian pacifist to join him. He glanced at Wyrd. Another scale turned to gold. He wondered if the old wise woman knew.

By riding until dusk, Jarl crossed the valley that day. He felt a sense of urgency. The Shadowlord was a powerful wizard with aspirations that went far beyond this alternate Earth. If magic were unleashed on Jarl's world, science would be powerless against it. Earth couldn't win if the leaders refused to acknowledge magic. Some scientists still insisted that although there might be other intelligence in the universe, it would never contact the Earth. He couldn't see scientists accepting the powers of the Shadowlord very easily. Plus the military . . .

Jarl made camp that night under the shelter of an overhanging rock. He felt relatively protected, but he missed Mirza. According to the directions given him by the villagers, it would take him another two days to reach the Black Mountains. If Fafnir knew what he was talking about, Wyrd would point the way to the dragon he sought. Jarl placed his hand gently over the bracelet. The action reassured him. He slept deeply, without dreams, in the eerie golden glow that surrounded him. A stray moonbeam gleamed briefly on Wyrd, silently talismaning a protective shield of magic about Jarl and his horses. The searching black shadows that swooped saw only bare rock where the dragon bracelet kept vigil.

The next day saw Jarl walking about as much as he rode, because the highway became a dim trail, almost washed away in spots. Sometimes it wound around a mountain. The trail narrowed so that the saddlebags scraped the rocky wall while infinity dropped beside it. Jarl led the way and the ponies followed trustingly. Their passing dislodged an occasional rock, but he could not hear it land, so far below was the earth. The villagers called these foothills! At times both man and pony almost sat when the path dipped steeply. By the end of that day Jarl knew the hill ponies were a wise choice. Showier horses could not have been so loyal and surefooted as the shaggy animals he purchased from Trader Krom. He gave them an extra pat and a ration of oats from the saddlebags. The sparse grass wouldn't make a meal even if his ponies foraged all night. Jarl ate a piece of bread, a hunk of cheese, and an apple for his supper. Lighting a fire was beyond his strength.

As he slept, the Wyrd-glow warmed as well as protected. The dragon bracelet watched over his companions soundlessly.

Jarl awoke refreshed. He searched beside the trail until he found the thin trickle of water that filled the basin his horses had drunk from the previous night. He refilled his water bottle, a gift from the innkeeper. The depredations of Fafnir had almost ruined his business, and so Rumpf had expressed his appreciation with the water bottle.

For a time the trail wound more or less levelly through the mountains. The rock gradually changed from a light shade to a gray so dark he understood why the mountains were called black. He couldn't identify the stone. On this, the last day before he reached the heart of the range, he noticed the strata getting darker and darker. By late afternoon he was surrounded by pitch-black rock. A chill wind sprang up, making travel uncomfortable. Jarl walked, leading the ponies, until he came to a narrow defile that ended in a level patch of ground that looked like the remains of an amphitheater. Across the open space he saw what looked like an unroofed building that could shelter him and his ponies for the night. As he reached the end of the narrow passageway through the rock, Wyrd tightened. Jarl stopped immediately. He sensed this place was old, but no message of his senses warned him of evil. The ruins lay quiet, seemingly deserted by whoever—or whatever—had made them. He decided to step cautiously into the open just as a laser beam swept the path ahead of him where he would have been but for Wyrd's signal.

He pulled out his sword while his brain scrabbled to find a reasonable explanation for a futuristic weapon in so ancient a location. He dropped the pony's reins, hoping its training included standing when the reins fell to the ground. His eyes widened in surprise as his enemy stood before the opening, blocking his vision of the ruins.

One look at the humanoid, metal-encased alien before him told him what he faced: a monstrous robot warrior. A creature from human fiction, it had no natural place in this alternate universe. For the first time he had personal experience to prove Rory's story of human creations incarnate in Realm.

"Halt, human," the robot voice commanded.

"Robot, explain your presence in this world."

"I am the loyal servitor of the Almighty Metallic Leader. I will kill you."

Jarl wondered who programmed the robot. Its words sounded ludicrous. "Are you such a slave that you can't answer the question a human asks you?" Jarl taunted, trying to think of a way to save himself.

"I destroy all humans. You are human," the machine said tonelessly and raised its weapon.

Jarl had no choice but battle. He had more brains than to stand still and await his annihilation. He didn't want to risk the chance of a beam ricocheting off the unknown black rock of the defile and wounding or killing him or his ponies, leaving him afoot, perhaps wounded, alone and miles from nowhere.

His reaction was immediate and final. His sword swept up at the light lanced toward him. The blade of the sword caught the brilliant ray. The sword emitted a high keening that affected Jarl like the sound of fingernails on a blackboard. The jewels on the hilt glimmered with unearthly fire. His sword was drawing power from the laser—how, Jarl never knew. He advanced as the robot's weapon emptied itself of its charge. The metal warrior dropped it and raised its arms to grapple with its human adversary. One incandescent touch of the sword turned it to fine white ashes blowing on the wind, powdering the nearby black rocks before disappearing.

Jarl realized Wyrd had taken no part in the battle. The power of the sword was incredible. Its might differed from his talisman's, but its capability for destruction was awesome. No wonder Mirza wanted him to take the sword from the spriggan! Now it vibrated with life as he held it in his hand. The jewels had seemed beautiful before, but now they flashed coruscating fire, which danced within their colorful interiors. Some great battle in the past must have used almost all of its power. The force of the laser had returned it to its former glory.

As he watched the gems, the faint thread of Mirza's voice seeped into his mind. He concentrated fiercely, but the message was a mere mental whisper.

The Shadowlord is furious with you! There is little time to lose. You need not go to Realmgate after all . . . Come!

The urgency Jarl felt behind the words worried him. *Mirza! Mirza!* He tried mindspeech, but he knew it was useless. Even though the sword's enormous boosting ability amplified his attempt, he was not a good enough telepath to reach through the veils of evil that shrouded Mirza from him. The effort must have cost her a great deal. He barely understood her thoughts.

The dying sun perched atop the mountains that ringed the ruined amphitheater. Its rays turned the rock an ominous red, and Jarl rode his pony to the remains of the roofless building. The stillness of the vast area magnified the small sounds of Jarl's making camp. Any material used by the builders had long since moldered into its component elements. Jarl wondered who had built so well in such an inaccessible location. What possible purpose could there be for such structures as had once dominated this level miniplain deep within the mountains' fastness?

Wyrd clasped his arm lightly, so Jarl knew there was no present danger. It was safe—or at least as secure as any other place on Realm.

When the last rays of the sun disappeared beyond the rim of the farthest mountain, a pale phosphorescence lit the area. Tiny sparks advanced and retreated under the light of the strange stars, but Jarl did not see the dance. He was far too tired to know or care.

Wyrd watched for a time. Then on impulse—the first one he'd had in a millennium—his mind swiftly rearranged the atoms that composed his body. He had no wish to frighten the younglings, but the music they danced into the air reminded him of his youth, when his species was still bound within corporeal bodies. As his form danced, the young ones formed an awed circle around him. He beckoned to them by changing colors and adding delicate scents of plants long forgotten. Colors flashed, aromas wafted, and music tinkled in a dance whose figures filled the very air with the essence of joy.

Jarl slept. He didn't stir when Wyrd rematerialized a metallic body around his arm.

The next morning Jarl awoke as dawn broke over the rim of the black, snowcapped peaks that surrounded the amphitheater like a jagged wall. After a meager meal, he and the hill pony circled the open space while he searched for the continuation of the path he had followed. He stood deep in the Black Mountains. Why had Wyrd offered no direction? Jarl raised the bracelet to eye height and thought distinctly and strongly: "Wyrd! I want to talk with you." He received the mental sensation of a lazy reply.

Yesss, Dragon's Pawn?

"You can talk to me telepathically?"

Only a human would ssstate the obvious sso sstupidly.

"You've been on my wrist for days and never spoken to me. Presumably you understand the rules of this crazy place, and you made no effort to communicate with me." Jarl spoke aloud, giving his bracelet a disgusted look.

Thought sendings are dangerous when evil lurks to listen. You respond well to pressure.

Jarl noticed that Wyrd was managing his s's better as he continued to talk, although a faint hiss appeared from time to time in Jarl's mind. Jarl had the distinct feeling that the dragon was making a joke, but he didn't think much of Wyrd's sense of humor. "Would you mind telling me how to find Fafnoddle, since Fafnir promised you would aid me once we reached these mountains?"

Of course. As Wyrd thought the words, his diminutive head negligently moved so his nose pointed to a fallen rock. *Sstraight ahead.*

Jarl rode to the indicated boulder. By standing in the stirrups, he could see over it. Years before, it had dropped from the rim above, covering the dim path. Without Wyrd's suggestion, Jarl knew he might not have found the continuation of the path. "Thanks," he murmured aloud, but he received no reply.

"How far is it?" His bracelet kept silence, as if it were no more than an ordinary piece of metal. He tried several more questions, but his talisman ignored him. "All right. No more conversation," Jarl said, giving up his attempt to get more information. He settled himself comfortably in the saddle and patted his mount. "Just me and my trusty cayuse," he drawled, tugging on the lead rope of the other pony that followed.

Several times he dismounted to lead his ponies around rockfalls that partially blocked their way. No bird broke the blue of the sky. The chill air bore no scent. The mountains were lonely sentinels. Jarl felt his living presence made him an alien intruder into the vastness of the natural fortress around him. He stubbornly refused to speak to Wyrd—the dragon probably wouldn't answer anyway, he reasoned to himself.

Sstop, Pawn, Wyrd hissed within Jarl's mind.

"Why?" Jarl asked as he pulled on the reins to halt the obedient pony. "I don't see anything to stop for—unless you want me to go rock collecting."

There. Wyrd's head pointed upward to a ledge.

The increasing nervousness of his mount should have alerted Jarl to the proximity of the dragon. He was exasperated with himself. He really would have to stop depending on other people—or creatures—if he intended to rescue Mirza from the power of the Shadowlord.

He scrutinized the boulder-strewn side of the mountain before him. "Wyrd, I don't see the opening."

The bracelet remained silent. Jarl dismounted and soothed his skittish horses with handfuls of oats from the saddlebags. Food was going to be a problem if he didn't make contact with Fafnoddle soon. He looped the reins over a convenient rock. He gazed at the landscape around him. Did a boulder hide the mouth of the dragon's cave? There were a great many rocks to check, so he decided to begin. As he worked his way around the first rock, he heard the crash of glass.

A giant opening in the side of the mountain appeared as if by magic. An irritated roar and billows of smoke erupted from it.

Jarl had found the dragon.

CHAPTER ELEVEN

As soon as the smoke cleared, Jarl wiped his watering eyes and climbed to the ledge outside of the cave.

"Is anybody home?" he called. He wished he felt comfortable beginning a conversation with a dragon.

"No!" hissed a voice from inside.

"Fafnoddle, are you in there?"

"No!"

"I'm coming in." Jarl took a deep breath and stepped forward.

"In that case, be careful. There's some very nasty stuff crawling over the floor."

Once inside, Jarl looked around in wonder. The roof of the cave emitted a gentle golden glow. Along both sides of the gigantic cavern enormous stone beds of flowers and greenery flourished. The place was a gardener's paradise.

"Well, seeing as you've come uninvited, don't just stand there. Help me!" a petulant voice hissed.

Jarl looked past the banks of greenery to the rear of the cave. On a natural shelf a bronze dragon perched. His tail twitched ominously, reminding Jarl of Minou, his cat, when she was angry. The dragon's wings were furled because the back of the cave was too narrow for flying. A poisonous orange glow came from a puddle of viscous material that spread questing pseudopods even as Jarl watched.

"Hurry!"

"What do you want me to do?"

"Take a pinch of that herb on your left and throw it into the mess on the floor."

"You mean the moley?"

"Yes. Hurry!" A thin line of neon trickled upward toward the saurian. "Be careful. Don't let it touch you," the dragon warned.

The puddle appeared sentient, because it began to send out thin feelers in Jarl's direction as he approached. Jarl took the generous handful of moley that he gathered and tossed it into the puddle while Fafnoddle muttered words in a strange language. At least Jarl thought they were words. They were, unless the dragon was gargling. The puddle turned brown, then black, shrinking upon itself until it winked out of existence. An ululating shriek echoed shrilly from the walls.

"What was that?" Jarl asked, shaking his head to clear the last traces of the unpleasant sound from his ears.

"Another experiment gone wrong." The dragon sighed, hopping down to turn the pages of an ancient book propped on a rock. One long claw ran across the page as the dragon read aloud to himself. He seemed to have completely forgotten his visitor.

Fafnoddle was absentminded as well as being a pacifist and an evident vegetarian, Jarl noticed. Jarl perched on a stone to wait.

Finally the dragon turned and noticed him. "Oh, are you still here?"

"Did you think I'd come to rescue you from your predicament with no other reason?" Jarl smiled. He could understand what bothered Fafnir. There was nothing intimidating about this dragon. In spite of his tremendous size, he was too scholarly to frighten anyone. He reminded Jarl of some of his college professors. No wonder the old fire breather wanted his son to change. From a dragonly point of view, Fafnoddle was a travesty of dragonhood.

"Well, not really. If you wait long enough, something usually turns up," answered Fafnoddle.

"So I noticed," Jarl said, remembering the thin line of fluid climbing the rock where Fafnoddle sat earlier.

Fafnoddle clearly remembered, too. "I suppose you're expecting a reward—dragon's treasure and all that?" Fafnoddle lowered his head until it was level with Jarl's. He tilted it inquisitively.

"No, I'm not."

"That's a relief." Fafnoddle blinked owlishly. "Most humans would, you know."

"I don't want any dragon gold."

"Good. I don't have a red cent. All the money I collected during my youth I spent for my garden and magic lessons."

"I see. You're not materialistic like most dragons."

Fafnoddle shook his head disparagingly. "I haven't an avaricious bone in my body," he mourned. "I'm a great disappointment to my father."

"Speaking of your father—Fafnir sent me."

The dragon's head shot up in surprise. "You know my father? You met him and lived to tell the tale?"

Jarl nodded.

"He must be mellowing in his old age, then. Time was when he simply ate all the humans who crossed his path." The dragon's head speared down to eye level. "You didn't hurt him, did you?"

The rapidity of the dragon's movement reminded Jarl of a rattlesnake's strike. For the first time he felt a twinge of awe. A young dragon was quite a different proposition from an old one. "I wish you'd stop that. It makes my head swim," Jarl complained before answering the dragon's question. "I didn't ruffle a single scale. Fafnir sent me to you."

"What for?"

"Don't be so suspicious."

"My father . . . I only wish you could have heard all those lectures about the glory of the family, the Fafnir honor, the joys of treasure hoarding . . . " He absentmindedly scratched a magical symbol on the floor with his index talon. Impressed, Jarl noted that the mark was incised in inch deep into the rocky floor. Fafnoddle shook his head sadly. "I'm afraid I'm a big disappointment to my family."

Jarl looked at the length of the dragon and imagined his wingspan. Anything this beast did would be giant economy sized. "Your father would like you to accompany me," Jarl repeated patiently.

"Knowing my father, he probably wants me to shake the fertilizer off my scales and go out and bathe myself in blood." Fafnoddle shivered, sending tiny ripples of brown dust to the floor.

Jarl noted a strong barnyard smell even as his vivid imagination painted a picture of a rapacious dragon attacking humanity. He sincerely hoped he would never earn the enmity of a dragon. "Not exactly. I'm going on a—quest. Fafnir though it would be an interesting experience for you to go with me."

"What do you expect of me? I'd better warn you, I'm a dragon of strong convictions. I'm a pacifist. I abhor violence. I certainly don't have either the time or inclination to fly around the country doing dragonly deeds of derring-do." Fafnoddle stopped. "That was quite clever of me," he complimented himself. "Dragonly deeds of derring-do," he repeated theatrically, in case Jarl had missed his verbal tour de force.

"Very alliterative, but let's return to the subject at hand. I'd like you to be my companion."

"I hate to be repetitive, but why should I? Past experience tells me my wily sire has something up his scales."

"He has your welfare at heart, I'm sure. A leprechaun told me I'd need a dragon ally," Jarl added honestly.

Fafnoddle slowly lowered his head until it rested on the floor.

Jarl found this movement more disturbing than the quick lowering. There was a certain inevitability that produced a zero at the bone when a dragon's head came to rest within inches of an all-too-mortal human body. Be careful what you ask for, Jarl thought. You might get it.

Wise golden eyes studied Jarl silently. "Well, you look all right—for a human," Fafnoddle amended.

"There is a beautiful woman—" Jarl began.

"Isn't there always?" the dragon interrupted.

"—named Mirza," Jarl continued, ignoring the remark.

"Mirza?" Fafnoddle's head shot up, narrowly missing a stalactite in his surprise.

"Do you know her?"

"She's highly thought of in Realm. Everyone knows her."

"I'm going to free her."

The dragon's eyes widened. "Who would dare to lock her up?"

"The Shadowlord. She's at his castle. I had a message that said I should come to her."

"The Shadowlord, you say? That upstart. The last I heard he settled at Fellkeep in the south. Miserable location. Nothing but marsh and sea."

"Well, over the years he's gained power. He's recruiting non-Realm creatures created by the human minds of Earth."

"Earth? Bless my scales, I haven't heard that place mentioned in years. When the Keepers' Council rejected Shadow, he swore he'd become their master, but nobody actually believed that he meant what he said. How could it be possible? The Keepers range the alternate universes at will. They have powers beyond belief at their command."

"Somehow or other, something is fouling up their plans. From what I've seen, the Keepers have quite a battle on their hands."

"If he's dared to capture Mirza, he's become bold indeed," the dragon inadvertently punned. "Her mother was very good to me when I was a dragonette. I'll have to go along and see what I can do."

"Good. I can use your help." Jarl wondered how old Mirza was.

Fafnoddle eyed the bracelet on Jarl's wrist. "Hmmm. I see you must be the current Dragon's Knight."

"Not Knight. Pawn," Jarl corrected him. "That's why I need your assistance."

"That's true. If you were Dragon's Knight, you wouldn't need me. You and Wyrd would be an unbeatable combination. Since you're only a Pawn as yet, I'll come." Fafnoddle paused and glanced around at his garden. "I must make a few preparations."

Jarl watched as the dragon slithered over to turn a golden knob. Fafnoddle peered under some plants. Small droplets of water were forming on the underside of golden piping.

"That should do it." The dragon picked a glowing globe and popped it into his mouth. "Would you care for some fruit?" His taloned claw delicately picked another and offered it to Jarl. It was slightly larger than an orange.

"Thanks." Jarl bit into his, and the taste surprised him. "It's steak!" he said, taking another bite.

"No, it's fruit, created to taste like steak. Even under these special lights, it's hard to grow. I'll set my watering system on steady drip. I've studied for years to become a master mage, only to find out once a new variety is growing, the plants respond best to ordinary care."

Ordinary care? Jarl glanced at the steady golden glow being emitted from the high ceiling. He noted the pipes of precious metal and the oddly colored fluid that produced so prolific and wonderful a crop. What would Fafnoddle consider extraordinary? Like any gardener, the dragon pinched here and discarded a leaf there. He tilted his head and seemed to be listening.

"What are you doing?" Jarl strained to hear, but could discern no sound.

"Listening to make sure the plants are growing well." Fafnoddle noticed Jarl's look and said apologetically, "You have to be very careful with transplanted sunshine. There's so much of it in the desert region of Realm, no one cares if I move a little of it here. It's not really very complicated magic."

"Maybe not for you, but I'm impressed. My grandmother was quite a gardener, and she would have gone berserk over your setup."

The dragon fluffed his scales with pleasure at the compliment and then shivered. "Please don't use such harsh terms. Berserk indeed. The very thought of a berserker swashbuckling around, lopping off heads with indiscriminate abandon, petrifies me. Rescuing one young witch shouldn't be very dangerous—should it?" He looked at Jarl for reassurance.

"We can handle it together," Jarl told him, hoping he wasn't uttering the largest lie of his life.

"Well, I'm ready."

Jarl preceded him to the mouth of the cave and slipped his way down to his mount. All was well until Fafnoddle jumped off the ledge and landed directly in front of the startled and outraged ponies. At once Jarl found himself the chief performer in a bucking-horse act appropriate for any rodeo.

The dragon backed off a few paces and curled up, bracing his head on his looped tail. "Bravo!" he hissed.

Jarl couldn't take the time to decide if the commendation belonged to him or his horse. The word seemed to encourage his pony to more frenzied exertion. Jarl was unabashedly holding on to the high-carved cantle with one hand and the pommel of the saddle with the other.

The amused snorts coming from the dragon were not helping make Jarl's ride any easier. Each time the dragon emitted a sound, the horse bucked higher in the air. His one thought was to rid himself of his rider and leave the vicinity of the dragon, which his instincts told him was a hereditary enemy. His dam hadn't reared any weak-witted foals!

Finally sheer exhaustion stopped the pony's rebellion. He stood, shaken, eyes rolling, obedient to the pull of the reins because he had no strength remaining to disobey. His lathered sides heaved and his heart galloped.

"That was some show," the dragon told Jarl admiringly.

"I'm glad you enjoyed it." Jarl was quite as shaken as his mount by the unexpected exertion. Seeing how large the dragon was when he spread his wings to land before the pony made Jarl appreciate his horse's reservations about having a dragon as a traveling companion. "We aren't going to be able to travel together unless my horse accepts you." Jarl dismounted and urged his mount down the path.

"It's a good thing I've given up smoking. That would have disturbed the poor beast. Don't worry. I'll take care of it." He waved a scaly forelimb and the horse quieted at once.

"How did you do that?"

"A little magic. He doesn't see me as I really am now. He's also forgotten ever seeing me in my true form."

"What does he see when he looks at you?" Jarl's curiosity forced him to ask. Fafnoddle still looked like a dragon to him. In fact, Fafnoddle looked magnificent in the sunlight. Each separate tooth gleamed whitely like an extravagant toothpaste advertisement. Jarl could easily imagine such a creature carrying off a sacrificial maiden for a luncheon date. No one would ever guess he was a vegetarian by looking at him.

"Oh, he thinks I'm a hummingbird," Fafnoddle said modestly.

"That will help. We've still got a problem to solve."

"My spell will last. He'll see me as a hummingbird for as long as I will it," the dragon said huffily.

"That's not the trouble. I can see that walking isn't your strong suit, Noddle." Without thinking, Jarl used the shortened version of the dragon's name.

"Do I call you Pawn?" the dragon hissed in an injured tone.

"I'm sorry if I hurt your feelings," Jarl said quickly. The thought of an enraged saurian set his teeth on edge. "It's just that Fafnoddle seems such a mouthful."

"Call me Faf, then, if you must shorten my name. Noddle makes me sound a bit of a fool, you know."

"A fool is the last thing I'd think of calling you."

"Well, I haven't involved myself in human affairs for several hundred years, and I wouldn't want any humans to think I was lacking in brains. Normally I wouldn't hurt anything, but if I lose my temper, I'm apt to let off steam like anyone else." he said.

Jarl hid a smile. "Faf it is, then. Call me Jarl."

"Very well, Jarl."

"Now, back to the business at hand. Could you actually transform yourself into something that could travel with me more comfortably?"

"Probably, but I'd rather save my magic in case we really need it later during this adventure. Magic is a resource that requires conservation. If I use my powers too often, my scales tarnish."

"Oh, I see. Well, then, could you fly ahead of me and meet me later?"

"Surely. Let me show you the hidden path. It starts at the top of this mountain."

Jarl blanched. The mountainside was almost straight up, and he already had some experience in climbing it to reach Fafnoddle's lair. "I might be able to make it, but the ponies can't."

"Hmmm." The dragon stretched his wings as he thought. Then he walked to the horse, spread his wings, puffed a hot breath under himself, and rose, clutching the horse in his talons.

Dragon and horse disappeared above and Jarl stared. What was Faf doing? In a few minutes the dragon returned, dipping low in a controlled power glide, to scoop Jarl up in his claws and ascend once more into the air. Jarl's stomach almost emptied itself in surprise, but luckily the trip was short. With his feet firmly on the plateau at the top of the peak, Jarl's stomach flopped into its accustomed location. His mount grazed on a small patch of grass beside the mountain lake. He seemed skittish. Jarl didn't blame him. Did the animal believe a hummingbird had carried him? The pony paid no attention to the dragon, so the spell must be holding.

"What about my pack pony?" Jarl asked.

"He'll only be in the way. If you'll permit me, I'll send him over the mountains into a meadow. You can pick him up later, if you decide you want him."

Jarl nodded his agreement. "Just bring me the saddlebags," he requested.

The dragon disappeared downward. In a moment he returned. He dropped the saddlebags beside Jarl.

"Thanks," Jarl said, loading them on his mount. "How does a lake come to be here at the top of a mountain?"

"A little hocus-pocus. In the north there's a vast lake brimming with water. I merely helped myself to enough to fill this basin."

No matter what the dragon said, it looked like a great deal more than hocus-pocus to Jarl. He mounted and rode around the water to the break in the plateau. He could see the remains of a road that lead gently downward. Who leveled the top of the mountain? Then he saw the pentagram incised in the smooth stone at the side of the lake.

Faf gestured negligently. "Old Ones. Real magic workers. They were here and gone long before my ancestors emigrated from Earth."

When Jarl and Faf reached the downward slope, the dragon said, "I'll see you at the bottom." He unfurled his wings, caught an updraft, and sailed like a surrealistic kite until he began some fancy flying.

Jarl was almost certain the act was for his benefit. One graceful maneuver followed another. "He's showing off just like a little kid," Jarl murmured to himself. "It's some show."

His bracelet, which up to this time had kept complete silence, allowed a faint hint of gentle agreement to insinuate itself into Jarl's mind. Jarl smiled. Another scale had turned to gold.

CHAPTER TWELVE

The sturdy-footed pony picked his way carefully down to the point where the little hummingbird he could see awaited them.

In this manner a hop, skip, and jump system of travel evolved. Faf would name a place ahead some little distance and amuse himself cavorting in the air until Jarl was almost there. Then the dragon would swoop and land, awaiting his partner in the adventure. He absented himself when Jarl made camp. He left his friend to the joys of a carnivorous meal that turned his vegetarian stomach. Sometimes human beings were too ferocious to believe. He didn't mind Jarl's catching the fish—they were ugly when removed from the water. How could Jarl bring himself to snare and eat those cute rabbits? Faf shuddered when he thought about it as he soared. After dinner Faf returned and settled his tail carefully in the midst of the coals of Jarl's fire.

As he explained the first time he did it, "Sorry, but I can't abide a cold tail. A dragon could catch pneumonia sitting about all night with his tail chilled."

Several days later Jarl arrived at the bank of a broad river. He needed to cross it to make his next rendezvous with Fafnoddle. The road was over-grown. No one had passed this way for a long time. Jarl supposed it was because of its proximity to Fellkeep. The Shadowlord made an unpleasant neighbor. Jarl remembered the desolate look of the abandoned cottages he passed. So far, he hadn't met a soul.

While he studied the water to see if he could detect a place to ford the river, he heard splashing and wicked squeals of glee. He waited, prudently keeping concealed until he knew what creatures were coming down the river. A flat raft came into view. A dull brown lizardlike animal poled it. Or was it an animal? Surely that was suffering he saw when it raised its eyes to meet his. It sensed where he was, although he knew he was out of the line of sight of anything on the water. Then he noticed the heavy ropes that bound the creature to the raft.

The other beings on the raft were vaguely human in general outline, but their pale, misshaped faces and ugly bodies were travesties of human form. At three feet, they were almost a full foot shorter than the lizard-person, but they were so hunched over they appeared shorter. One urged the lizard to greater effort by scratching it with catlike claws. It kicked the lizard. When Jarl saw its goat's feet, he knew what it was. His grandmother had told him tales of the korred, a truly nasty species of dark elf.

The current was strong. In spite of the efforts of the lizard, the raft swung close to shore where low-growing creepers trailed over the korred. Although the sounds they made were strange, Jarl could understand what they said. Jarl wondered how this could be until he remembered Wyrd. It was important for him to know what was happening, so Wyrd had made him fluent in the creature's speech.

"Push, wyvern, or we shall not bother to take you home!" the korred rasped with a scratch on the lizard's hide that left four streams of blood seeping.

The wyvern was doing all the work involved in rafting wherever they were going. Not one korred attempted to assist the wyvern, although several offered taunts and further claw marks. At closer range Jarl saw the creature's tattered back. The hot sun beat down as the rope bonds rubbed across the cuts with every movement of the pole. Jarl dismounted silently and drew his sword. The raft was almost ready to touch the bank. As it passed Jarl's hiding place, he swept his sword over the ropes, which parted easily under its keen blade.

In a flash the wyvern disappeared into the water. Jarl used his foot to give the raft a healthy shove into the main current. He followed on the bank, watching the antics of the korred as they tried to regain control of their craft. He smiled as he thought of the rapids Faf warned him about that morning. He heard the angry screeches of the korred turn to howls of fear as the raft began its journey through the rock-strewn rapids. They were afraid of the water. Jarl hoped they couldn't swim.

He retraced his steps to his horse. The hill pony had not moved from the spot where he left it. Jarl was about to ride farther upstream searching for a shallow place when he felt a faint message begin to form in his mind.

Help . . . me . . . Man-one, or . . . I perish.

Something was commanding about the weak sending he was receiving. A wyvern must be some type of magical being. He walked to the spot near where the wyvern disappeared.

I hear you, he thought strongly, not certain if he could communicate in mindspeech.

This water . . . is not home to me. My wounds call hungry ones . . . to feast. I must get out of the water . . . welcome though the cool kiss of moisture is to me . . . .

The voice trailed off, but Jarl saw a pale green trifingered hand clasping the bank almost at his feet. He reached down and grasped it, drawing the wyvern onto the bank. It weighed surprisingly little. Chameleonlike, her color had changed to match the leaves around them. The most unexpected thing about his new friend was her sex. Although he saw nothing to suggest her femininity, he knew she was female.

That is so . . . .

Could everything—one, he mentally corrected himself—read his thoughts here in Realm?

Only when you think strongly about me.

The wyvern's head drooped. Jarl caught her before she fell to the ground. The pony made no demur when he climbed into the saddle with the wyvern clutched in front of him.

Jarl didn't think it was a good idea to wait around. There was always a chance that those korred might return. Any friends of theirs were sure to spell trouble. They outnumbered him even if they gained no help. He couldn't protect both himself and the wyvern from attack.

Upstream the river narrowed and Jarl was able to cross. He headed inland, searching for the open space Faf had found in one of his aerial surveys. Faf scouted at least a day's journey ahead and told Jarl about it each evening. It gave him something useful to do while he waited for Jarl to catch up to him.

Jarl watched for the open space amid the oak trees where he was to make his evening camp. Faf mentioned a small stream that wound through the glade. Somehow Jarl sensed the wyvern would want to be near water.

The sight of several squirrels alerted him to the proximity of the oaks. "It must be around here somewhere," he muttered to himself.

Ahead and to the left, Man-one, the wyvern's thought touched him briefly.

"How do you know?"

There is power in the oak. Ahead you will find a giant tree. You may leave me at its base.

"You're so weak . . . ."

There will be help for me. Do not worry, Man-one.

Jarl reluctantly agreed to the wyvern's wishes. He placed her carefully under the oak she indicated. Then he walked on, leading the horse, in the direction she pointed out to him.

It was only a short way to the open space Faf had mentioned.

Jarl and Faf arrived at the same time. Jarl knew Faf was a vegetarian. Still, it was unnerving to wait below and see something so huge zeroing in on the same little clearing where you stood. Jarl still marveled that the pony should believe Faf was a hummingbird. Without the dragon's spell, the pony would bolt through the woods while Jarl fought for control.

"Sorry I'm a little late," Faf greeted him. "I bought you something for dinner. I didn't think you'd be able to catch anything in these woods."

Jarl caught the knapsack Faf dropped from between his claws. It held steak fruit and some bread.

"How did you get this? Do the steak plants grow in other places?"

"I made a lightning trip home today. My plants are fine."

"It's taken us days to get this far. Can you really fly that much faster on your own?"

"Let's just say we dragons have a few secrets up our scales," Faf said mysteriously.

Jarl could tell from Faf's manner that he had no intention of satisfying Jarl's curiosity. "You said you expected me to be unable to catch anything in these woods. Why?"

"This is one of the last safe places near Fellkeep. It's a dryad colony. Each dryad protects her tree and the creatures that live in it. In large numbers dryads are capable of relatively strong magic. Creatures inimical to life and peaceful pursuits are not welcome here. I used to come here as a dragonette because most dragons can't enter here."

"When things got too tough at home?"

"You might say that. I feel that someone else is sheltering in this grove beside us. Do you know anything about him?"

"Her," Jarl corrected. "It's a wyvern."

"A wyvern! How did she get here? I've never seen one of them so far north. They used to live in the marsh near Fellkeep."

"I brought her."

"They don't think much of anything masculine. How did you meet her?"

Jarl told him what happened.

"That makes sense. The korred are usually only minor annoyances. I suppose if the Shadowlord is all the things you say, they're in league with him. They've never been kind in their dealings with humans. They lump anyone who looks human together and hate them all equally. Most dragons have nothing to do with them. We don't like prejudice. Many perfectly adequate beings don't have scales," he said, somewhat weakening his protestations of tolerance.

Jarl offered to share his steak-fruit with the dragon, but he claimed he was full. There was enough fruit in the bag for several more meals.

"Thanks for the fruit. The wild game is sparse lately."

"I imagine the Shadowlord and his allies misuse the animals for their pleasure."

"They hunt in these woods?"

"Not exactly. I want you to wear this special moley and carry this," Faf said, reaching in the knapsack and taking out an odoriferous lump.

"Whew! What a stench!"

"Never mind the smell. You must keep this with you at all times. I'm not sure how much protection Wyrd can give you from the mockers."

"Mocker's?"

"The Shadowlord's creatures can call a human to them in spite of their desire to stay away. They can call other creatures, too, more's the pity. Some of them don't know enough to wear garlic or carry moley as a safety charm."

"I'll carry the moley, but the smell of the garlic would draw attention to me."

"Some of my grimoires say mockers feed on the life essence of living creatures. It is rare to find the desiccated husks of the mocker-called. On those occasions, every bone in their bodies is the same—broken." Faf proffered the garlic again.

Jarl shook his head. "Not for me, Faf. Wyrd ought to be some protection."

"Very well. I tried." Faf said before he dug a hole with one talon and buried the small lump.

"What do these mockers look like?"

"No one has ever seen them. On the way home I stopped off at a friend's cottage to learn the latest news. If the Shadowlord gains control of Realmgate, he can invade any world he chooses.

"When I heard about the mockers, I thought you might need a little extra protection. Some magicians theorize they are demons called from another plane of existence. They only operate in the dark. With any luck, I hope never to see one." Faf's scales rippled.

Jarl added the second piece of moley to the one the witch had given him.

"Oh, you already had a piece."

"You never can tell when an extra bit of moley will come in handy—and now I have a spare." Jarl wrapped himself in his cloak, more for a sense of comfort than because he needed the warmth.

The dragon sprawled out in a half circle around the fire with Jarl on the opened side. Faf positioned the tip of his tail in the glowing embers. "Ah," Jarl heard him murmur, "all the comforts of home."

The next morning Jarl felt a flurry of leaves on his face. He opened his eyes, but he saw no one. Puzzled, he rubbed them and looked again. Then he heard a giggle.

"Here," a soft feminine voice called.

"Where?" Jarl asked, checking to see if someone was behind Faf.

"Here, mortal! In the tree above you."

Jarl dutifully peered into the branches over his head. Careful searching showed him the form of a young girl. She stood in a crotch many feet in the air.

"Be careful! You might fall."

"Pooh. Not me!"

"If I were your father, I'd tan your hide, young lady. You'll break every bone in your body if you fall."

Faf's chuckle reminded Jarl that he and the girl were not alone in the glade. Jarl turned to glare at his friend. "A big help you are! Wouldn't you worry if that was a young dragon up there on that limb?"

"Not particularly." Jarl's expression spoke for him. Faf hastened to explain himself. "Dragonettes are born knowing how to fly."

"All right, all right. So I picked a poor example, but you know what I mean. You're still amused. What's so funny? I'd like to be in on the joke."

"That—er—young girl is a dryad."

"Dryad or not, isn't she a little young to be climbing so high?"

"What a nice compliment," the dryad commented, having materialized at the foot of the tree.

"Hello, Windflower."

"Good morning to you, Faf. What brings you to my woods? I haven't seen you for four or five hundred seasons."

Then Jarl remembered his mythology. A dryad was as old as her oak. This tree would need half a dozen men to encircle it. As usual in Realm, looks were deceiving.

"Jarl Dragon's Pawn and I are going to rescue Mirza from the Shadowlord."

"I will send word to my sisters. Mirza has always been kind. We did not know she was imprisoned. If ever Oak can aid you, you have only to ask."

"Thank you," Faf and Jarl said in unison.

"How are you involved in this rescue, Faf? The last I heard, you were secretly studying magic far from your father."

"I'm still studying. This is a vacation for me. I thought a little exposure to magic in the real world might prove edifying."

"You must be very watchful. There is a degree of protection for Jarl because he is the Dragon's Pawn, but his protection probably doesn't extend to you, Noddy dear."

Now is was Jarl's turn to smile. The dragon's scales on his neck and head shifted slightly, showing their well-burnished edges in the light of the morning sun. Jarl realized he was seeing a rare sight. Faf was blushing.

"Hrumph!" Faf choked back a warm reply. "I'll be careful."

"The Shadowlord is evil beyond knowing. We have set up wards in each oak glade to protect the innocent. Trapped, taken, or destroyed before they can reach our sanctuaries is their usual fate."

"Jarl's talisman grows in strength every day as Jarl grows in wisdom. When the testing time comes, he will succeed." Faf's golden eyes gleamed with surety as he spoke.

"I almost forgot my original reason for coming here," Windflower said, looking over her shoulder with one hand and leg melding into the oak. "Seabreeze sends her thanks."

Jarl wondered who Seabreeze was, but the dryad's next words answered his question.

"She left this morning for the wyverns' cave by the Marshy Sea. The Shadowlord's accomplices are damming the great river in an attempt to dry up the marsh. He wants to destroy the wyverns because they command sea magic.

"I see Wyrd's scales gain gold as you help the wyverns. Good-bye." With her last word she disappeared into the tree.

"Are all dryads as beautiful and abrupt as that?"

"I've known a good many. They're just like anyone. Each is an individual. Windflower is a Keeper and the ruler of the Oaken Circle. The press of her duties at this dangerous time makes her a little abstracted."

The dragon stretched like a cat and pounded his tail upon the ground. "Kinks. I'd better get airborne and let the sun limber me up. Keep going due south. Wait for me at the top of the first hill you come to this afternoon. If you look sharp and there's no mist, you may be able to see Fell Forest. We're in the land of King Caeryl already."

Jarl watched his friend shoot into the air. Wyrd fitted his wrist closely as he mounted, prepared to face whatever the day might bring. Wyrd wasn't uncomfortable, but Jarl felt warned that the price of life was constant vigilance.

CHAPTER THIRTEEN

The day passed uneventfully until the lengthening shadows of the misshapen trees that lined the path reached across the slender open space Jarl traveled. The path wound steadily upward. Jarl thought he would reach the meeting place by late afternoon. It was lonely traveling by himself, but having the dragon reconnoiter each day's journey before he made it was helpful.

Jarl's hand felt cold; Wyrd gradually tightened in warning. As soon as Jarl became alert to the possibilities of peril, Wyrd loosened the pressure. Jarl's eyes scanned the vegetation on both sides of the path. In some places vines straggled from treetop to treetop, forming a canopy over the trail. From time to time a huge tree branch overreached the narrow ribbon of road. Jarl entered one such dark patch just as his horse bolted. The first lunge of the horse was his only warning. As he clung to the saddle, he leaned forward and the rope noose aimed for his head trailed over his back harmlessly.

The brigands hidden beside the path had no chance to stop him now that his horse had gained its stride. Jarl urged it on, knowing that he needed a relatively clear spot to face his enemies. The arrow that whizzed by him strengthened sounds of pursuit. He planned to stop his mount when he got to a place where he could swing his sword. If luck was with him, it would be a large enough area for Faf to land. The tiny circling dot in the sky was almost sure to be his companion—he hoped.

"Catch him! Don't let him get away!"

The words rang in Jarl's ears. His horse faltered. The trail was so overgrown he couldn't see the sky. His only chance lay in escaping the never-ending green tunnel. He hesitated to leave the path. All he needed was to find himself lost in territory his searchers knew well. As if sensing his desperation, his horse put on one last burst of speed, temporarily outdistancing the rain of arrows that followed them. This last effort brought them to the top of the rise Faf mentioned earlier.

Jarl pulled on the reins and dismounted, giving his horse a hurried slap to move him out of harm's way. He drew his sword as the first of the robbers reached him. The jeweled hilt soaked up the rays of the sun, sparkling. The first robber's eyes widened when he saw the sword. His greed to claim Jarl's weapon caused him to underestimate Jarl's swordsmanship. His careless attack left his neck vulnerable. Like a striking adder, the sword separated the robber's head from his body. Jarl had no time to regret his actions. He was battling the second and third robbers consecutively. A fourth was trying to circle around him from behind. A fifth skulked, jackal-like, at the fringe of the battle as he worked his way around to Jarl's horse with the valuable saddle.

So intent on reaving was this last bandit that he didn't pay attention to the huge shadow that swept the clearing. Faf's first burst of flame charred him neatly dead. The shock of the dragon's arrival gave Jarl the edge he needed. A lunge finished off one of his attackers. Faf darted across the open space and picked up the horrified robber who had been trying to position himself behind Jarl. For a while the air rang with the clang of swords in use. Jarl managed to get inside his opponent's guard. The only brigand remaining found himself firmly clutched in Faf's talons ten feet in the air.

"Bravo!" Faf hissed as he settled gently to the ground.

"I thought for a while that you weren't going to make the fight," Jarl gasped. "I could have used your help a little sooner."

"You were doing so well—"

"I know you hate violence." Jarl panted slightly.

"Exactly. And what are we going to do with him?" Faf opened his giant talon, which curled gently—for a dragon—around the surviving attacker, who hit the ground with a thump.

On seeing the plate-sized eye within a foot of his face, the brave robber fainted.

Jarl remembered his meeting with Faf's father. He couldn't help feeling some sympathy for the robber, who looked rather young to be a hardened criminal. "First we'll revive him. Then we'll find out why they attacked me," Jarl announced.

A little water from Jarl's canteen brought the youthful criminal around, but no sooner did he open his eyes than he fainted for the second time.

"What the—" Jarl ejaculated in puzzlement. He turned to see what had terrified the robber. Faf stood right behind Jarl. His head was poised over Jarl's shoulder. During his association with Faf, Jarl had become used to the dragon's looks and idiosyncrasies. He had forgotten how a normal human might react to so imposing a specimen of dragonry. When Jarl tactfully explained this to Faf, the dragon nodded and moved out of the robber's sight.

This time when the would-be robber revived, Jarl began to question him. "Who are you?"

"Will Fletcherson," the youth said, unobtrusively trying to see if the dragon was still present.

"Why did you attack me?"

"We needed food and a way to get back into the king's good graces."

"King?"

"King Caeryl. We were cast out of his kingdom for laziness and petty thievery. We thought it would be easy to steal for a living. We were wrong. These deserted lands belong to the Shadowlord. We lived hand to mouth, glad to find a patch of berries or an abandoned fruit orchard." A tear rolled down the boy's face, leaving a clear track in the dirt that covered it.

"Go on," Jarl commanded, impatient to have his questions answered. At least these men were not in the Shadowlord's pay.

"It was your saddle that decided us. We recognized it."

"Oh, you mean Prince Leon's saddle."

"Did you take it from him?" Will faced his captor with an angry look.

Impressed by Will's clear loyalty to the young prince, Jarl told him quietly, "No, I did not. It was in the treasure of Mog, the ogre."

"Ogres are mean. They spell trouble for any man. Did you outsmart him?"

"No." Jarl glanced at Faf. He had learned to read the dragon's expressions from their daily conversations. When the amused nostrils of the dragon quivered, Jarl knew the cause. Now he was answering the prisoner's questions.

The curt monosyllable intrigued Will. "Then how did you come by it?"

"I killed him," Jarl said.

A look of admiration lit Will's face. "I knew we shouldn't have tried to rob you. I was kind of glad when you escaped my noose. We might never

CAROL L. DENNIS

have chased you but for the saddle. Gilly, our leader, told us if we took the saddle and you to the king, he might forgive us. The prince was kidnapped before we were exiled."

"The lad's learned his lesson. Mayhap we should make a slight detour and tell King Caeryl the probable whereabouts of his son."

Will turned and, recognizing the dragon, paled.

"Don't worry. He won't hurt you. He's my friend."

"Dragons aren't usually friendly," Will said, trying to look brave and failing.

Faf snorted, and Jarl said hurriedly. "Where's the best place to make camp?"

"Around those rocks is a sheltered area. It isn't safe to build a fire in the open. We met an old hermit who warned Gilly and the rest of us that strange things range this area in the dark."

"If you'll give me your parole, I'll trust you. Tomorrow we'll set out for the palace. I'll let you have credit for rescuing the saddle, and perhaps the king will readmit you to the kingdom."

"I promise," Will told Jarl with shining eyes.

Jarl noted his prisoner's changed demeanor. The youngest member of the band, he probably was just lazy, not a hardened criminal. Jarl set Will to gathering an evening's supply of wood.

"What were you saying about the prince? Do you know where he is?" Jarl asked Faf when they were alone.

"I have reason to believe he's at Fellkeep."

"How do you know?" Jarl kept an eye on Will as he spoke.

"I saw an ill-assorted group of creatures delivering a young man who was bound and gagged to raiders wearing the Shadowlord's cloaks."

"You saw and didn't try to rescue him?"

"How was I to know it was a prince? An updraft brought the name Leon to me, but I didn't hear any honorific attached. Besides, there were a great many of them and only one of me. If they were connected to the Shadowlord, some of them were probably magic workers. I'm still learning. I'd promised to meet you—and a good thing it was, too—I dislike violence."

After listening to Faf's catalog of excuses, Jarl said, "All right. I hear you."

They camped under a rocky overhang that held the fire's warmth and yet shielded the light from possible enemies. There was enough room for Faf, too. Will enjoyed the last of the steak fruit with Jarl and Faf. His eyes bugged when he saw the dragon bury his tail in the embers of the fire.

"Do you really think the king will forgive me? It will make my mother happy to have me back. Especially since I've decided to work for a living."

"I've never met the king, but I'll try," Jarl promised. He decided Will was a good enough lad, although not very strong-minded.

Jarl and Will fell asleep, but Faf only drowsed. There was something—something evil—in the air. Being a magical creature himself, he knew that Wyrd's protective aura was not fully effective. Ponder though he did, he could not understand what the problem might be.

"Faf! Are you awake?" Jarl whispered. He could see the up-and-down movement of the dragon's eyes that signified a nod. "What is it, Wyrd?" Jarl thought sleepily as the bracelet tightened on his arm.

"So, as I promised, we meet again, meddlesome one," a silky voice wafted through the darkness. "You have led me a merry chase. For days I have searched for you."

Jarl recognized the voice from his previous meeting. He heard it the night Mirza and he were protected by the pentagram of the well. He didn't answer. Faf's eyes narrowed to slits, but he, too, was silent.

"What—what is it?" Will's scared question broke the silence.

"It's a minion of the Shadowlord's. We've met before," Jarl answered grimly.

"The power of your talisman is weak. You are a Pawn indeed."

"In deed, in deed, in deed," a tiny chorus answered.

"What do they want?" Will's voice broke on the last word.

"We were called. You called us to you."

"I never did!" Will's frightened voice shrilled.

"We know you didn't mean to, but you must have a summoning token if you're telling the truth," Faf said. "Search your pockets." Faf's tail poked the fire, encouragingly the embers to blaze briefly.

Will's first pocket yielded a pit from the steak fruit plant and a few breadcrumbs. His second contained a flat stone with runic engraving.

"What's that?" Jarl asked.

"It's only an unusual stone I found on the road this morning," Will whined.

"Toss it in the fire," Faf commanded as he removed his tail, stirring the embers into a larger blaze.

The stone sailed through the air. It landed in the center of the small blaze, which immediately went out.

"Oh," Will gasped.

"Isn't it a little dark around here?" Jarl's hand tightened on his sword, but his words sounded confident.

"Yes, I agree," the dragon's measured tones answered Jarl. Faf emitted a pure blue stream of flame directed at the dead ashes. At first nothing seemed to happen, but at last a light formed and sprang into flame, casting a golden glow around them.

"So you can work magic as well, dragon?" An irritated sigh from the darkness followed the rhetorical question.

Faf refused to answer verbally. He flicked the charred calling stone into the darkness with his tail.

"Why do you not join us, dragon? You are a seeker after power, as we are. Join us. We offer all the dark knowledge you wish and unlimited power. Come!"

"Come, come, come," the echoes urged.

In answer, Faf beamed a hot blast of flame into the darkness. For a second both Faf and Jarl were wholly absorbed in peering into the blackness. They saw a faint outline of a cowled figure surrounded by amoeboid blobs of utter darkness.

"Come," the voices tugged at Jarl, but fortified by Wyrd and the moley, he resisted.

Will, however, was unprotected. While the summoning stone could call evil, those truly untouched by evil doings could resist within the protective aura of fire which Wyrd and Faf created. Will had spent too long a time with the brigands trying to survive. Even if he was unwilling, he had participated in following those who did wicked deeds; therefore, he was vulnerable. Before either Faf or Jarl could hold him, he leaped into the darkness and disappeared. His howl of utter despair rang in the air. Jarl was ready to dash forward, but Faf stopped him.

"It is too late already. I'm sorry. I've read of such visitations. I assure you there is nothing you or I can do for him now," the dragon said sadly.

"My—associates—thank you for the donation," purred their shadowy visitor. "Perhaps we shall be victorious the next time. You will have further opportunity to join the shadows."

"Shadowss, shadowss, shadowss." The mockers' voices faded.

The black pall gradually thinned to let the sharp light of the stars shine through. A clean, cold gust of air dissipated the last of the fetid odor.

Faf looked at Jarl. "That's as close to evil as I ever want to get."

Jarl agreed.

"At sunrise I'll have to look at my scales."

"Why?"

"They're probably tarnished. Goodness only knows what pollution those creatures brought with them," the dragon complained. He stirred the fire languidly with his tail. "I'll add a few sticks. This early morning chill is the worst possible thing for a dragon's health."

Jarl welcomed the light and warmth himself. Faf's concern for his health added a touch of normalcy that Jarl needed. He blamed himself for Will's death. Resisting was difficult, and the struggle had exhausted him. He should have given the extra piece of moley to Will. Wyrd at least seemed satisfied. There was no sense of constriction from the bracelet. With this in mind, Jarl fell into a deep sleep.

Faf half closed his eyes and meditated on the nature of the evils so lately encountered.

CHAPTER FOURTEEN

The morning's sunrise pinkened the eastern sky as if to expunge the memory of evil from the minds of the two adventurers. After a short discussion, Faf persuaded Jarl it would only take one extra day to deliver the saddle to the king. Along with it, they could also tell the king what Faf had seen.

"Take the left fork in the road," Faf advised. "If you hurry, you may arrive at the city by noon. Make that pony trot a little. He's getting spoiled—fat and sassy. If he snorts at me one more time, I'll remove the spell and show him a thing or two." Faf blustered.

"I've taken good care of him. I can get to Mirza faster on horseback than by walking. I'm still not sure this is the right thing to do. Maybe you could go to the king and I could keep on. As fast as you fly—"

"From now on, we're sticking together. Look what happened when I was a little late yesterday." Faf pouted. "Now there's some action starting, you want me safely out of the way."

"I thought you were a pacifist."

Faf snorted.

"Oh, let's go on, then." Jarl kicked the astonished horse into a trot. Faf sailed lazily overhead, keeping a close watch for danger.

The trail let steadily downhill, so Jarl made good time. He clattered over a wooden bridge and passed a rude marker that said "Green Valley." Within minutes he saw signs of human habitation. Neat fields lined the roads. Prosperous farms alternated with smaller holdings. Once Faf saw Jarl safely past the running water, he flew higher and higher, leaving Jarl to his own devices. Faf's infallible magic sense told him every inch of that river was warded with potent spells to protect humans from the machinations of the Shadowlord.

Precisely on the hour of noon the bells in the city rang in joyous cacophony. Jarl dismounted at the castle gate to which friendly citizens directed him.

"That's why I must see the king," Jarl finished explaining to the portly man who claimed to be the king's seneschal.

"A fascinating tale. We must see that Relnot, the royal magician, hears it." He clapped his hands and a liveried servant arrived.

"Send for Relnot," Jarl's listener commanded.

"Yes, Your Majesty." The servant executed a military about-face and exited the room.

"Your Majesty!" Jarl gasped. Jarl expected a king to look the part. This man dressed richly, but he wore no crown. No courtiers were in evidence, either.

"Sorry, but it simplifies matters if people don't know who I am when they're telling things. I hate formality, and if there's one thing that brings out the awkwardness in people, it's speaking with a king." He smiled kindly at Jarl. "A king is an ordinary man in an extraordinary position. You can't imagine how boring all that yes-Your-Royal-Highness, no-Your-Royal-Highness, yes-sire, no-sire, three-bags-full-sire form of address gets to be. I hope you'll forgive me my little impersonation."

"Of course, sire."

"See? Now you're doing it, too. Ah, well, it was fun while it lasted."

A much-bemedaled man in a uniform hurried through the door. "Tsk, tsk, Your Highness. Up to your little tricks again?"

"Meet my seneschal, Pomfret Pompuss." The king waved his hand carelessly in the direction of the man whose purple pantaloons and yellow velvet jacket warred lustily.

Jarl half bowed in response to the other's gesture. The comfortable atmosphere stiffened. A veneer of court superficiality overlaid each procedure. Jarl saw why the king played truant from formality when he had the chance.

"His Majesty's royal magician, Relnot," a servant intoned.

Jarl turned to watch as a tall, thin man in white robes bordered with cabalistic designs glided into the room. His lined face and silver beard made him look old at first glance. His blue eyes sparkled with intelligence. In one look Jarl judged him trustworthy. The magician's sharp eyes lingered for a second on Wyrd, then passed to the king.

"You called for me, Your Majesty?"

"Who else commands you, Relnot?" Pompuss said.

The king ignored his seneschal. "Jarl, here, has news of Prince Leon. He's the prisoner of the Shadowlord."

"The Shadowlord would like to pass freely over your domain. Kidnapping the prince is his way of encouraging you to join him as an ally." Relnot shook his head.

"Never! Not so long as I am king. He and all those connected with him reek of evil. Even to free my beloved son, I will not betray the trust of the people in this kingdom. What legacy would I leave my boy if I joined the Shadowlord?"

"But—but—" Pomfret Pompuss began.

"I will promise to be neutral, to take no action against him if he frees Leon. Become his ally? Never!" The king threw back his shoulders and placed his hand on his sword.

"Sire, is it wise to be so hasty?" Pompuss interjected.

The king waved him away. Relnot took no notice of his exit, but Jarl was more willing to believe this man was king when he saw the instant obedience he commanded.

Relnot ran his aristocratic hand over his beard. "I will send your message, sire. The Shadowlord has been of interest to me since he first appeared here in Realm. No one knows where he comes from, and he has no friends. My long study of him leads me to believe he will spurn your promise and demand you join him."

"When you first suggested the possibility that Leon was a hostage of the Shadowlord, I thought many days upon what I must do. Now there is proof, nothing for it but to become reconciled to the loss of my son." The king's face remained stern and calm, but Jarl saw his right hand clench into a fist as he spoke.

Jarl said, "Is there anything I could do to help?"

Both the king and the magician had almost forgotten Jarl.

They turned to him, surprised that he should offer his aid.

"An ordinary person has no chance battling our evil neighbor. His allies destroy every living thing they come upon. They befoul the very air where they pass. I can send no stranger into danger on a fool's errand," the king said.

"Wait, sire," Relnot commanded. "Perhaps Jarl is not an ordinary stranger after all." He pointed to Wyrd. "How came you by that bracelet?"

Prepared for their disbelief, Jarl answered, "It appeared on my wrist after a visit from Rory, the leprechaun."

"Let me see it," Relnot said, holding out his hand for the bracelet.

"I cannot remove it. I have worn it constantly since I received it."

"I have read of an ancient talisman which the heroes of Realm possessed. Supposedly it selects its wearer and remains with him until the need for its aid ceases. Its wearer is the Dragon's Pawn until he masters the talisman's powers for himself."

"That's me, all right," Jarl admitted.

"Then there's some danger to the whole of Realm. The old records tell of an evil demon from otherwhen, defeated by Andronan, the last wearer of Wyrd."

Jarl nodded. "Clearly the Shadowlord is bypassing the normal gates between alternate worlds. His magic is causing the creatures that humans on my planet imagine to become real in Realm."

The magician's eyes flashed. "He swore years ago at the Keeper's Council that he would have vengeance, because they would not allow him to become a Keeper. We have heard little of him until lately. Protected as this kingdom is by my magic, it makes us insulated from his depredations. We have heard terrible tales of his doings. The Keepers were wise to refuse him free passage between worlds."

Jarl told them about Will's death.

The king shook his head. "It did not occur to me they would not go north when I exiled them. You can see why I must refuse your offer of aid. Even wearing a hero's talisman might not save you if the Shadowlord himself decided to harm you."

"Well, at least I can return the prince's saddle to you."

"You have the royal saddle?" Relnot asked.

"It's the one I used to ride here."

"Have it brought to my chambers immediately. Let us see if a little magic can give us further information about the prince."

A servant hurried to get the saddle while the king, Relnot, and Jarl mounted the marble steps to the tower room of the magician.

Relnot's quarters at the top of the main tower were light and airy. Not one cobweb hung from the wooden shelves that held calfhide books. The tops of the tables that curved along one sector of the wall gleamed spotlessly. The embers of a neatly tended fire warmed the room. Jarl looked out the window. The magician had a panoramic view of the southern border of the kingdom. Jarl wondered where Faf was.

"Magic is like anything else," Relnot said into Jarl's ear. "It's not enough to do a good job occasionally. The real work is seeing to it that things stay in a proper fashion." Relnot turned at the respectful knock at the door.

"Come in, come in," he said. "Put the saddle on the round table in the center of the room." Relnot approached the table as the servant bowed himself from the room. "Ah, yes. It is the royal saddle."

A shadow passed over the tower, momentarily darkening the room. Relnot whirled, looking for its source. He raised his hand preparatory to hurling a spell at the huge dragon now seated on a neighboring tower.

"Wait! That's Faf, my friend," Jarl said.

"A dragon for a friend? You keep strange company," the king muttered irascibly from his spot near the door. It looked suspiciously as if he was planning a little magic of his own—a disappearing act.

"I'm Fafnoddle von Fafnir. It's a pleasure to make your acquaintance," Faf said to Relnot. By stretching, his neck bridged the gap between the towers and his gargantuan head rested on the stone windowsill of Relnot's room. "I've seldom seen so neat a bit of magic as that border ward you have in place."

"You recognize the spell?" The compliment clearly pleased Relnot.

"Oh, yes. I work a little magic myself from time to time."

Fearing the meeting was going to turn into a magical shop-talk session, Jarl interrupted. "This is King Caeryl, Prince Leon's father. The gentleman you're talking to is Relnot."

"Your Majesty," Faf intoned politely, dipping his nose in what passed for a bow with a dragon.

The king smiled graciously. Then he approached the table. "What do you plan to do with it, Relnot?" he asked, indicating the saddle.

"I'll see if it will speak to me when I place my hands upon it," Relnot said. He reached out to lightly touch the saddle.

"Psychometry. I've heard of it," Jarl said quietly, to avoid disturbing the magician.

"Well?" the king asked impatiently. "Is it speaking to you?"

"I see a cave . . . Mog, the ogre, dwells within . . . It is dark . . . The prince and his retainers have made camp . . . Something evil approaches . . . There is fighting . . . The campfire dies . . . There is no one left alive to tend it . . . the saddle, picked up by Mog and carried to his cave . . . ."

"What of my son?"

"That is all I can see. I also received the impression of a black dragon carrying off a maiden . . . Can't see how it's connected with Prince Leon, sire."

"The maiden is Mirza, a friend of mine," Jarl interjected.

"I was not certain of her identity. Mirza enjoys changing her shape from one creature to another. It is difficult to recognize her."

"That's Mirza, all right. The black dragon that took her is a creature of the Shadowlord. Faf and I are going to Fellkeep to rescue her."

"You do well to carry moley," the magician said. "Sire, if Jarl Dragon's Pawn is already going to Fellkeep, perhaps he could aid us."

"Well, if he's already decided to risk his life, we would be glad to accept any help he offers." The king smiled at Jarl.

"Jarl, I have a potent spell that weakens me for days. I hesitate to use it unless I know for certain it will bring results. I can have the prince here in this room in a twinkling—but to bring him, I must know exactly where he is. He must also have this in his possession." Relnot reached deep into his robes and removed an ordinary-looking acorn.

"I shall try to see that he gets this. How will you know exactly where he is?" Jarl placed the acorn in his pocket.

"Wyrd will respond if you're willing to expend the power of your talisman in our behalf. From here, Fellkeep is three days' hard ride."

Faf hissed. "I've been checking the roads. The Shadowlord has made a great many nasty little arrangements for us. Traveling on horseback will be too dangerous, Jarl."

"Then you won't be going to Fellkeep?" The king's face expressed his disappointment.

"I'm going!" Jarl insisted.

"Of course you are," Faf soothed. "As the arrow flies, the journey will only take about a day."

"Are you going to ask Relnot to turn me into an arrow?" Jarl asked, unmollified by Faf's manner.

"Not at all. I'm going to carry you as I did once before."

"But—" Jarl began. He remembered the swooping sensation all too well. If men were meant to fly, they would have scales, he mentally paraphrased an old Earth saying, fitting it to Realm.

"I'm in my prime. I should be able to do it easily. It will mean less fighting and a faster trip to Mirza. It's the one avenue of entry that looks clear. There are suspicious blank spots just over the border on every road, path, and trail that leads out of this kingdom. The Shadowlord means business. Only a master of magic has the power and art to produce so much nothingness. Who knows what each may hold?"

"Nothing good, I'll wager," the king said, hoping his attempt at levity would ease the tension he saw Jarl was under.

Relnot and the king were nodding agreement to everything Faf said.

Jarl surrendered. "All right. If you say so, I'm game." Sorry about this, he apologized silently to his stomach.

"Stay the night," the king said expansively. "We'll see you both have plenty to eat and a place to sleep." He looked at Faf estimatingly. "How many cattle will we need to slaughter for your meal?"

Faf's wings flew wide, ready to snap together and create a gale of indignation. Jarl recognized the signs. He hurriedly said, "Faf is a vegetarian, sire."

"A vegetarian dragon? How very—"

Faf expected the next word to be *odd* and he raised his head to vent a stream of fire and smoke into the air above the tower. It narrowly missed a pigeon that landed on the windowsill of the other window in the room.

"—er, interesting," the king concluded prudently.

Relnot lost all interest in dinner preparations when the bird landed. He soothed the bird as he untied the small role of paper from its leg. "Sire, this is one of Prince Leon's messenger pigeons." Relnot skimmed the writing and passed the note to the king.

"It's from my son! He's alive." The king straightened as if an invisible millstone had removed itself from his back. "You were right, Relnot. I'm to have three days to remove the magic barrier and welcome an envoy of the Shadowlord's who will bear an alliance treaty."

"Now there's no time to lose." The magician gave the nervous pigeon a last stroke and placed him in a cage. He dropped a cloth over it to blot the sight of Faf from the fluttering bird. "Speed is necessary now. The only way to get Jarl to Fellkeep is by dragonflight. At the end of the three days the Shadowlord will feed the prince's soul to one of his demon allies. If we ever see the prince after that, he will belong to the Shadowlord."

Relnot's words seemed to linger in the air after he spoke them. His listeners understood that his study of the Shadowlord made his gloomy forecast all too probable.

"Faf, are you ready? We could start now and—"

"No, Jarl," interrupted Relnot. "It's madness to begin a journey that will bring you from safety during the deepest hours of night when the powers of the Dark are at their zenith. At sunrise, with the Light fully on your side, is the time to begin such a venture."

"Relnot is correct. I also feel a sense of urgency, but we need to begin our journey in the morning," said the dragon.

"I thank you both," the king said quite humbly, considering his rank. "Now I will go to order our meal."

"If you need to talk to me, stand below in the courtyard," Faf said. "My neck's getting stiff from all this stretching."

The day waned. Beyond the warded border the many inexplicable shadowy areas deepened to ebon with a darkness that was no mere absence of visual light.

CHAPTER FIFTEEN

The bright yellow ball of the sun lit the sky. It drove the clouds away as Faf carefully clutched Jarl.

"Well, we're off," Faf said joyfully as he cast himself from the top of the tower and hurtled toward the ground with wings outspread.

The king's good-bye still echoed in Jarl's ears. He was happy he had refused breakfast. It proved to be a fortuitous decision. Twenty feet from the ground, Faf caught an updraft and soared into the blue, and Jarl felt rather green. He swallowed. "Faf, was that necessary?"

"What?" Faf banked neatly and flew blind. He curved his head to hear Jarl better.

"That grandstand takeoff," Jarl shouted into the teeth of the wind.

"Oh, that."

"What if that updraft hadn't been there?" Jarl had visions of himself on the bottom of two feet of dragon paté spread over the courtyard stones under the tower.

"Oh, I practiced that takeoff twice this morning before you arrived. I knew that we'd get airborne. I wouldn't risk splattering a Dragon's Pawn all over the king's courtyard. You know how—"

The huge circle Faf was making dizzied Jarl, so he finished the dragon's statement. "Yeah, I know how violence appalls you. Let's get moving. Flying in circles isn't getting us any closer to Fellkeep."

"I'm not actually flying. This is resting. The thermals are doing all the work. Don't worry."

Jarl felt the dragon's claws clutch his harness through the pad he wore.

He looked down at the rapidly passing earth below him and glanced at the vast bulk of the bronze dragon above him. "Oh, no. I won't," he lied. Then he shot a thought at Wyrd. "I suppose you think this is the only way to travel."

Yess, drifted through his mind, followed by a chuckle.

Great, Jarl thought to himself. A vegetarian pacifist hypochondriac and the joker of the ophidian set, how could I get so lucky?

A ghostly chuckle brushed his mind in reply. At least Wyrd had a sense of humor. Jarl wondered what had happened to his.

They passed the border without any problems. Faf soared cloudward on a giant thermal, then leveled out, approaching the great Fell Forest with bulletlike speed. Wind stung Jarl's eyes. He didn't see the two birdlike shapes that approached rapidly from the south.

Fortunately, Faf did. "Hmmm. Company," he muttered.

"What?" Jarl shouted.

"Company," Faf roared, making all speed toward a grove of oaks that he could just see on the horizon. "I'll have to put you down for a while."

"Drop me, you mean?" Jarl's eyes widened. Would Wyrd be able to save him?

"I'll land you in those oaks. There's something very strange about those things ahead."

Jarl squinted. "They look like birds to me."

"They're not like any birds I ever saw before. They come from the south, and I'll bet the Shadowlord sent them. When I meet them, I'd like to be free to maneuver—in case."

"All right, but you're acting like a little old lady. We're over halfway there because of the tailwind you found, so I guess we can spare the time."

Faf skimmed the tops of the trees as Jarl unloosed the safety loop he had harnessed to the dragon's leg. When Faf opened his claw and dropped him, Jarl floated gently to the biggest tree in the grove. Jarl expected a rough landing, but Faf—or Wyrd—had taken care of him. He arrived as lightly as thistledown.

"Welcome," a friendly voice said behind him.

Jarl carefully held on to some branches near him. He edged his way from the swaying outer portion of the oak to a fork where two branches formed a sturdy crotch. He sat gingerly and looked for the source of the words.

"Here I am!"

Jarl peered toward the sound of the silvery laughter. A lovely woman stood on a bough so slender it moved gently with every passing breeze. The age of the tree he rested in told him the dryad was a mature magical being.

"Hello. I hope you don't mind my being in your tree. I do have a good reason," Jarl told her with a smile.

"I know. I see your friend fighting above us."

Jarl's unique position had temporarily caused him to forget about Faf. Above the forest Faf was quite literally flying for his life. The birdlike shapes in the sky were an enigma to Jarl, until one of them emitted a beam of light that narrowly missed Faf. Faf was doing evasive maneuvers through the air that made his previous stunts look like movements of a timid field mouse. Jarl's forehead creased. Faf couldn't keep it up forever. He was outmaneuvered at every turn. Beams of light crisscrossed the air. Sooner or later he would make a slight error in judgment. That mistake might well be his last.

Jarl looked at Wyrd. He would have to try to awaken the power he knew lay within his talisman. He began to concentrate.

"No, Dragon's Pawn." A soft hand touched his arm gently. "If you use your power here, you will call the Dark to my tree. I do not wish to see it destroyed. I am responsible for it and the life it shelters, you see."

Her green eyes were strangely luminescent in the dappled light that filtered through the branches. Jarl looked into them. He admitted the wisdom that lay behind her remark. "But I've got to do some—"

"Look!" The pale fingers gestured toward the sky. Three more ominous shapes had joined Faf's first two enemies. Faf belched a cloud of smoke and disappeared behind it. The strange birds clustered, centering their fire upon the cloud. Faf burst through the lower edge of the smoke and headed straight into the midst of his enemies.

An agonized "No!" burst forth from Jarl. Faf acted as if he were a kamikaze pilot. One part of Jarl wanted to cover his eyes. The other part kept him watching, hoping for something—anything—to happen that would save his friend.

A strange clap of distant thunder sounded. Faf and the birds disappeared together in an instant.

"Do not grieve. All will be well."

"How would you know? You've lived by this tree all your life," Jarl said bitterly. Jarl felt as if he had a stone in his chest. His eyes scanned the sky, hoping Faf was still there, somewhere, just waiting until the time was right to swoop down and get Jarl. Slowly the realization came to Jarl that he would never see Faf fly again. He had not known the dragon for long, but the emptiness he experienced was vast, far larger even than the dragon himself. He knew rescuing Mirza would be much more difficult without the aid of his friend. For the first time he felt a personal sense of hatred for the Shadowlord. "How could you possibly understand how I feel?"

"Leafshine is my name, and I do understand. It is true I do not travel, but there are ways of knowing given to our kind."

Jarl regretted his inability to help his friend. He knew he was incapable of taking an action that the dryad assured him would call the Dark and destroy her tree. Leafshine and her oak were innocent bystanders. Jarl would never forgive himself, never. These black thoughts passed through his mind when Wyrd tightened ominously.

"What I needed now," Jarl muttered. "More bad news."

Leafshine paled to a shadowy pattern among the leaves.

Jarl sat still on his perch, nothing moving but his eyes. Where was the danger? In what form was the Dark approaching? Jarl looked at the dryad and formed a question in his mind, but she gestured for silence and pointed downward.

On the path far below he could see a line of chained prisoners. Guards rode up and down the line urging speed with flailing whips. A man fell, temporarily slowing the group. A rain of blows fell on him and his luckless companions who could not escape the lashes of their captors. Desperately they tugged at him, half dragging, half carrying him as the line began to move at last.

"Be careful, Kurs," one of the bestial guards said.

"I know the way to keep the scum moving," Kurs growled his reply.

"We've been pushing them hard. If one dies before the changing, we'll have to answer to the master."

A look of fear passed over Kurs's face. "No more whipping," he agreed, "but they are moving faster now."

"This will make our quota. We'll get our reward tonight."

"Yeah, women! There's one of them female prisoners ... "

Kurs's voice faded as they followed the staggering line.

The green hand that had been restraining Jarl from action dropped. "I am sorry. The Shadowlord is master of monstrous evil. Many of your kind have passed down this path."

"Women, too?" Jarl asked through clenched teeth.

"Children also," was the sad answer that accompanied Leafshine's nod.

"I've got to get to Fellkeep. Are there many of these slave parties on the roads?"

"The number grows daily. The total is unknown. The raiding parties must now go long distances to find unprotected humans, but there are dozens who search."

"How are these prisoners changed? What is the changing referred to by the slaver?"

"I do not know. Many go into Fellkeep and few come out," Leafshine told Jarl. "There are no oaks around Fellkeep. The ground is swampy. The wyverns have made most of the clear portions of the swamp poisonous so that none can travel there. That way they can better watch the comings and goings of the Shadowlord's servants."

"Is there no safe way to proceed?"

"There is one narrow way though the oak forest made by the Old Ones. With your talisman you may be able to sense it. The old magic guards it well. Evil will not touch him who follows it."

"I'd better get started. There is nothing I can do about my friend, but I can still rescue Mirza." Jarl looked down at the ground far below. Then he started searching for a place to tie the section of rope that had bound him to Faf's leg.

"That won't be necessary," Leafshine said.

"I've got to get down somehow." The oak was large. The spaces between its mighty branches were too wide for Jarl to climb down unassisted.

Leafshine gestured to the other side of the tree. Jarl looked and saw a series of branches sprouting at convenient intervals.

"Will they hold me?" he asked the dryad.

"Of course. I created them for your use."

He tested the first branch. It held, and he began his trip earthward. There was no exact way of telling how far he had come, for the branches disappeared as he finished using them. He didn't bother checking below him. He supposed that the dryad was materializing them under him as he needed them. He reached the ground without incident. Solid earth felt unexpectedly good under his feet.

He jerked as he heard a distant thunderclap. "What was that?"

Leafshine smiled. "It is your friend returning."

"Faf?" A shower of tree leaves answered his question as the dragon arrowed down through the branches to join him on the ground under the giant tree.

"Sorry, Leafshine, I'm wounded and my control isn't all it should be." Some leaves fluttered around Faf as he spoke.

"I understand," the dryad said.

Faf sprawled in exhaustion.

Jarl examined the long scorch mark on the dragon's wing. "Faf, that was a close call. I thought—I thought—"

"I know, Jarl, but aside from my flying's being pretty erratic, the injury is minor."

"What happened up there? It looked as if you and those birds disappeared."

"I just flew home."

"You make it sound so easy. What do you mean you flew home? Your cave is miles from here."

"We dragons have the ability to return home instantaneously from anyplace where we may be. When I got there the birds weren't with me."

"What do you think happened to them? Did the Shadowlord recall them?"

"I don't really care, Jarl. They disappeared, and I for one, am quite happy to see the last of them. They may look like birds, but magically created weapons is what they are." Faf drew a ragged breath.

Jarl and Leafshine looked at one another. They knew Faf's wound must be serious.

"Leafshine, can Faf stay here with you until he's healed?"

Faf raised his head proudly. "I'm going with you."

"I'd like you to come, too, but it just isn't possible. You're already wounded. You can't fly correctly. The only way to reach Fellkeep is to walk—and you know how you hate walking!"

"I won't be able to get airborne for several days. I'll try to walk. At least until I get to the Wyvern Marsh."

"What will you do there? Swim?"

"I'll get them to help me. My mother was a friend of the wyvern's queen. For old-time friendship, they may cure me with some of the mud from their cavern."

"You'll never be able to walk all that way."

"Perhaps I can help, Noddy." Leafshine patted Faf as if he were a small child.

Too tired to blush, Faf just rolled his eyes and then closed them.

Leafshine melted into her tree, but returned in a few seconds carrying a cup-sized acorn full of a dark green liquid. "Drink this!"

"Do I have to?" The dragon raised his head so it was too high for the dryad to reach.

Leafshine stamped her foot. "Fafnoddle von Fafnir! Stop this nonsense!" She stood directly in front of the dragon as he lowered his head reluctantly. The tip of his red tongue forked out of his mouth slightly. "All the way now. I don't want to waste any of this," she commanded. The tongue inched out a bit more and she grabbed its tip, pouring the entire dose on it as Faf quickly retracted it.

"See? That wasn't so bad," she soothed as Jarl watched, fascinated. "There's a good dragon," she praised as she kissed him on the snout.

"Bitter stuff," he complained.

"You're feeling better already, aren't you?" she teased.

"Drat it, yes, yes, but—"

The reply reminded Jarl of old Fafnir. Clearly Faf was a scale off the old hide—at least in some ways.

The dryad looked at Jarl. "You'll need some help, too."

"I'm not wounded or exhausted," he assured her hurriedly. He didn't want any part of her dosing.

"Not medicine. Magic." Her lips twitched, but she managed not to laugh.

"Oh," Jarl breathed, well aware of Faf's ill-concealed grin.

Leafshine held out her finger. It swiftly grew into a twig with one sturdy green leaf at the tip. She broke it off and handed it to Jarl. "Use this to find your way."

"Oh, you mean the Old One's path. What am I supposed to do with this? Jarl looked at the twig. It certainly seemed ordinary enough.

"Simply hold it in front of you. It will activate the spell as you pass. Start to your right," she instructed, fading swiftly from sight before Jarl could thank her.

"Are you ready, Faf?"

"Lead the way," Faf said in a falsely hearty manner. He wasn't very good as hiding his pain, but he tried.

Jarl started to his right. He held the branch in the air. He didn't need to hear Faf's snicker behind him to know he looked odd walking through the woods waving a branch like a fairy wand. He was too glad to have Faf safe to get really annoyed. He was about ready to suggest they find their way to the road and take their chances with the Shadowlord's raiding parties. The woods around them became brighter with a pleasant glow.

A golden avenue almost ten feet wide appeared before them. Following the branch as if it were a dowsing rod, Faf and Jarl trod the Old Ones' highway, safe from the detection of the Shadowlord. They made good time. By nightfall, Faf insisted he could smell the marsh ahead. They camped on a piece of mosaic that held the faded outline of a pentacle within its perimeter.

They ate fruit and bread for their meal. It was the last of the supplies the king sent with them. Faf seemed satisfied, but Jarl entertained a fleeting thought of the old witch's magic bag. A hot meat pasty, a steak sandwich, even a hot dog would have been more filling than bread and fruit.

Jarl watched the moon. He remembered camping trips he took when he was a boy. He felt the quiet peace of the night. This reminded him of other nights sleeping under the stars—except, of course, on former trips he didn't have a dragon curled up around the fire. The heat radiated off Faf's scales. His tail poked the fire if it showed signs of dying down too far.

Jarl had a nagging feeling that Mirza needed him. The king had three days to decide about joining the Shadowlord. What might have happened to Mirza in the days since being captured worried him. What did her captor want from her? Jarl didn't know exactly how powerful or important Mirza actually was here in Realm. He did know enough about her to be sure she would never join the forces of the Dark. Were her powers protecting her in spite of her being in the clutches of the Shadowlord? The first time he rescued her she was bound by a magic chain, but she wasn't suffering. She was simply a prisoner. She had not confided in Jarl. How did she come to be a captive? Why was she kept in the desert? What part did the Shadowlord want her to play in his evil schemes?

Faf said he could smell the marsh. Fellkeep was close. Jarl knew he had twenty-four hours to get to the prince and rescue Mirza.

He concentrated on Wyrd. He formed a question in his mind.

Sssleep, a forceful thought came. And Jarl did.

Faf dragon-napped throughout the night. His wound was becoming more painful as time passed. The dryad's restorative gradually wore off. He looked forward to meeting the wyvern queen. Surely when they entered the marsh that was part of their watery domain, they would contact the wyverns.

Twice during the night he roused to see the wand and the pentacle blaze with power. He dimly sensed evil within the wood. He thought a question in his best High Dragon, the tongue that dragons used only when conversing among themselves.

His reply came in the same tongue. *Sleep.* And Faf did.

The next morning's light found Faf and Jarl following the Old Ones' highroad. Jarl eagerly forged ahead. He wanted to rescue Mirza.

Faf was just as impatient to travel, but his reason was the pain from his wound. He always eschewed violence on moral grounds, but now he had an even better reason for his avoidance: violence could hurt. He had no intention of telling Jarl how weak he was becoming. A powerful dragon shouldn't feel like sitting down in the road and crying. He gritted his magnificent teeth and blanked his pain from his mind. He recited basic cantrips and then advanced to more esoteric spells. Right in the middle of a particularly difficult one, he bumped into Jarl, almost forcing him into the slimy pool that lapped the shore on which they stood.

Faf and Jarl watched, dismayed, as the oak branch flickered, paled, and died.

CHAPTER SIXTEEN

"Well, that's it, Faf. No more magic in the wand. No more path."

"This is the wyverns' marsh. I know where we are now."

"Looks like a swamp to me, no matter what you call it. Now what do we do? I don't relish wading in that." Jarl poked the withered branch into the murky ooze. A few bubbles popped on the surface. Several feel from the bank the water undulated as if something moved beneath the surface.

"Swamp adder," Faf said, cocking an interested eye at the ripples.

"Poisonous?"

"Not very. A little moley will cure most bites. It only chases things that are smaller than it is anyway."

"That's good news."

"Not exactly," Faf hissed. "Swamp adders have grown to a length of fifty feet."

"Fifty feet!"

"Don't worry. I'm with you," Faf consoled his friend. "Besides, although it's been years since I was last here, I seem to remember a series of pathways." Faf craned his not inconsiderably long neck to the left and the right. "Ah, here it is. A dragon never forgets. The footing here will be tricky. Give me a sprig of your moley. It will ease my pain temporarily and give me strength." Jarl silently passed his friend the herb.

Faf led the way to a half-sunk stone, placed the moley in his mouth, raised his tail over his back, and stepped out. *Follow me*, he advised mentally over his shoulder.

Jarl had always heard that elephants didn't forget. He could see a definite similarity between elephants and dragons.

Faf interjected a mental *Humph!* which made Jarl jump.

Another glance at the half-sunk stone and he sincerely hoped that on Realm dragons remembered. As Jarl started out, he wondered about how many of his thoughts Faf picked up. Jarl also worried about getting through the swamp before the moley's power to invigorate the dragon ran out. If Faf slipped, Jarl envisioned the dragon being swept into the nearest swamp adder's coils and ending up as a snack.

Jarl hopped carefully after his friend. For Jarl the gaps between stones were large ones, but to the dragon they were small spaces. Jarl was so busy following Faf he didn't even spare a smile at the odd sight Faf made, mincing along from stone to tussock, tussock to stone.

"Are you all right back there?"

"Yeah," Jarl puffed. "I'm fine, but could you go a little slower?" Jarl marveled at the power of the moley. Faf seemed fine.

"This particular piece of the swamp remains deserted because there are always some—let us say—unpleasant denizens in this part of the marsh."

"Great," Jarl muttered under his breath. "That's me, a hopping hors d'oeuvre for the unfriendly neighborhood monsters."

"Not such farther. There's a waiting place a short distance ahead."

"Glad to hear it," Jarl answered, more to let Faf know he was still alive and hopping than to carry on the conversation.

When they reached a moss-covered flat ledge some inches above the surrounding muck, Faf swung around to view Jarl's last hop to relative safety. He expelled a short jet of fire at a creeping tendril that writhed toward his friend. It withered from the blast.

Jarl dropped his sword back into his sheath. "Thanks. I'm glad you haven't given up smoking. What do we do now?"

"We wait."

"We don't have time to stand around. We must go on to Fellkeep—"

"It has been long since one of your kind has come to us. What do you and the Man-one desire of the wyverns that you wait upon our Judgment Rock?" The sibilant voice of an unseen listener interrupted Jarl as if the human's comments were unimportant.

"What—" Jarl began.

"Quiet. The success or failure of our mission may rest upon what we say in the next few minutes," Faf warned.

"Speak," that voice commanded.

"I, Fafnoddle von Fafnir, grandson of Draka of the Flame, claim guest right of Lythyr, your queen."

"What gives you this right, dragon?"

"I do not claim it on distant cousinship, but because of the friendship which my mother shared with Lythyr in the days of her youth before she became your sovereign."

Faf sat like a graven image, awaiting the verdict. Jarl wondered what they would do if the wyverns refused their aid.

"I acknowledge your right." From the mist that clung to the south side of the rock came a raft poled by two lizard people.

"Come," the disembodied voice invited.

Jarl and Faf boarded the raft, which settled lower with the addition of the combined weight. Jarl moved to the center when he saw ominous ripples in front of the raft. For once he found Faf's great size a comfort.

The strange craft moved silently through the marsh on a watery byway that was not clear to Jarl. On the north side, at least, the wyverns were impregnable to attack from any ordinary source.

"How far does this swamp spread?" Jarl wondered aloud.

"Several days' journey in all directions except to the south," Faf answered.

The lizard beings said nothing, but steadily propelled the raft forward to a destination known only to them.

"What's to the south—besides Fellkeep, I mean?"

"The Southern Sea and the home caves of the wyverns."

"How do you know so much about them? I thought you said they didn't like males."

"They don't, but my mother used to tell me stories about her dragonettehood. In the old days Lythyr and my mother adventured together."

"Have you met this—Lythyr?" Jarl's human tongue was about six inches too short to give the name the correct pronunciation, but he tried.

"Once when I was just out of the egg, she came to visit. She told my mother I would grow into an unusual dragon." Faf chuckled. "She was correct, but my mother took small comfort from the accuracy of her prediction."

"Are we prisoners or something? Why don't those fellows talk to us?"

"They're male wyverns," Faf explained.

"So what? They could still pass the time of day."

"Wyvern society is matriarchal. One of the reasons wyverns so seldom come into contact with humankind and the other denizens of Realm is they deeply disapprove of our system of allowing the males to be the dominant members of our groups."

"Can't they talk?"

"After a fashion, and then only to wyverns in their clan."

Faf smiled at the outraged expression on his companion's face. "It is their way and has been for so long as any can remember. They are as they are."

"That is wisdom indeed, oh fiery one." The words interrupted the conversation.

Faf began to speak to the wyvern who stood on the bank that loomed out of the mist. "This is Jarl—" He stopped in midspeech.

"Yes. Follow me." The green body of the humanoid wyvern glistened emerald. Their guide wore no clothing except a tin belt from which hung various implements.

Jarl was unable to recognize most of them. He would appreciate the sharpness of the small dagger that hung, unsheathed, at the wyvern's side.

This path reminded Jarl of the Old Ones' road in many ways. Could the Old Ones have been wyvern ancestors? Jarl had received no hint of the shape of the revered legendary Old Ones from the conversations in which they were mentioned. There were so many things in Realm of which he was ignorant. So far he had been fortunate in his mentors.

He wondered how long Faf could keep moving with his wound. Perhaps the Old Ones' way had healing properties like their sanctuaries. The wound looked inflamed to human eyes, but how was one to know with a dragon? Faf's deliberate pace was halting, showing signs of the strain he endured. Jarl marveled at the bravery of his friend. For an ardent pacifist, Faf put up quite a fight when he had to. Jarl expected a scholarly dragon to be persistent and intelligent. Now he realized Faf's courage and stoic endurance of pain. The blood of his lineage made a difference.

His father had a son he could be proud to acknowledge when told of this adventure. If they successfully returned after they bearded the Shadowlord in his keep, Jarl amended his thoughts silently.

Their guide passed under the last of the huge vines that snaked across the few trees hardy enough to perch themselves on grassy hummocks and survive.

Jarl trailed after at a distance of several feet. His eyes no longer had to adjust to the change in the light. Thus it was that he saw a shadow pass above the wyvern a split second before the creature realized the danger. Jarl's sword sprang to his hand automatically. It sliced the head from the repulsive mottled green and black attacker, spraying its yellow blood liberally. It writhed on the ground as the three watched from a distance. Finally a last few flops drained it of its remaining pseudolife and it lay still.

Jarl approached, but the wyvern halted him after the first few steps.

"No, Man-one. Even in death such things are dangerous." The wyvern gestured to the withered leaves of some plants that blood from the dead attacker had touched.

"What was it?" Jarl asked. He thought it was a good idea to know the name of anything he killed. He marveled at how proficient he was becoming with the sword.

"We call it Death-that-flies. It is only one of the many reasons for our enmity to the Shadowlord. Such were not seen here until he became Lord of Fellkeep."

The wyvern hurried them through the open spaces and at last turned between two rocks that seemed riven by some giant force. Jarl and Faf passed through the entrance to the wyvern's home cavern.

The smell of sea air and the brightness of daylight gave way to cool darkness as they traveled deeper. The low ceiling made it necessary for Faf to bend his neck to traverse the route. Jarl felt concern for his friend. How much longer could the dragon bear the added strain of a somewhat unnatural position? A draft of warmer air heralded their arrival at a main cavern.

Jarl could see no source of the dim illumination in the vast chamber. Many wyverns passed silently on errands. He received a whispery sensation just out of his comprehension range. The denizens of the cavern were only silent to the human ear. Jarl's mind felt the touch of the wyverns as they greeted their guide. Two wyverns, obviously guards, stopped them when they reached an opening on the other side of the vast hall-like room.

"The queen summoned," their guide explained. The guards moved aside, giving the party leave to proceed.

"Here is the Man-one you requested, Queen Lythyr."

"Welcome."

The word, spoken in deference to their male state, was unnecessary. Jarl sensed the ancient wisdom behind the quiet dignity. A slender silver chain hung around her neck. That and the aura of power that emanated from her were the only signs that differentiated the queen from her subjects. On the chain was a circular crystal disk, rimmed by a thin silver band. Something in the nature of the disk kept Jarl from gazing at it too closely. Yet it was compelling in its beauty, gleaming in the glow that came from the walls of the room itself.

"This one saved my life again," their guide told the ruler.

"So, my daughter, this one rescued you from the korred. I am much indebted to you," she said, turning her huge eyes on Jarl.

"Jarl is Dragon's Pawn," Faf said, as if that explained everything.

"It has been long and long again since Wyrd selected a human as champion. Long-lived though we are, it was in the time of my mother's mother that such happened last."

"Can you help me reach Fellkeep?" Jarl asked. He felt awkward when they talked about him as if he were not present.

"What purpose has the wearer of Wyrd in the lair of Evil?"

"I go to rescue Mirza." Jarl said the words simply, not realizing he had fallen into the diction of the wyvern queen.

"Know you of the evil powers of the Shadowlord? To enter his domain is foolishness indeed unless you are most careful."

"There is great need. Mirza is my . . . friend." Friend wasn't the exact relationship he wanted, but it was the only word that fit. There was no word in his language to express the idea of woman-attracted-to-but-male-has-not-yet-responded.

The queen nodded. "I understand, Man-one. Why ask help from us? Know you that we do not enter into the quarrels among men?"

"This isn't a quarrel exactly," Jarl began.

"Queen Lythyr, the Shadowlord makes war upon us all. His birdthings attacked me," Faf said, sounding almost indignant at the idea. "The actions of the Shadowlord indicate that he considers anyone not on his side to be either his enemy or his prey."

"To our recent sorrow, we know. Six of my warrior maidens died, and still the korred captured Seabreeze. Your saving Seabreeze allowed us warning of the evil planned for our race."

"Does he want to force you to become his allies?" Faf asked.

"Seabreeze discovered that the Shadowlord plans to go far upstream to the source of the mighty river that forms this marsh and block it."

"Then the marsh will dry . . . " Jarl thought aloud.

"Yes, our natural protection would vanish. Our magic workers are too few to guard our borders successfully on four sides. Evil will flow against us from every direction."

"Won't the Keepers aid you?" Faf asked quietly.

"Our calls have gone unanswered. It is many days' journey to the north. The way is long and dangerous after we pass King Caeryl's land."

"His kingdom, too, is in danger of being sucked into the power of the Shadowlord," Faf said gloomily.

"What mean you, fiery one?"

"Prince Leon is now a prisoner in the castle of Fellkeep. Jarl here has a magic talisman he needs to deliver to the prince if he can. If Jarl fails, King Caeryl must become a vassal to the Shadowlord or lose his son forever."

"May I see the talisman?"

Jarl dropped the acorn into the tree-fingered hand of the queen.

"Ah, it is a transportation spell that Relnot intends. His border magic is excellent, but this will not be effective within the confines of Fellkeep. The Shadowlord would be instantly alert to any good magic within the walls of the castle."

"Then it is hopeless?" asked a disappointed Jarl. Did he now have two people to rescue?

"Not worthless if you can get the prince here to Judgment Rock. It is a place of power to the Old Ones. Enough yet remains, to animate a spell for Good."

"Do you make a practice of rescuing the innocent, Man-one?" Seabreeze's question had a tinge of amusement.

"Well, not until lately," Jarl said honestly. "Wyrd is a good influence on me."

"As Dragon's Pawn, will you carry word-of-mouth of our circumstances to the Keeper?" the queen asked as she returned the acorn to Jarl.

Faf focused his half-closed eyes on the queen. "Didn't you and my mother venture into Fellkeep during the years when it was empty?"

"You have not outgrown your habit of questioning, fiery one," the queen began. "So you know the tales of your mother's deeds. Many times we searched where wiser heads would have forbidden us entry had they known. Perhaps it was part of the great design that we should seek knowledge which seemed to have no usefulness save that it was perilous to gather."

"Did you find anything that might help me gain entrance to Fellkeep?" At any other time Jarl would have enjoyed listening to the wyvern's tales, but now the urgency of reaching Mirza took precedence over all else.

"It is many years since the way had travelers. I can draw a map, but whether it would serve you as it served us remains hidden."

"Mother, can you not use your scry stone to look?" Seabreeze suggested hesitantly.

"What you ask may be dangerous, but with proper precautions—perhaps."

"The Man-one aided me . . . " Seabreeze's reminder trailed into silence.

"Very well. I shall try." The queen passed through a low doorway, beckoning for them to follow.

Jarl ducked to enter the small room where Lythyr seated herself on a throne, submerging the disk on her neck in a circular pool. Scenes passed over the surface of the water.

Fafnoddle, unable to enter because of his size, satisfied himself by peering from the doorway.

Lythyr's voice spoke in the minds of her watchers. "Two will search the ancient passages . . . One returns, the other travels onward . . . A door opens . . . Within the room lies . . . "

Jarl! Is that you? I sense the power of the Light. Who is it? Mirza's thought reached them clearly. She was mind-sending through the wyvern's disk.

"She is indeed One of Power," Lythyr whispered. "Answer quickly, Man-one. To hold power within the circle is difficult."

Jarl looked at the blurred image in the submerged disk. *How can I find you within the Keep?* He hurled his thought with all the force he possessed.

Mirza winced. Jarl was becoming adept at mindtalk and didn't realize he need not shout mentally to make himself heard. *I'm within the south tower. The evil here insulates me from Realmgate.*

"Hurry!" hissed Lythyr. "I sense the Shadowlord. He has begun tracing the link!"

Jarl, come quickly! I've found out—

"Is she all right?" Jarl said. "What happened?" He looked into the swirling mists of the disk.

"I do not think your mate suffered any physical damage when the Shadowlord destroyed the link," the queen told Jarl gently. "Sometimes the stone tells more than present things. Within the stone, time is of no consequence. Perhaps my visions were of incidents yet to occur."

"Could you see Mirza?"

"For me, she was shrouded by mist, battling some evil I can only sense.

The danger to her is of the Dark. It is well you hurried to her aid, Man-one. I fear the Shadowlord knows you come. The time grows short."

Lythyr turned from Jarl to Fafnoddle. "Fiery one, you are in great pain. Why did you not tell us of your wound?"

"It is only a small scratch—"

"Do males ever admit the truth? Turn and go to the other side of the main cavern, bender-of-truth," Lythyr said, shaking her head at Faf's folly. She pointed. "There you will find a pool of heal mud, one of the wonders of the ancient dwellers that still serves the Light."

Faf withdrew his head, allowing them to exit the room that held the submerged throne. They watched him stagger to the heal mud. They heard him grumble, "It's a great deal of fuss over nothing." He sank into the mud. Only his head remained on the bank. His great eyelids closed in a blissful expression. "Very comfortable," he managed before falling asleep.

"He rests. That is good," Seabreeze said.

"In a day or two he will recover his full strength," Lythyr added indulgently.

Jarl knew the queen had a soft-scaled place for the child of her old friend. "Poor Faf. He wanted to go with me to Fellkeep."

"He will sleep until healed. When he wakes, he must feed. Then we will see. We must have many fish prepared."

"Not fish, Your Majesty." Jarl explained. "Faf's a vegetarian. He eats mushrooms, fruits, nuts, and berries." Jarl enumerated the things he had seen the dragon eat.

"That simplifies matters. There are many edibles that grow in the marsh if one knows how to look. Your friend may eat his fill when he wakes."

"Will you not share a meal with us, Man-one?" Seabreeze asked.

"I can't wait to begin my trip to Fellkeep." Jarl excused himself.

"Some little time has passed in the outside world. Now the Dark rules. It's better to begin our journey tomorrow," Seabreeze told Jarl.

"Our journey? You can't go with me! It's too dangerous for a—" He searched for a word. If he said female he'd probably get lynched. "Wyvern." He felt a chuckle from his bracelet. Clearly Wyrd understood what was happening although he chose not to play a part in events.

"I, too, can use the disk—even when it's worn by my mother," the wyvern explained. "The two figures she saw were you and I."

"But—"

"The disk sees truth, Man-one. I will be your guide."

"Far be it from me to resist both magic and female logic." Jarl snorted.

The wyverns nodded, accepting his words as a simple statement of fact.

Seabreeze looked at Lythyr, who stood silent during the conversation between her daughter and Jarl. "After dinner, we will study the map my mother has made for us."

"I will start my journey to Fellkeep as soon as I have seen the map," Jarl insisted.

Lythyr's three-fingered hand lightly touched the device at her neck as she looked at Seabreeze. A silent message passed between them.

"It shall be as you say, Man-one. We shall assist you on your way. Tomorrow I shall join you, and I shall be your guide," said Seabreeze.

Womanlike, the wyvern had the last word.

CHAPTER SEVENTEEN

Jarl stood on the bank and watched the raft that had brought him to shore disappear in the evening mists over the wyverns' swamp. Somehow the darkness of night seemed deeper here on the bank so near to Fellkeep. Jarl walked carefully, looking for the large tree that the wyverns had told him about. It would give him some protection from the Death-that-flies and the other weird creatures that infested the area the Shadowlord controlled. Jarl's confidence in Wyrd's powers had amused the wyverns, but Jarl felt he couldn't wait. Tomorrow was the third day of the three granted to King Caeryl. Jarl felt he needed to get to Fellkeep and find the prince as soon as possible. The wyverns had told him where he would find an entrance, and he expected to be there long before Seabreeze caught up to him.

Looming ahead of him, he saw the huge tree, covered with moss that almost touched the ground. It made a darker blot in the darkness that seemed to clutch him with palpable fingers. Jarl took a deep breath and entered the space between the roots. Inside, the darkness was less dense. Clearly the appearance of the tree was a clever disguise meant to ward off evil. There the wyverns could rest safely right under the nose of the Shadowlord—if he had a nose, Jarl thought grimly.

Everything depended on what he could achieve the next day. He was honor bound to try to rescue Prince Leon. As soon as he delivered the boy to the wyverns for transportation to Judgment Rock, he would try to rescue Mirza. No, he amended to himself. I *will* rescue Mirza.

Jarl reached into his pocket and brought out the fire-stone the wyverns had given him. It looked like an ordinary piece of coal to Jarl. If the wyverns said it would start a fire at his command, he was ready to believe it. Too much evidence had piled up to prove magic existed here on Realm. At home, placing an unlit piece of common coal upon the ground and telling it to light mentally would have earned Jarl free room and board at the local funny farm. Here, the coal lit a cheery blaze out of nothing.

Jarl sat and absentmindedly rubbed Wyrd. He felt a little lonesome. The bracelet sent no sense of communication into Jarl's mind. It was as if the bracelet were exactly what it pretended to be: an odd piece of jewelry. Jarl wondered if Wyrd feared the Shadowlord. Or could it be that the dragon was merely saving his vast powers for the rescue attempt the next morning? Jarl had almost dozed off when he saw the hanging moss at the edge of the re-created clearing begin to move.

His hand clutched his sword. Had Seabreeze changed her mind? Just like a woman. She had promised to join him later. How late was later to a wyvern? Jarl had the impression she had stayed to finish off some magical mumbo jumbo, wyvern style. He knew it was nowhere near morning. Wyrd remained relaxed on Jarl's wrist, so he knew whoever came was a friend. He sat, alert, waiting.

A human hand brushed the hanging moss aside. A dark-haired man entered the open space. He wore a black belt over a dark outfit. His clothing marked him as a martial arts master of some kind.

The stranger smiled at Jarl and gestured to the small fire. "May I join you?" he asked.

Jarl glanced at his bracelet. Wyrd had not tightened; therefore, this man, whoever he was, must be a friend. "All right."

"I suppose you wonder what a decent human being is doing so close to Fellkeep," the stranger began conversationally.

"And?" Jarl replied.

"Sent here by some mutual acquaintances, you might say," replied the stranger.

"Mutual acquaintances?" Jarl repeated. "Who?"

"One of them is a little old lady," the stranger began.

"Say no more." Jarl smiled. "Is she as enigmatic with you as she is with me?"

"I don't know if I'd choose that word exactly. Since most of what she says must be nonsense, you could say she didn't come across as much of an explainer."

"Yeah. I know just how you feel," Jarl said, accepting the man without reservation for the first time.

The man covered his mouth to hide a yawn. "If you don't mind, tomorrow is time enough to talk. Let's catch a little shut-eye, okay?"

Jarl noticed the use of the term shut-eye. "You're from Earth, too, aren't you?"

The man nodded. "Got it in one," he murmured, settling down on the other side of the small blaze.

Jarl smiled to himself. Well, he thought silently, even if Wyrd is strangely silently tonight, I've still got friends pulling for me. A martial arts expert would make a fine ally, if he would join Jarl. Why else would the old wise woman send him if not to help? Cheered, Jarl fell asleep.

A shadow moving across the dappled sunlight woke Jarl from his sleep. Jarl started to stand and then realized he was trussed like a Thanksgiving turkey. His hands were tied behind him. The stranger was minus his black belt, so Jarl knew what restrained him. "Traitor," he hissed, sounding more like Wyrd than he knew.

"No, not traitor," the man said. "Ally."

"Is that how a friend behaves on Realm?" Jarl pulled at his bonds futilely.

"If I could figure out how anything in this damn place works, I wouldn't be here. I am the Shadowlord's enemy, not yours."

"So you tie me up so near his keep that he could send a little old lady to drag me in and succeed?" Jarl's lips thinned mockingly.

"Can't you just take my word?" The question seemed anguished.

"Seeing is believing. Take off these bonds if you're so friendly, and then I'll believe you."

"It's necessary that you stay tied for a while. You'll work your way free eventually."

"Liar." Jarl spat the word angrily.

"I can prove myself the Shadowlord's enemy," the stranger said sadly. He reached up with his gloved hand and pulled the rubber mask from his face.

Jarl stared in horror. The warty green visage that stared at him contained human eyes, but the dripping fluid that seeped from the creature's face radiated a sickening green glow.

"The Shadowlord did this to me. I was to be the hero and rescue this crazy place from the Shadowlord. I brought modern weapons and all my tactical skills to the battle."

"Then why did they need me? How could you lose?" Jarl asked, trying to settle his stomach by looking into the creature's eyes and ignoring the horror of his face.

"I lost because I can't believe in magic. The Shadowlord asked me to join him. I still think I'd have to be nuts to start taking orders from some charlatan in a hooded robe. He looks like some monk out of the Middle Ages. He must have some mental powers, but he can't be a magician because there aren't any such things!" He pounded his clenched fist into his other hand.

"How can you doubt that magic works here? There are too many strange events for logic to explain away. I didn't believe at first myself, but after meeting dragons, and a unicorn, and the old witch—" Jarl shook his head. "I know I sound crazy, but magic does exist, and on Realm magic works."

"I didn't believe in magic when I came and I still don't."

"Then how do you explain what has happened to you?"

"It's some kind of germ warfare. It must be."

Jarl felt sorry for the man turned creature. Not being able to accept the reality of Realm made him even more vulnerable to the powers of magic. The poor guy had never had a chance. Jarl thought of the many times magic—or magical beings—had saved him.

The man took a second mask out of his small pack. Jarl watched as the creature pulled it on. He removed a bracelet in the shape of a dragon from the pack and put it on his arm. "Now I'm ready," he said grimly.

"Ready for what? Halloween? Let me go and we can team up. I have to enter the keep and free—"

"No, don't tell me. It's better if I don't know. In case the Shadowlord tries to pick my brain, there won't be any information there that will help him."

"Wait!" Jarl called softly. "Where are you going? What are you going to do?"

"I'm going to leave you tied, for starters, and then, like the hero I'm pretending to be, I'm going to keep an appointment."

"An appointment?" Jarl mentally cursed his tendency to repeat parts of a statement when he didn't understand. He thought he sounded like an idiot when he did it.

"The Dragon's Pawn must die," the creature said calmly. "My condition is not correctable—or so the old woman says. Once the green grue gets over your head, nobody can do anything. I choose not to live my life as a mutant or whatever the Shadowlord has made me into with his strange drugs and rays.

"So the Dragon's Pawn shall die in battle, taking as many of the enemy with him as he can." The Jarl mask smiled down at the tied man. "Wish me luck, buddy. Once the Shadowlord thinks you're gone, you should have an easy time thwarting him." With a wave of his hand, the Jarl impostor disappeared through the moss.

Jarl lay on the ground, struggling silently with his bonds. In the distance he heard the noise of battle, but he couldn't get free. *Wyrd!* Jarl thought. *Why don't you help me?*

Wyrd gripped his arm tightly but made no reply.

"You must know all about that poor guy. I don't even know his name," Jarl muttered through clenched teeth.

Wyrd remained inanimate.

"I trusted you! What's this lesson supposed to teach me? Don't even trust your allies on Realm?"

The sounds of battle stopped abruptly.

Jarl sighed. "That's it. Scratch one human."

The tree moss swayed as a body forced itself into the open space underneath the moss.

"What the—"

"I told you I would be your guide, Man-one," Seabreeze said. "I mourn our loss."

"Our loss? Yeah, our loss. My loss, you mean. Why didn't you help that poor guy?"

"Because we wyverns are magical creatures—and he did not believe in magic. Many allies he had if he could only believe in our powers. He destroyed himself by refusing the aid of the magical beings that were his friends," she concluded sadly as she untied Jarl.

"Now we go to rescue our friends." She folded the black belt and offered it to Jarl. "Perhaps you would like this," she added as she turned and left the shelter of the tree, knowing Jarl would follow.

Jarl didn't want to remember the trip to Fellkeep. The wyvern quickly deserted solid ground for more marsh. Jarl felt safer within walls than he did passing through the marsh on foot or on the wyvern's craft. That morning he saw more ripples than before. He watched the giant black and gold reptiles slide like animated branches from half-sunk tree limbs. He prudently kept his hand on his sword the whole time because of their water coming and going. He wasn't certain if the adders were so active because it was breakfast time, the end of their night's hunting, or because his giant companion had intimidated them the previous day. He knew that feeling the hard rock of the shore under his feet was a distinct relief.

Brush and boulders screened the opening to the passages. Only someone looking for the entrance and knowing its probable location could find it. Jarl's skin tingled as they passed within the confines of the castle.

"It's raw power," Seabreeze said. "The Shadowlord draws it from other worlds regardless of what he does to the energy balance. It may well be that some sun is being depleted to feed his insatiable machines. If the gate he forged here collapses, my people and our home will disappear in a burst of ravening power that may well split this world. Do you now see why my kind shun men?"

"All men are not like the Shadowlord," Jarl protested.

"Where you come from all men are peaceable and rational?" The wyvern cast him a sly look.

Jarl did the best he could without actually lying. He ignored the question.

"Follow," she said. "Past this point, only necessary talking lest we stir trouble best left alone."

"Agreed," Jarl answered. He acted as yes-man for the wyvern, and he didn't like the idea much. It didn't fit his picture of a hero.

"Indeed," she added, having the last word as usual. "When one enters the mouth of the mercat, one does not prod its tongue."

Their way led forward into the bowels of the keep. The walls showed no breakages once past the entrance. The dry walls glowed with the form of light Jarl recognized as a hallmark of the Old Ones' construction. A barrier of stone blocked their path. He stopped, but Seabreeze kept walking. She faded into the barrier and disappeared.

Jarl gulped and followed. Anything a wyvern could do, he could do, too. After a cool sensation, the darkness was total.

"Ssss," Seabreeze whispered her caution as she opened the pouch on her belt and took out what seemed to be a live coal. She dropped it on the unlit torch she carried. It responded with a warming light. Again she let the way.

Now the air cooled. The light flickered, illuminating half-visible scratches on the wall a good six feet from the floor. Small scurrying noises told them they were not alone in the passages. Seabreeze never faltered as she led them past openings that were the beginnings of other corridors. The torch glow was strong. Against the wall Jarl saw a misshapen skull. Tiny scurriers had carried off the smaller bones of the creature years ago. The larger bones remained as mute witness to one adventurer who had entered and found death.

Jarl and Seabreeze ascended a series of steps. He was certain the curved walls meant they were within the tower stones themselves, but he saw no signs of any openings. Were there no windows in Fellkeep? Were they cleverly hidden under the treads of the stairs they climbed?

"We are near the one you seek." A three-fingered hand pointed ahead.

"Is there an entrance marked on the map?"

"There are many ways to tower rooms from this passage. We must use care that we do not enter a place where Evil awaits. It is possible that Relnot tuned the acorn you bear to the presence of the prince. If this is so, we can tell when we are near him." The whisper of the wyvern was as soft as her name.

Jarl took the acorn from his pocket. Seabreeze touched it briefly and nodded. He felt a flicker of life within the magician's token.

"I sense the Powers of the Dark within."

Within where? Jarl thought. He could see no differences in the stones which formed the walls of the passage way.

"I use the deep sight of my people. To me, there are doorways. We have passed many such, but their contents were not meant for us. Now I sense a young manling who may be the one you promised to aid."

Jarl willingly gave the acorn into her hand. When she raised it to the wall and traced a path against the stones, it began to glow greenly.

"The one you seek is within," Seabreeze said with certainty. She traced patterns that glimmered in the air. A door-shaped crack appeared in the stone. Jarl bent his head and passed into the room.

A flaxen-haired boy sat on a rough cot pushed against a bleak wall. His eyes rounded in wonder as Jarl beckoned to him. The boy's head raised proudly at Jarl's gesture. His resemblance to King Caeryl was plain.

"Who are you?" he asked with a great deal of dignity for so young a person.

"A friend. Your father wants you to come with me." Jarl smiled as the prince bounced off the cot.

The prince didn't look behind him as he slipped easily through the narrow door. "Hello," he said courteously to the wyvern. Behind them the door closed silently.

"So, young Man-one, it may be that you are a worthy successor to your father." She handed him the acorn. "This is from Relnot. Used properly, it will take you home. It may not be safe to use it yet."

"Isn't my father all right?" the boy asked anxiously.

"I did not mean to alarm you. I spoke of future happenings. You are brave for so small a human."

"I'm as tall as you are. I'm quite normal for my age," Prince Leon assured her seriously.

"Come, then, Evil-slayer. We have no time to waste," Seabreeze told the boy.

"Wait!" Jarl hissed, sounding like Faf. "What about Mirza? I won't leave without her."

"My sight tells me the young one and I are to leave. Before nightfall, he will be at the Rock of Judgment. It will amplify Relnot's spell and carry the prince home. You must continue your quest alone." With these words, she handed Jarl the almost consumed torch. "Good-bye, Man-one." From her pouch she took a silver circlet that glowed when she placed it on her head. She motioned to the boy; they descended the stairs.

CHAPTER EIGHTEEN

Jarl deplored the rapidity of her exit. She hadn't even told him if the trick for finding the doors would work with Wyrd as the activator. A slight tightening on his arm reassured him.

Hurry, Wyrd's thoughts echoed in Jarl's mind. *There still lurk in these secret ways creatures it would be well not to meet.*

Agreed, Jarl answered mentally. *And now that Leon is on his way to safety, there's always the possibility that someone will check and find he's missing.* Adrenaline flowed through Jarl. He was preternaturally alert. He and Wyrd were on their own again.

Jarl stepped upward, stair by stair, until Wyrd signaled the place of Mirza's confinement. Jarl held his arm next to the wall and somehow he knew the correct movements to make with the bracelet. The pattern he traced was not exactly like the wyvern's, but it produced the same result. The solid wall shifted silently. Jarl mentally applauded the architects of the Old Ones. They certainly knew how to build. Not for the first time Jarl considered what might have happened to so talented a race. They had mastered everything they set their abilities to do. What would cause such a race to disappear from Realm?

The shaft of bright light that lit the stones before him showed the layer of dust that had accumulated since anyone had opened the door. Jarl cautiously stepped into the light, and Mirza almost knocked him down, running into his arms.

"Jarl!" she cried.

Despite the danger of their position, Jarl was gratified by the exuberant reception he received. Could Mirza have grown more beautiful during their separation? Their long-delayed embrace was everything to Jarl imagined—and more. Facing the Shadowlord would be a small price to pay to regain Mirza's company. He held her tightly for long seconds, wishing he never had to release her.

Mirza recovered her composure too rapidly to suit Jarl. She shook her head and gently pushed herself away from him. "Do you know a way out?"

"Yes. It's the same way I got in." Jarl grinned. Wyrd tightened on his arm. "Come," Jarl urged, drawing Mirza to the narrow opening.

"No!" a cool voice said from behind them as the opening disappeared in a puff of sulfurous black smoke.

It's the Shadowlord, Mirza thought to Jarl before they turned to face their enemy together.

"How foolishly brave you've been, Dragon's Pawn." Although the setting sun lit the room, a curious haziness existed under the hood where the face of the Shadowlord should have been.

Mirza and Jarl stood together before the naked evil of the wizard.

"I thought you were dead—more punishment for those demons who reported you killed. I also did not know that a human could master the power of the talisman so quickly." He peered at their clasped hands. "Or can it be that you gallantly came to the rescue of the fair damsel without mastery of your only weapon?"

"I have my weapon—" Jarl started to reply.

"Silence! In Fellkeep there is little that I would use against you that so common a weapon as a sword could destroy."

Jarl looked at it. Common was the last thing he would say about it, but to his surprise it no longer glistened with gems. A plain metal guard protruded from its sheath. No wonder his enemy made light of it! "Perhaps," he said quietly.

"You have caused me considerable annoyance. The prince escaped because of your meddling. I am not yet ready to attack Relnot, so the kingdom will remain independent—for now."

"Good," Jarl said, certain another of Wyrd's scales had turned to gold.

"I will remove those puny border wards when I am ready. You are quite resourceful for a mortal. Because of your potential, I will make you a generous offer."

Jarl said nothing. Mirza clasped his hand wordlessly.

"Aiding the enemy, my dear? In the fullness of time, you, too, will join me."

The remarks rang in Jarl's ears. The words were freighted with menace. He knew Mirza would never willingly aid Evil.

The Shadowlord turned slightly to focus on Jarl. "I offer you the opportunity to join me. I will give you the rulership of Earth."

"What's the catch?" Jarl asked. Perhaps this offer would give him a clue to the Shadowlord's plan.

"There would be certain little tasks given to you—and of course, some minor contributions to our cause."

"Minor! He means letting earthlings become slaves!" Mirza burst in hotly.

The Shadowlord ignored her words. "What is your answer—Pawn?" Jarl's title sounded like an insult coming from the mouth of the wizard.

Jarl wanted to return to Earth, but now that he heard the offer, he knew rather than take it, he would remain in exile forever. Jarl gave his answer deliberately. "No."

"They named you well. You are a pawn of the Keepers in a vast game you do not understand. Why should you care for the citizens of alternate earths? If you join my cause—you can protect the majority of the citizens on your world. Isn't Earth one of those places with democracy? Isn't the majority most important?"

The insidious logic of the Shadowlord washed over Jarl. In a strange way, the Shadowlord was right. By joining, Jarl could partially mitigate the evil magic of the empire the wizard would create. Jarl thought about the denizens of Realm. These creatures—no—these people were real. Some of them were his friends. He could not allow them to perish without trying to save them. Wyrd must be a lot more powerful than he thought for the wizard to offer power as he had.

"No," Jarl repeated.

"Stubborn, too? Even the powers of the Light must use flawed tools." The Shadowlord laughed. "I will give you until tomorrow to reconsider. If I do not like your final choice, both you and your companion shall know the force of my wrath." The wizard delivered this threat in pleasant tones that underscored his power.

Jarl welcomed a respite. "I will reconsider your offer only if you leave Mirza with me."

"So bold? You are a sparrow bargaining with a hawk, but I will grant

your request. Those who follow me get all they desire—within reason."
The Shadowlord glided close to Mirza. "Perhaps you will use your charm
to encourage him to make a wise decision. You might wish to offer yourself
as an object lesson on the folly of noncompliance."

Jarl watched, astounded, as Mirza turned pale. The Shadowlord
laughed wickedly. Then he literally winked out as a puff of air extin-
guishes a candle flame. Nothing of him remained in the room except a faint
scent of brimstone that a breeze from the tower window soon dissipated.

"Mirza, are you all right?" Her pallor concerned Jarl. What hold did the
Dark have over her? Or was it just his imagination? Most of the women he
knew would have had a screaming fit after a scene with a person like the
Shadowlord. They needed to escape. Jarl supposed it was a forlorn hope,
but he walked over to where the door to freedom had so lately closed. He
raised his bracelet. Jarl waited for the surge of knowledge that would tell
him how to move his arm to activate the mechanism—or magic—that
would open the door for the second time that day. Nothing happened!

Mirza smiled ruefully at him. "Did you actually think our enemy is so
inexperienced as to leave a way open to our powers? If that were so, I
would have returned to you long since."

"Then you've made no progress in discovering a way to escape?"

"I've tried every kind of magic I ever learned, but all of my spells failed.
I can't even change my shape to fly away. My best efforts were the
moments of mental contact with you."

"So at least one thing does work." Jarl pondered. "What happened to
the black dragon that brought you here?"

"You mean Ebony?"

"Ah, you know his name?"

"Not his—her," Mirza corrected.

"So Ebony is a female dragon . . . " Jarl imagined a scenario in which Faf
recovered, wooed the dragon, and managed an airlift out of Fellkeep. He
shook his head. He must be getting desperate. A scenario like the one he
envisioned wouldn't even make a good plot for a grade-Z movie.

"She is ensorcelled by the silver chain about her neck. So long as she
wears it she is bound to do the bidding of the wizard. She has no choice in
what she does."

"Do you talk to her mentally?"

"Oh, yes. Sometimes she flies to that tower over there." Mirza drew Jarl
to the one window in the tower room. Looking out, he could see another

tower, twin to the one they were in, across the paved courtyard many feet below. He gazed down with interest. From this height it was difficult to make out details, but groups of nasty-looking creatures passed through the courtyard on various errands. Some of them reminded him of nightmares he'd had as a child. The others were worse.

"They are truly horrible, are they not, poor creatures."

"You pity them when they propose the destruction of your world?"

"Of course I do. Recruited from many places, dependent on the powers of the Dark for their daily food. No chance to return to their own worlds, they are worthy, but many are mere shells, kept alive only by black magic. Others found themselves displaced from their homes in Realm and elsewhere."

"Well, you're more charitable than I am." Jarl slipped an arm around Mirza's shoulders to take the sting from his words. "I only want to find a way to get us out of here. Does your dragon friend fly up here to talk to you?"

"She perches on the top of that tower and then we mindtalk."

"Doesn't anyone have the power to hear your conversations?"

"Mindlink is rather rare between species. Sometimes there is an affinity between beings. I have such a one with Ebony. Perhaps it's because I have flown as a dragon."

Jarl's eyebrows shot up.

"Only when the moon is full," Mirza teased.

Somehow her effort at humor relaxed Jarl. "Can you call her now?"

"Perhaps."

"Well, call!"

"Why?"

"Trust a woman," Jarl muttered. "Look, Mirza, the only avenue we have open is your telepathic power. Wyrd refuses to respond to me. Perhaps we can use the dragon as a messenger."

"Oh. And have you acquired an army that will come at your call?"

"Not exactly, but I may just have a dragon or two up my sleeve. So please call!"

"Very well," Mirza replied, a puzzled look on her face.

Jarl couldn't hear a thing. "Are you trying?" he asked.

"Yes," she snapped. "How can I carry on a conversation if you keep interrupting?"

"You're talking to the dragon now?" Jarl cast an injured look at his bracelet. Wyrd lay inert on his wrist. Why wasn't he helping? Was the bracelet saving power until they really needed it? Or was the Shadowlord's magic stronger?

Jarl started thinking—hard. How was he going to free the black dragon from the silver bind chain? He looked out the window. Silhouetted against the gray dusk of the evening was the twin tower. As he watched, a great shadow glided in and perched on it. The whole scene looked like a cutout from a child's Halloween card. Far in the background the globe of the moon inched over the horizon. The view was oddly beautiful, if menacing. Far below, shrieks, bellows, and some unclassifiable noises, best left unidentified, drifted upward to the tower room.

"Feeding time at the zoo," Jarl said, wondering if he and Mirza would get a meal. He decided they would not be able to eat it for fear of drugs—or something worse.

Mirza gave him an inquiring glance, but he shook his head, indicating he had not really meant the comment for her ears.

"Jarl, Ebony is willing to help—if she can. She will try to fly a message, but if the Shadowlord finds out, he may kill her." Mirza frowned, worried about her new friend.

Jarl eyed the top of the window. It was tall. A plan began to form in his mind. "Ask your friend to fly over and sit on this tower. Then I want her to lower her neck through the window." Jarl hoped Ebony's neck was as long as Faf's.

Across the courtyard, Ebony opened her wings. An updraft floated her from the tower. She guided herself to where Mirza and Jarl waited.

"Is there always an updraft near these tall towers?"

Mirza nodded.

"Well, that explains why so many of the old castles had towers. They're really takeoff sites for dragons."

"Everybody knows that." Mirza snorted, reminding him of the brown mare's shape she liked to wear.

"On Realm, maybe. On Earth, I thought towers were used for defense."

The winged form settled over them, blocking out the moonlight. Shortly, a huge nose and one plate-sized eye appeared outside the window.

"Ebony wants to know what you expect her to do."

"Wait until I climb on the sill. I need to get closer to the chain on her neck." Jarl put his hand on the side of the opening, jumped up, and landed, surefooted.

Mirza gasped. A slight miscalculation and he would have fallen into the courtyard. She watched as he looked at the silver links that were clasped around the neck of the dragon, much as a pretty girl might wear a necklace. The silver was beautiful against the iridescent black scales.

"May I touch it?" Jarl asked. Without his association with Fafnoddle, voluntarily approaching anything with a mouth of teeth the size of the dragon's would have been the last activity on his list of things to do.

Yes, Ebony replied mentally, moving her neck closer to ease Jarl's exploration. In the stress of the moment none of them realized the oddity of Jarl's being able to hear the dragon speak.

"There are no breaks in any of the links. I can't find a single weak spot."

"Naturally not. It was forged by magic power," Mirza reminded him.

"The chain's not tight. Perhaps I can cut it off with my sword—if it's retained any of its magic with its change in outward appearance." Jarl drew the sword, held the chain as far as possible from the dragon's body, and brought the sharp edge down directly on the metal.

Ebony's eyes were closed, but she bravely held steady. At the moment of impact, a high keening sound assaulted their ears.

Mirza put her hands over hers.

Jarl gripped the window's edge tightly as vertigo assailed him.

Ebony herself blinked her watering eyes.

"I'm sorry," Jarl apologized.

Do not be sad. At least you tried to release me. The dragon's tones were grave and showed her resignation to her fate.

"I'm not ready to quit yet. I haven't tried Wyrd."

"Do you think it's safe to activate Wyrd again while we are here in the citadel of the Shadowlord?" Mirza touched the bracelet with gentle fingertips.

"If that noise didn't bring a guard, probably nothing will. We'll never know till we've tried." Jarl looked at Wyrd. He received no sign that the circled dragon was anything more than an unusual piece of jewelry. Jarl held the bracelet close to the chain, commanding with all his mental force, *BREAK!* A bolt of energy sparked across the gap, and the chain disappeared.

"Free at last," the dragon hissed happily.

"Wyrd broke the spell," Mirza said, smiling.

"Thanks, Wyrd," Jarl told his bracelet. He received no reply, but Jarl noticed another scale had turned to gold.

"I am yours to command, my lady," Ebony said to Mirza.

"Then listen to Jarl's plan," Mirza urged, certain he would have one.

"I'd like you to fly to Judgment Rock in Wyvern Marsh. Do you know where that is?"

"It is a landmark fliers know well, the only bare area in the marsh."

Jarl almost sighed with relief. He hadn't the slightest idea of how to direct anyone to find the rock. Perhaps their luck had turned. "Someone will communicate with you if you land there. Ask them to send Faf back here with you."

"What will this—Faf—do?" the dragon asked.

"Faf is a dragon like you. He has carried me in the past. If you can carry Mirza on your back, he can carry me. We can mount from this window."

"Do you mean Fafnir? He's too old," Mirza said.

"No, his son, Fafnoddle."

"What changed him? I haven't seen him for years, but he was always a peaceful creature."

"Some birdthings burned him in a fight."

Mirza looked surprised at the news but said, "Perhaps he'll be unable to carry you."

"If he can't, Ebony will take you to safety at least. I'll wait here alone. I'll still have my sword, and perhaps if things get bad enough, Wyrd will help me." Jarl forced a smile to his face, trying to cheer Mirza.

"I won't leave without you."

"Don't be stubborn. It's not ladylike," Jarl teased. "Anyway, I bet you'll find a ready Faf—wounds healed or not. You'll see."

"I shall fly to the rock. Tomorrow, as the sun's rising, we will come," Ebony promised.

"We'll be waiting," Jarl said.

"Be careful. May the Light protect you," Mirza wished. The giant head disappeared from the window. Jarl and Mirza watched as the saurian sailed away, a black silhouette of hope against the waxing light of the full moon.

Jarl sat on the crude cot with Mirza nestled close to him. No words were needed between them. The kindly eye of the night looked down; Jarl was amply rewarded for his heroism.

CHAPTER NINETEEN

The long night paled in the east. The evil inhabitants of Fellkeep slept while two mighty dragons flew above. When Ebony landed on Mirza's tower, Faf did the same on the other.

Seeing the inquiring eye of Ebony at the window, Jarl woke Mirza. "It's time to go," he said softly.

"I won't leave—"

"Yes, you will, and so will I. Faf's across the courtyard on the other tower. There's no time to waste. So far our luck has been phenomenal. Let's get moving before our cowled friend reappears."

Jarl helped Mirza onto the window ledge. The wyvern queen must have used her magic disk to see the need for a safety harness. The harness and a rope were attached to Ebony. It was the work of moments to secure Mirza to the rope the dragons held. Ebony slowly drew her to the tower top.

As soon as Ebony took off, flying slowly to the north, Faf arrived. His great head snaked down to the window.

"Hurry, Jarl! We have little time. The spell thins."

"What spell?" Jarl asked as he climbed the rope Faf held for him.

"The one Wyrd and the wyverns have woven for you two this night. It was some kind of false-seeming. The Shadowlord thinks Ebony still wears her collar and that you two are sound asleep." Faf checked Jarl's readiness, held out his wings to receive an updraft, and sailed into the relative safety of the sky.

Faf flew as well as he ever had. The two dragons arrowed north for the border of King Caeryl's land. Once past that magic line of power, they would be safe. The dragons seemed tireless. They soured on the air currents like hawks, and like hawks they watched. Not for prey, but for the enemies they knew searched for them.

As they traveled, Mirza and Jarl spoke to each other telepathically.

Mirza, can you tell what's happening behind us?

You should link with Wyrd to get that information.

Won't it distract him if he's doing something? Faf said the wyverns and Wyrd cast a spell to help us escape.

Don't concentrate hard. Merely look at Wyrd and allow your mind to drift. Perhaps you can become an onlooker because of your proximity to him. It shouldn't disturb him to have you see his handiwork.

I don't understand his ability to cast spells with the wyverns. I get the impression they didn't think much of humankind and that they wanted to remain neutral.

The Shadowlord provoked them. He would not leave anyone alone. He boasted of the things he's accomplished, like his isolating them from contact with those at Realmgate. Then there's his plan to dry up the wyverns' ancestral marsh before attacking them. He wants to be the only remaining entity with magic powers of any consequence. The wyverns are extremely powerful if the ancient tales are true, Mirza told Jarl.

Why do they accept Wyrd so easily?

In the legends of the time when Wyrd appeared here, the first wearer of the bracelet was a wyvern.

Oh, so wyvern males do get to be heroic? Jarl said before he thought.

The Dragon's Pawn was a female priestess-warrior, Mirza told him with an undertone of feminine satisfaction she did not try to hide.

Does that legend say anything more about Wyrd?

A fragment of an old tale says Wyrd was once mighty, but he misused his powers and punishment followed.

What did he do?

We have lost that part of the story. It may be somewhere in the Dragon Chronicles in the library at Realmgate, but I've never seen it. Mirza said.

Well, I suppose it's not important—except to Wyrd—after all this time.

Jarl's curiosity led him to focus on Wyrd and try to day-dream. Gradually the blowing winds and the fast-moving earth below him faded from his consciousness. There was a lack of light and a sense of the Dark. He felt raw emotions. Anger. Dread.

At Fellkeep the Shadowlord was trying to remedy their escape. Fearful workers hurried to loose the birdthings. A vision of the tower room would have shown a place bare of everything. It looked as if a giant fist had obliterated all the material articles in the room, which still echoed with the anger of the sorcerer. The Shadowlord didn't like being thwarted. He believed the magical seeming that had been insinuated, ever so carefully, into the tower room during the long night while Jarl and Mirza awaited the return of the dragons.

Jarl felt a sense of satisfaction that could only have come from the wyvern Queen Lythyr

Yes, echoed in Jarl's mind. *Now we prepare to face the wrath of the Shadowlord.* Abruptly Jarl was high in the sunlit air, flying north to escape the Shadowlord's power.

Jarl told Mirza what he had experienced. *I hope we haven't been the cause of the Shadowlord's attacking the wyverns.*

Remember he was already using his dark powers to plan their destruction, Mirza sent. *His agents captured Seabreeze. If you had not rescued her, she might well be in his power now. That outweighs any inconvenience we caused.*

You may be right. At any rate, Queen Lythyr is enjoying her retaliation against the Shadowlord.

She is surprisingly bloodthirsty. Faf added his thought to the conversation.

How so? Jarl asked.

I was there to see the beginning of the preparations her people are making to defend themselves, and they plan some extremely violent surprises. If the Shadowlord thinks he will have an easy conquest because the wyverns have always been peaceful, he has made a major error in judgment. Faf chuckled.

What's so funny?

The marsh holds many of Realm's nastier creatures. When Evil enters that marsh, it may well find itself in the position of the fisherman who sits on one of his own lures.

Are you tired? Jarl asked, remembering Faf's wound.

No, but I'm worried about Ebony, Faf answered. *She's never carried anything so far before.*

What about when she stole Mirza?

Oh, the Shadowlord used some machine to transport her to Fellkeep instantly. They were only airborne for a few minutes.

How did you find out about that?

You don't think you and Mirza are the only ones who can talk together mind to mind, do you?

Oh, Jarl said rather lamely, chagrined to find he hadn't thought of a telepathic link between the two dragons.

Actually, all dragons prefer to mindspeak. We sometimes speak aloud for humans because it disturbs most of you to converse dragon-fashion. You're a refreshing change from the average human.

Perhaps Wyrd had something to do with my acceptance. I always thought of myself as quite ordinary. When you talk to a bracelet—and it answers—well, let's say it's an experience that changes one's way of thinking.

You've done nobly, Faf complimented. *Coming from a world which has largely rejected magic for technology . . .*

Jarl got the feeling that Faf stopped talking to save his pride. Perhaps science was wrong in refusing to believe in magic. He couldn't imagine Earth if magic became a normal occurrence. Take telepathy . . . what if people could know what their friends actually thought of them?

Wyrd tightened around Jarl's wrist. *Faf, something has disturbed Wyrd. Do you see any danger?*

The dragon obligingly turned his head to look around. *Your talisman is correct. Those birdthings that kill with light beams trail us.*

Relnot's border spell should protect us, Mirza said.

Will you have to set us down to fight or can we beat them to the border? Jarl twisted in his harness. The birdthings were gaining.

Fight? With what? You must save Wyrd for special occasions, but I think my magic can help us now.

Faf clearly held mindspeech with Ebony, who let Mirza tune in to the conversation. Mirza looked at Jarl.

What do you suggest I do? she asked.

How am I supposed to know? I'm not sure what your powers are. Can you turn birdthings into butterflies?

Mirza shook her head. *No. Because they are Darkforged, I couldn't. Have you another suggestion?*

Could you turn them into jet planes? Jarl asked, forgetting Mirza wouldn't know what a jet was.

What's a jet plane? she asked.

Never mind. I don't have time to explain. Where are they now? Jarl struggled to turn. It was difficult because Faf and Ebony were no longer gliding, but actively flying, which created a fierce wind.

Behind us and closing in, Faf thought grimly.

Can you conjure a—a large storm close behind us? One with plenty of lightning bolts. Jarl suggested to Mirza.

Jarl could see Mirza's lips moving. Her hand sketched a strange pattern that etched a design on the wind. Behind them, thunder boomed. White fluffy clouds clumped together, turned gray, darkened, and hung, green-black, in the air. Faf and Ebony circled so Mirza could complete her spell as they watched.

That's some storm, Jarl commented admiringly.

Storm magic is one thing I'm not very good at. I did conjure a brief shower once, but I had a headache for days afterward. I'm impressed, Faf told Mirza.

They heard the roar of the wind behind them. The strange storm advanced on the attacking birds. The birdthings did not emerge from the clouds that shrouded them.

"That did it!" Jarl shouted into the wind.

I hope so. I took a great deal of energy. How far is it to the border of the kingdom? Mirza asked, closing her eyes.

Only a few minutes flying time, Faf answered.

That's good. Carrying me is tiring for Ebony.

Yes, but I'm using every thermal I find to help me, and I will take you as far as necessary. The quiet thought entered the minds of Faf, Mirza, and Jarl.

Soon we cross Relnot's magic protection spell. Then we can rest, Faf told her.

We should travel directly to the castle. Mirza isn't in shape for camping out overnight, Jarl said.

Mirza turned a frightened face toward him. *Why do you say that? Have I not been with you before?*

I meant being a prisoner and all, it would be nice to be coddled a bit. Had he offended her? He only wanted her to be comfortable. Her face seemed so white. Perhaps she only seemed frail in comparison to the huge dragon who carried her.

Thank you, she told him softly. *It will be good to be clean and to sleep in a warm bed.*

We can fly the added distance easily, Ebony and Faf assured her.

Are you certain, Faf? Jarl asked. *Those burns you had were bad ones.*

That wyvern mud bath cured me completely. When I awoke, I found that you had left without me. That disturbed me.

I couldn't wait. I only had three days. Prince Leon needed rescuing and I wanted Mirza out of there. We reached them through some almost forgotten tunnels that the Old Ones made. The wyverns knew of them. You couldn't have passed through them.

I know.

You knew about the tunnels? The statement surprised Jarl.

No, but I watched all that happened to you through Lythyr's crystal disk. There was great rejoicing when Seabreeze returned with the prince. As soon as they were safely on the rock, the prince used the acorn and disappeared. The wyvern's queen said the spell was a success and he was home with his father.

I'm glad to hear that. Fellkeep is no place for anyone who is decent, let alone a youngster.

Look, Jarl. Isn't that the castle ahead?

That's it. I can't understand why the major city is near the southern border. I'd rather have my capital as far as possible from Fellkeep.

When the city was built, there were cordial relations between the keep and the castle. When the old wizard who lived there died, it stood empty for a long time. One day when the Shadowlord is overthrown, the wyverns want peaceful humans at Fellkeep and may resume trade. The Meander River wanders over much of the landscape. It eventually drains into the sea near Fellkeep. It made a natural highway for traders. Mirza finished Jarl's brief history lesson.

Jarl looked down at the river below. *We're over the border now, but I don't see much traffic.*

No, Ebony answered him. *When I began wearing the collar of Darkness, I harassed the shipping. Finally, the few people who lived in the region once governed by the Keep fled. The Shadowlord forced me to do other—things.* The pause in Ebony's explanation showed how much she regretted serving the Shadowlord.

Her listeners wisely refrained from asking for more details. Ebony's unhappiness was clear.

When they reached the castle, there was not enough room for both dragons to land on Relnot's tower, so they elected to settle on a wide, clear area that was the field for jousting contests and fairs. Jarl and Mirza removed the harnesses from the dragons. Jarl carried them over his shoulder.

"Ebony and I will be leaving now. We'll return to this spot in two days to fly you to Realmgate."

"You're not staying?" Jarl had become fond of Faf. He would miss him.

"I've been away from my cave for too long. Ebony will come with me for a visit."

Wasn't that a twinkle in Faf's eyes? Jarl looked at the black dragon for confirmation. She lowered her head almost coyly.

"Thank you both. Be careful. Being north of Relnot's magic barrier seems to be some protection, but I know it's not perfect. Jarl and I will see you in two days." Mirza waved as the dragons beat their mighty wings and sailed into the sky.

"What was the matter with Ebony? She seemed a little—weird." Jarl said. He guessed he still had a lot to learn about dragons.

"Silly! You can't see romance when it's right over your nose." Mirza gave him an indulgent smile.

"You mean—" Jarl looked at Mirza wide-eyed.

"Of course," she answered complacently. "Now, if you're ready, our ride to the castle is coming."

CHAPTER TWENTY

Jarl turned as a magnificent coach, pure white with gilded wheels, approached.

"Welcome!" the king's familiar voice said. Relnot and the prince were with him. The coach had barely stopped when the king hopped out. "Come, come," he said, motioning for them to enter the coach. "Leon told us every-thing. We've been expecting you." He stood aside courteously as he helped Mirza in. Then he motioned for Jarl to precede him. "Don't stand on cere-mony, Jarl. You're a hero to everyone in the kingdom. That's why I came for you in this behemoth. It's a blasted nuisance, but on occasions of state, it's tradition to use it."

"Your Majesty is very kind," Mirza said, every inch a lady.

"Have to be, have to be. Jarl here saved my boy. I know your grand-mother, too. I'd not want her to think I'd slighted her favorite grand-daughter."

"Only granddaughter, you mean," Mirza teased gently, responding to the real warmth of the king's personality.

"How is your grandmother?" the king asked.

Jarl wondered about Mirza's family. What kind of weird relatives would she have? If he and Mirza ever got any time to themselves, he decided he would have to ask a few questions. Was the old wise woman related to Mirza? If she was Mirza's grandmother, that would explain why she was so helpful. Jarl wished he had more answers and fewer questions. Mirza and the king seemed to know each other well, judging from their conversation.

Mirza answered the king. "Hale and hearty, busy as ever."

The coach bowled swiftly into the city where cheering crowds lined the streets. The king waved to the populace. Under cover of the excitement, Relnot said quietly to Mirza. "Are you in need of help?"

She glanced at him quickly before replying, "Later, please."

Short as the exchange had been, Jarl heard it, but decided it was not the time to ask for further information. At the palace they separated.

"You must have time to refresh yourselves before dinner," the king decreed.

Jarl was glad of a chance to wash. One of the things he missed most from Earth was the modern plumbing. The steaming tub of water the servants carried into his room would never replace a hot shower. Still, it was a far cry from the cold washes he had been taking daily as the terrain allowed.

For the first time he dressed in the clothing of Realm. From the large selection at his disposal, he chose a soft brown leather jerkin and matching breeches. Since the servant looked scandalized by the color he selected, he added a brown velvet cape with dragons embroidered in thread of gold. His high boots glistened with polish. While the colors were much quieter than those of the other courtiers he had seen, Jarl felt comfortable in his choice. At least he wouldn't disgrace his host with his clothes.

He followed a servant to the royal banqueting hall, which resembled a scene from a medieval tapestry. The large T-shaped table at one end of the hall stood burdened with food. Servers scurried about, bringing more as he watched.

Rushes were strewn on the floor. Jarl hoped the tapers that lighted the room would not fall and ignite the substitute for carpeting. Small groups of courtiers stood talking. Jarl was certain they waited for the king. As he stood silent and alone, Mirza joined him. Her golden dress glittered, as did the ornaments she wore in her hair.

"You are very beautiful, my lady," Jarl said, bowing over her hand.

She smiled. "I feel dressed like a queen. I wouldn't care for it all the time, but for tonight it's pleasant." All signs of tiredness had disappeared. She tucked her arm in his and began walking toward the table.

The king entered from the far door. He spoke briefly to a servant who approached them.

"His Majesty awaits your company at the table."

"Honored," Jarl said before he and Mirza joined the king.

During the meal Jarl watched the other guests. Their clothing was so brightly colored that he began to understand why the servant had looked shocked by his somber color selection. From his place at the king's right hand, Jarl was able to see everyone except Mirza and Relnot, who both sat on the king's left. He did notice that Mirza and the magician spoke together. He wondered what she found so interesting in the conversation, then decided that it was probably an interest in magic. Mirza looked like a young woman. He reminded himself that she was the granddaughter of a witch. Did that made her a witch, too? What of her mother and father? She had to be older than she looked or they wouldn't let her wander around shaped like a fennec. Everyone knew her. Most referred to her as "my lady." Did that mean her father was a king or lord or something? Jarl made a mental note to ask her when they were alone sometime.

It was late the next morning before Jarl awoke. No sooner had he stirred than a servant tapped on his door. Later, suitably dressed for the day, he went to find Mirza. She was not in the room assigned to her, but her maid said she had gone to see Relnot.

Jarl finally found the steps leading to the tower. When he stood outside the heavy oaken door, he thought he heard the sound of sobs, but upon his knocking, they stopped. Relnot himself opened the door.

"Good morning," Jarl said.

"Come in," Relnot answered with a quiet smile. His measured invitation did not match his visitor's cheery words.

"Is something the matter?"

"No, Jarl," Mirza answered, but her eyes were suspiciously bright.

"My lady," Relnot began.

"Relnot and I were investigating an interesting piece of spell work together," she told Jarl.

Relnot spoiled his agreement by shaking his head. Jarl caught the gesture out of the corner of his eye.

"Have you eaten yet?" Mirza asked, ignoring Relnot entirely.

"I wanted to see you first."

"Let's descend and find our meal together," she suggested. "Do you want to come with us, Relnot?" she asked courteously.

"I have some work to attend to before this afternoon's conference with the king. So, thank you, no."

Jarl and Mirza found their way to the breakfast table with the help of Prince Leon, busy enjoying a few days of freedom from his tutor. His bright chatter livened the atmosphere as Jarl finished a large breakfast. Mirza ate very little, he noticed.

"When I am older. I shall have one of the stallions for my very own," he heard the prince telling Mirza.

"So you like horses?" Jarl asked, unsure how to speak to a royal child.

"This kingdom raises the best horses in Realm," Mirza explained. "'To ride a southern horse' is a proverb here."

"It means to have the very best," the prince added, gratified to be able to tell a grown-up something.

"Oh," Jarl said, rather less than brilliantly.

"Would you like to see the horses?" The boy was eager to show them, so Mirza and Jarl followed him to the stables.

An army of servants—far more than were in use in the castle, an amused Jarl noted—cared for the horses. No burrs were visible in silken manes and tails. The liquid eyes of the animals watched the visitors, and several nickered as if they knew the prince. One golden stallion especially caught Jarl's attention.

"You have a good knowledge of horses," the prince said, sounding just like his father. "Oromon is the best horse we own. My father has trained him as a battle stallion in case we ever have to go to war," he seriously. Leon unconsciously aped the stance and manner of his father. "Here, you can feed him today, if you're not afraid." The boy offered a carrot to Jarl.

Please remember that I need to conserve my strength, Wyrd's voice hissed through Jarl's mind.

I didn't call on you for anything.

I can't very well sleep if you are going to do foolhardy things every time I close my eyes. That brute of a horse has large teeth. You'd better be sure he doesn't decide to bite the hand that feeds him. You won't be able to hold a sword with half your fingers missing.

Don't be such a worry-Wyrd, Jarl teased. *This time I know what I'm doing.*

I hope so. Don't call unless you're in real need, and I'll take a short nap.

Agreed, Jarl thought. The whole mental exchange had taken place with such rapidity that the prince was still waiting for Jarl's answer.

"All right," Jarl agreed, unaware that all work stopped while the stable boys watched him feed Oromon. He held out his hand, saying, "Here, boy." The horse bowed his golden neck graciously and accepted the offering. "Good fellow," Jarl said as he stroked Oromon. The horse munched contentedly.

The grooms made small sounds of amazement among themselves. The prince exclaimed, "You fed him!" and then quieted. He knew he should not raise his voice around the excitable thoroughbreds.

"Sure. Why not? Doesn't he like carrots?"

A groom bowed low before Jarl. "Oromon is the king's mount. He is very particular about the people he allows near him, yet he accepted you."

"Well, perhaps today is my lucky day," Jarl answered off-handedly, not impressed by his performance.

"I must tell my father that Oromon accepts you. Perhaps the stallion knows you are a hero. Horses are very wise."

"He's a fine animal. Perhaps he senses my admiration for him," Jarl answered aloud. Mentally he wondered if his bracelet had anything to do with his affinities for the inhabitants of Realm.

"You do have a way with horses," Mirza said as they walked back to the castle.

"Oh, I've had some practice riding fiery mounts. One of them in particular was very headstrong, but I could tame her." He flashed a mental image of Mirza in the brown mare's shape to her.

Mirza tossed her head and snorted. He laughed at her equine gesture.

By the time they reached the castle, Prince Leon, had run ahead, telling his father about Jarl's feeding Oromon. "—Oromon likes him, Father."

"Oromon is a very wise animal, my son. I will consider his opinion of Jarl when making my decision."

"What decision, Father?"

"Matters of state, Leon. Today you may join us for a meeting of the Council. Then you shall know." He ruffled his son's hair, noting how tall he had grown. It was time he learned more of how to govern the kingdom.

Jarl thought the council hall was a bit austere. Battle armor hung on the high gray walls. A long U-shaped table dominated the room. A plain gold throne filled the open end of the figure. The king, who sat on the throne, wore navy-blue robes of state and a golden circlet upon his brow. Jarl knew the king well enough to guess he didn't enjoy the trappings of his office. King Caeryl's grave visage set the mood for the meeting.

Pompuss sat on the king's right hand. Beside him sat the prince. Jarl and Mirza sat beside Relnot, close to the king.

King Caeryl raised his hand, and the low murmur of voices ceased. "We gather today to discuss a matter of importance to the kingdom," he began.

Heads nodded in agreement. All knew the subject of this meeting.

"The Shadowlord abducted Prince Leon and ordered me to join his cause."

A few gasps of surprise and lifted eyebrows greeted this announcement. The fact was news to some of the Council.

"Jarl, the Dragon's Pawn, whom you met last night, rescued the prince with the aid of Relnot's talisman and the wyvern Queen Lythyr." The king looked steadily at his advisors. They were attentive to his words. "Now we must choose: war or peace?"

Pompuss, resplendent in green, spoke in an excited voice. "This means war! How dare this upstart wizard detain a royal personage?"

"War is a very serious undertaking. Can we not make use of Relnot's magical defenses and remain inside the kingdom?" The thin man in gray who spoke rubbed his black beard in agitation.

"How stand our defenses, Relnot?" a third asked, leaning his stout body over the table until his buttons threatened to pop.

Relnot answered after the king signaled him to do so. "For now, the defenses hold." A collective sigh of relief came from the advisors. Relnot raised his hand in admonition. "I must warn you that the power of the Shadowlord, once a minor aggravation, is waxing stronger every day. There are vast amounts of energy being channeled into his projects. Eventually he will be able to overcome my best magical efforts unless we stop him or keep him busy elsewhere."

The advisors sat stunned by this news. "What then shall we do? Begin war immediately before he is too powerful to stop?" The black-bearded man spoke for all of them.

"It is already too late for that. We have two choices open to us," the king said. "We can close our borders with Relnot's most powerful spell and hope the Shadowlord ignores us, or we can ally our kingdom with his enemies."

"Who are they?" Pompuss asked, so absorbed in the information he forgot to act injured because he didn't know about the Shadowlord's enemies beforehand.

"Jarl, can you tell us of the conditions outside of our kingdom? Since Relnot created the border ward, few of our people have left to travel in the outside world."

"I have recently been both north and south of here," Jarl began. "The Shadowlord has enough power to command the evil tribe of korred to do his bidding. He has enslaved a number of peace-loving creatures, one of which, a black dragon named Ebony, freed of his bondage, helped us escape."

"A black dragon, you say? We have been raided by a vicious dragon who disrupted our shipping and trading," a red-faced man said.

"Ebony had no choice in what she did. While she wore the collar of the Shadowlord, she was his slave, forced to do his bidding by an evil spell," Mirza explained. "Many creatures from many lands form his forces."

"Why should we care? Evil creatures cannot cross our border now," another said.

"If a dragon can be enslaved," Relnot answered, "a man most certainly could be ensorcelled."

Jarl added, "He is calling creatures from another world to do his bidding. There are metal men, flying machines that use rays of light to maim and kill, and other monsters, such as a flying thing called Death-that-flies by the wyverns." Jarl ignored the whispering around him and went doggedly on with his information. "I have been under the walls of Fellkeep, and it vibrates with a strange power. The Shadowlord calls more and more evils to the keep. When he is ready, he will attack any on Realm who do not offer him absolute fealty."

Silence fell on the group as they considered his words. Only a few advisors looked disbelieving.

"This is true," Mirza spoke quietly. Her words dropped into the pool of silence around the table. "During my imprisonment in the tower at Fellkeep, I learned the Shadowlord means to attack Realmgate itself." Ripples of disbelief touched each listener.

Jarl could see this news astounded the Council. Their surprise made him realize how important the gate and the Keepers must be to this society. Attacking them seemed to be sacrilege to the men seated at the table.

"I will carry a warning to Andronan, the Elder Keeper. The hosts of the Shadowlord will march before the summer ends," Mirza concluded solemnly.

The king studied the faces of his councilors. "Will we abjure the neutrality we maintained during the reign of my father and go to war?"

The answer was obvious.

"Tomorrow Jarl and Mirza go north to Realmgate. They will carry my message to the Keepers that we will send what help we can. Pompuss, raise and equip the kingdom. By the next new moon, our army must march to Realmgate!"

CHAPTER TWENTY-ONE

Jarl and Mirza stood waiting on the field where the dragons agreed to meet them.

Mirza expressed her concern. "I hoped they would join us before it was too late. Many of the races of Realm have pledged to support the Keepers in their fight to keep Realm free. If the Shadowlord gains control of Realmgate, he may pass between worlds unhindered."

"How could anyone who knows the Shadowlord ignore him? Thinking he could force King Caeryl to join him and deliberately alienating the wyverns may be the very mistakes that win the battle for us." Jarl told her soberly.

Two specks appeared in the sky. Ebony and Faf produced an amazing aerial performance before landing.

"Don't they look happy?" Mirza commented as she and Jarl watched.

"I don't see what for," Jarl said. "Here we are planning a war effort, and two of our best weapons are acting like a couple of teenage show-offs."

"Well, dragons don't take honeymoons, and some celebration is in order," Mirza said, defending them.

"Honeymoon!"

"Yes! This event will please Fafnir. He's worried about the family name dying out, and now, given enough time, he'll be a granddragon."

Jarl stared at her. "How did you know about all this?"

"Any woman could tell. You men just don't have enough romance in your souls." Mirza scolded him gently. Her face saddened momentarily, then brightened. "I'm very happy for them."

"Do we say congratulations or anything?" Jarl wondered.

"I doubt it. I don't know all the dragon protocol. Faf marches to a different drummer anyway. In the great library at Realmgate there is a set of fifty volumes containing the dragon etiquette. Thick ones," she added when Jarl looked as if he was having trouble believing her.

They had asked to leave quietly. Only Relnot, the king, and Prince Leon stood waving at the edge of the field when the dragons took off bearing Mirza and Jarl. Gradually the neat fields below gave way to forest, then to wild land. Finally Mirza announced they had passed the northern border, guarded like the others by Relnot's magic.

Jarl touched Wyrd, appreciative of his watchdog qualities.

All is well, Wyrd whispered in Jarl's mind. Then he perversely refused to answer any of Jarl's questions. It was almost as if Wyrd did not reside in the bracelet at all times. When Jarl came to consider it, this odd thought was no more unbelievable than wearing a talking metal talisman. Just so long as Wyrd was present when Jarl needed a warning . . .

Where are we now? Jarl asked Faf after they had flown for several hours.

Over Feraland. The Old Ones ruled here, the legends say. Then one day they left—disappeared, Faf said.

Doesn't anyone know where they went or why?

No being now living, Jarl, Mirza chimed in on Faf's history lesson.

My great-great-grandmother said an old legend told of their desire to change and be something they were not. The Old Ones couldn't reach their objective so long as they stayed on Realm, Ebony said.

I never heard that. I spent a great deal of time studying the Old Ones when I was a student. None of my teachers mentioned that information. In fact, none of the books in the library carried that tale, Mirza replied.

My family handed the information down, said Ebony. *One of my ancestors was a special friend to the Old Ones. As many dragons are interested in history as magic. We live long lives and see how most thing work out in the end.*

Feraland looks like wild country to me. I hope King Caeryl can keep the promise he made to the wyvern messenger, Jarl said.

We left before they settled everything, but I'm sure Seabreeze and her companions will come to a satisfactory arrangement with the king. Together they will see that the Meander flows, unblocked and in full spate, to keep Wyvern Marsh as wet as it has always been, Mirza replied.

Oh, but it wasn't always wet, Ebony said, matching her glide perfectly to Faf's.

I know. Don't tell me. Jarl grinned. *The information was part of an old family story.*

Faf fixed one enormous eye on Jarl. If Ebony had shown any sign of being upset by Jarl's teasing, Faf would intercede.

Jarl made a mental note not to tease Faf's dragonlady—or wife, or mate, or whatever one called the female half of a pair of dragons. If he got the chance, he planned to find out how long dragons lived.

That night they made camp deep in Feraland. The tall trees fought for a ray of sun. Because of the many trees, Faf and Ebony had difficulty finding a place large enough for them both to land. When they spotted a clearing, they settled into it gratefully. It had been a long day. Jarl and Mirza were stiff from their time in harness. They hobbled around, getting their land legs. The earth seemed strangely still after the constant movement of the wind, the dips and glides of the dragons, and the updrafts that carried human and dragon into the clean blue sky.

Faf watched amusedly for some time and then asked, "Do you think you'll be all right if Ebony and I go for a short flight?"

"Yes," Jarl answered, and Mirza smiled her agreement. Both couples would enjoy a little privacy. Ebony rose first, with Faf flying after her in a gigantic game of aerial tag. They were much more agile without riders, Jarl noted.

"They're like two children," Mirza said.

"Better them than me. How anyone would want to fly after the day we've put in, I don't know."

"Remember the air is their natural home. It's wonderful to fly lightly without an unnatural weight," she added thoughtfully.

"Watch out who you're calling an unnatural weight," Jarl warned her mock-seriously. He enjoyed being alone with Mirza.

"Night will come early here. If we plan to have a fire, someone must search out branches."

"Someone hears and will obey, m'lady," Jarl told her.

He gathered a sizable number of suitable dead branches quickly. The trees were so thick there was little or no undergrowth. The deadwood was easy to find lying on the bare ground.

When Jarl dumped the first load in the clearing, he stopped a moment to ask a question. "Are there dryads in these woods?"

"Can't you tell?" Mirza counterquestioned. "If dryads rule over a forest, it is a living thing, filled with the sounds and sights of life. Birds fly between the branches and roost in nests. Squirrels frolic from tree to tree. Ground creatures like rabbits and badgers make holes at the foot of trees, and owls inhabit openings in large trunks. This forest is dead."

"I hadn't actually thought about it before, but if I compare this forest to the one near Fellkeep, I can tell there is a difference. It's as if it's waiting for something. It's an eerie sensation, but we should be safe. Wyrd hasn't tightened at all."

"Most people feel uncomfortable in Feraland, so it is sparsely settled. This used to be one of the main areas for the Old Ones. Some say Feraland waits for their return."

Jarl cleared a space for the fire and placed some sticks ready for the match he didn't have. He supposed they would have to wait for Faf or Ebony to start their fire.

"This land has had a pretty long wait, if you ask me. Even long-lived creatures like the dragons have never seen an Old One. What did they look like?"

"Old ballads say they were surpassing fair with moonbeams woven in their hair and sunlight in their hearts."

"Sounds a little uncomfortable to me. Using that description, it would be hard to recognize one," Jarl said.

"The Old Ones were teachers. They shared their magic gladly. At one time, the humans on Realm could do almost as much as the Old Ones themselves. To be in contact with them . . . changed people. The foolish became sensible; the intelligent became wise." Mirza looked wistful.

"Too bad they're gone. We could do with a little of their magic. Think what it would mean if the old places were reactivated with their former magic powers." Jarl didn't like the look on Mirza's face. She seemed sad. He was just about to talk to her about whatever was bothering her when she spoke.

"It would lighten Realm with joy. Speaking about light, we have very little of it left. I suggest that we both gather as much wood as we can in the next few minutes. Long before the sun actually sets, we will be in darkness because of the thickness and height of these trees."

The two of them gathered a few more armfuls of wood. Jarl and Mirza sat on their cloak-blankets. Each was more sumptuous than the one Jarl had purchased from Trader Krom. The king had spared no expense in outfitting their party. He wished they didn't have to sit in the gloom waiting for the dragons to return to light the fire. Just then Mirza started the blaze with a negligent gesture.

"Boy, it surely does beat rubbing two sticks together," Jarl said, warming his hands in the cheery flames.

"Bring me a food pack, so I can prepare a meal," Mirza commanded Jarl with a smile.

"I'll do that, Mirza, if you can set a magic border around this place like Relnot did around the kingdom."

"It is small magic to hide two people. I will make us unnoticeable."

"Why not make us invisible?" Jarl asked.

"That takes more power. With this glamourie we shall be unnoticed by anything that might pass or fly over. It is much easier and just as effective. Tomorrow may bring a need for my strongest magic, and I want to have a reserve."

"How will Faf and Ebony find us?"

"I don't expect to see either of them until tomorrow. They like to be alone together, too, you know."

"That makes good sense. Besides, Wyrd will be watching." Jarl opened the pouch containing the food. "Hmm. Bread, cheese, a flask of cider, and fruit. It looks as if Faf chose the food."

"I didn't know what the conditions would be. If we were unable to light a fire, I wanted us to be able to eat something decent," Mirza explained.

"Well, I'm so hungry anything would taste good," Jarl said before biting into his bread and cheese.

After eating, he prepared the fire so it would burn as long as possible. Then he and Mirza wrapped themselves in their cloak-blankets. He wasn't sleepy and would have been glad to talk. However, Mirza breathed deeply almost as soon as she stretched on the ground, so he was quiet. Being the prisoner of the Shadowlord was an ordeal to weaken even a hardy soul. Moreover, flying north via dragon express was not a particularly refreshing way to spend a day, either.

Jarl awakened to the snapping and crackling of a brisk fire. Early dawn tinted the sky above, and the earth smelled as if it were invigorated from the cool night breezes.

"Time to get up, sleepy one. I've already found a stream through the trees. Go splash a little water on your face and you'll get alert fast," Mirza promised him.

He watched for a moment. From somewhere she produced a small pan into which she was sprinkling herbs. The resulting tea smelled delicious. The idea of breakfast galvanized Jarl into action.

The small spring that fed the stream bubbled clean and cold from between two rocks. Jarl was shaking the water from his hair when he heard the sound of swords clashing. Wyrd had tightened, but his hands were so cold he hadn't noticed.

He arrived at the clearing on the run. Mirza was slashing valiantly at two men, but Jarl could see she was tiring. His sword leaped to his hand. The first cut severed one robber's head. The second was unnecessary, for when the remaining robber saw an armed man instead of a woman before him, he fled into the trees. Jarl started after him, but stopped when he noticed Mirza's white face.

"Are you all right?" he asked, kneeling beside her.

"Yes," she told him gamely, looking down at the damp patch that was forming on the breeches she had chosen to wear, saying earlier they were more comfortable for traveling.

"No, you're not. Let get those breeches off so I can assess the damage."

"No," she said. She turned even paler as Jarl watched. "I'm all right. I tell you," she insisted.

"Little liar," Jarl chided gently. "No more nonsense now. Let me see the wound."

"No!" This time she sounded mule stubborn. She clutched the breeches to her possessively.

"Mirza, the stain is getting larger and larger. At this rate you'll faint from lack of blood, and then I'll take off those pants and care for your wound. Wouldn't it make good sense to let me help you before that happens?"

"Oh, Jarl, no," she moaned.

"Don't be shy of me. I've seen you in next to nothing, and you've never been like this. Remember the night you wore that green dress you insisted I bring from Mog's treasure hoard?"

A small smile was his only answer, but it told him she would allow him to help her.

She slipped out of the boots that covered her feet. Jarl schooled his face to show no shock, for human feet were not in those boots. Instead he saw hideous splayed paws—or were they hoofs? Jarl had never seen anything like them.

When she removed her clothing, he saw the full extent of her deformity. From the waist down she was a monster. What had happened? That night in the glade when he first saw her she had human feet.

Mirza must have read some of what Jarl was feeling from the look on his face. "Now you know," she told him flatly.

"Now I know what?" he repeated.

"What a monster I'm becoming!" she flared through her tears.

Jarl ignored her words and began to bind her wound with a piece of cloth he found in their provision bag. "How did this happen?" he asked gently.

She didn't pretend to misunderstand. "It's a spell of the Shadowlord," she admitted tiredly. "When I refused to join him, he said some words I've never heard before and he laughed. Every day it creeps higher on my body. When it reaches my face, it will be permanent and impossible for anyone—even the Shadowlord—to remove."

"Is there nothing that can be done?"

"That's what Relnot and I were checking the morning you came to his tower. Relnot thinks that the heal spring north of Realmgate may be able to cure me."

"We'll go straight there," Jarl announced. "Where is it?"

"I'm afraid not," Mirza countered in her quiet voice. "The rate of the transformation has increased now that I'm away from Fellkeep. Even on dragonback we cannot travel fast enough to reach the magic spring before it's too late." Her brave smile almost broke Jarl's heart.

A shadow swept over them, followed by another. Jarl half drew his sword, then replaced it. The dragons had returned.

"Faf!" Jarl shouted as his friend landed in the clearing, "Can you fly any faster than you have been?"

"We're not that late," Faf answered. Then he looked around carefully, noting the headless human corpse. "What happened here?" A gout of steam showed his concern.

"We were attacked, but Mirza fought them off."

Faf and Ebony saw from the cutaway portion of Mirza's clothing the unnatural green and gray color of her warty hide.

"No, Jarl, Ebony and I can't fly any faster," Faf replied slowly, trying to understand what his air speed had to do with Mirza's affliction.

"This—stuff—is creeping upward each day," Jarl explained, putting his arm around Mirza's shoulder. "We have to reach the heal spring north of Realmgate before she's totally changed. The spell may be reversible until then."

Faf looked at Ebony, who nodded. "If you and Mirza are willing to take a little risk, we can travel faster."

"How?" Jarl asked practically.

"Both Faf and I have discovered we have a new talent."

"Talent?" Jarl and Mirza chorused.

"What Ebony means is that we can think of where we want to go when we're airborne, and then somehow we're there instantaneously."

Mirza shook her head. Evidently the unauthorized gate of the Shadowlord was awaking strange new powers in the beings of real magic. She explained her theory to Jarl.

"Well, dragons have always been somewhat of a mystery. Multidimensional transport seems pretty farfetched, but on Realm anything can happen. If Faf and Ebony can fly to places they can visualize, we'd better make use of their newfound ability. The Shadowlord has not only opened the gate to the Earth monsters he's recruiting. Somehow other attributes have slipped through, too. That's why you can fly in this new manner," she told the dragons.

"It's true that no dragon we ever heard of ever flew like this," said Ebony, accepting her new ability easily.

"I'm not altogether sure we can carry a passenger while we do it," Faf said.

"I'm willing to try it, if Ebony will carry me," Mirza said with a look of hope on her face that cheered Jarl.

"Let's pack up. Ebony carried Mirza before. Both of you should be able to take us with you."

Jarl helped Mirza get ready. He fastened the last buckle on her harness and kissed her quickly. "Don't worry. This is bound to work," he assured her, hiding his doubts.

"You can kiss me after what I've become?" Mirza said in wonder.

"I've liked you as a fennec, admired you as a unicorn, and been in tight spots with you in a horse's shape. The form you wear doesn't change my feelings for you," Jarl told her stoutly. The shine in her eyes repaid him handsomely for his avowal. "I'm always yours, m'lady," he said, giving her hand a squeeze.

As soon as Jarl was in the harness, Faf joined Ebony in the air. They flew north for a little distance and then separated.

We'll see you in Realmgate, Jarl sent a final thought winging to Mirza and Ebony.

Agreed.

BLACK. COLD. LIGHT.

CHAPTER TWENTY-TWO

Jarl looked down. "I guess it was a failure," he told Faf in disappointed tones.

"Look ahead on the left," Faf advised.

A series of iridescent towers and domes filled the skyline in the distance. It was Realmgate, the citadel of the Keepers. "Where are Ebony and Mirza?"

"Behind us." Faf chuckled. "You can't let females get too far ahead."

"You're right. If they did, we'd never catch up."

Faf wheeled in a giant circle so Jarl could see Ebony and Mirza coming. They swooped by and Faf rose on a giant thermal to glide close behind them.

"Where are you going to land?" Jarl asked.

"Outside the wall," Faf answered.

Ebony and I are flying into the hills to the spring first, Mirza said.

Shall we come with you? Jarl asked.

No need. Show the gatekeepers your talisman, and they'll tell you where to go.

When Mirza finished speaking, Ebony flew on and Faf started down.

"Are you sure we shouldn't go with them?" Jarl asked.

"The healing spring was originally the shrine of a goddess. Women have always gone there. Males are only tolerated. I've never actually been there myself, but I remember my mother talking about it."

"Is there any place on Realm your mother didn't see?" Jarl asked, really curious.

"She only admitted to four thousand years, but even if she was that old, that's enough time to visit a great many places."

"What did your father do when your mother traveled?"

"She hadn't chosen him yet. He was busy pillaging around on his own, to hear him tell it. With daring parents like mine, you can understand what a disappointment I always was to them."

"Your father will be proud when you tell him about your adventures."

"After Mirza visits the spring, I want Ebony to meet him."

"That's a good idea. Give him my thanks for suggesting we be partners."

"After we see my father, we'll return," Faf promised, landing softly on a grassy meadow outside Realmgate's walls.

Jarl loosened his harness and shouldered it and his pack. "Are you coming with me?"

"I'll scout around a little. I haven't been here since I was a youngster. Things change in a few hundred years, you know."

Jarl waved, then turned toward the city where he hoped to get answers to some of the questions he had. The high walls of gray rock were imposing. The heaviness of the architecture reminded him of ancient Egypt. The walls looked as if the Old Ones built the citadel.

He trudged down the stretch of road that led to Realmgate. Several farmers with carts preceded him, and a merchant's caravan passed him. He stepped off the road to allow the dust of the horses to settle before continuing.

"What's happened to that fine mare you rode when last I saw you?" a hearty voice inquired.

It was Krom, the master trader. Jarl recognized his portly form at first glance. Thrown over his shoulder was his dark brown travel coat. Jarl noticed he wore a sword.

"She's changed a bit since you last saw her," Jarl joked in his turn. The twinkle in Krom's eyes when he asked his question told Jarl the trader knew Jarl's mount had been a were-horse.

"Were you and your horse—" he chuckled,"—being carried by those two dragons I saw fly by earlier?"

Jarl grinned. "That was Mirza and I."

"I take it you've given up riding and become a certified walker," Krom looked down from the back of the gray gelding he rode.

"Well, it's a change from flying, I'll admit, but now I have no horse and the gates are near, so I suppose I'll survive."

"If you should be in the market for another horse, I have two fine ones for sale. One is a perfect mount for a lady." Krom added as an afterthought.

CAROL L. DENNIS

"Where will you be staying, Master Krom?" Jarl saw Krom raise his eyebrows at the question. "In case I should decide to buy a horse or two."

A laugh escaped from Krom. "My caravan will be north of the city. Ask anyone for me and they will tell you."

"Can you recommend an inn where I can get rooms?"

"There's no place that will board two dragons," Krom warned. "Even in so cosmopolitan a city as Realmgate, they have their little idiosyncrasies, and harboring dragons inside the town is one of them."

"Faf and Ebony will take a holiday while we're here. I need a place for Mirza and myself."

"Since you have a lady with you, you'll want better accommodations than many of the inns in town offer. I'd try the Unicorn and the Dragon, if I were you."

Jarl raised his hand to wipe the dust from his face. Wyrd's scales caught the light of the sun and reflected it.

The trader gave a small gasp of recognition. "Is that not a talisman?" he asked, pointing to the bracelet.

"Yes, that's Wyrd."

"Then you're the Dragon's Pawn, the hero who is to help Realm in this age!" he said excitedly. "That explains your sword and your ability to kill Mog."

"I'm afraid so," Jarl said ruefully.

"You will have no need to find an inn. As Dragon's Pawn, Andronan will find rooms at the castle for you."

"Who's Andronan?"

"The main purpose of Realmgate is the keeping of the gate between the worlds. The university here trains the Keepers, and Andronan is the Elder Keeper."

"How do I find the university?"

"It's the largest building in the city. See the triple spires that reach the heavens?"

"I can't imagine how they were built so tall."

"Magic."

"Don't tell me. The Old Ones?" Jarl guessed.

"This gate is the only operational one remaining on Realm, and for that reason it is precious. Only the will of a master wizard can harness the energies needed to open a gate."

"One person could do all this?" Jarl's tone expressed his disbelief while his eyes swept the triple spires in awed appreciation of their iridescent beauty.

"One Old One," Krom corrected. "Today the art of gate creation is beyond our knowledge. No one now living knows the secret. Considering how dangerous a gate can be, it is well that Realm only has this one."

"What's dangerous about a gate?"

"Sometimes strange things appear in the center of the triangle formed by the spires. Then the Keepers must establish communication or send it back to whence it came, if it is bestial and had only stumbled on a gate in its own world."

"You know quite a lot about gate-keeping," Jarl observed.

"Keepers do not always stay here in the citadel. Sometimes they journey far. On such a trip they may well need allies and friends. I have known many Keepers."

Judging from the reception he got, this hardly counted as a first trip for Krom. The watchman waved Jarl and the trader through respectfully. The people in the streets were about their business, and Jarl noticed that many greeted Krom. Krom stopped before an oaken gate set in a marble wall. It opened before he knocked.

"Welcome, master," a young man in a brown cassock greeted Krom.

"Here is one Andronan will be glad to meet," Krom said quietly. With a friendly nod, he gestured to Jarl to enter. "This is Tieron, who will take you to the Elder Keeper. I'll see you later."

Jarl followed his guide. Outside the oaken door the cobbled street had been rough under Jarl's feet. Within the walls of the university, a marble mosaic composed of intricate designs paved the courtyard. It reminded Jarl of the other pavements of the Old Ones. Flowers, bushes, and trees bearing apples, cherries, pears, and oranges graced the neatly kept walk. Strange fruits and blooms in a myriad of colors swayed gently in the breeze that ameliorated the heat of day. A bush covered with blue roses scented the area.

"I see you appreciate our garden," Tieron said.

"It's unusual to see so many different plants growing together in one place."

"Here under the influence of the gate, we are able to grow species from a thousand worlds. When we Keepers become sojourners on the planet we adopt as our own, we search out the best to add to the garden. Each planet with a gate has only one plant here. Only old Earth has more than one specimen in the garden."

Jarl felt like a country bumpkin as he gawked at the sights. The fruits were of every hue and shape; the flowers called for attention by scent and color. "Where are you taking me?" he asked at last, when Tieron showed no signs of pausing.

"We've been expecting you for some time. Andronan wants to see you."

"Tell me about him," Jarl said.

"He is the Elder Keeper," Tieron answered, as if that was all the identification needed.

"What does he want with me?"

"I do not know. You have learned much as Dragon's Pawn. Perhaps it is time for you to take the final steps to becoming Dragon's Knight. My appointed task is to bring you to him." Tieron entered a low door and led Jarl up a long flight of stairs. They stopped outside a small room. "This will be yours. You may leave your pack here."

Jarl felt lighter when he put his pack in a corner of the room. "Er—" He stopped, not sure what to say.

"Yes?" Tieron inquired politely.

"I have a friend with me. She'll need a room, too."

"The Lady Mirza?"

"You know her?"

"Indeed I do. She is often here at Realmgate. Her room awaits, always prepared for any time she chooses to use it."

"Fine. Then I'm ready to see Andronan."

The hall they trod was light, although windows were few. The walls themselves seemed insubstantial, subtly shifting in some way that Jarl could sense but not see, although he stared.

"In here," Tieron said.

Jarl crossed the threshold of the doorway to a small closet-like area. To his astonishment, they began to rise in the air. His stomach gave a queasy rumble.

"This is a gravity well." Tieron smiled. "I didn't think to warn you. Many of the artifacts of the Old Ones affect humans in odd ways."

"I should have known." Jarl found floating upward with no support, an unusual experience. They passed openings that led to other floors, but no passengers joined them.

Tieron said in a low voice, "We get off at the next level." He took Jarl's arm and pulled him over the doorsill onto solid floor. Jarl almost stumbled.

"Sorry," he said.

"Do not worry. The first time anyone exits a gravity well is somewhat awkward. You'll probably not have any trouble the next time. My first exit was without help. I fell flat on the floor. Most upsetting," Tieron said solemnly.

Jarl couldn't help smiling. Tieron's words and actions were those of a much older man and sat oddly on the young guide's shoulders.

A few short steps brought them to another door. Tieron knocked discreetly. The door opened silently, showing them a monastic room furnished with a bed, a table, and a chair.

"Come in, Tieron," the aged occupant of the room commanded quietly.

"Yes, sir."

"I see you have brought the Dragon's Pawn. Thank you. You may leave," he said kindly, for Tieron's awe was palpable. Tieron bowed and left, closing the door behind him.

Andronan looked at Jarl and said, "So you are Jarl Koenig, Dragon's Pawn."

"Yes, sir." Jarl found himself answering respectfully, understanding the guide's actions better now that he was under the bright gaze of the old man's deep purple eyes.

"I am Andronan. I serve Realmgate as Elder Keeper."

"I've heard the name before," Jarl said.

"More years ago than I care to count, I too, was Dragon's Pawn."

Jarl heard Wyrd speak. *Greetings, Andronan.*

"Ah, Wyrd. You, at least, have not changed."

If all goes well. I am nearing the end of my—-servitude.

Andronan smiled. "You have done well in choosing your companion."

Wyrd made no reply. The talisman gave Andronan the silent treatment, which surprised Jarl. The old man, however, seemed not to notice that his last statement went unremarked.

"The Shadowlord waxes while the magic of the Old Ones wanes. The coming battle between Light and Dark here on Realm will be a decisive one. We shall need your willing help. Do you give it freely?"

"I do," Jarl said, feeling that some ceremony had occurred. "After the battle, will I be able to return to my own home?"

"In that battle you shall be Dragon's Knight. As Knight you may pass unhindered to any location in the alternate universes that the gate serves."

"When do I change from Pawn to Knight? In the battle?"

"You shall be a full-fledged Knight before you face the Shadowlord. Only as Knight will you be able to withstand the tests of battle."

"What do I have to do to become Knight?"

"Your eagerness gladdens me, Jarl. Soon I shall have word of the activities of the Shadowlord. I feel the time of battle approaches on swift feet. In these days that yet remain before the testing, you will study here in the university."

"Do I learn battle tactics?"

"You might call it that, but the easiest word for it is magic."

"You mean I'm going to become a magician?" Jarl's mind jumped to the incongruous picture of himself pulling rabbits out of a hat.

"No," Andronan said, looking deeply into Jarl's eyes.

In Jarl's mind the rabbits turned to dragons in midhop and flew away into the air. "I didn't think that!" Jarl said.

"No," Andronan assured him, "but the power to make others see the visions you create is one of the weapons you may well face in the coming war."

"I'll learn to do that to others?"

"You will have many abilities that you do not now envision. To withstand a magical assault, you must know how to wage one yourself. To have the power to do a thing, however, does not mean you must use that power—except in defense or extremity. As the Champion of the Gate, or Dragon's Knight, you must master the magic of Realm, even if it is a poor remnant of the glorious wizardry which existed before the Old Ones vanished."

"I should like to know more of them."

Andronan looked pleased at Jarl's interest. "The library will be open to you. Wyrd will make it possible for you to read the Old Ones' tongue and any other language you may find in the books that are here."

At this point the door opened and Mirza rushed into the room, crossing it rapidly. "I'm back, Grandfather," she said to Andronan, while a startled Jarl watched her kiss the old mage. "You look tired. Why are you standing?" She pulled up a chair, and he sat, shaking his head. With a flick of her hand, a stool materialized. She sat, arranging her skirts carefully.

"What of our guest?" Andronan reminded her. "He has no chair."

"Oh, he can make one for himself," she said.

"I can?" Jarl asked.

"Of course, silly. Just concentrate on the spot where you want a chair to appear. Think of the shape of chair you want, and Wyrd will help you form one," she said patiently, as if she were teaching a child.

"Okay. Here goes," Jarl said, following her instructions carefully. If she thought he could, he would. He pictured the overstuffed chair he had in his den, complete with a handle that put up a footrest. The air shimmered. With a dull pop the chair appeared. Jarl sat.

"Very good!" Mirza clapped.

"I have never seen a chair like that," Andronan said as Jarl pulled the handle that raised the footrest.

"They're very popular where I come from," Jarl said.

"You need Grandmother here to take care of you." Mirza fussed gently at Andronan. "Sometimes I wish she wasn't so powerful. Neither of you can enjoy her guarding the whole southern border," Mirza muttered.

Andronan turned to Mirza. He ignored her outburst. "What have you been up to since your last visit?"

"I've been making friends with Jarl and helping him get here," she said, making it sound very unexciting.

"Good, I'm glad to hear your madcap ways have not brought you any difficulty."

She squeezed his frail hand gently. "I've been very good. You've nothing to worry about at all."

"Then shall we forget about your being a prisoner of the Shadowlord—twice?" Andronan said roguishly.

"Oh, Grandfather, don't be so fussy. Everything was quite all right. Jarl came to the rescue both times." She looked at her rescuer and added, "He's very good at heroing."

"You're a minx, just like your mother and grandmother."

"Have you heard anything from Mother and Father?" she asked.

"No, they are still off Realm on an assignment. Perhaps you can visit them when this is all over."

"You're becoming too tired. I'll take Jarl with me and start him on his basic lessons."

"Very well. I shall see you both later."

"You will rest, won't you?" Mirza said.

"Go along, and we'll see," he half promised.

Mirza took Jarl's hand, and like two children they left the room together. As they closed the door, they heard the sound of the lever on the chair raising the footrest.

"So that's the way of it," Andronan muttered to the empty room after they were gone. "Like her mother . . . "

CHAPTER TWENTY-THREE

"Well?" Jarl asked as they floated gently downward in the Old Ones' version of an elevator.

"Well, what?" Mirza countered.

"Are you all right? I mean, did the heal spring break the spell?"

Her eyes met his seriously as she gave him a sad smile. "No."

"What do you mean, no!"

"The Shadowlord's spell is more powerful than the residual magic of the goddess. All over Realm the old power is fading. There are no Old Ones to revitalize the magic, and the Shadowlord must be the single most potent magic worker on this world."

"What do we have to do to cure you?"

"I don't know." Mirza sounded resigned.

Jarl couldn't understand her calm. Perhaps her ability to shape-shift had made her more tolerant of strange forms. If she turned into a warty gray-green monster, surely it would bother her. He tried to ignore how much the idea worried him.

"But—-but you know all about magic. Surely there must be something we can do! Maybe Andronan would know . . . "

"He's old. He won't allow himself to die until he's seen Realm in safe hands. He limits his magic to the gate and its uses. It can't aid me in this. I cannot burden him with my problems."

"Not my—our," Jarl told her, placing his hand in hers when she reached for it.

"Our problem," she amended, pulling him onto another level.

"You're certain there's nothing you or anyone here on Realm can do?"

"I'm certain."

"Then I have an idea that may work," Jarl said.

"What is it?" Mirza's grip on Jarl's hand tightened. Becoming a monster bothered her more than she was willing to admit to Jarl.

Jarl had forgotten how lovely she could look when she felt excited. "Well, since the dragons only have to visualize a place to fly there instantaneously, perhaps if they visualized a time as well as a place, then they could take a rider back in time itself."

"How would that help me?"

"If a dragon envisions a place in the past, the dragon may be able to fly to that place and that time. The Old Ones existed in the past. Surely they could break the spell if Ebony can time travel."

"I'll ask Ebony if she'll try."

"Is she still around? I thought she and Faf were going to visit Fafnir."

"She's found a comfortable cave in the mountains. She and Faf weren't leaving to see Fafnir until tomorrow. If I mindcall, I'm sure she'll come."

"I'm not certain I want you to take the risk. It may be that on Realm, dragons can only fly from place to place instead of from time to time. Perhaps Ebony isn't strong enough, or—"

"Don't be silly. She's coming now. She'll meet us at the north gate," Mirza called over her shoulder, running down the corridor.

"Wait for me." Jarl dashed after her, watching her long auburn hair flow behind her as she sped into the street.

Jarl marveled that no one in the city stopped him. Everyone knew Mirza. She called greetings as she hurried by, with Jarl following her as closely as he could. She was amazingly fleet of foot (perhaps because she understood the movements of animals). He stopped twice to make apologies, but she never bumped anyone.

The guard smiled indulgently as they flew by him. It occurred to Jarl that the people they met must think he and she were lovers. The fatuous look on the gatekeeper's face confirmed Jarl's suspicion.

In an open space on a small hillock outside the city gates, Faf and Ebony perched like two overgrown canaries. The dragons had the advantage of being able to fly straight to the meeting place instead of dodging through winding city streets filled with half the population of Realmgate.

"Are you ready?" Ebony asked when Jarl and Mirza drew close and stopped to rest.

"Oh, yes. Can we go now?" Mirza asked, advancing to stand beside her friend.

"Wait a minute!" Jarl and Faf roared in unison.

"We've got to discuss this first," Jarl said.

"Where exactly are you and Ebony going?" Faf asked Mirza.

Mirza was almost incoherent because of her excitement. "Not where! When!"

"Not so fast," Jarl cautioned.

"Haste is imperative," put in Ebony. "Show him," she commanded Mirza.

"I don't want to—"

"Show me what?" Jarl asked belligerently. Things were moving too fast for him.

"Oh, Ebony, I hoped he wouldn't ever have to see." Under Jarl's scrutiny, she opened the top of her dress a fraction. A few inches from her neck a scaly green patina marred the whiteness of her skin.

Jarl's protest died a sudden death. Wordlessly he gathered Mirza close in his arms.

"You're right. There is no time to lose," Faf said. "I'll fly you into the past."

"I'm afraid not, Faf. There should be a special bond between rider and dragon. There is a better chance of that between Ebony and Mirza."

Mirza withdrew from Jarl's arms and stood next to Ebony. Without further speech, Ebony seized Mirza in her claws and rose into the air. Faf and Jarl were unprepared for their departure. The dragoness barely cleared the ground before she and her burden vanished.

A chill wind enveloped Jarl and the remaining dragon. *Goodb*—echoed in Jarl's mind amid a sensation of otherwhereness.

"They're gone," Jarl said flatly.

"We can follow," Faf hissed as he always did when he was genuinely disturbed.

"Where? or rather, when? Mirza didn't tell us where—or when—she intended Ebony to take her. Did Ebony tell you?"

"No, and there are too many places and times for us to be able to check."

"Were you linked to Ebony when they disappeared?"

"I had a sense of total blackness and cold, but nothing else." Faf's huge wings beat the air in frustration.

Jarl braced himself until Faf settled down again on the ground. "What are you going to do now?"

Faf shrugged his wings in an almost human gesture. "I'm not sure."

"Will you return to the cave Ebony found?"

"I'll nip back to my own cave and check my plants, work on a few spells, and wait."

"How can I get in touch with you so you'll know if they return?"

"Not if, Jarl. When. You don't know Ebony as I do. She's a very determined dragoness. If she sets her mind on going back in time, she'll arrive. We've talked about the Old Ones. In her family they remember many stories of which I knew nothing—and I am something of a historian. She, perhaps better than any living being that now exists, can visualize Realm as it was in the time of the Old Ones."

"I'm happy to hear it, but I can't help worrying. You still didn't tell me how to reach you," Jarl added as an afterthought.

"Every day at noon I'll return here for an hour. If Mirza and Ebony return, I'll be here."

"Very well, take care. If the Shadowlord figures out who helped Mirza and me to escape, he may want to gain revenge," Jarl warned.

Faf's next words proved how much adventuring had changed him. "I have a well-protected cave. One advantage of flying this new way instead of the regular way is instantaneous transportation. At Realmgate it should be safe enough—until his army attacks."

Jarl watched silently as Faf rose into the air, flapped his wings once, and disappeared. Now the long wait for news began. Jarl trudged to the city. His enthusiasm for learning had dimmed. He scuffed his feet occasionally as he walked and took no note of the brightly hued garments of the populace. He started when someone placed a hand on his arm.

"Jarl, what happened out there?" Krom asked.

"Mirza and Ebony are seeking aid for a spell the Shadowlord cast over Mirza when she was his prisoner."

"Who has the power to lift an enchantment of that strength?"

"The Old Ones."

"The last Old One disappeared from Realm ten thousand springs ago!"

"I guess that's when they've gone," Jarl said.

"When they have gone? Don't you mean 'where'?" Krom's bushy eyebrows twitched while he struggled to understand.

"No. When. Ebony and Faf have discovered they have some abilities they didn't have before the Shadowlord began opening his version of a gate to admit the fantasy creatures from my world to Realm."

"They can fly into time itself?" The ends of Krom's mustache quivered with interest as he heard Jarl's information.

"Yes. In addition, they can fly instantly from one place to another in some kind of shortcut through—" Jarl groped for words, "—somewhere."

"By the Bright Ones! That's wonderful news. Their ability will be of great help to us in battle."

"Yes. I'd be feeling optimistic myself except for one thing."

Krom looked at Jarl expectantly, his inquiry written on his face.

"I'm not sure whether Ebony has the ability to fly back in time, Krom."

"Then where are they? I saw them disappear as I was searching for you."

"That's a good question. I only wish I knew the answer."

"When will you know for certain?"

"They set no time for their return. If they fly into the past, if they find the Old Ones, and if the Old ones can cure Mirza, then they will return."

"What you need is something to take your mind from this while you wait for news. No amount of worry will help, you know."

Jarl shrugged. "What do you suggest?"

"Some study about the powers of Wyrd, for one thing."

"How do you know about that?" Not for the first time Jarl felt as if everyone on Realm knew more about his business than he did.

"Andronan is my master," Krom said simply.

"I should have known. Are you some kind of Keeper, too?"

"You might say that." Krom's eyes twinkled. "Let us return to the university," he suggested, taking Jarl's arm just in time to pull him out of the way as a cart rumbled by.

"Agreed. Perhaps if I can command Wyrd's full power, Faf and I can search for Mirza."

"If she and her dragon find themselves trapped in a time corridor, there is no hurry."

"What's a time corridor?"

"One of the old books mentions something of the sort . . . "

"What are we waiting for? Come, show me where the book is," Jarl commanded, glad to have something he could do besides wait.

Krom hid his smile as best he could and accompanied Jarl along the streets of Realmgate, hoping to get him interested in his studies through the old manuscripts. The trader tossed a coin to a passing street vendor to pay for the two fruits he selected, then strode after his young friend to share his purchase.

Two weeks passed as Jarl immersed himself in learning all he could. His spare time rushed by. While he spent time perusing the old books, his main task was mastering his bracelet and the power he could summon with its aid. Every day at noon he strolled outside the city to meet Faf, who never failed to come, bringing steak fruit or some other proof of his horticultural prowess. The cook at the university appreciated the additional provender. So much so that a steak-plant seedling reached to the sky in the garden.

Jarl sat by an open window facing into the garden, when a messenger brought word that Andronan wanted to see him at once. Jarl closed the dusty tome respectfully and returned it to the old librarian, who could find any book at will, using some system known only to antiquarian librarians.

The man seemed as ancient as his volumes. Jarl believed he probably had read them all. The librarian was old enough. The rules for finding books in the library made little sense to Jarl. He was not the only student who found it easier to ask for help rather than search the shelves himself.

"Thank you, Librisald," Jarl said, handing the book to the librarian carefully.

"You are most welcome, Jarl. I have noticed with satisfaction your joy in the old histories of Realm. So few appreciate them, you see," he added sadly, pushing his long eyebrows out of one eye. His gnarled fingers touched a binding fondly.

"They're very interesting, but now I am summoned by Andronan." Jarl bowed his head in leave-taking as did all the other students who used the library. Everyone treated the old librarian with great respect.

Jarl located the gravity well with ease and walked out onto seeming nothingness with confidence. His rise was faster, for he found that by standing in the exact center one could almost double the speed of ascent.

Andronan's door was ajar, and yielded to him before he knocked. Within he saw a wyvern, Master Krom, and the Elder Keeper himself.

"Welcome, Man-one," the wyvern said, identifying herself as Seabreeze by her tone of voice and way of addressing Jarl.

"Good day to you all." Jarl smiled and turned to his host. "Andronan, is there something you wanted of me?"

"Yes, but Krom will tell you much you need to know." Andronan sat in the chair Jarl had created, but he motioned Jarl to another chair that faced them all.

Krom began without wasting any time. "The Shadowlord is massing an army on his northern border. Seabreeze brought us word. Relnot's magical powers have sealed the borders of King Caeryl's kingdom to all. The result is to protect the citizens and to force our enemies to detour, giving us several days' delay in the arrival at Realmgate. By tomorrow, a regiment of the King's best fighting men will be at our gates. The wyverns will hinder the Black Legion to give us more time to set up our defenses."

In the middle of his report, Krom started pacing as if he could not bear inaction, but he stopped, glanced at Andronan, and sat abruptly. "I'm sorry," he apologized to the older man.

"Years ago when I was assistant to the Elder Keeper. I also had difficulty in showing composure at all times," Andronan told Krom.

When the Elder Keeper finished speaking, Jarl asked, "What do you want with me?"

"You will lead our army in battle."

"What army?" Jarl had spent long hours at his studies and was unaware of the large force that mustered during his days and night of study.

"Each kingdom of Realm has sent a number of men. King Caeryl himself has sent a thousand," Krom said.

"The wyverns have sent three mistresses," Seabreeze said.

"Mistresses?" The word puzzled Jarl.

"You would call them adepts or workers of magic," Andronan told Jarl in serious tones, although his eyes twinkled at Jarl's lack of understanding.

"If you'll excuse me, it's almost noon. I'll need to speak to Faf when he comes. Then I want to see some of the troops I'll be leading and talk to their captains," Jarl said with sudden decision. He had never been a battle commander before, but he was a good chess player. He would not surrender Realmgate to the Shadowlord without putting up the best fight he was able to produce. The Dragon's Pawn now had the knowledge to become the Dragon's Knight.

Correct, a sibilant voice hissed in Jarl's mind.

"Give my flying cousin my regards, Man-one," Seabreeze said.

"I will," Jarl promised.

"You'll find the troops massed on the plain south of the city. I shall see you there this afternoon, I trust." Krom nodded shortly.

"Krom, I begin to have hope of victory," Andronan said as Jarl strode from the room, an excited gleam in his eyes.

CHAPTER TWENTY-FOUR

The icy lightlessness swirled around Mirza and Ebony.

The dragon's thought penetrated her companion's wonderment. "Picture with me the healing spring," Ebony urged. "See the day when the Green Lady presided over a newly created mere."

Mirza joined her thoughts to the dragon's. Ebony had a clear visualization of the spring area, complete with rose garden massed alongside a temple that was in ruins in their time. In a dim corner of her mind Mirza realized that this was a seeing passed down from mother to daughter for generations to insure the memory of the glory of the past. Then, with a wrench of the senses, they were there, a part of the scene they had envisioned together.

"We did it!" Mirza said jubilantly, enjoying the panoramic view that spread below them.

"Of course we did," Ebony replied with the saurian equivalent of a chuckle. "Was there any real doubt in your mind? Once you gave me the idea, I realized I could do it. So long as we can see the place and the time to which we go, I can take us anywhere and anywhen you choose." The quiet confidence of Ebony was cheering.

"Do you think the Old Ones or the Green Lady will be able to cure this?" Mirza's hand crept to her throat and withdrew hastily as her fingers touched rough scales.

"In the old stories I learned as a dragonette, there were miraculous healings—believe in a cure."

Ebony swooped in a vast circle searching for a smooth spot on which to land her rider. The courtyard behind the temple was small, but of adequate size to land if the flyer were careful and competent. Ebony alighted swiftly, releasing her claw grip of Mirza at the precise moment to let her stand upright on the pavement. Mirza staggered and would have fallen but for an assist from the dragon's tail which curled gently about her waist, giving her time to regain her balance.

"All in one piece?" Ebony asked.

"Yes, thank you. Do you—" Mirza began and stopped abruptly as she saw a tall, willowy form approaching. The Green Lady, legendary goddess of the pool, drew nearer. In the faded murals on the interior walls that were still standing in Mirza's time, artists had faithfully depicted the attributes of the goddess. No artist, however skillful, could do justice to the serenity of the wise green eyes of the Green Lady. The color reminded Mirza of every spring she had ever seen. Also brought to her heart were the first real rays of certainty that her plight was curable. Without her volition, Mirza's hand opened the top of her robe, exposing the scabrous ugliness to the view of those calm orbs which saw into her very soul.

"Come, daughter," a leaf-cool voice commanded softly. "You have almost left it too late. There is little time to waste."

"Don't you want to know—"

"Later, child, later. Now you need the water's power, pure and good. Bright Ones can work through the waters here," she continued, leading Mirza in the direction of the shimmering basin.

On the bank Mirza quickly divested herself of her clothes and slipped into the water, feeling it close over her fevered body with a caress of returning normalcy. The Green Lady entered the water, which seemed not to wet her robes. Her slender hand reached out in benediction and touched Mirza's head, indicating she should submerge herself completely. When Mirza regained her breath, the lady touched her head a second and then a third time. Her serene face lit with gladness. Mirza knew she had been freed from the spell.

The Lady returned to shore. She waved her hands in an intricate movement that caused the very air to become visible. In her hands she held a robe of the finest cloth. The iridescence of the material resembled the pale color in the buildings of the Old Ones in present-day Realmgate.

"Oh, is that for me?" Mirza said, when the Green Lady offered it to her.

"Woven from the dreams of the Bright Ones is this robe, and therefore it can be anything its wearer wishes."

Mirza was not able to imagine wishing it to be anything else than what it was. It clung to her body lovingly. In it she had the fragile beauty of a butterfly.

"Come. There is much for you to learn in your allotted span here with us. Only a most powerful being could so twist a spell of the Bright Ones to produce the enchantment that brought you here." The Green Lady's voice chimed against the slight breeze and interwove itself with a nearby bird's song.

Mirza marveled at the manner in which the lady blended into the natural beauties of the landscape. All of the harsh destruction that the years would wreak on the site had not yet happened. A springtime freshness was evident in every flower and blade of grass. The shapes of the blooms were subtly different, and the colors had a vibrancy of hue that had not survived into Mirza's time.

"Can you tell me who the Bright Ones are? I always thought it was another way of referring to your people."

"Ah, no, my daughter. The Bright Ones are the stars themselves, more mighty far than we. In their infancy they had physical bodies as do we, but now they are pure thought. We are their inheritors as you are our heirs."

"Do you serve them, then?"

"In a way. It had long been our task to guard the gates, those lines of communication made possible by the will of the Bright Ones. We may, if it is needful, pass between the children of the Bright Ones."

"Then the children of the Bright Ones are suns!"

"Correct," the Green Lady answered.

"How wonderful that you are able to open and close the gates."

"It is both our blessing and our curse. Some of us are even now using our power to enslave and toy with the fortunes of the simpler beings that inhabit the worlds which circle the suns."

"Why don't you stop the evil ones?"

"Because it is not in our nature to kill, only to heal and help."

"We are much in need of your powers in my time. There is in Realm an evil one who serves the Dark—-the Shadowlord," Mirza explained simply.

"I have seen your coming and the future of Realm in the face of the moon. I am to teach you to strengthen the gate magic, now weakening for lack of understanding.

"We have the university at Realmgate, where all the old books are. Some of us study all our lives to keep the gates."

"Does it not take at least three of you in your time to open the door between the worlds?" The lady's smile took most of the sting from her words.

"Yes." Mirza looked down at the ground, and then she raised her chin defiantly. "We do serve the gate," she said proudly.

"You keep the gates. Pleased are we with the Keepers."

"Why did the Old Ones leave Realm? Surely you could have stayed to keep the gates if it was your wish."

"In my vision I see the natural abilities of the human race twisted, dwarfed, and stunted because of the powers that we used, meaning only to help them. Soon I must tell our Council. They will agree that we must move from Realm so that your race may grow and prosper."

"But—" Mirza began in denial.

The Green Lady raised a finger for silence. "It is time for us to move to another existence in another reality."

Mirza frowned, trying to understand.

"Those of us who elect to obey the Council will become . . . " She searched for words which would have meaning for her curious listener, " . . . things of the spirit, totally free of our material bodies, free to wander not only from one world to the next, but also free to move in the spaces between universes and in the stream of time itself."

Mirza's silence showed her degree of incomprehension.

"It is of no matter. Those of us who most helped the creatures of this world will not vanish without preparing a gradual withdrawal of our gifts. I was the healer. This spring will cure physical ills and give peace to twisted minds for many years after I have gone."

"You look sad. I am sorry," Mirza said.

"There is no need, daughter. For us, the millennia we have enjoyed physically were a type of childhood. It is no easier for an Old One to become mature than it is for your kind," she said with a wry smile. "Since you have come all this time, I must teach you some of the magical skills you will need to set your universe aright. The forces of the Light must triumph over the forces of the Dark this time."

They walked to the center of the rose garden where Mirza smelled a lavender blossom with delight. She flushed guiltily. "I forgot. Where is Ebony?"

"I mindcalled her ancestress to offer her hospitality while we are together. You would not want her to lose the opportunity to learn more legends for her vast store of knowledge."

"Do you know everything?" Mirza burst out, awed by the revelations of the lady.

"I am the Green Lady. I weave the web of life for many. The thoughts of all things living I can see," she sighed. "Because that is my curse, I dwell far from most of those you call the Old Ones."

"Curse? It would be wonderful to have your ability!"

"You speak as a child. Would you want every evil idea that hatches in the dark reaches of the minds of those around you to be your burden? You would know every lie, every greed, every perversion of the good that existed. Those who were not perfect in their thinking would shun you. Do not wish for such an ability."

Mirza felt the rebuke keenly, but she said nothing, for she knew she had wished foolishly. How could the lady teach anyone as thoughtless as she?

"Do not take on such a burden, daughter. Your judgment of yourself is too harsh. I will teach you many things that can only enhance your natural abilities and help to make you a force for good."

Mirza basked in the ray of the Green Lady's smile. Threaded amid her excitement was the humble desire to be worthy of the lady's teachings.

"Let us enter the temple and begin," the Green Lady said, drifting over the ground like mist. She entered a small door outlined by a cascade of roses red as blood.

Mirza wished Jarl could know she was free of the Shadowlord's spell, but she dared not return until she learned all the Green Lady wished to teach her. The scent of the roses clung to her dress as she entered the door in her turn.

Jarl wearily dismounted from Oromon, the magnificent war stallion that was the gift of King Caeryl. "Give him a good rubdown, will you?" he said. He waited for the freckle-faced groom's acknowledgement of his order before adding, "Add an extra measure of oats. He deserves them." Jarl stroked the velvety nose that nudged his chest. "Yes, boy, rest well. Tomorrow night the moon will be a silver sickle in the sky. In the waning of the Light, the powers of the Dark will rise and do battle."

"Are—-are we ready, sir?" the groom asked timidly, which surprised Jarl because, as a normal thing, every freckle on the boy's face danced with mischief.

Jarl smiled at him grimly. "As ready as anyone can be for a Lord of Shadows," he said as his hand gripped the groom's shoulder in a reassuring contact. "If each of us does his part, we shall make a good fight."

He watched as Oromon tamely followed the groom to his stall. Realmgate bulged at the seams. Each building housed some of Jarl's army. The citizens regarded it a honor to host the Legion of Light within their walls. Remembering how people in his world felt about quartering soldiery, Jarl couldn't help but appreciate the hospitality bestowed on his soldiers. He realized that most of the fighting men would revert to being simple citizens themselves after the battle.

In his room he stepped into the marble tub already prepared for him. He was seldom alone and had less time than that for reflection, but as always his thoughts went to Mirza. She and Ebony had been gone for weeks. Would they return? There was no way of knowing until Faf was free to begin their agreed search in otherwhere—or otherwhen, he amended his thoughts.

Faf roosted in an empty tower above the university. He kept the old librarian rummaging through long-undisturbed stacks of tomes for books to delight his taste for ancient history. If Librisald liked Jarl, he positively doted on the dragon. The elderly man and the saurian spent many interesting hours researching and sharing their finds. The more obscure the item was, the more pleasure it gave them to find it.

One piece of research made them aware that Wyrd was more of an amplifier of power than a source. For that reason, the person who wore the bracelet had to understand the basic tenets of magic. Under the direction of the Dragon's Knight, Wyrd could lend strength to the power of other, more magically talented people.

Jarl blessed Lythyr for sending the three mistresses. He couldn't tell them apart. When they united to accomplish a task, they evinced all the paranormal abilities known on Jarl's world plus a few he had not known existed. Magic seemed to consist of an ability to turn probabilities into realities.

Jarl enjoyed the new room he had been assigned by Andronan. It shielded him from the common coming and going of the myriad of people that overflowed the main building and filled the town. He was a light sleeper and found the responsibility thrust upon him caused him to awaken at a hint of noise, of difference, of change. He didn't understand how he almost slept through his first meeting with the Dark Forces. Now the slightest tightening of Wyrd would bring him to his feet, alert and ready for whatever came.

He padded to the bed, where a clean tunic and breeches rested as if put there by invisible hands. Tieron, his servant, was as awed of Jarl as he was of Andronan. He appeared instantly at Jarl's call, but otherwise he served silently and unobtrusively. Jarl fastened his belt around his waist and pulled on his boots. He was ready to go down for his evening meal.

Wyrd tightened on his arm.

"Well, this is it," Jarl said aloud. "A day early, too!"

Not sso. Mirza returns. Wyrd's words hissed in Jarl's mind.

"When? I mean, where?" Jarl asked, striding down the hall and jumping into the gravity well that would take him to the lower floor.

At the place where you left her, Wyrd answered.

Jarl paused to say to a student, "Send word to Faf in the tower. The Lady Mirza has returned!"

Too preoccupied to notice the shadows that gathered in dark pools in relatively protected places, he raced out of the university and through the streets of the city. He nodded and waved briefly to citizens he knew. They stood talking in small groups after he passed them on his way to the north gate.

Scouts' reports from the west told of vast windstorms over Gran Desierto. The sun was shrouded by the amount of flying sand in the air. It reposed, blood-red, on the top of the low range of mountains to the west. Jarl judged the sun would set in two hours. He increased his pace. He wanted Mirza and Ebony inside the walls of the university before nightfall.

A heat haze rose from the bare rocks which formed a portion of the northern plain. Wyrd clasped his wrist firmly, as if to remind him of the nearness of the dark. Occasionally Jarl's peripheral vision caught hints of filmy shapes. One resembled a giant lizard, but not exactly. Another vision was an amorphous blob, an animated mouth, complete with yard-long fangs. If the massing horrors took part in the attack on Realmgate, the mistresses from Wyvern Marsh would have enough to slay. Even their bloodthirsty instincts for revenge would be sated, Jarl thought as he jogged onward.

In the distance, silhouetted on the ruby disk of the sun, the gigantic black form of a dragon appeared in a wink. It increased in size as Jarl watched. A shadow passed overhead. Jarl drew his battle sword. He reluctantly turned his eyes from Ebony to face the new danger, only to relax with a sigh. It was Faf, who settled beside him and hissed a greeting that was almost unintelligible. Jarl observed that in moments of great emotion, Faf's precise human mindspeech became more reptilian.

Where was Mirza? She had left clutched in the talons of the dragoness. Now he could not see her. Had something gone wrong? "Faf! Can you see Mirza?"

Faf gazed at him with one plate-sized orb. "She is safe."

"I can't see her!"

"Wait and you will," Faf advised. "Why not try mind-talk?"

Jarl called mentally, then looked at Faf. "You see—-"

We're coming. Don't be so impatient, Mirza's thought reached out to silence Jarl.

Welcome home, Faf said as Ebony made a two-talon landing beside the watchers.

I'm hungry, Ebony said as Mirza slid from her seat between her wings. When she rode, Ebony's neck hid her.

Jarl gathered Mirza in his arms. Faf showed his joy by ecstatically blowing a series of smoke rings into the air.

"You weren't really worried about us, were you?" Ebony said. She was astounded at their relief. "I wouldn't put Mirza in danger. I knew I could do it," Ebony told them modestly. Only Faf seemed to hear her, so she gently nudged Jarl in the back, almost knocking him down.

"Hmmm? Oh, yes, of course," he said. His mind was on other things than conversation.

"There was no danger," Ebony repeated.

The words registered this time. "Well, I'm glad to have you both back safely."

"If the reports we've been getting are correct, there will be danger in plenty as soon as it gets dark tonight," Faf said grimly.

"You're right. We'd better get these two inside the gates." Jarl kept his arm around Mirza as they talked.

"Can't we go to our cave in the hills?" Ebony asked.

"Not tonight. Realmgate is the focus of the Dark Legions. The mistresses from Wyvern Marsh have seen a host of evil slowly closing in on the city," Jarl answered.

Faf snorted a jet of fire. "Let them come. We're ready to fight."

"Weren't you a pacifist when we left?" Mirza looked puzzled by Faf's warlike air.

"Still am," he averred. "However, if you had been here and heard about the kinds of outrages the Dark Legions have perpetrated on anyone unlucky enough to fall into their power—well!" He emphasized his point with a three-yard burst of pure blue flame.

"What about the wounded?"

"Come with me. You can see the casualties that survived to shelter with us," Jarl told Mirza. "We've hauled barrels of the healing water. That cures some of the minor wounds, but others are beyond the water's power." His clenched teeth told her how badly hurt the worst cases were.

"Show me the water. There is something I can do to increase its strength," Mirza said, walking rapidly toward the north gate and safety.

"I'll see you in the tower after dinner," Jarl called to the two dragons that rose into the air behind them and quickly passed above them.

CHAPTER TWENTY-FIVE

An icy blast scudded black clouds toward the half disk of the sun that was still visible above the mountain peaks. As Jarl and Mirza entered the gates, the huge portals closed silently behind them. They turned to watch the clouds occlude the sun as preternatural twilight closed over Realmgate.

"We'll not have long now before their first attack, sir," the gate guard said, hefting his war ax in his hand.

"Send word at the first sign of attack."

"Yes, Sir Jarl!"

Mirza covered her mouth with her hand. "Sir Jarl?" She giggled.

"I've asked them to call me plain Jarl, but I seem stuck with the title."

"Don't worry," she told him with mock seriousness. "I'll call you Plain Jarl if it will make you happy."

"I'll call you plain minx," he said, giving her a hug as he guided her through the almost deserted streets.

"Where is everybody?"

"We thought it best if the women and children remain indoors. Some women are tending the sick in the refectory at the university. The men are waiting in their assigned places. We're ready to repulse an attack."

"It sure does feel warm," Mirza commented, lifting her long hair from her neck.

"You're right. Every night until tonight it's been cold. Now it's warm." As Jarl spoke, the heat increased. "Get inside," he said, shoving her gently through the outer gate to the university. "This is part of the attack. I recognize it," he finished bitterly.

"What is it?"

"It's a fire storm. If the wyvern mistresses and Andronan can't extinguish it or shift it or something, we'll all be very dead shortly." He turned his back on her abruptly, running toward the south gate. He knew it would only be a matter of time until every combustible thing burst into flame spontaneously. Sometimes he almost regretted the amount of knowledge he gained from reading those books that Librisald gave him to study.

"My Lord Jarl," a sweating guardsman said. "Look!"

Jarl didn't need the pointed finger to show him the direction of the bright ball of flame that raced toward the walls. It expanded from its white-hot core to a gigantic size as they watched. Despite their bravery, the heat overcame some men. Jarl felt nauseated himself. His armor was hot to the touch.

"All right, Wyrd. Now what?" he asked.

Wyrd glowed with a phosphorescent light that spread downward onto the iridescent walls that surrounded Realmgate. A cool breeze sprang up and rushed to meet the blazing air. From the walls themselves a vapor misted, smelling of fresh spring rain, diluting the scent of charred wood. Before the eyes of the startled defenders, a huge whirlpool of disturbed air formed. Thunder boomed and lightning cracked. The walls emitted a soft, white vaporous moistness that spread a protective layer over the entire city.

The storm raged in a pyrotechnical display that was a thousand times the equivalent of any fireworks Jarl had ever seen. When heavy rain began to fall, he managed a weak question. "Wyrd, did you do all that?" He expected no answer to his rhetorical question, but this time his talisman was almost garrulous.

The Old Ones built the city. Thought you that unrealmly science could breach its walls? The walls themselves were their own defender. Now the Shadowlord must wage war fairly and in the proper manner. The smug complacency to Wyrd's mental message chilled Jarl. Who but an alien creature would think that wars were fought according to some etiquette?

After Jarl checked the guard posts along the walls, he was certain the attack was over—at least for a time. The hard rain pelted the ground, splattered wetly, and filled the streets with water, then ran along the ancient cobblestones and exited the city via great conduits. Gradually it slackened to a fine mist that stopped after a final wisp over the city.

Jarl saw the faint gray line in the east that presaged the dawn. He believed the light brought safety, but in that assumption he was incorrect. Almost within minutes of the sun's rising, the heat combined with the watery mist that saved Realmgate to form a heavy blanket of humidity. The heat and humidity made every breath an effort. The heat brought with it a feeling of despair. Jarl didn't see how anyone could fight well under the conditions that prevailed in the city. His only hope was that the Shadowlord's forces would suffer as well. He forced a smile at the tired defenders he saw as he headed for the refectory at the university.

"You were magnificent!" Mirza told him excitedly as he snatched a hurried bit of food.

"I was?" Jarl mumbled between mouthfuls.

"The way you held Wyrd and he called the stones of the walls to save us . . . " Her voice died when she saw the look on his face.

"Where were you during the attack that could give you such a vantage point?"

"Up in the tower with Faf and Ebony."

"In the tower! You little—muttonhead! What do you think I shoved you into the university for? I thought you'd have the sense to stay with Andronan. Why in the name of the Bright Ones did he let you go into that tower?"

A ghostly chuckle echoed in his mind. Faf's precise mental message was succinct. *Do you think any being could stop her if she decided to do something?*

Jarl paused. *You're right,* he thought in the dragon's direction.

We wouldn't let anything happen to her, Ebony explained in mindspeech. *Besides, she is a powerful mage herself.*

It wasn't the first mental communication Jarl received from the dragoness, but it surprised him that he recognized her so easily. Magic and mindspeech were psi abilities he was coming to take for granted.

"What could you do against a menace like that fire storm?" he said aloud. He wanted to give his message maximum clarity, and hearing the words helped him to focus his thought.

The dragoness's answer made his mind feel as if it had just received a sharp tap. *I would have flown her to another time or place.*

"Taken her to top of the tower with you, I suppose?" Jarl lasered a thought upward in exasperation.

Oh, I didn't think of that.

Jarl felt the mental anger of Faf building. Therefore he said, "Well, you should. It would upset Mirza if you destroyed the university. I do appreciate your care of her."

"I would much prefer it if you three would stop talking about me as if I were a wayward child," interrupted Mirza.

Jarl eyed the curves the iridescent dress outlined so faithfully. "Wayward, I agree with you one hundred percent. Now, as to the child part—"

"Men!" Mirza snorted in exact imitation of Ebony.

A messenger rushed into the room, bowed respectfully to Mirza, and said, "Sir Jarl, strange visions are appearing outside the walls."

Bidding Mirza a quick good-bye, Jarl hurried after the messenger. He joined a group of men on the wall. Strange shapes swirled from a ground-hugging miasma that seeped into the air. It smelled like stagnant pond water. The men watched silently. They knew that if the nightmare shapes materialized inside the walls, they would have to fight them in hand-to-hand combat

"They are demons from another world," Mirza said in Jarl's ear.

"You get inside someplace," he commanded as he slipped his arm around her waist for a quick hug.

"Don't be silly. If these demons are materializing from the Earth, they may be capable of appearing anywhere inside the walls as well as outside. Where do you suggest I go?" she asked sweetly.

Jarl knew when she used the saccharine, submissive style of speaking she was most stubborn. "Well, at least you could stay near Ebony," he growled.

"I shall go help the wyverns," Mirza announced. "I know when I'm not wanted." She pulled free of Jarl's encircling arms and descended to ground level so rapidly she disappeared into the unnatural darkness as if by magic.

"Jarl, trying to keep the Lady Mirza out of danger is a hopeless task," Krom said as he stepped up beside the younger man on the walls.

"Can't she see—those things out there are becoming more solid by the minute and they'll rush us," said Jarl. "I've better things to do than worry over her hurt feelings."

"I've known her since she was born. She doesn't hold a grudge—-usually," Krom added an admonitory condition to his comforting words.

The sun's rays poured from the sky, sucking the water from every puddle and adding to the humidity s as a mass of unbelievable horrors became carnate before Realmgate. The demons came in many colors, all evoking sensations of discomfort when Jarl tried to look at them closely. None of the shades were normal. They hurt human eyes when they forced themselves to look at them. They called forth the basest feelings men were capable of experiencing. As soon as human minds registered their unnaturalness, they shifted into something worse. Some resembled the paintings of Hieronymus Bosch. Some were composed of portions of animals that seemed vaguely familiar. Some resembled Jarl's choicest nightmares, and others bore no likeness to anything describable. No matter what the form, sullenness and total enmity radiated from each.

Wyrd grew steadily tighter until Jarl gasped, "All right. I'm alert. If you keep tightening, I'll be a one-handed fighter. My fingers are cold as it is." Wyrd relaxed in response to Jarl's complaint.

Hopping, skittering, crawling, scuttling, the nightmare attackers came at the walls. The rain of arrows from the defenders did only slight damage, and few of the demons were stopped by the barrage. Jarl moved to the ladder that descended near the south gate where the major attack massed. He drew his sword and felt the strange life that pulsed within, eager to slay. Then the first of the shapes touched the walls of Realmgate. Howls of pain and terror rose from the demons. They melted away like ice upon a warm hearth.

"Wyrd," Jarl began.

It is the wyverns and Mirza. They have powered an ancient defense built into the walls. Mirza must have learned of it when she went back in time, Wyrd answered, before Jarl had voiced his question.

The cheers of the defenders rose over the mewling caterwauling of the demon horde. Jarl knew the battle was far from over, however, for Wyrd had not loosened his firm grip of Jarl's wrist. Jarl turned to speak to his men and looked behind him for the first time. The demons, who had disappeared from before the walls of Realmgate, had rematerialized inside the walls, behind the row of resolute defenders.

"Don't desert your posts," Jarl cried. "Pass the word. Work in pairs." Jarl sent a messenger to inform Andronan of the latest calamity. He summoned the few reserves that remained, men he had allowed to rest. While his losses were not as great as the Shadowlord's, there had been a steady attrition as the wounded had disappeared into the university for care. Jarl felt the heavy sense of doom that hung over the battle sites. He forced himself to advance on the demons who attacked the defenders far inside the walls. They outnumbered Jarl's forces. When the next wave attacked from the outside, Jarl knew they also would breach the walls. What he needed was a new weapon. Where was he to find one? His forces stretched thinly around the walls. He didn't have an inexhaustible source of manpower, or demonpower, he thought sourly.

Drive them over here, to the square in front of the tower, Faf mentally commanded. *They are creatures of the dark, and they can't stand against fire!*

Jarl commanded his men, "Light the torches that line the walls. Use them to drive the demons!"

Every spare man—and some that weren't—began driving the demons before Faf and Ebony.

The dragons spouted long gouts of flame that effectively dispersed the demons.

Jarl and the other sweating defenders stood victorious. They were so enervated by the heat and the humidity, they could only turn and slog grimly back to their posts on the walls of Realmgate.

"Count off by threes. Excuse every third man for a break to drink and cool off," Jarl shouted.

Jarl's command sobered the ebullient spirits of the battle-weary men who had yet to face the minions of the Shadowlord at close quarters.

"What is he likely to send against us next?" Jarl asked Krom, noticing the sun flickered, then resumed shining, but not as brightly. The day darkened much as it does before a major storm when heavy clouds cover the sun. Only now there was not a cloud in the sky. Jarl worried. How dark could it get? There was still light enough to see by, but he preferred the full light of the sun. What damage was being done to the sun by the Shadowlord's illegal gate? Jarl hadn't studied enough to know all the details, but he knew there were limits beyond which it could be fatal to steal energy from a sun.

"Otherworld science failed, as did otherworld demons. Now he will use the creatures he has created in his laboratories," replied Krom.

Krom's estimate of the situation proved to be correct. The last of the demons disappeared in a red haze. In their place marched regiments of human beings.

"Are there so many renegades who would desert humanity?" Jarl asked bitterly, thinking of the men who would die at his command.

Before Krom could answer, the men on the walls began crying out, "That's my neighbor who disappeared two years ago," "There's my brother," "I see my sister's child, killed in a battle with the Dark Ones . . . "

The voices carried anger, pity, and grief. Jarl understood the Shadowlord's plan. His men would face the forms of those they knew or loved. "Don't panic, men," Jarl called. "Those who approach are only shells, the outer husks of those whom you knew. They have been reanimated by the Shadowlord's necromancy."

Mutterings greeted Jarl's announcement, but each man kept to his post.

The human forms ran the short distance to the walls and began hoisting the scaling ladders that they carried. A giant of a man hacked at the oaken gate, uttering bestial roars.

"That's Hugh, the blacksmith. He's the strongest man in King Caeryl's kingdom," a youth said with awe in his voice.

"Aye, that he was," his grizzled companion agreed.

The very gate itself reverberated to the powerful blows being rained upon it. With an earsplitting sound, the gate that had protected this section of the city for years gave way. Jarl came down from the walls and faced the blacksmith, unconscious of his rapid descent.

The sword in Jarl's hand glowed with the heat of battle. It parried the thrusts of the immense Hugh, who did not seem physically hindered by being a living dead man. Jarl's sword flashed, gashing great wounds in the pale flesh of the Shadowlord's creation, who fought on bloodlessly. All around him, he could feel the battle rage. In a daring move, Jarl ducked under the arms of his enemy and beheaded the one-time blacksmith. He paused a fraction of a second and almost lost his arm when the giant fought on, minus his head. Unable to see, the monster cut a wide swath with his weapon. Jarl dismembered the body piece by piece. Not until Jarl hacked the legs and arms from the torso did the body give a final twitch and melt away into an oily black spot. It exuded the foul stench of corruption. The day seemed to lighten fractionally as the evil creatures died, Jarl noted. He hoped it wasn't just wishful thinking.

Jarl led the soldiers sent by King Caeryl. Although the group was only half its original size, they burst through the gates in the walls of the city in the forefront of the group that attacked the Black Legion. The solid thud of the repaired gates behind them reminded them there would be no turning back until the battle ended. The defenders of Realmgate had learned that dismembering the enemy brought an end to their unnatural lives. Grimly, with a sense of purpose, they fought the not-men, who had once been their friends and loved ones.

As Krom remarked to Jarl later, "Each man felt he was allowing those he fought to obtain a clean death at last, so that they might rest in peace."

The vast number of living dead dissolved before the eyes of the war-weary defenders. Only a few pockets of resistance remained, and they were widely scattered.

Jarl allowed his fingers to loosen on the hilt of his sword. He was bone tired. Looking at his men, he realized how exhausted they were. He was just about to order the gated reopened when he noticed the faint shimmer that always preceded the arrival of more of the Shadowlord's hellish allies. The sun itself paled. What now? Jarl thought to himself wearily. He watched in disbelief as characters from man's vast array of fiction began to appear on the battlefield and engage his weary men.

Over half of his men were gone. Hundreds of new allies of the Shadowlord kept appearing before him. *Faf*, he called mentally. *Can you and Ebony help?*

Sorry, Jarl. We're all flamed out from the last wave.

For the first time Jarl considered the possibility of actually losing to the Shadowlord. His sword arm ached. How could the rest of his men keep fighting? They didn't have magic swords to keep them. *Wyrd*, he called in desperation.

Wait, Knight.

Knight? Jarl clenched his teeth. Now was no time for a battlefield promotion. They were about to lose the war! Jarl hacked grimly, lopping off the limbs of the indescribable creature that faced him, hoping each stroke could be his last.

Behind him he heard the great gates of Realmgate swing open. He didn't have the time to turn around and look to see who was joining his side. There couldn't be many, that was for sure.

A huge wolf, easily three times Faf's size, had materialized on Jarl's left along with a laughing man with fire-red hair. Jarl recognized them both: Fenris the Wolf of the World's End and Loki, the Trickster, from Norse mythology. They wreaked havoc among Jarl's thinly spread troops.

Jarl began to work his way toward them when two huge men passed him, running easily. Jarl did not recognize them at first. When he did, he shouted for joy. The one-handed warrior was Tyr, the legendary enemy of Fenris. The other man was Prometheus, from Greek mythology, long the friend of man as Loki had long been man's enemy.

"How did this happen?" Jarl said aloud.

CAROL L. DENNIS

Andronan and I worked together, Wyrd hissed happily in Jarl's ears. *If the Shadowlord could bring evil creatures, why could we not summon good ones?*

Jarl sensed the satisfied tones of his bracelet. He glanced at it and could have sworn it wore a smirk. He picked up his sword to join the battle once more.

Rest now, Dragon's Knight, Wyrd commanded. *We may have need of your talents later.*

So Jarl watched the miraculous battle unfold. Arrows thunked into the carcasses of strange beasts. The Lincoln-green of the archers told him Robin Hood's band was on his side.

The one-eyed Egyptian who battled another must be Horus and his legendary enemy, Set, the Egyptian god of evil. Jarl didn't see any modern characters from fiction that had come to the aid of Realm's defenders.

Need science to fight, hissed Wyrd.

Jarl guessed the two huge men with the curly black hair and hooked noses were Gilgamesh and Enkidu from Babylonian mythology. They were superb fighters, and Jarl admired their technique. Two ogres who were even uglier than Mog struggled with a giant blue ox and another man who was even larger. Jarl recognized Paul Bunyan as the giant ax flashed, lopping limbs. Paul's laughter boomed across the battlefield.

As Jarl scanned the battlefield, Wyrd tightened. Jarl felt the cold chill of danger behind him. He swung around, sword ready to strike.

The Shadowlord stood, enigmatic as ever. His hooded robe hid any humanity the Shadowlord might claim. The long-nailed fingers started to move in an intricate pattern, forming a black hieroglyphic that hung in the air as if it were written on paper.

Jarl stood, mesmerized by the magic of the Shadowlord. Time slowed and the Shadowlord's actions commanded all of Jarl's attention. His muscles locked into rigidity. He strove to wield the sword, but his body was immobile. Only his mind raced, desperately searching for an answer.

A gray mist enclosed Jarl and the Shadowlord. The sun became a red ember as the Shadowlord tried to destroy Jarl. He realized he couldn't defeat the Shadowlord alone. *Wyrd!* Jarl mindcalled.

Strike! Wyrd commanded in a voice loud as thunder, which blew through the strange symbols, leaving tattered rags of black.

The symbols faded even as Jarl's sword glistened and hummed its way directly through the body of the Shadowlord. The mist disappeared abruptly and the Shadowlord himself paled and blew away on the wind.

Jarl watched dumbly, unable to believe he had defeated his enemy. He looked back at the battlefield, but he could see no trace of his adversary. It was too easy. Was the Shadowlord destroyed? Jarl wasn't sure. Where was he?

Wyrd did not respond to Jarl's repeated questioning, so Jarl assumed his talisman was searching for the elusive wizard. In the distance he heard the booming laughter of Paul Bunyan as his giant ax destroyed another evil creature.

This laughter seemed to be the actual turning point in the battle. The enemies of Realm were gradually winking out, recalled by the Shadowlord, who must have realized he was losing.

"Jarl!" Mirza called, running through the gate. "Come! The Shadowlord is escaping!"

Until their meeting, Jarl had seen no cowled figure on the field. He decided the Shadowlord must have retreated to Fellkeep, the nexus of his power. Jarl saw the Shadowlord's birdthings destroyed by Faf before he flamed out, but shadow magic could have enabled him to see through the eyes of any of his creatures. He knew Mirza's knowledge resulted from wyvern magic.

Ebony and Faf were already aloft as Mirza said, "The Shadowlord has withdrawn all his power from his creatures and allies. He is using it to force another gate at Fellkeep."

Faf swooped, clutching Jarl unceremoniously in his talons. At the same instant, Ebony snatched Mirza, who seemed better prepared for Ebony's actions. Great wings beat the air. The two dragons rose above Realmgate and disappeared.

There is no time to lose, Mirza mindspoke grimly into the black otherness in which they traveled. *If he forces a gate, he will escape.*

Jarl felt a queasy stab of vertigo as Faf dropped from the air above Fellkeep.

Mirza warned, *Back! It's too late!*

As Faf and Ebony wheeled away and upward, a coruscating light blazed below them.

It's the unchaneled power of the sun the Shadowlord harnessed. Help me close his gate or all of Realm perishes!

Jarl received a psychic picture of a vast yawning maw, incandescent with raw fusion. While Mirza veiled the light with a green shield that flickered insubstantially, Jarl concentrated on reinforcing her command of the shield, picturing a solid, nonpermeable substance. As his mental eyes "saw" the shield, his physical vision fixed itself on Wyrd, calling on the store of magic to which the dragon bracelet was the key.

The green orbs of the dragon grew. A lambent coolness bathed the mental projection that Mirza and Jarl shared. A slight tremor passed through Jarl's body. Almost at the end of his endurance, he wondered how Mirza was able to continue. Her chalk-white face was masklike with concentration. Then when Jarl could stand the tension no longer, the linkage they shared snapped just as a solid green shield extinguished the last escaping gleams of raw force.

Mirza turned her pale face toward him. "That gate closed. It can never be reopened." Then she smiled wearily. "Look at your bracelet. All the scales have turned to gold!"

During the excitement of sealing the gate, Jarl had forgotten where he was. The tight grasp of Faf reminded him that he and Mirza were hundreds of feet in the air, firmly clutched in the talons of two dragons. The dragons had circled the scene of the action while the gate sealing took place.

How about returning to Realmgate—if we're finished here?

Have you the power, my friends? Mirza asked.

A mental snort from Ebony was the answer.

Jarl had one moment to glance down at the blasted, smoking gate ruins that covered the top of the cliff with rubble. Then they were otherwhere. The black nothingness was a welcome relief after the raw power they had battled. Suddenly they were above the city. They landed gently on the clock tower of the university. A great cheer rose from the populace when they recognized Jarl and Mirza.

EPILOGUE

The cool hall of the university, once so strange to Jarl, now seemed like home. He watched Mirza's color return to normal as they rode the gravity well to Andronan's room.

"Hail, Dragon's Knight," Andronan and Krom intoned together as Jarl entered the room.

"We sealed the minigate the Shadowlord created, Grandfather," Mirza announced.

"That was only a minigate?" Jarl gasped.

Krom and Andronan smiled at Jarl's flash of naiveté. Mirza grasped his hand firmly and nodded.

"We owe you a great deal of thanks. You both have done a very brave thing," Krom spoke quietly.

"The Shadowlord got away," Jarl said.

"To face the unharnessed power of a gate, even with the help of Wyrd, takes courage."

"We didn't have a lot of choice." Jarl grinned, giving Mirza's hand a squeeze.

"Faf and Ebony would have taken you otherwise. Had you chosen, you and Mirza could have escaped Realm and left us to our fate," Andronan said as he laid an approving hand over their clasped fingers.

"What would have happened if we hadn't been able to close the gate?" Jarl asked, feeling curiosity now that he had time to think.

"The gate would have absorbed Realm, and the sun would have died," Andronan said.

"How can a sun die?" scoffed Jarl.

"We do not understand exactly, but whatever sun was powering the gate would have disappeared from its logical place in all the universes. We do not know where such suns go," Andronan told them.

"You have done well," Krom told Jarl seriously, from his seat near the window.

Faint sounds of revelry came through the opening, reminding Jarl of the people below. "How are my men?"

"All who have survived are well or are being tended by the wyverns. Mirza revitalized the spring of healing during the battle. The water saved many lives. The cures it now fosters are miraculous."

Andronan looked from Jarl to Mirza. "It is time for your reward, Dragon's Knight," he said.

"Reward?" Jarl repeated.

"Was not your greatest wish to return home?"

"Well, yes, at one time, but—"

"Earth needs you. The Shadowlord will not rest or know satisfaction until he masters the universes. The keepers on all planets will watch. Now that we now no longer need face evil here on Realm, we will be free to train many of our young as Keepers. For now, however, we are woefully short of watchers."

"What do you have to do to be a keeper?" Jarl asked, knowing he was going to volunteer to watch over Earth, before he heard what he must do to qualify. There was no way the scientific community could counter the magic of the Shadowlord, should he decide to invade. After all, people will not fight something they don't believe in—or in this case, something they believe doesn't exist.

"You need to understand the gate system," Krom said.

Jarl nodded yes, vigorously. Part of his study time had taught him gate lore.

"Also you need a partner," Andronan added slyly.

"Oh." Jarl's face fell. He didn't think Faf would leave Ebony to go with him.

"Let us go to the gate area. With three of us, we can open the gate and send you home. We will send someone—suitable." Andronan's eyes twinkled. "When we can."

The gravity well moved them down slowly, probably because all four of them were in it at the same time. Jarl wanted to stay on Realm, but he realized it would be impossible to let Earth be unprotected. How long would the Shadowlord take to recoup his losses? Where would he appear next?

The gate covered a huge, flat area behind the main tower that housed the clock. Faf and Ebony perched on the tower's crenellated edge, much like a pair of giant economy-sized lovebirds. Jarl suspected they had been mentally eavesdropping, but he didn't care. Faf was one of the reasons why he would miss Realm.

I learned much in my adventures with you. Faf's words echoed in Jarl's head as he took the place Andronan indicated near the center of the golden star that marked the portal.

I'll miss you, Jarl thought back. *You, too, Ebony,* he added.

I owe you thanks, Ebony spoke in his mind. *Without your removal of that cursed necklace, Faf would still be in his cave alone.*

Jarl caught a flash of Faf's horror at the thought. *Goodbye, you two,* he spoke to them mentally for the last time. "Good-bye, Andronan, Krom." He bent his head toward each man briefly. Then Jarl turned to Mirza. "I'll miss you, too."

"For goodness' sake, why?"

"Well, you'll not be a very easy person to—-forget," Jarl ended weakly. "You'll be here, and I'll be on Earth, and—" He stopped because Rory and the witch materialized next to Andronan.

"Hello, Grandmother," Mirza said calmly.

"I thought it was time for good-byes, so I picked up Rory—"

"Without so much as a by-your-leave, as usual," the feisty leprechaun spluttered.

"Didn't you want to come?" the old woman asked him teasingly.

Rory's face flamed another shade brighter, but he ignored her and said to Jarl, "You be careful. Don't let that bracelet get you into any trouble." Rory offered his hand to Jarl along with the advice.

"I'll be careful," Jarl promised, shaking the Rory's small hand.

The students and faculty of the university had gradually gathered. Now they called their good-byes. Jarl felt angry. They were all smiling, except for Rory, whose grin literally went from ear to ear. Probably, they would be glad to see the last of him, Jarl thought to himself.

"Well," he added lamely, trying to be a good sport to the end, "good-bye, Mirza."

"You don't think I'm letting you go alone, do you?" Mirza said standing beside him, her face lit with the iridescent glow the star was beginning to cast. "Come on." She laughed, pulling him into the center of the star and through the gate.

"But—" Jarl began.

"No audience," Mirza assured him gaily.

"No audience?" Belatedly Jarl realized they stood under the old oak tree near his cabin.

She pulled down his head, snuggled close, and warned, "You'd better make this worth my while."

"Always happy to oblige you, my lady. I expect we'll have a little peace around here to get to know one another better."

"Much better," Mirza whispered in agreement.

On Jarl's wrist, the golden Wyrd relaxed his awareness of the pair and prepared to wait until he was summoned. One eye closed in a gentle wink, and his tiny gilded tongue curled into a dragon's version of a smile.

DRAGON'S KNIGHT

PROLOGUE

Four beings of pure energy joined in a preordained meeting, shaping a vast hall from the dust of interstellar space. Then, simply because they had the power to do so, they recreated the forms they had once worn.

The time for vengeance is at hand, Oron, a tall golden plume of light, intoned in the minds of the others.

There is a threat to the young Bright Ones. We must keep vigil, agreed Cronal, the second Watcher, smoothing his star-pale beard with an aged hand.

Is there no other avenue open to us? The Lady, the only female Watcher, stood lapped in silver. Her lucent skin and shining hair glowed, as did her robe. Her argent eyes looked sadly at the first two speakers. *Can we not hold our hand yet a while? No race grows strong enough to join us without making some errors. Let us give the keepers and Wyrd more time to contain the evil one who has sprung up among them.* Her soft words echoed telepathically with hope and patience.

"Yess," hissed the dragonoid shape out loud that was Drakon, "we must allow the keepers more time, lest we repeat the mistake made by Wyrd and destroy what we mean only to protect. Wyrd has tried to expiate his guilt by serving lesser races. He has worn the form of a dragon bracelet for centuries. He will work with the humans to contain this threat to the Bright Ones. He has never forgotten that his experiments with the Old One's gates destroyed a Bright One."

"The Bright Ones are few; the humans are many. I will defend the young ones," Oron said.

"Would they want that protection at the price of a whole world's destruction, Oron?" the silver Watcher asked quietly.

The golden plume wavered, indecision written in a shifting column. "Perhaps not, Lady."

"Realm is an important gate. Once closed, hundreds of worlds will be shut off from communication with one another," Drakon inserted into the silence. "This action will sacrifice many opportunities for trade and mental growth if those worlds must exist alone."

"In my visions of the future, I note that our brother Wyrd will play a part," Cronal added.

"Are we agreed to wait before making final judgment?" Drakon asked, his red eyes flashing.

"Yes," Cronal said. "The Keepers deserve a chance to save their worlds."

"I too, would watch before acting." The Lady smiled her approval.

"Then I will wait also—but I watch! If there is an endangered Bright One and no one else to save it, I shall cast the uncontrolled gate and the planet that holds it into the Black Universe. There it will never threaten another Bright One," Oron said in a voice that mirrored the cold between the stars. He winked out with no further ceremony.

"Oh, dear," the Lady sighed.

"Oron has little patience with those of flesh and blood," Cronal said. "His kind never knew the burdens of a physical body; therefore, his race has the greatest kinship with the Bright Ones who approach the energy form he inhabited before he joined us on this plane."

"Wyrd has successfully aided younger races before this crisis. Let us place our faith in him once more," Drakon said, bowing his head before taking wing and fading silently into ruby dust.

"What of us, old friend?" the Lady asked Cronal.

"We shall do as we have done for eons, my Lady. We shall watch." The hand he raised in blessing faded gradually as the Lady he addressed became a million silvery motes that scattered into otherwhere.

CHAPTER ONE

"I'm bored!" Mirza announced to her friend, Ebony.

The huge black dragon perched on the tower above, but her long, snaky neck allowed her to drape herself down the building and rest her head on the window ledge of the tower room where Mirza stood.

Mirza pushed her red hair back and looked out the tower window.

Where are the children? Ebony asked in mindspeech.

"Argen is with Librisald, the old librarian, down in the book storage area of the university library," she said. "They are trying to catalog the books the Old Ones stored there."

That task should keep him safely busy, Ebony said, *considering there must be fifty rooms packed floor to ceiling with books.*

"Now, how did you find that out?" Mirza looked at the dragon. "Oh, I know. Seren is off with Fafnoddle, poking around on Realm. I bet he told Faf, and then Faf told you."

It would be difficult for two dragons bonded as we are to keep secrets, Ebony said, and ruffled her scales with satisfaction. *Where is your little daughter? She is younger than the twins and must take more care.*

"She's staying with Grandma Cibby in her cottage in the woods." Mirza paced restlessly. "So here I am without a matronly care. Instead of doing something exciting or interesting with my vacation, I'm just standing here."

You'll think of something, Ebony told her. *I must return to the cave. First Egg's little sister is ready to hatch any day now and I want to be there.*

"How is First Egg?"

He's at the awkward stage. He pokes his nose into everything and refuses to study. I wish he were more like your Argen. Someday he will be wise—for a human, Ebony added. "First Egg may have to be bespelled into a cavern for a few centuries with the **Dragon Chronicles**.

"Oh, surely not," Mirza said.

You sound like his father. 'Dragons will be dragons,' he says. He's sure the boy will finally settle down and be a credit to the family. Although how that will happen with that old rogue Fafnir pouring wild tales into his ears, I can't imagine.

Mirza smiled, remembering the ancient dragon who had been a terror to all during his prime. Somehow, she didn't see First Egg being violent. Times had changed. Since the dragons had been allies during the Great War against the Shadowlord, most people on Realm accepted them. "Seren is pretty adventuresome himself. I don't know why they aren't together now."

Probably because my foolish husband is out skylarking with Seren like a young-ster himself. Come to see me at the cave, she invited with a show of teeth that passed for a smile in dragonkind.

Mirza watched the black dragon vanish into the sky. "Now that looks like fun," she muttered to herself. She swiftly changed herself into a large hawk, fluffed her feathers, and sailed out the window. A few short wingbeats took her to the other side of the university where the library was. She landed on the window ledge and hopped onto the floor before changing back into her human form. She paced through the huge, deserted room. Usually only Andronan, her grandfather, the Head Keeper, used the Room of the Book of Worlds.

The Book of Worlds, a creation of the Old Ones, kept a constant record of the happenings on all of the worlds that contained gates to alternate earths. Mirza went to the stand that held the giant book and began idly turning pages, skimming the news. She stopped as a footnote caught her attention.

"Rogue gate?" she muttered. Now that interested her. She knew of no one capable of manipulating the energies involved in gate creation besides herself and one other—the Shadowlord. All of the resident keepers on the various worlds served by the gates watched constantly for the presence of the evil mage. His continued existence endangered Bright Ones and younger races as well. No one reported any trace of the wizard. Now, Mirza realized she had probably located their enemy. She didn't want to be responsible for a false alarm. She decided she would use the master gate at

Realm to look into their gate on the planet. What was its name? Achaea. She knew about the world although she had never visited it herself. Achaea was the home world of the beings that earthlings knew as the Greek gods. It would be a fascinating place to search, she was certain.

She hurried to the courtyard of Realmgate, smiling and returning the greetings students and faculty offered her as she passed through the many corridors. Since winning the great battle she and her husband Jarl had fought with the Shadowlord, most of the students studying to be keepers knew her. The Shadowlord had almost destroyed the Bright One that nested in the sun of Realm. If she and Jarl had not stopped him, the Bright One would have died within the sun and the resultant nova would have destroyed Realm. As she wished the twentieth student a cheerful, "May the Bright Ones smile upon you!" she reflected that anonymity had its advantages.

The long stone corridors would have been forbidding except that the ancient builders had added large windows that looked out on beautiful gardens filled with wondrous plants from all the alternate worlds that the gates served.

Mirza moved from the cool shadow of the corridor into the bright light of the courtyard where the gate pulsed, waiting the will of a traveler to choose a destination.

"Hello, milady," the assigned keeper of the gate said, smiling at Mirza. His wrinkled face lit up. Mirza was a favorite of his. He had known her since she was a child.

"May the Bright Ones be with you, Guardy," Mirza replied. "Is it all right if I use the gate?"

"Of course," he assured her. "In what way may I assist your trip?"

"Oh, I'm not actually taking a trip. I just want to look in on a few places."

"You'll be here for some time?"

"Yes, I think so."

"Then perhaps you would finish my watch for me. I have a few minutes left before the end of my vigil, but I have some errands to do."

"That's fine with me. I'll keep watch until I'm relieved. If any strange animal or being blunders through the gate by accident, I'll give him forgetfulness and send him home. You go ahead," Mirza said.

"Thank you."

"No problem," Mirza replied, and then wondered if Guardy had understood the Earth slang she used.

CAROL L. DENNIS

"Of course there's not a problem, milady," Guardy said. "I would not leave my post if there were."

"It's just an expression. On the world where I live now, people say that when they mean everything is all right."

"That's fine then." He waved and walked quickly to the exit.

Mirza could hardly wait. She moved to the observation square and positioned herself safely in its center. The star-shaped mosaic that outlined the gate itself flickered, then adjusted itself to the planet Achaea as Mirza thought about the scenes she wished to view. The gate could offer views of many places easily, but each gate had only one location where travelers could move between worlds.

When Mirza looked on the landscape the gate offered to her view, she thought how much it resembled the country Greece on Earth. Sleepy villages, olive groves, and herds of goats and sheep dotted the country-side. She grew aware that the quality of the light shifted strangely. That meant there was a disturbed Bright One in the sun of Achaea. She decided to take one more peek to double check her findings before she went to tell Andronan. If a Bright One was in trouble, they would probably need both Jarl and Wyrd. She thought about Achaea's great Isle of Atlan, a kingdom of great majesty and power. Everything seemed normal from a distance. She wanted a closer look, so she concentrated on a gray fortress on the northern end of the island.

The gate pulsed wildly, emitted a high keening noise, and created a great wind that sucked her from her vantage point.

"Rogue gate!" Mirza called a warning, realizing no one would hear her even as she disappeared.

The gate of Realm returned to normal seconds before the appointed keeper entered. "Hmmm," he muttered to himself. "Guardy isn't here. It's not like him to leave early." He glanced around the empty courtyard. "Oh, well, no harm done," he said softly as he sat on the stone bench to guard the portal of the gate.

CHAPTER TWO

Jarl Koenig missed his family. Only a week earlier his wife Mirza had volunteered to take the children on a visit to her home back on Realm. He stared blankly at the computer screen. The silence in the house irritated him. Jarl accepted the idea that his wife had special powers which some would call magical. After twelve years of married life, he still found something strange about Mirza's method of going home. Her relatives lived on an alternate earth accessible only by using a gate. The Old Ones had created a system of gates between worlds using a science so advanced that it resembled magic. The artifacts of the Old Ones—still functioning, for the most part—showed Jarl how far twentieth century technology had yet to go before it could rival that of the gate's designers.

He glanced down at the dragon-shaped bracelet on his wrist. "What the—" he muttered aloud. Something had awakened the pseudolife of Wyrd. The dragon's coils tightened, a sure sign that something was about to happen.

The dragon's words formed in his mind. *Ssomeone comes.*

"Who comes?" Jarl said aloud. He could communicate with his golden bracelet mentally, but he still preferred to speak when he had the opportunity. Mindspeech was only one of the talents that had developed since he became the wearer of the bracelet. Some of his abilities seemed so strange to him he still had trouble believing what he could do.

"Fafnir," Wyrd answered.

"The Dragon Fafnir?" Jarl pictured his huge saurian friend materializing under the ancient oak tree in the forest behind his house. The tree was the gate between Earth and Realm, Mirza's home. If his nosy neighbor, Mrs. Dzingleski, saw the dragon, he mused, she might stop being so infernally curious about his business. Then he imagined the monumental task of convincing her she had not seen what she had seen. This brought his errant sense of humor to a halt. He hurried out the back door, wondering where he was going to put the dragon now that he had arrived on Earth. It was near Halloween. Perhaps he could convince anyone who saw Fafnir that he was some kind of animated monster for a mythical business promotion.

The small bushes at the edge of the clearing disappeared behind him as he entered the main part of the forest. Actually, it was small, as forests go. The grove was necessary to protect the location of the old oak, the focal point for the magic of the gate on the earth.

"Fafnir," he called softly. Somehow, it didn't seem proper to yell in the Forest of the Gate. "Where is he, Wyrd?"

Not here.

"I can see that for myself. Fafnir is too big to play hide-and-seek. Where has he gone?"

An amused chuckle was his answer.

Jarl knew from experience that when Wyrd decided to be enigmatic, he might as well forget his question. If Wyrd, his bracelet, answered anything during a secrecy fit, the remark was so cryptic it made no sense at the time.

Jarl retraced his steps, noticing the patterns the leaves made of the bright moonlight that bathed the forest floor. The dragon had probably flown directly to the house. Jarl picked up his pace as he smelled toasting marshmallows. Had the children returned with Fafnir? He entered his back yard through the swinging gate that Mirza insisted on to keep the children safe. He thought the gate was a good idea, but he felt it protected his neighbors more than it protected Seren, Argen, and Lealor. A witch's children were pretty durable. His lower jaw dropped as he viewed the scene.

In the light of a brisk blaze, First Egg, the grandson of his dragon friend from Realm, was carefully toasting marshmallows—one on each talon. The pony-sized reptile enjoyed the warmth. The jack-o-lantern grin on his face indicated huge satisfaction. The inky spaces at the front of his formidable mouth awaited his adult fangs, which would grow in soon. He was teething early. First Egg was only seventy, and Jarl knew that dragons weren't mature until they reached one hundred. Jarl's twins, being human, were only twelve years old, but time on Realm moved differently. The gates twisted the skeins of time, as well as space. Sometimes when he returned to Earth, the date was the same as when he left—which was impossible, he always told himself, thinking of his adventures during the absence from home.

"First Egg!"

"Uncle Jarl!" The dragon hissed happily, turning to face Jarl so rapidly he forgot about the burning marshmallow stuck on his fiery tail. He pounded his tail on the ground, preparing to run to his human friend.

Whoosh! The dry leaves that littered the yard caught fire. Jarl dodged the awkward embrace of the sticky dragon and raced for the hose, which he directed on the fire. First Egg watched with salad-plate eyes, alternately cheering Jarl and licking marshmallow from a talon.

Jarl directed a mental probe to his bracelet: *I thought you told me Fafnir was here.*

A gleeful chuckle ticked Jarl's mind. *Sso I did.*

First Egg busily raked smoldering leaves into the center of the yard where a small blaze still flickered unsteadily. Jarl relentlessly turned the hose on the fire. The look on the dragon's face was ludicrous.

"I want to toast more marshmallows!" First Egg said like a petulant kindergartner.

"Not tonight, First Egg," Jarl said, surveying the beleafed and sooty dragon with disgust.

"I'm not First Egg anymore."

"Why not?"

"Because I've got a baby sister ready to hatch at home. I'm all grown."

"Have I lost count somewhere? As your godfather, shouldn't I have been part of your naming day?"

"I decided to call myself Fafnir, after my grandfather."

"Sorry, Wyrd," Jarl muttered. "I thought you were kidding."

The bracelet winked a lazy eye at him before closing both emerald slits for a nap.

"Well, First—I mean, Fafnir," Jarl said, "I didn't even send you the traditional piece of gold to begin your hoard."

"Oh, that's all right. I'll get some gold from here," Fafnir announced confidently.

"From where?" Jarl's eyes widened. He smelled trouble. Dragons were notoriously stubborn. He hoped he could talk this one out of whatever scale-brained idea he had.

"My granddragon told me about the gold on this world. Now that the other dragons have moved to Realm, all I have to do is take it from the humans who stole—" Here he pressed a talon over his lips. "Sorry," he apologized. "From the humans who got it from our hordes in the first place."

"Where will you find it?" Jarl repeated his question.

"Fort Knox, Uncle Jarl," Fafnir answered. "Don't you even know where your world's own hoard is? Grandfather told me everything."

Jarl swallowed, took a deep breath, and counted to ten mentally. He reached nine before he saw the lights of a car coming up the road. All he needed now was Leocadia Dzingleski to show up, snooping for gossip. "Time to come in, Fafnir," he said with commendable panache, turning the hose on the dragon. Tiny bits of soot and leaves washed into the grass of the yard.

"That's cold," Fafnir hissed, exhaling a warm draft of air to dry himself.

Jarl noted the temperature of the exhalation. Yes, Fafnir was definitely maturing. Any day now he'd be belching flame and destruction all over the place. Jarl hoped he could convince his guest to return to his home as fast as possible. He didn't approve of children smoking, and he certainly didn't want a newly flamed dragon lighting up his home.

"I'm cold, Uncle Jarl."

"Fafnir, I'm not your uncle. Besides, I feel old when you call me uncle. Just call me Jarl."

"My mother told me it wasn't polite to call my elders by their first names." The little dragon's righteous nod aggravated Jarl.

"All right, but you're actually older than I am."

"I am?" Fafnir's head shot closer to Jarl as the dragon peered at his human friend.

"Yes, you are." Jarl gritted his teeth. "Come along. I want you in the house before the neighbors park their car and see you." Not for the first time Jarl damned the luck that caused the Dzingleski's to buy the land next to him. When the previous owner died, Jarl had been in Realm. He returned to find the land subdivided into plots that cost an exorbitant sum. Neighbors would have surrounded Jarl except that his land adjoined a national forest on two sides.

He needed the privacy. Mirza, his Realm-born wife, was not only a witch, but also a shapeshifter. While ordinary husbands lectured their wives on not wearing their nighties in front of unshaded windows, Jarl had to contend with a wife who liked to take strolls sky-clad. Somehow, that sounded much better to Jarl than stark naked. The first few years of their marriage they had no neighbors, so it didn't matter. Later, one of the little neighborhood girls swore she had taken a ride on a real unicorn, and another neighborhood boy said he saw a winged lady dancing in the woods. Then Mirza had to cease her excursions.

Jarl closed the kitchen door with a sigh of relief. Fafnir barely made it into the house. Jarl stood looking at his guest, wondering how he would keep him entertained until he could send him home. A sharp knock on his front door interrupted his reverie.

"You stay here until I call you," he told Fafnir. The dragon opened the refrigerator as Jarl hurried to the front part of the house. Thank goodness Mirza had left enough food prepared for an army —it ought to hold the dragon for a while, anyway.

"Hello," Jarl said, opening the door. Mrs. D. stood in the doorway in full panoply. She had swathed herself in clothes she deemed suitable for what she referred to as a "cultural evening." This meant her long-suffering husband had driven her into the city to the opera or theater.

Her inquisitive eyes swept around as much of the room as she could see through the half-opened door. "Homer and I smelled smoke. Is something on fire?"

"I had a little trouble earlier when I burned some leaves. Everything is under control now. I was just getting ready to go to bed."

His visitor's sharp gasp was his first intimation that "things" were not under control. As he glanced behind him, the door swung completely open. Fafnir stood in the hallway, an apple pie balanced on one talon. A fleck of whipped dairy product sat jauntily on one nostril.

"May I eat this?" the dragon asked.

Jarl's head nodded an affirmative while his mind broke the speed of light, thinking how he was going to explain Fafnir to his fainting neighbor as he caught her.

CHAPTER THREE

Jarl looked down at the huge woman who sagged in his arms. "Don't stand there, Fafnir! Come and help me get her on the couch."

"You told me—" the dragon began in righteous tones.

"Never mind what I told you." Jarl almost snarled the words. "My back is breaking, and if she ever gets stretched out on the floor, we'll need a derrick to lift her."

"It's a nice clean floor, Uncle Jarl—"

"Don't call me Uncle!" Jarl dragged his neighbor's dead weight over to the couch and draped her unconscious form there.

"What's this?" The dragon offered Jarl a folded sheet of paper.

Jarl glanced over his shoulder. "Fafnir, I don't have time to read to you. I've got to decide what to tell Mr. Dzingleski. He's parking the car now, but he'll soon be at my door. How do I explain this?" He gestured to the prone form on the couch.

"This has a picture of a dragon on it! It's not a very good picture, of course . . . ."

"A dragon? Let me see that." Jarl snatched at the paper, which turned out to be a program from a Wagner opera. "The Ring Cycle! This is the answer to my problem."

When the knocking on the door started, Fafnir moved to open it.

"No, Fafnir. You go hide in the kitchen and don't come out—no matter what happens. This man mustn't see you." Jarl hustled the puzzled dragon into the kitchen and hurried to open the front door.

Mr. Dzingleski stood in the doorway, a look of inquiry on his face. "I wondered if my wife was here," he began in his soft voice. "She wanted to check about the smell of burning leaves, you know. Ever since she joined the volunteer fire department, she's been really alert to fire." His voice trailed off as Jarl motioned him to enter.

The first thing he noticed was the recumbent form of his wife. "Oh, dear," he whispered, as if he feared waking her. "What happened?" He stood in the center of the room watching his wife.

"She's probably overwrought. What with all those speaking engagements to local groups about fire safety," Jarl said lamely. His neighbor was such an ineffectual person that it made Jarl feel awkward. He had no doubt as to who was the boss of the family next door. If Mr. Dzingleski were the one on the couch, the administration of smelling salts and the calling of the emergency ambulance by Leocadia would be history by this time.

His neighbor approached the couch gingerly. "Leocadia, my dear," he began in his soft voice as the huge body stirred, then sat up.

"What in the world," she said, correcting her unladylike posture immediately. "The last thing I remember . . . " Her eyes widened. I saw a . . . " Her confident voice faltered as the glanced around the room. "I mean, for a moment there, I thought I saw . . . " She paused.

Jarl watched the change come over her face as she remembered clearly what she had seen. He smiled comfortingly. "Yes?" he offered.

"I . . . I . . . "

Mr. Dzingleski stared. He obviously had never seen his wife at a loss for words. "Perhaps we should go home, my dear," he said quietly. "All that rousing music, valkyries and dragons . . . " He stepped back as she lumbered to her feet.

"Dragons," she muttered, looking at the long hall that led to the kitchen.

"Wagner's very heady stuff," Jarl said. "I have strange dreams after seeing his operas. I guess my imagination runs away with me."

"Yes," she agreed. "There's no telling what the imagination of a truly sensitive patron of the arts might create after an evening at the opera."

"Come, Leocadia. We are keeping Mr. Koenig from his rest." Mr. Dzingleski gently shepherded his wife to the door. As proof of how shaken she was, she said not another word, but went quietly.

"Good night," Mr. Dzingleski said for the pair of them as they exited the room.

"Good night," Jarl echoed into the soft dark, before he closed the door behind them. He saw Fafnir peering from the shadowy hall. "Well, I'm glad that's over."

"Is it safe to come in now?" the dragon asked.

"Sure."

"Why did I have to hide? The man seemed very nice. He wasn't an evil wizard or anything, was he?"

"Fafnir, haven't you learned anything about modern Earth?"

"Well, there is some stuff written in my father's books, but they're so boring! He told me to read about Earth so that someday I could come to visit you." The dragon gave a self-satisfied smirk. "I didn't have to wait for him to bring me, did I? I came all by myself!" Fafnir thumped the floor with his tail. In his enthusiasm, he was apt to forget how large he was.

Jarl jumped to the rescue of a lamp that tottered from the force of the small quake the dragon had raised, expressing his pleasure at the trick he had played on his father.

"What do you think your father will have to say when he learns you have used the gate to travel here without his permission or an invitation to come?" Jarl asked, hoping some sensible thoughts might keep the rest of his furniture from imminent destruction.

"Oh, kippers! I never thought about that. You aren't mad at me because I popped in to see you, are you?" The dragon's eyes filled with tears.

"No, no," Jarl hastened to reassure him before he drenched the carpet past redemption. "Come on. Let's go to the kitchen and see what we have to eat." Jarl herded his uninvited guest down the hall.

"I'm glad you're not mad at me," the dragon said, wiping his eyes on a tea towel that was quite inadequate for the mopping exercise.

Jarl rummaged in a drawer until he found a large terry cloth dishtowel. "Here," he said, handing it to Fafnir. "I'm not angry at you, of course, but it is always a good idea to check before you visit someone."

"When I decided to come, I flew to the gate and used it." The dragon hung his head.

"Don't you remember how Mirza had to cast a spell on you so people would see you as a human the last time you were here?"

"Now I do. It's so hard to keep in mind what a strange place you live in. Imagine! A whole world that thinks dragons are only legends! People here must be pretty stupid. We dragons have always liked to travel. When the Old Ones opened the gate system between worlds, practically every dragon who was important traveled through them. It says so in the **Dragon Chronicles**."

"Didn't your **Dragon Chronicles** also tell how you dragons joined the other magical creatures that moved to Realm when men started turning to science instead of magic?"

"I haven't read everything in our history books. They're so boring. I skipped around, here and there, reading anything that interested me."

"I wouldn't let your mother find out how you've studied them," Jarl warned. "She takes the past very seriously."

"Why would any dragon find all those old boring tales interesting? Besides, my mother can quote for hours. I guess before my granddragon died, she made my mother memorize almost all of the **Dragon Chronicles**. Mother said that was how they kept young dragons out of mischief . . . " A horrified look passed over his face. "Jarl." He inhaled a great amount of air. The top slice of the bologna Jarl was using to make a sandwich flew through the air and plastered itself over Fafnir's nearest nostril. His pink dragon tongue licked it off and jammed it in his mouth. He chomped once, then continued. "Do you think she'll make me learn it all by heart, too, because I came here without her permission?"

"Perhaps. I really can't say. What do you suppose your father is going to do?" Jarl asked the question with clinical detachment. He thought some punishment was in order. He shuddered to think what would happen if Fafnir started dropping in on them with no warning. That would strain even Mirza's magic skill—trying to keep the neighbors from finding out about Fafnir!

There were always hordes of kids running in and out of the house to Mirza's magic cookie jar that was always full of fresh cookies. The refrigerator that she enchanted to be full of fruit juice and fresh milk, no matter how often thirsty children opened it, made their house a prime stop for the youth of the neighborhood. The neighborhood mothers probably hated his wife. They must think she spent most of every day baking and shopping.

Fafnir opened a frozen package of croissants. He delicately stuck one to each claw, and then flamed them briefly. His tongue raked the strawberry filling from one before he tossed it into his mouth and swallowed.

"Do I have to think about what my father will do? I'd rather have Auntie Mirza come home with me and help me explain. Then maybe he won't turn me into a jar of coralberry jam."

Jarl smiled. He couldn't help it. Fafnir would make the largest jar of coralberry jam anyone had ever seen. He'd heard Fafnoddle threaten his son with just such a transformation in moments of stress. Ebony, his wife, wouldn't let him smoke in the home cave. She said it made her feel ill. So Fafnoddle found himself forced to express his feelings verbally.

"Well, can she?"

"Can she what?" Jarl asked between bites of his sandwich.

"Can she come with me to help explain?"

"She who?" Jarl had lost the thread of the conversation as he watched Fafnir spear giant dills with his tongue. Jarl hoped pickles and strawberry croissants wouldn't disagree with his guest. He had no idea how to soothe a dragon with a stomachache.

"Aren't you listening to me?"

"Yes, but who are you talking about?"

"Auntie Mirza, of course."

"Mirza's not here. She's back on Realm with the children."

"No, she's not. I looked for her before I came. I can't find her."

"She has to be there! She wouldn't leave Realm without telling me. I'm to join her there tomorrow."

"I tell you, she's not there. I looked. I thought she'd come home for a while. That's why I decided I'd visit and pick up a little gold from Fort Knox, then return with the start of my hoard. I knew she'd help me."

"You must not have looked everywhere. She's probably turned herself into a unicorn or something and is traveling around incognito."

"I know I'm right. Mother said she hasn't been able to contact Mirza and mindspeak for two days. So she must have gone someplace."

Jarl knew about the special bond that his wife and Fafnir's mother had formed. If Ebony couldn't reach Mirza, then she was not on Realm.

"How exciting!" Fafnir said, wrapping his tongue around the pickle jar and holding it close to his saucer-sized eye to make sure he had not missed any pickles.

Jarl automatically cleared away the mess in the kitchen as he puzzled over the situation. "Exciting?" He finally asked when the dragon's comment registered.

"Why, yes. It's not every day that someone disappears, especially an adept like Auntie Mirza. I bet that dreadful Shadowlord has his cowl in it somewhere. Aren't you worried, Uncle Jarl?"

Jarl, too busy being concerned, didn't bother to correct the dragon. "We'd better use the gate and return to Realm."

"Before I get a chance to find any gold for my horde?" Fafnir wailed his disappointment. "We have to go now?"

"Now!" Jarl said firmly.

CHAPTER FOUR

Jarl and the dragon stood beneath the great oak that marked the gate's position on Earth.

"Are you ready, Fafnir?" Jarl asked.

"Couldn't I fly someplace close and pick up a few gold items?'

"Absolutely not," Jarl said in his firmest voice. He had no way to enforce his preferences on Fafnir. Jarl wanted to have him safe in Realm before the young dragon figured it out. He hoped he would never have to cover up the presence of a live dragon on Earth. With Mirza's help, they might manage. She had a very innovative mind. Alone, he shuddered to think what might happen. You could always discredit what people said about what they saw, but most places where Fafnir could find gold readily had security cameras. How could you fool a photographic negative? Now that he had managed to distract the dragon from his Fort Knox idea, he wanted them safe on Realm before Faf thought of it again.

"Visualize the star at the university on Realm," he commanded. He hoped the dragon would follow his advice. If Fafnir decided to be cute, no telling what place he might envision. While Fafnoddle and Ebony were friends, they were like most parents. They would probably hold Jarl responsible if anything happened to their little darling, although only a dragon could consider anything as large as Fafnir "little". Then seeing that Fafnir had closed his eyes, Jarl made the appropriate magical passes to activate the gate.

After a brief moment of vertigo, Jarl opened his eyes. They were both safe in the great Courtyard of the Gate. Jarl heaved a sigh of relief. Now, if he could just get Fafnir to return home of his own volition. He turned to the dragon and said, "It's important that you go home now."

"Do I have to? Things are just starting to get interesting."

Jarl was astounded to notice that young Dragons wheedled exactly like young humans. He hoped child psychology worked on dragons, too. He decided to try.

"Well," he began, "I suppose you may stay—but you'll have to explain to Andronan about using the gate without his permission."

"Couldn't you do that for me?" The dragon's eyes widened. If there was one human he was in awe of, it was Andronan, the Master Keeper.

"I could if you weren't here. However, if you insist on staying, then you'll have to talk to Andronan yourself. In fact, he should be ready to see us any minute. I had Wyrd call him as soon as we got here. He's waiting in his study for us."

"Please explain to him for me that I really had to get home. My mother will be worrying about me, I'm sure," the dragon said dutifully.

"Very well. By the way, here is a piece of gold for your hoard. This way, you didn't waste the trip." Jarl handed the dragon a gold coin that he had palmed from Seren's coin collection before they left Earth.

"Oh, thank you! Now I'm officially an adult!"

"Weren't you before? You said you were."

"Not quite. The first real piece of gold a dragonette gets turns him into an adult officially."

"Congratulations, then," Jarl called as Fafnir rose into the air. For a brief moment, Jarl wondered if he had broken dragon protocol. He had a feeling there should have been some type of ceremony with Ebony and Fafnoddle present. He didn't have their permission, either. Then he shrugged his shoulders, greeted the gate watcher politely, and hurried up the steps to Andronan's study.

"Come in, Jarl," Andronan called, just as Jarl reached the door to his study. How the old Keeper always knew when someone stood outside his room had always puzzled Jarl. Jarl's bracelet alerted him to company, but the old mage had nothing but his magic talent to tell him of visitors. Of course, there were still things Andronan did that Jarl could not duplicate even with Wyrd's aid.

He strode through the door, noting that Andronan was sitting in the tilt-back chair Jarl had created for him some years earlier. That was one innovation that he had taught Andronan. He wondered if there was any other way in which he really affected Realm. The land seemed changeless. Since they had defeated the Shadowlord, no major threat had developed in any civilized portion of the country. He smiled at Mirza's grandfather.

"It's always good to see you, Jarl. I don't know where Mirza could be. She's never missed greeting you when you arrived here before," he said. A slight frown, almost lost in the wrinkles, briefly marred his ancient face.

"There's nothing to worry about, but I did come to check on my family," Jarl replied.

"Oh, they're all fine. Argen and Librisald are thick as a bookshelf jammed with those old dust catchers they love to peer at together."

The old man's tone sounded slightly mocking, but Jarl knew what a bibliophile Andronan was himself. Indeed, Andronan had carried the young Koenigs with him on visits to the library on more than one occasion. Seren and Lealor enjoyed making houses with the old volumes. Argen would sit patiently in a corner, leafing through books carefully in hopes of finding a picture or two. He never seemed to tire of the library.

As the children grew older, Lealor became an animal lover. She spent as much time as possible in the woods that were so abundant on Realm. Jarl never worried because he knew that Rory, his leprechaun friend, kept an Irish eye out for her. He had appeared more than once with Jarl's daughter riding leprechaunback. It said a great deal about the bond between the two. Few existed on Realm who had ever touched Rory, but in the tiny hands of Lealor, he became almost gentle. Most knew the leprechaun as a feisty, fiery-tongued individualist who hurled imaginative invective as easily as he gulped whiskey. They would have to see the sight more than once to believe it.

Jarl smiled to himself as he pictured his eldest, Seren. The boy and the dragons on Realm had taken to each other instinctively. Before Jarl thought Seren was old enough to ride horses on Earth, Seren and Fafnoddle had been sailing around on Realm updrafts. "Just checking things over," as Fafnoddle explained calmly when a horrified Jarl first saw his small son kicking his heels and shouting, "Faster, Faf, faster!" Seren would be all right so long as he stuck with the dragons. Jarl quailed mentally as he considered what young Fafnir and Seren could think up together. Maybe a word or two with Fafnoddle might save both sets of parents hours of concern. With a son like young Fafnir, Jarl imagined Faf's scales would tarnish centuries earlier than normal.

Jarl continued the conversation. "I wasn't thinking of the children this time. I had an unexpected visit from Fafnir—the dragon we used to call First Egg," Jarl explained, knowing Andronan probably thought he meant the young dragon's grandfather, Fafnir.

Old Fafnir was the dragon Jarl met on Realm during his first visit. He might never have met Fafnoddle, Fafnir's son, if it hadn't been for Jarl's promise to make Fafnoddle go with him to rescue Mirza. Things had certainly changed! While Fafnoddle was still a vegetarian, his pacifist tendencies had totally disappeared since the battle with the Shadowlord's Dark Legions. Old Fafnir, delighted with his son's prowess, loved telling how his son and Ebony had seared demons into fine ash to protect Realm.

Andronan nodded to show he understood. Jarl said, "Young Fafnir said Mirza was not on Realm."

"Are you sure?" Andronan stood. "Let us go to the gate and ask the keeper there if anyone has seen Mirza. He always tells me if anyone has seen Mirza leave. She always tells me if she plans to go gallivanting."

Although Andronan usually talked just like everyone else, occasionally his great age showed when he used some charmingly dated word or expression. Jarl filed "gallivanting" away in his mind. Somehow, the term was exactly right for the restless flitting his wife had a tendency to do when she became bored. On Earth, membership in a half dozen volunteer groups kept her busy. Jarl wondered what she had done on Realm before he married her. He had never thought to ask.

They passed through the corridors to the gravity wells that served as elevators in the university. Andronan acknowledged the reverential bowed heads with his kindly smile as they passed the students and faculty who thronged the halls. Jarl raised his hand in greeting as he saw people he knew.

They crossed the well threshold and sank decorously to the ground floor. Jarl wished he could understand the engineering skills the Old ones had used to create the wells. No moving parts were evident. Whatever form of energy powered the wells still worked perfectly. Jarl thought it might be some use of solar power, but he had never been able to find the book that explained the system. Librisald had been cataloging books all his life and still had not reached the end of the tomes the Old Ones had left behind. Jarl had seen the stacks in the library. Over fifty rooms remained, piled from floor to ceiling. No one expected Librisald to live long enough to complete the cataloging. Argen was already a help, but he didn't read enough languages to be very efficient. When his son grew older and came to the university to study, Jarl knew what he would become. Seren's voice echoed in his father's memory: "There's no hope for Argen. He even smells musty like those old books he and Librisald carry around all the time. Phew."

Andronan led the way out of the gravity well into the beautiful courtyard. There, the Realmgate pulsed with a soft radiance among flowers and trees of such colors, shapes, and scents they almost defied description.

He approached the current Keeper who watched the gate. "Have you seen my granddaughter, Mirza?" Andronan asked.

"No, sir," the young keeper answered with the traditional nod of respect. "Guardy was talking about seeing her here the other day," he added.

"We will stand watch for you. Please find Guardy and ask him to join us here." The politely worded request had all the force of a royal command, to judge from the keeper's hurried exit.

In a very short while, Guardy entered the courtyard, followed by the younger keeper. "How may I serve you, Andronan?" he asked.

"We wondered if you saw Mirza leave Realm by the gate the other day."

"She was here, looking into one of the worlds, but there was no warning she intended going anywhere," Guardy told them. "She came almost at the end of my watch: Why, she even volunteered to finish my vigil for me," he added as he recalled the afternoon.

"When you left, Mirza was still here, using the gate to look into another world?" Jarl asked.

"That's correct. Right here." Guardy nodded as his finger pointed out the spot.

"Did you know which world she was watching?"

Guardy said, "No, I didn't think to ask."

"Who had the watch after you that day?" Andronan questioned.

"Why, it was Vigan, the young keeper you sent after me."

Andronan gestured for Vigan to approach. "Very well, Guardy. You may return to your studies now, if you wish."

"I'll stay, if you don't mind. Is there some problem about Mirza? I well remember what shenanigans she could pull when she was a girl."

Andronan gave the old keeper a mock look of disapproval. "As do I, and I also remember who helped rectify her minor mistakes and mitigate the punishment for some of the catastrophes she almost caused, old friend."

Guardy chuckled softly. "Me and every other keeper on Realm," he said, being deliberately ungrammatical.

Andronan and Jarl turned their attention to Vigan. "Do not fear, my son," the Master Keeper said kindly. "Did you see what world my grand-daughter Mirza watched the other day?"

"No, I never saw her. I remember the day because I passed Guardy as I reported for my turn as watcher. I thought it was odd that no one was on duty, but it was only a matter of minutes. I knew Guardy wouldn't leave his station unless all was well."

"Then we'll have a long search. There are thousands of worlds that have gates. Without a clue, it may take days to find out where she went." Jarl glanced at his bracelet, but Wyrd said nothing. Wyrd had never been exactly talkative. However, in the past, the dragon had helped many times. As Jarl gained control of the powers that Wyrd possessed, the dragon intruded less and less into human affairs, seemingly content to be an ornament on Jarl's wrist.

"She may be in danger and have need of you. We must find out which world drew her interest." Andronan smoothed his beard as he thought out loud.

"Excuse me, but I may be able to be of some assistance." Vigan's interruption surprised them all.

Andronan's raised eyebrows encouraged him to continue. "Ruel, one of my friends, saw a bird fly from the window where the **Book of Worlds** is. He said it flew here to the Court of the Gate. There is neither food nor water here. Perhaps the Lady Mirza shape-shifted herself and came here. Might she not have left some clue in the room?"

"It's the only lead we have." Jarl started out of the courtyard with no further ceremony.

"We thank you both for your assistance," Andronan said to the two keepers before he, too, headed for the room where the **Book of Worlds** lay opened.

CHAPTER FIVE

Jarl waited impatiently for Andronan to join him at the shaft that would bear them to the upper levels of the building.

"If we are fortunate, Mirza left the **Book of Worlds** open to the page where she was reading, Jarl."

"I can't imagine why she would leave without telling someone. After all, the children are here. It isn't like her to go off without letting someone know."

"If she was in as great a hurry as we think, she may well have left the book open," Andronan said, as he left the shaft slightly ahead of Jarl. The room they wanted was only a short distance down the corridor.

When they entered the room, they saw the **Book of Worlds** resting on its lectern—and it was open. Jarl's sense of relief was palpable. Andronan and Jarl both noticed the name of the place at almost the same moment: Achaea. Even as they gazed, a footnote was being added to the bottom of the entry on the page.

"A rogue gate is being used?" Jarl said, puzzled. "Who would take the risk of using a rogue gate?"

The SShadowlord hissed Wyrd.

Jarl was skeptical. "Why would he want to create a rogue gate on a planet ruled by the ancient Greek gods? If I remember my mythology correctly, the old gods of Greece didn't think much of mortals who meddled with godlike powers. It doesn't make sense that Mirza would rush off to help Zeus and Company." Jarl paced around the room as if he needed to be taking some kind of action.

"I know why she may have gone so hurriedly. Look at the addition to the footnote." Andronan's long index finger pointed to the lines he meant.

"That says the gate is becoming unstable. It's sure to unbalance the nearby star. Does it harbor a Bright One?"

"Yes. The worlds where gates are possible all have stars that host Bright Ones. The Old Ones probably understood why this is so, and several of our most intellectual mage/keepers are studying the issue. Yet we do not understand." Andronan shook his head. "The universe is so large, and our minds are so small. One lifetime is scarcely enough to begin to unravel the secrets that wait for us on this plane."

"I'll need to check on the children. I don't like to leave them, but Mirza could be in danger. The last thing I need is to try to watch the kids and look for Mirza at the same time. I'm not sure they'll be safe here. Perhaps I should take them home to Earth."

"Surely they would be safer on Realm. We understand magic and Lealor, at least, has magical powers. On Earth most people do not believe in magic and wouldn't know what to do to counteract it if Lealor forgot and shapeshifted or mis-spoke a spell," cautioned Andronan.

"That's right. I'll have to make arrangements for the children to stay on Realm. I don't like to bother any of my friends here . . . "

"It is no bother. You locate the children, and I'll be responsible for them while they are here. The children's visits are far too short as it is. It will be good for the keepers to have some lively young ones about the place again."

While Jarl appreciated the offer, he had his doubts about allowing the children to run wild on Realm with only the keepers to act as watchmen. The younger keepers needed to continue their studies, and the older keepers were immersed in various projects and might well forget the children for days on end. Just as Jarl was about to make his decision, Wyrd spoke in their minds. *I will arrange protection for the children.*

Jarl was about to question his magic talisman, but Andronan said quietly, "We would appreciate that. We know that the Shadowlord feels no compunction about involving innocent family members in his plans. We have not been able to find any trace of him in all these years. I often have a feeling that he takes an interest in what we are doing." Jarl looked as if he intended to ask a question, but Andronan answered it before he had the chance. "I have never been able to trace him by any means at my disposal."

"We would appreciate your help." Jarl hated to admit it, but he still had many things to learn about the powers that those familiar with the gates could summon. He could now accomplish many feats that he previously believed to be impossible. Jarl knew enough to realize that no matter how much it humbled his pride, he probably would need all the help he could get.

If Wyrd said he could protect the children, then he undoubtedly was capable of doing something to keep them safe.

"To create the protection, I must be near the children." Wyrd's strange, gemlike eyes glittered, a sure sign some paranormal or magical thinking was occurring. "Excuse us, Andronan. We go." With these words, Jarl felt the familiar jarring wrench and moment of vertigo that always accompanied Wyrd's version of traveling. It reminded Jarl of the gate trips. However, it was impossible to believe that a small bracelet could unleash or control the vast powers of a gate at will.

Jarl glanced around him. They were upstairs in one of the large rooms of the library. The piles of dusty books, layer on layer, made clear the origin of the librarians' term, stacks. High windows illuminated the room. A stray beam of light accented millions of dusty motes stirred up by Argen, his son. He staggered along under a miniature mountain of books.

"That is you under there, isn't it?" Jarl asked, taking the top foot of books away to reveal his son's flushed face.

"Hi, Dad. What are you doing here? Librisald was just talking about you yesterday. I'm helping him catalog. I've finally learned the Old Ones' numbering system, so I'm pretty sure these books are a set."

Jarl glanced at the spines of the books. "You're right. You'll be about three feet closer to finishing the cataloging when Librisald tells you where these belong."

"It's so frustrating. All I really am is a go-fer."

"A gopher? I realize you dig around a lot, but I don't think you really deserve to consider yourself a rodent," Jarl teased.

"You missed a pun. G-o-f-e-r, Dad. Get it? I 'go-fer' this book and then I 'go-fer' another." Argen's grin made him seem younger than he actually was.

"I got it, but I wish I hadn't. Your mother's gone through the gate to Achaea, and Andronan and I believe that she may need a little help. Before I go, I want to make sure there is protection for my children, including you, my son."

"Seren and I are old enough to manage on our own. Lealor's the only one you have to worry about."

"Nevertheless, Wyrd has offered to give you a little extra protection, and he wants to see you."

"Me?" Argen's eyes rounded. Their father never spoke of his relationship with Wyrd, but many of the people on Realm told tales of the eldritch power Wyrd could summon to aid Jarl.

Do not fear. Wyrd's voice echoed in Argen's and Jarl's minds. *You will appreciate my gift.*

A silver glow began to emanate from Wyrd's scales. It grew to basketball size, then began to shrink until there was only a silver band pulsating in the air. Then the band slowly flew to Argen and settled gently on his wrist.

Argen looked down. A silver replica of Wyrd rested on his arm. Within a few seconds, it felt as if it had been there forever. "Wow," Argen breathed.

Not Wow. My name is Nyct, the voice of Argen's bracelet said in his mind.

"Nyct," Argen repeated dutifully. He looked at his father. "Its name is Nyct," he told him.

Jarl, who up to this moment had no idea of the method Wyrd would use to give his children protection, looked a little bemused.

An audible hiss came from the silver bracelet. *I am not a thing,* he told Argen. *Please refer to me as 'he' or use my name.*

"Sorry," Argen managed.

Apology accepted, Nyct answered.

"Dad, are you sure—"

This is my son. Wyrd's voice reached all three of his listeners. *I had not thought to ever have another, but now I make you a partner, so you shall not face adversity alone.*

"Thank you. I'm honored," Argen managed to say, rising to the occasion.

You are considering the disadvantages of wearing a talisman. You are young to bear the burden, but you have not thought about the advantages of your new partner, Wyrd said, in the softest tones Jarl had ever heard him use.

"Advantages?" Argen repeated.

Jarl remembered his feelings when he first came to Realm. He also remembered how dumb he felt when his best reply was a repetition of something someone else said. Like father, like son, he thought whimsically.

What books is your father holding? Wyrd hissed.

"Why, he had volumes one through four of **Interstellar Maps of the Sky as Seen from Realm.**" Argen paused. "Hey, I actually read the titles!"

Argen placed his pile of books on the floor and took the stack from his father's arms. Sitting on top of the nearest pile, he began to leaf through one of the books. Within seconds, he was so immersed in the book he was holding he almost didn't hear Wyrd speaking to him.

Advantage number one, Wyrd told him. *Nyct is young, but he has powers he can share with you. The two of you will grow up together, and each will profit from the other's strengths. Now we can go again*, Wyrd said to Jarl.

Jarl never had time to say goodbye. He found himself on the plateau above Fafnoddle and Ebony's cave.

Jarl looked around, but he didn't see Seren anywhere. It was a relief to know that Argen, at least, wasn't going to cause any problems for anyone. Now that he was able to read the books in the library, Librisald would have an energetic helper. Jarl hoped the old librarian could think of ways to keep Argen from trying to read all the books they had to catalog. Or perhaps Argen would sift through and find the books in Librisald's special areas of interest. Jarl could picture them together poring over musty volumes in some corner of the library.

The clouds, which scudded ahead of the playful wind, made shadows move over the ground. Then a pinpoint in the distance grew larger and Jarl could make out the form of a dragon. It was his old friend Fafnoddle. The huge dragon swooped down at a tremendous speed, however briefly, and landed, feather-soft, next to Jarl. Jarl greeted his friend with a smile and his usual queasy stomach. There was something about seeing a house-sized being literally dropping in on you that never failed to evoke a state of panic.

"Hello, Father," Seren said from his place on Fafnoddle's back.

"Were you responsible for Faf's diving demon routine?" Jarl asked.

"Not me. Fafnoddle wanted Fafnir to see how much he had to learn about flying." Seren's eyes shone as he remembered. "What a ride it was. Loops, in and out of the dark, and speed! Well, Fafnir hasn't showed up yet. He is still behind us—isn't he?"

"I set him quite a pattern to follow. He was getting a little big for his talons. It doesn't do any harm for a father to show his son a thing or two." Fafnoddle's eyes glowed green. "It will be some time before young First Egg thinks he is big enough to wear that name he chose for himself." Fafnoddle lowered his head so Seren could walk down his neck and jump to earth. The rumble that Jarl recognized as the dragon's chuckle sounded like old Fafnir's. "Blowing a little fertilizer off my scales," he hissed happily. "Beautiful day for a spin, isn't it? Care for a ride, Jarl?"

"No thanks. I came to check on Seren." Fafnoddle didn't seem to be angry about Jarl's unscheduled gift of gold to his dragonette. Jarl decided he might as well not raise a fuss over the possible dangers of carrying Seren into what must have been quite a duel between the two dragons. Neither Seren nor young Fafnir appeared harmed by their experience, judging from the streaking form in the air that was now aimed right where they were standing.

"How good is Young Fafnir at pinpoint landings?" Jarl asked in what he hoped sounded like a casual tone. While Jarl had been around dragons for years, he still had a healthy respect for their size, even small ones. He preferred not to be the landing pad for Fafnoddle's son.

"Quite good, father," Seren answered. "I help him practice."

Jarl tried to remain calm as he imagined those practice sessions. "How do you do that?"

"Oh, I ride up here on his back. Then I get down and stand someplace. He flies off and sees how fast he can go and still land right next to me."

Seren's smile sent shivers down Jarl's back. "Oh," Jarl managed weakly, seeing a mental picture of Seren in the hospital with casts on every limb.

"No need to fret, Jarl," Fafnoddle said. "I put a spell of protection on the boy, so even if my lead-winged son landed right on Seren, he'd bounce off safely."

"Thanks," Jarl said, wondering who the spell really protected.

Both of them, Wyrd said in Jarl's mind.

At this moment, Fafnir sailed under his father's nose, hugging the ground, and landed right beside Seren.

"Not bad, Faf," Seren congratulated his friend.

The older dragon's head jerked to hear his nickname applied to his son.

"He did do well, didn't he?" Seren asked the two surprised fathers.

Fafnoddle rumbled and hissed an answer while Jarl nodded his agreement.

"Darn. I wish you wouldn't speak dragon. I never can seem to remember the words, no matter how hard I try. Faf laughs at my pronunciation."

"Perhaps I can remedy that," Wyrd said out loud so they could all hear him.

"You can?" Seren said, confident that Wyrd's powers could do anything.

Fafnoddle's plate-sized eyes focused on Jarl's bracelet. "You would give a man-child the power to speak to dragons in the language we brought from the stars?" He seemed slightly incredulous.

Yess. In years to come, the abilities I now make available to him may tip the scales and avert catastrophe, Wyrd answered mysteriously. Suddenly, a golden glow formed around the tiny form of the dragon. It grew, pulsed several times, almost as if it were breathing, then formed into a golden shape that flew to Seren and wrapped itself around his arm. As they watched, the shape became more definite. Finally, a perfect golden replica of Wyrd himself rested on Seren's wrist.

"Oh—" Seren began, looking carefully at the bracelet. "Thanks, Wyrd." He returned to the study of his bracelet.

Fafnoddle said a few short words that his son echoed. The strange syllables of dragon talk hissed on the air. Seren muttered an answer distractedly, then looked astounded. "Hey, did you hear that? I spoke perfect dragon, didn't I?" He looked at Fafnoddle for his answer.

"Indeed you did."

"What shall I call my bracelet?"

Why don't you ask him? Wyrd suggested. *You need not speak aloud.*

CHAPTER SIX

Seren looked at his bracelet, which glinted in the sun. *What shall I call you?* he asked, following Wyrd's suggestion.

The tiny bracelet opened both green eyes and focused on Seren. *My name is Soladon,* he answered. *By what name shall I call you?*

Seren. Seren Koenig.

Very well, serenserenkoenig. The bracelet carefully repeated, syllable by syllable, what the boy had told him.

Not serenserenkoenig. Just Seren. Koenig is my father's name.

Seren?

That's it. Seren.

Seren looked at the dragons and his father. He seemed surprised to see them waiting for him to speak. Then he realized how swiftly the mental exchange had taken place. It was almost like carrying on a conversation with himself. He smiled down at his bracelet. "This is really neat."

Soladon is my son. He will learn to unleash his powers as you learn how to command yours. You have a great affinity with the dragon races. For a human, you are surprisingly adaptable to the dragons. In time you will be able to aid your friends and others of their kind when trouble comes, many years hence . . . . Wyrd's voice trailed off as if he were seeing the future. He said abruptly, *Now we go to find Lealor.*

This time Jarl had prepared himself. When Wyrd said the first two words, Jarl raised his hand in goodbye, and so was able to bid farewell as he winked out of sight.

Perhaps it was just as well that he did not hear Soladon ask, *What shall we do now?*

Young Fafnir replied, "Oh, Seren and I have many things we want to try."

Fafnoddle shook his head and flew back to the cave where Ebony awaited him. His last view of the three showed them huddled together, obviously planning the day's activities.

Jarl and his bracelet appeared in a grove of trees. He waited a moment for the dizziness to abate, then looked around him carefully. He could tell from the health of the woods that it was under the protection of dryads. Only they could achieve the perfect balance between tree, grass, and flower that produced meadows of such surpassing beauty.

"I thought we were going to where Lealor was," Jarl said quietly to Wyrd.

We are, Wyrd answered, allowing his amusement to show in a dragon grin.

"Hi, Daddy!"

Jarl looked around him, searching for his daughter.

Silvery laughter came from above, causing him to look up and catch a glimpse of the dryad who must live in the gigantic oak that dominated the clearing. He looked up twenty feet to the first limb, which stretched its protecting branches out over a portion of the meadow below. He stifled his gasp. Jarl didn't want to say anything to startle his daughter, who stood on the middle of the branch, at least ten feet from the trunk. She waved vigorously to him.

"Here I am," she announced. "Isn't it a beautiful day?" The precarious nature of her position didn't seem to bother her.

Jarl himself felt hollow inside. His overactive imagination conjured a picture of Lealor falling out of the tree. "You better come down from there, honey," he coaxed. "I need to talk to you, and I'll get a crick in my neck if you stay up so high."

"You're not worried, are you, Daddy?" Lealor peered down on him and grinned before stepping off the branch into thin air.

Jarl took a few quick steps forward, but found himself pushed aside by the racing figure of a leprechaun, who screeched out, "Don't be afraid, darlin', Rory will catch you."

Jarl noticed for the first time how the leprechaun had grown. Since he was a magical being, he could probably be any size he chose. He had grown over two feet since Jarl first met him when he had brought Wyrd to Jarl's home. Rory ran close to the tree, then sat down abruptly as he struck some invisible barrier. Jarl heaved a sigh of relief. No wonder Wyrd had done nothing. The talisman had sensed the wards around the tree and knew Lealor wouldn't come to harm. Instead of falling to the ground, Lealor descended what must have been an invisible staircase until she reached the bottom of the tree. Her father could not help smiling as he listened to the irate Rory sputter. His face was as red as his hair and he shook his fist directly under Lealor's nose.

"Oh, Rory, don't be silly! Flowerface wouldn't let anything happen to me." Rory was still sputtering as she leaned over and gave him a kiss. "Now, darling Rory, don't be an old grouchy spoilsport. Next thing you know, someone will take you for a human."

"Indeed! Whose fault would it be if they did? Scarin' a poor innocent leprechaun half to death and then insultin' him by suggestin' he's actin' like a human."

Lealor threw her arms around him and gave him a big hug. "I'm sorry. I won't do it again if it really frightens you. I didn't think anything could frighten a leprechaun. At least, that's what you always told me."

"Well, it was just a manner of speakin', you understand. Nothin' frightens Rory . . . ." The leprechaun blustered on until Jarl, noting that his thick brogue had almost disappeared, broke in on his monologue.

"Fortunately, no one was in danger, Lealor. You need to remember that it's not kind to upset your friends."

"I'm sorry, Daddy. I knew Flowerface would take good care of me, and I forgot that you might not know it, too."

"Wyrd has a present for you, honey."

"Oh, good. I like presents."

A faint mist formed in the air, swirled in an almost invisible pattern, and then settled on Lealor's wrist. "Hello."

"Look, Daddy, Rory. It's a baby Wyrd."

Yes. You are correct, Wyrd said, speaking telepathically to all three of them. Rory opened his mouth to say something, then shut it as he realized he was hearing Wyrd speak. *Your bracelet is my daughter, Myst. She will protect you and give you good counsel when you are about to do something foolish.*

Lealor looked at the glassy iridescence of the dragon shape that clasped her arm. "You mean I can't ever take it off?"

243

Not for many years, child, Wyrd told her.

"Thank you very much, but I don't want your bracelet, Wyrd. Take it back. It would be just like having Seren and Argen bossing me around all the time."

"Lealor!" Jarl warned.

"I don't care! It would be bad enough if it was just an ordinary bracelet, but if it's going to be telling me what to do all the time, I don't want it!"

Very well, Lealor.

The girl's eyes widened as her bracelet mindspoke.

I am sorry you don't like me. It is my destiny to keep you safe, and about that I can do nothing. However, I will not speak to you again.

Lealor regretted her hasty outburst when she saw two small tears roll down Myst's nose, but she was too stubborn to try to make friends. "Okay. I guess you can stay on my arm, then," she said.

I am sorry, Lealor. I thought my daughter would have a friend in you, but you have chosen otherwise. Myst, I sorrow for you. Protect, but do not speak. Do you hear the words of your father?

The head of the bracelet rose a fraction so it could nod. Myst accepted the burden of silence.

"Now, just a minute. I'm sure Lealor will reconsider when she's given this matter some thought, Wyrd."

This is no longer a matter for humans. Keep silence before dragonlaw. Finished it iss. Wyrd closed his eyes as if in pain. *She shall rue this rash decision in time to come,* Wyrd said solemnly. *We go.*

Jarl's last sight of his daughter showed her being comforted by Rory. He only hoped he would be able to get Wyrd to relent after Lealor realized the magnitude of her error.

CHAPTER SEVEN

Andronan smiled as Jarl materialized in front of the fire in his room. "Well?" he asked.

Not well, Wyrd answered, then closed his eyes in obvious withdrawal.

Jarl looked at his sorrowing talisman. It was easy to see that Wyrd had withdrawn himself from the company of humans. In the past, when Wyrd retreated like this, it took a call from Jarl to get a response and return Wyrd to a consciousness of this world. Jarl allowed himself the luxury of a small sigh before seating himself in the second chair drawn up before the fire.

It was a warm summer day outside, but within the university, there was often a sense of chill, almost as if the builders had preferred a colder climate. Andronan sat before the fire with his aged hands resting on his knees. Jarl supposed, at his age, he appreciated the warmth of the cheery blaze.

"What went wrong, Jarl?" Andronan asked. "We can talk now that Wyrd has so tactfully withdrawn his presence."

"I'm afraid it was more disgust than tact," Jarl admitted, running his hand through his hair. "The boys now have bracelets that are Wyrd's children. They provide both protection and friendship."

"Wyrd presented the boys with talismans like himself?" Andronan's eyebrows raised.

Jarl realized that it was the first time he had ever seen the old mage surprised. "Yes. And it looks like they will get along just fine. Wyrd clearly considered the natures of the boys before giving them the bracelets. Seren has a talisman named Soladon who started their relationship by giving him the power to speak the dragon tongue perfectly. Seren was in seventh heaven, chattering away to Fafnoddle and young Fafnir with a perfect accent. Trying to speak the ancient language of the dragons is something I never hoped to accomplish. I suppose Wyrd could have given me the power, but I always managed all right with everyday human speech."

Andronan asked, "And what power did Argen's bracelet bestow on his partner?" Then he chuckled. "No," he said, raising his hand. "Don't tell me. I'm sure I know. Argen can now read all the books in the library, right?"

"You got it in one guess, Andronan. When I left him, he was sitting in the stacks reading some old tome. I suppose you'll have to send someone to make sure he eats. Think of Librisald's delight when he discovers Argen's new ability. Between the two of them, they may well have the stacks catalogued in twenty or thirty years."

"What of Lealor? Did Wyrd not give her a talisman also?" The look on Andronan's face said as plainly as words that he could not believe the bracelet-giving didn't include Lealor. Jarl knew Andronan loved the boys, but he had always had a secret feeling that Lealor was the old mage's favorite. The look on his face proved Jarl's intuition to be correct.

"Yes, but Lealor thought the talisman was only a way to spy on her. She hates being told what to do. I suppose being the baby of the family isn't easy. I never thought before how many times Mirza and I correct her. Of course, you can't rear a child today on Earth without a good many cautions. Perhaps my mistake was allowing the boys to boss her around. That's what she told Wyrd. She didn't want a bracelet that would always be telling her what to do. She said it would be just like having her brothers bossing her all the time."

"Goodness! How did that strike Wyrd? I'm afraid there have not been many who contradicted anything he said. And for Lealor to actually refuse the bracelet—that is what she did, isn't it?"

"Yes, it is." Jarl looked into the fire, obviously remembering. He continued with his story after glancing at Andronan. His hands were clenched into fists. It was difficult for Jarl to believe the calm old mage could have emotion enough to actually feel antagonistic. Lealor was his great-granddaughter, and even an ancient mage must feel some of the family ties that bound regular mortals.

"Was Wyrd angry?" Andronan asked quietly, leaning forward to hear Jarl's answer.

"Anger wasn't the emotion he felt. He seemed surprised and

then—hurt, I guess, is the best word I can think of. After all, Wyrd has shown no emotion in all the years we have been together. I have no other experience with him to compare this one to. I tried to talk to Lealor, but while we both love her dearly, we know how stubborn she can be. When she gets one of those donkey streaks, talking to her is a waste of time. She damaged Wyrd's pride in his offspring. He forbade Myst to talk to Lealor. Myst agreed. Her feelings were hurt, too, because she cried two tears. Lealor saw them and was ready to be more sensible, but it was too late. Wyrd would not listen. The best thing to do was let the whole mess die down a little. I hope eventually Lealor and Myst can become friends. If Wyrd stops being so hard to deal with, the whole thing will blow over—with time."

"It appears that Lealor is not the only stubborn being involved in this. So long as Wyrd did not invoke dragon-law—"

"He did." Jarl watched Andronan shake his head sadly.

"In that case, there is nothing we can do. Dragonlaw is that ancient body of laws which binds dragons in all honor. For a dragon to change a command given under the law's binding would take a miracle. In all my studies of dragons, I have yet to hear or read of the law being broken. What did Wyrd tell Myst?"

"He told her to protect Lealor, but not speak to her."

"Did Myst agree?"

"Yes."

"It was a thoughtless question. Myst is Wyrd's daughter, and being newly created, she would agree like any obedient child. If she had only been older—"

"How can Wyrd have three children? Who is the mother of Soladon, Nyct, and Myst?"

"Dragons who are extremely powerful are capable of cloning replicas of themselves, complete with all the skills, but not the memories, of the creating parent. The bracelets will have all the power of Wyrd."

"Kids shouldn't have that kind of power at their command. Who knows what they may decide to have their talisman do?" Jarl began to sweat, and he knew the small fire in the grate had nothing to do with his feeling.

"No, you don't understand. While the talisman have the power, they will only come into it gradually, as they need it. It will be years before they are a match for their father in power. They are like children. They will remember what they experience, they can probably return to Wyrd's horde—wherever it is—and read in his books to gain knowledge, but they won't be creating mountains of ice cream or burgers on command. Their main function is to protect the children, and it is only when they are doing this that they will be at full power." Andronan smiled when he saw the look of relief on Jarl's face. He knew one of Jarl's strengths was his ability to imagine contingencies, but sometimes an imagination could be as much a curse as a blessing.

The two men sat in comfortable silence for a few moments. Then Jarl asked, "Do you suppose it's safe, checking on Lealor? I don't want to do or say anything further to upset Wyrd."

"Don't worry, Wyrd has withdrawn until you summon him to return," replied Andronan.

"Lealor should be safe with Cibby at her cottage in the woods even without her bracelet. I really need to find out what happened after Wyrd zapped me here," Jarl fretted out loud.

"That's easily done. We can use a little of my magic to check up on the girls."

Jarl hid a smile from his companion. Only an ancient mage would think of calling Cibby a girl. Jarl had met the witch on his first trip to Realm. She wasn't anything like the witches he had heard about in fiction. She seemed to be a one-hundred-percent-huggable old granny type. Nothing in her appearance or demeanor suggested how powerful she was. She seldom stayed at the university with Andronan. She spent the greater part of her time in the woods, helping the animals. Her healing talent was truly formidable. Lealor had obviously inherited her love of animals, and she already had learned several of the simple spells to alleviate pain and heal wounds. Jarl was not sure if she spoke with the animals, or only understood them so well it appeared she could speak with them. When questioned, she had answered, "Why, I just know. It's perfectly plain. Don't you know, Daddy?"

While Jarl was thinking, Andronan had opened a closet and brought out a crystal bowl, filled with what looked like pure mercury. "Now, let's take a look," Andronan said.

"What is that?" Jarl asked.

"This is a device we learned to build from some of the Old Ones' records Librisald finally deciphered. It works like a crystal ball, but the images are much clearer."

"What powers it?" Jarl asked after peering into the silvery depths of the liquid.

"I'm not absolutely certain, but the mind and determination of the viewer cause the liquid to reflect the scenes the viewer wishes to see."

"Then all we have to do is think about what we want to view?"

"That's correct. Stand here beside me and let's both envision Cibby's cottage."

As Jarl and the mage watched, the silvery surface took on color and began to reflect a picture of Lealor and her Grandmother Cibby.

"Not bad," Jarl commented. "With sound, it would be almost like watching television at home."

"Oh, sound," Andronan said, absently passing his hand over the liquid with a few murmured words.

"Grandma, I was pretty bad today."

"Why do you say that, child?"

"Well, when Wyrd made Daddy disappear, Wyrd was mad and sad all at once, and my daddy didn't act pleased with me, either."

"Was it because you refused Wyrd's gift?"

"That's not the worst thing I did. I made Myst cry. I could feel how sad she was inside, and she's still sad, but she won't talk to me. Rory said I'd just have to keep trying, that no female could stop talking for long, but he must be wrong. It's been all afternoon, and Myst still hasn't said a word."

"Well, come sit on my lap, and we'll talk about it," her grandmother told her, as she sat in her rocking chair.

"What about the dishes? We didn't wash them yet," Lealor protested.

Her grandmother waved her hand impatiently at the dishes, which disappeared.

"Grandmother, you told me not to use magic when the job was something you could do without spells."

Her grandmother smiled at Lealor's righteous indignation. "Well, child, there are times when even the best of rules needs breaking. That's what it means to be an adult. Adults know when to ignore rules."

Lealor climbed onto the old woman's lap, thinking deeply, "You mean like when an animal's hurt, helping the animal comes first?"

"Ah, then you remember the day you didn't come when I called because you were helping that little bird get back in its nest."

"I could have helped it faster if I could have spelled it into the nest instead of having to climb up the tree."

"You remember when you explained, I wasn't angry?"

"I know you like me to obey—but you understood."

"That's another thing grown people hope they do."

"Understand children?"

"Correct, plus adults and dragons, too. Now, let's talk about what's bothering you."

"Well, I was playing in Flowerface's tree, and perfectly safe, you know, when Daddy and Wyrd appeared. Wyrd made Myst come on my arm and told me she would take care of me and tell me what to do. I told him I didn't want a bossy bracelet, and—"

"Did you actually say the words 'bossy bracelet' to Wyrd?" The old lady pushed her eyeglasses up on her nose to hide her smile.

"Not exactly. I said something like it would be just like having my brothers along, telling me what to do all the time, and I didn't want his gift."

"Oh, dear," her grandmother sighed.

"Well, then Wyrd told Myst not to talk to me for ever and ever, and she said she wouldn't."

"Perhaps Wyrd will change his mind—especially if you ask him politely and apologize."

"Somehow I know he'll never change his mind." Lealor let a big tear roll down her cheek. "Myst promised not to talk, too. Myst is so pretty. She'd never break a promise."

"Ah, Myst. Let me see."

Lealor obligingly held up her wrist.

"Hello, Myst," her grandmother said kindly.

Myst nodded her head in greeting.

"I don't suppose Wyrd imposed dragonlaw on your promise and his command?"

The tiny bracelet nodded a vigorous yes.

"Why, Myst, you're talking to Grandmother," Lealor said with a smile.

"No, child, she's not. What she's doing is responding to what I say."

"Can you respond to what I say?" Lealor asked Myst, hope springing into her eyes.

Myst nodded solemnly.

"I need to tell you I'm awfully sorry for not wanting you at first. Wyrd made you sound all bossy and horrid."

"Wyrd didn't mean to do that," her grandmother said. "Dragons have different ways of looking at things, dear. Then, too, Wyrd was speaking human, which is not his native language."

"Like when I say something in Spanish to my friend Anita Morales, and she laughs because I said it wrong?"

"Yes, that's it exactly. Now I think it's about time for you to be in bed—don't you?"

"Not really, Grandmother," Lealor said, and then spoiled the effect with a yawn.

Jarl looked away from the scene. He started to say something, but Andronan cut him off. "Wait," he cautioned Jarl.

Lealor hopped into bed and her grandmother leaned over and gave her a gentle kiss. "Sleep well, little one. Tomorrow you and Myst have many hours to discover one another."

"Do you think Myst will ever forgive me for being so mean?" Lealor's conscience was still bothering her.

"Why don't you ask her and find out?"

"Myst, I'm awful sorry. Will you forgive me and be my friend?"

The flickering firelight barely reached into the corner where Lealor's cot rested, but Myst's glowing eyes moved up and down.

"'Night, Grandma," Lealor said, snuggling on her side with the wrist containing the bracelet on her pillow where she could see the slitted eyes of her new friend.

"Good night, dear." Lealor's grandmother watched her eyes flicker shut in sleep before touching her index finger lightly on Myst's head. Myst's eyes closed in satisfaction at her touch.

The old woman returned to her chair and sat quietly rocking before she said, "What is it you two want, peeking into my cottage this time of night?"

CHAPTER EIGHT

Jarl looked at Andronan, who was shaking his head ruefully.

"I apologize, my dear, for seeming to spy on you."

"Oh, I was sure you had a good reason—such as a concern over how Lealor was faring."

"Yes, that's it exactly," Andronan said, clearly glad to escape so easily.

Jarl smiled. "What do you think about the bracelet mess Lealor has gotten herself into?"

Cibby rocked a few times in silence before she said, "It isn't a mess—exactly. In days to come, not having full communication with her bracelet will cost Lealor. Now that Myst will respond to questions, the situation is not half as awkward as it might have been."

"It's bad enough, I can tell you. Life hasn't been very pleasant on this end with Wyrd's feelings hurt," Jarl said.

"I don't know if that is really the case. Dragons are an awkward lot at the best of times," Andronan said, carefully pulling his sleeve away from the silvery material in the bowl.

"You don't remember anything like this ever happening when you wore Wyrd all those years ago, do you?" Cibby asked.

Jarl saw that she was petting her cat, Greymalkin, who had jumped on her lap. While Jarl knew that Andronan had been the previous wearer of Wyrd, he had not heard all the details. "I've got a question, although it may not be the time to ask it."

"What, Jarl?" Cibby and Andronan said together. They chuckled gently at their mistake, for both had thought the question directed at them.

"Could either of you tell me why I am wearing Wyrd and Andronan is not? I mean, how exactly did Wyrd and Andronan separate? Is Wyrd so disturbed by my daughter that maybe he'll decide to disappear or something?"

Andronan shook his head. "No, Jarl, that is not how Wyrd works. Wyrd is bound to the mortal he chooses to serve, until the mortal has done all he can to vanquish the enemy Wyrd is defending against."

Cibby smiled at Jarl, rocking gently. "My hero," she said roguishly, "vanquished his enemy in a fierce battle, and Wyrd returned to his velvet box until the need was great again."

"Now, Sibyl, my heroing was all done years ago."

"You're still my hero," she said firmly, rocking her chair so positively that Greymalkin fled from her lap.

For the first time, Jarl saw a definite resemblance between Mirza and her grandmother. Thinking of Mirza gave him a sharp ache in his chest. "Then I'm not likely to lose Wyrd in the middle of my search for Mirza?"

"No," Andronan told him. "Clearly, Wyrd believes you will still need his aid to combat the Shadowlord when he reappears."

"During your first encounter with the Shadowlord, his power grew greatly. You will find it even harder this time to vanquish him than previously." Cibby's eyes went strangely black as she added, "At your next encounter, you and Mirza will need the help of others—perhaps Wyrd's visualization of the future tells him his children and yours together will win the next victory."

"Cibby, was that a prophecy? Is Mirza in danger from the Shadowlord?" Andronan asked.

"I hope not, but I fear she is," Cibby admitted, rocking rapidly. She took her knitting from a bag attached to the arm of her chair, pulled her glasses down from the top of her head, and placed them firmly on her nose. A log popped in the fireplace and the knitting needles clicked sharply as Cibby's old fingers cast stitch after stitch.

"Try not to worry about it," Andronan comforted. "Remember, I once wore Wyrd and I know how powerful he is."

Jarl added, seeing that nothing Andronan said was going to make much difference to Cibby when she thought of her darling great-grandchildren in danger, "We know Lealor is in good hands with you watching her. I didn't want to go off Realm and leave her all upset if I could calm her. I know she will be all right now. Don't you agree?"

"Yes, she should be reassured now. I'll try to keep her interested and busy during the next few days while you disappear."

"Thank you. I'll be leaving in the morning for Achaea."

"Yes, you shouldn't delay. I have a little niggling feeling that this time Mirza needs your help."

"The gate to Achaea is unstable and it, at least, needs attention now if the Bright One within is to survive. I'll see that Jarl starts promptly in the morning. Good night, my dear."

"Bright Ones keep you safe, Jarl." Cibby blew a kiss. "Good night." The silver mirror in the dish rippled once and the vision of Cibby vanished. A cold wind emanated from the bowl as Andronan passed his hand over it.

"Put it back in the cupboard, will you, Jarl?" Andronan walked to his chair and sat wearily.

Jarl replaced the bowl carefully, shutting and locking the door when the bowl was in its place. He crossed the room and sat down beside Andronan. "Say, there's no chance that it would show me Mirza, is there?"

"Sorry. It will only work here on Realm. If you had the time to master the spells, you could learn how to make one of your own and use it on Achaea by creating it there, but it would be a chancy business to try any magic there, unless you were really desperate."

"Why?" Andronan had studied for so many centuries that Jarl always felt like a child when he had to ask him a question. Still, Jarl knew the only way to find out things was to ask when you didn't know. Andronan always seemed eager to share the knowledge he had.

"Even as the wearer of Wyrd, you are still a mortal. The gods who lived on Achaea are, after all, the gods of your ancient mythology on Earth. While I don't know them personally, the old tales depict them as pretty harsh to mortals who tried to use magic that they felt was theirs."

"Yes, I can remember some pretty ghastly stories from the myths. Any mortal who got too big for his toga ended up punished severely."

"To the old gods of Greece, *hubris* was the only sin. Any mortal who thought his powers matched those of the gods found himself punished. I don't know if they would accept your use of magic or not. It would be more tactful for you to check and perhaps ask for permission before you tried any spells."

"Believe me, I'll be really diplomatic while I'm there."

A puzzled look caught the old mage's attention.

"What is it, Jarl?" Andronan asked

"Well, it just occurred to me. How is the Shadowlord disturbing the Achaean sun without the use of magic? Surely the gods should be aware of what's happening."

"Perhaps the Shadowlord is using the Old Ones' science instead of magic, and the gods have not paid any attention. Then, his base may be so far away from Olympus that the gods have overlooked his actions."

"You mean it's possible that the gods have had it all their own way on Achaea for so long, that it's impossible for them to imagine any opposition?"

"Perhaps. Achaea is far away and the gods have had little or no contact with the gates for centuries. I wish I could be more helpful. The only answer is for you to visit and find the answers for yourself."

Jarl watched Andronan smother a yawn. "You're tired, too. If I'm to start early tomorrow, I'd better get some rest as well."

"Yes, we must both be in good shape tomorrow morning."

"Are you coming with me?" Jarl asked, surprised that the old mage would even consider such a trip.

"No, but I can control the power of the gate so that it will not further disturb the Bright One in the Achaean sun. If we destroy the sun, you and everyone on the planet will die. Even slightly disturbing the Bright One might affect the power of the gate. You and Mirza would be marooned on the world forever. There is a great risk in what you attempt."

Andronan's quiet words dropped into the stillness of the room. For a moment, Jarl wondered where the chill breeze of discomfort was coming from. He glanced around for the source of his discomfort, but he saw the windows were closed.

CHAPTER NINE

Mirza had made many trips trough the gate system, but none like this. Instead of an instantaneous arrival, she felt herself slowly being stretched thinner and thinner. She felt the memory of her shout, "Rogue gate!" drawn out into an indescribable echo, "—aaaaaaaaaa." Her physical body gradually changed to an energy form, and some new sense told her she was approaching her destination. She became aware of hundreds of tiny grey, threadlike forces that converged on a point where great energy was being formed. Then she realized what she was experiencing: the actual forces that someone had created to make a gate. One end of each gray thread came out of blackness, but all without exception curled around an energy form almost cocooned in the threads. It moved weakly, similar to an insect in a spider's web.

In the strange state between gates, Mirza could feel the bewilderment of the creature; it was very young. Mirza extended her hands and tried to pull the grey threads, but they were like wires, unbreakable. In her physical form, Mirza had control of the molecules that formed her body. This made her able to shape-shift into any creature she wished. In this distorted state, she was not sure what would happen if she attempted to change, but she knew she had to try. She willed herself into a giant crab with huge claws. Her claws quickly severed the grey threads. As each disappeared, she felt a tiny shock. The threads slowly quivered before turning to dust and disappearing. Only one thread resisted her claws. It was a silver thread that gently spiraled around the area the other threads had covered. Mirza could feel herself coalescing, changing into a physical state, but she was sure she had saved the creature in the cocoon, now recognizable as a Bright One.

The tiny Bright One moved restlessly, like a child having a nightmare. Mirza found herself softly singing the words to a lullaby, lullie, lulloo." In the strange state between the gates, the song did not seem to be sounds at all. Instead, a series of multicolored ribbons flashed into being. They twined around the silver thread and slid around and around the coils, gently fluttering in the eddies of energy surrounding the infant Bright One. For a moment, Mirza felt a strangeness in her head. It was almost as if someone had rapidly thumbed through the pages of a book. Then, with a jar, she felt herself being delivered to the surface of Achaea.

A glance was enough to tell Mirza that she had made an unorthodox landing on the planet. For one thing, she was not at a gate point at all, nor was she upright. She rubbed herself as she prepared to rise from the ground. Then she slowly sat again, hoping she would not frighten the three creatures that came into the clearing where she rested, hidden by tall grass and flowers.

"Hurry up, Neso. We'll never find her if you keep dithering."

Mirza watched incredulously as a centaur pushed a sphinx into the little glade. A satyr capered behind them.

The sphinx half-unfurled her wings, reminding Mirza of her dragon friends. "Something's wrong. She didn't come through the gate."

"Well, I say if the Master can't deliver hostages for pickup where he sends us, then it's his fault, not ours!" The satyr leered at his two companions and blew a few notes on his pipes.

"Tootle away like a fool, Sylvor. No one expects a satyr to show any sense. How you ever tore yourself from that group of fun lovers that fawn around Pan I'll never know. Why the Master chose you escapes me!" The centaur lifted his feet daintily in a little dance pattern.

"How you can dance, Kiron, when things are in such a muddle, is what I don't understand. My mother always told me that we sphinx needed to keep a cool head on our shoulders. As the most famous riddler on the whole of Achaea, I can understand why I am a chosen one. My lineage is impeccable. What are you, Kiron the Centaur, but an adventurer, out to have fun? And you, Sylvor, come from a long line of satyrs—and everybody knows what kind of dryad chasers you are. I notice that neither of you playboys is nearly so brave when the Master is around."

"It would be foolish to irritate him. When he finally completes his work on the island, we will have a world to rule. I will take all the centaurs with me, to a world where we will be supreme. No more of this looking over your shoulder all the time to make sure you haven't upset some goddess or other." The centaur reared, pawing the air with his front hooves.

"I want to rule a world with many beautiful maidens, and not one dryad or daughter of any minor god or goddess. When you find a really lovely darling lost in the woods, she calls on daddy or mommy, and you're in big trouble."

"Are you going to take any fellow satyrs along or do you plan to be the only one in your kingdom?" Kiron asked Sylvor.

"While it might be fun for a while. I'd eventually get tired of ruling alone. Besides, if I didn't take some of my friends along, who would I have to drink with? Nobody can drink like a satyr." Sylvor struck a pose and then played a small fanfare on his pipes.

Neso touched a tree with her paw and left a series of long gashes with her razor-sharp claws. Her small exhalation of breath sounded faintly like a hiss. "Being the most famed drunkard would be something you would be proud of. Now, my family—"

"Spare us, oh wisest of riddlers," Sylvor teased. "Kiron and I have heard many times about your ever-so-great-grandmother and her stand outside of Thebes on Earth."

"Only a sphinx would boast of getting killed because some ancestor or other was slain by a human hero. Believe me, it's a lot more fun to be alive, partying with your friends. Don't be so uptight. Satyrs and centaurs are about the only kinds of beings that really know how to have fun."

Neso crossed the meadow in four bounds. "Come on, you two, we've got to find her."

"Very well," Kiron answered, mincing his way along in Neso's path.

"Wait for me," Sylvor called, producing a brief tune on his pipes. He danced his way after them, playing and following a pattern of steps that reminded Mirza of the dance down the yellow brick road. The children and she had often watched a videotape of the old movie.

Sylvor's perambulations brought him next to Mirza. He stopped blowing on the pipes and asked with a leer, "Who might you be, lovely one?"

"I'm Mirza," she told him, accepting his hand. She expected him to help her to her feet, but instead, he leaned over and kissed her hand. She tried to pull away, but he kept a tight hold.

"By any chance are you related to any of the goddesses or gods here?"

"Here? Of course not. I just got here."

"You don't look like a dangerous and powerful sorceress," Sylvor said, dropping her hand at last.

Mirza rose to her feet as regally as she could. "That," she told him, "is not the issue at hand. I want to speak to your Master."

"Oh ho! Not too proud to eavesdrop on the conversations of others," Sylvor said with an amused chuckle. "Well, follow me, and I will soon have you to a spot where you can converse with the Master."

"Sylvor," called Kiron, reentering the glade. "Oh, no, you fool. Now is definitely not the time to be frolicking about with this," Kiron paused to look closely at Mirza, "delectable wench."

"Wench, indeed," Mirza said crossly. "I want to see your Master. Take me to him now."

"Your wish is his command," Kiron said, unable to resist playing with words.

"Let us gambol on that, my dear," Sylvor said, resuming his piping.

With Sylvor leading the way and Kiron following behind her, Mirza left the glade. In only a few minutes' walk they caught up with Neso, who was somewhat chagrined to have missed finding their quarry. She stalked ahead, following a path that ran down to the water's edge. A small boat, tied to a rock, floated gently on the surface of the water. As soon as they entered, it skimmed rapidly across the water, leaving land far behind, proving it was a magical craft.

"Might I ask where we are going?" Mirza's long red hair spun out behind her like a banner. While she rather enjoyed the ride, she was curious.

Neither Kiron nor Sylvor answered her. Their clutch on the sides of the boat made her think they might be seasick. Neso, however, obviously enjoyed the ride. She lifted her wings enough to catch the cool breeze before answering. "Look at the great rulers, frightened of a little trip to Atlan."

"Atlan?" Mirza repeated.

"The Island of Wizards," Neso told her. "The Master is the mightiest wizard of them all. He will open gates to many worlds, and because we help him, our reward will be a world of our own to rule as we wish."

"What if these places already have rulers of their own, or the beings there have no wish for you to be their ruler—"

"The Master will have great armies to do his bidding."

Mirza didn't like the sound of what she heard. If one of the gods was responsible for the rogue gate, it was going to be tricky indeed to save the Bright One. While Mirza had special training and the ability to shape-shift her own body and other items under the right conditions, tackling a full-fledged god was more than a mortal with any brains looked forward to trying. She wished she had arrived at the gate. With what she knew now, she would have stepped back through to get Jarl. Having him near and the power of Wyrd to call on would have been comforting. She glanced over her shoulder at the centaur and the satyr. Her hair blew in her face and she pushed it back so it could flow with the wind. Both of them looked miserable. Neither was very well designed for boat riding. Ahead of her, Neso held her face to the wind.

"We'll soon be there," the sphinx shouted, and the wind obligingly threw the words to the three behind her.

Mirza watched carefully. She saw shore birds flying ahead of the boat. Then she could smell the land itself. Gradually, the island came into view. A tall mountain dominated the north end. To the south, great marble buildings sprawled, forming a city. Small cottages and occasional estates climbed the sides of the mountain. One long piece of land jutted out to sea. A large building housed an odd tower on the very end of the spit of land. As the strange craft in which Mirza and her captors rode drew closer, Mirza could see the tower was some type of celestial observatory. Somehow, it loomed over the rest of the building of which it was a part. In spite of the size of the city, the mountain and the observatory were the real focal points of power on the island. Mirza felt an odd ripple, like pages being rapidly turned in her head. She wondered how long the aftereffects of the strange gate trip would produce this weird sensation. She could only hope nothing had been permanently scrambled in her mind by her experience.

The water became shallower with each passing minute. As Mirza began to worry that the great speed the boat still displayed was going to dash them against the cliffs, the craft slowed. Then, with no steering from Neso that Mirza could detect, it headed of its own volition toward a deep fissure in the great granite cliff ahead of them.

Mirza looked around carefully as the boat entered the giant crack. The steep sides looked impassable. If she needed to escape the Master—whoever he was—she would have to fly, birdlike, or turn herself into a fish as she cast herself into the water. She saw men running along the sides of the cliff above. Ahead, the water opened out into a harbor which was obviously not natural, for a series of tiers stood tall, blasted from the rock. Here there were many steps, making the top of the cliff accessible.

Neso jumped lightly from the boat when it rested beside the dock. Mirza accepted the hand of one of the men who was there to moor the craft. She had no time to watch Sylvor and Kiron disembark, because Neso was urging her to hurry up the stairs. Mirza did not often regret her impetuosity, but this was one time she wished she had told someone back on Realm what she was doing. She had barely made it through the gate. How long would it take the Master to repeat his work, if she did not dissuade him? Would the gate work correctly now that the grey threads were removed? It had not deposited her at the regular gatepoint. For the first time, she realized that it might not be possible to reach Achaea through the gate at all. If that were true, she was quite literally "on her own," for Jarl might not be able to reach her, even using the power of Wyrd.

Neso, walking behind her, kept urging Mirza forward, up the steps, until they reached a great open space before a door in the building. The size of the doorway dwarfed Mirza, which did not add to her feeling of security. Because she was able to shape-shift, she understood that size wasn't everything. She did hope the Master wasn't going to be as large as the doorways she was seeing, while Neso hustled her down one corridor after another. Why did trouble always seem to come in such large packages?

The guards standing before each of the doors were ordinary humans. Mirza was sure. Except for them, the building reminded her of the university at Realmgate. Only three people passed them as they traversed the corridors, and two of those carried papers, while the third read a scroll as he walked slowly by, not even noticing Mirza and Neso.

"Open!" Neso commanded a guard at one of the great doors.

The guard followed her orders quickly without saying a word. Mirza could see that Neso expected obedience—at least from the guards in the buildings.

Neso did not give Mirza a chance to say anything to the guard. She pushed Mirza into the room and said, "Wait here." The heavy wooden door closed soundlessly behind the sphinx, leaving Mirza in a large room. Surprisingly, considering the heat of the sun outside, the room was cool. Mirza supposed it was because the walls were made of thick marble. The room was dim, with the only light entering from a small, barred window set in an outside wall.

Curious, Mirza walked over and looked out. The view spread out below the cliff, revealing the city at the south end of the island in detail. The clear air and bright light made it possible to see for a great distance. Mirza looked at the plan of the city: the four quarters, the canal system, the great buildings. She exhaled softly. "Not Atlan. This is Atlantis as it might be on Earth if the island had not sunk below the waves more than a thousand years ago."

CHAPTER TEN

She walked around the room, carefully noting everything. She knew she could escape from the window because the bars were set so far apart. If she changed into a hawk, she could easily fly away. The furniture was sparse: a chair, a couch, a table. In one corner a small fountain of water fell into a marble basin. When the basin was full, the water overflowed into a pipe set into the floor. The water made a soothing sound as it splashed into the basin. It was the only audible sound in the room. She looked at the murals on the walls. One showed a mountain scene; the second, a seascape; the third, a forest; and the last, an underwater scene. The room was pleasant—for a prison.

Mirza reclined on the couch. No sense in being miserable and pacing back and forth, she thought. She might as well save her energy for her meeting with the Master. Which god would it be? Apollo was reputedly interested in truth, but would he want armies to enforce his rule? Ares would love to mastermind human and inhuman armies. He was something of a coward, and Mirza doubted he had the brains to plan an invasion scheme. Could Athena, the goddess, have decided to use her wisdom to make a gate? Why would gods want another gate? They already had one that worked fine—until someone meddled with it. Mirza closed her eyes and tried to think.

The great door opened silently, but Mirza was aware that someone had entered her room. She opened her eyes and saw one of the guards standing in the doorway. She tilted her head and raised her eyebrows in inquiry.

"You are going to face the Master now," the guard told her.

She rose, brushed off her robes, and preceded him through the door. She turned to the right at his command and continued down the corridor until he indicated she should enter another corridor that led ever deeper into the center of the building. Finally, he stopped her at a door where he knocked sharply. The door opened into a room filled with scrolls, strangely shaped glass containers, and models of things Mirza didn't recognize.

Mirza entered the room and the door closed behind her. Through a doorway that led to another room, a cowled figure entered.

Before the figure had said a word, Mirza muttered, "I should have known."

"We meet again, Mirza Koenig," the Shadowlord said.

"Not exactly by my choice," Mirza answered, holding her head high. "We of Realm thought that you were so badly frightened by our last meeting that we would have years of peace before we had need to face you again."

"Not frightened, foolish woman. Injured! Now I have healed and grown more powerful than ever. You and your husband—even aided by that conscience-driven worm, Wyrd, will not be able to stop me this time."

"I wouldn't call a dragon with the power which Wyrd can command a worm, if I were you. Dragons can be touchy. If he finds out about your opinion, it may anger him."

"You foolish gatekeepers do not even know what Wyrd really is!" The Shadowlord half rose in anger from the chair in which he sat.

"You do, I suppose?" Mirza taunted. Perhaps now she could get the answers to some of the questions Jarl and she had puzzled over in the past.

"The reason I know about Wyrd is that I have collected within this building the greatest number of scrolls, books, and stone tablets anywhere in the universe."

"Then I was right. This is some kind of university or school."

"Yes." The cowled head nodded briefly, as if it pained the great wizard to grant her being correct about anything.

Mirza wished the Shadowlord would throw back his cowl. She could see nothing of his face except an occasional silver flash, which she gathered must come from his eyes. She wanted to hear the story of Wyrd, but she also wanted to see the face of her adversary. He almost radiated energy. She could sense it. At least he was not lying when he told her his power had increased. Somehow, she wished he had been exaggerating about that.

"I bet that you didn't gather all of the material that's here," Mirza baited, trying to get as much information as she could.

"Not personally, no. I was able to add to this library significant information about the gate system. The Old Ones were not gods. They were wise because they were so ancient, not because they had better minds than we do."

"They certainly had a better system of ethics. They didn't harm any Bright Ones when they formed the gates."

"Ethics! That is a word for the weak who do not dare to do anything they wish. Look where ethics has got the Dragonlord Wyrd."

"Yes—you were going to tell me about him."

"Long before you were even a gleam in your misbegotten father's eye, Wyrd was as ancient as the Old Ones themselves."

Mirza swallowed. All the Keepers had thought of Wyrd as an animated power source. They had vastly underestimated him, if what the Shadowlord said was true. "That seems pretty farfetched. Why, Wyrd is only a few inches long."

A dusty chuckle emanated from the Shadowlord. "In your dimension that is his size. However, there is a great deal more to Wyrd than meets the eye. He allows only a small part of himself to enter this universe. He didn't want to destroy your frail egos. He targets enough matter in this universe to focus his power. He made the rules himself, thousands of years ago."

"Why would any being that powerful allow himself to become the servant of an ordinary human?"

"Quite simple. He is atoning for destroying a Bright One."

His quiet words hit Mirza like a bomb. On the one hand, she didn't think Wyrd would do such a thing, but on the other, the Shadowlord's flat recital had the ring of truth. He had nothing to gain by lying about Wyrd. Indeed, he had admitted Wyrd was more powerful than anyone thought.

"Do not look as if I have told an untruth. Wyrd was the highest dragonmage in his dimension. The gates left by the Old Ones fascinated him, once he discovered this dimension. He wrote that the gates were the only things in our universe that had any worth."

"If he felt that way, then why did he consent to become a bracelet and help the beings here?"

"His race considered the Bright Ones to be a life form equal to theirs. When they discovered his gate studies had caused an infant Bright One to die through his negligence—which I admit was caused by ignorance, not intent—they banned him from their midst until he could redeem himself by saving a Bright One from destruction."

"Then why is he still sticking around? He saved the Bright One in the Realmsun by helping us drive you away before you could finish forcing your version of a universal gate."

"That is the joke of the universe. In all those thousands of years aiding the heroes of the lesser races, he came to believe that they, too, were worthy. He could now return to his dimension in full honor—but he refuses to go."

Mirza was having trouble accepting all the information about Wyrd. She had always thought of him as a cute little bracelet, an artifact of the Old Ones, left behind to aid their younger races. She was glad she wasn't wearing the bracelet. When she was younger, she wanted the bracelet to use her as the hero to protect Realm from evil.

"That's interesting, but it's not the reason I'm here," replied Mirza.

"Spare me your lectures. This time, my gate will be even more powerful than those of the Old Ones. Not only will my gate be universal to every world, but it will also be able to choose the time I want. I will have the greatest army of heroes and warriors selected from every time and world that exists!"

Mirza wouldn't give her enemy the satisfaction of knowing what an impression his latest news had created on her. Instead, she flew to the attack. "I suppose if you destroy the Bright One in Acheasun, it is of no account?"

"Don't you who live on that backwater world of Realm have a saying about having to break an egg to make an egg pasty?"

"Backwater?" Mirza's red hair almost crackled with her wrath. "Realm and its inhabitants were good enough to send you fleeing when we defeated all the foreign beings and evils that you could call to help you."

"Admitted. I was not fully prepared. Now I am. There, I had no allies. Here I do. There are some very good minds here on the island."

"That's another thing. How have you kept from having trouble with the gods of Achaea? They don't like mortals usurping their powers."

"I deliberately chose a place where the gods would not interfere. Atlan has long had an agreement with the gods. So long as they only use their powers on the island, the gods allow it."

"Eventually they are going to find out you are tampering with their sun, and when they do, I have a feeling you will be sorry—very sorry!"

"Before they find out what I am doing, it will be too late. I have planned long and well. This time my gate will be universal and multitemporal."

"In that case, you have no need of me. I'll just go back to Realm—"

"Your tampering with my gate has caused a further imbalance in the sun. The Bright One seems to be resisting our attempts to reset the gate. However, I will allow you to join us. Your gate knowledge, added to my own, should allow us to complete the project with little damage to Achaeasun and its pulsing Bright One."

"What you are really telling me is that there is no way for me to get home using the regular gate." Mirza hoped her dismay at the prospect of staying on Achaea did not show.

"There is a way off Achaea—but you won't be using it. I remember how unreasonable you were the last time we discussed joining forces. So before we talk further, I'll have to make a few preparations." He waved his hand and Neso appeared in the room. "You and Kiron and Sylvor are to go collect those three . . . items I thought I might need. Send Mirza to her new home. She'll not escape my jailer, Medusa."

Neso's face paled. "Won't she be in danger?"

"Now, would I send a prospective ally into danger?" The black-cowled figure asked. "Don't worry yourself over her. A powerful spell by one of the Old Ones protects her. It is not worth my time to try and break it. Mirza will be joining us of her own free will when you have finished bringing me her children." He gestured a second time with his hand and Neso disappeared.

Mirza gasped. "A spell prohibits you from returning to Realm!"

"Now, my dear, there is no rule that says visitors from Achaea may not come to Realm. If they each bring a souvenir with them when they return, who is to stop them? The minigates they will use are so small we power them from here on the island. When they leave Realm, they'll siphon power from your gate to return. Then we'll talk. I look forward to your future cooperation."

The last sound Mirza heard was a rasping laugh. The Shadowlord's negligent wave sent her into darkness.

CHAPTER ELEVEN

Sylvor capered under the canopy of trees in the Realmforest. It was hard for him to believe that he actually stood on another world. It wasn't his style to worry or make a close examination of the trees; therefore, the slight differences in the forest made no impression on him. He knew he would meet his quarry soon. The star that he wore around his neck to activate the gate grew warm, as his Master had promised. The child was near. Sylvor played a captivating melody on his pipes. His tune worked as if he were the Pied Piper of Hamlin. Seren appeared almost magically.

"Hello. Who are you? I've never met you before." Seren said to Sylvor with a friendly smile. He recognized him as a satyr, a being he had never seen on Realm until this moment. Many afternoons spent in front of the television with his father and his brother had familiarized him with most types of monsters and unusual beings from fantasy. His mother said she knew more fabulous beings than any on what she called "those tasteless children's programs." When he met more of the beings on Realm, Seren agreed with her.

"My name is Sylvor." The Master had not told him how big this child was. He was almost as large as Sylvor himself. There was no way Sylvor could force Seren to go with him, but the satyr thought he could trick him.

"I'm glad to meet you," Seren said politely. Then his enthusiasm took over. "Wait until Faf sees you. I bet he's never met a satyr, either. I can't wait to see the look on his face."

"Who is this Faf?" Sylvor didn't think the minigate would transport three people at the same time. The essence of the whole operation was to get the child on Achaea before anyone who had the power to stop him from going appeared.

"Oh, he's a dragon. He's one of my best friends. Soladon is my other friend."

"You mean the bracelet you wear on your wrist is Faf?"

"No. That's—"

Soladon tightened on Seren's wrist. *Do not tell this strange satyr who I am.*

Seren thought his bracelet was being overly suspicious, but he didn't argue.

"What?" Sylvor asked.

"Oh, nothing." Seren tried to change the conversation. "I'm going to the ruins of Fellkeep to meet my dragon friend, Faf. Would you like to go along?" While it would be good to tell Faf about the satyr, it would be even more spectacular if Seren could actually produce Sylvor to show him. It wasn't very often that Seren saw anything before Faf did, because Faf could fly.

Even when Seren rode on Faf's back, he usually was so busy holding on he didn't see much unless Faf pointed it out to him. Fafnoddle, the dragon's father, had a much smoother ride. Seren had not thought about it much before, but riding Faf was a lot like bike riding on someone's handlebars. He was probably a pretty heavy load for the young dragon. Maybe that was why they only flew on short trips. Seren meant to ask his friend about his new discovery. He didn't want to be too much of a burden. On the other hand, without Faf's power of flight there were a lot of places they couldn't get to. That meant missing new experiences, giving up some of the adventures they might have. Seren didn't think Faf would want that any more than he did.

"Fellkeep? Is that a local landmark?"

"You mean you haven't heard of Fellkeep?" Seren was astounded.

"Not that I remember."

"You must really be from the deepwoods if you don't know about Fellkeep."

"Realm is wide. Is it really so strange that I would not know of this Fellkeep?" Sylvor realized he had made an error, and he was groping for a way to keep the boy from noticing it.

If Sylvor had thought to look, he would have seen that Soladon's eyes had become green chips of ice. Soladon listened and watched carefully. Perhaps this was a creature that would menace Seren. The small talisman gathered his power, ready to strike if he became aware of the slightest danger. It was not only that Wyrd had created and set him the task of guarding Seren. He really liked the boy and his hulking dragon friends, especially the young Faf. Existence on this level with these life forms was interesting, very interesting.

At night, when Seren slept, Soladon made use of the time to study the dragon lore in Wyrd's huge library. The talisman didn't notice anything strange about going someplace else with his mind when only a small portion of it had to watch the sleeping boy. For all he knew, Seren himself was studying human lore during the sleep periods.

Seren, excited about his new friend, paid no attention to the significance of Sylvor's ignorance. For once, he would get to tell someone about his parents' exploits. "Fellkeep is where the Shadowlord lived. It's where my parents defeated him in a final battle for the safety of Realm!" Seren paused in his breathless recital to see if he had properly impressed Sylvor.

"Oh, that Fellkeep!" Sylvor nodded wisely.

Seren continued. "Come on, and I'll tell you as we walk."

The satyr nodded and took a place beside Seren on the path. This was fine. His minigate had deposited him near the ruins of a great castle fortress. The place must be Fellkeep.

"In the old days, the Shadowlord used Realm as a gathering place for his armies. He set up a rogue gate. That's one not authorized by the Old Ones. It stressed Realmsun, which was about to explode when my parents took a hand. Faf's mother and father carried my parents to Fellkeep in time for them to use magic. Wyrd, my father's—"

Keep silence about the power of the dragon bracelets, Soladon warned mentally.

There's nothing wrong with Sylvor. Why shouldn't he know about your father's part in saving Realm? Seren's thought flashed.

Now the satyr believes I am nothing, a mere ornament on your wrist. It is best so. Someday the ignorance of your enemies may be to our advantage.

We don't have any proof he means me harm. Rapid as this exchange of mental conversation was, Seren could sense he was losing the argument.

Do you expect those who mean you harm to announce their villainy upon meeting you? Humor me. Let us wait to tell Sylvor of my real identity until there is more of a reason.

Well, okay, Seren agreed, still certain his friend pushed the guardian business to its farthest limit.

"Wyrd, your father's what?" Sylvor asked.

"I was trying to think of a word to describe Wyrd. His name means fate in some old language. Wyrd is a powerful magic user. Somehow, he's able to augment the magic powers of my father. Without him and the wyverns who live in the marsh, the humans on Realm would not have won the war."

"Why do you meet Faf at Fellkeep?"

"Oh, Faf and I like to have adventures and find out things. His mother had some terrific adventures when she was younger. My mother had fun, too, but now both of them are always worrying about Faf and me. If it wasn't for Grandma Cibby, I wouldn't know half of the neat things my mother did when she was young.

"Faf's grandfather told us about the wonderful adventures the dragons in his family had. Faf's grandfather is the only one who encourages us to explore. He likes to hear what we find out about. We fly there every so often to report. He knows a lot of interesting things. Some of our best adventures started with interesting bits of old stuff he told us about. Fellkeep is one of the places we think our parents would worry about. So, we meet there and then we don't have any grown-up asking, 'Where are you two off to today?'"

"Aha! It keeps you from lying!" Sylvor leered his understanding.

For the first time in their brief acquaintance, Seren got a glimpse of the satyr's real nature. He found the passing expression disturbing, but he told himself it was his imagination. That's what comes of listening to Soladon, he thought.

"We wouldn't lie to our parents, Sylvor. We wouldn't do anything they expressly told us not to do, either. We don't want to worry them. Sometimes we've been in pretty narrow squeaks, but we managed to get out of them." Seren's eyes shone with the memory of how they had outwitted several of the odd denizens of Realm.

"Somewhere around here is Leafshine's oak. That's one of the things Faf and I want to do someday, find Leafshine and let her tell us about the aerial battle that Faf's father fought with the mechanical birds the Shadowlord created. My father never wants to talk about it, but we found out about it from Faf's grandfather."

"How much farther is it?"

"Not far now. We have to skirt the marsh before we reach Fellkeep."

"Is there no path through the swampy ground?" Sylvor asked, piping a brief tune.

"Well, yes, there is, but we'd have plenty of trouble using it."

"Isn't it much shorter to go through the swamp?"

"Sure, it's shorter, but we're males," Seren said, as if that explained everything.

"What does our sex have to do with passing through the marsh path?" Sylvor asked between short bursts of music on his pipes.

"The wyverns live there, you see," Seren explained. "They are strange beings. The lady wyverns run everything."

The path abruptly came to an end at the edge of some murky water. Seren turned to the left and continued through the trees. The damp ground bore witness to their passing. Sylvor's hoofprints and Seren's footprints showed plainly where they had been and pointed their direction of travel. "How long will we have to go through this mud?" Sylvor asked. He was not in favor of leaving so clear a record of his passing. The minigate that would leave no trace of his visit to Realm was safely located on dry ground.

"We're very close to Fellkeep now. Any minute the ground will start rising and there will be much more rock." Seren turned around and grinned at Sylvor before continuing his monologue. "The wyvern ladies are super magic users. They're very attractive, too. My father rescued one of them. Wyverns are not usually very friendly to men, but Fafnoddle's mother was the wyvern queen's friend. It turned out that the wyvern my dad rescued was a wyvern princess, so they helped cure Faf's father of the wounds he got fighting the bird-things.

"While he rested, the wyvern princess guided my father into Fellkeep, where he rescued my mother. My father said the wyvern princess was very brave and awfully intelligent. The magic they used impressed my father, but he wouldn't give any details. He said maybe the wyverns didn't want other people to know how they worked their magic. I'd sure like to meet one of those wyverns, but they seldom stray far from this marsh."

Sylvor hoped the boy was right. One of the last things he wanted to meet right now was a wyvern. Especially, he didn't want to meet any being who was a friend of the boy's father. Wyverns sounded like a group of creatures Sylvor could well do without.

Through a break in the trees, Seren and Sylvor got their first sight of Fellkeep. Sylvor hopped gratefully onto a large flat rock. He could tell they were very close to the minigate. He was almost certain it rested behind a large rock to the right. Now, how could he best get the boy to cooperate?

Seren solved the satyr's problem for him.

"Faf's not here." Seren's face fell. The satyr probably had things to do and wouldn't want to wait around until Faf arrived. "If you don't have anything important to do right now, we could look around while we wait for my friend," he said, delighting Sylvor.

"That sounds like a good idea to me," the satyr agreed. Luck was with him. In a few minutes, he would have the boy positioned, and then he could activate the minigate and finish his task.

Seren hopped from rock to rock like a mountain goat. Sylvor was unused to young humans and expected him to fall momentarily. It was all he could do to keep from calling out a warning. The satyr had enough sense to know his only hope of manipulating the boy lay in his being a friend, not another parental figure. The satyr hurried to the place behind the rock where he thought the minigate waited. He was right. He turned and shouted for Seren.

"Seren! Come see what I found!" The star on the chain around the satyr's neck pulsed redly. The proximity to the gate activated it.

"Where are you, Sylvor?" Seren looked around for his friend.

"Over here behind the big squarish rock," the satyr answered.

Seren examined the many blocks of stone that littered the area. "Call again," he urged. "There must be a million of these squarish rocks," he muttered to himself.

"Here!"

This time Seren was able to pinpoint which rock Sylvor meant. He clambered down from his rock and worked his way in Sylvor's general direction.

"Stop, young manling," a quiet voice said.

Seren turned and saw a green lizard step from behind a boulder. "You're a wyvern!" he said.

"That is correct."

"Something's wrong, Wyverns don't speak with human males."

"That also is correct, young manling. However, in this case, something is owed."

"You don't owe me any money," Seren said, bewildered. How could a strange wyvern owe him anything?

"Money is one of the curses your race bears. No wyvern has such a debt."

"Why stop me?" asked Seren.

"The wyverns owe a debt to Jarl Koenig. My own honor repays. I offer safety in place of danger."

"What do you mean by that?" Seren understood that wyverns were weird creatures, but this one didn't even make sense. "What danger?"

"The danger that comes from traveling by an unauthorized gate."

"There's no gate here now. My father and mother destroyed it when the Shadowlord fled Realm."

"Think you that we watch not the area around our home? We learned not to ignore the activities of humans in our area. If we had watched the strange one you call the Shadowlord, he who was our great enemy, we would have stopped his evil long before it grew past simple containment."

"Then, I'll bet you know my father."

"Yes."

"Are you Seabreeze?"

A nod was his answer. Seabreeze pulled a sharp dagger from her belt and motioned Seren to stand where he was. Sylvor came from behind the rock and motioned Seren to come to him. He did not see the wyvern who had stepped into the shadow formed by the narrow crevice between two stones.

"What's keeping you? Don't you want to see what I've found?"

"Sure I do but—" Seren took one step forward, then halted.

Seabreeze stepped from the crack and stood between the two.

"This is my father's friend, Sea—"

Soladon hissed, *Shhh!* in Seren's mind.

"We do not give our truename to our enemies, Young One," the wyvern said.

Seren looked at the satyr and the wyvern. He didn't know what to believe. His bracelet and the wyvern both warned him, but nothing about Sylvor seemed dangerous.

"You doubt me, Young One?" the wyvern asked.

"Not exactly, but—"

"Speak, Hoofed One. Tell Jarl Koenig's son what lies behind the rock and why you desire his presence so urgently."

"I want to show him something." Sylvor almost whined his answer. He could tell Seren was beginning to doubt him.

"See the star around his neck, manling? It pulses with the energy that will activate another gate that leads to great evil."

"Hey, Sylvor, she's right. Your star is shining. It wasn't dimming and brightening like that when I first met you."

"Very well. Yes, there is a gate, and you will come to me now." With these words, he began playing a strange little tune on his pipes.

Seren tried to resist, but the very notes pulled him forward.

"Stop, or you are doomed!" Seabreeze commanded.

"I'm trying!"

"Look at your bracelet!"

Seren tore his eyes away from Sylvor and looked at his bracelet, even as he advanced ever closer to the satyr. Soladon's eyes seemed to grow larger and larger, then, with a wrench, everything disappeared in a golden haze. Seren heard the wyvern speak farewell in his mind and everything faded to black.

CHAPTER TWELVE

Jarl arose before the sun on the morning he planned to go to Achaea. He wore boots, his ever-durable jeans, a shirt, and his cowboy hat. No Texan was ever more ready for adventure than he was that morning.

He passed through the silent hall of the university to the great refectory. A short stop at the window brought Calor, the head cook, with a plate of steaming pancakes.

Calor gave him a wide smile, showing the gap in his front teeth, for the cook liked fighting almost as much as he did cooking. "Sun rises early, doesn't it, Jarl," he boomed, his voice filling the empty refectory.

"Indeed, my friend," Jarl answered, "but not early enough to catch you unawares." Jarl gestured to the heaping plate.

The cook beamed and handed Jarl a glass of freshly squeezed coralberry juice. "Coffee will be ready in a minute," the cook promised. "So sit down and begin to eat or cold pancakes will be your fare this morning."

"Nobody makes these like you do, Calor. I don't know where you got the recipe," Jarl told his friend, sitting at the table nearest to the food window.

"It was your own good wife, the Lady Mirza, who brought the recipe to me. She told me how fond you were of these strange cakes baked in a skillet. The children always eat better breakfasts when I make pancakes. Well I remember the first time I served them good oaten porridge. You'd have thought I planned to poison them. Seren and the little miss still won't eat porridge, but if I put plenty of coralberry jam on the table, Argen will."

"I remember the fuss when he started the fad. Now almost everybody mixes coralberry jam with their porridge."

"I find I prefer it that way myself—" Calor stopped abruptly, his wide eyes looking comical in his broad face.

A leprechaun had materialized on the end of Jarl's table. "Bewitched I am," he sputtered. "Sent hither and yon, Bright Ones know where, at the flick of a finger!" He thumped a small knapsack on the table. "Well, this errand's done." He said this more cheerfully, as he looked longingly at the pile of pancakes on Jarl's plate.

"Good morning, Rory," Jarl told his friend.

"Top o' the mornin' to you," the leprechaun answered.

"How are you today?"

"Well, but I might be better if I had a little somethin' to stick to my ribs." He eyed Jarl's plate, which was rapidly being emptied.

"Calor." Jarl raised his voice slightly. "Have you a few more pancakes going begging in the kitchen?"

"Coming up, Jarl." Calor came to the window and shoved a small mountain of pancakes through.

Rory made a magical pass with his hands, and the plate sailed over to rest in front of him. He wasted no time in digging in.

Calor came to the window with a pot of coffee and two cups. Jarl hid his smile with a large hand. Calor's lower jaw dropped open, and he stared at Rory. The leprechaun paid no attention to the cook. He kept shoveling pancakes into his mouth as if he had had no food for months.

Jarl couldn't resist a chance to tease his friends. "Didn't you get a chance to have any breakfast this morning?" he asked, winking at Calor.

"Of course I did! Didn't Cibby just send me with a provender bag for your trip?"

"What did you eat out of the bag?" Jarl asked with real interest.

"At Cibby's I had eggs, bacon and fresh bread. I found myself with a real thirst. I knew you wouldn't mind if I conjured up a small potation to wet my whistle as my granny used to say." Rory reached into his back pocket and pulled out a small flask. He tipped it up and allowed a stream of amber liquid to cascade into his throat.

"What would that be?" Calor asked, not knowing Rory as well as Jarl did.

"A taste of old Ireland." Rory smacked his lips and took another drink.

"You're drinking alcohol for breakfast?" a scandalized Calor asked.

"I'd not drink just any old thing with so delicious a meal. Nothing but the finest Irish whiskey. It gives a zip to pancakes that coralberry jam never did!" Rory rubbed his stomach, which stuck out in an alarming fashion. It reminded Jarl of the way a small pup looked after finishing a bowl of food. "I'll have to be off, Jarl. Give my regards to Mirza when you find her. Look!" he commanded.

Both Jarl and Calor glanced over at the door where Rory pointed. Andronan entered, chuckling.

"You two let Rory get away with his pot of gold again, didn't you?"

"If that leprechaun has any gold, it's spent at the first tavern he materialized next to," Calor said, picking up the empty plates Jarl set on the window.

"He likes to keep his hand in, he told me once," Jarl said. "So I always pretend I'm fooled when he points. It pleases him to slip away behind my back."

"What can I get you for breakfast, Andronan?" Calor asked.

"Nothing, thank you." Andronan raised his hand in negation. "Don't lecture me, Calor. I will come and eat something after Jarl has gone. I promise."

Calor stood, arms akimbo, "I won't lecture you, then, but one of these days the wind from some spell will blow you over if you don't eat regular meals."

"You stay after him about eating, Calor. Mirza and I trust you to keep him from starving himself."

At the sound of Mirza's name, Andronan's face lost its look of amusement. "Mirza," he said softly. "Yes, Jarl, now is the time of your departure."

Jarl pushed in his chair, took up the provender bag, and told Calor goodbye. Then he followed Andronan through the door and down the hall to the Courtyard of the Gate.

Vigilan stood and stretched when Jarl and Andronan entered the courtyard. His shift was over, and someone would be replacing him shortly. He bowed respectfully to Andronan and nodded to Jarl. "Good day to you both," he said.

"To you, also," Andronan replied. "I know how very tired you are, but would you stay and help anchor the gate for Jarl's trip?"

"Of course. I would be honored." Vigilan's thin face flushed with pleasure.

Jarl moved to stand within the star that formed the gate. Andronan motioned him back.

"Why?" Jarl asked.

"We do not know the condition of the receiving gate of Achaea. First, we must test the gate. I don't know what would happen if you transported yourself into the gate matrix without having a reception point that would receive you."

"Then you believe there is a damaged gate at its terminus on Achaea?"

"All may be well, but sensible precautions should be taken before trusting a gate blindly, when we know there has been trouble on the other end."

"So how do we test the gate?" Jarl asked impatiently.

"First we need someone at each point of the star. We three must have two others to stand watch."

"Are we too late to see Jarl off?" the welcome voice of Guardy asked. With him was Argen.

"Dad's still here, Guardy," Argen said. "Hi, Dad."

"What brings you out to the gate so early? Usually you'd be sleeping until noon."

"That's not what I do when I'm here. At home things are usually pretty boring, so there's no hurry to get up on a Saturday. Here, Librisald and I have lots to do, and I get up early. Besides, Calor won't make pancakes after ten. He says it interferes with lunch preparations."

"Are my other two children going to grace my leave-taking with their presence?" Jarl asked in mock solemnity.

Argen, who did not have much of a sense of humor, took his father's words at face value. "Lealor is with Grandma Cibby, and Seren and Faf are off together somewhere. I'll be the only one here this morning."

"Argen, do you think you could hold one of the points of the star?" Andronan asked quietly.

"Me?" Argen's voice rose in a squeak of excitement.

"Are you sure this is safe for him to do, Andronan?"

"It's to give balance to it. There should be no danger to him. Mirza was about his age when she started working with the gate."

"Okay, then," Jarl said, hoping the old mage knew what he was talking about. Jarl was glad his children wore the bracelets. To him they made an extra margin of safety.

Nyct opened sleepy silver eyes and spoke mentally to Jarl. *Do not worry. While I am on guard, nothing truly evil can come to the child.*

Does Argen hear you speaking to me? Jarl asked curiously.

No. The reassurance was for your mind only.

I just wondered. If Argen heard you call him a child, he'd probably be angry.

*I shall remember and call him—*Here, Nyct obviously searched for a word.

Try calling him youth or young man if you must, Jarl suggested.

Thank you. I master your language slowly, although I can read all the languages in the library, Nyct said, puzzled by the gap in his ability.

Don't worry about it. Spoken language and written language differ greatly. Your father, Wyrd, is probably a master at written communication, but he doesn't speak all the languages he reads. If you share his abilities, learning to speak the languages of the worlds will be something you must learn to do, in addition to Wyrd's talents.

During this time, Andronan had placed everyone but Jarl around the star. He motioned to Jarl to take his place, which he did quickly.

The sun gilded the Courtyard of the Gate with mellow sunshine. The four robed figures stood like statues. Argen wore the robes of a novice Keeper while he was on Realm. Only Jarl wore pants. Somehow, in spite of the fact that this was the first time Argen had stood in a star, he looked more at home than Jarl did.

"You are all familiar with Achaea?" Andronan asked.

"Yes," they answered.

"Raise your arms, palms downward, and concentrate on that world."

They did so, and Jarl was astounded to see hazy gaps form in the lines of the star. He knew the star mosaic was solid. Suddenly, it was only a shell with so many gaps that Jarl would not have known it was a star if he hadn't seen it before.

"Drop your hands now!" Andronan commanded.

They did. Jarl looked at the faces around him. Guardy shook his head and muttered to himself. Vigilan's face was white with strain. Argen looked puzzled. One look at Andronan's face brought Jarl to his side. He helped the tottery old mage to a bench against the wall.

"What is it? What happened?" Jarl asked.

The others drew around. "The gate—the gate—the gate to Achaea. It's gone!"

"Then how is Dad going to rescue Mother and bring her home?" While the question was childlike, Argen's face had taken on the maturity he was not due to deserve for many years.

Guardy said, "Go get the healer. Have him bring a restorative."

"Yes, sir," Vigilan said, hurrying off on his errand, relieved to be able to do something.

Andronan sat quietly, taking deep breaths. He seemed normal, except for his talc-white features. Jarl sat down beside him and took one hand, while Argen sat on the other side and leaned against his great-grandfather. Guardy stood before them, shaking his head. No one said anything for some time.

Jarl asked, "Is there no way we can reach Achaea?"

The healer bustled into the courtyard and went directly to Andronan. "So, my old friend," he said, "you are ill?"

"The gate to Achaea is inoperative," Jarl told him while the healer poured a small amount of golden powder into a vial and offered it to Andronan. The old mage took it silently. Color gradually returned to his face.

"Are you all right now?" the healer asked. "You must rest."

Andronan rose with the aid of Guardy and the healer. He left the courtyard without saying anything to Jarl and Argen.

"Now what do we do?" Argen asked, sure his father would have some plan of action.

Jarl put his arm around his son's shoulders before saying, "Son, I don't know." Jarl and Argen both jumped when they heard the loud "pop" which echoed in the courtyard.

"Uncle Jarl, Uncle Jarl!" young Faf panted. "My father will be here any minute. Don't let him turn me into a feather duster."

"What in the world—" Jarl began just before a second loud popping noise came from the courtyard. Argen drew his knees up on the bench to make more room and Jarl moved his legs until they hung over the side of the bench. The Court of the Gate filled with dragons. Faf was trying to get as close to Jarl as he could and Fafnoddle, his father, filled the rest of the area. In fact, it was such a tight squeeze that Fafnoddle's tail wrapped around a pillar and draped over the second floor balcony that ran around the courtyard.

Smoke poured from Fafnoddle's nostrils. He lifted his head so his friends didn't suffocate and tried to control his temper.

"Uncle Jarl, save me!" Faf screeched, almost crushing Jarl in an attempt to get as close as possible.

Only on Realm, Jarl thought wearily to himself. Over my head in dragons. How in the world am I to protect Faf from his father—especially since he's a full-grown dragon? What is Fafnoddle so angry about?

"First Egg, you are within a scale of being turned into a coralberry tartlet!" the irate Fafnoddle hissed.

"I'm not First Egg any more. That's a baby name. I'm Fafnir, like my grandfather! I'm not a baby any more."

"Don't you dare stamp your foot, Faf. It will crack the tile in the yard," Jarl warned, trying unsuccessfully to push Faf away so he could get a breath.

"Jarl, why are you calling this child by an adult name?"

"Well, he told me he had grown up. Just look at the size of him! You certainly can't go around calling anything that large an egg," Jarl explained.

"Oh, scales!" Fafnoddle shook his head. "I'm afraid it's all a misunderstanding. My son has to study the **Dragon Chronicles** and learn a great deal of dragon lore before any dragon will consider him even half-grown."

"I'm sorry if I contributed to the misunderstanding—"

"But, Father," the little dragon broke in, "I have a piece of gold for my hoard, too."

"What did I teach you about breaking into adult conversations? You apparently haven't learned about basic courtesy. Why can't you keep silent like Argen, here." Fafnoddle flicked his tongue in the boy's direction. "He probably knows more dragon lore than you do, too!" Here Fafnoddle raised his head to expel a cloud of smoke in his indignation.

"I'm afraid he does have a piece of gold, Fafnoddle," Jarl said. "If it makes any difference," Jarl drew a deep breath and added, "I gave it to him. It came from Earth."

"Well, I'm glad to hear he hasn't taken up lying, along with his disobedience. However, he is still mistaken. It is true he can select an adult name and that he must have gold to start his own hoard. If he had studied a little more diligently, he would have found out there is a test and ceremony he must pass through to make everything official. One piece of gold is a piddling amount to begin a hoard with, my son," Fafnoddle said, partially mollified by Jarl's explanation.

"Thank you, Father. Then I can use my grown-up name—Fafnir?"

"Well, perhaps not around your mother. What she will do if she ever hears of your behavior tarnishes my scales just to think of," Fafnoddle concluded.

"It's permitted to add to my hoard?"

"Yes, I suppose so. A dragon can't have too much gold. I suppose you and Seren will be adventuring all over Realm looking for hidden caches of gold," Fafnoddle grumbled. "Remember, now—no stealing. This gold has to be unclaimed!"

Jarl didn't have to be in mental contact with Fafnoddle to know what he was thinking. All he needed was to have irate denizens of Realm showing up on his cavestep complaining about their missing gold.

"One other thing. You have to spend at least two hours a day studying. Dragon's honor." Fafnoddle solemnly scratched a large "X" on a chest scale with a claw.

"Oh, father—" the little dragon began.

"Oh, father me not!" Fafnoddle roared in a truly magnificent bellow. "Home! Now!" he commanded.

A "pop" and the courtyard was missing one small dragon.

"If I had known what a bother a family was, I might have stayed a bachelor," Fafnoddle said. "If it isn't one thing Ebony wants fixed around the cave, it's another. First Egg would be Last Egg if I had my way. Only Ebony wants a big family. I do nothing except get the boy out of one scrape after another. When I really need to concentrate, I come here to the university to think. Andronan lets me use that big pool at the back of the grounds to soak my tail when I study." Fafnoddle looked at his friend. "Jarl, here my family has been fretting you and something's wrong. I can tell."

"You could say that," Argen put in. "The gatelink between here and Achaea is now broken. Dad doesn't know how to get Mother home."

The huge saurian raised his eyelids, turning his eyes dinner-plate size. He asked Jarl mentally, *Is this true?*

Jarl nodded.

"Well, then Wyrd will have to take a hand," the dragon said.

"I'm afraid not," Jarl answered. "He seems to be sulking. When Lealor refused his bracelet, he really got—" Jarl paused, looking for an appropriate word.

"Ticked?" Argen said helpfully.

Perhaps not exactly, Nyct said to Argen mentally, *but very disturbed. He is considering the Cosmic All and may stay like that for days.*

"Whatever Wyrd feels, he is not communicating with me at present," Jarl said. "I need to get to Achaea, and the gate can't take me."

"I have been doing a little experimenting with the dragon ability to travel dimensionally. If you are sure of where you want to go, I'll attempt to take you there."

"Yes, I'll gladly accept your offer. Argen, tell Andronan that we have gone to Achaea. Tell him not to worry."

"Sure, Father," Argen said with a smile. He didn't let it fade from his face until he was hurrying down the hall to Andronan's room. Sometimes Argen thought he knew where his brother Seren got his tendency to follow through his hare-brained schemes without calm deliberation. Argen would have felt better about the trip if his father had taken time to put a safety spell on himself and the dragon. What if Achaeasun had exploded? Argen didn't have the slightest idea what happened to travelers who arrived at the place where a gate had disintegrated. Somehow, he didn't think his father had even considered that scenario. Maybe that's why Seren was so brave. He didn't have the brains to think about all the things that could go wrong.

Back in the courtyard, Faf popped in. "Greeks had gold, didn't they?" he asked.

"Home!" his father's voice roared as again a small dragon form popped out.

CHAPTER THIRTEEN

Argen scuffed leaves with his feet. How could Andronan send him out to play? He had held a point of a star that morning, and this afternoon Andronan had sent him away like a child.

He couldn't even work in the library until the next day. Librisald had been adamant, too. All the adults had ganged up on him, saying it was for his own good. He took the thick book out of his inner pocket. Thank the Bright Ones, he had something to read. He looked around for a convenient log to sit on and became lost in the history of Realm.

Argen raised his head at the sound of hoof beats. Who would be riding here in the woods, off the path?

"Hello, young man," said Kiron when he noticed Argen seated on a log.

"Hello." Argen looked at him carefully. "You're a centaur, aren't you?"

"How well read you must be to recognize me." The boy's friendliness delighted Kiron. It would be easy to transport him to Achaea.

"My name's Argen. What's yours?" Argen asked, plucking a sprig of greenery and sticking it in his book to mark his place.

"I'm Kiron."

"What are you doing here?"

"My master sent me on an errand into this part of Realm. You know it well, don't you?"

"Pretty well, I guess. My brother Seren is the one who knows all about Realm. I like to read, but he's an adventurer."

'You mean you never have adventures?" Kiron sounded astounded.

"None to speak of. My brother doesn't sit still long enough to read anything. He likes to run and climb and fly around on Faf's back. I get a little airsick when I ride Faf. Besides, Faf is Seren's special friend. My special friend is Librisald."

"Is this Librisald a dragon, then?" Kiron asked.

"Only if he catches someone not taking care of the books in his library." Argen smiled at his joke. "Actually, Librisald is the old librarian at the university."

"Well, if he's an old scholar, he wouldn't make a very good person to have an adventure with. We centaurs, on the other hand, can climb, run, jump—" The centaur cocked his head to the side. "I've just had a marvelous idea. Why don't you come along with me to seek the cave I need to find?"

"I don't know if I have the time. They'll worry about me if I'm not back for dinner." Argen stood and thought.

"No wonder you never get to have any adventures. You spend so much time thinking, you never venture anywhere."

Argen frowned. Next, he looked up into the centaur's face. "You know, you're right. I'll go and help you look."

"Fine!" replied the relieved centaur. "Our quest would go much faster if you would ride on my back. You have ridden horses, haven't you?"

Not for anything would Argen admit his experience consisted of pony rides around the ring at the local fair at home. He swallowed and ignored the question. "How will I get on your back?"

'If I kneel down by the log over there, you can mount easily." Kiron suited his actions to the word, and Argen climbed on.

Kiron walked carefully through the woods. He had no intention of breaking a leg in some burrow or other. His cautious movements also allowed Argen to get the feel of riding a tall mount. Kiron could tell the boy was a novice rider from the death grip the boy's legs kept on his body. The boy worked harder to stay on than Kiron did to keep moving.

"Say, Kiron, what exactly did your master send you to bring to him?"

"My master said I was to find a cave containing some old books he left there for safekeeping."

"Seren and Faf were talking about some caves north of Realmgate. They explored a couple, but they said there were too many to waste time looking in all of them."

"Oh, that's no problem. When I get close to the cave, this star I wear around my neck will start to shine. That's how I'll know I'm in the right place."

Nyct spoke in Argen's mind. *I do not like the star. Something tells me it is evil.*

I'm sorry, Nyct. I thought you were asleep. I'd better introduce you to Kiron, Argen mindspoke to his bracelet.

No, it is better not. I will introduce myself when the time is right.

Kiron finally reached a road. "Hang on to my waist. Now I will really give you a ride." With these words, Kiron began to trot with Argen struggling to stay upright, fighting the strange rhythm that put his bottom in position to slap into Kiron's back with every step. "Here is an easier pace, Argen, but it's faster." Kiron began to gallop.

The wind blew in Argen's face. He thanked the Bright Ones that he had tucked his book securely inside his robe. He wasn't sure what Librisald would do to him if he damaged or lost it, and he didn't want to find out.

Kiron galloped tirelessly, while Argen held on as if it were a matter of life or death.

"See that path to the left?" Argen called.

"Yes," the centaur answered.

"That path cuts around Realmgate and leads directly to the hills." Argen didn't want people to see him hanging on for dear life. Besides, someone was sure to stop him because it was almost time to eat. He deserved to have an adventure.

"Very well. Whatever you command," Kiron said, aware that it was a joke he couldn't share with the boy. It suited his purpose also to avoid the city. His master had sent him to Realm through a minigate, and he knew taking Argen with him would depend on his swiftness and his secrecy.

Kiron could feel the star warming against his chest. They were approaching the minigate.

"Kiron, after we find the books, will you have time to meet my brother and Faf?"

"Perhaps. Who knows? We may meet sooner than you think," the centaur answered, certain he would meet the boy's twin brother when the boys were imprisoned on Achaea.

"I'd sure like to show him he's not the only one who can meet new people and have adventures." Argen remembered that sometimes Faf and Seren had been in danger on their adventures. He asked cautiously, "Er, Kiron, there won't be any monsters or anything guarding these books, will there?"

Kiron could tell what his answer should be from the tension in his rider's body. "No. Of course not."

Argen relaxed. "At any rate, I've done something my brother's never done."

"What is that?"

"I've ridden a centaur. Why, Seren's never even met one."

"He's never met me," Kiron said. "In fact, if you're looking for records, I've never allowed a human to ride on my back before. Riding a centaur is a great honor. Several of us have been famed teachers, but we don't go giving rides to just anybody, you know."

"Would you do me a favor?"

"Depends on what it is."

"My little sister Lealor is a real nut about—" Here, Argen paused. He knew better than to say animal to the centaur. "—rare creatures. If she sees you, I know she'd love to have a ride." Argen plunged on before Kiron could say no. "It wouldn't have to be a very long one. A walk up and down the road, you know. She's kind of little, but she's a real fast learner, and I know she wouldn't be afraid."

"If I meet your little sister and it is possible, I'll give her a ride," Kiron promised.

The ground had been gradually ascending, and now the path became a rough track. It dawned on Argen that it must be hard for Kiron to keep carrying him up into the hills.

"Hey, I bet you're tired. Why don't you let me down and I'll climb for a bit?"

The centaur thought for a moment. They hadn't seen a soul all afternoon. The boy could never outrun him. Back on Achaea the centaurs played tag in the rocky mountains. If the boy tried to run away, he would grab him and take him to the gate. They must be very close because the star was almost too warm to be comfortable. It wasn't very likely that anyone would be able to stop him from abducting Argen now. He hoped Neso and Sylvor were doing half so well as he was.

"How thoughtful of you," Kiron said, stopping so Argen could dismount.

"There are two caves ahead," Argen said.

The centaur approached, but neither affected his star. "Neither is the right cave," he told the disappointed boy.

They continued their search.

The sun was an orange ball low in the sky before they finally found an opening that caused the star to flicker.

Argen had been getting a bit worried. Soon night would come, and how was he to get home? Andronan might ask for him and would be concerned if he was not at the university. Everyone expected Faf and Seren to be out late. Argen didn't think it was fair, but very few things on Realm were large enough or dangerous enough to bother a half-grown dragon. With Faf to protect him, Seren had more freedom than Argen. He, however, knew that everyone expected him to be safe in the library in the evening.

"I'm sure glad we've found the right spot. I'd better be starting for home pretty soon," Argen said.

Kiron threw up his head. "Why, you wouldn't want to leave now, would you? You haven't seen the books that are in the cave. I am to bring two books with me—I'm sure my master wouldn't mind if you read the rest."

Books to read? Books that were not in the library? Perhaps some new ones that someone could copy and add to the collection? Argen made his choice. Nothing would stop him from seeing those books, even if he had to climb all night.

"I'd really like that," Argen said. The centaur stood at the mouth of the cave, urging Argen to climb up and enter.

Stop, Jarl Koenig's son, Nyct said in Argen's mind.

Argen could tell what Nyct had to say was important because he called him Jarl Koenig's son. That sounded like some kind of official dragon pronouncement. *Stop what?* he asked, pausing a few feet from Kiron.

Do not approach the centaur. He means to do evil to you.

What makes you think that? Argen puffed a little before taking another step upward.

It is not what I think, but what I know.

"Argen," Kiron said, "are you coming or not? Do you want me to help you up?" Kiron held out his hand. It was inches away from Argen's if he held his out.

Argen! Nyct hissed imperatively.

The boy had never heard his dragon sound so—so dragonly.

Do not take Kiron's hand. Look into my eyes. Look now!

Kiron stepped down to come close enough to take the boy's hand. He was only seconds away from success. He saw the boy glance down at the bracelet he wore. The strange eyes of the creature seemed almost alive. Then Argen vanished.

CHAPTER FOURTEEN

Argen blinked his eyes. He was in Cibby's cabin. Seren stood in front of him, looking bewildered.

"Nyct, what happened?" Argen was still recovering from his dizzy spell and spoke aloud.

"I'll tell you what almost happened," Seren broke in. "You almost got yourself transported off Realm by an agent of the Shadowlord."

"Oh, coralberries! You have to be out of your mind. I just met this centaur named Kiron today. We were having an adventure. He had to retrieve some books from a cave north of Realmgate and I was helping him."

"You certainly were!"

"Yes, I was! Why not? Do you think only you and Faf deserve to have adventures? I had Nyct with me. I wasn't in any danger. You've got to stop acting like I'm a baby. I'm only five minutes younger than you are, anyway. That doesn't give you the right to boss me around and treat me as if—"

Seren pushed his brother into Cibby's rocking chair. "Listen a minute, that's all I ask."

"That's all I've been doing since I got here." Argen rocked angrily back and forth while Seren looked at him silently.

Seren knew his brother was stubborn. There was no use trying to reason with him until he calmed down. So Argen rocked and Seren waited.

"Come to think of it, how did I get here?"

Seren relaxed. Everything would be all right. Argen was thinking again. He wasn't so bad—for a brother—and he was really smart when he wasn't being dragonheaded. The only creature Seren knew that was harder to reason with was Faf. After one of their disagreements, Faf's father had told Seren to be patient with his son. In spite of his size, Faf was really a very young dragon. Seren had said "yes sir" respectfully. You didn't argue with anything that weighed over a ton and breathed fire. Still, Seren noted that Faf's granddragon, old Fafnir, acted a lot like young Faf. After that, Seren went to great lengths to make sure nothing got wedged in Faf's mind that required changing later. He'd have to remember to treat his brother the same way. They were getting too old to settle everything as they had when they were younger—in a fight.

Soladon spoke. *Brother, have I your leave to tell Argen what we found out?*

Yes, Nyct answered.

Both Argen and Seren heard the exchange. It was a mark of the difference in their characters that Argen thought the courtesy was nice and Seren thought it was rather overdone.

I will mindspeak, for my voice is weak in this form.

It occurred to Seren to wonder what other form Soladon possessed, but the thought vanished when the dragon bracelet continued.

The wyverns used their scrystone to understand the situation we have here. Someone wants to abduct you two humans and transport you to another world. The wyverns say they are certain this person is the one your parents call the Shadowlord. Magic spells barred the Shadowlord from ever returning to Realm, but the spell casters did not think to bar his agents from this world. Therefore, Kiron and Sylvor entered Realm. Because these two creatures are like those in the mythology of Earth's Greece, the wyverns think the destination planned for you two is Achaea, the world from which the ancient gods came to civilize the Greeks of Earth.

"Wait a minute, Soladon." Argen leaned forward in the rocking chair. "If someone tried to kidnap us, maybe they are also trying to capture Lealor."

"I never thought of that!" Seren said, jumping up from the bench and striding to the door.

"Hold it," Argen advised. "Let's use our heads before we rush off in six directions."

That is wise, Soladon commended.

"Do you two know anything more than what you have told Seren and me?" Argen naturally took command.

There should be no reason to worry. The wyverns are great mistresses of magic.

They have placed a spell that will keep all three of you Koenig sibs on Realm unless you wish to go to another world, Nyct said.

"Oh, then I guess I worried over nothing." Seren returned to his seat on the bench.

"Perhaps not, brother," Argen said. "Is there any way to get in touch with Lealor's bracelet? You know what an animal lover she is. If we were attracted to a satyr and a centaur, maybe some strange beast will entice her. I was willing to go with Kiron until Nyct zapped me here." Argen shot a private thought to his bracelet. *Thanks, Nyct.*

Appreciation acknowledged, Nyct replied to Argen alone.

Our sister has been forbidden to speak. I do not think she will respond unless there is dire danger to her small charge.

"Isn't there anything you can do?" Seren stood again.

We will search for her thoughts, but there are many who think in Realmforest. I will alert the wyverns as well. Being female, they may have a greater affinity for her thoughts than we do.

Seren agreed with the sentiment, but Argen, really thinking now, noticed that although they were four males, they were hoping that a group of females could help them with their problem.

Lealor was deep in the twilight forest. She carried a whole fistful of moley in her hand. She sat very still under a tree, hoping that the unicorn she had tracked for most of the afternoon would finally decide to trust her and come to make friends. The beautiful white beast took dainty and hesitant steps toward Lealor at last. Lealor was glad. Her arm felt ready to drop off. She knew that if she moved it a fraction, the unicorn would probably run away. She was certain that once the unicorn ate the moley she could persuade it to give her a ride.

The unicorn advanced. Only a few feet separated it from the girl. Its delicate nostrils quivered, catching the moley scent. The wild unicorns loved moley above all other plants. Lealor had tried before without success to tame a unicorn. She almost always carried some dried moley in her pocket, but this time she was having wonderful luck with the fresh green leaves. She also had a half pocketful of moley seeds. When she saw a promising patch of ground, she planted a few seeds. Her dryad friends gave her the idea. They promised to tell the unicorns who was responsible. Lealor loved unicorns best of all the creatures on Realm.

The pure white coat of the unicorn stood out in the dimming twilight.

Lealor hoped Cibby wouldn't worry. Cibby knew Lealor could understand the animals and was safe in the Realmforest. Also, Lealor had the
protection of Myst, the dragon bracelet given by Wyrd.

The unicorn looked at Lealor out of its wise eyes. Lealor watched the
beautiful animal. She could tell it was going to eat out of her hand. Another
two steps would bring the magical beast close enough to eat. Lealor held
herself stone-still.

Suddenly, the unicorn raised its head and shied away. It looked to the
left, whirled, and trotted away into the uncertain light of the early
evening.

To say Lealor was vexed would be an understatement. She jammed the
moley into her pocket. Then she blew her long bangs out of her eyes. She
wiped her moley-stained hand on her apron, knowing a small spell would
remove the marks later. Now whatever caused the unicorn to go away was
going to be sorry! It was probably one of the boys sent to look for her.

Brothers were a constant bother and older brothers were the worst.
They thought they knew everything. Someday she planned to turn them
into toads. Not permanently, of course. She knew her parents wouldn't
like that. She had already turned a small pebble into a butterfly, but she
couldn't turn it back. She felt embarrassed that she had to get Cibby to
help. The older witch had given her a good lecture on not working magic
until she was sure she had mastered the entire spell, both change and
return. Lealor knew Cibby wouldn't tell on her. How her brothers would
laugh if they knew about some of her mistakes. Witchcraft was like
anything else. You had to practice. She didn't want anyone but Cibby to
know all the things she could do. She was afraid her father would forbid
her to practice—and then how could she ever become a witch like Cibby?

Lealor's ears were not as keen as the unicorn's, but now she heard something approaching. She looked into the trees and saw a sphinx silvered by
the moonlight. Lealor was not a bit frightened. The sphinx delighted her.
She knew there were many unicorns on Realm, but she had never heard of
a live sphinx. Neither of her brothers had seen one, either. Of that she was
sure, because they would have told her all about it if they had.

Neso spoke softly so as not to frighten her quarry. "Hello."

Lealor looked at Neso, who padded closer, wings furled to look as small
as possible. "I'm Lealor. What's your name?"

"My name is Neso. I am a sphinx."

"Yes, I know that. I've seen pictures of wonderful creatures like you in storybooks. I didn't know there were any of your kind here on Realm. Do you live in the desert?"

"Not exactly. I do live far away from here, though," Neso told the girl. She crouched down next to her. "What are you doing here in the forest at night? Don't your parents worry about you?"

"I should be going home now," Lealor admitted. "I'm staying with my great-grandmother. She has a cottage over there." Lealor waved a hand in the general direction of Cibby's home.

"I'm on a quest," Neso told her. "Somewhere very close to here lies the magical casket that Snow White slept in. I have a magic talisman to help me find it. Wouldn't you like to join me?"

"It's funny that I haven't discovered it already. I've been in these woods many times," Lealor said, frowning.

Myst tightened on her arm to warn her, but Lealor didn't pay any attention. Since Myst didn't speak, Lealor often forgot all about her dragon bracelet.

"Oh," Neso said, thinking fast. "You couldn't find it unless you had my magic talisman. See?" Neso allowed a claw to flick the star that she wore around her neck on a chain.

"How does it work? My—" Lealor broke off. Myst was so tight her wrist hurt. She guessed the little dragon didn't want her to mention their relationship. After all, not being able to speak was pretty terrible. No wonder people said that a being that could not talk was dumb.

Neso almost purred her satisfaction. Imagine! The child was asking the very question Neso wanted to answer. It was going to be easy to trick the child into the magic box her master had fashioned to look like the glass-lidded casket in the fairy tale. Neso, of course, had not known the tale, but her master assured her that little children on Realm all knew the story.

"If you would help me find it, I would let you try it if you were brave enough."

"I'm very brave," Lealor said matter-of-factly. "My brother Seren rides dragons and Argen, my other brother, knows everything in the library at Realmgate. I'm friends with all the animals in Realmforest."

Neso looked around her warily. If the child had so many friends, perhaps it might be well to lead her to the minigate immediately. "Will you help me?" she asked.

Neso impressed Lealor. She wanted to aid the sphinx. "Yes, I'll help. I hope it won't take very long."

The catlike creature turned and paced off in the direction of the minigate. Within a few minutes, her direction finder, the star, began to glow. "See," she told Lealor, who hurried to keep up with her. "We are getting very close."

Lealor was so intrigued by Neso, she paid no attention to Myst, who was feeling very agitated indeed. The little girl wouldn't even look at her bracelet, so Myst could not transport her to safety. The glow of the star mesmerized her.

"Aha!" Neso said triumphantly. "Here it is!"

The disguised minigate rested in a forest glade bathed in soft moonlight.

Lealor approached the glass-topped casket with awe. "Are you sure this was Snow White's?"

"Why would I lie? Doesn't it look like the one in your storybook?" Her master has assured her it did.

"Yes, it does. Will you open it? Please?"

"I'd be glad to," Neso said. She opened the casket and boosted Lealor, who was too short to climb in the high box by herself.

Lealor stretched out on the satin bed within. "My, I feel just like Snow White. So you suppose if I stayed here long enough a prince would come for me, too?"

Myst's senses were so alert to danger she actually hissed aloud. It was this sound that drew Soladon and Nyct's attention to their sister's predicament. They saw the danger instantly.

Make her look at you! Soladon advised.

Myst gave a frustrated hiss. Didn't they realize she had tried that already?

Use your eyes to transport her to Cibby's cottage! Nyct commanded.

It was too late. With a lightning move of her paw, Neso snapped the lid of the box closed. The star at her throat exploded with light. Neso, box, and Lealor vanished, leaving only silver moonlight in the abandoned glade.

CHAPTER FIFTEEN

Jarl looked around in surprise. Fafnoddle and he stood on a great plain. The Courtyard of the Gate had vanished. A bright yellow sun bit the dried grasses that struggled to survive in the dusty soil.

"Good heavens, Faf, that was fast! I didn't feel anything."

"I should hope not. I've been studying for some time. I have improved since those first few desperate trips we took together."

"Will you be able to stay with me, or will you have to return?" Jarl rather enjoyed having Fafnoddle with him again. This world looked tame enough, but Jarl had experienced magical places before, and he knew that innocent surroundings might well hide dire dangers. With Wyrd still communing with his Cosmic All or whatever, Jarl liked the idea of a fierce, magical friend's company—just in case. Wyrd's present behavior reminded Jarl of his children when they were sulking, which was rare.

"I'll stay around for a while, at least," Faf said. "They should be able to manage without me at home. First Egg will be studying, and Ebony is perfectly capable of taking care of our cave and the egg." He delicately scratched his back with the end of his tail. "You know, this is like old times! It's been far too long since we've had an adventure together, old friend."

Jarl nodded his agreement even while he smiled at the thought of being called "old friend" by a dragon, who was over a thousand Earth years of age himself.

"Which way shall we go?" Faf asked.

"I have no preference, but those mountains in the distance look promising," Jarl answered, settling his pack on his shoulders.

"Shall we walk, or would you like to fly?"

"Why don't you do a short reconnaissance flight to help us get our bearings? I'll start north. You'll be able to find me easily enough. This grass is only about six inches tall."

Very well, Faf thought in Jarl's general direction, as he unfurled his wings and let the breeze raise him.

Jarl watched his saurian sidekick float upward as if he weighed nothing at all. It was a wonder what magic could do. Jarl had felt the solidity of his friend. There was no way a nonmagical creature that large could get airborne, yet Fafnoddle flew as easily as any bird Jarl had seen. One thing Jarl had learned from his magical encounters—if it works, don't try to figure out which laws of physics are being broken. That was a sure way to get mental indigestion.

He remembered trying to understand how his wife shape-shifted. She had to have control of the molecules of her body somehow. There were billions or zillions, for all he knew. When he asked her how she shifted, she said, "It's easy. All I have to do is think what I want to look like, and my body takes that shape. Anyone should be able to do it." When he told her she had to be able to explain her ability better than that, she answered, "Tell me exactly how you lift your arm." Jarl thought a moment, then said, "Let's just forget the whole thing, okay?" That was the last time he had tried to really understand magic. Sometimes he could will impossible things to happen, and if they did, well and good. He comforted himself with the thought that a person didn't have to understand a car's engine to drive, either.

Fafnoddle made a lazy circle above him, then landed directly in front of him. Jarl looked into the dragon's dinner-plate-sized eye, for Faf lowered his head to talk to his human companion. "Well, there's a slit place ahead in those mountains that looks as if it goes clear through to the other side of this world. I'm a little large to fit, but you could enter it easily. This whole place reeks of magic, by the way."

Pop!

"What was that?" Jarl asked, whirling.

"First Egg!" The look on Fafnoddle's face was one Jarl had never seen before. The dragon's bottom jaw dropped until it hit the ground with a thud. Jarl mentally noted that a dragon's jaw was like a snake's. That explained why some dragons were reputed to eat whole elephants in one gulp.

"As I asked before, Greeks used to have lots of gold, didn't they?" enquired First Egg.

"What has that got to do with your appearance here?" Fafnoddle said in parental stern mode. Jarl understood his feelings. He could almost hear Fafnoddle reciting to himself, "Stay calm."

"Well, there I was, studying my scales off for hours—"

"Hours!" Fafnoddle roared. "Thirty minutes haven't passed yet!"

Jarl could tell his friend was steaming—literally. He moved to the side to be out of possible parboiling range. In moments of stress there was always a chance Fafnoddle might forget that Jarl was a human and didn't have any fire-resistant scales to protect his tender hide. Jarl, however, had reckoned without considering he was the little dragon's godfather, and as such, considered a protector by Young Faf. Somehow, he had managed to insinuate Jarl between himself and his irate father. Jarl wondered if Wyrd would protect him from incineration, because Fafnoddle was almost bursting with rage.

At the last possible moment, when Jarl contemplated finding out first hand how charbroiled steak felt, Fafnoddle raised his head and emitted a truly impressive sheet of red-hot flame.

Jarl thought he heard Young Faf breathe an awed "Wow!" but he couldn't be certain.

"I'm going to warm some scales around here if you don't go home this instant!"

The little dragon's "Yes sir," was followed by the popping sound that Jarl was beginning to associate with Young Faf's precipitate arrivals and departures. He was almost certain he heard a thought as well—*Adults get to have all the fun.*

Fafnoddle let off a few more brief flares into the air. "Didn't want to start a fire in all this grass," he commented. "Look, Jarl, much as I'd like to stay, I'd better go home and keep an eye on First Egg. He'll probably have a mountain of gold stored before he's learned enough of the dragon history and law required for recognition as an adult. It's getting so it's not safe to take your eyes off him. Now that he's learning basic travel he'll be even worse. I despair of keeping him at his books." Fafnoddle gave Jarl an apologetic look.

"I understand, Faf. Remember, I'm a father, too."

"Yes, and you have three children." Fafnoddle gave a delicate shudder. "Sorry. Good luck." Faf disappeared silently.

Yes, Faf certainly had been practicing. As huge as he was, not even the smallest sound occurred to mark his transition to Realm.

When Jarl heard the slight pop from behind him, he didn't even turn around. Oh no! he thought to himself.

"Say, Uncle Jarl, you don't need a little help finding Auntie Mirza, do you?" Young Faf stuck his neck over Jarl's shoulder, which brought "uncle" and "nephew" nose to nose. Jarl noticed that Faf had taken time to grab a few kippers for a snack. Jarl abominated kippers second hand. Partially digested fish smelled almost obscene.

Trying not to inhale, Jarl mouthed, "Your father just went home to help you study."

"Oops! Guess you'll have to do without my help." Young Faf disappeared almost as soundlessly as his father.

Jarl stood alone on the vast plain. Achaea resembled the Greece that Jarl had visited once on Earth. The bright blue sky and clear air made distant objects like the mountains seem closer. Jarl remembered that no place in Greece was more than fifty miles from the sea. He decided he would look when he got higher in the mountains. He believed it was the same here. He began his lonely walk toward the northern range.

He made good time, and by nightfall was in the foothills. He made a fire, ate, and slept. So far, Wyrd showed no signs of life; however, Jarl felt relatively secure. The night passed uneventfully. The next morning, he continued his climb. It wasn't until noon that he discovered the slit in the mountains that Fafnoddle had seen the previous day.

It didn't look very promising, but the landscape appeared deserted, so Jarl felt he had no choice. It was almost as if he was compelled to continue. Something about the slit made him feel uneasy, but he had Wyrd, so he decided to enter. After all, if he made a mistake, he could simply turn around and walk out.

The path into the slit seemed worn to the point of feeling smooth, as if many footsteps had passed that way before Jarl. The walls of the place were rough, as if riven from the rock. On Earth, Jarl would have thought the rock formation resulted from an earthquake, but on Achaea, he supposed the natives would say the thunderbolt of Zeus, Ruler of the Gods, had caused the giant crack.

The bright sun no longer shone on his shoulders. He welcomed the cool feel of the shade in the cleft. He took several steps into the natural passage before deciding he did not want to continue. He turned to retrace his steps, and he found the sunny opening filled with the largest dog he had ever seen. Usually Jarl liked dogs, but this one set the hair on the back of his neck straight up. The huge beast had three heads.

"There, there, fellow," Jarl said in his most disarming fashion. "Move aside like a good boy."

The dog looked at Jarl with all six eyes and stood, rocklike, blocking the opening.

All of a sudden, the sunlight that Jarl had been so glad to get out of seemed very attractive. He approached the dog. While the animal made no threatening movements toward him, it didn't move out of his way, either. Jarl patted one of the heads and tried leading the dog to the side, but he couldn't budge the gigantic canine.

"How about a little scratch behind the ears, mortal," the dog said.

Jarl looked at the beast in surprise. "You speak?" He scratched the indicated place.

"Why not?" the dog said. "You won't be leaving here any time soon, so who's to hear about it?"

"I don't think he knows who we are," the second head said, nudging Jarl with his nose so Jarl would scratch him behind the ears as well.

"Perhaps we should introduce ourself," the third head said.

Jarl reached over to scratch the animal's third head. It couldn't hurt to try to keep on the beast's good side. Perhaps if he were friendly, he could get it to move aside.

"We're not here to make friends with the dead, you know," the first head said.

"You're not going to tell Hades we talked to you—are you?" The second head made a soundless snarl. The sharp white teeth impressed Jarl mightily.

"Of course not. Do I look like the kind of person to do that?" Jarl told the head he was scratching.

"He can't tell Hades about us. He doesn't know our name," the first head said.

"Ignorant one," the third head turned to look at the first, "we are famed throughout the land. All mortals know Cerberus, the Guardian of the Gates of the Land of the Dead."

Jarl agreed with the third head. If he had seen the dog before entering the slit, he would have realized he had arrived at the Land of the Dead. Cerberus had been a monster in several movies, but none of the copies came close to the real thing. Jarl swallowed.

"Ah, pleasant as this scratching is, we can see you must be thirsty. Travel down this path only a short way and you will come to an icy brook of clear water. Someone created it to satisfy the thirst of mortals." The first head smiled wolfishly. The sight of all those teeth did little to reassure Jarl.

"Indeed, waste of water," the second head added.

"We tell you this because you are the first mortal to scratch our ears in such a long time," the third head told Jarl.

"I'm not nearly as thirsty as I am anxious to get out of here. How about letting me pass back into the light?" Jarl asked.

All three heads growled. "Not allowed. Pass on."

Jarl had no way to compel Cerberus to allow him to return to the Land of the Living. He remembered enough mythology to know getting out would take permission from the King of the Dead himself.

Jarl noted that as he stepped deeper into the Kingdom of the Dead the path became ever broader. Smooth, seamless, it wound ever deeper. By the time Jarl came to the brook, he really was thirsty. He knelt, prepared to slake his thirst. Wyrd tightened on his arm. Jarl looked around him. Where was the threat? He saw nothing and bent for the second time to drink, lowering his cupped hands into the icy water.

This time Wyrd hissed, *No!*

"I'm thirsty," Jarl complained. "Why not drink?"

No wonder Rory calls you a lackwit mortal fool in his anger, Wyrd told Jarl mentally. *Do you not know of the waters of Lethe?*

"Lethe?" Jarl repeated, cursing himself as he did it. He had really tried to break his habit of repeating a word when he didn't understand.

Those who drink these waters forget everything. The piteous dead of Achaea do not spend eternity remembering their lives.

Jarl lost all desire for a drink. He let the water trickle through his fingers and wiped his hands on his pants, jumped over the stream and continued to follow the path.

Now it began to wind about, and Jarl felt lost. It was almost a relief to come to a river. On the far side he could see a boat poled by a shrouded figure. "Who's that?" he asked Wyrd.

Charon, the Ferryman of the Dead. This is the River Styx. Charon will take you over.

Jarl hailed the boatman, who turned to look at him. A shiver ran down Jarl's back. Charon was a skeleton. Jarl watched the thin figure manipulate the pole as he brought his craft around. Once pointed at the bank where

Jarl waited, the boat moved smoothly through the water without any movement on Charon's part.

"Ho, mortal, where are your pennies?"

"My pennies?" Jarl was at a loss. Pennies? He practically never carried any. What could you buy for pennies in this day and age?

Charon extended his skeletal hand, palm up. "Your fare, mortal."

Then Jarl remembered. The dead had two pennies placed over their eyes. It was to pay for the ride into the actual Land of the Dead. Jarl fished in his pocket. He found the first penny easily, but he had no other. He dropped it into Charon's hand.

"Where is the other?"

"I don't have another," Jarl told the ferryman. "I'm sorry."

"This is most irregular. I don't make a practice of hauling people around for half fare, you know. It is hard enough to make a living in such a dead-end job." Charon heh-hehed at his macabre witticism.

"What do you suggest I do now?"

"You could wait until someone comes along with an extra penny," Charon suggested, not very helpfully.

"That would take too long. Could you take a dime or a quarter? They're worth more than a penny."

"This first copper you gave me is debased metal. I'm already being generous. No penny, no boat ride."

Jarl watched as the current began to pull the boat further from the bank where he stood. He found himself trapped between Charon and Cerberus. How was he going to produce another penny? Then he remembered the magic provender bag Cibby had sent. It was still in his pack. The spell she put on it made it produce food at the request of the owner. Would it produce a penny? Jarl knew it was dangerous to use magic on Achaea, but he hoped magicking a little food and a penny would be forgiven.

"Well, here goes," he said to himself, as he reached inside. The bag seemed empty. In frustration, Jarl tipped it upside down and shook it. He thought *penny* as hard as he could. The bag obligingly dropped a thin copper piece onto the rocky bank.

"Charon, I have the other penny."

The boat returned to the shore. Charon held out his hand, which still held the first coin Jarl had given him. When the second penny joined the first, Charon nodded his acceptance, and Jarl entered the boat. On reaching the other side, Jarl stepped from the craft and looked at the boatman. "Where do I go now?" he asked.

Charon waved a bony hand in an all-inclusive sweep up and down the bank.

"I need to find the King of the Dead next," Jarl explained.

"No need to hurry," Charon's dry voice whispered. "You have eternity, you know."

Jarl stared at Charon as an awesome thought occurred to him. What if the boatman was right, and Hades, King of the Dead, would not release him?

CHAPTER SIXTEEN

Jarl turned abruptly and began walking along the path that had been behind him. As he passed, he noticed that the dim blue light in the long corridors had no source. It simply existed. He heard soft whispers like the rustling of leaves as he passed. Others traveled the same path, but they seemed as insubstantial as the almost-understandable voices that existed just out of Jarl's range of hearing. Even when Jarl looked directly at one of the shades, it remained shadowy and indistinct. Jarl wondered if some quality of the blue light made his eyes useless for clear vision. As he considered the problem, he realized that he was the only living person in the corridor. The shadowy people led half-lives, and only by drinking the waters of Lethe could he join them in whatever kind of existence was possible here in Hades' dread kingdom. He shivered. No wonder they were called the piteous dead.

The indistinct, whispery voices grew in number until he realized he must be approaching a place of some importance. When he turned the next corner, he saw the vast Hall of the Dead where Hades and his queen, Persephone, held audience.

The dim blue light that permeated the corridors grew somewhat brighter here. The grey and blue exasperated Jarl. When he looked at the two thrones centered against the far wall, he saw a beautiful woman seated alone. Her pale hand beckoned him closer.

"Who are you, mortal, who dares to invade the Kingdom of the Dead without permission of its royal master?"

"I am Jarl Koenig. I seek my wife, Mirza."

"Mirza? There is no shade present here who bears that strange name."

"Actually, Your Highness, I came for information. I thought that perhaps here in your kingdom, I might find it."

"If this Mirza is not here, how would you expect me to know where she is? I have not been with my mother for some months. She is free as I am not. Oh, to return to the Land of the Living!"

Jarl heartily agreed with that sentiment. "Perhaps your husband might be able to send me to a place where I could find out."

"I doubt that. The last time he tried to help a mortal it turned out badly. Orpheus played so beautifully, too."

"I need the information as soon as possible. My wife is being held captive."

"How exciting! A hero on a quest for his wife. So many interesting things happen on the surface. Here, it's just boring, boring, boring." An almost imperceptible pout marred the perfection of her features.

"Don't you get to spend some time on the surface?" Jarl asked.

"Well, yes. You see, I was abducted by my dread Lord Hades when I was a young girl." Her eyes widened as she remembered. "I was terrified. When Hermes came to tell Hades he had to release me, Hades offered me a pomegranate seed. Like a fool, I ate it. Hades said I had to spend half the year with him because I ate here in his Kingdom."

"Your mother must miss you when you are not on the surface."

"Yes, she mourns for me. The humans call her time of mourning winter. She was so clever to think of a way to free me. And then I ate that seed and spoiled it. She spoke quite sharply to me about it. I can still recall what she said to me after all these centuries." A sad smile passed over Persephone's face.

"I'm sorry that you are so unhappy here, but—"

"Please don't think that! I've grown quite fond of Hades. He'd do anything for me. It's not every girl who gets chosen by a god, you know. When I get tired of bathing, and trying on my new dresses and combing my hair, Hades allows me to pick somebody and he causes them to remember about when they were alive. I've heard many interesting stories."

"Isn't that kind of cruel? I mean, to make people remember their lives—" Jarl shivered. Personally, he thought it was a gruesome idea.

"After they've told their tales, Hades makes them forget. He's really very thoughtful. If I ask to have someone remember a second time, they don't even know they've talked to me before."

Jarl thought Persephone was still very young, as goddesses go. The centuries seemed to sit lightly on her. While she looked beautiful, she was obviously not an intellectual. He wondered if Hades considered this before he kidnapped her. To live eternally—even for only six months a year—with someone without Mirza's quick wit and keen intellect would have been hell, no matter what the Achaeans called it, in Jarl's estimation. Where was Hades, anyway?

"How long will it be before your husband returns here to this chamber?" Jarl asked Persephone, who was looking in a small polished hand mirror that she had attached by a ribbon to her waist.

"He won't return here," she began, then stopped speaking to gather her hair to one side and gaze into her mirror again.

"He's not coming here for some time?" Jarl questioned, aghast. How was he to contact the god if he did not return to his kingdom for years? Jarl had forgotten that to an immortal, time meant nothing. After all, gods had forever to get things done.

"What a silly question," Persephone said. "To get him to return all I need to do is call him."

"Will you please call him now?" Jarl was fast tiring of Persephone's company. Maybe that was why Hades made himself scarce, he mused.

"Do I look all right?" Persephone peered anxiously into her mirror. "I always try to look my best, you know. Mother said even if I had to live down here, it was important not to let myself go. In a few more months, it will be spring and I can return to the surface."

"Yes," Jarl assured her. "Could you call him now?"

"Oh, very well. I don't see what all the hurry is for. After all, you'll be here forever."

Jarl fervently hoped Persephone was wrong. He listened as her sweet voice called for her husband. Within seconds, a chill wind blew through the hall. Hades had arrived. He strode to the front of the room and sat upon his throne. He did not seem to notice Jarl.

"Did you call, my dear?" Hades asked, smiling at his wife.

Jarl went unnoticed as Persephone gazed deep into her husband's eyes. Jarl couldn't really blame her. The marble perfection of the god's skin and his handsome features compelled attention. His curly dark hair and beard reminded Jarl of the handsome Greek young man he had seen on his trip to their country. Perhaps there was more of an immortal admixture in the Greek population than anyone admitted. Hades' short chiton bared his knees, which were perfectly formed. Any artist would have loved having him for a model. The Lord of the Dead possessed the same imposing looks as the old ruined statues of the gods of Greece on Earth.

Persephone finally remembered to speak. "Yes, I summoned you. We have here an unusual case. A mortal has come to visit."

Hades' penetrating eyes fastened on Jarl. "A mortal, hmmm?"

Jarl nodded. He seemed to have lost his voice somewhere.

Hades returned Jarl's nod and smiled, which relieved Jarl greatly. Hades was one person he didn't want to annoy.

"Well, mortal, do you have a name?"

The rich tones of Hades' voice soothed Jarl. "Yes, sire. I do. My name is Jarl Koenig."

"Isn't that an odd name, dear?" Persephone interjected, as if Jarl had no feelings at all. Perhaps she forgot that ordinary people would feel insulted. It would make no difference to the remembering dead. Jarl thought that hearing of the lives of the dead must be like television was back home. Many people said things to the set that they wouldn't repeat to the actor's or umpire's face. He'd done it himself.

"It is not an odd name on Earth, his world of birth," Hades explained patiently.

"Yes, I do come from Earth. I am seeking news of my wife, Mirza."

"Did she get her funny name from Earth, too?" Persephone asked like a little child.

"Originally, it was the name of a star visible from Earth," Hades told her.

Hades' answer surprised Jarl. He had not known that fact himself. Evidently, the gods were as knowledgeable as they were reported to be.

"Now, tell us your tale, for it will amuse my wife," Hades commanded.

Jarl did not like being in a position where Hades could order him around so cavalierly, but he appreciated that in his position he had little choice. For one thing, if he was ever to leave the Kingdom of the Dead, it would be with Hades' approval.

"I have come from Realm, the home of the keepers." Hades nodded, gratifying Jarl. Clearly, the god knew of the gate system. "My wife was investigating a rogue gate that someone is creating here on Achaea."

"Are you certain, mortal?"

"Yes. You might not have noticed here beneath the earth, but Achaeasun is not behaving normally."

"What difference does that make to us? I don't get to go to the surface for months yet."

Hades seemed to be thinking. He ignored his wife's statement. He muttered, "The Bright One."

"The Bright One does not seem permanently harmed. When my wife arrived, she did something to hinder the rogue gate."

"What god dares tamper with the gate? Notify Father Zeus at once!"

"Sorry, but I believe the person creating the gate is not a god."

"Punish the hubris of this mortal immediately." The words of Hades chilled Jarl. Mirza had certainly placed herself in the middle of a class-one mess this time. Would the gods of Achaea think that mortals who tried to stop the tampering were also guilty of overweening pride? If Jarl recalled correctly, hubris, which was just a fancy name for what Cibby called "getting too big for your britches," was the only thing mortals could do to really bring the gods down on them with a vengeance.

Persephone noticed the change in Hades' mood, too. She fanned herself with her mirror and paid no attention to the disarray it caused her hair.

Jarl didn't really want to call any attention to himself, but he needed to get out of the Kingdom of the Dead. Hades might just hare off to Olympus or wherever the gods on Achaea stayed, and then he would find himself locked up for the duration.

"My wife and I saved the Bright One in Realmsun," Jarl said with an almost unnoticeable quiver on the last word.

"Mortals did such alone?"

"Not alone," Jarl was glad to say. He didn't like the look on Hades' face.

I aided, Wyrd said, just as Jarl prepared to turn into a shade himself.

Hades peered at the dragon bracelet. "Is that you, old friend?"

The chilly atmosphere warmed perceptibly. Jarl could tell because the sweat running down his back felt less like ice water.

Yes. This mortal is under my direction. It is his task to stop the transgressor. Wyrd's thoughts filled everyone's minds.

"In what way can I aid you?"

The mortal must be reunited with his wife. Can you assist him in this?

Hades replied, "Such a trifle! Is that all you ask? Done—" and the King of the Dead began to wave his hand.

"Oh, dear, and he was just coming to the interesting part," Persephone said. "You'll send him off, and I never will find out what happens."

"Perhaps I was making it too easy for him," Hades said, dropping his hand while he thought. "I know. I will give you a sword and shield. Whoever heard of a hero without weapons? Wyrd, you must promise to let him do everything—until the actual confrontation, that is—by himself."

Agreed, Wyrd intoned in his dragonlaw voice.

"I want to help, too," Persephone said. "I'll send his wife a box of my famous beauty salve. She'll probably have frown lines from her captivity." Persephone waved her hand and a box appeared. She offered it to Jarl.

Jarl stepped forward awkwardly to take her gift. He held a sword in one hand and a shield in the other. Which one dared he drop to take the box? Either choice could bring down retribution. Would Hades think he preferred the box to the weapon he dropped? On the other hand, what if he didn't take the box? Would Hades feel offended, believing his wife slighted by a mere mortal? *Wyrd*! Jarl thought adamantly. A soft snore was his only answer. The dragon really meant it when he said he would not help Jarl. Jarl felt frustrated. What business had a mortal mixed in with the touchy gods of Achaea? His hesitation amused Persephone.

"Here, mortal," she said, rising graciously to place the box in his shirt pocket and button the flap. "What odd clothes you wear." She shook her head. "Do not feel bad, though. You look ever so much more normal than you did when you arrived. The sword and shield are very becoming."

"Are you quite finished?' Hades asked abruptly.

"Don't be jealous of an ordinary mortal," Persephone laughed, a silvery tinkle on the icy air.

Jarl's blood pressure dropped and he felt like hypothermia had set in. Was Hades the jealous type? Surely not, Jarl hoped.

"Oh, my dear," Persephone chuckled, "if you could only see the look on your face. This has been a most diverting experience. Now it's over," she said, her merriment disappearing.

Noting her sad look, Hades said, "Would you like to be able to watch what happens to Jarl and his wife?"

Persephone clapped her hands. "Oh, could I?"

"Surely. Mortal, kiss her mirror."

Jarl felt relief that the command wasn't anything worse. As he kissed her mirror, he saw that it now reflected a miniature of the audience hall.

"You may watch until he has freed his wife," Hades promised.

Hades' wife had been right. The god was thoughtful. Jarl gave thanks that his actions would not continue to be royal amusement during his entire time on Achaea.

"Ask your questions of the Graiae, who, with only one eye, see all," Hades advised with a wave of his hand.

Jarl found himself back on the plain, bearing the heavy sword and the awkward shield. The fact that both seemed made of pure gold made him doubt their practicality. He considered dropping the weapons until he remembered that Persephone watched. "Ye gods," he thought to himself before continuing in the direction he faced. He hoped it was a clue to the whereabouts of the Graiae—whoever he, she, it, or they might be.

CHAPTER SEVENTEEN

Mirza paced before her window, frustrated by the powerful isolation spell her old enemy had placed on her room. The Shadowlord was waiting for something, she was sure. Did he really mean it when he said he was sending those creatures to kidnap her children? She and Jarl had many friends on Realm whose magical power could protect them if the Shadowlord tried any outright type of kidnapping, but deviousness and stealth were the Shadowlord's middle names. If he did manage to have his creatures infiltrate Realm, they would operate from the shadows, barely noticed by any who would protect the children. Mirza allowed Seren, Argen, and Lealor the freedom of Realm because those who lived there knew they were protected. The most evil creatures that conspired with the Shadowlord had died in the battle at Realmgate. Any who survived did so on sufferance and were unlikely to call attention to themselves by an act against the children.

Mirza reluctantly admitted that the Shadowlord would try to steal the children, but he would be facing two main obstacles. For one thing, Mirza knew her children were intelligent. Even considering her possible motherly prejudice, they were well above average not only in intelligence, but in resourcefulness. Mirza and Jarl still had many discussions about the degree of freedom the children had. Mirza carefully monitored the first excursions of the young Koenigs. Had they not proved worthy of the trust they desired, no amount of pleading would have secured them their freedom.

Mirza had carefully watched Lealor. While the youngest, she had the most magical potential of the three. Not until it was clear that she would neither hurt, nor suffer hurt, was the young witch given freedom from supervision. Then, too, the strong bond between Cibby and the girl was another safety factor. Mirza stopped pacing and shook her head ruefully, remembering. Lealor would go to Cibby with her problems and questions before she would ask her mother. The second obstacle faced by the Shadowlord was the actual transportation of his allies and their prisoners—if they should capture the children. Mirza paced and pondered.

The room grew noticeably dimmer. From force of habit, Mirza glanced out the window to see how dark the clouds were. Then with a shudder, she continued pacing. Achaeasun itself dimmed and brightened. Mirza feared greatly for the development of the Bright One inside. No one now living had seen an infant Bright One, but there were descriptions left behind by the Old Ones, the original creators of the gate system. Mirza was almost certain the cocooned shape within the power nexus was Achaeasun's infant Bright One.

She wondered how much of a setback she had managed when she cut those strange strings. She hoped what she had done was a major defeat for the Shadowlord. For at least a brief time, the Bright One was unbound. Was it old enough, wise enough, to take steps to keep itself safe? Mirza doubted it greatly. Somehow, she had sensed contentment when she had sung the multicolored lullaby to the infant. The baby needed more than an infantile appreciation for a lullaby to protect itself from the magical machinations used against it.

Her fists clenched. She strode to the window and pounded on the stone sill. Her magical senses stretched to the fullest, she searched for some chink, some tiny flaw, that would give her an entryway to freedom. Once out of the Shadowlord's prison, she would shapeshift to a hawk's form and fly to the gate. Willing to try anything, even risking her life using the unstable gate, her motherly instinct took over. She didn't care if she offended the gods of Achaea by shapeshifting. She wanted to alert the keepers of the danger to the Bright One. She wanted to ask them to join her on Achaea. Together they would attack and defeat the Shadowlord. The ache in her hands alerted her that she was pounding the stone sill rhythmically. Common sense said her dream was impossible. If the gate was weird enough to give her an unusual passage, who knew what might happen if many people tried to pass?

Dejected, she sat on a bench, positioned so she could look out the window. She wanted Jarl. He had always been beside her in the past, but she knew that this time, his presence might not be possible. Her eyes focused on the shape flying outside the window. In the past, the black dragon, Ebony, had been another being she could trust. If only it were Ebony, but it was not. It was the sphinx, Neso. The sheer beauty of the flying creature comforted Mirza briefly. Although she could not shapeshift while in the Shadowlord's power, she could remember the feeling of the wind beneath her wings and the joy of riding an updraft.

She heard the door open. It was not time for a meal. What would the Shadowlord want now? She was growing tired of his daily harangues. Didn't the mage know the meaning of the word no? She used it so often, she sometimes felt as if it were the only word in her vocabulary. With a weary sigh, she turned to face the door.

One of the guards stood in the doorway. "You are to come immediately."

Brilliant, Mirza thought. All the emotion of a grade Z movie. She rose, however, and prepared to follow him. Perhaps today she could pry some answers out of her wily opponent.

Mirza entered the Shadowlord's vast audience hall unannounced. Mirza's womanly intuition, which had nothing to do with magic, told her the Shadowlord was in a towering rage. Neso the sphinx stood before him.

"You have failed me, Neso," the Shadowlord said. His voice sent ice cubes skittering through Mirza's veins.

"But, Master, I brought you the box—"

"Oh, yes, you brought me the box, but somehow you allowed it to malfunction. I cannot open it to get at the contents!"

"But, Master—" Neso's wings quivered. "My part was to fetch the box with the child within. It is no fault of mine if you cannot open it."

A child within a box? Could it be one of her children? Mirza wondered. If so, which one? If the Shadowlord could not open the box, there must be some magical spell protecting its contents. For this, Mirza was glad.

The Shadowlord glided across the floor. It looked as if he had no feet, Mirza noticed. What a foolish observation to be making at a time like this, she chided herself mentally.

He glided across the floor several more times, reminding Mirza of the way she paced in the room that was her prison.

Finally, he spoke. "You are right, sphinx. You have completed a part of the task I set you. Therefore, you may choose. You may go to the room in which Medusa waits and see her in all her beauty—"

Neso gasped. "I would turn to stone! It is the doom Athena pronounced on her centuries ago!"

"—or," the wizard continued as if Neso had not spoken "you may allow me to choose an alternate punishment that will allow you to live."

Neso's bunched muscles relaxed. "Anything except turning into stone, Master."

"You are content with your choice?"

"Yes, Master." Neso's voice was barely audible.

"Indeed." The Shadowlord's voice held a satisfaction that frightened Mirza. She was glad the spell the Lady had given her protected her from the magical evil she sensed in the room.

The Shadowlord nodded to two of the guards who stood at the door. "Take this creature to the labs and tell those who work there to remove her wings for study." He added, "Painfully!"

Neso's catlike eyes glowed. Her muscles tensed to spring, but a negligent wave of the Shadowlord's hand changed her demeanor to docility. She seemed to go willingly with her guards after that.

Mirza hoped her shudder was not noticeable. The powers of the Shadowlord had grown indeed.

"Guards," he commanded. "Send in Kiron and Sylvor."

Mirza watched curiously to see what manner of men or creatures these two might be. She had already figured out that they were probably the ones sent to kidnap her other children.

"Kiron," the guard announced as a centaur entered the room.

Mirza recognized him immediately. He was one of her original captors. In her concern over her family she had forgotten all about meeting the centaur and the satyr when she had met Neso. She made a mental note to keep alert and try to remember everything that happened. Any scrap of information might prove useful if she got a chance to battle the Shadowlord.

Kiron sidled and pranced nervously, but said nothing.

"Sylvor," the guard announced as the satyr entered. The satyr seemed more self-possessed. He waved his syrinx at Mirza, but he did not speak.

"Well?" the Shadowlord said.

Sylvor spoke first. "We came, Master, as you wished."

"As I wished?" The silky tones of the wizard's voice alerted Mirza and she stood as still as if she had been the one to see Medusa and turn to stone.

"You have both failed. Your quarry escaped you. I shall be merciful—this time. I have an errand for you. You are to go to the room at the end of the corridor, enter, and tell the woman who awaits my orders she is to come to me here."

The relief of Kiron and Sylvor was palpable. They nodded and turned to leave. Kiron and his companion both flashed smiles at Mirza because they thought them hidden from the view of the Shadowlord. They exited the room promptly, obviously relieved to have escaped punishment and eager to do their master's bidding.

Mirza felt sorry for them. They were small ciphers compared to the prime number who remained in the room with her.

"Oh, Great One," one of the guards spoke.

"Speak, captain." The geniality of the wizard thickened Mirza's blood. She did not understand exactly what was happening, but she felt it was terribly important.

"May I and my guards retire until your guest leaves?"

Mirza could feel the fear of the men.

"So, you do not like Medusa? You fear her power?"

"Yes, Great One," the captain replied, not caring if he appeared cowardly.

"Then begone!"

The guards turned on their captain's command and marched double time from the room.

Then Mirza understood. Sylvor and Kiron had gone to order Medusa to come. When they spoke to her, they would look at her and turn to stone. Such was the Shadowlord's mercy.

He had always been powerful, and his powers had definitely increased. However, Mirza found his newest trait, that of conscious cruelty, to be even more daunting. Her powers and Jarl's had grown also, but their adversary was more formidable now. In their first meeting, he had seemed detached in some way, but now his active malice was truly frightening.

Mirza stood alone in the chamber with her enemy.

"Are you not afraid of Medusa also?" he asked in a mocking tone.

"No," Mirza answered, looking straight at the Shadowlord.

"One can admire your spirit, even as one seeks to tame it," he replied.

Mirza was about to find her pride and inquire about the box, when Medusa entered the room.

"Greetings, Great One," Medusa said. "Am I called to turn this red-haired woman to stone?"

"No, Vain One, a spell protects her—at least at present."

"If you remove it, I shall be glad to show her my unusual beauty face to face," Medusa said, careful not to look directly at Mirza.

"To remove the spell would take a great deal of magical power and more important, time. I have uses for her before turning her to stone. She is a most foolish female, but I have hopes of convincing her to join me yet."

"Why should you need her? You have my powers at your command," Medusa said.

"Your vanity is showing," the Shadowlord told her. "Her powers are far different from yours. Allow me to introduce you. Mirza, meet Medusa."

"Without her, ye shall never shine. True power be yours through witch's line," Medusa murmured.

"I beg your pardon," Mirza said, "I don't understand."

"Nor do I," Medusa answered. "It's a shred of an old prophecy that came to mind for no reason."

"Foolishness! Success does not wait on prophecy," the Shadowlord said angrily.

"Perhaps I misunderstood. I thought the foolishness of which I spoke was the reason you are so patiently awaiting this one's change of mind, when you could have me as your willing ally."

Mirza looked at the strange being who stood before her. She had the body of a beautiful woman. The material of her robe was rich and intricately patterned. Her head, however, was horribly adorned with a number of writhing snakes of various kinds. Their constant hissing was nerve-wracking. Mirza wondered how the poor creature stood it. Did the poisonous kinds never bite her? Mirza wondered. While she felt only pity for the hideous parody of womanhood that stood before her, Mirza sensed that Medusa felt a kind of jealousy. How vain the creature was! She had evidently decided to cope with her affliction by accepting it and being proud of her difference from normal women. Mirza smiled. Hadn't Medusa used the term *unusual beauty* to refer to her looks? That was coping, with a vengeance. Even the Shadowlord took care to cater to her vanity in his conversation.

That thought brought another to Mirza. When she first had faced the Shadowlord, there had been no humanity in him at all. Now he had somehow acquired a sense of power, an enjoyment of cruelty for its own sake, and the ability to understand the creatures about him. She reminded herself to be very careful what she said and did around the wizard. If he sensed the slightest weakness in her, he would use it to the fullest extent. It was not a comforting thought.

"She seems to be a harmless mortal type," Medusa said. Her hair hissed an agreement.

Mirza listened, astonished as Medusa said, "Be still, my darlings. Mother is busy now."

The tenderness in Medusa's voice was heartbreaking. Medusa would never have children. What man or creature could have an interest in someone whose face, no matter how pretty, remained framed forever with a wide selection of slithering serpents?

"Beware!" the Shadowlord said in a stern tone. "Do not underestimate this flame-tressed witch. She will use every wile she knows to lull your suspicions so she can escape. Do not trust her—ever."

He really makes me sound like a dangerous force, rather than a person, Mirza thought. On the other hand, she admitted to herself, he had reason to fear. She had been part of a group of magic users who had trounced the Shadowlord thoroughly, when he had tried to use Realm, her homeworld, as a base for his illicit gate. That gate was part of the plan of the Shadowlord to move the evil armies from one alternate earth to another. Somehow he had gained the knowledge to attempt a gate that not only transferred people spatially, but temporally. Mirza fought to keep her hands from clenching as she thought about all the damage the Shadowlord might do if he were free of time as well as space.

"I shall watch her carefully, Great One."

Mirza noted that those the Shadowlord considered to be creatures addressed him as Master, while humans addressed him as Great One. Had the wizard developed prejudices, as well? Both terms indicated a subservience that Mirza deplored. He had learned pride, too. Mirza only hoped it went before his fall.

"That is well. I will do what I can, however, to see that she gives you little trouble." At this point, he waved his hand and a curtain across the corner of the room opened, displaying a glass casket. Within lay Lealor in a semblance of sleep.

In spite of her resolution to do nothing to alert the Shadowlord to her feelings, Mirza gasped and took a swift step forward.

"Would you care to have a closer look?" His hand made a sweeping gesture that urged her forward.

Medusa stepped forward too and looked within the box. Mirza was happy the casket was tightly shut. She hoped Lealor wouldn't wake up and see Medusa. Mirza had no idea what form of spell held her daughter, but she had no wish to see Lealor frightened or turned to stone.

"The young one looks like her," Medusa said in a disgusted tone of voice. She moved back of her own volition.

As she retreated, Mirza advanced. She looked down at her sleeping child. Her color was good. Her chest rose and fell normally. She was breathing. Mirza put her hands on the transparent top. Some-thing—someone, she mentally corrected herself, within the box was powering the spell that held it shut. It did not seem like human magic. Where on Realm had Lealor learned such a spell? Mirza gazed carefully at her daughter. Then she noticed the almost invisible crystalline bracelet on Lealor's arm.

Unknowingly, Mirza must have given some sign of what she saw because the Shadowlord said, "Ah, is there something there that a mother might sense that I, master mage that I am, cannot?"

"I doubt it," Mirza said dryly. The Shadowlord became more human by the minute. Perhaps, Mirza thought, his newly acquired humanity might be the agency through which defeat was possible. She felt that she had learned much about her adversary. She hoped he had not learned as much about her.

Her gaze returned to the tiny dragonoid form. She mindspoke to the bracelet. *Who are you?*

Never had Myst felt more like breaking dragonlaw. She bit her tiny tongue to keep from replying. Her eyes flew open. She allowed her tongue to flick out and in once to show Mirza she was alive and sentient. Myst could only hope that Mirza would continue trying to communicate with her. If only Mirza would ask a yes or no question that Myst could answer with a nod or a shake of her small head!

Somehow, Mirza seemed to understand Myst's desire. Her next words proved it. *Are you connected with Wyrd?*

A tiny nod, almost imperceptible, was her answer.

Are you holding this box under a shut-spell?

A second nod.

Is my daughter all right?

A third nod.

Mirza wanted time to stand and ask many more questions, but the Shadowlord moved beside her. She realized it was dangerous to try to keep communicating, even on a tight mental band, with her enemy near. She stepped back and looked at the Shadowlord.

When her hands moved from the box, they trembled, so Mirza deliberately held them still at her sides by an effort of will.

The Shadowlord must have noticed, for there was satisfaction in his voice as he said, "Ah, all that folderol about a mother's love is true."

Not for the first time, Mirza thought that perhaps the Shadowlord was literally inhuman as well as inhumane. Mirza gazed at him, silent. Why, by all the Bright Ones, did he wear his cowl so his face was always in shadow? No wonder he was the Lord of Shadows! In a confrontation such as this, being able to read an enemy's face was invaluable. Mirza felt quite vulnerable, and though in the past she had scorned veils, she wished quite desperately that she wore one now.

"Please note the small air holes at the foot," he said in a voice that reminded Mirza of the one he used when talking to Neso.

Mirza looked. It was true.

"In a few days, I shall pour the contents of this vial into those holes. I'm not sure how long I shall wait, but a few days at least."

A noxious green liquid that Mirza recognized with a shock of horror filled the vial. It was the same green liquid that had threatened to turn her into a monster on Realm when she had refused to join the Shadowlord and had not yet received the protection of the Lady.

"I see that you remember. After I pour this liquid in those holes, it will begin at Lealor's feet and move to her head. The same conditions will prevail as when you were enchanted. If the green growth reaches the child's head, the transformation will be irreversible. If I should hear of an escape attempt—" The Shadowlord was silent. He could see that Mirza understood.

"I will not attempt escape," she said reluctantly. His planning ability had grown as well. For how long had his spies gathered data on her family? He knew her daughter's name and Bright Ones only knew what else. Why had they believed it would take many years for the Shadowlord to regain enough of his power to challenge them again? In a few short years he had not only regained his powers, but increased them. Their inability to believe in his fast recovery was likely to cost them dearly, Mirza thought. She almost despaired.

"Good. I see you understand. Remember, in a few days more I will call you for another audience. You would like to see me pour the elixir—wouldn't you?"

Mirza could sense his fiendish joy. Truly, the Shadowlord was now a greater threat than ever to the peace of the worlds and the safety of the gates. Mirza's only hope lay in the thought that Jarl had to be searching for her.

With an almost casual wave of his hand, the Shadowlord sent the two women to Medusa's cave, almost half a world away.

CHAPTER EIGHTEEN

The huge dragon spread its wings over a cowering Seren. This was no Realmish dragon! Its teeth filled its cavernous mouth, a forest of ivory daggers, each one serrated to rend and destroy. The sulfurous stench in the air proved the fire-breathing capability of the dragon, as did Seren's smoking clothes.

Seren raised his weaponless hands to ward off the next breath of the evil saurian. "Please," he begged. "I have done nothing to you." He gestured to the dragon's horde, a mixture of gold and human bones. "I have not touched one treasure that is yours. I came to see the mightiest dragon on this world. I mean you no harm."

The dragon's eyes glittered his hatred of everything human. It ignored the frightened boy's words. Its snakelike head reared high, then swooped down on the helpless human, mouth opened to take one bite and rid the universe of another hereditary enemy.

Seren faced his doom bravely. He stood with his hands at his side, a grave look on his face.

"Motherrr!" a shrill voice screamed. Argen, chained high on the wall, called out in agony from the dungeon. His arms seemed too frail to hold the weight of his body. The moldy walls could just be discerned in the feeble light of the one candle that guttered, close to its end, on the rickety table across the cell. The sickly smell of long imprisonment and despair radiated through the air.

With a hollow boom, the great door to the huge torture chamber opened to admit the evil wizard who had imprisoned Argen. "Now will you tell me of the ancient book you found in the library? It contains the most powerful spells of the Old Ones' greatest wizard, Alchemor."

"Alchemor was evil. It was largely through his spells that the Old Ones almost destroyed all the lower life forms on Realm, including the human race. No one must ever have the opportunity to learn those spells. The book, guarded by the most powerful magic enchantments known on Realm, wasn't even catalogued. If I told you where to find it, you could not read it," Argen whispered through dry lips.

"I will be the judge of that," the angry wizard thundered, making Argen cringe.

"May I please have a drink of water?" Argen asked. He had thirsted for two days. If he had any thought other than the pain in his arms, it was of the constant thirst he endured.

"Water?" The wizard smiled. "You shall have more water than even a thirsty prisoner can drink. This is your last chance. Will you speak?"

"Never!" Argen said proudly. Although there was small chance that the wizard could open the book to learn the spells and live, yet Argen would not take it. He tried vainly to moisten his lips with his dry tongue. Finding no moisture, he closed his mouth and looked as resolute as he could.

"Guards!" the wizard called.

Two monstrous creatures entered the room and awaited the bidding of their master.

"Throw this prisoner into the moat!"

"The moat, master?" the larger of the two creatures rasped.

"Do you not have ears?"

"Yes, Great One, but there be hungry water swimmers in the moat. This small boy will be but a snack for them."

"Indeed," the wizard said with a smile. "Then he will have no further need of our hospitality, will he?"

The two creatures grinned at their master's macabre joke before advancing to take Argen from the wall. The wizard left the room. The candle guttered futilely, then went out . . .

"Oh, it's so dark here," Lealor said. "I don't like the dark. Mommy? Are you there, Mommy? I want to go home."

A huge roar echoed in the chamber where Lealor stood. "Oh, mommy, I don't know what it is, but it's big and hungry. Mommmmmy!" The child's voice shrieked her terror.

Mirza sat upright in her bed, wide-awake. She couldn't think what to do. She needed freedom to help her children. Where was she? The rough stone walls of the cave she slept in flickered in the light from the small fire in the center of the chamber. She lay down again on the crude cot that was her bed. While the Shadowlord spared no expense on his lodgings and work areas, the places prepared for the imprisonment of his enemies were lacking in all but the most rudimentary comforts.

Mirza closed her eyes and remembered the three dreams that had awakened her. Her magic told her they were only dreams and not reality. She wished she could have a few minutes to talk to her Grandmother Cibby, who had true sight. Mirza's own power in that area was slight, coming unbidden and leaving only tantalizing fragments of information which might be true or not. Cibby's own power to foresee came unbidden, but what she saw was true. Mirza, however, had one power her grandmother did not. Sometimes Mirza was able to clear her mind of all thought and "see" what was happening to those she loved. During all the days of her imprisonment she had never lost hope that Jarl would come for her at last. So sure was her faith in her husband that she had never tried to use her powers to find out what he was doing. Using magic on Achaea was dangerous unless one had the permission of the gods. At this point Mirza was willing to take the risk of offending the powerful beings who ruled this world. She closed her eyes and relaxed her body. She had the strange feeling that someone watched over her, and yet it was no being she could actually recognize. She set the intriguing puzzle to one side and widened her search for Jarl. If he was on this world, she would know it.

Jarl walked on a treeless plain. His backpack looked familiar. Many times Mirza had seen him like this on camping trips. She could not recognize the place, but she knew he was searching for her. She mindcalled, but Jarl showed no signs of hearing her. Nevertheless, she smiled as she saw First Egg pop into sight. The young dragon and Jarl talked animatedly. Mirza wished she could hear the exchange, for she had carried on conversations with the spritely dragon herself. Finally Jarl nodded, and First Egg sprang at him, clutched his belt in his claws, and shot into the air, after which both disappeared abruptly. Clearly the young saurian had mastered basic travel. Mirza was certain First Egg's parents had no idea he was popping in and out from hither to yon. Mirza hoped he wouldn't stunt his growth by overusing his powers. Remembering the dragon's precipitate ascent and disappearance, she could only hope Jarl's belt was up to the trip. She sat on the edge of the cot before lying down again. Her lips curved in a smile as she remembered the look on Jarl's face when the dragon had taken off.

The little dragon set Jarl down gently, considering the way he had so abruptly picked him up and flown off with him.

"Sorry, Unc—I mean, Jarl. I can't spend much time here. My father and mother are taking turns checking on me. I've got an alarm rigged that lets me know when they are coming. So far, it's worked because they only peek every forty-five minutes or so. That gives me enough time to pop in and see what's happening here."

"Wouldn't it be an even better idea to study those **Dragon Chronicles** and learn the material? I can manage without you. If your parents ever find out you're popping in and out like this, I dread to think what they might do. Have you considered that not only do you face the danger of traveling from Realm to Achaea, you also may have to brave your father's wrath? I've never seen him as mad as he was the last time he caught you here."

"Uncle Jarl—oops, sorry. It's a hard habit to break, you know," the dragon apologized. "What would you do without me? It might have taken you days to find the Gorgonian Plain without me to help."

"That's true. But there are some things you don't know."

"What, for instance—the location of a small treasure in gold?" Faf asked, cocking his head inquisitively.

Jarl admitted to himself that the little pipsqueak was cute—if a half-ton or so of anything could pass as cute. "Fact one: Hades' wife, Persephone, is watching all I do through a kind of magic mirror."

Jarl watched in horror as Faf preened a little and waved insouciantly. "Hello, there," Faf said in his most polite voice, "Isn't this exciting?"

Jarl half choked and decided his best bet was to ignore the whole thing. "Fact two: Wyrd has promised not to help me. Perhaps Hades will be angry if you do."

"I bet Persephone will think I'm interesting. You don't get a chance to see a Realmish dragon every day, you know."

Jarl decided to try one more time before he gave up. "Maybe so. Dropping in as you do could get you into trouble. Don't you think you should stay at home?"

"What! Miss all the action?" With a rather endearing wink of one huge eye, the little saurian disappeared.

Jarl caught his final thought. *Gotta fly!*

Jarl stood a city block from a singular mountain. He could see the cavelike opening in its face. "Gotta fly, indeed," he murmured to himself as he started walking toward the mountain.

CHAPTER NINETEEN

Seren and Argen stared at one another. Their sister had vanished. Through the rapport they had with their talismen, the boys had experienced their sister's disappearance simultaneously with Soladon and Nyct. Finally Seren managed a weak, "Now what?"

"Don't look at me for answers. Lealor has done some weird things in her time, but allowing herself to be trapped in that box—"

"Yeah," Seren said, clearly still awed by what he had witnessed. "How could anybody be so dumb?"

Soladon hissed his distress. *To think that our sister failed in her care of her charge!*

Nyct's mental voice spoke to all three. *Now is not the time for bewailing what is done. Gone is a scale fallen. Only time will replace the loss.*

"What have falling scales go to do with anything?" Seren said, plunking himself down on the bench near the table.

"Nyct only means that we shouldn't be crying over spilled milk," Argen explained.

"Where do you hear all that strange stuff, anyway?" Seren asked with an exasperated look on his face. "That's what comes of spending all your time with those greybeards at the university. You sound like some weirdo. Don't ever talk like that in front of our friends, or they'll think you're a freak," he warned.

"There's more to life than television and videos," Argen rejoined heatedly.

Let us put our heads together and plot what we must do to free our sister and yours. If they are speedily returned to Realm, perhaps our father never need know, Soladon said, tightening on Seren's wrist to assure his attention.

Argen paused to wonder where the dragons learned to speak English. Sometimes they sounded strange, but their meaning always came through. He said aloud, "Well, one thing's for sure."

"That's a relief. You sound like you've got our problem all solved." Seren smiled at his brother.

"Don't relax too soon. What I mean is, we've got to handle this by ourselves."

Would it not be wiser to inform Andronan or Cibby and let them aid Lealor and Myst? Nyct said.

"No!" both boys said, in agreement for once.

Then what would you have us do to aid you? Soladon asked.

"You mean you haven't got any ideas?" Seren's raised eyebrows showed his astonishment.

Argen, who had probably worked more closely with his new friend and protector, had a more realistic view of what might be possible with the aid of the dragon bracelets. "Sere, they're not supposed to do our thinking for us. They'll be glad to help, but we need to offer them a plan and then find out what they can do to help us."

That is correct, Nyct said, obviously proud of his charge.

Right on, Soladon said, trying to use the language he heard Seren use with Faf.

Nyct shut his eyes and reprimanded his brother privately.

Soladon gazed at his brother with amber eyes and then stuck out his tongue so quickly that neither Seren nor Argen noticed.

"Our first job is to find out where Lealor and Myst are now."

Sensible, Soladon told his charge.

"I bet they're on Achaea. That seems to be where all the action is. If the wyverns are right and the Shadowlord is at the bottom of this mess, Lealor and Myst are sitting right on top of the pile."

"How can we make sure, Argen?" Seren asked.

"Well, if Nyct will zap me into the Room of the Book, I can check the changes added about Achaea during the last few hours."

Done! Nyct said as Argen and he disappeared.

"Soladon, now that we're alone, can you explain to me how you dragons get from here to there so quickly?"

It's quite simple. Space doesn't really exist for us as it does for humans. There-fore, we need only envision where we want to be and we are there.

"Somehow that doesn't make sense to me."

Do not worry. There is much in the life of humans that makes little sense to them. It is not enough that we are capable of 'zapping' you when it is necessary? Must you understand everything? Can you not just accept?

"I'd still like to know how it's done. After all, I'm the zapee, so to speak."

Soladon emitted a dry chuckle. *Indeed you are.*

Argen and Nyct reappeared as swiftly as they had vanished. Argen said, "Achaea it is. Lealor and Myst are there, all right."

It will please you to know that Lealor is safe, but imprisoned in the magic casket. Myst has been able to seal it so that the Shadowlord may not harm Lealor.

Good. She has done well, then, Soladon said. *Keeping the girl safe may well shield our sister from the wrath of our father should he find out about this.*

"Even I can figure out our next step," Seren said. "How are we going to get to Achaea?"

"Using the gate is out," Argen told his brother. "The Book of Worlds says Achaeasun is destabilizing."

"What exactly does that mean?"

That something continues to disturb the Bright One within the sun, Soladon hissed, clearly somewhat disturbed himself at the news.

If the rogue gate is not quickly brought under control or allowed to disinte-grate, Achaeasun may nova, destroying the Bright One, Nyct clarified.

"Crisping our parents and sister to a cinder," Seren added, showing his comprehension of what the bracelets had told him.

Argen shuddered. Sometimes his brother's choice of words lacked finesse. "We must act now." Argen knew his parents had special powers, but his reading of heroic histories told him that even with magical aids, sometimes evil triumphed over good. Seren didn't really believe anything bad could happen to his parents. Argen understood the situation better and realized that his parents were facing a much more serious situation on Achaea than they had on Realm. For one thing, there was no way to deter-mine the level of disturbance that would cause a sun to nova.

For another, the power of the Shadowlord must have increased to allow his allies to steal Lealor, protected as she was by Myst. Argen almost wished he didn't understand what could happen. Knowledge could make an uncomfortable companion.

Agreed, said Nyct.

Soladon's tiny head nodded.

"Okay, fellows," Seren said to Soladon and Nyct. "We're ready to go. Zap us there." He waited in complete confidence.

Our powers limit us to Realm, Nyct said sadly.

That is not quite true, Soladon said. *We have the absolute power to protect you anywhere, but our father did not give us the immense amounts of power necessary to transfer humans from one world to another.*

"If our bracelets can't zap us there, can Faf take us?"

"I'm not sure. I haven't seen him for a while. His parents expect him to study a lot. You know how much he wants to become an adult! Well, mastery of the dragonlaw and **Dragon Chronicles** is part of the grown-up deal. He's had his nose buried in a book every time I wanted to see him. I get the idea that I'm not any too welcome in his home cave right now," Seren said.

"You can't mean Faf wants to study! From what I've seen of him, he probably needs to work hard. Still, I can't see him turning down a chance at adventure for a bunch of old laws and the complete history of dragonkind from year one on."

"Faf's not the problem. It's his mother, Ebony. She can be pretty chilling without saying a word. When I ask if Faf can come out and play, she's terribly polite. I can almost feel her eyes boring into my back if I try to walk into the side chamber where the library is. I mean, a couple of tons of annoyed mother can be pretty hard to take, you know."

"Well, this is an emergency. At least we've got to try. If Ebony won't let us go, we may have to tell her about Lealor."

"Moral lackwit!" Seren said in his best leprechaun imitation. "There's got to be a way."

Perhaps you two should talk to Fafnoddle, Soladon suggested.

"Fafnoddle? Whatever for?" Seren asked.

Fafnoddle took your father to Achaea. Could he not also take you two? Nyct said, unwilling to allow his brother to take full credit for an idea he too, had harbored.

"No!" both boys said simultaneously, in perfect agreement for once.

"I understand that it is your job to protect us and maybe Fafnoddle would be safer transportation than his son, but you don't know what grown-ups are like," Argen told them.

"They take over everything," Seren said. "Why, I bet in no time at all, we would be told to go play with our marbles or something while a bunch of grown-ups took over." The face Seren made showed his opinion of the dragon bracelets' idea more clearly than his words. "We could get in trouble for not taking care of Lealor."

"Besides, Mother and Father are both busy already. Even your father, Wyrd, might be pretty upset if we distracted him over this," Argen said.

A look of surprise passed over Nyct's face. *I had not considered fully the results of our suggestion.*

Nor had I. Soladon flicked his tail. *Perhaps we should save telling our father until there is no other way of managing,* Soladon hissed.

"Now you're showing sense!" Seren told his talisman. "We haven't even challenged anyone yet. We'll save any parent-type help for a last resort."

The two dragons nodded. At least they had tried to make their charges see sense.

"Let's go to Faf's and try before we give up," Argen said.

CHAPTER TWENTY

No sooner had Seren nodded his agreement than both boys found themselves standing at the foot of the mountain where the von Fafnirs lived.

"Thanks, fellows," Seren told the bracelets.

"Yes, thanks," Argen added, wishing his stomach didn't react so badly to being zapped from one place to another without any warning. He wanted to seem like his father, capable of doing anything. He didn't realize from whom he had inherited his queasiness.

"Faf!" Seren called.

Ebony's huge head snaked from the cave. "Who calls my son?" she asked.

"Ah, hello," Seren said, managing to sound apologetic. "I'm sorry if we came at an inconvenient time—"

Ebony's huge eye glittered greenly as she lowered her head closer to the boys.

"—but we were hoping to play with Faf for a while," Argen finished his brother's sentence, a thing he hadn't done for years.

Seren shot his brother a look that said plainly as words that he didn't appreciate the verbal rescue.

Argen tried to hide his exasperation. Seren often rushed into a situation without thinking. He then hoped the right words would come to him in time to avert disaster. It would serve him right if Argen left him to extricate himself from the mother dragoness without any help. Then Argen remembered how important it was for them to contact Faf and he said, "It's—" he floundered momentarily himself, before continuing, "—well, to tell the truth, we're lonely. With mother off Realm we just wanted someone to be with. I guess," Argen said, trying to look like a deserted child. If dragons had maternal instincts, Argen planned to take full advantage of them.

Seren nodded, a smile of relief on his face.

"Oh, you lonely boys, I hadn't thought of that. Come in, come in," Ebony offered expansively, grabbing Argen by his belt and hoisting him up to the ledge where she stood.

Argen tried to look happy while he told his stomach to settle, or else. How could Seren be so friendly with dragons, of all things? Even when they did you a favor, meaning only kindness, it turned into a disaster.

"Thank you," Seren said with a small bow to Ebony, who placed him gently beside his brother.

"It is well to see your mother reared you to be polite," Ebony said. "You are a credit to her." She cast a disapproving glance at Argen as if she was making a comparison in which Seren came out much better than did Argen.

"You'll have to excuse Argen," Seren offered. "He hasn't been lucky enough to be around dragons much and he's kind of shy. Dragonkind are pretty magnificent to ordinary humans, you know."

"Botheration!" Ebony said, clearly not as taken in by the flattery as Seren hoped. "You just want me to offer you a few steakfruit, don't you?" The dragon chuckled. "Go on with you. You know where Faf studies. Go and get him. He can go out for the rest of the afternoon. He's been studying hard for hours," his proud mother said.

Seren lost no time in entering the cave. Argen, looking at the imposing bulk of his companion on the ledge, smiled what he hoped was a polite smile and entered the cave rapidly. He wasn't exactly afraid of dragons, but he doubted he'd ever get used to them towering over him with mouths full of daggers that seemed ready to rend and tear any moment. Seren chose dragons over any other creatures on Realm. Argen hurried after his brother. Sometimes he thought Seren was a bit of a fool.

"Have some steak fruit," Ebony bellowed after them. "Help your-selves."

Argen felt the warm exhalation on his back. He shivered in spite of the warmth. Catch him making a buddy of a dragon. No sir. All he asked of life was a room full of interesting books to read. This adventure stuff was already palling on him.

Seren reached into one of the trays that held greenery. The walls were lined with row upon row of hydroponic plant holders. Seren tossed a glossy fruit at his brother. "Catch," he said with a smile.

Argen hadn't been in the home cave of the dragons for years. He remembered coming when he was younger, but now he was awed by Fafnoddle's gargantuan horticultural effort. At any other time, he would have enjoyed talking to Fafnoddle about his indoor garden. Now, however, knowing the real purpose of their visit, he just wanted to convince Faf to come with them and leave. What, he wondered, could an irate dragon do to a human who tried to coax her young into a dangerous undertaking? Argen firmly suppressed another shiver. He sincerely hoped that he, for one, would never find out.

Seren had already entered the huge corridor that led to another cave. Argen hurried after him. The hallway seemed long to Argen, but when he compared the relative sizes of the dragons and humans, he realized that for a dragon, it was only a few short steps.

Faf and Seren were already talking when he entered the room. Argen looked around him in awe. This part of the cave was as large as one of the huge rooms in the University library. There were hundreds of books piled on shelves, stacked on a table, and resting on a ledge that ran around the room.

"Come on, Argen," Seren urged. "Faf will fly us to the plateau that's above the cave. We don't want to stand around here all day, do we?" The last two words were said with special emphasis, as if to remind Argen of the real purpose of their visit.

"Oh, yes. That's right. We have only a few hours before dark, and who knows how long—" he broke off because Ebony entered the room. "—it will take us to finish our game," he said, somewhat lamely.

"You children run along. First Egg needs plenty of fresh air so his scales don't tarnish. A growing dragon has to take care of his health," she explained to the boys.

"Oh, Mother," Faf complained.

"Well see he has a chance to get plenty of fresh air," Seren promised, almost pushing Argen into the hallway.

"Thank you for the fruit," Argen said.

"You're very welcome. We have a great deal of it to harvest right now. We're always glad to share with our friends," Ebony said with a wide smile that sent shivers down Argen's back.

"Hurry up. We don't want to waste any of this lovely afternoon," Faf said for his mother's benefit.

The three hurried out of the cave. Once on the ledge. Seren let out a large laugh. "Bright Ones in a basket," he hooted. "All you needed was a teacup in your hand to sound like some of the ladies my mother has over to the house to play bridge."

Faf let out a small puff of smoke, and while Argen coughed and hacked, he said, "You did want to get out of the cave—didn't you?"

"Okay. You're right. It always pays to keep your mother happy. If a little fancy politeness will do the trick, I guess it's for a good cause."

Argen had waved enough of the smoke away to take a breath of uncontaminated air. Smoke always nauseated him.

"Upsa daisy," Faf said, grabbing Argen in one claw and Seren in the other. Argen very nearly disgraced himself as they rose rather unsteadily into the air. He blessed the fact that he had saved his steak fruit to eat later, rather than gobbling it down as Seren had.

"Hey, Faf," Seren complained, "you should be more careful."

Argen longed for the feel of the ground beneath his feet as he mentally applauded his brother's attitude. The awkwardness of their ride and the indignity of being hauled up by his belt should be avenged, Argen felt. Seren liked flying with dragons. He simply had to be crazy, that was all.

"Why?" Faf asked, carefully dropping them both at the same time with a small thump. He flapped his wings once more, landing beside them.

"You might hurt yourself trying to lift both of us at once. We're pretty heavy," Seren said, making a fist and socking his friend on a mammoth front leg in a friendly gesture.

"Dragons are a hardy lot. You don't have to worry. If two of you had been too much to handle, I'd have dropped Argen."

Argen's eyes flew open. "What?" He gasped.

"Well, you've got a magic bracelet, just like Seren. It would have saved you," Faf explained with panache.

"Gee, thanks," Argen muttered, glad the dragon couldn't read his mind at that moment. The words he was thinking would have earned him a stern lecture from his parents if they had heard him. He knew some terms his parents definitely would disapprove of. It was one of the benefits that came from wide reading.

Seren explained what had happened to Lealor and their reason for needing Faf's help. "So," he concluded his story, "would you be willing to risk helping us? If you can't travel like your parents, we'll just have to ask their help."

"Not be able to travel like my parents? Naturally I can. Since my parents discovered their ability, all adult dragons on Realm can travel the way they can."

"Yes," Argen said, feeling he owed Faf a semi-setdown, "but are you adult enough to travel to Achaea? You'll have to take the location from my mind. I'm the one who knows all about the place. I understand you and Seren are a team, but can you work with my visualization?"

"I'll take you both on my back, and we can go," Faf said, taking the matter so casually that even Seren looked at him, estimating his chances of success.

Argen saw the look on his brother's face. He felt relieved to know that his brother did have some sense, after all. Argen had feared that Seren would want to rush into this adventure without proper safeguards.

"Climb on my back," Faf said, stretching himself out on the ground.

Seren wasted no time in mounting his friend. "Come on, slowpoke," he teased. "The air up here is great. You're gonna love dragonriding."

Obediently, Argen started to climb aboard the dragon.

"Not back by my tail," Faf commanded, "In front of Seren. You're the navigator," he said with a twist of his head and a smile.

Argen thought the bravest thing he ever did was dismount almost in Faf's mouth and clamber up in front of his brother. He fully expected to have nightmares about this flight.

Faf's takeoff was not reassuring. He lurched into the air with full power, said, "Here we go, ready or not," and disappeared from Realm.

The coldness cut through Argen's robes and he thought he heard his brother warn him to hold on. Blackness turned into bright sunlight so rapidly that he didn't even have time to worry about falling off.

"Hey, Faf," Seren called. "Where are we?"

"Where do you expect?" Faf said silkily.

Argen shivered. Sometimes Faf did seem like an adult dragon.

"We've got to get to Achaea," Seren explained.

Faf rippled his scales, depositing both boys on the dry ground. "Achaea," he said proudly.

"But—" Argen began, stopping to swallow firmly. "You didn't get any images from my mind. I didn't have time to think about Achaea."

"Oh, that," Faf said, with a wink to Seren. "I thought I'd give it a try on my own," he told Argen, who had turned pea green.

At this bit of news, Argen did deposit the contents of his stomach on the grass.

"I'm sorry, Faf," Seren apologized. "He's supposed to be housebroken and relatively civilized."

Faf giggled. "Frightened humans are so funny. It really doesn't take much to scare your brother, does it?"

"Much to scare me?" Argen turned to face his detractors. "Because I have the brains to understand how dangerous this form of dragon traveling is, you two idiots make fun of me! Let me tell you, if Faf had made an error, history would find us scattered over twenty different places of reality. No one with the tiniest atom of sense would consider traveling as we did unless the need were exceptionally great. I consider rescuing my sister to be worth risking my neck for, but you two set out as if this was an afternoon picnic! Faf, 'fess up. How many times have you made the trip to Achaea before?"

"Oh, scales! I thought I'd surprise you both. How did you ever find out my secret?" Faf pounded his tail on the ground to show his chagrin.

"The transition was too quick and so smooth. The very fact that you were so sure that this was Achaea told me you'd been here before," Argen said.

"Maybe I'd better start spending some time in the library myself," Seren admitted. "I didn't think about the danger of making the trip. Besides, the talisman we wear would protect us."

No, two sibilant voices spoke in three minds. One voice continued speaking to the three. *On a world, especially Realm, we have power. In that space between one world and the next, only the gates offer any certainty of safe harbor.*

Argen and Seren looked at each other in horror. They realized how much they had come to depend on the protection which Wyrd had provided for them both.

"Well, that's not our problem now," Faf told them. "On Achaea, even Wyrd limits his powers. The gods who live here are extremely proud of being the only major magic wielders."

That is true, Soladon said.

Yesss, Nyct agreed, the hiss in his voice showing his concern.

"Now what are we going to do?" Faf asked Seren.

Seren glanced at his brother.

"Don't look at me. You're the adventurer in the family. You tell me," Argen told him.

CHAPTER TWENTY-ONE

Argen, Seren, and Faf looked at one another. They stood in the middle of a vast plain on Achaea, but not one of them had given any thought to what they would do when they got there.

"Oh, boy. We may have really messed things up," Seren admitted.

The sunlight dimmed and returned.

Argen glanced skyward. "Yes," he said. He hated to have to agree with his brother, but this time Seren was right. Mess was a rather tame word to use to describe the predicament they were in.

"Hey, fellows, I don't mean to cause any trouble or anything, but I can't stay here too long. Any moment my mother is liable to start looking for me. If she can't find me on Realm, you may be looking at a grounded dragon."

"How can she ground you, Faf?" Seren was intrigued by the idea.

"Oh, mother dragons can bespell their offspring so that they must stay in the home cave." Faf shuddered. "It gives me the horrors thinking of it. If my sister hatches and I'm cooped up like some Realmish fowl, I'll go crazy."

"What's so bad about your sister hatching?" Seren wondered aloud.

"Well, dragon mothers sing to their new hatchlings as they dry."

"So what's so bad about that?"

"Have you ever heard my mother sing?"

"Well, to be honest, no. I wouldn't have thought her voice was that bad, though. She sounds fine when she talks."

"Oh, it isn't how she sings. It's what she sings—the **Dragon Chronicles**."

"Deadly," Seren said.

'Hour after hour, hour—"

"Look, you two, time is passing. We've got to think this thing through," Argen broke into their conversation.

Okay. So think, brother, think."

"Why me? Whenever the going gets tough—" Argen began.

"—the tough get thinking!" Seren finished brilliantly.

For the first time, Argen understood why it irked Seren so much, when he finished his sentences for him. He made a private vow never to do it again, then continued trying to reason with his two fellow adventurers.

"Are you both agreed that we can't handle this alone?"

"You mean that we need help?" Seren said.

"Assistance?" Faf added.

"Help, aid, assistance—whatever you call it, we can't manage here without some kind of magic." Argen looked at them, obviously expecting them to see the wisdom in what he said.

"Magic, huh?" Seren said.

Argen privately thought his brother could be thickheaded sometimes, but he didn't say anything about it. All they needed now was one of those brotherly arguments that went on for hours.

"Magic?" Faf said, as if he had never heard of the word before.

"M-a-g-i-c," Argen spelled in exasperation. He wondered how high an ax would bounce off his companions' thick skulls.

"Mortals can't use magic here. They get in big trouble with those guys on Mount Whatchamacallit," Faf said.

"Brilliant, Faf," Argen said under his breath. "Right," he said aloud. "So who do you think we need to get to help us?"

"The gods themselves!" Faf and Seren echoed each other.

"Yes. There is a temple on Achaea. It's called the Temple of the Oracle. The gods sometimes answer the petitions of mortals who visit there. It's our best bet."

"How far is it?" Seren asked.

"I'm not sure, but it's near Mount Olympus," Argen told him.

"I think I know where it is," Faf offered tentatively.

"Then you have been making unauthorized trips to Achaea!" Argen said.

"Well, yes. I followed my father and yours the first time. It's such an interesting place, and the gods gave the Greeks all that gold . . . so I kept coming."

"Why aren't you in big trouble with the gods, then?" Seren asked.

"I don't know. I haven't found any gold yet. I never gave it any thought." Faf frowned in puzzlement.

"I know. Flying is a natural dragonly ability. Even those trips through the dark are natural. That's why. Just let a mortal whisk through the air on his own and see what happens. I've read some really horrendous stories about mortals who were punished for being what Grandmother Cibby calls 'uppity.' The Greeks call that kind of overweening pride *hubris*. Boy, do they punish mortals who show any. Arachne, Tantalus, Ix—"

"Okay. Cut the mythology lesson, Argen. Let's get going," Seren said, climbing on Faf's back.

Argen carefully considered the possibilities. On the one hand, he could stay here. Faf and Seren might foul things up and then the sun would nova. That was one option. Then, on the other hand, he might climb on Faf's back for another ride. He was on the horns of a dilemma. Or, to be more in keeping with his location, he was between Scylla and Charybdis, the devil and the deep blue sea.

The sunlight dimmed. Argen clambered aboard Al Fafnir Airlines.

Seren handed his brother his not-too-clean handkerchief. "Try to hold on to everything until we get there, okay?"

Argen took the proffered hanky.

"Is everybody ready back there?" Faf inquired in bright tones. He reminded Argen of the stewardesses on real airlines.

"Of course," Seren called to his friend.

"I guess soooo," Argen managed as they winked out of sight.

Faf did a shrug that deposited both Argen and Seren on the ground. "Sorry, but I gotta fly," Faf explained as he popped out of sight.

"Some friend he is," Argen commented.

"Let's be fair. If our mother was on our tail like Ebony is on his, wouldn't you make sure you didn't get caught doing anything she would disapprove of?" Seren defended his friend.

"Yeah," Argen grudgingly admitted, "but can you see either one of us being so rock-headed that our folks had to make us study?"

"Not you, maybe, but Mother has had talks with me." Seren peered around them. "Let's start walking on this path Faf set us near. It goes up into those mountains." Seren started out, not waiting to see if Argen followed.

"Okay. Okay." Argen puffed his way behind his brother. He'd had more exercise in the last two or three days than in the previous two months. He longed to return to the safety of the library. Even riding on Faf beat all this walking uphill. Earlier, Argen had been tempted to tell his brother that these were only foothills, but now that they had climbed awhile, mountains did seem a better word. He swore to himself that if they came out of this adventure with a whole skin, he'd never envy his brother again. Argen much preferred his adventures between the covers of the books in the library. He liked reading about daring feats—heck, someday he might even write about them. He was most definitely cured of any wish to partake in the excitement firsthand. He noticed that he wasn't puffing so much any more. He hurried to catch up with Seren, who forged ahead as if he wore seven-league boots.

The next bend in the path gave them a full view of the Temple of the Oracle. "Wow!" Seren mouthed silently. Argen's small gasp of awe showed his state of impression, too.

"Oh! So there you are. I was about to stop and wait for you to catch up."

"So I noticed," said Argen dryly.

"Well, here we are. Now what do we do?" Seren asked, expecting his brother's hours of reading to pay off now that they had arrived at the temple.

"I think the next thing to do is to stand on the porch and wait for someone to come speak to us."

"You think? You mean you don't know for sure?"

"How could you expect me to? I've never been a suppliant before."

"Suppliant? What's that mean? Be careful what you say about me."

"A suppliant asks the gods for help."

"Same as a beggar, isn't it?"

Argen winced. Trust Seren to put things in their proper light. No fancy face-saving words for him. "I suppose so."

"I know so. Fafnir says calling a digging tool a digging tool simplifies things."

I bet he does, Argen thought. Then he asked, "I wonder where Faf heard that expression. It's a pretty old one."

"Not Faf, Old Fafnir, Fafnoddle's father."

Argen nodded. He should have been able to figure that out on his own. While Seren's young friend was a bit of a kook, his English was some of the best Argen had heard spoken by a dragon. Quite idiomatic. His association with Seren probably accounted for it. Now old Fafnir wouldn't see any difference between a digging tool and a spade. In fact, if he were corrected, he'd probably flame someone's eyebrows off.

"Come on, Argen," Seren interrupted, as if ascending the stairs to the porch had been his idea in the first place.

"I'm coming."

While Seren peered inside the huge open door, Argen turned around to enjoy the scenery. It was magnificent.

"Do you suppose we should just go in?" Seren asked.

"I don't think so." Argen shook his head. "The open door allows a breeze to blow through the temple. How would you feel if someone walked in our kitchen when Mother was airing it?"

Seren shifted his weight from side to side. Patience was not his strong suit. Argen stood quietly, glad for a chance to rest and think about what he was going to say when someone did come.

The boys did not wait long. An old man dressed in a white robe appeared and spoke to them in a language neither understood.

"Uh oh," Seren said. "Now what do we do?"

Do not worry. We will help you, Soladon promised. As suddenly as that, the boys understood the old man's words.

"Who stands before the Temple of the Oracle?"

"We do," Seren said.

Argen cast his eyes upward briefly and replied, "Argen and Seren Koenig, suppliants to the gods."

The old man peered at them. "Suppliants to the gods? Young boys such as yourselves?"

"Yes, sir. We have lost our sister and need to find her. She's very young," Argen explained.

"Ah," the old man said. "Now I begin to understand. Were you two not asked to watch over her and take care of her?"

"No, sir," Seren replied. "We thought we should take care of her since our parents . . . " His voice died down. How was he to explain travel between the worlds? Would the old man believe them anyway?

While Seren sweated for an answer, Argen filled the breech." . . . would expect it of us, I'm sure." Argen gave a small sigh of relief.

"Perhaps you two would like a small meal before you visit the oracle," the man said.

"Yes," Seren answered. He felt as if he hadn't eaten in days. He was sure he could eat more than Faf at that moment.

"If you please." Argen nodded his answer.

"Then follow me." The man walked through the huge door and turned left down a narrow corridor. At its end was a kitchen containing a huge table. "Sit, and I will see what I can find for you to eat."

Argen and Seren watched the man get milk, bread, and cheese. They were so hungry everything tasted delicious.

"My name is Palemon," the old man said as he sat.

"We're very happy to meet you, sir," Argen said.

Seren nodded. His mouth was full.

"Now, tell me more about your sister. What did you say her name was?" Palemon broke a small crust of bread and chewed it slowly while he waited for their answer.

"Lealor," Seren answered, taking another bite of cheese.

"Did she wander into the hills or woods by herself?" Palemon's shrewd eyes watched the boys in turn. "Or did someone take her away?"

"If she wandered off, we probably could have found her ourselves," Argen said.

"Sure," Seren put in with his mouth half full of food.

"Was Lealor taken away in a boat?"

"Not exactly. She rested quietly, locked in a box, the last time we saw her."

"Locked in a box? The last time you saw her?" Palemon frowned. "Boys, if I am to help you, I must hear the story in full. Something tells me you are not trusting me with the whole tale."

Should they trust Palemon? He seemed all right. Argen looked at Seren, who shrugged.

"It's clear we have to have help from someone, Palemon. The box Lealor entered was magic."

"There was a sphinx, too," Seren added, trying to be helpful.

"A sphinx, you say?" Palemon looked surprised. "It's not often that ordinary mortals get to see magical beasts."

Seren raised his head quickly at that.

"We're not really so ordinary, Palemon," Argen explained.

"Would it be those dragon bracelets you wear that make you different?" the old man asked.

Argen waited a moment to see if Nyct or Soladon would forbid talking of them, but nothing happened. "Yes, sir. The name of my talisman is Nyct."

Nyct raised his head and bowed to Palemon.

"Mine is Soladon," Seren said.

Soladon repeated Nyct's gesture of respect for Palemon.

"They remind me of a powerful dragon mage named Wyrd," Palemon said after looking carefully at the dragons.

He is our father, sir, Nyct spoke directly to Palemon.

"Indeed." Palemon ran his long-fingered hand down his snowy white beard while he considered that piece of information.

Argen felt himself relax. Here was someone he was sure would really help them—or put them in contact with someone who could. For the first time since his adventure on Achaea began, he felt safe.

"Do you know about the gates?" Argen asked.

Palemon nodded.

"Our mother, Mirza, came from our world, Realm, to Achaea through your gate. It's quite possible that someone—we think it is a wizard called the Shadowlord—is tampering with the gate. That's why your sun is acting so strangely. There's a creature that lives inside it called a Bright One. The Bright One in Achaeasun is young. If it gets disturbed enough, it will—" Argen paused. What did Bright Ones do that exploded their suns? He had never thought to wonder before.

When he got back to the library—if I ever do, he thought—he wanted to ask Librisald. If Librisald didn't know himself, he could tell Argen where to look, or who knew the answer.

"Yes?" Palemon's soft voice urged Argen to continue his tale.

"Argen's always drifting off like that, sir," Seren explained. "He's not weird. Honestly. My dad says that he thinks long thoughts sometimes, that's all."

Palemon struggled to repress a smile. He understood Argen and Seren far better than either knew.

"Sorry, sir," Argen grinned, looking sheepish. His father would tell him to get to the point, he knew.

"Go on," Palemon suggested.

"Well, when a Bright One gets disturbed enough, it does something and the sun explodes."

Palemon raised his eyebrows.

"Yes, sir. It's true. I swear," Seren put in.

"Your sun brightens and dims like it does is because the Bright One is roused. I don't know how much longer it will wait. So it's really important that somebody stop whoever is tampering with the gate. Before we were born, our mother and father saved the sun of Realm. That's why our mother is here. Our father came after her. We were to stay on Realm and wait for them to return."

Seren rushed in with the rest of the story. "But Lealor, our sister, climbed in this box and a sphinx closed it on her, and they disappeared. We think Lealor is here on Achaea someplace. That's why we need to speak to the gods."

"Indeed," Palemon said. "Your cause is worthy. Shall we go to the Hall of the Oracle?"

"Oracles are pretty weird, aren't they?" Seren asked.

"Sometimes, my boy. Sometimes. When they are not entranced to see the future, they can be relatively normal, like anyone you might meet." Palemon rose from the table.

"Shouldn't we help with the dishes or anything?" Argen asked.

"No," Palemon smiled. "A serving girl from the village in the next valley will come up later to cook my evening meal and she will clean up then."

He walked slowly from the room and the boys followed him to a huge hall with a hole in the center of the floor. A three-legged stool sat next to the opening. The hall was open on two sides, but Argen and Seren could see some vapor coming from the hole. The gentle breeze dissipated the fumes, but Argen wrinkled his nose.

"Smells like sewer gas to me," Seren said sotto voce.

"Shhh!" Argen hissed, sounding like his bracelet. "Sir," he said aloud to Palemon, "where is the oracle?"

Palemon's answer was to sit on the stool and smile at the boys.

"You?" Seren managed.

'You're the oracle?" Argen asked.

Palemon nodded and, bending low over the vent in the floor, began to breathe deeply.

CHAPTER TWENTY-TWO

Jarl trudged toward the mountain that loomed over the plain. It was as if there were a perpetual eclipse. In the half twilight, Jarl peered upward for a glimpse of the sun. Surely Achaeasun had not actually dimmed to this extent? If so, he was probably almost too late to rescue Mirza and confront the Shadowlord before the sun went nova. Jarl felt a moment's pity for the small Bright One who would probably end up destroyed or, at least. deformed by the tampering the Shadowlord was doing. He shrugged. No sense worrying about things he couldn't change.

He looked down at his bracelet. *Wyrd*, he thought as strongly as he could, *would you please give me a hint as to where this Graiae is?* Jarl fully expected no answer, but to his surprise, Wyrd raised his dragon head and nodded to the mountain. "You mean that's where I must go?"

An almost imperceptible nod was his answer.

"Thanks," Jarl breathed, wondering if Hades and Persephone were both watching in the magic mirror.

Distances were deceiving on the plain. After only a few minutes' walk, Jarl found himself looking upward at a cave large enough to contain two good-sized barns. The ledge outside the cave was so wide that Jarl was unable to see inside. Wyrd's whispered, *Here*, told him he had at last reached the dwelling place of the Graiae. The name seemed familiar, but he couldn't quite remember where he had heard it before. After all, those Greek names could be confusing. No wonder people back on Earth said, "It's Greek to me," when they didn't understand.

Jarl checked his sword before starting to climb the short inclines to the cave. He felt prepared for any kind of monster Achaea could throw at him. He didn't put it past Hades to send him on this quest to keep Persephone amused. His sense of being watched formed cold prickles at the back of his neck. One of the side benefits of being reunited with Mirza was the idea that Persephone's mirror would stop operating at that point. At least, it would if Hades kept his word. Somehow, the idea didn't reassure Jarl much. There were many cases where gods had broken promises to mortals. In fact, the only god who always told the truth was Apollo.

For a moment, Jarl wished Apollo had told him about the Graiae. Then he remembered what happened to Cassandra. Why couldn't Mirza have adventures at home, on Realm, where things were normal? Jarl heaved himself onto the ledge with a smile on his lips. Normal? A place that dripped magic from every bough? He had come a long way in his beliefs when he could regard Realm as normal!

A strange rock formation blocked his way into the cave. He would have to work his way around it. He checked his sword for the second time. There was enough room along the ledge for Jarl to stand comfortably without fearing the edge. It was as if the rock was a marker for a hiding place. It was easy for Jarl to peer around the edge and look for the Graiae. When he did, he sheepishly took his hand from his sword. Three little old ladies with gray hair sat in rocking chairs, busily knitting.

"Same old thing, dears," said the tallest of the women.

"The gods are busy partying, the peasants are working, and those strange people on the Isle of Atlan are making weird thingamabobs and doohickeys or whatever you want to call them."

"Whatchamacallits, Deino," said the oldest-looking of the three. Her hooked nose reached almost to her chin. "Whatchamacallits is what I call 'em."

"That's nice, Pephredo. Whatever you do, don't fuss," said the third old lady with a smile.

"Why shouldn't I raise a ruckus? It's my turn to see now. Deino always wants to have more than her share of time, and you always take her part. I'm the oldest and so I ought to have the longest turn with the eye." Her long fingers scratched the wart on the end of her nose.

"Oh, very well. You can be so hard to get along with. Now, Enyo is always so charming, I'm glad to relinquish our eye to her." The tall woman's hand reached up and removed her eye from its socket. She carefully placed it in the hand of the old crone, who almost snatched it from her. Her shaky fingers pushed the eye into place.

"Now, that's more like it," she said. Her head moved from side to side as she peered into the distance. "I can see so many more interesting things that you two," she said. "I'm always glad to have my turn so we can get some real news of the world. Times aren't what they were in our girlhood, I can tell you. Did you notice, sisters, that even the light seems to come and go out there? Didn't used to do that in my day, I can tell you! Crops are all in. Looks like it's been a good year. Cattle have increased, too. Say, girls, do you remember that rich farmer outside of Delphi?" She glanced to each side, making sure her sisters were paying proper attention. "Well, he's got himself a new wife. Pretty little thing, she is. New coat of whitewash on the house and all. That must be in her honor. He's still got her working, though. She's minding the goats. Bet she's going to make some of that goat's cheese—you know, the soft kind I like best. Haven't had any in centuries, seems like."

"Well, it's your own fault. When Daddy had us placed here, he told us to ask for any supplies we wanted. You never thought to ask for a goat!" Deino rocked back and forth. "I, however, did remember to ask for fruit trees and berry bushes."

"Don't be pompous, my dear," Enyo warned. "None of us could know that we'd be waiting here forever, you know."

"Should have known, should have known," Pephredo muttered, intent on her watching.

"We were remarkably silly when we were girls, weren't we?" Enyo said. "Father thought he was doing the best for us all, I'm sure."

Deino sniffed. "You don't have a cross bone in your body. You should have taken the offer that old shepherd made for you. Daddy would have been happy to see at least one of us married."

"We'd have been in a fine pickle, if she had."

"Oh, surely Daddy wouldn't have made us marry one of those sea monsters. He was threatening us to make us consider some of our offers."

"But, sisters, although it's hard to remember, we were born looking old. What personable men were going to offer for our hands? It must have been such an embarrassment to Daddy. Even offering the best of dowries, he couldn't interest any young men. There were so many handsome ones." A tear rolled down Enyo's cheek at the memory.

"Don't sit there blubbering," Pephredo's harsh voice said. "Won't change a thing. Why, we've been sitting here in this blasted cave longer than some mountain ranges have existed." She cackled briefly. "It's far too late for us. Lucky we weren't spring chickens. If we'd have married, we'd have gone to Hades' realm by now. Yes, long gone by now, dead and buried."

"Can't you tell us what's happening out there instead of doddering on?" Deino's sharp voice broke the brief silence. "You're supposed to tell us what's going on. That was our bargain when Zeus gave us the eye. With only one eye and one tooth among us we have to share."

"That's so, sister. If we had married, though, perhaps we might have had children."

"Well, I've always thought we were most fortunate. We were never subservient to any man—except Father, of course," Deino said.

"Well, you were too proud to wed, and I never took any man's fancy. Daughters of Phorcys and Ceto, we were. Sea gods don't find it easy to marry off their girls to mortals—and we all had human shapes right from the start."

"You're keeping the eye far too long. It's Enyo's turn now, I'm sure."

"She hasn't said anything, has she? Let her ask for it when she thinks it's her turn. At least she never rushes me for her time with the eye." Pephredo rocked and looked, making no attempt to pass the eye.

"If I wasn't here to encourage you to share it, she'd probably never get a turn."

"You can't resist a chance to harp, can you, Phredo?"

"Don't call me Phredo! You know I hate it!"

"Oh, my dears, don't fuss so. You know it always upsets me when you argue."

Pephredo glanced at her sister's agitated face. "Now, Enyo, you know we don't mean it. Here, it's your turn. Take the eye and see what you can find to tell us what you see." Her aged hand removed the eye and passed it to her sister.

"About time," Deino muttered, but so softly that only Pephredo could hear.

"Oh, how wonderful it is to see! I love to hear you both telling about all the things you see, but being able to see oneself is so much nicer."

"No argument there," Pephredo said, rocking back and forth as her hands resumed their knitting. "I suppose now we're going to get the latest report on all our little feathered and furred friends." She sighed.

"Of course we are," Deino put in. "If ever the Fates slipped up, it was when they made Enyo our sister. She should have been a nature goddess. Then she'd have been happy."

"The Fates don't often ask a body what they want to be. As for being happy—" Pephredo snorted. "Hah! Just look at all the miserable mortals the Fates bedevil."

"Not just mortals. Consider the plight of our sister, Medusa, poor girl."

"Yes, she's a good case in point. Why, on that miserable little ball of dirt—what was its name? Earth, I think they called it—the Fates actually let one of those mortal heroes kill our sister."

"Wouldn't you rather hear about all the lovely animals in the woods?" Enyo asked. "You do want me to tell you about the animals, don't you?"

"What I wish we had was some of that goat's cheese," Pephredo said.

"What I wish is that we could have an adventure ourselves. Why, the last important thing that actually happened to us was that time when Perseus came to us for help. Since we moved back home to Achaea, we haven't had one hero come to visit us. Those were the days." Deino sighed.

"Oh, I wish you could see! There's the cutest little squirrel. His cheeks are full of nuts and he's carrying them into his tree home." Enyo smiled happily, but neither of her sisters saw her look of joy.

"How exciting," Deino said, not meaning a word of it.

"Don't be snippy, sister dear." Pephredo said. "It will be your turn for the eye soon enough."

"I can't get used to it, sitting here day by day. Somehow, I still wish I could play a part—even if it was a small one—in the real happenings on Achaea." Deino sighed again.

"Fat chance," Pephredo answered. "No one even remembers us except the gods. Even the gods forget us. Only Hades comes to visit once in a great while."

"I'm sure he only remembers us because we will never enter into his kingdom. It's no fun being a symbol of old age."

"Excuse me, ladies," Jarl said in his politest voice, "but I would like to have some information." He stood directly in front of Enyo, who still retained possession of the eye.

"Oh, my dears, if you could only see what I see!" Enyo's mouth dropped open as Jarl bowed to her. "Oh, my. So handsome, too," she breathed, as if she was afraid she would scare Jarl away.

"Who spoke?" Deino commanded.

"Who, indeed," echoed Pephredo. "Give me the eye, sister." She fumbled for it, but Enyo made no effort to remove it from her socket.

"Give me!" Pephredo commanded.

"No, wait," Deino said, "Remember what happened the last time we tried to pass the eye with a stranger present?"

"Indeed I do," Enyo said. "We all sat here blind, having to bargain with the handsome young man—what was his name? Pericles? Persuit? Persimmon?" Her murmurs fell away as Pephredo broke in.

"Perseus, that was it."

"Well, whoever, we mustn't trust this one," Deino said.

"Weren't you just wishing to have part in an adventure?" asked Jarl.

Pephredo chuckled softly. "There speaks an adventurous spirit."

"He looks perfectly lovely, sisters," Enyo assured them. "Quite trustworthy."

"I'll believe that when I can see him myself. How can we be sure it's safe to pass the eye?"

"Let me assure you I have no desire for your eye, being fortunate enough to possess two myself."

Deino said acidly, "We supposed as much when Enyo didn't introduce you as a cyclops."

"What if you get ready to transfer your eye and then I walk way over there near the edge while you change?" Jarl offered.

"That sounds fair," Pephredo said. "If we don't trade the eye, I won't get a chance to see him, sisters."

"Very well," Deino grudgingly agreed.

Enyo took one last look at Jarl and handed the eye to her sister.

"Well for once, Enyo, I agree with you. He is a very comely mortal."

"Deino, give me a quick turn with the eye. I want to see him, too."

"Only if you promise to return the eye to me after you look. You always want to have the longest turn."

Pephredo reached out with her scrawny hand. "I promise. I promise," she said. "One quick peek and then I'll give it back."

Deino handed the orb to her sister, who popped it in and then looked at Jarl. "Fine-looking fellow, sisters. Now, we'd like to know what you are doing here. I'm sure you didn't make this visit because you know us. Someone must have sent you. Who was it? Why have you come?" She leaned forward in her chair, peering at Jarl.

"Sister, you promised," Deino interjected.

"Oh, indeed I did. Here." Pephredo reluctantly removed the eye and gave it to Deino.

"Now, that's better," she said, positioning the eye in its socket. "Did someone send you?"

"If I may have your permission to approach," Jarl began.

"I wish I could still see him. How polite he is!" Enyo said, rocking very fast in her excitement at the thought of an actual visitor.

"Come closer," Deino commanded.

Jarl obeyed. He took off his sword and shield. Turning his shield upside down, he sat on its padded interior. The shield made a noise as he sat upon it.

"Oh," Enyo said, jumping at the sound.

"What was that?" Pephredo asked suspiciously.

"Nothing, sisters. Our visitor sat on his shield. I must say he certainly isn't acting much like a heroic type." Then she turned to Jarl. "Don't you know you should be ready to fight at all times? Who knows what kind of a monster might materialize any moment?"

"I rather hope not," Jarl said. "I've been very busy ever since I arrived on Achaea, so I could use a little rest."

"You've not told us yet who sent you."

Jarl found it interesting. Whoever had the eye seemed to be the spokeswoman for all three sisters. "Hades sent me."

"Hades? Whatever for?" The other two old ladies rocked and nodded their agreement to the question.

"He told me to find the Graiae. That is you, isn't it?"

"Grey women, that's us." Pephredo chuckled.

Deino cast her a look. "I was talking with this hero, sister."

"Humph. Doesn't mean the rest of us have to sit dumb as stones, does it?"

"Well, no." Deino admitted. "I do have the eye."

"Don't have to be able to see to speak," Pephredo said with some logic.

Enyo said, "Sisters, we are ignoring our guest to bicker among ourselves. He will think us rude," she added gently.

"No," Jarl told her with a smile. "I can understand it's quite upsetting to have a stranger pop up on your doorstep as I did."

"Quite right," Pephredo said.

"So Hades told you to find us, did he? Why would you come on such a quest?"

"My wife has disappeared. I know she is somewhere on Achaea."

"You want us to help you locate her? How romantic!" Enyo sighed.

"That's it," Jarl confirmed.

"Why did Hades send you to find us? It can't have been very easy. Hades knows where we are. Why didn't he come and ask us himself?

"His wife wanted to watch me find Mirza, so he created a magic mirror for her."

"You mean she's watching us now?" Enyo's hand went up to smooth a stray curl from her forehead.

"Yes, I think so," Jarl told her.

"Oh, dear me."

"Don't fuss so, sister. What if she is watching? You know yourself, looking can't change things. If it could, we'd have some soft goat's cheese here every time I wore the eye. Maybe Persephone will take the hint and send us some, now that she knows."

"He didn't say she could hear, sister. Only see."

"Hearing is part of the enchantment. Perhaps I have some cheese in my pouch, here." Jarl rummaged in the magic provender bag Cibby had given him and found a neatly wrapped parcel of the cheese. He offered it to Pephredo, putting it in her hands.

"What's this?' Her hand patted the package, then unwrapped it. She lifted it to her nose. "Goat cheese, as I live and breathe!" She pulled off a morsel. "Thank you, stranger," she said, before putting a piece in her mouth.

"Tell us what you want. Giving us gifts won't gain you our good will." Deino frowned slightly.

"Gained him mine!" Pephredo contradicted, chewing busily.

"My name is Jarl. I've already told you I'm searching for my wife. I know she is being held a prisoner against her will. She has long red hair," he continued.

"Ha! We already know where she is!" Pephredo said.

"You do?"

"Yes, indeed," Deino added. "Our sister, Medusa, is her warder."

"Then you did see her with the eye!"

"Of course," Enyo said, nodding. "She's a very beautiful woman. No wonder you search for her."

"Wonderful! Tell me where I can find Medusa."

All three shook their heads.

"You can't tell me where she is?" Jarl was thunderstruck. "Yet you have seen her?"

"Yes, Jarl, we have," Deino said. "But we won't tell you where to find our sister Medusa."

"We've sworn a pact," Enyo said.

"We won't tell," Pephredo added. "Does this mean I've got to return the rest of your cheese?' she asked sadly. "We'll never tell."

CHAPTER TWENTY-THREE

"What do you mean, you'll never tell! I can't find my wife unless I find Medusa."

"It's the fault of that Persimmon person," Pephredo explained, still clutching the package of cheese. "We'd tell you except for our oath." She held out the package to Jarl. "Here's your cheese," she said gruffly.

"Oh, keep that," Jarl told the old woman. "What I'd like to know about is this Persimmon."

"Not Persimmon. Perseus," Deino told him.

"Oh. I've heard about him. He killed Medusa."

"Yes. You would do the same if you saw her."

"Just a minute," Jarl said. "If Perseus killed Medusa, how can she be alive here to hold my wife captive?" He looked at the three old women, awaiting an answer.

"The gods restored her when we left Earth," Enyo offered.

"Then why are you worrying? Besides, I won't hurt her."

"It was a terrible experience. Imagine having your head lopped off when you really hadn't done anything wrong." Enyo shook her head sadly, unable to understand such wickedness.

"She was the only mortal sister, you see," Pephredo said. "She was young and beautiful when she offended Athena. Always a mistake to offend a goddess, mortal. Remember that!" She rocked silently a moment before adding, "Must be getting old. Giving free advice when it's not wanted."

"You may be sure I will remember what you have said. It rings true."

Jarl sat, perplexed. How was he going to get these old women to tell him what he wanted to know?

"It was so sad," Enyo told him. "She had the most beautiful curly black hair."

"Down to her waist, it was," Pephredo nodded. "Some goddesses can't stand to see a lovely mortal. That flame-haired woman of yours had better be very careful."

Jarl's heart skipped a beat. He had not thought that Mirza might excite the envy of any goddess, although she was strikingly attractive. He remembered the first time he had seen her. One glance and he loved her. Looks like hers might well attract the attention of one of the philandering gods. Then what would he do?

"Alas!" Deino rocked back and forth, her old hands clasping the wool she was knitting. "Athena turned her hair to snakes, ugly repulsive things that writhed and hissed when anyone approached."

"Medusa almost went mad the first few days. She stayed in her room, moaning and carrying on. Not that she didn't have reason, you understand."

"Pephredo, it was a fortunate thing that she did. Remember that shepherd boy who saw her out on the hill the next morning?"

"That I do, Deino. That I do. His blood froze up in him. Stone cold, that's what he was."

"No, sister," Enyo's gentle tone broke into the discussion. "Cold stone. The boy turned to stone."

"Yes, I remember. We covered her head, but it was so awkward. When the neighbors came, wanting to see her, she sometimes took off the covering."

"Right. Got so statues of horrified neighbors covered the place. Father sent her off to live with her sisters, Stheno and Euryale on the shores of Oceanus, near—"

"Pephredo!" Deino warned. "You almost gave away Medusa's location."

"Ladies, knowing my wife's location is much more important than simply finding her. There is a sorcerer here called the Shadowlord. He is trying to force a gate from this world to others. My wife and I stopped him on Realm, where we come from. He must be vastly more powerful now than he was years ago when we first encountered him. Already this tampering with a gate disturbs the Bright One in your sun. The light elsewhere on your world dims and returns. When this has happened often enough, your sun will become a nova and explode, destroying everything on this planet. I'm not sure how far the process has gone since I began talking to you. Believe me, it is important I find my wife as soon as possible."

Deino, who had the eye at the time, said, "He looks like he's telling the truth, sisters."

"Could I please see?" Enyo asked, holding out her hand.

"Very well," Deino said, passing her the eye.

Enyo's hand shook, and the eye rolled from her fingers onto the floor. "Oh, dear," she said softly.

"Well, what do you think?" Pephredo asked.

Tears rolled from Enyo's empty sockets. "Sisters, I fear to tell you, but—"

Jarl found the eye and pressed it firmly into her hand. She gave him a radiant smile. "I think, sisters, that we can trust him."

"Well, let me see as well," Pephredo grumbled. "Have to be last all the time. Well?" Her voice cut the air like a knife. "Well?"

"I wanted to make sure I didn't drop it, sister."

"All right." Pephredo fitted the eye in her socket. "He does look like an honest sort. Are we agreed? Shall we tell him where Medusa lives?"

Deino said, "But our oath. What about that?"

Jarl could feel time rushing by. How many minutes had he wasted with these three already? "What exactly did you swear?"

"That we would never tell another hero where Medusa was so he could go and hurt her."

"And if I promised not to hurt her?"

"How can we be sure?"

"I can make you a promise."

"We never had suitors, but we know how easy it is for a mortal man to break his word when he wants something," Pephredo said.

Deadlock!

Jarl stared at the Graiae. They gazed back at him with their five empty sockets and the eye. Enyo offered timidly, "Do you suppose—" then she paused. "No, I guess not."

Jarl was ready to try anything at this point. "What?" he coaxed.

"If you would leave your shield and sword with us . . . "

"Good idea, sister." Pephredo turned to Jarl. "Leave us your sword and shield, and we will tell you."

"Agreed." Jarl placed his sword and shield at their feet. He hoped Hades would not be angry, and he also hoped he didn't meet anything he couldn't talk into a reasonable frame of mind. He decided he'd worry about how to handle Medusa when he came to her.

"Sisters," Enyo said. "We are not being quite fair."

"Not fair!" Pephredo said. "Remember that happened the last time we dealt with a mortal—that Per—what's his name?"

"Perseus," Deino supplied.

"Can't we allow him at least his shield? He cannot hurt Medusa with that, but it might protect him. Remember, he cannot look at her without turning to stone."

"Very well," Pephredo agreed.

"We must keep the sword," Deino said, having the last word.

"Now, where is Medusa?"

"You will find her near Tartarus, on the shores of Oceanus."

"Which direction would that be?"

Three arms raised, fingers pointing south.

"How long will it take me to make the journey?"

"Many days."

"I don't have that kind of time!" Jarl was ready to swear from frustration. Wyrd would refuse to zap him there, he was sure. Lealor's rejection of Wyrd's gift was costing her father dearly. "How am I to get there? I wish Faf were here."

Jarl spun around at the slight "pop" behind him.

"Did someone mention my name, Uncle Jarl?"

Jarl was so happy to see the small dragon that he didn't even bother to correct him for saying "Uncle Jarl."

Pephredo had the eye at the time. "Aha! So you finally come to see us again, Little One."

Faf reached under a wing tip and pulled out a bag, which he gave her. "I thought you might like these," he said.

"What is it, sister?" Enyo asked. "I love surprises."

Pephredo opened the bag. "More of that steakfruit. Good stuff," she said, taking one and passing the bag to Enyo.

Jarl's stomach heaved at the thought of riding with Faf, but he had no choice. "Can you take me to where Medusa lives?"

"Sure, but why do you want to go there?"

"That's where Mirza is."

"I think I've got the time. I can't stay, you know. My mother will be checking on my studies any minute. Besides, I brought you—"

"Later. Just get me there. Then you can go," interrupted Jarl. He turned to offer a courteous goodbye to the Graiae, but Faf wasted no time. He grabbed Jarl by the belt and popped them to the shores of Oceanus.

"Where's Medusa?" Jarl tried to ignore the queasy feeling in his stomach.

"I didn't think you wanted to drop in on her literally," Faf said. "You'd better figure out how you're going to talk to her without looking at her. You turn to stone if you look her in the face, you know. She's up the beach in a cave." One talon pointed the direction. "Gotta go, Uncle Jarl." With a cheery wave of his talons, Faf disappeared with a faint pop.

Jarl walked slowly in the direction the dragon indicated, holding his shield ready. If he thought Medusa was near, he planned to use the shield like a mirror. The conversation of the Graiae had reminded him of the story of Pereus, who used his shield in the same way Jarl planned.

The sun shone brightly on the golden sands. The waves curled in to the shore. A surfer would be in ecstasy in a place like this, Jarl thought. Ahead a cliff face that jutted out into the sand interrupted the strand, almost obliterating the beach. Jarl hoped he wouldn't have to swim. He didn't think he could and still carry the shield. And that shield was one thing he definitely wanted with him when he found Mirza.

When Jarl actually reached the narrowed part of the beach, he found a three-foot clearance between the cliff face and the water. If he were careful, he wouldn't have to get his feet wet. He had no idea what was on the other side of the cliff, so he stopped and listened. He couldn't hear anything except the sound of the water against the shore. To be on the safe side, he positioned the shield and advanced, looking into it. If Medusa awaited him, he wasn't going to look at her by accident.

A bronze shield does not make the best of reflective surfaces—even it if is a magical gift from Hades, Jarl thought. He saw movement above the cliff face. Was it Medusa? The wildly flowing locks might be snakes; however, he was too far away and the shield simply wasn't a good enough mirror.

"Jarl!" the figure shouted.

He recognized Mirza's voice. The figure was his wife, not Medusa. His happiness at being reunited with her almost made him cast his shield aside, but common sense triumphed. He clutched it awkwardly as she ran into his arms.

She leaned against him with her head fitting into the curve under his chin. "Where have you been? I sensed you a long time ago. It's the Shadowlord again," she said calmly. "What took you so long?" She planted a kiss on his chin by way of apology for her questions.

"I went through hell to get here," Jarl told her, not aware of his pun. Mirza was certainly taking it calmly, he thought. But then, who else would tamper with the gate system? Everyone had been so sure it would take the Shadowlord years to recover from his defeat on Realm. The power being used here was tremendous. It made the Shadowlord's former abilities seem almost insignificant by comparison.

"Do you mean it was hard to find me or that you actually went to the Land of the Dead?" she asked with a twinkle in her eyes.

"Both," he offered, hugging her.

"Tell me. Tell me," she teased him as Lealor often did when she wanted a story.

"Very well. We miss you on Realm. The opened **Book of the Worlds** was left turned to the page about Achaea, and that was our only clue. The Bright One in this sun is in a disturbed condition. I couldn't use the gate, so Faf brought me. I mistakenly wandered into Hades and Cerberus wouldn't let me out, so I begged my freedom from Hades himself. Either he didn't know where you were, or he wanted to use my odyssey in search of you as entertainment for Persephone."

"How could that be?"

"He created a magic mirror for her. It was like a handheld television."

"You mean she's watching us now?" Mirza looked around as if she could locate the video camera she suspected was taking pictures of them.

"Not now. Hades promised me Persephone would only watch until I found you."

"Did you come by boat or did you walk?"

"Part of the way I walked, but this last part of my trip I came by Air. Fafnir."

"What's Old Fafnir got to do with this? There's no way he could have made the trip."

"Not Old Fafnir—young Fafnir."

"Young Fafnir? Who's that?"

"First Egg," Jarl explained. "He's decided to be an adult and Fafnir is the name he chose for himself."

"I thought there had to be a ceremony and a horde of gold, and—"

"Faf has cut most of that short with my blundering aid. I gave him a piece of gold. When he arrived back home—by the way, dear, the refrigerator and freezer are empty and the pantry is pretty well decimated, too — he intended to remove all the gold he could carry from Fort Knox. He thought there were mountains of the stuff stored inside and that humans wouldn't notice if he took enough to start his hoard. I convinced him to return to Realm with me. We'll have to replace the gold piece in Seren's coin collection."

"You old softy, you gave it to Faf, didn't you?"

"Well, how was I to know that was the official start of his hoard? I'm lucky Ebony and Fafnoddle didn't roast me for it."

"They're pretty understanding, for dragons. If more dragons had adventures with humans, they'd all come around to more sensible positions."

"Speaking of sensible positions, where is Medusa? I had to promise I wouldn't hurt her and give up my sword to find out where this place was."

"She's resting at the back of the cave." Mirza brushed her long hair away from Jarl's face. The snappy breeze off the water cooled the air.

"Then why didn't you run away from her?" Jarl asked.

"I dare not leave. Sometimes I see her watching me in the evening when I comb my hair. Those snakes are truly hideous. She has such an ugly expression on her face, sort of soured."

"Well, I can understand why. You weren't very happy when the Shadowlord placed that enchantment on you years ago—remember?"

"Yes." Mirza shuddered.

"Why haven't you left already? Or is there some reason you won't help me foil the Shadowlord again?"

"No matter what the danger, I must help you, but I am afraid."

"You're afraid of Medusa?"

"No, it's not her. She's only guarding me so the Shadowlord will remove the snakes. No one else on Achaea would dare the wrath of Athena. Poor Medusa."

"Poor Medusa indeed! How is it you've stayed with her for days and not turned to stone?"

"Remember, the spell of the Green Lady protects me, plus I always carry a little moley with me—in case of unicorns, you know." Mirza reached into her pocket and pulled out a small sprig.

Jarl took the few leaves she offered and put them in his shirt pocket, which he firmly buttoned. "Okay. Now what?"

"The minute we leave here, we put Lealor in danger."

"Lealor? She's back on Realm with a guardian bracelet!"

"Not now. She was enticed into a magic casket by a sphinx and the Shadowlord has her—"

"Then what are waiting for? We'll go to wherever he's holding her—"

"No, Jarl. I have probed the magic of the Shadowlord while I waited for you. I was planning to try something—anything—if you did not come, and I needed to know his real power. It is tremendous. He can actually tap Achaeasun itself. All my instincts tell me to try to rescue Lealor right away, but I know we cannot succeed unless we have the power of the gods to aid us. Even then, defeat is a real possibility."

Jarl saw the shimmer of tears in Mirza's eyes. Mirza never cried, but now she seemed ready to weep like any silly heroine.

"How much time have we? Will Medusa report immediately to the Shadowlord?"

"Well, I told Medusa all about the Bright One. She's agreed to let me go because I've promised to take her to Realm and use the waters of the healing spring on her."

"Oh, I almost forgot. Persephone sent this for you." Jarl handed Mirza the opaline box. "Maybe Medusa won't have to wait."

Mirza opened the box curiously. The salve within emitted a flowery scent. "What is it?"

"Persephone said it was some kind of magical beauty cream," Jarl began, but Mirza was already running to the path up the cliff.

"I'll be right back." The words drifted over her shoulder to the astounded Jarl. "I want Medusa to try this. Persephone is so thoughtful!"

Mirza disappeared above. Jarl knew all about beauty routines. He found a dry patch of sand shaded by the cliff and stretched out for a nap. Mirza would return when she wanted him. He wondered how much time they would have to rescue the Bright One. Mirza hadn't seemed worried about the time element at all. Jarl couldn't really blame her. His concern about Lealor wasn't allowing any sleep or rest. Rescuing the Bright One might have to wait.

At that moment, the sun dimmed ominously.

CHAPTER TWENTY-FOUR

Jarl jerked upright. The dimness seemed to last fractionally longer than before. How were they to stop the Shadowlord? His power had definitely grown in the years while Jarl and Mirza reared their children. He remembered the prophecy, which said it would take the combined powers of them all to stop the Shadowlord. This time it was crucial that he not escape.

Jarl rose and started up the path Mirza had taken so short a time before. When he came to the opening in the cliff, he set down his provender bag and debated whether to trust the moley's power or not. Then, too, he had Wyrd. Even if he was still sulking, he probably wouldn't want Jarl to turn to stone. He felt like such a fool, maneuvering the shield. With a shrug, he placed the shield over the provender bag and entered Medusa's home.

The absence of light temporarily blinded him. He stood in the dimness and waited for his eyes to adjust. He could hear Mirza's voice within the cave. The beauty preparations were at a critical point, he could tell. The next few moments would be crucial. The possible nova would have to wait. He preferred facing it to facing Mirza if his interruption caused Medusa to refuse to try the cream that Persephone had sent.

"Well, hold still a moment. I need to cream this around your hairline. Do you suppose you could hold the snakes off your neck for me?"

Jarl shuddered. He imagined Mirza carefully creaming away the snakes from Medusa's scalp. She had a much stronger stomach than he did.

"There. That's done. Don't you feel much better now? Let me put a little on your face. Hold still. I don't want to waste any. Now rub it well to be sure you get the full benefit of the cream," Mirza advised.

"Am I really going to look the way I did before Athena punished me?"

Jarl listened carefully. The second voice must be Medusa's. It didn't sound as if she were a horrible monster. The tone of her voice was remarkably similar to Enyo's, even gentle. It wasn't so surprising. They were reputed to be sisters, after all. Phorcys and Ceto were supposed to be the parents of the gorgons and the Graiae. He wondered if they had any normal children. Ceto, their mother, must have been a really brave goddess. Who knew what the next batch of children would turn out to be or look like? Jarl's blood ran cold.

Maybe it wasn't bravery after all. He had married a shapeshifting witch and never given a thought as to what kind of children he and Mirza might have. Neither of the boys had showed much magical aptitude so far, but Lealor was already demonstrating witchly powers. That of healcraft for animals, for instance. The sound of someone approaching drew him from his thoughts.

"Jarl, dear, I want you to meet Medusa."

Jarl turned. Leave it to Mirza to be cordial to her jailer. The tall, curly-headed young woman next to her was lovely. Her black hair had a sheen that was spectacular. Her facial features were regular and her complexion was radiant. That beauty cream Persephone sent must have worked, he thought.

"I am most happy to meet you," Medusa said in quiet tones.

"And I you," Jarl answered, bowing. He hesitated to offer his hand but stopped because of the snakes that were wound around her arms.

"Do not be afraid of my companions," Medusa said. "We have been together so many centuries, I have not the heart to abandon them."

Jarl decided Medusa really wasn't monster material. Perseus must have stretched the truth a great deal when he retold his adventures. Didn't drops of blood from her severed head form Pegasus? Surely a truly evil monster couldn't produce such a wondrous creature. Perhaps the gods had engineered the whole thing. Hadn't Pegasus helped another hero kill the Chimera, the lion-snake-goat mixture of myth?

Mirza gave the gorgon a hug, snakes and all. "Jarl and I must go now. I hope shortly to have the Shadowlord so busy that he will not have the time to seek you out. If he should send a messenger to see how I am, say I refuse to join him and am staying with you. I bet no one will enter the cave to check. Stay in the shadows yourself. In a few days, I hope this whole adventure will be over for everyone."

"Thank you, my friend. May you have success in your enterprise." Medusa glided the few short steps to the opening in the rocks and waved as Mirza and Jarl descended the path.

"Isn't she lovely now? I don't know how long we can keep the news of my escape from the Shadowlord, but we really must get working on this." Mirza's hand sketched a gesture toward the sun. "That poor little Bright One."

"That poor little Bright One that has the power to destroy the entire sun to escape the machinations of the Shadowlord," Jarl muttered. Why was it that, when he was with Mirza he was unable to worry effectively? Was it because they had come through all kinds of scrapes in the past? He knew he didn't trust Wyrd's powers nearly as much as he did those of his wife. She often assured him that he was her equal in power, but he knew he was not yet her equal in knowledge. Power, without the knowledge of how best to use it, was almost worthless. Together, however, they made a formidable team. Why then was he so concerned over the increase in the Shadowlord's powers?

"Now to begin," Mirza said.

"You mean we're going to start the battle here? Now?" Jarl's voice rose in spite of his efforts to keep calm.

"Of course not," Mirza said. "First you have to get us to Olympus."

"Olympus?" Jarl swallowed. "What makes you think I can get us there?"

"Not you. Him." Mirza's finger pointed to a spot over Jarl's left shoulder.

Jarl turned to see what or whom she pointed to. Shades of the three o'clock monster movie! Winged sandals, funny hat, and caduceus, a staff with two snakes curled around it. Why, he thought to himself, do I have to get involved in so many adventures with snakes? I hate the loathsome things. However, he did recognize the god. Hermes, the messenger of the gods, always carried the caduceus.

"Are you looking for us?" Mirza asked the god.

"If you be Mirza, I seek you."

"Are you here to transport us to Olympus, or do you only bear a message for us?"

"I bear a message."

The god's admiring eyes made Jarl nervous. He wracked his brain to remember all the stories of Hermes he had ever heard—he was a trickster, a messenger, and insatiably curious about everything. The memory of a bubble gum wrapper he had collected as a child came to mind. The Greeks worshiped Hermes because he was the god of speed and gamblers. Not one of Jarl's recollections showed Hermes to be a womanizer. Probably, he didn't stay in one place long enough to attract feminine attention. Jarl hoped this was so. How was a mere mortal to compete with a god if the god decided he liked the mortal's wife? Remembering some of the stories about Zeus, Jarl rather hoped Mirza wouldn't get to meet him on this trip to Achaea.

"Well, don't you think you'd better tell us what the message is?" Mirza smiled.

"Gladly will I tell if you will but answer me a question first." Hermes zipped over to a rock in the shade and sat.

He reminded Jarl of a hummingbird. Holding still seemed to be an unnatural thing for him to do.

"Of course I will. You have only to ask," Mirza said.

Mirza was being her usual charming self. Jarl was busy wishing she was worn from her captivity. She looked ravishing to Jarl. Perhaps she had dabbed on a little of Persephone's magic beauty salve. Medusa hadn't said a word if she had. Even women born under different suns ganged up on men when it came to beauty secrets.

"Are you immortal that you dare to undo a spell placed by Athena? When she finds out how fine Medusa is looking these days, she will probably be quite put out, you know. You are the most courageous being I have met in some time."

"Pooh. There's no courage required. I didn't do anything or use one speck of my magic. Persephone sent Jarl, my husband, with the magical beauty salve. Could I do any less than share it with Medusa, who, you must admit, had suffered long and had a great need for the properties of the salve? Now how can Athena be angry with me? Medusa endured the punishment for centuries. I'm sure wise Athena can judge the measure of the gorgon's suffering. Why should her punishment continue? To dwell on the past would be less than wise—and I'm sure Athena sees no necessity for that."

Hermes watched Mirza with a grin. "Well said, My Lady," he agreed. "You are as clever verbally as you are in other ways. I can see that having you on Olympus is going to prove to be quite entertaining. I was planning on delivering my message and running off in search of some excitement.

Your arrival, however, may engender more adventure than that hide-bound band of old fuddy-duddies cares for."

"Have you the power to take us there with you?"

"Of course. There is one little problem . . . "

"That is?" Jarl put in. No matter how interesting the conversation was, he wanted to get on with the matter of the Shadowlord. Saving Lealor and the Bright One were his only two priorities. He would feel much better when he started the preliminary steps to curb the power of the Shadowlord.

Hermes shifted his attention to Jarl from Mirza. For a moment, Jarl felt very much like an ant at a picnic.

"What is the problem?" Mirza asked impatiently.

"I am not commanded to take you two with me, only to tell you to come to the meeting place of the gods . . . " Hermes considered the situation.

"Oh, come," Mirza said. "Are you not the god of gamblers? Are you not willing to trust to chance and take us with you?"

"Well said. Well said. I admit that what you say is true. With the possibility that Athena is angry or at least annoyed with you, is it worth bringing you unannounced before Zeus? I, naturally, will be on your side. We can count on Hera as well. Apollo will be glad to have help to straighten out our sun. I can't really speak for any of the others. You start your travels, and I'll just check back to make sure it's safe to bring you, then I'll return." Hermes stood, raised the caduceus, and disappeared in a flash. Literally.

"Well, now what? We don't seem to have made any progress there," Jarl said.

"Will Faf be popping in again?" Mirza looked at her thin sandals. They were not what she would have chosen for a long walk.

"Who knows?" Jarl's exasperation showed in his voice. "Too bad Hermes didn't leave us a little of that luck he's supposed to spread around. We have certainly had our share of unlucky happenings."

"What do you mean by that?" Mirza asked. "I thought you were pretty lucky to find me so fast."

The sun dimmed, brightened, and dimmed again.

"Do you know something about the Bright One that I don't?" He gazed skyward with his eyebrows raised. "Like, for instance, how long it is until Achaeasun goes nova?"

Mirza felt the strange rippling effect in her mind. What could it be? Was her trip through the flawed gate going to cause her permanent brain damage? She frowned at the thought.

"You may well frown." Jarl wiped his eyes tiredly. "You can't work magic for fear of offending the gods. Wyrd promised Hades not to help us until we actually face the Shadowlord. Lealor waits imprisoned in a casket. Faf is unreliable about arriving, and we can't be sure what kind of time frame we're got, before it's too late to stop the Shadowlord."

"We are in a pickle, aren't we?" Mirza laid her head on Jarl's shoulder.

"Did someone mention pickles?" a voice asked. "I'm quite hungry."

As Jarl started to turn, he and Mirza disappeared.

"Uh, oh!" said the little dragon, scratching his head. "How did they do that? Maybe it's time for a father and son talk." A large pop indicated a hurried departure.

CHAPTER TWENTY-FIVE

"Weird," said Seren, watching the oracle inhale the vapors from the opening in the floor.

"Wyrd rests, storing energy," Palemon said in a voice that raised the hairs on the back of Seren's neck.

"Lealor, our sister. Where is Lealor?" Argen asked.

"In a box."

"He isn't wasting any words, is he?" Seren looked skeptical. "I could have told us that!"

"That's the way an oracle works," Argen explained, trying to decide how to frame his next question.

"Where, exactly, is she?" Seren asked.

"In a box in the main audience hall of the Shadowlord's castle."

"Where is the castle?" Argen asked.

"On Atlan."

"Is Atlan another world?" Argen asked, hoping it was. If Lealor was on another world, she would be safe if this one blew up.

"Atlan is an island on Achaea." The voice of Palemon sounded dead, somehow. Both boys could hear the strangeness. It was as if the Palemon they knew, the kind old man, had left, and something or someone quite different inhabited his body.

"Can I rescue her?" Seren asked.

"You can retrieve the box. With help."

"Who will help me?" Seren asked.

"Call on the gods."

"Can you summon the gods for us?" Argen asked.

"They come not at mortal summoning," Palemon intoned.

"Oh, great!" Seren broke into the conversation.

Argen gave him his dirtiest look. "How then are we to get the help of the gods? How can we win their favor?"

"They come not at mortal summoning," Palemon repeated, "but they are here." With those words, Palemon fell from the stool.

Argen and Seren both rushed to help the old man up, but a luminous figure in a white robe materialized beside him. "Rise, faithful servant."

It was the most powerful voice the boys had ever heard in their lives. They couldn't have told what made them believe implicitly in the power of the figure, but there was no doubt of who was boss in the room.

Seren and Argen looked around them. A number of the luminous figures stood in a half-circle behind them.

Argen murmured, "Hera."

One of the beings smiled.

"Ares."

The well-muscled warrior set his spear on the floor sharply in answer.

"Artemis, the huntress."

Another silent smile.

"Athena, the grey-eyed."

A nod.

"Hephestus, master artificer."

The figure shifted slightly. The boys could see he was lame.

Seren looked in awe at the beautiful woman who stood next. He burst out, "I know her! Aphrodite!"

Seren felt a warm glow from the figure. It felt almost like a hug.

The next luminous figure stood with a small puddle of water beneath his feet. The air smelled faintly of seaweed.

"Poseidon, the Earth Shaker," Argen said.

"And I?" the hollow voice of Hades echoed in the room.

"Great Hades, Ruler of the Underworld."

Seren wondered where his brother found the courage to speak to the King of the Dead. In fact, he wondered how he found the courage to speak at all. The room was filled with power; he could almost feel the electricity in the air. He had always wanted to meet a Bright One, because they were reputed to be the most powerful creatures on this plane of being. After seeing the gods, Seren decided to give up his wish. This was about as much as he could handle.

Palemon stood beside the awesome figure of the silver-haired god.

"Father Zeus," Argen concluded. If anyone could save Lealor, it was this group. In fact, any one of them could probably transfer Lealor, box and all, to this place with a raised eyebrow. A light sweat covered Argen's forehead. If only Seren didn't put his foot in it. He understood Faf's worry about being turned into a coralberry crumpet now. He and Seren could become grains of sand on the beach, for all these magnificent beings might care.

"We heard," Zeus said.

Argen felt relief. The tone of voice was mighty, but not unfriendly. Perhaps the gods would help them.

"Let us destroy this Shadowlord, brothers," Poseidon said.

'Not without a battle, surely," Ares said.

Hades looked at the God of War. Argen was very glad he had not received that look.

"Yes. He deserves severe punishment," Zeus said.

"Impertinent mortal." Hera's cool tones made Seren feel as if he was standing in a draft.

"I agree," Athena said.

"That's a first," Hera said. Argen stifled a smile. So the old tales about the infighting among the gods were true!

"Are we not all forgetting about the innocent maiden in the box?" Artemis said. "I would not have one of my creatures trapped so."

"Bring the box," Hera commanded.

"I will," answered Aphrodite. She raised her hand in a commanding gesture, but nothing happened.

"Well?" Athena asked.

"Gods, the box is strangely heavy. It refuses to come at my command." A slight frown marred her perfect visage, before she remembered about wrinkles and ceased.

Seren looked stunned. What kind of force did the Shadowlord have at his disposal to thwart the wishes of a goddess?

"Let me try," said Hera. After a few seconds, her face fell.

"I shall bring the box," Ares said. At his command, a short buzzing noise sounded. He winced. "It bit me!" He pouted.

"No, it only resisted your command," Zeus said. "Let us play no more.

All lend your will. Let us show those upstart mortals the power of the immortal gods! At my command," he said, looking at the luminous figures around the room. "Now!"

The surge of force reminded Argen of an electrical storm. His skin crawled. He wanted this to be a bad dream so he could wake up. He glanced at his brother. Seren stood calmly, but Argen knew his brother very well. He could see the pounding of his pulse at his throat where his open-necked shirt lay unbuttoned.

The box appeared in the room, first as a shimmering outline, then in reality. Seren hurried up and looked within. "Yes," he said. "She's in there, all right."

"We thank you all," Argen said, half-afraid of what Seren might blurt out in his happiness.

"May I open the box?" Seren asked, surprising Argen. Maybe Seren did understand the danger of alienating the gods.

"If you can," Zeus said.

Seren took hold of the handle and tugged, but the lid remained immovable. The gods watched silently as he tried.

"Argen, come here and give me a hand," he commanded.

The combined efforts of both boys did not budge the lid.

"What's the matter? The sphinx only flipped the lid down, Soladon told me," he explained to Argen.

"Then why can't we open it?" Argen asked reasonably.

"A strange force—what you humans would call magic—binds the box from within and without," Zeus explained.

From within, we understand, Nyct said, speaking for the first time.

"Ah," said Zeus. "Do I not recognize the form of my old friend Wyrd?"

We are the children of Wyrd, created to protect these three young ones, Soladon continued. *We know that she locked the box with dragon magic from the inside.*

Myst is willing to release her magic, mighty Zeus, Nyct said, *but she does not know where the second spell came from. Since it intended no harm, and was meant to protect, she did not even know it was there until Argen and Seren tried to open the box.*

"It is the outer force that holds the box immobile. Is one of you responsible?" Zeus asked.

"Lovely as she is, I did not bespell the box," Aphrodite said.

"Although I rejoice that the little maiden is unharmed, it is not my will which holds the lid shut," Artemis said. She pulled an arrow from her quiver. "Shall I shoot at the lock?"

Zeus smiled. "No. Pure force is not the answer. What we need is the magical herb, long gone from Achaea, called moley."

"We have lots of that on Realm," Seren said.

"Yes, on Realm, but we are here, and have no way to get any," Argen reminded his brother. Argen felt frustrated. "I bet anything she's got a pocket that's full of the stuff, seeds and all," he said, kicking the heavy box with his foot.

The small thud of a book falling from a pocket was his only answer.

"By the Bright Ones," Seren said, "Couldn't you even come here without a book to read?"

Palemon said softly, "The youth seeks wisdom."

Seren bent down to pick up the book. "Hey, look. Something fell out."

Argen snatched it from the floor. "It's the twig I stuck inside to mark my place before I started my adventure with Kiron the Centaur."

"It's moley," Seren said jubilantly. He grabbed it from his brother and handed it to Zeus. "Is this what you need?"

The other gods gathered round to touch it.

"Link with me and the magical moley," Zeus commanded. "We will shatter the spell together."

Beware, sister, Nyct called out.

Protect Lealor as you were bid, Soladon advised.

Myst's head shot up at an indignant angle. It was as if she said, I know what to do.

Seren and Argen privately worried at the idea of their sister at the nexus of the force that the gods commanded. There was nothing for it now but to hope that Myst knew what she was doing.

The room filled with a strange green glow as the gods used the moley to focus their powers on the lock. With a small ping, it flew to pieces. The lid raised of its own accord at the will of the gods.

At a nod from Zeus, the boys went to the side of the box.

Argen called softly, "Lealor, are you all right?"

Lealor's chest rose and fell, but there was no answer.

Seren said loudly, "Wake up, Lealor!" It was the same tone he used when she didn't get up in the morning for school.

Lealor's eyes fluttered. Her small hand rubbed across her eyes. "Do I have to?" she asked Argen. "I was having the most wonderful dream about a sphinx . . . "

Then she noticed the faces around her. "Where am I? This isn't my bedroom on Realm."

"Don't be afraid. We're here to protect you," Seren said, just as he always did when he thought she was scared.

"Okay," she said, sitting up. "I'm not scared, am I, Argen? Not with the two bravest brothers in the whole world to protect me."

The adults in the room hid their amusement as best they could. The little maiden was unharmed.

"Now that item is complete," Athena said, "should we not do something about our sun?"

Hermes sped through the door. "Oh, Zeus, I have done as you commanded and watched Jarl and Mirza. They are free, having turned Medusa into an ally, and can come at your command."

"All is well, then." Zeus raised his hand and pointed to a spot on the floor where no one stood. A strange shimmer, like the heat on an asphalt road, began to form. Within seconds, Mirza and Jarl stood in the room.

"Faf?" Jarl said.

"No, dear, the immortal gods of Achaea," Mirza corrected him. "Look, they have saved Lealor for us!"

Jarl strode across the room and lifted Lealor from the box. She clung to him tightly.

"We are greatly in your debt," Mirza told the gods, addressing her words to Zeus. Her happiness at being reunited with her family was almost palpable.

A soft, silvery glow formed in the center of the room. Both gods and mortals looked at it in wonder.

"Is there a god missing?" Seren hissed to his brother.

"There's a bunch, so don't ask me. I don't know everything," Argen whispered back.

As they watched, the silver light slowly coalesced into the slender figure of a woman. It was the Lady, Mirza's special benefactress.

Mirza smiled. "You are most welcome here, my Lady."

"I thank you." Then she turned to Zeus. "O, Zeus, I greet you in the name of the Old Ones."

Zeus astounded Seren and Argen by inclining his head in greeting.

"What happening of great moment has caused you to appear before us, O, Silver Watcher?"

"Two things. First, you broke my spell on the casket, which alerted me to your involvement and Oron's growing anger. You were but young when first you knew Oron, Guardian of the Bright Ones' children."

"I remember him well. He wanted to destroy mortal man many times, but we stood as their protectors," Zeus said.

"Oron is vastly angered by the disturbance of the Bright One in Achaeasun," the Lady informed them all.

"Let him be! What business is it of his?" Ares said.

Zeus gave him a look that Argen wished he could learn to use on Seren when he was being especially exasperating.

The Lady answered, "If there is more disturbance to the Bright One, Oron has sworn to cast this world and Realm into the Black Universe!" Jarl held Lealor more tightly. Mirza moved to his side. The twins stood awed by the pallor on the faces of the gods.

"This Oron must be some powerful guy," Seren whispered to Argen.

Argen swallowed and nodded. He had a much better idea of the power such a feat would require than did his brother. The term 'guy' seemed ludicrous for so mighty a being. Not for the first time, Argen wished this was all a dream so he could wake up.

"You have little time to act. We who favor men have done all we can to restrain Oron. Now, unless you act in concert, you will disappear from this universe forever!"

"All of us?" Poseidon asked.

The Lady nodded. "Mortals and gods, Wyrd and his children."

Lealor wriggled and Jarl set her on the floor. She approached the Lady and looked up. The Lady raised her hand and placed it on her head. A shower of silvery motes bathed Lealor from head to foot.

"Oh," Lealor breathed softly. "And am I to help, too?"

"Yes, my child."

The Silver Watcher sketched an ancient sign of blessing over them all and faded into an argent haze which the breeze blew away.

"Surely not the children," Mirza burst out.

Yesss, Wyrd answered. *The Shadowlord is more powerful than any mortal has ever been before. Every hour that passes increases his strength, for he is tapping Achaeasun for power. It is his drain on the sun that causes the dimming. I fear the Bright One cannot last long under such a strain.*

CHAPTER TWENTY-SIX

The Shadowlord stood in his workroom, putting the finishing touches on a strange collection of wires. "There, now. That corrected Mirza's officious meddling. The power of Achaeasun is mine for the taking." Soon, very soon, he would create a gate that the Old Ones had considered impossible. He allowed himself a small feeling of satisfaction. All the years of sacrifice had been worth it. Those who thought him unfit to wield the power of the gates would bow before him. Perhaps he would destroy the Old Ones' gates, leaving his gates as the only access between worlds. His grandiose plans were interrupted by a knock on the door.

"Come in," the Shadowlord commanded.

His voice sounded so pleasant that it frightened the messenger who had been present when the genial tones of the Shadowlord ordered unspeakable magical acts performed. He, however, found himself committed to delivering the message, so he opened the door and spoke when commanded by the Shadowlord.

"O, Great One, a kraken has come to the undersea gate and we believe it wishes to speak with you."

The wizard moved to the door, saying nothing. The messenger hastily stepped back. There was something strange about being in close proximity to the Shadowlord. Whatever the sensation was, it went far beyond simple fear. Some of the workers swore the hair on their necks stood up when they approached too closely. The messenger heaved a sigh of relief as he exited the room. He, at least, had escaped the wrath of his master.

Far beneath the magical tower where the Shadowlord worked his arcane spells lay the seagate entrance to Atlan. In the past it had allowed whole ships to pass inside the walls of the fortress. With the arrival of the Shadowlord, however, stranger visitors than the ships of those from the far reaches of the sea entered silently and left, bearing various commissions from the master of the fortress.

The guards were all gathered near the door with weapons at the ready. They saluted as they moved aside to allow their master passage. The surface of the water was calm and inky black. Here and there the golden light of torches glimmered on the water, but many were close to burning out.

At the Shadowlord's command, the neglected torches sprang to new light, seemingly burning the very air that surrounded them. The wizard turned to his men and commanded, "Bring me two prisoners." Then he turned his back to them and faced the dark waters.

Those who watched later swore that the wizard listened and spoke softly to the water itself. No sign of the giant sea creature was evident. When the soldiers arrived with the two prisoners, the Shadowlord gestured for them to hurl the wretches into the water. That one of the prisoners was fair and female made no difference in his command. The soldiers hesitated, knowing what lay in wait beneath the surface. The Shadowlord made a sweeping motion of his hand. Lightning crackled, forcing the two hapless humans into the dark sea. The soldiers watched as the waters writhed and turned. Each imagined the horror of what must be happening beneath the waves. One young soldier turned a pale green, visible even beneath the light of the torches. His commander put a steadying hand on his shoulder, as if to warn him that the sea could hold three as easily as two.

After a time the movement ceased. The slap of the water against the stony walls of the manmade cavern stretched the courage of the soldiers to the breaking point. One veteran made up his mind to retire should he survive whatever was to happen next. As they watched, a giant eye slowly rose until it lay upon the surface. It filled the watery area.

Undaunted, the Shadowlord commanded, "Show!" and the eye of the kraken became a mirror of events the monster had witnessed. Thus the Shadowlord saw the joyous reunion of Mirza and Jarl, the visit of Hermes, and the departure of Mirza and Jarl. For a second, it was as if the heartbeat of the world stopped. The soldiers cringed from the anger of their master.

His raised hand gathered power from the air and cast it in the form of a fireball at the eye of the watery messenger. The vitreous fluid of the eye seethed, forming steam that carried the strong odor of sea wrack. The very stones of the fortress trembled. A miniature seaquake disrupted the area, dislodging stones, as the huge beast withdrew from the wrath of the incensed mage.

"How dare she escape!" The voice of the Shadowlord filled the area as if Stentor himself spoke. Stones loosed by the passage of the monster fell into the water, propelled by the sound waves the voice of the foiled lord created. A crack of lightning hurt the eyes of the terrified soldiers who watched helplessly, fearing their doom would be next. When a few blinks had restored their eyes, they looked in vain for the Shadowlord. He had disappeared.

The frustrated mage reappeared in the audience hall. The strong smell of ozone alerted the guards. One of them opened the door to check the room. The Shadowlord vaporized him before he could even ask if everything was all right. The door slammed in the face of the remaining guard.

The Shadowlord picked up the container that held the green liquid that would turn Lealor into a monster. With the speed of a striking bushmaster, he glided to the curtain that hid her box and disintegrated it with one wave of his hand. Nonplussed, he stared at the empty spot. Lealor and the casket were gone!

The guard outside the door did not repeat the error of the first. He stood at attention, jumping slightly as he heard the various crashes and tinkles of the Shadowlord's ire. Retorts flew from tables and crashed against the wall, spraying assorted contents all over the room. Some splashes ate the stones they hit; others ran down to the floor and writhed with pseudolife. Metal containers were squashed flat before disappearing, contents and all. Wood vanished in a puff of flame. The very air shimmered with the force the Shadowlord called upon, as he flew from one area of the room to another. The wizard who wanted to control the vast system of the Old Ones' gates could not control himself. The Shadowlord was throwing a tantrum.

After a time, the audience hall lay bare. Nothing remained but the walls, ceiling, and floor. At this point, the Shadowlord conjured a chair and sat. His sobs were too quiet for anyone to hear. Then a long period of silence fell. Finally the Shadowlord rose and faced the room. His mind, which had been overwhelmed by the force of his anger, began working once more.

Mirza was no longer his goal. He wanted Lealor. A child would be more malleable. Then the Shadowlord did something no one ever saw him do. He smiled. What better way to make Mirza pay than by taking her child?

They would see, he told himself. First he would locate Lealor . . .

"We must act quickly," Mirza said, hugging Lealor tightly.

"I'll shake the earth under Atlan," Poseidon offered.

"What will happen to the innocent humans who live near the shore? The tidal waves will kill many and destroy the fishing. You are as rash as ever," Athena told him.

"She is correct," Zeus said.

"What do you want us to do to help?" Jarl asked, not at all sorry that Zeus was to be in charge of the battle.

"First, we must move to the site," Zeus said. "Poseidon, raise up a promontory where we may stand and see the Island of Atlan, but not be on it."

"I obey, brother," Poseidon said.

"Now we must travel there," Zeus said.

"Won't that take too long?" Seren asked before he was aware he spoke out loud.

"No, child. I will take us." With those words, the walls of the room disappeared.

They stood upon an up thrust of rock on the coast. In the distance, a dark spot upon the blue water, lay the island where the Shadowlord made his headquarters.

Zeus turned to Jarl. "Your child is safe from the Shadowlord. Are you willing to help us in repayment?"

Mirza looked at Zeus. His question surprised her. The gods asked for their help? How could that be?

"You may well wonder how it can be that we need your aid. In our arrogance—" Zeus looked at the other gods "—all of us ignored the danger to our sun. It has been many centuries since anything threatened the peace of Achaea. We came to believe that never again would evil lodge here, on our world. When we chose to return home from Earth all those centuries ago, we swore not to advance man further, to allow him to live peacefully, without the growth that brought the beginning of science and the end of magic to Earth. That result was a surprise, and not desirable. Why, mankind even denied our existence once he embraced science."

"We have kept our vow," Athena said as the others added words of agreement to her statement.

"What do you know of the Shadowlord, this upstart mortal who somehow developed such power?"

Zeus naturally looked to Jarl for information. Mirza held her tongue. They would turn to her if Jarl could not furnish the facts they needed.

"He is a powerful sorcerer. He seeks power over others without counting the cost. Both my wife and my daughter have been his prisoners. He uses a mixture of machines and magic. Realm was the first place he tried to gain control of a gate. Now he not only seeks to be able to travel from place to place, but also from time to time. Isn't that right, Mirza?"

"Yes. He calls his gate a universal gate. If he should succeed, there is no place and no time that will be safe from him."

"Oh, Mother," Lealor said, standing as close to the edge of the promontory as she could. "Feel the pretty light!"

In the wink of an eye, a long, golden cone of force arrowed across the waves and homed in on Myst. In that brief instant, Mirza intuitively sensed the danger to her child, but quick as she was, Lealor and Myst vanished before their eyes.

"The little maiden," Artemis gasped.

"Gone!" said Hermes, stamping his foot in anger.

"How dare he!" Hera said, her regal eyes widened in shock.

"Because he can," Zeus answered her, "and his powers appear to be greater than ours."

Mirza turned to Jarl, who placed his arm around her shoulders.

"We're not going to let the Shadowlord get away with that, are we, Father?" Seren asked. He couldn't believe there was any situation his father could not handle with the assistance of Wyrd.

"Not if we can help it, son," Jarl answered.

"Now we have no time to waste," Mirza told Zeus urgently. "He knows I am working against him, and he promised he would enchant Lealor with an evil potion that will slowly turn her into a monster. We must not give him time to do that."

"Mortal woman, we will plan carefully," Zeus began.

Then the sun dimmed again. It was a bare outline in the sky. The darkness was greater than that of a total eclipse. The gods themselves stared in wonder at the sight.

Wyrd's voice hissed painfully through their minds. *Mirza is right*, he said. *The Shadowlord is now at the most crucial point in his manipulations. If he can succeed in channeling the power he has amassed, the sun and the Bright One within will release all his power at once in one great explosion which the Shadowlord hopes to form into a gate.*

"How do you know this?" Athena asked.

Because he has been studying my notes, which I thought were destroyed all those centuries ago. There was sadness in Wyrd's voice.

"Why weren't they at the library at Realmgate?" Argen asked.

I hid them at Fellkeep, deep within the earth under the castle, ensorcelled with the strongest magics at my command.

"He found them?" Mirza asked.

Wyrd nodded. The sun became even dimmer. *He may have too much power now for me to contain him*, Wyrd said, *Yet I must make the effort. Goodbye, Jarl, my friend.*

With these words, Wyrd uncoiled from Jarl's wrist and flew toward the island. As he flew, he grew larger and larger, until he was bigger than the island itself.

Jarl, Mirza and the children stared. Jarl tried to understand how a creature that huge could have coiled about his wrist for so many years. He hadn't known the immensity of the being who had voluntarily chosen to make himself a servant of an ordinary mortal.

Not ordinary, Jarl, Wyrd spoke within Jarl's mind. *You have the potential to become what I am over the centuries of life that I have granted you.*

"Centuries?" Jarl repeated.

Ask my children, Wyrd's mental voice grew until it commanded all who stood on the rock. *Form into a circle of power, hand in hand. I will endeavor to send Lealor to you.*

CHAPTER TWENTY-SEVEN

On the island, Lealor stood before the Shadowlord, firmly held between two guards. She looked at him, wide-eyed. "Why did you bring me here?" she asked.

"You are to help me, since your mother declined," the Shadowlord told her.

"I won't," Lealor said at her most stubborn. "You can't make me," she added for good measure.

"You certainly are your mother's daughter," the Shadowlord commented.

"What an odd thing to say. Of course I'm my mother's daughter," Lealor said, not understanding. "Tell these nasty men to let me go," she commanded imperiously, stamping her foot. "They're hurting me."

The door swung open and a harried man rushed into the room. "Master, we have a problem with—"

"I know," the Shadowlord said, already on his way out of the room. "I'll return shortly to deal with you, miss," he told Lealor over his shoulder.

As soon as the door swung shut behind them, Lealor shifted into dragon form. Her captors were so astounded, they let her free. She turned to face them, blowing fire in their direction. They turned and fled the room.

"Good," Lealor said, with no small satisfaction. "Now, what can I do to spoil the Shadowlord's plans?"

A red light blinked atop a mass of wires. Lealor scattered the wires with one blow of her talons. An intricate group of candles that burned on a table caught her attention next. One hot breath, and the candles melted. She charred an open book and many of the papers which lay out as if the Shadowlord studied them. Feeling she was getting into the spirit of the thing, she swung her tail and brought down two tables holding retorts and vials. The weak sunlight illuminated a metallic device in the corner. Lealor sensed power there, so she approached warily. The cone pointed straight up. She exhaled on it. Several of the small wires at the top drooped. The sunlight seemed a little brighter, so she drew back, inhaled, and prepared to incinerate the entire contraption. It was difficult holding a dragon shape and burning things. Her flame was almost nonexistent, but she tried. A few more wires drooped. She was almost ready to charge the corner and risk the power, when the Shadowlord entered the room.

"You little monster!" he said in a voice that gave Lealor goose bumps under her scales.

Lealor agreed; he was right. A dragon was a kind of monster, she supposed.

With a wave of his hand, he returned her to human form. Then he stood over her, radiating anger. "If ever again you attempt to turn yourself into another form than the one that is honestly yours, you will stay in that form forever. Do you understand?"

Lealor understood. Even though it was fun to take the shape of other things, there was no other form she preferred to her own. Her heart beat fast.

"Well? the Shadowlord thundered.

"Yes, I understand," Lealor said.

"Now, you must promise not to try to shape-shift again, for even I cannot remove the spell I have laid on you," he said.

"I promise," Lealor said.

"You must never tell anyone else about this, either," he went on inexorably.

"I promise," the frightened Lealor told him.

"Sit," the Shadowlord commanded.

"May I sit by the window?"

"Yes, but do not be so foolish as to try to escape. A sheer drop to the sea lies below."

"That was nice of you to care," Lealor said.

"You would be of no use to me dead. You do not yet realize it, but you have a marvelous gift."

"A gift? Where is it?" Lealor looked around the room.

"Where all the important gifts are, inside you."

'Inside me?" Lealor cocked her head like a little sparrow.

"When you are around magic, you steal bits and snippets for yourself."

"I do not!"

The Shadowlord chuckled, a rusty sound. "Well, then, let us say your gift is to gather extra bits of magic and add them to your magical store."

"Why are you so mean all the time?" Lealor asked.

"Mean, do you call it?" The Shadowlord glanced at the girl before returning to his work. He was trying to replace the delicate wires she had ruined.

"Yes," Lealor replied, undaunted. "When you were nice and let me sit by the window, I could see how pretty you could be."

"Pretty?" The Shadowlord gave a thin laugh.

"You don't laugh enough, either. When you do that, it lightens you."

"Child, I am the same grey old man I've been for as long as I can remember."

"No, I don't think you are a man. Or if you are, you surely are different from all the others I met on Earth and Realm," she told him. "Inside, you're half sparkly and half dim. You know, shadowy." A smile lit her face. "I bet that's why they call you the Shadowlord!" Lealor was proud of herself. She felt she had figured out the riddle of his name.

"Humph, sparkly, indeed. There's not a spark of light about me."

"Oh, no, Shadowlord. You're wrong."

The sorcerer turned to her and held out his hand. He pulled back his robe so she could see it clearly. His skin was old, wrinkled, and covered with age spots. "See, child, there are no sparkles there. So long as I can remember, I have been old and ugly."

"No," Lealor insisted. "I can feel inside you somehow. Inside, you are half sparkly and half shadows. When you were little, you didn't have all those wrinkles and funny brown spots, I bet."

"I don't remember," he said gruffly.

Lealor sat quietly, deep in thought. Then she said, "I know what must have happened! When you were just a little, little baby, someone must have magicked you into an old man. No wonder you're so unhappy. My mother says when we're unhappy, we like to see others miserable, so we mustn't let ourselves be grumpy."

"Enough!" The Shadowlord commanded, returning to his work.

"When you talked with me, you were getting more and more sparkly," Lealor insisted.

"Enough! Or I shall—"

Lealor gasped. The Shadowlord kept working feverishly, and did not turn again. He thought he had frightened her into stillness with his partial threat, but Lealor was not looking at him. She was watching the form of Wyrd grow larger as he approached the island. She sat quite still and gazed.

When Wyrd's magic pulled her through the window and hurled her onto the promontory, she shuddered as first fear, and then surprise washed over her.

"Oh, Mother," she said, safe in Mirza's arms. Then Mirza firmly put her to one side. "We are all holding hands to call power to help Wyrd," her mother told her. "You must be part of the circle."

"All right." Lealor happily stood between her mother and Artemis, who smiled down at her.

A little of the light had returned to the sun, but it was still dark enough to look at without hurting the eyes.

The oddly assorted bunch of gods, mortals, and children stood and waited for Wyrd's next command.

CHAPTER TWENTY-EIGHT

Wyrd hovered above the island, blocking out the light of the pale sun. He could feel the power of the sun being drawn down to Atlan through his body. His dragon sensory perception searched the building for the wizard, even as he broadcast a warning to the people of Atlan. If they heeded him, they would escape. When he finally became aware of the Shadowlord's whereabouts, he made a discovery. The girl-child had been right. The being all had assumed to be a mortal was not. He was the Bright One that Wyrd had searched for after his experiment had failed so many centuries before. Wyrd felt a pang at the thought of how the young Bright One must have suffered, hiding all these centuries as a decrepit old human. If only he had thought to check the Shadowlord when they battled on Realm! His search over the long years, with no clue to prove the Bright One's survival, had made him careless. He no longer expected to find the Bright One whose sun-nest he had made uninhabitable. At last he could right the wrong he had committed by telling the Shadowlord who he really was.

Wyrd sent out tendrils of thought and spoke gently to the flawed Bright One the humans knew as the Shadowlord. He tried to reason with him. *The child is right, you know.*

"Right about what?" the Shadowlord replied, making a few delicate adjustments to his apparatus.

You are not a man, Wyrd said.

"That's what everyone has always said. No one wanted me as part of their group."

I mean that you are a Bright One.

The Shadowlord laughed. "A Bright One, indeed. Why, then, do I stand here, old and misshapen?"

Because you were flawed when I tried the experiment you are trying now, Wyrd told him.

"Lies, all lies," the Shadowlord said. "If I were a Bright One, I'd throw every world I could into the Black Universe!"

Why? Wyrd asked, trying to understand the warped creature that stood before him.

"Because of the centuries I have spent like this!"

What are a few centuries compared to millennia? Wyrd asked.

"Lies!" The Shadowlord almost howled the word. "You think to make me stop or falter so that those overgrown gods can help the Koenigs save the Bright One in Achaeasun."

"Do not twist that last wire," Wyrd warned.

The Shadowlord reached out defiantly and adjusted the last small wire. Before he could even begin the chant to liberate the power, a fine humming began.

Back on the promontory, those in the circle, at Wyrd's command, channeled their power into the rapidly disappearing sun. Then, with no further warning from Wyrd, a vast shimmering area began to grow where the island rested in the sea.

Sweat formed on Jarl's brow. Mirza gritted her teeth. Lealor's grave frown of concentration showed her participation. Seren and Argen held hands even tighter.

The sorrowful voice of Zeus said, "We have no more power to give. Look!"

Out on the water, a great gate was forming. Through it the watchers could see scenes of life on many worlds, a kaleidoscope of shapes and events, swirling too fast to make coherent sense.

"Try harder, everyone," Mirza called in desperation. "We must help Wyrd!"

Jarl remembered calling heroes to fight the Shadowlord on Realm. Wyrd said he had powers of his own. So Jarl decided to try to call the mightiest hero he could think of—Paul Bunyan—to their aid. Jarl concentrated on the magic and the great woodsman appeared in the center of their circle.

"Hey, Jarl," his great voice boomed in greeting. "What did you call me for?"

"Paul, I want you to join in this circle and help call up power for Wyrd to tap. Come next to me and I'll let you in."

"Sorry, Jarl. My buddies and me won't be of any help in this battle. Now, if you needed someone to bash a few heads, why, I'm your man, but this heavy thinking isn't anything I do well."

Jarl received Paul's words with despair. He hadn't stopped to think that this was a mental, not a physical battle. All the heroes who helped on Realm were physical types. Paul was right.

Mirza squeezed Jarl's hand in sympathy. She understood what he attempted. She wished they could call on the wyverns for help, but she knew they would never leave Realm. This wasn't their fight.

"Can I go now, Jarl?" Paul asked.

Jarl nodded, and Paul faded from sight. They would have to fight the Shadowlord with the magic power on Achaea—and they had it all through the presence of the gods. He knew that all the power at their command was barely maintaining Wyrd. When Wyrd needed more power, as he was sure to do, they would fail.

Young Faf popped in. "Oh, is this a game?" When he attempted to enter the circle, he fell to the ground with a thud. He was, after all a young dragon, in spite of his size. The young dragon's arrival was a hindrance, rather than a help, because his plight distracted Seren. Jarl could almost feel the power level fall.

"Where is Faf?" Fafnoddle roared as he arrived, hot on his son's trail. He took one look around and joined the circle. "Shadowlord, eh?" He uttered, before concentrating and adding to the power being hoarded for Wyrd.

"Maybe you'd better check on First Egg, Faf," Mirza said.

"Later," Faf growled. "If we succeed in defeating the Shadowlord, we'll have all the time in Achaea to help him. If not—" Faf rippled his scales in the dragonly equivalent of a shrug.

If the prone form had been one of his children, Jarl knew he would not have been so calm. Dragons really were cold-blooded creatures, he decided.

Jarl assessed the power now present and calculated how much would be needed to assist Wyrd. Even with Faf's selfless help, they were still far short of success. Gods, humans, and dragon knew they would fail. There was no further power supply to call upon. The white faces of the gods and humans showed the strain.

Tears rolled down Lealor's face. Seren looked surprised. He had never considered that his father and Wyrd could fail. Argen looked years older than his age. He, too, understood they would be defeated.

Suddenly, a tremendous river of force poured into each of them. It was almost painful in its intensity. With a tremendous explosion, the gate flew apart. Wyrd spread his giant wings over the island in an effort to isolate the effects of the Shadowlord's magic. The second explosion was even louder. Wyrd, the Island of Atlan, and everything on it disappeared in a flash.

"Oh, my goodness," Lealor said, recovering her voice.

"Wow!" Seren added enthusiastically.

"Did we really defeat the Shadowlord?" Argen asked Hades as he dropped his hand.

"Yes," Hades answered. "My halls just filled with the newly arrived. I must go." He gave them a small bow and disappeared.

"We thank you," Zeus intoned.

"Was the Shadowlord really destroyed this time?" Mirza asked hopefully.

"Well, if not, it will take him some time to get up to more mischief, although Wyrd appears to be gone for good. The essence of his life form disappeared in the explosion," replied Zeus.

"If we destroyed the Shadowlord, Wyrd's demise would not be so painful," whispered Jarl. "The Shadowlord and Wyrd—both destroyed."

"Not the Shadowlord, Father," Lealor contradicted. "He went all silvery and slid through the gate as it disappeared."

"How do you know that?" Zeus asked.

"Well, sometimes I can see inside people. He was all sparkles and shadows usually, but when all that power poured through us, he used it to change somehow."

"What I would like to know is where that river of power came from," Mirza said to try and change the subject to ease the despair Jarl showed on his face.

It was me, a mental voice blasted in to the minds of everyone.

Lealor put her hands over her ears. Seren and Argen made faces. The mind shout made everyone most uncomfortable.

"Easy there. We hear you," Jarl said.

"Don't deafen us. It hurts our heads," Mirza explained.

I'm sorry, a quieter thought reached them.

"Who are you?" Lealor asked.

"Yes, who are you?" Mirza echoed her daughter's question.

You know. You saw me a lullaby.

"Sang," Mirza corrected automatically.

Well, then you sang me a lullaby and made those bad things stop squeezing me so tight. I'm Sweet Baloo.

"Sweet Baloo?" Mirza gasped.

"Who is Sweet Baloo?" Jarl asked.

"It must be the infant Bright One," Mirza said.

Can I come out and play?

"Not yet," Jarl said.

Pretty please?

"No," Zeus said firmly.

Everyone felt the sob.

"Where did he learn to speak?" Jarl asked.

"Probably from me," Mirza told him. "All during my stay here, I've felt watched. Sometimes I'd have an odd riffling feeling in my mind. I guessed it had something to do with the mess the gate was in when I arrived. I never thought it was the Bright One."

My name's Sweet Baloo, a petulant thought reached them.

"Now it is time for you to go to sleep," Mirza said. "You have many more years to sleep and grow. When you wake up the next time, you'll find yourself more stable and then you may come out to play—but only if you are very careful not to hurt Achaea and all the things upon it," Mirza warned.

But—

"Promise me," Mirza said.

Oh, I promise.

"Then good night," Mirza told Baloo.

Good night.

The faint tingles of power that had swirled around them ceased and Achaeasun returned to its former brightness. Then Mirza knew the Bright One had returned to sleep.

"Mother," Argen said, "You'd better check on Lealor."

Lealor stood in the center of a group of goddesses, explaining. "So then I simply melted the funny wires. I'd have done more, but I got tired, and the Shadowlord came and made me stop."

"You are a brave child," Aphrodite said, "therefore, I give you the gift of beauty."

"I," said Artemis, "give you the gifts of nature and the ability to understand animals."

"I give the gift of hearth and home," Hera said.

"I give wisdom," Athena said.

Before another goddess could say anything, Mirza stopped them. "Please," she said, "she is such a little girl. These gifts are much too grand for a child. She will not be able to grow up normally if so many wonderful presents mask her true potential."

"We cannot take back our gifts," Hera said.

"Could you sort of see she comes into them gradually, then?"

"We might manage that," Athena said.

"Done," said Aphrodite.

"Thank you all," Mirza said, relieved that she had not needed a major confrontation with the goddesses to make them see sense.

A sound caused Mirza to turn. Fafnoddle had revived his son, who seemed fine.

"Have I missed all the fun? I still haven't found where you store your gold. Seren, have you seen any gold?" he asked, looking around for his friend.

"By what right do you visit here on Achaea and look for gold without our permission?" Zeus asked.

Argen shuddered. One dragon wisecrack and they might all become coralberry crumpets.

"I didn't know I had to have permission," Young Faf said. "My friends were here and Uncle Jarl and Aunty Mirza—"

The gods had a sense of humor, but they tried to hide their smiles at the idea of a mortal being related to a dragon. Zeus was getting ready to speak again when an additional sauroid form materialized on the promontory.

"Is this how you study dragon history?" she hissed, ignoring everyone but her son.

"Study history? Why, Mother, we made history right here," Young Faf told her.

"I was hard put to trace you," she scolded. "If it hadn't been for your father following you, I might never have reached wherever this is."

"Achaea," Seren put in, anxious to help his friend.

"First Egg," Ebony said, ignoring Seren and shaking an admonitory talon, "how dare you sneak away from your studies!"

"Not First Egg, Mother," Young Faf said in a conciliatory tone, noticing the haze of smoke coming from his irate parent's nostrils.

"Ebony, my dear, we have enough problems without—" Fafnoddle told his mate.

"Oh, Ebony, how glad I am to see you!" Mirza said, effectively distracting the black dragon from her wrath.

"Is this where you have been? Ebony asked, looking around her in some disdain.

"It was the Shadowlord again. Your son and his father have been a great help."

"Well, that puts a different complexion on matters," Ebony snorted, partially mollified.

"Allow me to present you to the gods who rule Achaea," Mirza said.

Ebony nodded her head, as did Fafnoddle. "I remember that a great-aunt of mine, thrice removed, knew some of you," she said regally.

"Will any more of you be dropping through the skies?" Zeus asked.

"No, this is all of us," Ebony said.

Jarl sighed in relief. Old Fafnir wouldn't be coming, then. He asked Fafnoddle quietly, "Where's your father?"

"Oh, he's keeping watch on our egg, taking my turn. She's due to hatch soon," the dragon told him.

A ponderous thump punctuated his remark. There at the edge of the rocks sat the old dragon, Fafnir.

"Father, what in the name of dragon lore are you doing here?"

"Hi, Granddragon," said Young Faf.

"Fafnir! Why have you come? It's dangerous for you at your age!" Ebony said.

"Expected me to sit home like some overgrown lizard, watching that egg of yours hatch, did you? I'll have you know I was flaming cities and carrying off young maidens when you weren't even a twinkle in your father's eye!" the old saurian roared.

"My egg! Is it hatching?"

"Why else would I come rushing off at my age?" Fafnir growled.

"I must go!"

Mirza raised a hand. "Please, may Lealor and I come with you? I'm not too sure how safe the gate may be."

Seren sprang on young Faf's back and let out a shouted, "Wahoo! Dragonback, the only way to travel!"

Mirza said, "Jarl, do you think letting Faf take him is a good idea?"

"Don't fuss," Jarl said. "He brought both boys, but I wouldn't listen when he tried to tell me."

Argen was considering his choices. He remembered all too well his last ride. Which dragon would he have to ride?

"Come on, boy. I'll take you," the old dragon said.

Argen climbed on Old Fafnir's back. "My name's Argen," he said.

"Don't you worry. I'll have you back on Realm in no time," Fafnir promised.

"Don't just stand there, Jarl," Fafnoddle said. "We don't want to be last off." He lowered his head so Jarl could walk up his neck to a seat on his shoulders.

"Last off, is it?" Old Fafnir said. "Humph!" With no further warning he—and Argen—disappeared.

"Oh, dear," Mirza said as Ebony puffed them out of sight.

"It wasn't very fair of Fafnir to take off without giving us a chance, was it?" Seren said.

"Well, no, but it will do him good to win for once," Faf said, lowering his head politely to the thunderstruck gods the humans had totally forgotten. "I'll not visit again without permission, sir," he told Zeus.

"Well, see that you don't," Zeus told him.

"Ta ta, then!" Faf said jauntily and disappeared with Seren.

Jarl sat on Fafnoddle's shoulders among the gods looking down at them. "I thank you for your aid and hospitality. I'm sorry that the Shadowlord intruded upon you."

Athena spoke. "No, it has been most diverting. Your little maiden was right, you know. He whom you call the Shadowlord did disappear, and he is more than man—a great deal more."

The other gods and goddesses nodded their agreement.

"We'll keep watch for him," Jarl promised.

"Our world has fared ill because of him. The Island of Atlan is gone and with it, all the islands that were like it, and the allies of the Shadowlord's forbidden magic."

"What do you mean, and 'all the islands that were like it?'"

"He had recruited many times and many places, islands like this on our sister worlds on this plane," Zeus explained.

"Atlan—Atlantis?" Jarl breathed.

"On your world so was this island called," Athena told him.

"The power—" Jarl said.

"Tremendous, as we saw," Hera said.

"This Lord of Shadows," Artemis said, "will try his evil again, I fear. You will protect the little maiden, will you not? I have a great fondness for her. Give her this as a token of my friendship," Artemis said, taking an arrowhead from a small pouch and tossing it up to Jarl.

Jarl bowed his head.

Zeus said, "You have our leave to go."

"Thank you—" Jarl began, but he never finished, for Fafnoddle said, "I need to be at home!" and transported them back to Realm.

"Interesting creatures, aren't they?" Hermes commented.

"Yes, in the centuries, I had forgotten," Athena said.

"Perhaps it would be worth watching them—" Hera began, then stopped and amended her statement at the look Zeus gave her—"without their knowledge, of course."

"No interference, mind," Zeus said.

The others all agreed.

"Leave!" Zeus commanded.

The forms of the gods and goddesses dimmed and disappeared.

Zeus stood alone. "Mortals . . . worth watching indeed . . . " he murmured as he formed a bag of gold. A wave of his hand sent it to a cave on Realm where a single coin was hidden. Then he, too, returned to Olympus.

EPILOGUE

Jarl sat alone in the dark hours of the night. No matter how hard he tried, he could not get over missing Wyrd. Everyone else was back to normal—or as normal as they ever got, but Jarl missed the companionship of his magic bracelet. The silver moon shone through a window. The peace of the night was no consolation.

Jarl jumped as he heard a slight thump. Rory sat at the foot of the moonbeams, irate as usual.

"Meddlesome old witches," he muttered. "How is an innocent leprechaun going to get any rest? Dragon young and ancient crones bedamned!" The curse lost some of its force because Rory was rubbing his backside. Evidently, moonbeam riding resulted in a hard landing.

"Rory?" Jarl asked, unable to believe his eyes.

"How many other leprechauns do you know well enough to call friend?" Rory said irascibly.

"Why are you here now? It must be two or three in the morning."

"That's it exactly. I'm here because you're not in bed, sleepin' like any decent human."

Jarl stared. In all the years he had known Rory the leprechaun had never made him a visit without a reason.

"I'm here with a message."

"A message?"

"Wyrd says—"

"You have heard from Wyrd?"

"Not me. Cibby. Wyrd says not to be sittin' around mopin'. There are things you have to do, but he will see you again, after you have learned to do without him."

"If it were only that easy." Jarl ran his hand through his bronze hair.

"You think you've got problems?" Rory spluttered. "I just wish I knew how to get rid of a pesky dragon."

"What are you talking about? You're not making any sense."

"Young Fafnir, that's who. A leprechaun's gold isn't safe anywhere on Realm. Ever since Zeus sent him that bag of gold—what a waste! A dragon just hoards gold, you know."

"I know," Jarl answered sympathetically. "What do leprechauns do with it?"

"Why, any fool knows that! They buy sweepstakes tickets, my boy."

"Oh," Jarl said weakly.

"To get back to my problem—that overgrown lizard has been poppin' in and out and round about tryin' to find out where I've got my gold hidden! It's all I can do to stay one pop ahead of him. Not a moment's peace. If it weren't for my leprechaun perceptions, he might catch me. Then where'd I be? A pauper in my declinin' years, that's where. Any moment he'll be here, I suppose. So I'd better be goin'. Remember now, stop mopin'—grow!"

A whisker from Rory's brilliant red beard made a soft spronging sound.

"There's my alarm. Faf's near my gold again! He'll not get away with it!" With these words, Rory disappeared.

"Poor Rory," Mirza said, spoiling the sympathy of her tone with a silvery laugh as she entered the room. She held out her hand to her husband. "Come, am I not enough?"

Jarl rose from his chair. As he took Mirza's hand, he realized she and the children were more than enough to replace Wyrd until they should meet again as promised.

Wyrd stretched luxuriously. It was a relief to be able to extend himself fully. His mammoth form almost completely covered the huge ledge before his cave. He watched the shimmering energy forms that advanced across the broad valley below his mountain. He knew they came to greet him, for he had been absent a long time. He doubted he would ever become a part of the human plane again, now that his children shared his fascination for humankind. In time, they would help Jarl's children as he had helped Jarl. They had done well for being so young. Myst, especially, had succeeded in spite of the handicap Lealor had caused her to have. Wyrd's eyes clouded as he envisioned the future. Yes, when Lealor faced the Shadowlord for the final time, she would need all the help she could summon.

DRAGON'S QUEEN

PROLOGUE

Silver moonbeams illuminated the snakelike form as it moved over Lealor's wrist. Its glassy body reflected the moon-blanched colors of the covers. Lealor's red hair fanned dark against her pale features. In the air outside the tower window, a vortex of shadows whirled, then stabilized into the form of a huge dragon.

Wyrd had returned to Realm.

Lealor slept on, even as the voice of the huge saurian hissed, "Come, daughter." Silently, the glassine form of Myst, the only daughter of Wyrd, sped for the open window and freedom from her charge.

"Am I free to go now, Father?" she asked.

"Are you so eager to stop protecting this Jarl-child?" Wyrd replied, amused that Myst chose to stay the same miniature size she wore when she disguised herself as a bracelet on the arm of Lealor. Myst hovered before her father's face as if she were a hummingbird.

Wyrd softly exhaled a jet of flame, turning Myst into a pink figure as she basked in the glow of his affection.

"How nice," she said. "I often feel the chill clasped around Lealor's wrist."

"Is the task you have set yourself so onerous, youngling?" Wyrd's voice spoke the dragon mindtongue directly to his daughter.

"It was not exactly my wish to be born a talisman," Myst gently reminded Wyrd.

"Yes that is so. Twenty years ago I created you and your brothers to act as guardians to the children of my companion, Jarl Koenig."

Myst wondered if her father was at last becoming old. She had never known him to meander on about things they both remembered well. Still, she gave him her respectful attention.

"The peril of the Shadowlord hung close to those Jarl cared for. The guardian bracelets freed his human mind to address the rescue of his wife and to confront the Shadowlord once again." Wyrd lowered his head in shame.

"Do not feel sadness, father. You could not destroy the Shadowlord without endangering those you had sworn to protect—including that terrible infant, Baloo, the Bright One. Does the small Bright One still rest within Achaeasun?"

A look of surprise was an impossibility for a dragon, but Wyrd's eyes widened at Myst's question.

"Several times word has come that he is restless. Then Mirza rides Ebony, her dragon friend, to Achaea and sings a song to lull Baloo to sleep once more."

"I have been remiss. I should have watched Baloo's development."

"Oh, he is fine. It has been five years since he last woke."

"Have you decided whether to stay with Lealor, daughter?"

"Yes, father. I will stay. Until your search for the Shadowlord is successful, I must remain. My brothers are still companioning Seren and Argen. I would not leave my charge until I am certain she is safe. It would shame me. My teasing brothers would remind me of it for thousands of years."

Wyrd looked carefully at Myst. It saddened him that, of all his children, she must be the one to be unable to speak to her charge. If only Lealor had not refused Myst when he had offered her the protection of a talisman! Watching Lealor grow up, Wyrd had learned much more about humanity. Had he understood human children, he would not have invoked dragonlaw to silence his daughter. Both Myst and Lealor had suffered from his prideful command that Myst must never speak to Lealor, only protect her from magic. He nodded, and spread his wings, preparing to leave.

"Don't forget," Myst reminded him, "that Lealor and I are leaving Realm to act as gatewatchers for a year."

Wyrd nodded, wondering if he should tell Myst of his strong intuition that danger awaited Lealor. He abandoned the impulse, and rose into the air, fading into nothingness as he reached the top towers of the building. He comforted himself with the thought that facing peril built character in the young.

CHAPTER ONE

Lealor stood within the mosaic of the star, smiling at those who had come to see her go to her first post as gatewarden on another world.

The courtyard of the Gate had never been large and now it appeared full to bursting with well-wishers. Lealor looked around, nodding to the silent wavers and calling soft goodbyes to her more vocal friends. Her father looked agitated, but her mother was calming him. Andronan and Cibby, her Realmish great-grandparents, radiated their pride in their only great-granddaughter. Andronan's white robes and beard shone in the early morning sunshine while Cibby's hair, gathered in a generous bun, had a few wisps flying away in the faint breeze.

Be good, my dear, Cibby mindspoke a last admonition.

"Of course." Lealor answered her aloud. Lealor's grandparents had disappeared through a gate malfunction years before she was born, so she thought of her great-grandmother as the grandmother she had never seen. Lealor found it almost impossible to believe that Cibby was an extremely powerful witch. She had taught Lealor to use her own talents in spite of looking like an old woods-granny. *I promise, grandma*, she offered mentally, as she had when she was a little girl.

Lealor's momentary reversion to her childhood amused Cibby. She hoped being gatewarden far from home would satisfy her great-grand-daughter's yearning for independence. There was something so lovable about Lealor that Cibby, like the rest of those who had known Lealor since she was a child, sometimes treated her as if she were much younger than her actual age. She waved a hand and Lealor heard a faint plop as a magic provender bag joined her pile of baggage.

"Thanks, Gram," Lealor said.

"It's in case you get hungry for some goodies while you're away." Cibby gave her a wink.

"Don't forget me while you're gone," Fafleen, the young dragoness, called from her perch on the balcony. She fluffed her purple-blue scales and blew a delicate smoke ring. Her long, narrow tail twitched slightly from the excitement of seeing her friend leave.

"I won't," Lealor promised, feeling relieved that Fafleen's parents and brother had not come. Tons of dragon flesh hovering over Lealor had never appealed to her. Then too, young Fafnir, Fafleen's big brother, still had to gain control of his flame that shot out in all directions in moments of excitement. Lealor's mother, Mirza, threw a protection spell around everyone if Faf forgot to aim the flare upward. Still, it was nice not to have to worry.

Sure you wouldn't be wantin' a little company, bein' away so far and all? Rory, her self-appointed leprechaun guardian, wheedled mentally. The silver buckles on his shoes glinted from a recent polish, although his brown pants and jacket were the same as ever.

"Why, I'll be back before you can miss me. After all, it's only for one year. What could go wrong in such a short period of time? You know how easy it is to be a gatewarden. My parents wouldn't let me do anything dangerous. Don't be afraid for my welfare." Lealor smiled gently at her oldest and best friend. She knew she would miss his swift popping in and out to see her.

"Afraid? Now how could you think such a lackwit thing! Have you already forgotten everything I've taught you?" Rory drew himself up to his full two-foot height and stood, arms akimbo, a veritable classic picture of an outraged leprechaun.

"Sorry." Lealor apologized. "I know leprechauns are never afraid of anything, no matter what. It's the first thing I learned from you."

"Humph," Rory snorted. "It's gettin' too big for your mortal britches you are." Mollified, he waved before he winked out.

Lealor caught his last thought. *Too many mortals around for comfort. They'll be tryin' to steal my pot o' gold next.*

No one but Cibby and Lealor noticed the tiny teardrop that shimmered in the air before it splashed wetly on the ground.

Now you will be careful, won't you? Mirza mindcalled softly, knowing Lealor would never forgive her if she spoke out loud.

Bright One's sake, mother, I'm all grown up. I even graduated from vet school back home on Earth before I volunteered for this job. You know how short-handed we are since Argen discovered the **Book of Gates** *that lists the worlds that have portals and how to activate them.* Lealor's thoughts were sharp.

Try to be patient with your mother, Jarl warned his headstrong daughter privately in mindspeech, putting his arm around Mirza's shoulders. *No matter how you grow, you'll always be her baby.*

Yes, Dad. I'll try. Lealor added to herself that being out from under Mirza's smother love was one of the big attractions of being a gatewarden on Aurora. She was sorry to be leaving her family. Still, she couldn't help the flame of happiness that wavered inside at the thought of being an adult, on her own—at last.

"Are you sure you have everything you'll need?" Mirza asked, eyeing the huge pile of baggage piled at her daughter's feet.

Remembering her father's warning, Lealor stifled her first thought. "Of course, Mother. What could we possibly have forgotten? You insisted on my taking the magic medikit in case of injury, a ton of books to read, preserved rations, perishable items . . . " Lealor ticked things off on her fingers as she named them. She planned to give them to the poor as soon as she reached Aurora. *If they have any poor there,* Lealor thought to herself. A temple complex housed the gate on Aurora. Being in the care of the temple guardians was preferable to staying on Realm where everyone looked out for her welfare.

"I'm well provisioned," she told her anxious parent. Her foot tapped on the lumpy pack nudging her knees. "I even have that full-room decorator's setup you insisted I take in case I don't like my room or get tired of the way it looks." She smiled at her parent reassuringly. Lealor thought to herself that once she was off Realm on her own she'd never use half the supplies her mother had gathered for her. After all, Aurora was a civilized world. It was not one of the places that had dropped out of the gate system over the centuries since the Old Ones maintained the gates.

That was her mother. Prepared for fire, flood, and famine when it came to her children. She was bad enough with Seren and Argen. They were men, so Mirza finally gave in to their pleadings and let them do their own packing. Doing their own packing was just one of the things Lealor envied her brothers.

Seren and Argen had made friends of their talisman bracelets. Lealor never stopped regretting her refusal of Myst, the glassine dragon who curled around her wrist, forever silent as the dragon Wyrd had commanded. Seeing the daily interchange between her brothers and their dragon bracelets had rubbed a raw spot inside Lealor. Her quick refusal had branded her as headstrong forever. Bright Ones in a basket, she had been only seven when she told the magical dragon, Wyrd, that she didn't want a bossy bracelet. In all his centuries of life, no being had ever said *no* to a request from him. A cold chill went over Lealor as she remembered the event in detail. She'd been lucky. A dragonmage like Wyrd had the power to transform her permanently into anything he chose, or blast her to the Black Universe. Her father's face had looked so odd. That was her only clue to her danger. Thank the All she'd remained silent when Wyrd commanded his daughter to protect Lealor, but never speak.

Are you ready to go? Lealor asked Myst who gently clung to her wrist, silent as usual.

Over the years, the human and the dragon had worked out a primitive form of wordless communication. Myst reprimanded with a flick of her tail, making Lealor feel like she was being snapped with a rubber band. If Lealor framed a question, Myst could nod yes or no. Myst could tighten on Lealor's wrist to warn her of danger or suggest she should consider her actions more carefully. Lealor finally understood what a weak substitute they had, unlike the exchange of ideas Myst's brothers, Soladon and Nyct, shared with their charges.

Lealor had visited Aurora once before pledging to be gatewarden, so it wasn't difficult for her to begin visualizing where she wanted to go.

A loud thump disturbed her.

"Hey, you weren't going without giving me a chance to say goodbye, were you?" The rather pudgy young dragon that joined his sister Fafleen on the balcony peered down at her with one saucer-sized eye only inches from Lealor's nose. He curled his tail around his blocky golden body and used the end of it to polish some tarnish from his scales.

Lealor ignored the dagger-sized teeth in the dragon's huge head. "Er, of course not—" Lealor began to lie politely, wishing dragons used mouth-wash as she got a whiff of partially digested kippers, of which the dragon was fond. Privately she swore to herself, using the kind of oaths her parents didn't suspect she knew. If that wasn't just her luck! Trust Fafnir II, the densewit, to arrive just as she was about to leave.

"I'd have been here sooner, but grandfather takes a while to get ready to pop in, as it were," the dragon explained.

Fafleen gave a ladylike snort at her brother's remark, carefully directing the tiny flame skyward.

Lealor hid her smile. Talk about each child in a family being different! Probably young Faf would never get the **Dragon Chronicles** learned. His younger sister, Fafleen, had already memorized the hundreds of books that composed the history of dragons and their laws. Young Faf collected gold like a pack rat and hid it, under the fond delusion that his parents didn't know about it. His hoard was stashed in a dozen caves on Realm, waiting for his parents to declare him an adult. It was his hard luck that his mother was a stickler for the old ways and insisted on his continuing his studies. Faf would be older than his grandfather, Old Fafnir, before his mother would see him as an adult.

"Grandpa's coming," Fafleen warned in embarrassment.

Both Mirza and Jarl got ready to intervene in case the old dragon misjudged his landing space. Cibby, ever practical, wasted no time in putting a protective spell over everyone in the courtyard.

Bless her, Lealor thought, grandmother was always certain that safe was better than sorry. Lealor doubted the old dragon would notice the spell. He was really ancient.

A vast form shimmered over the crowd, drifted slowly to the spire, then slid to the balcony. It groaned with the weight of three dragons. Fafleen firmly anchored her grandfather's tail with one claw, and hid a pained look.

Lealor could sympathize with her. She knew how Fafleen hated to look foolish, and a brother and grandfather like hers almost guaranteed it.

Mirza cast a stabilizing spell over the building a second before her dragon friend Ebony, the mother of Fafleen and Fafnir, arrived with Fafnoddle, the young dragons' father.

The senior Fafnirs noticed the stress on the balcony and sensibly perched on a nearby pair of towers.

"We won't stay and hold you up, Lealor," the sensible Ebony promised, noticing Old Fafnir shedding scales on the courtyard. She levitated a small box into Lealor's hand. "A little remembrance," the dragon said.

"Why, thank you." Lealor felt guilty for wishing at first that the dragons had not come. They were her parents' and brothers' friends. They had fought the Shadowlord in the final battle on Realm, years before Lealor was born. If it had not been for their aid, perhaps every being on Realm—and who knew where else—would be the slaves of the master-mage.

Lealor had only met the Shadowlord once, and she still suffered silently from his curse. His words rang in her ears still: "If ever you attempt to turn yourself into another form than the one that is honestly yours, you will stay in that form forever."

She shivered, hoping no one would notice the goose bumps that rose on her arms as she remembered. The Shadowlord had also sworn her to secrecy. Lealor had not dared to break her promise in all the years since her vow. Although she had studied magic and searched for the counterspell, she had never found it. At first, Cibby and Mirza had commented on the young girl's refusal to shape-shift. As time passed, they decided shapeshifting was just a phase Lealor had gone through and then outgrown. They didn't know how often Lealor longed to allow her flesh to flow into another pattern. Nor had they any idea of how many times she cried herself to sleep. She felt imprisoned in the human form she was doomed to retain against her shapeshifting instincts.

She wrenched herself back into the present. Old Fafnir was offering her a small gold coin with his unsteady claws. Fafleen had a tight grip on his tail to keep him from falling headfirst into the courtyard. So great was the weight of the old dragon that Young Faf had coiled his tail around a projection on the balcony and sat on his sister's tail to keep her from joining the crowd of humans below.

"Thank you, sir," Lealor said, pocketing the tiny coin. She noted that as Fafnoddle waved a taloned digit, the coin grew much heavier. She smiled, thanking him for increasing the size of the coin with his magic. "Thank you all for coming, but now I must go to begin my adventure," Lealor told them.

Sunward, Baloo, the infant Bright One, heard her words. He had escaped from Achaeasun, his home, and was visiting Realm without anyone's knowledge. People and dragons interested him. He knew from past experience that if Mirza discovered he had left his sun-nest she would take him back and sing him to sleep. He wished Mirza would stop treating him like a baby. He liked Lealor and she had mentioned adventures, hadn't she? Baloo had also overheard her thought about wanting to break the Shadowlord's spell so she could shape-shift. Hmmm, Baloo thought. "I fix!" He whispered to himself, twisting the gate's power before he whisked himself to a far place only he knew how to find.

Before she could finish her sentence or visualize her destination, Lealor disappeared.

"Malfunction!" Fafleen hissed angrily as she flew into the powerfield before it dispersed.

Ebony hissed her distress, while Mirza stood in shocked silence. People and dragons stood as if spellbound, watching Fafleen also disappear. Everyone had experienced the strange ripple of energy as Lealor and Fafleen vanished. All the gate users knew they were in deep trouble. What they didn't know was what to do next.

An empty feeling settled over them as it dawned on them that Lealor and Fafleen were gone—perhaps forever.

CHAPTER TWO

Lealor looked around at the trees that ringed the cracked tiles of the gate mosaic on which she stood.

Fafleen narrowly missed her as she, too, landed on the faded patterns of the gate.

"Fafleen! What are you doing here?"

The dragon hissed in distress. "Wouldn't it be better to question what we are both doing here?" Fafleen carefully pushed aside a few of the bundles that formed Lealor's baggage. She settled herself more comfortably while she waited for an answer from her friend.

"Where is here would be an even better question," Lealor suggested.

"I wasn't the one visualizing the destination, you know," Fafleen replied, with some justification.

"Surely you don't think I had anything to do with this!" Lealor gestured to their surroundings.

"Well, the possibility had entered my mind." The dragon uncurled her tail carefully, letting it stretch into the trees that surrounded the gate.

"Believe me, I had nothing to do with arriving here." Lealor looked around them. "You don't recognize where we are, do you?"

"Egg's sake, no." Fafleen shook her head in a human way.

"How did you get here?" Lealor queried. "The last I knew, you were draped over the balcony, bidding me dragon's departure."

"At last a sensible question! Quite sensible," the dragon approved. "I felt—" Here, Fafleen paused to reflect. After years of human contact, she still had difficulty sometimes in conveying her thoughts in human languages.

"Yes, go on," Lealor urged, looking up while the dragon stretched her head high as if fresh air might help her to find words to speak.

Fafleen lowered her head to Lealor's level. "It was something strange . . . Almost as if something . . . or someone . . . interfered with the gate power. I swear I heard the thought 'I fix.' That's impossible. It reminded me of something . . . "

"Yes, and I know who!" Lealor interjected.

"You do?" Fafleen's eyes grew to dinner-plate size.

"Did you ever get to meet my mother's pet Bright One?" Lealor asked. She didn't stop to think how incongruous it was to call a being with the potential of wielding the tremendous power of a Bright One a pet.

The dragon closed her eyes as an aid to remembering. "Baloo?"

Lealor nodded.

"Loot and plunder!" Fafleen burst out in imitation of her brother's colorful vocabulary.

In spite of their predicament, Lealor chuckled. She knew what a trial her unscholastic brother was to Fafleen, a born scholar like her mother. How insulted she would be to learn she sounded just like him.

The dragon lowered both eyelids and glared at her human companion. "I caught that thought!" she said.

"Now, Faffie." Lealor took a step backward and hoped she could placate the dragon before she was incinerated.

"Faffie, indeed." The dragon snorted a little fire, but skyward, to show she was mollified somewhat.

"I've been to visit Aurora and, believe me, this isn't it. Do you recognize this world from any of your studies?" Lealor looked around her as if she could see through the vegetation that formed an almost impenetrable barrier around the abandoned gate.

"Let me take a short flight to check out the area from the air," Fafleen said. "This isn't any place I ever read about, but maybe from the air I can see some landmark or something that would be helpful."

A cool breeze made Lealor shiver. "Unless the sun of this world rises in the west, it won't be long until nightfall. I'd like to find some shelter for the dark hours. Keep a watch for a cave or something close, will you?"

The dragon wasted no time in words, but raised her wings and then brought them down in one mighty gesture that pulled her into the air.

Lealor wished dragons would remember how fragile humans were as she struggled to stay upright in the draft of the dragon's first wingbeat. She felt lighter here than she did on Realm. Perhaps Faffie had startled herself with her easy ascension, Lealor thought charitably.

Following standard gate practice, Lealor lugged her baggage out of the path of any incoming traffic. It was one of the first things new gatewardens learned: Clear the gateway immediately. No sense in moving into the woods. It would only make it harder for the dragon to find her when she returned. Lealor piled up some packages to form a rough seat and collapsed gracefully on top, prepared for what might be a long wait. Nobody understood dragontime because their sense of time duration was very different from humankind's. Even her brother Seren, who might as well have been born a dragon himself, considering all the hours he spent with his dragonoid friends, didn't understand. He found himself occasionally taken aback by the dragon's idea of what a "little while" was.

Now that Lealor relaxed, she was more in tune with the world around her. She noticed the prickly feeling you get when someone is watching you. It would have been relatively easy for her to cast a spell to make the unseen visible. One of the things she had decided before she left Realm was that she would not use magic. Other people managed fine without any hocus-pocus, and there was no reason why she had to use her witchy powers. Now that she was here—and who knew how long it would take until she could return home—she might as well begin the way she had planned.

She looked at her wrist circled by Myst, her dragon guardian. She felt the familiar pang of regret. She was reasonably intelligent, she had the healing gift as well as an affinity for animals, and she looked exactly like her attractive mother. Why wasn't she satisfied with what she had instead of wanting more? She didn't begrudge her brothers their dragon-bracelet companions, but she did wish Myst might speak with her.

That wish paled in comparison to her desire to shapeshift. Denying her true nature was a constant ache. The Shadowlord's threat that any further shifting would become her permanent form had made her a quiet, thoughtful person, never able to be fully joyful.

Turning up on the wrong world was the start of an adventure. Lealor meant to stay long enough to find out what this world was like. Judging from the state of the gate, it was one of the worlds that had been "mislaid" during the years when humankind had learned to use the gates the Old

Ones had abandoned. It would be nice to be able to reintroduce a world to the gate system all by herself.

First, Lealor knew, she had to find some shelter for the night. If worst came to worst, she could stay here near the gate with Fafleen. Although the dragon was only half grown, it would take a pretty formidable beast to attack a dragon.

A white bird with brilliant ruby eyes flew by and perched on a branch near Lealor. It bobbed briefly and tipped its head, watching her, but she knew it wasn't the bird that made her feel that she was being observed. Without a second thought, she whistled a few notes and called the bird to her. It flew to her hand as if compelled.

"Don't be afraid, birdie." Lealor reached into her pocket and offered a few seeds in the palm of her hand. She had never outgrown her habit of carrying tidbits in her pockets for her animal friends.

When the bird finished eating, Lealor tossed it gently into the air and smiled as it flew away into the green forest.

Lealor felt the prickles again. Where was that secret watcher? Suddenly she knew. He was behind her! She turned quickly and caught a glimpse of a little man peeking from a nearby tree bole.

"Hello," Lealor said softly, working a little magical spell that made her speak the tongue of this world without thinking. Then she remembered she had promised herself not to use any magic. Her visitor reminded her of Rory, except he was larger. She didn't want to frighten him away. He probably knew all about the area. His information might be more helpful than anything Fafleen saw from the air.

A slight pinging noise preceded the appearance of the little man before her. "Human, I suppose," he muttered to himself as if Lealor wasn't sitting there right in front of him.

She nodded in polite acceptance of his evaluation.

"Well?" he asked sharply.

"Well, what?" Lealor queried in return.

"Humph!" The little man snorted. "Humans are a dangerous lot. Berdu, perhaps you'd better vanish before she tries to capture you."

"Oh, I wouldn't do that." Lealor felt distressed and it showed.

"Why not?" He put both hands on his hips and leaned forward until his nose was only inches from Lealor's own.

Lealor was glad she had remained seated. If she stood, she would tower over the man by two feet or more. "Because it wouldn't be kind," she replied.

"Kind!" The man jumped back a foot. "When, pray tell, was any human kind to old Berdu?"

"Are most of the people you meet here in this woods unkind humans?" Lealor became concerned. She didn't mind spending time among uncivilized people, but she drew the line at unkind barbarians. If humans were unkind, she needed a place to hide until she could figure out how to get home. Although, she admitted to herself, if she could lay hands on that terrible infant, Baloo the Bright One, she might give him a good spanking for delivering her here without so much as an if-you-wouldn't-mind. He might think her action unkind.

"Berdu is all alone. No humans are friends with him, so Berdu doesn't show himself to most humans." He looked at Lealor with piercing green eyes. "You—you seem different, somehow."

"How'd you get here?" He glanced around carefully, running a hand over his long white beard that only missed dragging on the ground by an inch or so. "Sitting here on the old star. Used to be a gate. Yes, Berdu remembers. Used to be a gate to faraway places a long time ago. Very long time ago. Humans forgot this gate. Berdu watches. None of his people come any more. Poor Berdu. Berdu . . . " He shook his head.

Obviously the little man was very old. Lealor felt sorry for him, but she understood he had lost the train of thought he had been following. She gently reminded him she was there by speaking. "My name is Lealor."

"Le-a-lor? Funny name for a wicked witch. Even for a pretty wicked witch."

"I am not wicked!" Lealor jumped up in her own defense without thinking what effect it might have on Berdu.

He promptly disappeared.

"Berdu! Where are you, Berdu?" Lealor called and turned around, searching for him.

"Oh, I'm still here, missy. I'll stay invisible until I find out what kind of a wicked witch you are."

Lealor longed to stamp her foot at Berdu's stubbornness, but she realized she had to convince him she didn't mean him any harm. "Berdu," she said, in the tones that always produced compliance from Rory, her leprechaun friend. "I'm lost. I don't know anyone here except you and you keep calling me wicked. Can't we be friends? I promise I'll never hurt you, or take anything from you that you don't want to give me, or lock you up, or . . . "

"Careful what you promise. Promise breakers come to a bad end." A shaking finger materialized to her left, but the rest of Berdu stayed invisible.

Lealor hid her smile. "Back where I come from, it's not considered polite to hold a conversation without being visible."

Berdu pinged into sight with his finger still waving an admonition. "Where I come from, young one, it's not considered polite to correct your elders. Why," Berdu said, with the first smile Lealor had seen on his face, "I bet you haven't even seen your third century!"

Lealor's laughter pealed out. "Sorry. You're right," she apologized. "Can we be friends?" She held out her hand and waited.

Berdu took a step forward and placed his warm hand in hers. "Agreed." Then he stepped back hastily. "No nasty witchy tricks. Promise?"

"Cross my heart." Lealor smiled at her new friend.

A cloud crossed the face of the descending sun, darkening the clearing where they stood. The darkness reminded Lealor of her need for a place to stay. Where was Fafleen?

"Berdu, is there anywhere around here where I can find shelter?"

"Not at my place!" Berdu sputtered. "Not big enough for a giant. Not big at all. Little! Hidden! My secret!" he ended belligerently.

"Of course, I wasn't suggesting you would take me in for the night. I'd just like some place safe to sleep. What if it rains?"

"Your ringlets will be stringlets!" Berdu chuckled. "Ringlets to stringlets. Magic!" He stopped, suddenly silent for a moment. "Never use magic. Calls trouble. The bigger the magic, the bigger the trouble—tiny little spells clutter up the place until they call . . . "

"Call who?" Lealor never knew when her friend was going to drop a piece of important information.

Berdu put a finger before his lips in a gesture that commanded silence. "Bad. Not to talk about. Abandoned cottage that way." He pointed with a gnarled finger. "Next to the river in the oak grove, used to be magic, but not anymore. Never, never, no more. Bad happened there long ago. A good place now."

"No one lives there now?" Lealor didn't want to get into any trouble with the local people if she could avoid it.

"Good people lived there, but all gone now. All gone because—"

The huge shadow that was Fafleen soared over them. Berdu looked up and vanished.

"He was getting to the really interesting part." Lealor fumed a little, but calmed herself as the dragon landed. It wasn't Fafleen's fault the little man was so apprehensive.

"There's a village several miles to the north," Fafleen announced. "Farther north it looks like there's a big city, but it's so far away I couldn't see it very clearly. I thought it was just as well if I didn't go flying over. You know how touchy some ignorant humans can be if they see a dragon aloft."

Dragons were all alike in some ways, Lealor thought to herself. It never occurred to them that they were lacking in tact. They blundered on, saying what they thought. Lealor wondered how dragons in stories got the reputation for double-dealing and deceit. All the dragons Lealor and her family knew were forthright to a fault. They said exactly what they thought and let the scales fall where they would.

"Yes, I know, Faffie. Did you see an abandoned cottage that way in a grove of oaks?"

"Lealor, just when I begin thinking of you as sensible—for a human, that is—you say or do something really stupid." The dragon fluffed her scales in exasperation.

"Sorry. Don't tell me. You couldn't see the cottage because it was under the trees? Right?

"Much better. Logical."

Lealor hoped the dragon wasn't going into one of her lady dragon liberation speeches. Every dragon she knew had some individual quirk. Old Fafnir was into loot and plunder. Ebony, Faffie's mother, was a rabid historian. Lealor heard her in her mind's ear, "Those who don't know the **Chronicles** are doomed to repeat the errors of the past."

Fafnoddle, Faffie's father, was both a mage and a gardener. What could anyone say about his son, young Faf, sometimes called First Egg? He was a dragon materialist. Not for him the glory of the past, the wisdom of his kind, or the magic his father took such delight in. All he ever thought about was gold and how he could get more. Fafleen was a scholar like her mother, but she had lived in the shadow of her brother's sparse intellectual accomplishments so long, it had warped her into a real dragon's libber.

"Well, I met someone called Berdu. You frightened him away, but before he left he told me there was an abandoned cottage over in that grove of oaks by the river." Lealor pointed to make sure the dragon knew which direction she meant.

"Yes, I know the grove you mean."

"Would you be willing to airlift my luggage over to the cottage?" Lealor looked at the sun. It was quite close to setting.

"Surely. You had better get started if you want to get there before dark. Human feet are never as rapid as dragon wings."

Lealor ignored Fafleen's smirk as she grabbed several of the largest bundles and took off for the grove. Left alone, Lealor lost no time in hurrying after her friend. Fafleen would have to make several trips, and Lealor wanted to be at the cottage before it got any darker.

She could make out an overgrown path in the deepening twilight. Fafleen passed her, going back for another load. She was flying rapidly. If she finished quickly she could settle in for the night herself. A few minutes later Lealor noticed her airborne friend flying back to the cottage. Lealor hurried on. She had quite a way to go and Fafleen's flight would last at least fifteen minutes, judging from her previous trip. She skirted a clump of bushes, hoping the path would continue on the other side. She looked at the sky. Stars were beginning to be visible. She stepped back on the path with relief, almost feeling her way along in the gathering darkness.

She stopped abruptly when she heard a noise ahead of her.

"Who—who's there?" she questioned, afraid to move from the path.

A deep growl that sounded very unfriendly answered her. It came from the path ahead, between her and the cottage she hoped to reach!

CHAPTER THREE

Lealor took a deep breath. The animal—she couldn't see what kind—sounded large. She sensed waves of pain. She had a natural rapport with animals, but this one was big and hurt. Even humans were hard to get along with when they were in pain. It was so dark she couldn't see what to do. So she stood there, calming herself. She knew animals could sense when people were afraid and nervous. Lealor worked hard to appear calm and to project friendliness. She said softly, "I won't hurt you." At the same time, she mindcalled Fafleen as loudly as she was able. Then she waited.

What do you want? Fafleen answered her mentally.

I need a little help, here, Lealor mindspoke calmly. The animal growled again. ***Now!*** Lealor mindcalled in what would have been a yell if she had been speaking. To heck with dignity, she thought to herself.

"How rude! It wasn't necessary to mindblast me, you know," Fafleen said conversationally from where she hovered above. "I started coming the minute you called and I was almost over you anyway."

"You could have told me that," Lealor said quietly. Thanks a bunch, she thought to herself. "We've got a hurt animal down here."

We have? How did I get involved in your do-good scheme? Fafleen's thought carried some resentment with it.

Let's not split hairs—Lealor began mentally.

"Rabbits? A good idea. I'll go hunting for some," Fafleen said enthusiastically.

"Don't be dense, Faffie," Lealor said. "That was a metaphor. I meant let's not argue over small things."

"I'd have said it was a pun—"

A low growl interrupted her.

"Fafleen von Fafnoddle, help me."

"What do you want me to do? That bear seems quite cross."

"Bear? Then you can see?"

"Of course, dear girl. After all, dragons could hardly live in caves without good night vision. Mother was always feeding me balanced meals so I'd grow up big and healthy. Naturally I can see."

"Well, bully for you," Lealor said. "Try to shine a little light down here, won't you?"

"Why didn't you use mage light? I know Grandma Cibby taught you how."

The last comment distracted Lealor enough to wonder why it didn't seem at all strange to her that Fafleen and her brother called Cibby, who really was Lealor's great-grandmother, grandma. She put her errant thoughts in order and said, "I didn't want to startle the bear. Remember, I can't see him."

"Are you sure you really want to bother with him? I could take care of him for you. He looks delicious."

"Fafleen! Shame on you."

"It's all your fault. All that talk about rabbits. It's well past mealtime and I'm starving. This baggage handling is hungry work."

"Hold on until we can get to the cottage. I'll feed you from the provender bag grandma gave me before we left."

"Promise?"

It was amazing how something as large as a dragon could sound like a human child. Lealor had a tendency to forget that, intelligent as Fafleen was, she was still almost a baby by dragon standards.

"Cross my heart," Lealor said gently. "Now, a little light, please."

A jet of flame illuminated the night sky above the girl and the bear. Then it went out.

"What happened, Faffie?"

"I'm just tired out. I'll try a little mage light." A soft green glow shone down on the bear.

"Much better. Thanks." Lealor approached the bear, wondering why he hadn't made a sound while the dragon hovered above them. He hadn't seemed like a coward and she didn't suppose he was able to mindspeak like the animals on Realm. For a moment she was afraid he was dead. Then she touched his head gently. He had fainted.

"He's out like a blown candle," Lealor said aloud.

"Then could I eat him?" Fafleen said hopefully.

"No, you can't." Lealor hid her exasperation. Now all she would hear was "I'm hungry" every ten minutes or so until she fed the dragon. She ran her hands over the bear's body, feeling for damage. His paw was curled under him. It was in a trap.

"Can you help me open this?" Lealor asked.

"Do I have to? It's made of iron. I hate the stuff," Fafleen grumbled.

"All right. Just get me a stick a couple of feet long about this big around." Lealor indicated the size with her hands.

"Then we'll eat?"

"As soon as you carry him to the cottage," replied Lealor.

Fafleen hissed her exasperation. "All right."

The light disappeared, leaving Lealor standing in the dark. The bear made a noise. She stooped beside him, running her hands over his head in a soothing gesture. "It'll be all right, bear. Lealor is going to help you get well. Don't you worry."

The light returned and a stick plunked beside Lealor, who jumped. "Fafleen! You could have warned me."

"How was I supposed to know you'd forget all about me? You didn't forget you promised to feed me, did you?"

"No, Faffie. I didn't." Lealor sighed. She was feeling tired and hungry herself. She rose and poked the stick at the trap several times until she felt the teeth loosen fractionally when she pushed down. Muttering a prayer that the trap and the bear wouldn't bite into her, she finally pried the trap open.

"Now, Faffie. Grab the bear and carry him to the cottage."

"He's so heavy—" Fafleen began.

"I'll put a levitation spell on him so he'll be easier to carry. Hurry. This trap may close again any minute."

The dragon clasped the bear in her talons and rose into the air. *All this nice, fresh meat*, she mindthought, flying off into the darkness.

"Don't you dare eat him!" Lealor called, letting the trap spring shut.

I promise. Fafleen reluctantly sent the thought.

Dragon's honor? Lealor mindspoke.

"Human blood and bones, Lealor." The dragon snorted.

"Fafleen, you know your mother would have your hide for an ill-bred remark like that. Promise me again and don't forget."

"Yes, I promise. Dragon's honor."

Lealor heaved a sigh of relief. Dragons were hard enough to manage at any time, but a hungry young dragon at night, when she felt exhausted herself, was the limit. Now if only she could shift into the form of a bird or anything that could travel faster than a human. She wanted to shape-shift so badly. For the thousandth or perhaps millionth time, she regretted her promise to the Shadowlord not to shift her shape. It wasn't as if she had a choice at the time. She had been only seven when he cast the spell that would keep her forever in any shape she shifted to. Sometimes she wondered if she shouldn't choose some shape and shift into it and have the whole sorry mess over. If she had to stay in some shape, she guessed she would prefer to be a dragon . . . then common sense came to her rescue.

She felt tired and worried. She hurried on, blundering down the path. Didn't this misbegotten world have a moon? A cold wind blew. Above, almost as if her thought were being answered, the clouds parted and pale-blue light shone along the path. She made much better time with the light. She slogged on through the underbrush.

Finally, just as Lealor was about to give up and call Fafleen to come to her, she got to the river. "Bright Ones give me strength," she muttered. "You'd know the cottage would be on the other side of the water." She looked around. No sign of any easy way over. She didn't want to use magic unless she absolutely had to and she knew she would dry out eventually. She took a deep breath, ready to plunge into the water. She put her foot out and felt herself grabbed by the back of her pants. Before she could even frame a thought or yell to Fafleen for protection, she was on the other side.

"Now can we eat?" Fafleen asked plaintively, dropping Lealor within a few inches of the ground so she landed with a thump.

"Bright Ones in a bucket!" Lealor said, making the phrase a curse. "Don't ever lift me like that without warning me, Fafleen."

"You wanted me to wait until you were soaked?" Fafleen asked. "Temper, temper. What do you suppose your mother would say if she caught that thought?" Fafleen shook her head in a surprisingly human gesture. "A little while ago, you were correcting the way I talked!" The dragon cocked her head and sat squarely in front of Lealor. "Don't I get an apology or thanks or anything?"

Lealor gritted her teeth and smiled politely. She wasn't able to see the expression on Fafleen's face, but she remembered dragons could see at night so she smiled. Fafleen moved to the side to allow Lealor to pass.

"You're welcome," Lealor replied, stamping her way to the cottage door. Damn dragon, she muttered to herself. Oh, dear, she was even more tired than she had thought. She knew the only reason people swore was an inadequate vocabulary. It was also ridiculous. She really didn't want anything bad to happen to Fafleen, who was probably her favorite dragon of them all.

She had to do something about being so exhausted. She had a bear to help, a dragon to feed, and a shelter to get ready before she could sleep. She could always start doing without magic tomorrow, she told herself. She lifted her arms in the moon's pale-blue light and willed moon magic into energy. It wasn't much, but it would help for a while.

She pushed the cottage door open. Adequate in size, but filthy, this room had not held anyone for years, yet it was still weatherproof. She entered, feeling acceptance. Now why would that be? A spell? Her witchy senses explored. Yes, an old spell protected the building. She had promised herself to manage without magic, but she was just too tired to clean tonight, when a wave of the hand would take care of everything. She'd definitely start not being a magic user tomorrow. With a gesture, the room sparkled. "Not bad," Lealor muttered to herself. "Good as grandma could do it, I bet."

"Now can we eat?" Fafleen asked, putting her head next to the doorway. She was too big to enter the cottage. "You didn't forget, did you? I'm awfully hungry."

"Can you find the magic provender bag?"

Fafleen turned her head for a second and then thrust the bag into the room, holding it by one talon. She knew only Lealor could make the bag work.

"That was fast," Lealor commented.

"I took the liberty of locating it while you were coming," the dragon admitted.

"What would you like for dinner?"

"Well, I'm kind of homesick. Do you suppose I could have eight or nine bushels of steakfruit?"

"Eight or nine bushels? Are you sure you can eat that much safely? I wouldn't want you to get sick tonight. One patient is at a time is enough."

"You don't want me to starve, do you? I'm still growing," the dragon explained.

Lealor couldn't help chuckling. Of all the problems she expected to have as a gatewarden, this was one she never could have foreseen.

"It's not funny," Fafleen said, looking injured. "I suppose I could break my word and eat the bear, but I did promise . . . "

"Just tip the bag up and the steakfruit will come out, Faffie."

Lealor could hear the steakfruit being chewed. She didn't bother watching. Dragons were never neat eaters. She didn't think anything could diminish her own appetite, but she wasn't taking any chances. Outside the door, she saw the magical package that would decorate a room. She brought it in, and wished for the cottage to be furnished just as it was before someone abandoned it. She made the proper magical wave of her hand. A brief puff followed. The room was rather rustic, but comfortable. Lealor didn't waste time looking around. She reestablished the levitation spell on the bear and pulled him gently into the room. She put him beside the hearth. Even her gentle pat didn't rouse him.

His huge skin hung loosely on his body. His nose was hot, too. "Dehydrated, I bet," Lealor muttered. She saw a pot on the other side of the hearth. "This could hold water." She carried the pot to the door and handed it to the dragon, who was still chewing vigorously. "Are you still eating?"

"It's not my fault," Fafleen protested. "Mother read about chewing your food thirty times and made me promise I'd eat correctly."

"That a good idea. While you're chewing, take this bucket to the river and fill it for me, please," requested Lealor.

"I'm still hungry."

"Take another bite, then, and get me the water while you're chewing."

"If I do, can I have dessert?"

"Yes, I promise."

"Anything I want?"

"Get me the water and you can have anything you want for dessert."

"Deal," the dragon said, dropping gobbets of partially masticated steakfruit from her mouth.

"Don't talk with your mouth full," Lealor admonished the dragon, who skimmed along the ground with the bucket in her talons. She returned in less than a minute.

Lealor poured some of the water into a dish for the bear to drink. The rest she set over the fire that had come into being when the cottage was bespelled.

"Lealor," the dragon called from the door.

"Yes? What do you want now?" Lealor checked the water in the pot. It wasn't hot enough to clean the bear's swollen paw.

"You promised," Fafleen reminded her.

"Promised?" Lealor said. Only a small part of her mind was on her conversation. She came out and picked up a bundle of linens her mother had insisted she take along. It was one of the things she thought she'd be able to give away when she reached her destination. Was there some universal law that mothers always had to be right? she wondered as the dragon handed her the magic bag.

"Dessert," Fafleen demanded.

"What would you like?" Lealor regretted her rash promise. She would bet an old dragon's hoard that Fafleen's dessert order would be unusual. Whatever the dragon asked for, she would grant the wish and hope Fafleen would never tell her mother what Lealor had fed her.

"Ten triple-layer chocolate cakes with double fudge frosting."

"On top of all you already ate?"

"I'm not through yet. I want a ring of smoked kippers on each one for topping." Fafleen could see Lealor was having second thought. "You promised!"

"All right. So I did. In the interests of saving you from a tummy ache, how about three cakes?"

"Seven," the dragon bargained.

"Five," Lealor countered.

"Done."

Lealor reached into the bag and pulled out the first cake.

"Just toss it here," the dragon ordered.

One by one, Lealor brought out the cakes and threw them into the air. Fafleen's long neck snaked out and her opened mouth caught every one. The dragon lifted her neck into the air like birds do after a drink of water and belched loudly.

"Fafleen!"

"I couldn't help it. I'm pretty full, you know."

"Whose fault is that?"

"Why, yours. My mother would never have let me eat that much at one time. She doesn't want me to get my full growth too fast."

"You didn't see fit to tell me that before I fed you," Lealor said. She made a mental note not to let the dragon's size make her forget her real age. "It's time for you to go to bed. Where do you plan to sleep tonight?"

"In that big oak tree over there. I'll stay close in case you need some help."

Lealor, who had been quite put out with Fafleen's gluttony up to this point, felt touched by her consideration. "Goodnight, Faffie," she said quietly.

"—Er, Lealor?" the dragon said. "Could I have one more thing? Then I'll go straight to sleep. Dragon's honor."

"More food?"

"Oh, no. I'm quite full now. I wouldn't want to stretch my stomach. Could you reach into the bag and get a teddy bear for me to sleep with—for tonight, 'cause I'm kinda homesick."

Lealor noticed that ordinarily the dragon spoke excellent English, but now that she felt tired she sounded like a little girl. "Of course," Lealor said, reaching into the bag and producing a huge pink teddy bear with a white bow around its neck.

"Thank you. Pink's my favorite color." Fafleen took the teddy bear and clutched it to her like any human child. "Goodnight," she said. Then she flew to the old oak. Leaves rustled. "Night again," the dragon whispered.

The gentle snore of the sleeping dragon drowned out Lealor's reply. "She really is an exhausted dragon," Lealor said to herself as she entered the cottage and shut the door. She could bring in the rest of her belongings the next morning.

Now, to clean the bear's paw. She turned and looked upward into two large, glaring eyes.

CHAPTER FOUR

The bear stood in the center of the room, reared to his full eight-foot height. He swayed, and his injured paw dangled limply before him. He opened his mouth to roar his displeasure.

Lealor made a warding gesture. She drew in a breath. The room had augmented her spell. It surprised her, but she felt the addition to her warding as a kindness. She was almost sure this cottage was what remained of a former gatekeeper's home. Since all keepers were trained in healing, this probably wasn't the first time the home increased a spell to help a healer work on an injured animal.

Lealor knew the bear did not like being trapped indoors, but he needed her skills. She sensed waves of pain from the furry, brown body. "All right, bear. Let's get this straight once and for all. I'm the doctor, you're the patient. As soon as you're well enough to leave, I'll let you, but for now, you need my help more than you need to get out of here."

The bear tipped his head to the side as if he was struggling to understand her. He swayed again and almost fell.

"Now, my foolish pooka, you stretch out here where I had you so I can tend that paw." As she spoke she put her hands on the bear and pushed him gently. The levitation spell had not entirely worn off, so he was easy to move. Soon she gently bullied him into his former position. She kept talking as she worked over the bear, as much to reassure him as to reassure herself.

"Pooka. That's what I'll call you, I guess."

The bear growled softly.

"You don't like Pooka? Do you have a better suggestion?"

The bear looked at her with pain-filled eyes.

Lealor rested one hand on the bear's head in sympathy. She offered him water and he lapped it weakly. "Well, Brownie seems a bit mundane and Bear Mountain is a little awkward. No," she said as she prepared a basin of warm water and the cloths to clean the wound. "Pooka sounds too small. I guess I'll just call you Pook."

"Now, this may hurt a little, so I'm going to cast a teensy spell to keep you from feeling much pain." Lealor sat on the floor beside the bear. She muttered and gestured, then took the bear's paw into her lap, which she had covered with a clean cloth.

The bear growled softly, as if warning her.

"Don't be such a baby. I haven't even started cleaning yet. I'll have to see how much damage you've done to yourself." Lealor kept on talking as she worked. She didn't expect the bear to understand her, but her talking did soothe him somehow. She mindtouched the wound. Festered. She cleaned it gently and started the healing process, imagining healthy flesh where the trap had left wounds. Her hands shook a little as she finished. She felt so tired. She cast herself into a light trance and checked the wound and the bear's whole leg. She sighed with relief. The bear's eyes looked at her with an almost human look of inquiry. "We were lucky. I got it before the infection spread."

The bear dropped his head in what almost seemed like a nod of agreement.

Exhausted, Lealor failed to notice the nod. Her hands added a healing powder and wrapped the paw. She had done this many times in the veterinary clinic on Earth where she had worked. Her body was on automatic. She fetched the bear a pill and coaxed him to take it. "Good bear, Pook," she congratulated him when she finished. "This is your water dish. Try not to tip it over. Now, you stay there until morning, you hear? I expect you'll be much better when you wake up tomorrow."

Lealor took a cup from the cupboard on the wall. She filled it with milk from the provender bag. Next, she reached in and retrieved an apple. She crunched away for a moment, considering the sleeping bear. It was an effort to chew. She was simply too tired to eat any more. She decided she would rest on the cot in the corner for a minute before checking on her patient again.

She set the provender bag in the corner and stretched out on the cover of the cot. It was small, but comfortable, Lealor thought briefly. "So tired," she murmured before she fell asleep.

The fire on the hearth flared briefly, blown by the tiny draft of air that accompanied the opening of the door. The moonlight fell across the floor, making a gigantic shadow of Lealor's visitor. The bear's eyes opened. He watched as the intruder entered the room and looked around. When the shadowy figure approached the sleeping Lealor, Pook limped silently until he was behind the figure.

The firelight illuminated the glassine form of Myst. The visitor showed an inordinate curiosity about the bracelet.

Pook waited, taking no action, until the intruder reached out to touch the bracelet. Before any contact, the bear's giant paw shot out, claws extended, and pulled the intruder away. Pook pushed the intruder down on the floor and stood over him with one paw above his chest. He rumbled softly.

Firelight flickered over Berdu's face. "You stupid bear," he whispered. "I wasn't going to hurt her or take anything. I was just curious, that's all."

Pook moved his paw so that it didn't threaten Berdu. He watched as the little man rose from the floor. When Berdu tried to approach Lealor for the second time, Pook positioned himself between them. He shook his head from side to side in an unmistakably negative gesture.

"Move, you hulking brute," Berdu whispered. "I want to take a better look at that bracelet."

Pook stood guard as immovable as a boulder. Berdu gestured him away, but the bear ignored him. The little man tried to walk around Pook, but the bear used his body to block Berdu.

"You fool! She's an obvious witch. You're not old enough to remember what happened the last time folks around here tried to use magic. Bad things. Evil. No place to hide. All changed. All gone. No more. Poor Berdu. The last, the very last . . . " Berdu shook his head. "Oh, dear. So bad. Alas. Power gone. All changed . . . " The little man stood, lost in memories of the past.

Pook used the time Berdu spent in reverie to push him gently to the door. When the door closed behind him, Pook positioned himself directly between it and Lealor, sighed, and slept.

Across the room on Lealor's wrist, Myst relaxed her vigilance a fraction so she could dragonnap through what remained of the night.

The moon shone brightly over the cottage as if to guard it from any shadow of evil. The forest itself rested, waiting for the first rays of the morning sun to gild the cottage.

Pook raised one sleepy eyelid when Lealor arose and fumbled her way around him to the door. Her fists rubbed her eyes. She stretched and yawned, outlined in light, unaware of the bear's watchful gaze.

"No different from home," she murmured to herself. "Mornings come too early as usual. How can anyone enjoy them if they're not awake?" She turned and saw the bear looking at her with his large brown eyes. "Oh, so you decided to stay! I left the door ajar so you could leave if you wanted to. I'll make us some breakfast after I wash up." She propped the door open with a chair before picking up her towel, washcloth, and soap. "You might want to go out too, this morning," she said pointedly. On the one hand, talking to the bear was probably a waste of time. On the other, she always talked to animals as if they could understand her. If nothing else, it soothed them.

Somehow, she felt as if this bear was different. His eyes seemed to hold human intelligence. The bear was quite handsome, for a bear. She could almost imagine the strong square jaw and soft brown eyes he would have if he were human . . . She gave herself a mental shake and proceeded out the door. She had too much to do. Standing around imagining the might-have-happened only wasted time. She scolded herself as she hurried down the path to the water.

She returned to the cabin to find the bear gone. "Oh, dear," she said. "I hope he has the sense to return. I need to look at his paw again."

A soft woof from the doorway told her that the bear had not gone far.

She turned and smiled. "Oh, there you are. Shall we eat now, or do you want me to look at the paw first?"

The bear proved his intelligence by shuffling to the corner where the provender bag sat. He nosed it gently.

"It's all right. You may pick it up and bring it to me if you want, Pook," Lealor told him, impressed in spite of herself by the animal's actions.

The bear shook his head with disgust as he heard her call him Pook. Then he picked up the bag and carried it to her in his teeth.

"Thank you," she told him, wondering if he had been someone's pet. "I'll get you a nice bowl of cereal—" she began.

The bear growled softly.

Lealor raised her eyebrows.

Pook growled again.

"Fussy, aren't we?" Lealor teased. "Now how can I find out—Oh, I know. I'll name some things and you can nod to me. Okay?"

Pook lowered his head in agreement.

"Very well. Berries, biscuits, and honey, fish, eggs . . . " Her eyes widened as the bear's head moved up and down vigorously at each mention of food. Lealor continued, curious to see if he really understood her. "Big fat grubs?"

Pook signaled a definite negative with his head.

"Cookies?" Lealor tried again, and got another affirmative motion. She put her hand into the bag, rapidly producing the items, which she placed on the table.

The bear came over, favoring his hurt paw, and sat on the floor. The top of the table was in easy reach of his mouth. He began to eat ravenously, yet neatly.

Lealor sat to eat her cereal and berries. As she finished her meal with a piece of steakfruit from the bag, Berdu entered the cottage.

"Good morning, Berdu. Come in," Lealor said unnecessarily since Berdu had already seated himself at the table.

"Morning," Berdu replied, eying her steakfruit hungrily.

"Would you like some breakfast? Or have you already eaten?" Lealor asked.

"Already ate," Berdu said and hastily added, "but I could always manage an extra bit or two," when he saw the girl begin to clear the table. "What's that?" A long, bony finger pointed to the steakfruit Lealor offered to Pook.

"Oh, it's just some steakfruit." Lealor offered him one.

"Don't mind if I do," he said, finishing the fruit in two bites. "Well?" he asked, obviously expecting more.

Lealor, astonished to see a person that small eat so fast, reached into the provender bag and pulled out a large bowl, filled to the brim. She placed it near Berdu. "Help yourself," she said. Then she watched as he picked up the bowl, tipped its entire contents into his mouth, somehow managed to swallow all of the fruit, and burped loudly. "Not bad—for a snack. Unusual flavor. Don't think I ever ate anything like these before. Steakfruit, you say?"

"Yes. In my"—Lealor paused in thought—"country they are everyone's favorite fruit. So large, you know, and with no pit or seeds."

"How do you grow new ones, then, if they have no seeds or pit?"

"I have a few starts of the steakfruit plants, but I really don't know. They were created by Fafnoddle, a dragon friend of my family's—"

"Dragon created? Magic! No dragons seen in these parts for years . . . " Berdu seemed to lose himself in thought. He muttered disjointedly. Lealor couldn't catch everything he said, but some phrases made sense. "Weren," Berdu muttered. "Shapeshifters. Magic users. Bad times. Dragons all gone. Bad magic. Magic bad. Dragons. Gone. Weren. Enemies. Trouble." He looked at Lealor. "Never use magic. Dangerous. Berdu knows. Berdu remembers. Berdu remembers dragons . . . " Then he snapped out of his trancelike state. "Dragons?"

"Yes. Dragons. At least, a few. Fafleen, my dragon friend, is here with me."

"Here on Widdershins with you?" Berdu's eyes widened.

"Yes," Lealor answered her agitated guest. Widdershins, she thought. What an odd name for a world!

"Dragon! Here? Now?"

"Yes," Fafleen's voice came through the window. "I'm hungry, Lealor. Can you feed me some breakfast?"

Berdu shrieked once and vanished.

"Oh, dear." Lealor rose from the table and took the provender bag outside with her since Fafleen was too large to fit into the cottage.

Pook left the table as well. He stood in the door of the cottage and watched, fascinated, as Fafleen poured a never-ending system of edibles into her cavernous mouth. She ate without swallowing or pause. Finally, after several minutes elapsed, the dragon lowered the bag and returned it to Lealor.

"I wouldn't want to overeat," Fafleen explained. "Mother wouldn't approve."

"I should guess not," Lealor said. "In the future, I expect you to chew your food."

"Pish tush. Dragons don't have to chew their food. Our digestive systems are built for swallowing prey whole if we want to—"

Lealor interrupted her, not wanting to be the recipient of a long lecture on dragonly anatomy and life style. "Manners."

Fafleen blew a puff of smoke upwards. "You sound just like my mother."

"Never mind who I sound like. You know I'm right."

Fafleen seemed inclined to argue the point, but she stopped in astonishment as Pook uttered a warning growl. "My goodness, who, pray tell, do you think you are?"

Pook growled again. He limped over to a spot midway between Lealor and the dragon.

"Quite the protector, aren't you?" Fafleen hissed her amusement. "Imagine a bear doing battle with a dragon! It would be no contest, bear."

"Pook," Lealor corrected.

"Named him, did you?" Fafleen lowered her head. With her jaw on the ground, she was eye to eye with Lealor. She blinked her eyes like a simpering maiden. "Oh, my dear, you're not getting fond of him, are you? I mean with your witchy powers you could always zap him into a handsome young man. If all he did was growl like the hero in those barbarian books, he would be the strong, almost silent type—"

"Faffie Fafnoddle!" The pink-cheeked girl faced the dragon in exasperation. "I never!"

Seeing her truly embarrassed, Fafleen ignored being called Faffie and reassured her. "Of course not. I was just teasing. Can't you take a joke?" Little wisps of smoke drifted upward as the dragon chuckled gently.

"It was kind of clod-witted. More the thing I would have expected from your brother than you."

Fafleen winced. "Point taken. Bright Ones forbid I should sound like him." She blinked once. Then she said, "If dragon minds were all like his, none of us would ever find the doors to our caves so we could come outside to eat."

"Oh, come on, now. Even though he's no great literary light, he's still a pretty nice dragon. Don't exaggerate his weak points."

Fafleen snorted steam in the air, wilting some tree branches that were overhead.

"He's still young. First Egg may mature into a more thoughtful dragon later." Lealor wondered how she has ever got herself into the position of defending young Faf, who was not only ignorant, but seemingly gloried in his stupidity. Any mental acuity he possessed ended up spent in planning how to get more gold for mini-hoards he had stashed all over Realm, and Bright Ones only knew where else.

"We can only hope to be so lucky," Fafleen said.

Pook, who had listened to this exchange, watching first one and then the other speaker, relaxed. The dragon really was the friend of the girl, odd as the situation was. He huffed in satisfaction before wandering away from the cottage.

"Wait!" Lealor called. "Your paw! I didn't get to change the bandage on your paw."

Pook kept on going. He disappeared into the woods.

"Oh, fiddle!"

Fafleen's eyes twinkled. Humans were a never-ending source of amusement to dragonkind. "You want me to go and get him and bring him back?"

"Not now. He's got the sense to return when he's ready." Lealor looked into the sea of greenery where the bear had disappeared. "He's not limping much this morning. I guess I did a good job last night, even tired."

Fafleen ruffled her scales and shifted from one foot to the other, for all the world like a child who needed to use the restroom. "Er—uh . . . "

"What's the problem?" Lealor looked at her dragon friend and smiled.

"Well—" The dragon paused, undecided.

"You may as well tell me, Fafleen. You never look like this unless there's something on your mind. I can see it's worrying you."

"All right. Remember last night when I returned from my flight?"

"Yes. Go on."

The dragon raised and lowered her wings before settling down close to Lealor. "There were mountains to the west. Some of them might have caves. It's the perfect place for dragons to live—if there are any dragons left in these parts."

"Dragons had to exist here at one time. Berdu mentioned them at breakfast this morning."

"Why hasn't he ever stayed around to meet me? Every time I come around he disappears. Is it my breath or what?"

The dragon's injured tones carried a whiff of partially digested breakfast. In spite of this, Lealor said, "Oh, no. I'm sure that's not the reason. He's such a strange little man. He's afraid to use magic and he usually disappears if dragons are so much as mentioned. Whatever his problem is, I'm certain it has nothing to do with you, personally."

"I'd like to go exploring today. I don't want to leave you all alone and unprotected—"

"Bright Ones forever!" Lealor broke in. "This is just what I was so happy to leave home for. I wanted to be an adult, not everybody's child. Surely you can understand that, what with your folks forever glorifying every random fact your brother manages to absorb and totally ignoring your mastery of literally hundreds of entire books—including the **Dragons Chronicles** with the entire history of dragonkind listed, date by date—"

This time it was Fafleen's turn to interrupt. "All right, all right. I'm sorry if I treated you like a child. I didn't mean to, you know."

"I'll be just fine. Truly I will. Besides, Pook will return after a while. You saw how protective he was. I really don't need two gigantic bodyguards when I am out here alone in the woods."

"You have Myst to guard you as well." Fafleen nodded toward Lealor's bracelet. "I almost forget about her because she can't talk. Imagine a dragon oath-bound to silence! I'm glad my father didn't do that to me."

"Yes. I've often thought how unfair it was. There's nothing I can do about it. My brothers' talismens are their friends, but Myst and I don't even know each other because she promised her father not to speak to me. She could have taught me so much . . . "

"Dragons are good sources of information. If I can find any, perhaps I can answer some of the riddles about this place." Again, Fafleen rested her head on the ground so she was eye to eye with Lealor.

"That's a great idea! It would be a good idea to know more about Widdershins before I meet the local people." She could see her reflection in Fafleen's silvery eye. Seeing eye to eye with a dragon was quite an experience.

"What do you plan to do about returning home? They'll be worrying about us both. I've never attempted to transport myself from one place to another instantaneously because mother always said I'd stunt my growth. This does seem to be an emergency, and I do think I can do it." Fafleen scratched her chin reflectively.

"Perhaps, if we get into a real jam, you might have to fly home. The gate worked once, and I may be able to get it to work again. Dragon travel is kind of dangerous. Your folks haven't given you any practice flights or anything. I'd rather save your special traveling abilities until we really need them. After all, things are pretty peaceful here. Let's wait."

"That's a good idea. I'd like to meet some new dragons and have a few adventures before we have to go home to our mothers."

Lealor made a face at the idea of returning to their parents. "I want to gather enough data about Widdershins to bring this gate back into the system. Each of my brothers has found new worlds. I don't know of any reason why I can't do the same."

"Good." The dragon flexed her muscles preparatory to takeoff. "Look out below, I'm going up!" Fafleen sprang into the air with the first beat of her huge wings. "I'll return this evening. Save some steakfruit for me," she called as she barely cleared the tree branches above them before she arrowed west.

Lealor waved one last time and then turned and entered the cottage. "Now what shall I do first?" she muttered to herself. It was an old habit she had retained from childhood. Her brothers had done things together, but she was "the little one" in the family and usually played by herself.

Because she had promised herself to try not to use magic, she spent an hour tidying up the cottage, trying to remember where she placed the supplies she brought with her from home. "Maybe mother has something. If she had not helped me pack, I'd probably find there were a lot of things I wished I had brought. What is it about mothers anyway? They always have to be right. It must be some type of maternal magic that goes with the job."

She saw a fly buzzing at the open window. It didn't come in. "I wonder what's keeping it out?" she said. She walked over and put her hand up to the window. She could see sunlight and feel a gentle breeze, for there was no screen. The fly buzzed, blocked by an invisible barrier. "Hmmm." Then she extended her senses and noticed the shimmer of magic. "A very competent person set this spell. It's quite old, but it still works. Sunlight triggers it. I bet moonlight makes it work at night. Clever. I'll have to remember this." The disappointed fly buzzed away.

Sunlight glinted on Myst, her dragon bracelet, turning the talisman into a rainbow-hued circlet. It was rare for Lealor to notice her bracelet. Usually, Myst called attention to herself only when she warned her wearer to think before doing something potentially dangerous. Between those times when Myst tightened on Lealor's arm, she almost forgot about her.

"Myst," Lealor softly addressed her bracelet. "I need to talk to you a bit. You know I'm trying to manage without magic . . . "

The tiny dragon head moved up and down, indicating she knew.

"Well, I wondered if you could become invisible. You're very beautiful and people think you're an unusual piece of jewelry. They notice me because of you. I'd like to be very ordinary during my stay here. No magic, nothing special that anyone else couldn't do with training. You do understand, don't you?"

Myst closed her eyes in resignation. If Lealor wanted her invisible, then no one should see her. It broke her tiny dragon's heart. Somehow, she'd always hoped that Lealor and she would make a pair, have the special bond that had developed between her brothers and the girl's. Now she accepted the death of that hope. She would not act until her charge was within seconds of disaster. Lealor wanted to manage without her and so she should. Myst hardened her dragon's heart. No longer would she ache to speak with Lealor. She would guard as her father bid her. Nothing else.

As Lealor watched, Myst faded into nothingness. Only the slight feeling of weight remained to remind Lealor of her guardian.

Pook returned and Lealor tended to his paw, which was responding to her treatment remarkably well. A slight limp was all that remained of the injury that would have killed the bear if she had not helped it. She felt good about that.

The day passed rapidly. Lealor didn't even think of Myst. She wouldn't realize what she had lost until it was too late.

CHAPTER FIVE

By the time the sunset gilded the waters of the nearby river, Lealor had explored the area around the cottage. She looked anxiously towards the west, squinting as the sun blinded her.

"If that isn't just like a dragon," she muttered to Pook, who had returned and followed her as if he were a large dog, except he took short journeys to forage in the mass of berry bushes that flanked the rear of the cottage. Pook had discovered them. His happy woofing noises had led Lealor to the patch. The bushes were badly in need of care, but nevertheless produced a bumper crop of juicy fruit. Lealor filled a container for dinner and made a mental note to take cuttings back to Realm with her.

"Where is Fafleen? If anything happens to her, I'll be dead meat—literally—when her mother and father find out." She never stopped to consider how ridiculous it was for her to worry about defending a ton or so of healthy young dragon who could have gobbled her up in one gulp if Fafleen so desired.

Pook reared up on his hind legs and growled.

"What is it?" Lealor asked.

Pook dropped to the ground in a rush and hobbled over to knock Lealor down and stand over her, growling. Lealor looked up into the bear's ferocious face, wondering if she was going to become his dinner.

"Pook, let me up, you big lump!" Somehow, even in her undignified position, she managed to sound indignant and in control of the situation.

A shadow blocked out the sun for an instant, and Fafleen power-dived almost on top of them. She was in such a hurry that her talons actually skidded on the grass and her nose was within inches of hitting the ground. Lealor sputtered and Pook growled.

"Faffie von Fafnoddle, explain yourself!"

The dragon paid absolutely no attention to the words. Instead, she began speaking at a breakneck pace.

"Oh, Bright Ones in a bucket, you'll never, never, never, ever, never, ever guess what I've found in those mountains, Lealor—you'll be so proud of me and at last I've done something my older but obnoxious brother has never accomplished—my parents will have to admit I've done something really worthy for once and for all—and maybe even let me become an adult officially—"

"Bright Ones indeed, Fafleen! Slow down! I can't make talon or tail of what you're trying to tell me. Go back to the beginning and tell me again. For Bright One's sake, this time slow down!"

This impassioned speech lost something because Lealor was still flat on her back half under Pook, who had finally stopped growling. He nuzzled Lealor, leaving bright-red berry juice over her face.

"Let me up this instant, you overgrown—"

At this point, Pook carefully put a gigantic paw on Lealor's middle. She felt protected and not hurt. She did get his point.

"May I please get up? I appreciate your trying to save me from being squashed, but Fafleen would never do that to me."

Fafleen watched the lesson in courtesy with interest. "It never hurts to be polite, my mother says. Besides, I did make that landing a little too fast."

Pook made a noise that sounded suspiciously like a snort.

Fafleen peered at him. She was a bit nearsighted from all the reading she did in the dim light of caves. No one dared to tell her about it. "Lealor, are you sure this bear can't talk? I have a funny feeling in my scales about him. He's much too bright to be an ordinary bear."

"I've never heard a word out of him myself," Lealor said reaching over to ruffle the fur on Pook's head. "Now, what is this wonderful news that almost annihilated us all?"

"Teeth and talons! I've made a find!"

"You mean you've found some dragons willing to help us get home?"

"Something more important than that." The dragon blew three perfect smoke rings in the air and looked very satisfied with herself.

If there was anything Lealor hated it was a smug dragon. Her friend showed definite signs of getting too big for her scales. "If your mother saw those rings, you know, she'd probably forbid you to read for a whole day. You must have spent hours practicing. All that smoke isn't good for your lungs, you know."

Fafleen ignored her comment and continued. "I found a cave!"

"Well, goody for you. Do you propose we move there?" Lealor wondered why dragons took forever to come to the point.

"Not just any cave. It was a treasure hoard, but long abandoned."

"Gold and jewels aren't going to be very useful unless you plan to pay someone to help us." Lealor felt disappointed. Usually her friend was a very sensible creature, but she seemed to have lost her wits over an old cave. Surely she wasn't old enough to start thinking about nesting—or was she? Admittedly, dragons grew faster than humans. Her brother was so fixated on treasure, he hadn't started scale chasing. Girls were usually ahead of boys in the romance department. Fafleen was definitely female, so maybe . . .

"Better than gold and jewels." Fafleen snorted a jet of flame upward, careful not to start a forest fire. "Books! Old books full of stories and history I never heard of."

"Congratulations, Fafleen. Your folks will be proud of you. I hope you made certain that you're not intruding on any dragon's lair." The whole adventure was too good to be true. That a bibliophile should discover some abandoned library just didn't seem real.

"Best of all," the excited dragon continued, "there's a really old copy of a book that I think is the **Dragon Chronicles**."

"You think? Are the cover and title pages gone?"

"No, they're there, all right. I just can't read them."

"Why not?" Lealor was astounded. Fafleen read a dozen or so languages and spoke several fluently.

"I can recognize a few of the symbols, here and there. They look like some of the very oldest symbols of dragonkind. If I've found an unimaginably ancient copy of the **Chronicles**, Mother will be wild to find out about it."

Since Ebony and Fafnoddle, the dragon's parents, had the second largest library on Realm and had been book collectors for years, Lealor felt Fafleen's opinion was understated. In fact, Lealor had heard her brother, Argen, lamenting that scholars from the university went to the dragon's cave to study since Ebony wouldn't hear of lending her books. Once she got a book in her possession, she never let it far out of her talons. Argen himself had traveled to her cavern to pursue some arcane volume that he found mentioned in the main library on Realm, but couldn't locate there.

Lealor reminded herself not to get too interested in dragon tomes, when the real problem facing them both was finding a reliable way to return home. She knew both sets of parents would be frantic, trying to find them. If, she thought, they realized what had happened to them. "Did you happen to see any dragons in those mountains?"

"Well, no," Fafleen admitted.

"I bet you forgot all about our getting home, didn't you?"

A nod was her answer.

"That's all right." Lealor reassured her friend. "Tomorrow I suppose you'll be returning to your books. I'll wander downstream and see if I have any better luck in finding someone with information."

"Up," the dragon said.

"Up?" Lealor repeated, puzzled.

"Upstream."

"Why not downstream?"

"Because there's a village of sorts upstream and nothing but solid trees in the other direction. I noticed when I flew in."

Lealor sincerely hoped Fafleen's flight had gone unnoticed by the villagers. She didn't want to cope with aroused and fearful neighbors who might decide on dragon hunting. Berdu hadn't made clear exactly why magic was dangerous or what caused the dragons' disappearance, and she felt responsible for Fafleen.

However, she didn't think it would be a good idea to tell her friend. Every so often Fafleen became all dragon, stubborn and bloodthirsty. If the dragon became angry and declared doom on the village, life would become very complicated very rapidly. So Lealor only nodded and kept her thoughts to herself.

Lealor used the provender bag to provide a meal. She never consciously realized she was using magic. To her, the bag was simply a gift from Grandmother Cibby. Fafleen liked eating too well to point out Lealor's inconsistency. After dinner, which the magic bag produced in abundance, Fafleen asked Lealor to come out and talk to her. It was awkward, with Pook and Lealor eating inside the cottage and the dragon guzzling down kippers, steakfruit, and chocolate cake outside the door. She was too large to fit inside. Lealor didn't like the situation much better when the dragon stayed outside the window and looked in. Her eye filled the whole window frame. It made Lealor distinctly uneasy to look into the pupil when Fafleen made a comment. So she cheerfully dragged a chair outside. It really was too nice an evening to spend inside anyway.

"Talk away. I'm listening," said Lealor.

"Well, you did wonderfully well all by yourself today."

Lealor grimaced. She had given all her old university texts to Fafleen, earning her undying gratitude. She recognized the psychology behind the statement and waited for the unpleasant part that she was sure would follow.

"So . . . " Fafleen took a deep breath.

"Don't exhale!" Lealor warned. The cottage, sturdy as it was, would have a hard time withstanding the dragon's exhalation from a distance of six feet. Lealor had visions of flying shingles and downed trees. Sometimes Fafleen forgot her own strength. Years before, Ebony explained calmly to a wide-eyed little girl that dragons were very powerful and had to learn to use their might in moderation.

Fafleen had exhaled on a picnic one time and blown the food a half-mile away. "After all, dear," Ebony had hissed with some pride, "she is very young to be so powerful."

Fafleen's cheeks swelled as she held her breath and Lealor frantically signaled upward with her finger.

Pook, ready to pull Lealor to the ground and shield her with his own body, relaxed as the dragon obligingly followed Lealor's directions.

A shower of green leaves and twigs rained down in response to Fafleen's action. Lealor gave a sigh of relief. She had been right in assuming her friend was still too excited over her find to think straight. "So," she said, to urge Fafleen to continue.

"So I'd like to stay there." She paused and slowed down when she noticed Lealor's raised eyebrow. "I'll check in here once and a while. You could leave messages for me by my tree."

"Your tree?" Lealor tried to hide the amusement she felt by gesturing to the forest around them. The clearing in front of the cottage was so small that Fafleen's tail went snaking off into the brush. Within a few paces, twenty trees were near enough to touch.

"You're not teasing me, are you?" The dragon lowered her head until she was eye to eye with the girl.

The dragon's silver eye acted like a mirror. Lealor could see herself seated in the chair with the ever-vigilant, Pook curled by her right side. "Not exactly. It's not like you to be so vague. Those old books have you really excited."

"You don't understand, Lealor. When dragon historians get as eyeful of the old book I found, it will delight them. It's like discovering the missing link would be for you humans."

Clearly, Fafleen read and absorbed all the books anyone gave her. Every time members of Lealor's family came back from Earth they brought boxes of discards. The neighbors dropped off books for Argen after he told them he sent them to foreign countries. At first he was in big trouble with their parents, but Jarl finally saw the joke. What country could be more foreign to Earth than Realm?

"Well?"

"Well, what?" Lealor responded.

Fafleen raised her head and stamped. Lealor could hear the dishes rattle in the cottage.

"Can I?"

Lealor knew better than to say, "Can I what?" or worse yet, "May I."

"Okay by me. How long do you plan this period to stretch?"

"Only a few days. I'll come back for snacks, if you don't mind."

Lealor could picture those snacks. Five or six bushels of steakfruit and enough baked goods to stock a small shop.

"Sure."

"You can leave any messages for me by my tree," the dragon's head pointed to the tree she slept in.

"Let's leave messages for each other under the door of the cottage. With so many trees around, I might forget which one."

"Very well." Fafleen tried to sound adult and responsible.

Lealor remembered how young she was for a dragon. "If you should get lonely or anything, you know I'll always be glad to see you."

"Oh, I won't get lonely now. Not with all those books to read. I haven't even taken the time to look at all of them. For all I know, hidden in the piles, there are several more really important finds."

"Well, remember to let me know if you decide to explore any more. It's always a good idea to let somebody know where you will be in case you get into trouble." Lealor took the dragon's nod to mean she agreed. "Tomorrow, I'll wander downstream—"

"Not downstream. Upstream. The village I saw is upstream."

"Right. Not down, up."

A soft snore from Pook made them both look at the bear.

"Tired him out, we did." Fafleen chuckled, but softly, so the bear could sleep on.

"Well, he's still recovering from that paw wound. I'll let him stay here. It's not good for him to walk too far and overdo. Then, too, if I meet any villagers, I really don't want to have to explain a bear."

"Good night," the dragon said, waiting expectantly.

"Good night," Lealor answered, wondering what else Fafleen wanted.

"My teddy, please," Fafleen said, sounding exactly like a little girl in spite of being a good-sized dragon. Lealor had caused the teddy bear to disappear after Fafleen woke up. Evidently she still felt a little homesick.

"If you don't mind, can you make Pinky permanent? Then I can take her with me to the cave."

Lealor gave the dragon the pink teddy and watched the huge dragon settle herself awkwardly in the old oak.

Soon, soft snores from the bear and dragon told Lealor was time for her to go to bed as well.

Later that night distant thunder woke Lealor. The cold wind told her a storm was coming. Pook ambled in and settled by the fire. "Just one more reason for Faffie to have a cave of her own," she murmured. Lealor frowned. "I guess it's all right to use magic in a case like this," she told herself. With a wave of her hand she cast a protective spell over the dragon and the tree. "Now at least she'll stay dry," she said softly as she pulled the covers up to her chin.

Outside, the wind herded silver clouds together until they turned black and raced across the face of the moon. Soon rain flooded down. The runoff gathered into rivulets and hurried to the swollen river that increased its pace to the sea.

CHAPTER SIX

The sound of rushing water woke Lealor. Before she went to the bank of the river, she had a good idea of what she would find. The river was almost over its banks. "Well," she told Pook, who appeared behind her like magic, "I guess I picked a poor day to go adventuring. I need to ask Fafleen which side of the river the village is on. If it's across this"—here she gestured to the rushing water—"I'm not even going to try to visit."

Fafleen flew to check possible flooding before she would eat breakfast. "I'll earn my keep today," she told Lealor, "by making sure your exploring is safe." When she returned, she gave her permission for Lealor's expedition, but she added, with her mouth full of steakfruit, "You know, if you weren't so pigheaded, like all humans, I could fly you over anything you might want to see in half the time it's going to take you to trudge to that village."

Lealor winced. Never let it be said that dragons were tactful. In the stories she read, dragons were sneaky, sly, terribly wise, or didn't speak to humans at all. In the real world, however, her experience proved dragons to be forthright to a fault, impatient, sometimes foolish, and far too willing to give unasked-for opinions of the humans they knew. It was no use trying to convince a dragon that many, if not most, people were afraid of them. If Lealor really intended to live an ordinary life while she was here, starting out as the companion of a dragon, when the species was probably legendary in these parts, was not especially bright. So she clenched her teeth and smiled, as if she were not irked enough to give Fafleen a good whack with her broom.

It didn't help much that Pook had both paws over his mouth, for all the world as if he were trying to hide a grin.

"We've made our plans. Let's stick to them," she said. "After all, I don't want to keep you from those books. Be sure you remember I'm here and check in with me from time to time."

"That's another thing, Lealor. How long do you want to stay? I'm quite content, but I bet you're worrying about your folks. As the youngest egg—I mean, person—in your family, I bet your mother is pretty distraught."

"What about yours?" Lealor shot back. "I've seen her lose her equanimity more than once over you and your brother!"

Fafleen giggled. "Yes, she goes off every so often like one of those rockets you humans keep shooting off back on Earth."

Lealor couldn't help returning Fafleen's grin as she pictured a dragon in orbit after a launch. "As for how long I want to stay, I guess several months, at least. It's not going to be easy to get the gate functioning."

"Are you sure you know how?"

"Well, yes, I'm sure I have the knowledge. The trouble is, I've never actually done it. I always just watched."

"I understand," the dragon offered in a soothing tone. "Grown-ups never let us dragonettes do anything difficult either."

Lealor had a momentary desire to argue that she was a grown-up, but she throttled it. She offered two pillowcases filled with food to Fafleen. "Now, you come back when that's gone."

"Oh, I'll be back. Don't worry. This will be plenty." At Lealor's raised eyebrows, the dragon said airily, "I'll be living off the land, you know."

Lealor shuddered. She knew what that meant. The game in the area was going to be decimated on a regular basis. Berries and wild fruit didn't hold much interest for her friend.

Fafleen held her teddy bear between her sharp teeth and gripped a loaded pillowcase in each set of talons. "I'm off," she hissed through clenched teeth before rising straight up like a lightning bolt in reverse.

Lealor checked the cottage. There was food out for Pook. She didn't bother with water. With the river in full spate, she figured he could get all the fresh water he needed. When she left the clearing, he followed her. She commanded him to return, but he refused. Finally, she stopped and talked to him as if he were a person.

"I don't know how much of this you understand, but I'm going to try to reason with you. I don't want to seem weird—I mean, unusual—to the villagers. If I let you come with me until we meet some people, will you hide so they don't see me with you?"

Pook nodded vigorously.

"You do understand me, don't you? Fafleen was right."

Pook nodded again.

"Very well. Remember, you promised."

Fafleen had told her the village was close to the river on the cottage side. Lealor decided to follow the river to find it. They had walked for some time before the bear growled, then faded into the brush beside the overgrown path she had been following.

"Pook, for heaven's sake, what got into you? First you insist on coming along, and now you've vanished."

A low growl told her Pook was still close by, although she couldn't see him. Then she heard it. A faint cry for help.

Lealor listened. "There it is again," she said, knowing Pook was close enough to hear her even if he was in hiding. At least he was keeping his promise, she thought as she hurried toward the sound. When she arrived at the bank of the river, she looked for the source. In the middle of a flooded area, she saw a small tree hung up on a piece of boulder that was visible because it disturbed the rapid flow of water that rushed by it. Clinging to the tree's branches like a wet kitten was a boy of eight or nine.

After studying the situation for a few moments, Lealor acted. She began by taking off her boots.

When Pook saw that she was preparing to jump in, he growled.

"Pook, stop worrying. I'm a strong swimmer. It's not very far. That boy looks as if he's about ready to let go, and if he does, maybe I won't be able to save him."

Pook came out of the brush and stood beside her, nudging the magic provender bag, which she always carried with her, tied to her belt.

"Go away, silly bear," Lealor said, trying to push Pook from his position between her and the water. "I've got to go and get him." The bear stood, solid as the rock that was holding the tree. He growled and nudged the bag again.

She sighed. Bears could be as stubborn as dragons or men. "Okay, boy. What is it? You must be trying to tell me something."

Pook nodded and put a paw on the bag, nearly knocking Lealor over in the process.

"You want me to use the bag?"

Another nod.

"What do you want me to ask for?" she wondered aloud. Pook scratched a long line in the dirt with his paw.

"A rope?"

Another nod.

She reached in the bag and brought out a long nylon rope, light, but strong. "Now, how are we going to use this?"

Pook nudged his head into the loops that the rope made.

"You mean you're going to swim out to the boy?"

Nod. Nod.

"Pook, you'll scare him to death. You're pretty impressive, you know."

"Help," the boy's voice, perceptibly weaker, called. Pook growled impatiently.

"All right. All right. I hear you. Wait until I make a slip knot in this end of the rope." Her fingers worked busily as she talked. "Now I'll keep hold of this end. Are you sure you can get the loop over his body? Not his head, mind you. We don't want the poor child strangled before I can reel him to shore."

"Don't be afraid," she called to the boy, who watched with wide eyes. "I'm sending the bear out with a rope. Put it around you and I'll haul you to shore. Can you do that?"

The boy stared. He was petrified.

A loud crack came from the water. The tree had broken. Only the small net of branches to which to boy clung was upstream of the boulder. Pook sized up the problem instantly, and ran, carrying the looped rope around his neck. It was not easy for the bear to swim to the boy. He had to dodge floating bits and pieces of fallen trees and other debris without catching the rope in them. Swimming against the current tired Pook, but he had to come to the boulder from downstream so he could reach the child. When he finally got to the boy, he had trouble getting him to help place the rope around his body. He nudged and woofed encouragingly until the boy understood. The bear draped his body over the top of the boulder, and rested while he watched Lealor pull the boy to shore like some overgrown catfish.

The child was too weak to scramble up the bank and Lealor had to pull him to safety herself as the bear watched. The remainder of the tree washed loose with a crack, and floated by, narrowly missing the bear who was almost scraped from the rock.

"Come on, Pook," Lealor called. "Everything is all right at this end."

The bear, still recovering from the wound in his paw and the strenuous swim he had made to reach the child, had weakened considerably. He woofed with the effort it took to shove himself off the rock. He paddled as little as possible, trying to angle himself so the current would carry him to shore. He would have made it without trouble except for a huge log that bobbed loose from a pile where it had been snagged and rushed past, almost on top of him. The surge of water swamped him, dragging him under. His soaked coat weighed him down. He clawed his way to the surface. Only his will to survive kept his legs pumping. That and hearing Lealor's frantic cries.

"Pook! Keep swimming! Come on, Pook!"

The bear was at the end of his strength. He made one final effort, and felt his hind paws touch bottom. Then his head dropped and everything went black.

"Oh, Pookie. You've got to be all right," Lealor said as she and the boy dragged the bear farther onshore. "Come on, wake up. Wake up enough to help us get you all the way out of the water." She begged, and she tugged, and she pulled. The bear managed a few weak steps before collapsing on the grass.

"I'm pretty tired," the boy told Lealor. "I never rescued a bear before," he explained.

"Oh, yes. What can I have been thinking of?" Lealor said. "We'll have to stay here for a while until my bear recovers. Why don't you curl up here in the sun and take a little nap. I'll wake you when we're ready to go."

"I'm not going home," the boy said.

Lealor looked at him curiously. "We'll have time to talk about that later. You sleep for now." She helped him find a comfortable position on the grass and waved a minor sleep spell over him to assure that he would rest. She could think of no way that did not entail magic to get them both to the cottage. She had sworn off magic, so it was just as well, she thought. She was unaware that she had used magic to invoke the sleep spell.

She went over to the recumbent bear and curled up beside him. His fur was drying rapidly in the warm sun. He looked at her tiredly by raising one eyelid.

"Oh, Pook, you were a very brave bear. I'm so proud of you," Lealor told him, kissing him on the nose. Both his eyes flew open. "No, bear-of-mine," she told him, "I can't turn you into a handsome prince with a kiss. Go to sleep." She patted him gently on the shoulder before snuggling close to him.

Some time later, she woke. The sun's position told her it was early afternoon. "All right, sleepyheads," she called gently, "it's time to wake up."

Pook groaned and raised his head. His exhaustion showed in the way he pulled himself to his paws. The boy, pale beneath his tan, was not in much better shape. Lealor felt the strain of all that pulling and tugging herself. She forced a smile before speaking. "Come on, you two. It isn't very far to the cottage. Then I can give you something to make a new bear and boy out of you."

"What cottage?" the boy asked, too young to consider politeness when he wanted the answer to a question.

"The old place in the woods over there," Lealor gestured, "that I've fixed up to live in."

"The old witch's place?" The boy's eyes were round and seemed as big as a dragon's in his tired face.

"I wouldn't know about that," Lealor told him. "There was no witch inside when I got there. It was an abandoned place that no one wanted, so I moved in."

"Oh," the boy said, before moving on to his next question. "Are you a witch?"

Lealor didn't want to lie. Many people would call the magic she knew witch's magic, so she evaded the question with one of her own. "Do I look old enough to be a witch?"

The boy still didn't look satisfied, so she continued, putting her hand to her nose. "Is my nose hooked with a wart on it?" She rubbed her nose with the tip of her finger. "I don't think so."

The boy laughed as Lealor had meant him to. He changed the subject with his next question. "Is that your bear?"

"Not exactly. He hurt his paw and I helped him get better. He's kind of adopted me. He's pretty protective."

"Oh." The boy thought about it for a moment then said, "Like a dog?"

"Yes, a little like that."

Pook growled, and the boy jumped.

"A whole lot better," Lealor reassured them both. "He's an ever-so-nice bear who wouldn't hurt anyone who wasn't trying to hurt me."

"Did you train him to be a rescue bear?" was the boy's next question.

"No. He's just very smart." Lealor felt surprise as she realized how intelligently the animal had handled the boy's rescue and return to shore. Pook's own return to the bank showed he understood river currents and was able to plan and make use of them. Fafleen had certainly been correct in her assessment of the bear's brainpower.

"Oh," the boy said again, frowning with thought.

It amused Lealor to see how first he stopped to assimilate new information, then asked another question. Someday this boy would be rather wise himself. Realizing another query was forming in his mind, she asked one of her own first.

"I'm called Lealor, and the bear's name is Pook. What's your name?"

For an answer, she received another question. "You don't know my parents, do you?"

"I don't believe so," Lealor answered. "I'm new around here."

The boy smiled. "That's good. I wouldn't want you to start thinking of taking me home, 'cause I'm never going home."

Now it was Lealor's turn to say, "Oh." The boy looked like he was ready to run away. "Let's talk about that after we've had a little time to rest and get cleaned up." She gestured to her muddy clothes and boots. The boy and bear were muddy, too.

The boy looked undecided about whether to accept her hospitality. Then Pook nodded several times, which made the boy laugh. "All right, Mrs. Lealor."

"I'm not married, boy."

"My name's Aldon, miss."

"Glad to meet you, Aldon," Lealor told him. "Are you coming with us?" she asked him as she turned and started back the way she had come.

"I guess I could come for a little while. I never met a real live bear before," he said. "He won't eat me?" he asked.

"Not even a small nibble," Lealor promised, trusting that an intelligent bear would know little boys were not on the menu.

"Good," the boy said, the matter settled in his mind. He walked slowly up to Pook, unable to resist touching the bear, now that he knew it was safe.

Lealor watched, ready to act if the bear didn't like the touching, but Pook gently rubbed his head against the boy, which delighted him.

"Good bear," he said.

"Better call him by his name," Lealor told him. "You wouldn't like it if people just called you 'boy,' would you?"

"Guess not," Aldon said.

Lealor led the way back to the cottage, followed by Pook and Aldon, who had draped his arm around the bear's neck. Signs pointed to a friend-ship, Lealor thought when she glanced behind her to check on her companions. Aldon was a lot like she had been at his age, loving animals so much, he took them on trust. As they had with Lealor, animals usually accepted his good will and would not hurt him.

She planned what she was going to say to Aldon to find out why he was running away from home. So much for the idea of seeming normal, she thought to herself. Aldon thought of her as a kind of bear tamer. All she needed now was for Fafleen to fly in with some kind of news. Or perhaps Berdu would pop in, literally, on her and her guest. No sense fretting over calamity until it happened, she told herself, opening the cottage door and waiting for Aldon and Pook to enter.

CHAPTER SEVEN

It took eight buckets of water from the well to sluice Pook down. Aldon needed a bucket and Lealor used one on herself. When she pulled the tenth, and final bucket, she flexed her shoulders that felt as if they were asking for a divorce from her body. "Thank the Bright Ones that's over," she muttered.

In the cottage, Pook and Aldon were finishing off the last of the steakfruit from the bowl on the table. Lealor stood at the door, watching. Aldon would offer a fruit to Pook and then take one for himself. The boy left a row of stems neatly placed on the edge of the table.

"This fruit is really good. I've never had any before this," Aldon told her, wiping his mouth on the sleeve of a shirt Lealor had given him. It hung down enough to decently cover him.

She handed him his pants that a little sun magic had dried super fast. She didn't seem to be able to do without some magic, but she was trying to break her habit of using spells without noticing.

Myst stayed invisible as Lealor had requested earlier, so the dragon bracelet's look of disgust went unnoticed each time Lealor broke her vow to do without magic.

"Do you have any idea how far it is to the village upstream?" Lealor asked.

"It's only a candlemark or so," Aldon answered, having no idea that his questioner didn't know how long a candlemark might be.

The boy's curious eyes were taking note of everything in the cottage. Lealor didn't know if anything there might lead him to find out too much

DRAGON'S QUEEN

about her. She didn't want him to stay too long, in case Fafleen returned unexpectedly.

Lealor wanted to ask why he had run away from home, but she thought the question might disturb Aldon. So she asked instead, "Could you guide me to the village?"

"Why do you want to go there?" His voice showed he didn't think much of her choice of places to visit.

She knew better than to tell the boy she was looking for someone to help her, so she gave him an answer she hoped he would accept. "Well, for one thing, those people are my neighbors."

"Nothing ever happens there. It's feed the chickens, milk the cow, bring in firewood, day after day. I hate getting firewood worst of all."

From his tones, Lealor could hear the boy's unconscious imitation of his taskmaster.

"You don't like cows, chickens, and warm fires?" she asked with a smile.

His look was answer enough, but his next words confirmed his opinion. "How can anyone have adventures in a place like Riverville?"

"Oh," Lealor said, understanding instantly. Her brothers still teased her about wanting to ride her tricycle to Hawaii when she was a four-year-old runaway. "Then it's pretty boring there, I guess."

"Nothing special ever happens. The most exciting thing is when my big sister comes home for the harvest festival."

"Well, if it's so dull in Riverville, I suppose it would be safe for me to visit, if, that is, I can find it."

"Oh, you'll be able to find it, all right."

"You wouldn't want to be my guide?"

"I'd like to help, but if I go home, they'll make me stay."

Lealor gave no sign that he had just told her where he belonged. Instead she said, "Well, if it's so ordinary, anyone who brought a stranger to town would be a hero, wouldn't he?"

Aldon looked surprised, but after a moment's reflection, he said, "Yes. Maybe I could take you there."

"That's good. I was a little worried about finding it alone."

"Will your bear go with you?"

"Not this time. I don't expect I'll have any more adventures today. I'd like to meet my neighbors and perhaps trade for some eggs."

"My mother had the freshest eggs in town. Our hens are the best layers of all. Everyone says so."

"Then do you suppose she'd trade some eggs for these berries that I picked?" Lealor uncovered two small tin pails filled with glistening berries.

"They look delicious," Aldon said.

"Would you like some?" Lealor asked, marveling at his capacity for food. He must have eaten seven or eight steakfruits before she came in.

"Maybe a few." He started eating the handful Lealor gave him. "I was awfully hungry."

"You left before breakfast?"

Aldon finished the last of the berries and wiped his hands on his newly cleaned pants. Lealor did not envy his mother the task of keeping him clean.

"I left while it was still dark."

"My goodness, that was brave of you."

"Not really. I often go out when the birds wake me up. My uncle is a hunter and he says no good comes of staying in bed until the sun rises."

Lealor hid a shudder; she could hear his redoubtable uncle saying the words. One of her greatest pleasures when she was on Earth was staying in bed after her alarm rang. "Do you want to be a hunter when you grow up? Is that why you get up with the birds?"

"Usually," he admitted, "I like to stay in bed until I have to do chores. If you're setting out on a day's adventure, you need to get an early start."

Again, his unconscious mimicry spoke volumes for his absent uncle. Lealor felt she would know him if she saw him. "I think we'd better start, don't you?" she asked, handing Aldon one of the buckets and taking the other herself.

Pook waddled over to the door, obviously planning to come with them.

"No, Pook. Not this time. You stay here and rest. I don't want you sick again. Remember how sore your foot was? You stay," she said firmly, hoping her stern voice would convince him she could manage without her self-appointed guardian.

For a moment, the bear looked as if he would defy her. He took a step forward and winced. His paw hurt.

"See?" Lealor said, resting her hand on his head. "Dear Pook, stay here and wait for me." She gave him the smile she reserved for her leprechaun friend, Rory. It never failed her.

In answer, Pook limped over to the fireplace and stretched out to make a living bear rug.

"He's really a big bear," Aldon said admiringly. "I bet my uncle—"

"You better warn your uncle that nobody is to harm my bear," Lealor said, fiercely protective.

'Oh, no. Of course not. He wouldn't hurt a pet bear," Aldon assured her.

"I should hope not!" As she stamped out the door, Lealor's back showed her opinion of any hunter who would dare try.

Pook's eyes shone with an inner light. He absentmindedly rubbed his nose with one paw, looking very human as he did so. Then he stretched out in front of the banked fire and dozed off.

The passage of Lealor, Aldon, and Pook had cleared the old trail. At one time, many feet must have come this way, Lealor thought. In a few short minutes, she and Aldon passed the spot where she'd hauled him to the shore. She patted her magic bag, remembering the stout rope. Good old grandma, she thought, wondering how she would have managed without it.

Aldon went ahead of her from that point on. "If I'm your guide, I'd better go first," he told her. She could tell from his walk that he took his job seriously. In fact, she could almost see the hunter-uncle who probably taught him to travel through the woods.

She followed silently, wondering what kind of people lived in Riverville. She knew she could have asked Aldon questions and gotten some valuable insights on the villagers, but somehow it seemed sneaky, so she didn't.

She thought she caught a glimpse of Berdu in the underbrush beside the trail, but when she peered more closely, there was nothing. "What an imagination I've got," she muttered to herself.

"What did you say?" Aldon asked.

"Nothing important," Lealor told him. "How much farther is it?" Her legs were almost as tired as her arms. She was definitely out of shape for long forest walks following a river rescue. By the time she got home that night, she knew she'd be asking the magic bag for some liniment.

"It's just around that bend up ahead," Aldon pointed.

In a few more moments, they rounded the bend. Nestled in the curve of the river like a contended tabby, lay the village. Its peacefulness made it very attractive to Lealor, who missed civilization more than she realized.

Aldon led her straight to his home, one of the cottages on the outskirts of the little town. He opened the gate and let Lealor enter first.

A motherly figure bustled out the door and clasped a wriggling Aldon tightly to her. "Aldon Smithson, where have you been all day? We've looked everywhere for you. Your uncle said if you didn't turn up for supper, he'd start looking down river for you in his boat, flood or no flood."

"Oh, mother," Aldon said, pulling himself loose from her embrace with difficulty.

Then Lealor's presence finally registered with Aldon's mother. "My bright stars," she said. "Aldon, you've brought us a visitor."

"I'm very pleased to meet you—all," Lealor said, looking at the two men and little girl who came out to see what was happening.

At this point, Aldon felt he was well on the way to being forgotten, so he introduced the members of his family. "My Uncle Gren, my father, my mother, and Jessa," he said, pointing them out for his guest.

The introductions really weren't necessary, except for politeness' sake. Dressed in green, Uncle Gren, the hunter, looked as if he were one of Robin Hood's merry men. Aldon looked exactly like his father, except his father was more muscular and clad in a leather apron such as all blacksmiths wear. Dame Smith reminded Lealor of the pictures of the Old Woman Who Lived in a Shoe in her nursery rhyme book.

"Who might this be?" the blacksmith asked with a smile.

"This is Lealor—" Aldon paused at a look from his mother. "Miss Lealor," he corrected himself. "She lives downstream in the old witch's cottage and she and her bear pulled me out of the river and—"

"Hold on, youngster," his uncle said, in a voice Lealor recognized from Aldon's recital of his maxims. "Start your tale at the beginning—and tell it slowly," he cautioned.

So Aldon told how he met Lealor. He didn't realize how dangerous his situation had been. The looks on the faces of the adults who heard him showed they appreciated the danger he had been in. His mother gave him another hug when he finished and his father clapped him on the shoulder. From the way Aldon's eyes lighted up, this was a rare accolade. His uncle tousled his hair. The brief ritual of touching him reassured his family that he was alive and well.

"What are we all doing out here?" Dame Smith said, obviously flustered by the unexpected company. "Come in, come in," she said, gesturing vigorously toward the door. "Surely you're tired after your long walk." She led the way inside.

This cottage was larger than Lealor's. It had an upstairs loft and a side door led to a blacksmith's work area and forge. The members of the Smith family had earned their name. No wonder Aldon hated getting firewood worst of all. In busy seasons, filling the immense woodboxes would be almost a full-time task.

Dame Smith seated Lealor at the long table that dominated the room. "Now, it's not long until supper, so I won't spoil your appetite. A cool drink and a bite of cookie wouldn't hurt a flying buzzer," she said as she filled a mug from a stoneware jar wrapped in wet cloth that stood on the windowsill.

The cool fruity drink tasted delicious to Lealor. Everyone had a mug with her, even the little girl, Jessa.

During the conversation that accompanied the cool drinks, the story of the rescue retold by Aldon with graphic gestures and many childish exaggerations, earned Lealor the gratitude of her hosts. Aldon explained that Lealor wanted to trade for some eggs. His mother was adamant that she was giving Lealor a basket of eggs and some of her sweet fruit jam to go with the home-made bread she had baked that morning. Then Lealor insisted she couldn't carry those buckets of berries home and would have to leave them for the children's breakfasts. Uncle Gren, who hadn't taken his eyes off Lealor since he first saw her, said he would walk her home when she was ready to go. Lealor worried about his offer because she didn't want a confrontation with her bear. Pook looked really formidable, and since they thought she was an ordinary person, they wouldn't know Myst and Lealor's own magic was all the protection she would probably need.

Somewhere during these neighborly exchanges, Jessa had a coughing fit. Dame Smith fed her some sweet herb syrup, which didn't seem to do much good. Lealor reached into her magic bag, tied to her belt, and took out several kinds of herbs. She selected two small bunches and told Jessa's mother how to prepare them. "If you give her a spoon of this before she goes to bed, she should have a good night's sleep," Lealor said.

"I'm so glad you're an herb woman," Dame Smith said. "Our local healer, Fialla, is ill herself. No one in Riverville knows what to do for her. Would it be too much of an imposition if I asked you to stop and see her before you leave today?"

"I can't promise to do much but look. I may not have what I need in my bag," Lealor said. "I'd be glad to try."

As they walked through the village, Dame Smith introduced her to everyone they met. Lealor had enough invitations for dinners to keep her dining out for several weeks. Lealor thanked everyone, but said she needed to settle in before she could start socializing. Everyone understood. They were getting ready for the winter. In another few days, the harvest would be in full swing. Everyone she met invited her to the harvest festival. Dame Smith never intruded on anyone's invitation, but she filled Lealor in on each person they met. Several of the women who wanted her as a guest had young, marriageable son. The herb woman, Fialla, was old, Dame Smith explained. If Lealor married into a Riverville family, her talent would be a blessing to the village.

Dame Smith's information was never malicious, but it was honest. By the time Lealor reached Fialla's cottage, she had a good idea of what the village was really like.

Fialla, however, was a total surprise.

When Lealor entered her cottage, she smelled the herbal scents of all the good plants that were drying in the racks along one wall and in the bundles overhead that hung from the rafters. The whitewashed walls made the interior of the room bright.

In spite of Fialla's age, she was an imposing figure. Her fine, pale hair wisped around her face, which was round and wrinkled as one of the apples from the barrels in the root cellars people dug to store fruits and vegetables throughout the winters. Because she was six feet tall, she bowed her head when she passed under her rafters.

Dame Smith introduced the two women, then pleaded work at home as an excuse to leave. Fialla and Lealor watched her go. When the door closed behind her, the old woman turned to Lealor and smiled. "Welcome to the world of Widdershins. I suppose you're from the gate," she said.

CHAPTER EIGHT

"You know about the gate?" Lealor asked in astonishment, admitting by her question that she also knew about the gates.

"Oh, yes, I know about it." Fialla sat in her rocking chair. Lealor relaxed on the bench beside the fire, which burned bright and hot although only a small amount of wood rested on the grate. Minor fire magic, she thought. Fialla is more than a simple village healer.

"I'm glad to know you have not forgotten us," Fialla continued, her gnarled hands grasping the arms of the chair. "It's been a long time since last we had a keeper on Widdershins."

"How long?" Lealor asked.

"Seven generations of my family have lived and died since the destruction of the gate," Fialla said with a sigh. "People in my family have long lifelines," she added as an afterthought.

"What happened?" Lealor did not ask the question from simple curiosity. If she understood what kind of forces distorted the powers of the gate, she might better be able to return it to its original state.

"A new group of priests arose in the temples, almost overnight. Soon they controlled all the big centers of worship. The temples were rebuilt, and the Lady had only a niche in the corner instead of the main altar. The god that they replaced her with is cruel and avaricious, judging from the tithes his priests demand from the people. Under the Lady, gifts given helped the needy and ill. Now, the greedy priests tell the people that the new god demands money and goods. The Lady never needed gold or silver. This god takes his share—some think more than his share—of

457

everything bought and sold. Priests stay in every village of over a hundred people. When so many live in one location, it is their privilege to build an impressive place of worship to honor the god. Then the priests will gladly take over the matter of the tithes for those towns fortunate enough to have one."

Fialla rocked sadly for a moment. Lealor, used to dealing with older people, waited patiently, knowing there must be more to the story.

Fialla's eyes twinkled. "Funny, there haven't been over ninety-five people in Riverville for generations."

"Since about the time that the priesthood told the people about that rule, right?" Lealor's grin showed her understanding.

"We couldn't have a temple so near to an abandoned gate, could we?"

"Abandoned?"

"Yes. Over the years, forgotten by the villagers. We thought it was safer so."

"We?" Lealor probed gently.

"Village elders and the keepers."

Lealor brightened. "Keepers, here? What a relief. I thought I'd be all alone."

"You are . . . almost," Fialla told her with a sigh. "I am the last keeper trained in the village, but I'm not really a keeper. Over the years we were so busy hiding the gate to keep it from total destruction like the others on Widdershins that information became forgotten or never taught. By the time my ancestors realized how much, it was too late."

"So the priesthood destroyed everything?"

"Everything they could find."

"They have a lot to answer for," Lealor said, clenching her fists.

"They alone could not have come to power. If the magic users would have banded together, they could have withstood the priests. What weakened the magic wielders was their fighting among themselves. Only the keepers used magic sparingly, and only they were willing to share what they knew without thought of gain. The priesthood was able to convince the general populace that all magic users were evil."

"I know," Lealor said. "Only a few bad experiences with magic sets ordinary people against all use of it."

"The magic users and the folks who didn't use magic fought a tremendous battle west of here in the mountains. The magic users begged the dragon king to join them and fight the priests, but he refused. His great

magical powers and those of his subjects would have made a great difference. One legend claims destruction. Another says he was transformed.
No one knows for sure what really took place over there." Fialla waved in
the direction of the mountains.

"What happened to the dragon king's subjects?"

"They disappeared."

"How sad."

"Not as sad as if they'd stayed," Fialla said, shutting her eyes as if that
would keep out the grim pictures that formed in her mind.

"What else did the priests do?" Lealor leaned forward in her effort to
hear.

"They began persecuting the weren."

"The weren?" Lealor wasn't sure what weren were, but she remembered Berdu's mentioning them.

"A race of shapeshifters. Most weren't really magic users. The weren
folk simply had the ability to change their shape. The priests convinced the
people to kill any they could catch. They preached that all magic was evil,
and people believed them. They forgot about what good neighbors the
weren had been and all the times magic users had helped, and not harmed
them." Fialla shook her head. "For a while, many weren died, then
suddenly almost overnight, according to my granny—no one saw any
more. They didn't come in to the villages to trade, and they abandoned
their homes in the forest. I don't see how they all died, but whether they
took wing and flew away like the dragons, I couldn't say." Fialla, who had
stopped rocking as she told her tale, began rocking again.

While the old woman talked, Lealor had listened too intently to notice
how tired she was. The healer was so pale that it was hard to see when she
became even more ashen. Finally Lealor noticed.

"I'm sorry," she apologized. "I didn't mean to tire you when you're ill."

"Nonsense. If you're here to mend the gate, most people will welcome
you with open arms. Folklore remembers the gates and their keepers as
good and the times as a golden age. It's only the priesthood that want all
new things stamped out. My mother said we made almost no progress in
any field after the gates were closed. The one here remained protected
somehow. All it will take is several powerful magic users to remove the
spells laid upon it, and it should work."

"The magic users didn't bespell the gate, did they?"

Fialla shook her head.

"Then who did?"

"The priesthood. They couldn't make the gates work for them and in their anger, they did their best to destroy them, telling the people they were evil."

"Hold on a moment. The priesthood? I thought they were against magic."

"Oh, they are. Except for themselves, that is."

"You mean they forbid others to use the power and then use it themselves?"

"I'm afraid so. By the way, let me warn you. Don't ever do anything that could be construed as magic use. It will earn you punishment as a witch."

Lealor laughed. "No one is afraid of magic anymore. Arcane lore is part of almost all of the gate worlds where science hasn't taken hold."

"Heed me, child. It will not be a laughing matter if the priesthood gets you in its clutches."

"What about you?" Lealor gestured to the fire, which burned merrily in the fireplace without any added wood.

"Minor fire magic requires almost no power. It is safe. Even I might be in danger if anyone noticed my abilities. So I'm very careful what I do. I use herbs in my healing. Fialla the old herbwoman, the healer, is how I'm known by the villagers. It would be a very different thing to be Fialla the witchwoman."

"Then magic is all right if no one knows you're using it?"

"To a degree, if a great many small spells take place in any one area, they leave a trace that a witch-finder priest might notice. It's best to leave magic alone unless great need drives you, child."

"All right. I'll be careful," Lealor promised. "Can I do anything for you? The villagers seem worried."

"Most of my problem is old age. There is no cure for that, I fear I've left it too long to choose a successor."

"Did you have no child to follow after you?"

"My husband and daughter died of a plague years ago."

"Oh, I'm sorry," Lealor said. "I didn't mean to remind you of sad things."

"After all these years, I feel resigned. I have looked for years for someone with the talent to become a healer. I think I can train the Smith's little Jessa. All I can do is hold on until she is old enough to learn. Already I have taught her some of the simpler herbs. She can identify them and knows what they cure, but she is too young to actually help any patients."

Fialla smiled, "There are the . . . other . . . things a healer must know." Her head nodded toward the fire. "Some knowledge is too dangerous for a little one to have."

"You're in pain, aren't you?" Lealor said gently, noticing how slowly and stiffly Fialla moved. "Back at my cottage, I think I may have something that will help you—"

A discreet knock on the door interrupted her.

"Come in," Fialla called.

"I came to get Lealor for supper," Aldon said. He placed a covered basket on the table. "Mother sent your supper and some fresh bread and sweetfruit jam." Wide-eyed, he looked around the room. Usually his mother brought food to Fialla herself, but with unexpected company, his mother needed every minute to prepare what his father called a respectable feast on short notice. "Can Lealor come now?" he asked.

"Yes, Aldon, she may come," Fialla said as she rose from the rocker.

"I'll try to get back here tomorrow," Lealor told the healer.

"Thank you. Thank you both," Fialla said, uncovering the heavy basket Dame Smith had sent. "Please tell your mother I am much in her debt. I shall not forget her kindness."

"I will," Aldon promised as he and Lealor went out the door.

The dinner was superb. Although Lealor did not want to admit it, the closeness of the family reminded her of her own. She stifled a twinge of homesickness as she walked through the woods with her guide.

"Is something the matter?" Gren asked, stopping to bend his head to look into her eyes.

Lealor originally had no intentions of allowing anyone to walk her home, but considering the eggs, bread, sweetfruit jam, and leftovers Aldon's mother had hospitably heaped on her guest, Lealor had little choice but to accept the offer of Aldon's uncle. So she smiled up at him and wondered what was wrong with her. Here she was with a personable young man who obviously liked her, and she couldn't manage a single romantic ripple. Even the huge moon shining down on them from a sky filled with stars didn't make a dent.

"No, nothing," Lealor answered. "I was thinking that this evening is cool." Before Gren could take that as an invitation to offer his cloak or put his arm around her, she hurried on to another topic. "How much longer will it be until winter?"

"Ah, that's a good question to distract my attention." Gren chuckled softly.

"I really would like to know the answer."

"We might have as much as a month before the first snow. However, if things go as usual, we could have it any time. The weather in these parts is notoriously sneaky. One day will be bright with warmth in the sunny air and cool breezes in the shade. The next morning you can awake to several feet of snow piled in front of your door."

"Once we have a snowfall, how long will it last?"

"We're lucky there. It will probably stay on the ground for about three months, then one morning you'll awake and find icicles dripping on everything. Within a few weeks, spring will be here again."

"That's unusual. Most of the time where I come from, winter is long and drawn out. It snows and thaws, then snows and thaws so you can never tell exactly when spring arrives. Sometime the weather fools the plants too. Then the little green shoots get their noses nipped when it freezes again."

"Some say it used to be like that here in the old days, but that some wizard named Keeper put a spell on the whole area and changed the weather forever."

"A wizard named Keeper?" Lealor wondered if Gren hated magic users.

"Wizards as a rule are a bad lot. Legends say that Keeper lived in the area where your cottage is."

Lealor laughed. "Then I guess it's safe for me. Even if Keeper returned, he'd probably not harm me."

"Seeing as it's been hundreds of years since anybody's heard from him, that big fight the magic users had with the priesthood probably destroyed him and the priesthood's armies over in the mountains."

"You hunt over a wide area, don't you? Have you ever found anything magical over there?"

"Sometimes I've had a wan chancy feeling while I've been hunting, as if something or someone is watching me, but I've never found anything magical. I wouldn't know what to do with it if I had," he said gruffly, "and you had better not be looking for any magical places or things either. You could stir up more trouble than any magic you found would be worth. We've been fortunate in Riverville so far."

Lealor looked at him with a question in her eyes.

"I mean, we've not got a temple there. We're situated near the river and could easily become a larger place if we wanted to. Anybody who wants to live in a bustling, thriving town may move to one. The elders of Riverville aren't foolish enough to want the priesthood setting up shop among us."

"What about the taxes—I mean tithes?"

"Oh, the elders send them to the priests every year. If the potatoes are small, and the fruit a little wormy, well, what else can you expect of a poor village like Riverville? Then too, we don't always count very well. What civilized priest wants to make a two or three-day journey over notoriously bad roads, to see how to help the poor villagers?" He grinned at his companion. "Sad, isn't it?"

"Oh, very," Lealor managed through her laughter. "You poor, poor people."

"Well, we're not nearly so poor as we'd be if we had a temple saddled on our backs, and you may take my word for that." Gren's voice turned grim. "I'm the tax deliverer for the village. I have to go in to the duke's castle to hand it over. The priest always gives me the shivers if he crosses my path. You may be sure I plan my visit so I'm never there when there's an obligatory service. I'm in and out of there quicker than a furkin taking a piece of cheese out of a trap."

"In your oldest hunting suit, I presume?"

"Threadbare," he said solemnly.

"It's not far now," Lealor told him, hoping to keep the conversation going.

"How do you know?" Gren marveled at her woodcraft. Most village girls knew little, and cared less, for the forest. Lealor had said she was certain she could find her way home alone, and she had proved it several times during their walk.

"The berry bushes. They ring the cottage. They're especially thick right behind it. There are no others between it and Riverville. I noticed today when I followed Aldon. I didn't know then I'd have a guide home."

"Sensible," Gren approved. He wondered how she would react to a crisis. Probably like most women and girls he knew, she'd panic.

"Here we are," Lealor announced triumphantly as she walked into the clearing before the cottage. In her joy to be home, she swung around without watching her step, tripped, and would have fallen if not for Gren's strong handclasp. She looked up at him, silvered by moonlight for a second before the moon went behind a cloud. She felt, more than saw, the huge ursine shape that reared up from the brush beside the path.

Gren pulled her behind him as he turned to face the roaring bear that towered over them both. "Lady bless," he murmured while struggling to pull his axe from its sheath at his waist.

The cloud obligingly scuttled away from the face of the moon, giving Lealor and her escort their first good look at the angry bear.

"Is this your pet?" Gren asked quietly, never taking his eyes from the monster, who must have been foraging for berries before they disturbed it.

"I'm afraid that's not Pook," Lealor told him, trying to sound much braver than she felt at the moment.

CHAPTER NINE

Gren swallowed, pushing Lealor firmly behind him. "When I raise my axe to strike, I want you to run for the cottage and shut the door."

"Stay there, too, I suppose," said Lealor.

"Get ready," Gren said.

"No." Lealor's reply was soft, but determined. "I'm not budging. Give me a moment to see if I can soothe the bear."

"Woman, are you moon-daft? Look at the size of that thing."

"I've got a way with animals. Let me at least try," Lealor said. She could feel the bear hesitating. She was sure she could control it if she had a chance.

"I'll count to ten. If you haven't convinced it to go by then, I'll attack . . . and you run! Agreed?"

"That's not much time—" Lealor began.

"Then I'll attack now." Gren raised his axe.

"All right, all right. Put down your axe."

"Moon-daft," Gren murmured. "Crazy as a necklace bird . . . " He slowly lowered his weapon.

Lealor paid no attention to him. Every ounce of her concentration centered on the bear. She projected friendliness, warmth, harmlessness. The bear did not respond. "Seven, eight," she heard Gren say.

The two humans were so intent on the bear, they missed seeing Pook as he entered the clearing. One look told him the situation. He heard the man say, "Nine." Why was the man counting instead of protecting Lealor? Pook charged.

The wild bear turned her head toward Pook as he reared to his full height between Lealor and her. Pook's fangs gleamed silver in the moonlight. He showed no signs of giving her any consideration because she was female. Pook knew the she-bear recognized that this was his territory, and he had no intention of sharing. She dropped to all fours, turned, and exited the clearing.

"Ten," Gren said weakly. He counted again. Pook, the she-bear, and her mate. Surely, there couldn't be three bears this gigantic in the same area. How had he missed seeing traces of their presence? Perhaps it was time to settle down in Riverville. Lealor would make a fine wife, he decided.

"This is Pook," Lealor told her human defender as she walked between Pook's paws and received a gentle bear hug from him before he backed off and dropped to the ground.

The astounded Gren managed to say, "Glad to meet you, Pook," before he realized he was talking to a half-tamed bear as if it were human.

Pook grunted. Then he turned and walked into the cottage.

"I can't say I'm sorry that's over," Lealor told Gren with a smile.

"Are you all right, lass?" Gren hoped the moonlight hid his pea-green complexion from his companion.

"Of course. I still think if I'd had more time I could have handled that bear. I bet in spring there will be a cub or two around here." She gave Gren a stern look. "Any bears around here are off-limits."

"Naturally, if I see any dragons shall I put them on my don't-shoot list?"

"Well, now that you mention it, yes."

"Lass, you're moon-daft for certain. If it weren't for the fact no one's seen dragons in these parts for years, I do believe you'd try to make friends with them."

"Why not?"

"Why not!" Gren exploded, throwing his hands in the air in a gesture of surrender. "To be so beautiful and not have the sense of a child," he said conversationally to the moon, which had returned to unclouded brightness.

"Piffle! Such a fuss over nothing." Lealor looked exactly like her grandmother as she repeated one of her favorite sayings.

"Lass, you may do fine here through the winter—although I'm coming to check on you from time to time—but in spring, you'd best plan to come to my sister's in the village."

"Why, pray tell?" Lealor stood, arms akimbo, the perfect picture of feminine obduracy.

"The she-bear and her cubs-to-come, for one, and that bear, Pook," Gren said, gesturing theatrically toward the cottage door where an interested Pook stood watching.

"Oh, come in and stop arguing, for Lady's sake." Lealor pushed her way past Pook.

Gren, however, was unable to enter the cottage because of the bear's bulk. "How?" Gren asked.

"Pook, move over," Lealor commanded.

Pook looked at her and stood his ground.

"Pook, did you hear me?"

"He hears you all right. He's just not about to move to let me in. Make a pet of a bear and he gets notions," Gren said, trying to push past Pook to no avail. Pook faced the hunter and yawned, showing his sharp teeth and huge fangs.

"Impressive, at that," Gren murmured, placing the basket on the ground and stepping back.

Then Lealor tried to get through the door. Pook wouldn't move for her, either. In fact, he seemed to fill the doorway completely. "Pook," Lealor warned.

The bear stood in the doorway like a stone statue, and as easy to dislodge as one, too.

"He seems quite happy with me out and you in," Gren remarked with a smile. The situation was not without its humorous side, and Gren had a well-developed sense of the ridiculous.

"Oh, drat," Lealor finally said. "Look, Gren, I'm tired. It's been a long day, and you still have to walk home. I'll see you tomorrow if you're in the village. I plan to bring some things to Fialla."

"Very well," said a somewhat amused Gren, noticing how pretty Lealor looked when she was provoked. I'll go." Then he turned to the bear. "You win—this time," he told the bear before he left.

Lealor stood in the doorway and returned Gren's wave as he walked from the clearing to return to Riverville. As soon as he was out of sight in the moon-dappled shadows, she turned her attention to Pook, who ambled over to the fireplace and sprawled in front of it, innocence shining from every hair in his fine pelt.

"You bad bear! Shame on you! Shame on you! What if Gren had insisted I return to Riverville with him because you wouldn't obey me?"

Pook growled.

"How would you have stopped him?"

Pook yawned, showing his teeth and fangs.

"You're as stubborn as any man I've ever met—and that's no compliment," Lealor told him as she felt his amusement. She took off her boots, and bent to rub her sore feet. 'I've walked a million miles today. I'm certainly tired enough. Tomorrow, I'll get some things ready for Fialla. I recognize quite a few of the plants here. It's harvest time for herbs. I'll try to select mine and some to replenish her stores as well." Lealor sat on the edge of her bed. I'll stretch out for a minute and rest," she said as she pulled the covers to the foot of the bed. "How good this feels!" Within minutes she was fast asleep.

Pook rose and padded over to Lealor. He nudged her with his nose. A ladylike snore was his answer. He moved to the foot of the bed and awkwardly took the covers in his mouth, managing to cover her before he returned to his place before the fire.

The next morning Lealor ignored her aches and pains. She breakfasted with Pook, packed some interesting small jars and boxes into a basket, and set off for Riverville. Several times she stopped along the trail to gather herbs she recognized. By the time she reached Fialla's, she had a load of things to share.

"Come in, come in." Fialla said. "I was expecting you."

"Good morning," Lealor greeted the healer. "I've gathered a few of the herbs I need and some extras for you. I'm surprised at how many different kinds flourish so near the path."

"I've limited my gathering to the sources nearest the village," Fialla explained. "Don't forget that the keepers were herbalists. A strong stand of any herb usually spreads if it's not harvested into extinction. Most people won't go downstream on this side because of the legends. Think it's haunted, they do."

Lealor joined Fialla in her chuckle. "Some of the spots felt warded against animals."

"You could well be right, child. A sun ward is almost invisible, but will last forever—or until some magic user deliberately destroys it. The last of the magic folk had better things to do with their time before they disappeared, and I made use of those herbs for years without any trouble." Fialla had been bundling the herbs Lealor divided as she spoke. She placed hers in baskets that hung from pegs on the walls of her cottage.

Lealor replaced her bundles carefully in her basket. "I'll dry these when I get home." She reached into a corner of her basket and brought out a salve. "If you try this, it will help you."

Fialla took it and sniffed it inquiringly. "What herbs go into this?" she asked.

"Some that don't grow here. At least I haven't seen them yet," Lealor told her. "Part of the ingredients are special and don't exist here, so I've put a small duplicating spell on the box."

"Thank you. The spell is very well done—for an herb-woman."

The two healers smiled at one another in the understanding that two masters of a craft share.

A knock on the door announced Aldon's arrival. "Those old leaves cured Jessa's cough overnight," he said, "Now some people would like you to look at them . . . " He glanced at Fialla. "Mother says if Lealor can help those folks, you can husband your strength. Nobody here has anything seriously wrong with them."

Lealor spent the rest of the morning dosing the villagers and their animals. She felt much more secure with the animals than the people, but her veterinary training helped her handle all her patients. The main difference between the two kinds was that animals couldn't tell her what was wrong with them. Her special abilities came in handy. She could sense the pain her patients felt and that made a true diagnosis possible. She sighed with relief when the last woman left with cream for her cow's udder. She had given the woman a generous container full, sure that some of it would find its way to the woman's hands when she used it and saw how well it worked.

Over the next few weeks she made a practice of going to Riverville every two or three days. She really didn't want patients trouping out to the cottage if she could avoid it. For one thing, she was never quite sure what Pook might do since his unsociable behavior the night Gren walked her home. Second, it was just as well if no one saw Fafleen on her infrequent visits to pick up more steakfruit and pastries. Her visits dwindled in inverse proportion to the hundreds of books she was finding secreted in the cave.

The weather continued to be perfect with bright, crisp days of cloudless skies which turned to cool nights, star-spangled as a rule. No matter how long Lealor studied the skies, she was unable to recognize a single constellation. After the first few weeks, she quit trying. At night she felt most lonely. She was glad when Berdu dropped in. Steakfruit remained his favorite refreshment, but he developed a real fondness for root beer. Lealor hoped her sparse use of the magic provender bag wouldn't cause trouble later. She had taken Fialla's warning very seriously, after she had given it some thought.

The day of the harvest festival dawned, bright as a newly minted realm coin. Lealor felt ready for some fun. She had spent hours studying the few magic books she had brought with her. She finally decided what to do to reestablish the gate. Unfortunately, she needed at least three others able to wield the powers to effect a repair.

The keepers who disconnected the gate had done so thoroughly. The priests had not damaged any truly important part of the gate, because they did not understand how it actually worked. Only someone keeper-trained would be able to handle the energies necessary to make the gate function again. Today at the harvest festival she planned to ask Fialla how to find others qualified to help her restore the gate. No matter what the answer was, however, she planned to have a good time.

"Lealor!" Gren called out as he entered the clearing in front of the cottage.

It was only the second time he had visited. Pook took an extremely dim view of Lealor's having the hunter around. She decided that perhaps the bear sensed Gren was a hunter. That would account for his animosity toward him.

"Wait there, Gren. I'll be right out." She remembered the past few weeks as she poured a generous helping of steakfruit into a bowl and left it on the table. Pook often foraged on his own, but Berdu would miss the fruit if he stopped in. The fact that she wasn't home would not deter Berdu. Root beer filled the crock she kept cooling in the small stream nearby. He would find it, she was sure.

The children also knew the whereabouts of the root beer. Aldon and Jessa came once or twice a week. Their mother would only let them come when Lealor invited them. She would have been appalled to realize the children shamelessly asked to visit.

After Gren tracked the she-bear across the river and into the mountains, there was nothing in the area to fear except Pook himself. Lealor had an excellent reputation among the villagers. If she said Pook was safe, then Dame Smith believed her. The children used the bear as a backrest when they got tired and a pony when they wanted a ride. He listened to Jessa sing songs and Aldon tell stories of what he would do when he grew up. He became, in fact, the perfect sitter for the children, who loved him.

Gren knew that Pook waited on the path outside the village whenever Lealor was visiting. So long as Lealor had some protection, Gren kept his distance from the cottage. He repeated his call once he reached the door.

"I'm almost ready," Lealor said, pulling a warm shawl off the hook where she kept her outdoor clothes. "Now you do understand I won't be home tonight, don't you, Pook?"

Pook, sprawled in front of the fire like a furry teenager, raised one eye to show he was listening, not bear-napping.

"Lady bless us. Surely you don't expect that stupid bear to understand you."

Pook growled softly, startling Gren.

"Don't be so growlly. Gren didn't really mean it. You're quite the smartest bear I've ever known," Lealor assured Pook with a kiss on the top of his head.

The two humans set out for Riverville, followed at a distance by the bear. Neither Gren nor Lealor said a word about the bear until they were close to the village. Lealor turned and called softly. "Pook, I know you're there. Everything's fine. You go home now."

Gren strained his ears and managed to hear the bear moving off in the bushes. "You know, that's amazing. I didn't realize he was behind us until you spoke to him. How do you do it?"

"I know Pook, that's all. He's more stubborn than most men I know."

Their first stop was the blacksmith's house. Lealor gave each of the children a piece of candy.

"Now don't let that spoil your noon meal," she warned.

"Oh, we won't," Aldon said, turning to his sister for confirmation. She nodded in shy agreement, her mouth being too full of candy for her to answer.

"You spoil them dreadfully, you do," Dame Smith said.

"May we go over to the meadow?" Aldon asked.

"If you promise to take good care of your sister, son."

Aldon grinned, seized Jessa's hand, and pulled her out the door. He didn't want to wait around for someone to find a chore for him to do.

"Gren, can you help me for a moment?" The blacksmith's voice boomed from the forge.

"If you'll excuse me, lassies," Gren said, bowing low before he exited the room.

"That man! He'll be the death of me," Dame Smith said, laughing until the tears came to her eyes. Then she explained to Lealor. "He's the very image of that foppish courtier that took Nelda back to the duke's court last winter when Jessa was so ill. Our Nelda is a favorite of the duke's wife," she told Lealor with pride.

"One of these days Uncle Gren will get himself into trouble with those impersonations. You mark my words, mother."

Lealor turned to look at the pretty girl who just climbed down from the loft.

"This is my other daughter, Nelda. Aldon's probably told you all about her. She works at the castle."

Nelda smiled at Lealor. "Oh, dear. If Aldon has told you about me, you've heard truly dreadful things, I bet."

"Only nice ones about his big sister."

All three women laughed at this, for Nelda was barely five feet tall. Even Dame Smith, whose diminutive size was noticeable, was taller than her daughter.

"Nelda, why don't you take Lealor over to the meadow? There are all sorts of holiday booths set up for the fair."

"If you're sure you don't need anything, mother . . . "

"Why don't you stay and help if you want to?" Turning to the older woman, Lealor said, "I can pitch in too, if you want me."

"No, things are well in hand. You young ones go along and I'll follow later." Dame Smith crossed to the fire and stirred the pot that bubbled there, filling the room with the aroma of one of her justly famous stews.

"Come on, then," Nelda urged, taking Lealor's hand and pulling her through the door as if they were little girls again. "Hurry, before mother changes her mind." Lealor went willingly. Evidently, Aldon had learned the vanish-before-they-find-something-for-you-to-do trick from his older sister. As they passed Fialla's door, one of Nelda's friends hailed her.

"Excuse me," Lealor said politely. "I need to see the healer. I'll meet you in the meadow."

Nelda nodded in agreement and waved to her friend. Lealor knocked on Fialla's door.

"Who is it?" Fialla called, immediately following it with "come in," without waiting to see the person she had invited inside.

"It's only me," Lealor assured her, belatedly aware that she really hadn't responded to the question asked.

"Lady's blessing on you, Only Me," the healer teased. The medication Lealor had given her had restored much of her mobility. Today she sounded as cheery as the first bird to return in spring.

"I can see you're in what my granny calls 'fine fettle,'" Lealor told her.

"Indeed, I haven't felt so well in months. I've even planning to hobble over to the meadow to see the fair." The old healer looked to the corner where her walking stick rested.

"Hurray for you!" Lealor said, and meant it. "I have some good news and some bad news."

"This sounds like one of the jokes the children tell," Fialla said, playing along by asking, "What's the good news?"

"I've found out how to restore the gate."

"Wonderful! The bad?"

"I'll need three others who can use the power to help me."

"Oh my stars and whiskers," she said, rubbing her soft and hairless chin. "You do have a problem."

"With you and I to make two, we only need two more."

Fialla's face grew serious. "Child, I do not have the power."

"But—-but—-but, the fire magic and the healing . . . "

"That is not the same as the power to work a gate. Not everyone has it, you know."

"Do you know of anyone else?"

"Give me some time. Perhaps today I'll see someone I can use as a messenger. It's been years since I needed to speak to anyone with that kind of power. Those with magic power have to stay well-hidden."

"I know. How long do you think it will take to find someone?"

"I really couldn't say. Perhaps by next summer . . . "

For a moment Lealor felt a pang of homesickness so strong she felt tears well into her eyes. Then she mastered herself. She had wanted adventure, hadn't' she? Didn't Grandma Cibby often say to be careful what you asked for because you might get it? What difference would a few more months make? So she smiled. "Very well. I'll try to be patient. You will let me know how the search is going, won't you?"

"Of course, child. Now run along. I'll be over later."

When Lealor went outside, she found Gren waiting for her. The sunlight sparkled in his short golden beard. He looked exactly like one of Robin Hood's men to Lealor.

"Are you ready to go, lass?" Gren asked, offering her his arm.

"I am, kind sir," Lealor said. She curtsied and let him escort her to the meadow.

They walked past the stalls where animals were for sale.

"No bears here for you to rescue." Gren made a pretense of being vastly relieved.

"Oh, you!" Lealor made a face at her companion as if she were Jessa's age.

They stopped before a battered tent. Lealor held her breath. She scented evil magic within. That was impossible on Widdershins. Myst didn't tighten on her arm. That was strange. Lealor looked at her bare wrist where the dragon talisman curled, but she saw nothing. Well, she'd told Myst to keep out of things, more or less, and she was getting what she wanted.

Gren strolled on for a step or two and then turned back to Lealor. "Surely you don't want to have your fortune told by that charlatan," he said. "He's an absolute fake."

"I believe you," Lealor responded. 'No one can really tell the future—at least, not on demand and certainly not for money."

Two giggling girls had joined them at the front of the tent. A talking bird chained to a post announced from time to time, "Lorsham, Master of the Future, tells all. Lorsham! Lorsham!"

Lealor stood before it with a disapproving twist to her mouth. "Balderdash!" she muttered.

Gren took her hand, preparing to move on.

"Healer, do you not believe in the powers of the Far South?" One of the girls, a blonde with braids crowning her head, gazed up at Lealor, trusting her to tell the truth.

"We just wanted to hear him for fun," her dark-eyed friend put in, looking at Gren shyly.

"Why, Lealor here, can probably tell you the future herself," Gren spoke spontaneously, without thought.

"Yes, I can," Lealor said, amused to see the shocked look on Gren's face. Then she passed her arms theatrically through the air and said in a solemn voice, "I can see through the mists of time, two girls passing into this tent and being told lies. When they come out, they will be poorer than when they went in."

The girls and Gren laughed, understanding her joke at once. Lealor, however, had a blank look on her face. Her voice died to a whisper. "You,

Talin," she addressed the darker of the two girls, "will marry a rich merchant." Lealor's face froze. Then she blinked. "What?" she asked.

Talin watched Lealor with awed eyes. She was dumb-struck.

The blonde shook her saucy curls. "What can you tell me?"

Gren shot a look at Lealor and wondered what was the matter with her. "You girls are silly. No one can prophesy. It would be magic and you know that's evil," he told them. "Go along now."

The girls hurried off as Lorsham, the fortune teller, came out of his tent. Lealor took an instant dislike to him. She felt that same heart-stopping cold within that she experienced when she saw a snake. Wasn't she a trained animal doctor? She wished she didn't have this prejudice against snakes, but she did. Her eyes focused on the long finger with dirty nail that shook under her nose.

"—I'll thank you, young lady, if you'll kindly go somewhere else and stop disrupting my trade," the scrawny man in the threadbare robe covered with stars finished what had evidently been a longer tirade. She had missed most of it, trying to hide her reaction to him.

"We are sorry," Gren apologized. Lealor was white as a snow flower. What had upset her so?

Lealor was still trying to place the man. He reminded her of someone . . . That was it! His lank, greasy hair and long nose reminded her of the Pardoner in the **Canterbury Tales**. That man had been a hypocrite and liar, too. She allowed Gren to pull her away. For a full dozen paces, they said nothing.

Finally Gren broke the silence. "What exactly was all that about?"

"What was what about?" Lealor's puzzlement showed on her face.

"That foolishness about marrying a rich merchant."

"She will," Lealor said with confidence as his words reminded her of what she had told the girls earlier.

"How in this world or any other would you know that?" Gren was skeptical.

"I—-I just know, that's all." Lealor knew she had made a major error in showing her talent for prophecy. Here, where magic was forbidden—except to the priesthood, she reminded herself—her words could bring her harm.

"Then why didn't you tell the other girl something?"

"Because she will die in childbirth." Lealor's voice left no room for doubt.

"You have the gift to tell the future?" Gren's normal baritone sounded as if he had borrowed his voice from someone else.

"More of a curse. It seldom happens to me, but when it does, it is true." Lealor turned her unhappy face to his.

With an effort, Gren shook off the icicles that ran up his spine. "Well, let's think no more on it. Today is our day to enjoy the harvest festival fair." His quick consoling hug took her mind from the incident because it so surprised her. Not many men would hug a woman they believed to be a witch.

Later, Gren won the archery contest he entered. Then he insisted Lealor have the tiny silver arrow that was the prize.

"Ah, pretty lassie," a voice cried out, "will you not be giving the man some thanks for the gift?"

Lealor stifled the pang the words gave her. She missed the leprechaun Rory. The man teasing her spoke just like her friend. She wanted—no, she needed to go home. A chill wind blew by her. Or was she fey? She shook off the feeling with action. The crowd laughed as Lealor gave Gren a quick kiss of gratitude.

As the afternoon wore on, she looked for a long time at the wares the merchants had for sale. One clever carving of a man with a wolf's muzzle so intrigued her that Gren bought it for her. A jeweler showed her cape pins decorated with strange stones as well as necklaces and rings. She knew better than to admire anything much. Gren would probably insist on buying it for her and she did not want him to feel proprietary. She would have scandalized everyone concerned if she had bought anything for Gren, so she satisfied her urge to spend by buying a toy soldier for Aldon and a rag doll for Jessa. She popped them into her provender bag to leave her hands free to eat the tartlets Gren bought them.

"These are delicious," she told him, licking a spot of filling from her lips. "Back home, we'd call these pasties." She watched Gren finish the last of his tartlet without spilling a drop on his mustache or short beard.

Gren swallowed the last of the treat and said, "In these parts, pastries are big. They have a bottom crust and an upper one. In between there might be any kind of fruit or some of my sister's meat, vegetables, and gravy."

Lealor didn't bother telling him she'd said pasty, not pastry. What he described to her she called a pie. "Where did all the people come from?' she asked. She knew most of the folks from the village and many strangers were looking at the wares for sale in the stalls from which gaily-colored streamers of cloth flew. The local women were outfitted in their best. Even the men had put on festive attire. Some children, who ran from stall to stall, stopped and began watching with wide-eyed delight as a puppet show began from the back of a wagon fixed as a stage.

She and Gren stopped to watch as he said, "Actually, most of these merchants come from Draconsgate."

Seeing her puzzled look, he added, "It's the duke's city."

"That explains the sellers. Where did all the buyers come from? Riverville isn't this big, is it?"

"Not officially, but there are many families who live to the north and east of here. They never miss the chance to celebrate harvest in town."

"I can't see, Uncle Gren," Jessa complained, appearing from nowhere.

"Better?" Gren asked after he placed Jessa on his shoulder.

"Much, thank you," Jessa said, already giggling at the actions of the puppets.

Lealor saw Aldon climb on a hastily erected fence beside the wagon before she directed her attention to the stage, too.

Both the children and nearby adults watched, completely absorbed in the antics of the characters as they thwacked at each other in mock battles. Lealor kept an eye out for Aldon, because the makeshift fence didn't look any too sturdy. He would sit on the top rail, she thought to herself.

Within the fence, a mettlesome horse shied away from the loud laughter of the audience. Then the dealer entered the enclosure. When Lealor saw the horse's ears flatten, she knew trouble brewed for the man. As the dealer approached the animal, it backed away, eyes rolling. The man cursed under his breath and grabbed for the rope halter. The horse reared, then wheeled, kicking the fence where Aldon sat.

Lealor didn't waste a minute. She pushed through the crowd, some of whom had not even noticed the boy's fall. Lealor ducked into the enclosure, where the man stood motionless. "Gren," she called. "Keep that horse away from here."

"Right, lass," he said.

Quick as she was, Lorsham, the fortune teller, got there first. His hands looked dirtier than ever against Aldon's almost white hair.

"I will care for him," he said.

The owner of the horse had led him away, freeing Gren. He knelt beside his nephew. He ignored the man's offer, "Can you help him, lass?"

"Let me see," she said. When Lealor looked at the boy's pale face, she knew he had a serious injury. She reached for his hand, feeling for a pulse. The weak beat was erratic. She sensed the pain in the child's head. Her fingers gently felt his skull. An indentation marked the spot where the hoof had struck.

The crowd made way for the old healer. Fialla came forward and knelt beside the boy. She and Lealor exchanged a look. This injury was not a simple matter for herbcraft to cure. Fialla shook her head. "The boy will die, child," she told Lealor.

"No," Lealor said fiercely. "He will not die." She ignored the tightening of the invisible Myst. In her determination, she rested her hands gently on Aldon's head and used her powers to move the bone outward so it no longer pressed upon the brain of the child. She raised her pale face to the old herbwoman and nodded.

"Someone help move the boy to my home," Fialla said.

Gren carried Aldon out of the meadow while another villager cleared a path.

The fortune teller watched them go. The look in his eyes boded no good for anyone concerned.

CHAPTER TEN

Lealor sat in a chair by Aldon's bedside. Fialla hovered nearby.

"Well, child?" Fialla asked.

"He will be well," Lealor said, pale and strained. It took energy to heal a major injury like Aldon's.

"I'm glad for that," Gren said. He noticed Lealor's pallor. "Are you sure that you're all right, lass?"

"Tired." Lealor summoned a smile, warm as a candle's glow on a dark night.

Dame Smith, her husband not far behind her, burst into the room. "Aldon!" she cried out as she saw the ashen-faced form on the cot.

Aldon's father asked a wordless question of Fialla. His wife was on her knees beside the cot, holding Aldon's hand in hers.

"He'll be fine after a bit," Fialla told him. Lealor nodded her confirmation.

"Lady bless him—and you," Dame Smith said to the healers.

"It will be best if he spends the night with me," Fialla said. "If he wakes, I'll dose him with an herb tea for the headache he will have. For now, he needs his rest."

"Thank you, lass," the blacksmith said. "And you, too, Fialla." He and his wife left the cottage together.

Lealor sighed. She had lost all taste for the evening's festivities. She only wanted to go to bed and sleep for a moon's turn.

"Ah, lass," Gren said, "you have worn yourself out. Come to my sister's and rest a while."

"It's going to take her longer than that, Gren," Fialla said as if Lealor were not present. "She needs several days of rest."

"It was healcraft, wasn't it?" he asked the old herbwoman.

Fialla only nodded. "Come, child, rest here."

"That's your bed, Fialla." Lealor's voice showed her exhaustion. "I want to go home," she said like a little girl. She found she didn't mean the cottage in the woods, she meant home on Realm.

"Will you not stay with us?" Gren's hand rested lightly on her shoulder.

"Home, please," Lealor said.

"Very well. Drink this." Fialla handed her a cup in which a cloudy liquid swirled.

"Wasn't this drink for Aldon?" Lealor asked, drinking as she was bid.

"I can make more." Fialla smiled at Gren, who hovered nearby like a mother greenwing protecting her nest. "It's only a restorative to help her make the trip home."

'Have you set your mind on this?"

Lealor nodded, too tired to waste strength in talking.

"If you will walk her home now, it would be a kindness. The restorative is powerful, but will only last an hour or two. She needs to be safe at home before it wears off," instructed Fialla.

"All right," Gren agreed.

Lealor rose from the chair and approached Aldon. She placed her hand on his forehead. All was well. "Lady bless, Bright Ones protect," she recited, too tired to notice how surprised both Fialla and Gren were by the pale-green aura that surrounded her and her patient.

She straightened. "Let's go now."

"Are you sure, lass?"

"Of course," Lealor almost snapped.

Without another word, Gren led her out of the cottage and down the street. He picked up her bundle from his sister's. Lealor left the soldier and doll with Nelda, who was getting ready for the dance that night. Lealor accepted her profuse thanks graciously and hurried off with Gren. She could feel the flush of the herb's power within her, and she realized it wasn't her own will that kept her going. She felt she'd made herself very vulnerable. If Lorsham's bird was a magical creature, perhaps it could report to its master. Who was Lorsham? Nobody good, she knew already.

Gren took her arm and walked close beside her on the path. He had to, for the trail between the cottage and town was still largely overgrown. Lealor preferred it that way.

In spite of the many questions that seethed within Gren's head, he kept his silence, recognizing Lealor's exhaustion. How had she managed to heal Aldon? He heard Fialla say Aldon would die. He remembered the determination in Lealor's voice as she insisted Aldon would live. As he reviewed the scene mentally, he recalled the form of Lorsham, hanging over Aldon and the two healers like some bird of ill omen. The fortune teller had watched the two women carefully, as if he needed to see exactly what they would do. Gren couldn't remember seeing Lorsham before at a festival fair. Fialla didn't act as if she knew him either. Why would a stranger, who had no actual wares to see visit a backwoods fair? Could the priests have sent him as a spy? Riverville had so far escaped having a temple. Could the priests be suspicious? Gren decided to talk to the elders before he took the next tax payments to the duke.

They reached a wide place next to the river, only a short distance from the cottage. Lealor smiled at him. To Gren, she was almost unimaginably beautiful in the pale moonlight.

"I can make it from here." She slipped her arm out of his and stood alone.

"Are you sure, lass? I'd feel much happier if I could see you safely within."

"I'm a little old to be tucked up like a child." She looked into his concerned face. "I'll be all right. I promise."

Somehow, he knew she would be.

"Besides," she teased, "I don't know what Pook would do if he caught you in the cottage, tucking me in."

"Yes, there is that." Gren's rueful smile showed he was imagining the scene. "Very well."

She took his hand. "Gren," she said.

"Yes, lass?"

"Thank you." Her voice was sincere.

He marveled that she could honestly thank him after what she had done for Aldon. "My family and I owe more thanks to you than you do to me."

"How could I not help Aldon when I had the power to do so?"

"Good night," he told her, turning abruptly and starting back the way they had come.

"Good night, Gren," he heard her call softly after him.

He had taken twenty or more paces on the pathway home before it occurred to him that perhaps he should check on her, without her knowledge. He would worry if he wasn't sure she made it into the cottage. If Pook caught him, he's yell for help, if the bear wouldn't accept his explanation. He turned, ready to go back. Then he saw the huge shadow of a dragon pass over the face of the moon. He watched as the dragon flew lower and lower. It landed in the clearing he and Lealor had stood in only minutes earlier and headed for the cottage. He started to run. Lealor needed him.

Then Pook appeared on the path in front of him.

"Let me pass! There's a dragon . . . "

Pook did not seem disturbed by the news.

He tried to pass. He had no time to waste. Pook blocked his every attempt to go to Lealor. He finally stopped and really looked at the bear. "Can you understand me?" he asked, feeling like a fool as soon as the words left his mouth.

Pook nodded yes.

"Is that dragon a,"—he paused, searching for a word, any word, that would express a relationship between a human and a dragon—"friend or associate of Lealor's?"

Another nod yes.

"She doesn't need me to protect her?"

Another yes.

Gren took a deep breath and tried to calm his racing heart. "Very well. Good night to you, then." Gren turned and retraced his footsteps silently.

Pook did the same.

As Gren walked the path to Riverville, he realized he had fallen in love with Lealor, brave, talented, desirable. What exactly was Lealor?

A special bond existed between Fialla and Lealor. The bear was as intelligent as a human. Perhaps he was a weren. Gren had seen many strange things in the western mountains, but he had noted them and passed on. He was a hunter, pure and simple. He had never, though, seen a dragon, a thing from legends, before this night. She was its friend. Was she a dragon, herself? Another shapeshifter—or, since this was the very stuff of folk tales, a weren? He told himself she couldn't be. Yet . . . no, he'd know somehow. He was only a simple hunter, a very good hunter. He knew when it was time to give up on a hunt.

On the outskirts of Riverville he met Lorsham, floundering along the almost invisible pathway to Lealor's cottage. "Good evening to you," he said, wondering what the man, obviously no woodsman, was doing away from the fair site.

Lorsham peered into Gren's face. "Oh, it's you. Where would your meddling companion be? I thought you two would be at the dance."

"I was out for a breath of air." Gren wasn't going to tell this man anything. Daylight didn't make Lorsham impressive and now the moonlight made him look almost sinister. Perhaps it wasn't only womanly vapors that made Lealor wary of this man.

"Alone?"

The tone of Lorsham's voice made the question an insult.

"Yes, alone."

"Abandoned by the Fire Hair, eh?"

Gren nodded.

"Where'd you meet her, boy?"

Gren clenched his teeth. It would never do to hit so old a man, but how he wanted to! "She came in on a wagon with her family, from east of here somewhere. They pulled out at sundown. She didn't give me any directions how to find her again, either."

"Troublesome sort, she was. You're better off without the likes of her. If you should find her again, I'd like to know where she comes from. No one in town knows anything about her."

Gren said the first true words he had spoken to Lorsham when he said, "I don't imagine I'll be seeing her again before the snows." He nodded politely to the man, thinking to himself that the villagers took care of their own.

The next morning Gren arose early, as usual, and packed for an extended hunting trip. Many times he wintered where he was if the hunting was good. The well-provisioned family stood ready for winter without any more help. In a few days the snow would come, and he would be miles away from town, too far to change his mind and come home easily.

After Gren left, his bewildered brother-in-law said, "But—but I thought he'd planned to spend this winter here with us."

"Poor boy, she must have refused him last night," his sister told her husband privately.

Gren crossed the river and headed west. He didn't plan to find any answers there, but he did need time to think, and he always thought better in the wilderness.

As he walked, he reviewed the happenings of the day before. He was only a simple hunter, he thought. A simple hunter who had fallen in love—with a witch.

CHAPTER ELEVEN

Lealor spent two days at the cottage, resting. She wanted to see how Aldon was progressing, so on the third day she walked into Riverville. Fialla answered her knock on the door with a cheerful, "Come in."

Lealor looked at the cot where she had left Aldon. It was empty. She turned white as a ghost flower. "Aldon—" she began.

"Don't worry. He's been at home since yesterday afternoon," the old healer told her. "He felt far too frisky to stay in bed another day. Since his headache left him after the first few candlemarks, I turned him over to his parents. They know how to keep an eye on him." She stood, looking out of the door. Then she motioned to her guest. "Come and see for yourself."

Lealor looked where Fialla pointed. A small group of children running down the street stopped to play a circle game. Aldon stood in the center waiting to break out. He stayed until the proper time in the song and then ran, reaching the freedom outside the circle.

"A complete recovery, I'd say," said Lealor, relieved.

"So do I. You have a great deal more healcraft than I do, child, but you may have made yourself an enemy."

"An enemy? Why would anyone be angry with me?" Lealor turned her astounded face to Fialla.

"You did nothing wrong. I'm afraid that Lorsham found the injury when he touched the boy's head. A serious wound like that usually causes death, but the boy survived."

"I couldn't let Aldon die, Fialla."

"Of course you couldn't, but I wish that Lorsham had not had the opportunity to find out how dangerous a wound it was."

"I didn't think about him." Lealor frowned, remembering the man. "Abominable cheat! Taking the money from those gullible girls. How dare he call himself a fortune teller? Isn't that against the priest's law? Prophecy is a magical gift."

Fialla busied herself making them a cup of tea while she answered. "True, but the priests' law reaches no farther than the temples, and many back-country places do not bother to give lip service to them and their god. The simple people remember the Lady, although many city folks worship the fashionable god of the priests."

"I have talked about him with Gren, but I still don't know his name. Who is this god?"

"It is best not to name him. A chance remains that use of his name might call the attention of his no-so-humble priesthood." Fialla handed her a cup of tea.

Lealor sat at the table, cradling the cup in her hands. The outside air had a decided nip in it so the warmth from the tea was doubly appreciated.

"Are you planning to stay in the cottage over the winter? You're most welcome to stay here with me if you wish."

"I'd rather be at the cottage." Lealor realized how ungrateful her refusal sounded, so she continued. "Actually, I not only have the bear Pook to take care of, but I have another friend."

"Aldon has been full of your doings since you first came, but he has never mentioned anyone else." Fialla stirred a second spoon of sweetherb into her tea.

"My friend, Fafleen, came with me through the gate. We didn't mean to come. Something—or rather someone—tampered with the gate while we were in transition and we came here, rather than my planned destination."

"Who is so mighty that he can meddle with a gate when it is working?"

"I only know of two people, or beings, who would dare. One is a man of great evil called the Shadowlord, and the other is a young Bright One called Baloo. Baloo, I suspect, is responsible for our being here."

"I have heard tales of the Bright Ones, passed down in my family for generations. I never heard of this Lord of Shadows. Is he from the old legends too?"

Lealor shivered. "No, I only wish he were a legend. He lives, some-where, and plots evil. On Realm, my father and mother fought him, but he escaped. On Achaea, he planned destruction again. I was his prisoner, but my parents and their friends rescued me." The tea wobbled slightly in her cup. No, the Shadowlord was very real. For a moment, she wanted to tell Fialla of Myst, and her early rejection of the talisman bracelet, and all the sorrow that came from the decision made when she was only a child.

"Then you are here to find this Shadowlord and punish him?"

"No, as I told you. I came here on the whim of an infant Bright One. My family always searches for the Shadowlord, but he stays well hidden. Many worlds have gates. The keepers can only watch and hope they find him before he spawns more evil." Lealor smiled ruefully. "Spawns more evil. How foolish and melodramatic that sounds, but it is the truth."

"What does he do that is so wicked?" Fialla sipped her tea while she waited for the answer to her question.

"On Realm he gathered horrible creatures from imaginary worlds to fight for him. They were to form his army, but my parents, dragons, and heroes my father called from Otherwhens battled them and caused him to flee. On Achaea, he convinced the scientists of Atlan to help him. He planned to forge a universal gate to all times and all places. To do this he needed the power of Achaeasun. Baloo, the infant Bright One cradled in Achaea's sun, awakened early and would have died without my mother's healing." Lealor's eyes clouded as she remembered her childish attempts to destroy the Shadowlord's machines. He had looked at her in dragon form and changed her back into a child with one wave of his hand. Then he had forbidden her to change shape on pain of being forever that animal or creature she changed into . . .

"And?" Fialla leaned forward, intent on Lealor's story.

"And what?" Lealor came back to the present with a rush.

"What happened next?"

"Sorry. I forget that everyone doesn't know about the Shadowlord. The gate he formed was unstable, nearly causing Achaeasun to nova. When the gate itself exploded, the force of the blast destroyed the Isle of Atlan on all the time lines where it existed. Mishandled gate power can backlash on all concerned without the proper wards."

"No one knows where this Lord of Shadows is now?"

"No, and it's been almost twenty years since he escaped the last time."

"I can understand why you might ignore a person like Lorsham after having experiences with a man like your Shadowlord."

"Fialla, that's just it. I can't convince anyone, but when I was a child and looked at him, I swear he was all sparkly and shiny inside. His body looked like an old man, but he wasn't. He wasn't," she insisted. Her fingers went white about the cup.

"I believe you, child. What do you think he is, then, if he's not a man?"

Lealor shook her head. "I'm not sure. My parents asked me that question, too. Then I didn't know. For years I had such nightmares about my experiences with him that no one willingly asked me anything to remind me. Now that I'm older, I think . . . no, what I think is impossible."

"Few things are impossible. Do you believe him to be a demon?"

"No. Something much more incredible than that." Lealor looked at Fialla and suddenly knew that the old herbwoman would not laugh at her. She took a deep breath and said, "I think he's a Bright One."

"Why would a creature of such power work with gates? Legends say the Bright Ones were never flesh. Their pure energy could manifest anywhere and any time they chose." Fialla poured her guest another cup of tea.

"What if he didn't know he was a Bright One?"

"If they truly rock the Bright Ones in star cradles as the old lullaby says, how could he not know, child?"

Lealor opened her mouth as if willing herself to speak would produce the truth. Then she sighed. "I don't know."

"Sufficient unto the day," Fialla said.

"You're right about that, at any rate."

"If we move the furniture about, we could make enough room for another bed for your friend," Fialla offered.

"My friend wouldn't fit in this cottage."

"Is your companion an ogre or giant, then?" Fialla's face showed a lively interest, but no fear.

"Fafleen is a dragon."

"Ah, that explains your unwillingness to have unexpected visitors. Does she lurk in the woods or turn invisible when someone besides you is present?"

"How she would hate the idea that she would 'lurk' so someone wouldn't see her! She is a very proud young dragoness. Because she's so young, I wouldn't expect her to become invisible for a very long period. Invisibility is a magical aspect." Lealor took another sip of her tea. "I really am trying to avoid magic as much as possible."

"That is wise. Taming a bear is something people can believe, but taming a dragon . . . "

"I didn't tame her." Lealor almost choked on her tea imagining how indignant Fafleen would be if anyone suggested that dragons needed to be tamed. "On Realm, where we come from, dragons are personages, highly civilized beings, and much more intelligent than the fortunate humans they befriend." Lealor smiled at the look on Fialla's face. She added, "At least according to Fafleen."

'What did you do with her when Gren came to the cottage?"

"Oh, she has interests of her own. She discovered a cave filled with old volumes of forgotten dragon lore. For one so young, she's quite a scholar."

"The Cave of the Dragon King," Fialla breathed.

"Then you know of it?"

"Indeed. The old legends say the king of the dragons loved learning. Some humans gained great rewards by bringing him books."

"Fafleen must be just like him. Since she found the cave, she only flies by to check on me. She feels she must protect me from harm." Lealor set her cup down with an audible thump. "It's ridiculous. I'm a perfectly capable adult," Lealor began. She flushed, realizing that was something an adult did not have to announce.

"Don't you feel a responsibility toward her also?"

"Yes, but—"

"Friends care."

Lealor did not try to answer. Fialla was right. Her fingers went to her wrist and touched Myst gently. After a moment she said, "I have another reason for wanting to be by myself for a while."

"Gren?"

"Am I so transparent?"

"This is a small place. Everyone noticed."

Lealor made a face. "I hate the idea of people spying on me."

"There is little news in Riverville. The actions of one of our most eligible bachelors interested many. You have no need to worry. The day after the festival Gren left at sunup. Aldon told me his uncle would spend the winter trapping."

"I thought he was staying in town this winter."

"So did Aldon."

"Oh, dear."

"If you plan to come, you need to do it soon. I feel winter in my bones."

"No, I'll stay at the cottage."

"If you are sure that is what you want to do. I'll care for the villagers. We will only send for you if we have need."

"I want to see Aldon before I go home to hibernate with Pook."

"If you have need, send Pook to me with a message."

"Don't worry. I have all types of food. The villagers insisted on gifting me after I healed them. I'm very healthy. Pook actually shows no signs of sleeping the winter through. At least not so far," she added as she stood. "He's all the protection any mortal should need."

"Lady bless," Fialla said, giving her a hug.

"Blessings be," Lealor added before leaving.

The Smiths were hospitable as always, but after seeing for herself that Aldon had recovered, Lealor left the village for home.

During the time she was in Riverville the sky had become overcast. Halfway to the cottage, she met Pook who paced back and forth on a short stretch of the path.

"Are you waiting for me?" Lealor touched Pook lightly on the head.

He nudged her gently with his nose before setting off at a rapid pace. He looked back at her once, as if urging her to hurry.

"Pook, wait. I don't intend to run."

The bear woofed and waited until she came closer before moving onward at a rapid pace.

"Oh, silly bear. Why are we rushing so?" However, she increased her stride as a chill wind blew from the west, bringing the first flakes of snow.

Lealor liked snow and would have stood to watch, but Pook hurried her onward.

Neither of them noticed the black bird that watched them with beady eyes and swooped after them for a time, until the wind almost blew it from the skies. With an almost snakelike hiss of triumph, it headed east, pushed by the snowstorm's winds.

CHAPTER TWELVE

Long before Lealor and Pook reached the clearing in front of the cottage, snow covered the ground. The wind increased until Lealor had to bend forward to keep going. When Pook saw, he got between her and the wind. It made it easier for her to move steadily. They plunged into the band of trees that sheltered the cottage and immediately, Lealor felt the difference in the force of the gale and the temperature. Although she used magic herself, the warding spell was so carefully interwoven with the nature of the forest, she had never realized that magic protected the cottage. For a moment, she worried that the craft of that warding would shout *magic user* and cause her problems, then common sense came to her rescue. If no one had noticed in all these years, this year would probably be no different. The snow, which whirled like a dervish outside the protected area, landed lightly on tree, bush, and ground. The snowflakes gently dusted the roof of the cottage. The sight reminded Lealor of holidays. If someone not sensitive to magic came, he might well think the haven around the building was natural. Lealor opened the front door and entered the comfort of her warm cottage. She struggled out of her boots and gloves, congratulating herself for having the forethought to prepare for colder weather "just in case", as her mother often told her.

She stood gazing out the warded window. Only a little cold seeped into the room; however, she knew she needed to pull the shutters closed before going to bed. She had blankets and didn't mind a little chill, but if anyone came and her window was wide open in winter, it would take more explaining than she was willing to do.

She pulled off her boots and left them by the fire. Then she shrugged out of her coat and padded over to hang it on its peg. Pook pawed her slippers from under her bed.

"Hint, hint, huh?" she teased, laughing as Pook put a paw over his nose. His eight-inch claws made the half of his muzzle uncovered by the furry paw look like a walrus mustache.

She untied the provender bag from her belt and moved to the table. "Magical or not, tonight we're having a good old-fashioned hot meal."

Pook lumbered to the table and stood at his place, waiting while she set out huge bowls of hot vegetable soup. She got a loaf of bread from the warming oven attached to the fireplace, and added a dish of butter. Pook picked up his bowl and drained it in one gulp.

"Pook, don't bolt your food," Lealor said, handing the bear a door stopper of buttered bread which he ate in three bites. She shook her head. "I suppose you want more?" She said this as she returned his bowl to the bag to be refilled. This time he lapped decorously at his dinner, the edge of his hunger dulled.

By the time she finished her soup and bread, it was quite dark outside. "Oh, fiddle," she muttered, knowing it was time to close the shutters. She lit the big lamp that hung from a beam in the center of the room. It started burning at her touch in spite of hanging for years, unused. "More unde-tectable magic," she murmured to herself. Next, she redressed and went out, Pook trailing along with her. In seconds she removed the pegs holding the shutters against the walls of the cottage and repegged them in the closed position. Pook stretched to his full height and sniffed the air. Like all bears, his vision was poor, but his sense of smell was superb. Satisfied that no danger lurked, he followed Lealor into the cottage.

She quickly readied herself for bed. The magical flame sprite that would keep the fire burning during the night danced and leaped over the wood, creating heat and a dim light that lulled Pook and Lealor to the edge of sleep.

"I know Fafleen hates the cold, so I don't have to worry that she's out in this storm. Ice dragons thrive in it, but Fafleen, like most dragons, wants to be warm and toasty in winter weather. I wonder what's become of Berdu . . . " she murmured before she drifted off.

The next morning, snow ruled the world as far as Lealor could see. Most of the trees had lost their leaves and stood, stark and bare like living icicles, against the slate sky. A solid pall of clouds covered the sun. From them, snow drifted down, quietly covering everything. Lealor carried out bunches of cut grass for the deer and swept a bare spot to hold sprinkled seeds for the birds. She remembered Aldon looking like an ambulatory haystack as he carried piles to the shed behind the cottage. Jessa had been proud as she collected apronfuls of seeds from the wild plants that hemmed the path. The rest of the day Lealor prepared herbal remedies and studied the books she had brought with her. She wondered how Fafleen was coming along on her translation, but she didn't worry about her. It was best if no one saw her. A blue dragon would stand out vividly against the snow. Fafleen might stay away all winter, for she had plenty of supplies and was very self-sufficient. She and Lealor had discussed this possibility earlier.

Almost a month passed before there was any change in Lealor's routine. Early one morning a messenger from Riverville broke a path through the fallen snow.

Lealor opened the door and saw Hugh, one of the farmers that lived outside the village. "What brings you out in drifts like this?" she asked, gesturing for him to come inside.

"Fialla sent me with a message. The duke's little son is ill and no one can cure him. Nelda told the duchess about you, healer, and now the duke summons you to his court. The messenger awaits in the village."

"Well, sit down by the fire and warm up while I get ready."

Hugh doffed his cap and went to stand near the hearth. He narrowly missed stepping on Pook, who sprawled before the fire in his usual place.

The bear rose with a roar of outrage that even frightened Lealor. Hugh turned as white as the snow outside and backed carefully to a spot just inside the door. No amount of urging on Lealor's part could induce him to move farther into the cabin, although Pook moved to one corner and sat, keeping an eye on their visitor.

Hugh watched the bear and Pook watched Hugh. Lealor thought they looked ridiculous, glaring at one another, but she gave up trying to make them act civilized. All she could do was hurry, so the awkward situation would last no longer than necessary. Bears and men, she decided privately, were the only two things as stubborn as dragons.

Pook growled softly as she collected what she thought she might need to help the boy. She talked to Pook as if he were another person. She always talked to animals this way, and even if Hugh thought she was crazy, she wasn't going away without trying to make the bear understand. She explained to Pook about the note she was leaving for Fafleen, just in case she should decide to come to visit. She tried to impress on the bear that she would be quite safe. but his growl showed he didn't believe her. When she was ready to go, he blocked her path to the door.

"Pook," she said, aware that Hugh never took his eyes from the bear, "You must move or you'll be sorry."

The look on Hugh's face said as plainly as words that he wanted to see how Lealor controlled an eight-hundred-pound bear.

Lealor was wondering about it herself.

"Pook, I intend to go. If you don't let me pass, I'll—I'll hit you on the nose!" she said, quite pleased with herself for thinking of something that might work and was not magical.

Pook, woofed once, then turned his back on her and settled down by the fire. Lealor had a distinct impression that if he could have talked, he would have said, "Don't say I didn't warn you!" Once the way was clear, Hugh and Lealor wasted no time in starting out for Riverville.

The walk to the village was difficult, for once out of the cottage area, the snow was almost thigh deep. Hugh had broken a trail so her walk was not as arduous as it might have been. Once in the village, she stopped to see Fialla and Aldon's family. The messenger from the castle tried to hurry her, so after Lealor spoke to her friends, she wasted no time in climbing aboard the sleigh the duke had sent. The messenger had fed the rested horses, making the trip to the castle as rapid as anyone might wish, considering the snow.

A change of horses and a relief driver awaited them at the halfway point. Snuggled in furs like a princess in a Russian fairy tale, Lealor slept in the sleigh. The next morning at sunup, they entered the castle courtyard. Lealor felt sorry for the horses, though they had changed teams a second time at a crossroads inn. They had given her time to eat and walk around briefly, before loading her up again and rushing onward. She felt so tired, she didn't remember much about the stop except it was a relief from the cold.

The servants woke her and helped her out of the sleigh before they hurried her inside the castle. The somewhat dazed Lealor stood in the huge entrance hall until Nelda, the Smith's daughter, came briskly down the stairway. Before Nelda smothered Lealor in a hug, Lealor had time to notice that Nelda's clothes were a good deal finer than anything she had worn to the festival.

'Oh, healer, I'm so glad you came. Little Reynal is so ill. We've tried everything," she continued, as they climbed the stairs.

While the hall below seemed warm, the halls they passed through felt distinctly chilly to Lealor. The grand tapestries on the walls impressed her although she knew they were there more to keep out the cold than to awe visiting healers. Nelda ushered her into a tower room, nodding to the guard outside the door. They entered a small chamber crowded with toys and people.

The boy is dying," a black-robed priest told the duke.

Lealor looked at the priest's cold face, specter pale. The poor child, she thought. Tended by someone who looked like he lived on curdled milk, what chance had he to recover? The smell! A scent of black magic filled the room. Was it, she wondered, meant to kill or to cure the boy? She took small breaths, intent on inhaling as little as possible of the noxious vapors in the room.

"That's the priest, Credolt," Nelda whispered in Lealor's ear.

"Very well," said the tall man with the silver hair and jeweled sword. Lealor guessed him to be the duke, not from his dress, but from his bearing.

"Perhaps if you made another offering at the temple . . . " Credolt said, attempting a smile, which only made Lealor dislike him more.

"No," the duke told him firmly. "You may leave," he added as Nelda and Lealor's presence finally registered.

The fire smoked fitfully when the door opened for Credolt and his three companions to leave. The duke waited until only Nelda, Lealor, and one other man were in the room.

"Your opinion, Dr. Small?" The duke muted his powerful voice, although the room seemed more spacious somehow without Credolt and company.

To give him credit, the doctor did not want to talk about the child's condition with the boy on the bed before him, but he was bound to answer his superior. He turned from the bed to face the duke and shook his head slightly from side to side. His sigh said more than words could have conveyed.

"Very well," the duke repeated. "You may leave." He waited until the door closed behind him. He smiled politely at Lealor, but he spoke to Nelda. "This is . . . ?" he asked.

"The healer, sir. Lealor," Nelda said with a curtsy.

Lealor inclined her head respectfully. She had never curtsied to anyone in her life and she did not intend to begin now.

"You are young, Healer Lealor."

Lealor nodded, standing quietly while every instinct said to go the boy.

"You have heard the prognosis of the priest and the doctor?"

"Yes."

"Are you willing to try to save my boy's life?"

"If I can, sir."

"Is there anything that I need to do before you begin?"

"Yes." Lealor's tone was grim as she moved to the side of the bed. "Have someone take out all these toys for now. Clear this room of smoke. Is there somewhere we can move Reynal while we clean?" She hurriedly put a stasis spell on the boy so his condition would not worsen.

"We've prepared a room for you next door," Nelda said. "We can move Reynal there. You go, too. You've had no rest since the trip. I had a meal sent up for you."

The duke lifted his son carefully and carried him from the room. The child's ash-blond hair and pale face seen against the rich brown of the duke's jacket gave Lealor a pang.

"I'll see to this." Nelda piled toys into the arms of the two women who appeared at the door like magic.

"Make sure you open the windows and air this room well, before we come in again." Lealor looked at the smoking fire.

"If there's no way to get that fireplace to draw correctly, we'll have to find another room."

"I'll take care of everything, healer," Nelda said, her manner showing her approval of Lealor's orders.

Lealor entered her room with a feeling of relief. Anything was better than that smoky, magic-filled room next door. She saw the duke sitting on his son's bed, holding the boy's hand. Reynal looked better to her already, but he was a gravely ill child.

"My lord, can you tell me what measures have failed to help Reynal recover?" Lealor placed her hand on the boy's forehead. He radiated heat. The special healer's gift the goddesses of Achaea gave her as a child told her all she needed to know about the extent of his illness.

"We've tried everything. Prayers in the temple, sacrifices to the god, potions, pills, leeches—"

"You allowed them to put leeches on the boy?" Lealor's fists clenched.

"Why, yes. Nothing else seemed to work, so Credolt talked to Dr. Small and convinced him to apply the leeches. You don't approve?"

"Have you ever seen what a bleeding wound does to a warrior on a battlefield?"

"Yes," the duke answered, considering her words.

"Isn't stopping the blood the first thing to be done in case of a bleeding wound?"

"Yes," the duke said, already seeing her point.

The door opened.

"Then why didn't your own good sense tell you that taking blood from a sick child was a bad thing to do?" Lealor entirely forgot to whom she spoke, she was so angry.

The woman who entered the room answered for the duke. "You must remember how ill Reynal is. We were ready to try anything."

"My dear," the duke said, rising to take his wife's hand.

Nelda bustled in. "The room is ready. It's cleared and aired. I had new logs laid on the fire, and it's drawing fine, now." Noticing the duchess, she smiled. "My lady, this is Lealor, the healer who saved my brother's life."

"We've been talking," the duchess said.

Nelda glanced at the tray on the table. "Why, you haven't eaten a thing!"

"All I'd like is a hot cup of tea for now," Lealor told her. "What's more important is getting this young man changed into clean clothes and in a freshly-made bed."

"You take time for your tea, healer, and I'll help Nelda with Reynal," the duchess said.

Lealor smiled. Evidently, Reynal's parents had been shoved to the side by all those quacks who were trying to cure him. Lealor thought it was most important for people who really cared about a sick person to help him. She would be glad for any assistance they would give her.

The duchess left with Nelda, following the duke, who carried Reynal. A maid appeared almost at once. Lealor sat wearily in a chair and allowed the girl to pull off her boots. She took the cup of tea the maid handed her, and she wiggled her toes in the thick socks she wore for the trip. The maid brought her soft slippers for her feet. Lealor spit out her first sip of the hot tea. Every sense warned her of danger.

"Is the tea too hot?" the maid asked.

"Where did this come from? Was it made for me?"

"Oh, no. I took if from the special foods prepared for the young duke."

"Reynal eats only these—special foods?" Lealor scrubbed her lips with the back of her hand. Something special was in the boy's food, no doubt of that.

"Is something wrong? Don't you like the tea? I can make fresh. There's a pot of hot water on the tray." The little maid was anxious to please, but Lealor did not entirely trust her.

"Bring me a cup of plain hot water," Lealor commanded. Once she had it, she reached into her provender bag for some tea laced with a special restorative herb. The bag delivered flawlessly. To take the maid's mind from what she had seen, she said, "I've clean stockings in my bag." Lealor sat, watching the girl retrieve them. She was content to save her energy for healing Reynal. She needed this brief time to recharge her own spirit for the fight ahead of her. She sipped her tea and allowed the girl to change her socks.

"How fine a wool this is, healer. What kind of stockings are these?"

"Orlon," Lealor answered without thinking.

"Or-lon? What kind of animal gives that wool? I've never seen an orlon."

Lealor was so tired she felt silly. She stifled a giggle. "Wild orlons are very rare, even where I come from," she said. She sipped her tea thoughtfully after she dismissed the maid. She knew she had a battle before her. She preferred resting before taking on a responsibility like this, but the boy needed help now, not when it was physically convenient for her. She rose and went to her charge. Nelda had the room aired and Reynal in bed. This time the duchess sat on the bed, stroking the boy's head. The duke stood beside her, watching.

"It's almost time for Reynal's medicine. Do you want me to give it to him?" Nelda asked, holding a vial in her hand.

"By no means," Lealor told her. She took the vial and sniffed cautiously. Nothing she had ever heard of before, but her magical sense told her it would not aid in the child's recovery. She reached into her provender bag. It was as well that her grandmother had modified it especially for her, or it would have produced only food. She remembered her father telling about the problem he had with his when he wanted it to produce a coin for a boat ride. She fished out a bottle of liquid antibiotic. She didn't know if using the bag would leave a magical residue or not, but now, she needed all the help she could get to start the healing process, so she risked being detected by some priestly snooper.

The duchess held Reynal's' head elevated so Lealor could spoon in the medicine that smelled like fruit.

"He'll sleep now," Lealor told the anxious parents. "I'll stay with him tonight. Please see that no one but Nelda comes in here until tomorrow."

The duke nodded his agreement. He and his wife had decided they trusted this flame-haired healer in spite of her youth. She was far from the aged granny they had expected. Both the duke and the duchess kissed the boy before leaving.

"Well, that's one improvement, at any rate," Nelda said.

"What?" Lealor asked, busy settling herself comfortably beside her patient.

"Letting his parents minister to him. Credolt and the rest of those men thought they should stay away." Nelda's sniff said as plainly as words her opinion of that policy.

"Nelda, I want you to personally prepare every bite that Reynal and I eat. Can you do it unobtrusively, so no one notices and makes a big fuss?"

"Why don't I keep bringing the special food up here, and then you can share yours with Reynal?" Nelda didn't need telling what Lealor was guarding against. "Do you want me to take turns sitting with him tonight?"

"No. For tonight, I'll sit." Lealor took Reynal's right hand in hers and placed her other hand on his neck. His pulse was stronger already.

"I'll bring you a meal later," Nelda said as she slipped out the door.

The rough panes let in a dim light. Lealor wondered where the day had fled, but realized it was only late afternoon. The dark gray outside the windows was only the harbinger of night. Leaden clouds dropped snow that the wind blew against the pane unrelentingly. Lealor smiled at the sleeping boy. She started pouring her strength into his body to help him fight the illness. Later Nelda came in to attend to the fire. Lealor slept bent over her patient, also sound asleep. A soft green light glowed from her and the boy.

"The Lady's blessing!" Nelda breathed in awe. She hurried off to tell her mistress Reynal was in very good hands indeed.

CHAPTER THIRTEEN

For Lealor, the next three days remained a hazy period in her memory. She sponged, dosed, and literally forced energy into Reynal. Her periods away from him were brief necessities. By the end of the time, she was pale and thin, but her much improved patient remained weak. Over the course of the next week he stayed awake longer and longer. Lealor remained close, just in case, but by the second week after her arrival, she was confident of the boy's recovery.

His parents showed their appreciation by showering her with gifts, since she refused the gold the duke offered. She took her meals with Reynal as a means of missing the formal dinners in the banquet hall; however, she did consent to ride the dappled grey mare the duke gave her as a present. Her herbal skills became open knowledge when word of the young duke's recovery became public. Castle servitors asked help for their ailments and for those of their relatives and friends. Since the duke requested that Lealor stay with them until spring, in case Reynal had a relapse, she was quite willing to give aid where she could. She carefully refrained from practicing on the members of the court. They could afford the fees of the doctors in the town. While it was sensible to avoid stirring up enmity by taking paying customers away from the local medical practitioners, she felt as if animals should be her real patients, and she only helped the poor because her care was better than none. Most of what she did was simple healing of sores, boils, cuts, coughs, and other minor ailments. She passed along a great deal of basic health information in the process.

Reynal studied part of every day with his tutor. This gave Lealor some free time for herself. She spent much of it in the stables, helping in the care of the animals. Some days were too icy or cold to risk injury to her horse, which she named Little Bit. Caring for the animals gave her a quiet pleasure that the constant company of the courtiers did not.

One afternoon as she came into the courtyard outside the kitchen, she saw a boy chopping wood for the fires. Lealor often walked through the kitchen on her way to the stables, so she recognized him as one of the cook's youngest helpers. The boys who helped the cooks were culinary go-fers, going for this or that at the cook's will. Lealor remembered how Aldon hated bringing wood for the forge. She wondered what he would think of the huge kitchen fires that never all went out. At least one fire burned heartily all night, in case some courtier or another awoke and wanted hot food. She didn't have a drop of noble blood. When she saw how hard ordinary folk had to labor to keep the nobles in the castle happy, she felt satisfied by her common antecedents.

Her stride took her across the courtyard to a back door of the stable. As she pulled it open, she heard a strange thunk followed by a yell. When she turned to look, she saw the boy swaying dizzily, propping himself on the ax. On his left legging a red stain grew exponentially. Lealor didn't need to see the wound to know the ax had hit an artery. The boy's life was seconds from ending. She sprinted across and ripped the cloth of the legging from the injury. He was in such a shocked condition that he was not even embarrassed. Lealor unhesitatingly put her hand over the gushing wound and began to heal. She probed deep with her mind, willing the flesh to close and begin to mend.

The cook waddled out the kitchen door and called, "Taydolf, you scatterwit! Didn't I tell you to hurry with that wood?" He continued scolding as he crossed the courtyard. By the time he finished speaking he stood next to the injured lad, and his voice changed considerably. "What on Widdershins happened? I sent the boy on a simple errand to get wood, and now he lies in a pool of blood."

"He hit himself with the ax," Lealor explained, turning her head briefly toward the cook, while inwardly she commanded, "heal."

"Oh, healer, it's you. Lucky for him that you were near. It must have been a fearsome wound." The cook wiped his hands on his apron over and over.

"I've repaired the damage. It isn't as bad as it looks," Lealor lied, not wanting the true extent of her powers to become known. "Let me have your apron to cover him. It's freezing out here."

"Who would have thought the lad would have had so much blood in him?" The cook shook his head and held out his apron. "He's such a little lad."

"Sending him out here to chop wood at his age wasn't a very wise idea," Lealor said with a grim look in her eyes. She always carried a few bandages and some healing herbs since news of her healing talents spread. For once, it was turning out to be an excellent habit. She reached into her coat pocket for a roll of cloth and bandages while she listened.

"I didn't send him to chop it, just to bring in a few armfuls. Old Tom is the wood chopper. He never should have left the ax out by the pile."

"Yes, besides being unsafe, it rusts the metal and ruins the edge," said Lealor, who had chopped quite a bit of wood since she arrived on Widder-shins. She brushed the boy's orangey hair out of his face and smiled at him. Too shocked to speak, he rested quietly, content to let the healer take care of him. The cook was thoughtless, but not cruel. "Make it clear when you send the small boys out that they are not to chop wood. If there is none ready, they must tell someone, not try to use the ax themselves. This boy might have been permanently maimed, trying to bring you wood." She frowned as she considered the situation. The cook looked so concerned that she added, "The boy will recover. This time we were lucky. He'll need a week or so of rest before he resumes his full duties." She looked down at the boy, awkwardly covered by the apron. "Send someone out with a blanket to take him to his bed, will you?"

Drundle, one of the serving men, arrived with a blanket. In moments, he wrapped the boy and carried him inside. It never occurred to Lealor to wonder who sent him. The priest, Credolt, who viewed the healing through an upstairs window, felt disturbed by the faint green glow he had seen.

"I wonder," he murmured to himself, "if there is any advantage in sending this upstart healer to the temple. In only a few more weeks we will need the spring sacrifice. She is both young and lovely. By the time we hold a trial, sacrifice time will be very near. I'll write a letter to my superior, Priest Lustven." His eyes gleamed with satisfaction.

Within four days, the spring thaw started. Everyone told Lealor that it would snow hard at least once more before spring really arrived, but the worst of the winter was over. The duke decided to take a fortnight's trip to inspect the northern defenses. Before he left, he specifically asked Lealor to stay until his return.

"Healer, usually I try to take my son with me when I make the rounds of the frontier posts. It's good for him to get away from court and learn a little about real life. The men like seeing him, too. When the day comes for him to take over, he will know the job and the men." He noticed Lealor's frown. "Now, I can see a much improved Reynal, but he's not well enough to come along with the chance of the weather's turning. If I wait much longer, the trip will be one long slog through the mud. The nomads don't normally raid until high summer, but I want to make sure all is in readiness," he explained to Lealor.

"I'll be glad to keep an eye on his health while you're gone," Lealor said, looking the duke straight in the eye as she said it.

The duke knew exactly what might threaten his son's health and his grim nod of agreement showed it. The astute duke remembered well how Credolt's ministrations had affected his son. He always protected his people from the depredations of the priesthood as well as he was able. Doing this had earned him the enmity of the priesthood, Credolt in particular. However, the duke never thought the priests would seek revenge by endangering a child. He had learned a great deal about the temple religion during his son's illness. He planned to redouble his vigilance over the priests in his domains and rear his son in his image.

During the next few days after the duke left, much coming and going kept the roads full. Everyone felt tired of being solitary. The merchants were moving all the goods they could before the roads thawed totally. The weather cooperated wonderfully, cold enough at night to freeze the roads, but with a hint of warmth and bright sunshine during the day to herald the coming season.

In the winter, few messages came from Mancy, the capital, where the King lived. With the approach of spring, a series of mail pouches arrived. Lustven seemed delighted with Credolt's candidate for the spring sacrifice. Every spring it was more difficult to find a suitable candidate for the ceremony. Having someone without a family to bewail her doom would be a welcome change from the usual political maneuvering that went on in Mancy every year when sacrifice time came again. The witch hunter would arrive within three days with a suitable conveyance to bring the witch who healed to face her trial at the temple in Mancy.

Credolt put down the letter. He rubbed his hands together as he considered the timing. With the duke gone, there was no one strong enough to oppose the arrest of Lealor. She would be in the capital before the duke returned home if his luck held. If the main thaw obliged, it would be weeks before the duke could arrive in Mancy to attest to Lealor's innocence. No one condemned for witchcraft had ever escaped the justice of the priests after the trial. For once, his lips managed a true smile, but while his face changed for the better, his eyes remained as cold as the snow atop Mount Neverthaw.

On the day the witch hunter arrived, Lealor got an early warning from Nelda, who had a series of informants which would have better suited the master of a spy network.

"Lealor, the witch wagon has come," Nelda told her friend with a worried look in her eyes.

"What's a witch wagon?" asked Lealor, who wondered why she should care as she picked up the beanbag she and Reynal had been tossing before the tutor came for the boy's chess lesson.

"When the priesthood has evidence of witchcraft, the witch wagon comes out to transport the accused person to the temple in Mancy. We've heard tales in Riverville about how cruel the witch hunters are. It's one of the reasons the elders refuse to let the town grow large enough to require a permanent priest. Who knows what he might send in his reports to the temple?"

"Oh," Lealor said lamely. She felt she couldn't stand by silently while obvious injustice happened. "Do you know who they are accusing?"

"Usually my sources know, but this time there is no word."

They looked at Reynal playing chess with his tutor. The boy almost glowed with health. A newcomer to court would never know how ill he had been so short a time before.

"He's much better," Nelda said approvingly.

"When the spring sunshine came, the last of the pallor disappeared," Lealor said, as she put her medicines in her magic bag.

"You talk as if most of the credit didn't belong to you."

"My healing powers are a gift."

"I have seen the Lady's green glow when you healed," Nelda said, not sure if she should mention the fact or not.

"A green glow?" Lealor felt surprised. On Realm and Earth she never glowed.

"Well, on Widdershins, those with true healing power from the Lady cast a green halo around them when they heal. It helps us tell if we're in the presence of honest magic."

"What do you see if the magic is evil?" Lealor asked out of curiosity.

"Oh, nothing. The old lore tells us that no evil magician or healer can cast a green glow, for that comes only by the will of the Lady."

"Then no one who is innocent should fear the witch hunters." Lealor smiled. One less problem to tackle. In a few days she should be able to return to her cottage. She wondered what news Fialla had for her. If no one could help her activate the gate, she was ready to let Fafleen try to take them home.

"Yes, but the trials do not have to be honest. In the past the accused have not wanted a chance to protest their convictions. No one can speak to the accused—"

"Whyever not?"

"The priests wish to protect people from the evil magic of the witches." Nelda pursed her lips briefly, then continued. "So we do not know why people refuse to defend themselves. At least that is what the priests tell us. They say the witches' guilt keeps them silent."

"Not exactly unbiased witnesses, are they?" Lealor could practically smell the corruption of the priesthood. Somebody should do something about them. The god they worshipped truly deserved better priests. Once a group of unscrupulous men got into the priesthood, they could manipulate events to their own interest. Even nonbelievers wouldn't want to fight against a god—in case they should be wrong and he decided to act against them. Suddenly, she wanted to return to her cottage in the woods where she had friends.

A knock on the door announced the messenger of the duchess.

"Come in," Lealor invited.

"Come to the audience hall at once, healer." Leydon, the messenger, spoke solemnly.

"Very well. Let me take time to change clothes so I'll be presentable."

"I said come at once. With no delays."

"What on Widdershins is wrong with you, Leydon?" Nelda asked. "Lealor will be there right away. Don't worry."

Leydon bowed and left without saying anything more.

"Very strange." Nelda frowned. "It's not like the duchess at all. Leydon and I have always been friends. He looks like he swallowed a pucker fruit."

"Oh, anyone can have an off day," Lealor said before she waved to Reynal and went to her room to wash her hands and face as quickly as she could.

For some reason the atmosphere weighed on Lealor as she entered the audience hall. Credolt stood next to a pair of men dressed all in black. A third black-clad man had his back turned away from Lealor. He was whispering to the priest. All color in the room seemed dimmed. The duchess sat in the duke's chair. She wore a worried look on her face.

"Healer," she began.

"Seize her," a voice said. It was the man with his back toward Lealor.

Lealor's eyes widened. She recognized the speaker before he turned to face her. It was Lorsham, the nasty fortune teller from the fair.

"Surely, witch hunter, you will give her leave to collect her possessions—" the duchess said, half rising from her chair, as if she sensed she needed all the authority she could get.

"No," Credolt said, gesturing to her to remain seated. "Search the witch's room quickly. If we allowed her to return to it, she might work evil magic or escape."

Behind Credolt, the door opened fractionally and remained open long enough for the secret listener to hear the priest speak. The door closed silently. Lealor doubted anyone else noticed it. All her senses were alert. She frantically tried to remember what she left in her room that might incriminate her. Worse yet, was there anything from Fialla that might catch her in this priestly net?

"Priest Credolt, if she must go to Mancy to stand trial, may she not go in a carriage? She did cure my son."

"No, never, not permitted. The witch wagon is specially warded to protect innocent bystanders from any evil spells." Credolt enjoyed flaunting his power, but he could see that the duchess, who had always been open to his suggestions, was changing her opinion of him. He therefore pretended to relent. "However, you may put clean straw in the wagon to cushion her and keep her warm in the cold. See to it," he commanded a servant.

The duchess looked ready to countermand the priest's order, but Lealor spoke. She did not want anyone here to get in trouble. After all, Myst would protect her from real danger, she told herself.

"That's all right. If I might have my cape . . . "

"No," Lorsham said. "The cape might be magical!" His smile paid

Lealor in full for her interference at the fair. She should have a cold, miserable trip to the dungeons of the temple. This thought caused him to smile.

Bright Ones, Lealor thought, noting the wintery grimace that the witch hunter used as a smile. He makes Credolt look positively benign.

"Then she shall have mine," the duchess said, motioning to a servant, who hurried to get it.

Everyone stood still. No one said anything, although the duchess looked as if she would like to speak privately to Lealor.

Credolt took the cape and examined it carefully before handling it gingerly to Lealor. He acted as if she had some noxious disease he was afraid of catching.

"Can you not wait a few days until my husband returns?"

Credolt's heart beat fast. The last thing he wanted was to face the duke for control of Lealor. The witch hunter came to his aid.

"No, that is not possible. We leave immediately for Mancy."

With a nod to his two burly subordinates, he bowed to the duchess, turned and exited the audience hall.

The two men took Lealor in charge and hurried her from the room. She could barely keep up with the strides of her captors, but as she took her last glimpses of the castle, she noticed Nelda on the top landing of the stairs, making the gesture Aldon had taught her that meant friends were helping.

CHAPTER FOURTEEN

Lealor was thankful for the cloak the duchess had given her when she felt the sharp bite of the wind in the courtyard. One of the stableboys was carrying a last load of golden straw to put in the iron-barred wagon. She looked at the pitiful few wisps of old straw on the ground. No luxuries for witches around here, she thought flippantly. She smiled at the boy as he exited the wagon.

He nodded to her shyly. "It's all ready, healer," he said.

The guard on Lealor's left released her long enough to strike the boy. "Not healer. Witch. Has she laid some spell on you?"

"Oh, no sir." The boy scurried off before the guard could correct him again.

Lealor silently gritted her teeth. She liked Olwen. They had worked together curing a lame horse. She taught him some of the herbs and remedies to use in healing horses. He was a quick learner, too. She couldn't blame him for hurrying away from the brutal guardsmen assigned to her. On Widdershins, witches couldn't afford popularity. It was too dangerous for other people.

With a shove and a curse, the men helped Lealor into the wagon. They closed the iron door and locked it. When Lealor heard it clang, she shivered. For the first time she felt cut off from her friends.

She looked around her prison. Crude but sturdy planks formed the witch wagon. One closed-in corner behind the driver's seat contained a chamber pot. From this, she deduced no rest stops were allowed her. Thank Bright Ones her provender bag looked worthless, and more important, harmless. She wondered if they would bother feeding her on the trip. While she wanted to see more of Widdershins, she had not planned to make a trip all the way to the capital city. She watched Lorsham enter a closed black carriage that probably contained all the comforts they denied her. With no warning, the driver of the witch wagon whipped the horses and Lealor's journey started with a jolt that would have left her on the floor had she not been holding on to the bars of her cage. She felt sorry for the horses who had done nothing to deserve the unfair treatment they were getting. The stablemaster had given the witch hunter two of the nastiest nags in the stable. Lealor remembered the boys complaining of bites and kicks when they tried to groom them.

Within a few miles, she had reason to be extremely thankful for the new straw. When she grew tired of standing, she tried sitting. The straw protected her body from the full effects of the constant jolts of the wagon. The horses kept a steady and rapid pace. If they showed signs of slowing, the driver whipped them. Lealor watched the scenery with interest. The rolling lands of the duke gradually flattened into a monotonous prairie, dotted here and there with small stands of trees. Lealor guessed from their size that they were probably fruit trees. The breeze was slightly uncomfortable, but the sun beaming down kept her from being really cold.

At sunset, however, they showed no sign of stopping. The terrain changed again. Many tall trees formed an unbroken forest on both sides of the road. They shaded the wagon from the last rays of the setting sun. Lealor felt tired and sore before they finally drew into an inn yard. The town around it was small and bleak. Lealor waited quietly for her captors to speak to her. To her surprise, no one said a thing to her. Lorsham did stop to give her a triumphant look as the servants led the horses into the barn, but he told her nothing of her future or the trip. After he entered the inn, the servants gave her surreptitious looks and a wide berth. They completed their tasks and hurried inside.

The driver had parked the witch wagon outside, next to the barn. The night was going to be cold, Lealor could tell, because she already felt chilled. She decided they had forgotten her when the nastiest of her guards brought her a battered tin cup containing water.

Lealor would not give him the satisfaction of asking anything. She already knew the news would not be good. She held the cup of ice-cold water in her hands and watched the man carefully.

"Well, why 'nt cha askin' me where supper is?"

For a moment, Lealor considered spitting in his face, but decided it would be below her. Even if her captors were brutal villains, she did not have to sink to their level. So she replied, "If you want me to know, I suppose you'll tell me."

A grudging spark of admiration lit the eyes of the man. "Ya got spunk, witchwoman. Too bad, wasting all that courage."

Lealor asked, "Why?" before she remembered he would use anything she said to mock her.

"The trial." He shook his head. "I can think 'a lots 'a things ya'd be good for besides priest's meat." He leered, leaving her in no doubt as to what use he had in mind.

"Priest's meat?" Lealor had not heard the term before, but it didn't sound good to her. She knew anything he told her would not be comforting, but some scrap of information might prove useful.

"Wouldn't want ta spoil the surprises awaitin' ya in the temple dungeons, Fire Hair." He laughed.

Shivers ran up Lealor's spine at the sound, but she faced him quietly. Pleading with someone like him was useless.

He stared at her so long she felt really uneasy. She trusted that Lorsham kept the keys to the witch wagon on his person. For that mercy, she was glad. Finally, the guard turned and left her alone.

"Oh, dear," Lealor sighed. She reached into her provender bag and brought out a sandwich. In for a penny, in for a pound, she thought, and blinked her eyes at the cold water in her cup that obligingly turned to hot tea with three spoons of sugar, just the way she liked it.

She heard a mouselike scratching sound, so small she could barely hear it. She looked at the straw carefully. "Come out mousekin. I'll not harm you." She placed a piece of her sandwich near the straw and waited. To her surprise, a small hand reached up from outside and grabbed the bite of sandwich.

"What in the world—Show yourself," she commanded.

"Please. You said you wouldn't hurt me," the boy said, rising to his full height, which brought his eyes on a level with the floor of the witch wagon.

"Of course I won't hurt you." Lealor was getting exasperated with the whole witchy business. Since being promoted to witch status, people acted as if she was going to turn them all into toads or something nauseating.

"Yes. You promised. I didn't know witches kept their promises."

Lealor didn't bother denying she was a witch. What would these people say if they knew her powers were gifts from some goddesses when she was a child, and that both her mother and her great-grandmother really were witches? She sighed. "No, I won't harm you. I promise." She saw his eyes on her sandwich. They looked like hungry eyes to her. "Would you like a sandwich?"

"A sand-wich?" he asked.

For a moment she thought, slow-witted boy, but then she realized that sandwiches were an Earthly invention. "Two pieces of bread like mine with meat inside," she explained.

He nodded shyly. She reached into her bag and pulled out a double-decker ham and cheese on rye with tomatoes and lettuce thrown in for good measure. The boy needed the calories.

He had to hold the sandwich in both hands. It was too big for him to get it into his mouth, so he nibbled it like a mouse. His eyes lit up when he got his first bite. He took several bites, but stopped before he finished it.

"Did I make it too big?" Lealor asked with a smile. She was right. The boy seemed half starved.

"Oh, no. It's very good, but I need to save some of it for later."

Lealor raised her eyebrows in inquiry.

"I ate more than my share, but my mother and little sister will still be glad to get this." He patted the little pouch he wore on his frayed belt.

"Hard times at home?"

The boy nodded.

She reached into her pocket and pulled out the only coin she owned. Aldon had given her a half-bit piece for luck when she left for the duke's castle. Lealor figured it wasn't lucky for her, and Aldon would never know she had given it away. Perhaps a small spell would make it lucky for this boy and his family. She waved a hand over it. A faint green glow lit the dark briefly, then dimmed. Now it would duplicate itself every time someone spent it.

She handed it to the wide-eyed boy. He took it without hesitation. Clearly he knew the story of the green glow. "This must be a secret. You understand?"

"Yes." He clutched the small coin in his hand as if it were pure gold.

"Now, put it in your pouch."

He obediently dropped it in.

"Every time you spend that coin, it will reduplicate itself, so you will never be without money. You must be careful. If you spend a great deal of that coin around here, someone might ask how you got the money and find out you have a magic coin. No one must know."

"They might think I stole it, too," he said.

"Right." Something bothered him. Lealor could tell. "What's the matter?"

"Please, Miss Witch, may I tell my mother?"

"Of course. Boys should never have secrets from their mothers." For a moment Lealor wished she could see hers, but she shrugged off the childish desire.

The boy was feeling more comfortable with her. "Your hair certainly is red," he said.

"Yes, it is," Lealor admitted.

"You came from the duke's castle?"

"Yes."

"I have something I'm supposed to give you."

Lealor's mouth dropped open momentarily. "What can you possibly have for me?"

"Some man had a message from Nelda for you." He rummaged in his pockets looking for it, while Lealor fidgeted. "I came because I'm brave and he gave me a whole penny piece." He fished out the crumpled note and handed it to her.

A yellow rectangle of light opened out from the inn. Someone was coming.

"Quickly! Run and hide. Remember to spend your money very carefully!"

Her only answer was another scrabble—gone into the bushes like the mousekin she had thought him to be at first.

The second guard stomped out, rattled the gate to the wagon and checked the lock. "Fool's errand," he grumbled, ignoring Lealor. "Told him nobody ever escaped the witch wagon. Made of iron, isn't it? Witches can't work magic surrounded by iron."

Lealor looked at him solemnly, but inside, her body felt light. Her magic did work, in spite of the witch wagon. She could still free herself, if she wished. She considered whether to melt the bars to slag, explode the wagon, or simply make it disappear. Then she realized why no one ever escaped the wagons. They were innocent victims without a shred of real power. She gritted her teeth. Well, she'd stay a prisoner until she knew the whole, sorry story—and then, they'd find out what happened to priests who messed with people who really did have power!

She had given up trying to do without magic, but she still thought it a good idea to hide Myst. She took a minute to talk to her bracelet, something she had been neglecting to do regularly, she reminded herself. It was easy to forget about the crystalline talisman, since she stayed invisible and had not tightened on Lealor's wrist in warning when the witch wagon came for her.

Without wasting any more time, she cast a tiny concealment spell and took out the crumpled paper.

"Dear Friend," the message began. "I've taken the liberty of moving some of your things out of your room. They are already on their way to your home. I'll see your friends hear about what has happened to you. I'm sure the duke will act when he gets back. Try not to worry. Lady protect. N."

The note cheered Lealor. She knew she could not save it, so she reluctantly blew on it, reducing it to ashes. A chill breeze nipped around the edge of the barn and scattered the ashes to the ground. Lealor curled up in the front of the witch wagon, pulling the straw over her. The large cloak covered her completely, once she drew her legs up. She turned the satin lining to the outside and snuggled into the rich fur, blessing the fierce vervel who died to keep her warm.

Even with the straw piled, the hard floor made sleeping difficult. Three more days to the capital, Lealor told herself, remembering Reynal's geography lessons. She fell asleep, not aware that the temperature around the wagon was a full twenty degrees warmer than the air in the remainder of the yard. The bright moonlight of the chill night made invisible the green aura that surrounded Lealor. Two silver tears rested on her cheeks.

CHAPTER FIFTEEN

The three days seemed long to Lealor. The constant jouncing of the witch wagon bruised her in places she had never been aware of before. The odd thundering sound of the wheels on unpaved roads became an irritation. The sick joke of ice water for her only meal also palled.

As they traveled nearer to Mancy, the little towns became more numerous. At each, priests subjected Lealor to public scrutiny. While a few gawkers filled with hate jeered at her, a number of the townspeople remained quiet, casting her secret looks of sympathy. These attitudes told Lealor that most of the population remained unimpressed with the priesthood. Sadness hung in the air. She detected an inverse ratio. The larger the temples, the unhappier the populace.

In spite of having a nourishing meal every night, she was hungry. Part of the softening up process made the accused witches physically miserable when they arrived at the temple. From the hate calls of the rude, she learned the name of the god the priests worshipped. Sardoom. Roughly translated it meant He Who Rules the Skies. Jumped-up impostors needed overblown names. The Lady, who was entitled to the name She Who Rules the Night, would never countenance being called by so grandiose a title.

Lealor was so aggravated by the time the wagon actually pulled into Mancy, she healed minor problems and cast a gentle good-luck spell on the poor who were jostled by the wagon as it pushed its way down the streets. The black coach containing Lorsham had hurried before them, eager for the comforts of civilization, Lealor bet. That meant only the guards might notice her magic. They showed muscle, not mind. They named her *witch*, so she might as well deserve it. If Lorsham were representative of the priestly clan, no amount of innocence saved anyone accused.

She hadn't expected the temple to be in the poor section of town they traveled through. When she thought about it, she knew why the witch wagon was taking so long to arrive at its destination. They paraded her through Mancy as a kind of object lesson. See the wicked witch we are protecting you from and thank the priests. If she looks innocent to you, fear the priests and give them no trouble. Sardoom's priests were capable of truly nasty scheming. Lealor ran her hand over her bracelet. Myst still clutched her wrist, although she remained invisible.

Finally, the witch wagon rattled through better sections of town. Imposing ranks of large stone buildings formed the last two blocks before they reached the Temple of Sardoom. The wagon wheels rolled easily across the level marble squares of pavement in the temple courtyard. Sardoom welcomed ostentatious display, judging by the temple grounds. No one spared expense in creating the temple environs.

The wagon rolled to a halt beside a small door in the side of a huge slab of pink marble. Incongruous, Lealor thought, watching curiously. She had never seen a jail or dungeon so pretty. She didn't enjoy the scenery for long.

A fresh set of guards wearing priestly vestments ushered her unceremoniously out of the wagon. All humanity vanished from their eyes as they looked at her. A cold psychic aura surrounded her and the priests. They said nothing to her, but pointed the way she must travel along halls that inclined ever downward. She passed rows of closed doors with peephole grates at eye level and food slits, also closed, a foot above the ground. She wanted the reassurance of Myst's presence, but the dragon bracelet did nothing. She did not dare to rub her wrist for fear of drawing attention to the talisman. She grudgingly admitted to the impressiveness of the trip to her cell, but she refused to admit her fright, even to herself.

The leading priest opened a cell on the left and stood aside, a bony finger pointing within. Lealor entered. The door closed slowly with a faint creak. The light from the corridor dwindled, then vanished as a hollow boom reverberated followed by the sound of the key in the lock. Lealor was alone in the darkness and silence.

"Is anyone in here with me?" she asked softly.

Her words echoed in the dark.

"Very well," she muttered before casting a warding spell against any priestly snooping. To her surprise, it worked. "My magic is unaffected by the priests' spells," she said aloud. She turned, ready to open the door. She gestured. The door remained closed. "Correction, Myst," she told her bracelet. "Some of my magic still works." Lealor lit mage fire so she could see her prison. Beside the door, two holders for torches stood empty, ready to light the small room if anyone cared enough to bring torches. A pallet lay in one corner, none too clean. It looked as if it might almost fit the iron bed frame that stood against the far wall. A bucket stood in one corner beside an open drain in the floor. "All the comforts of home," she mused.

She cleaned the pallet and replaced it on the bed frame with a wave of her hand. She sat heavily, surprised at how good it felt to sit without the sound of rolling wheels and the jounce of the witch wagon banging against her. She pulled a bowl of warm water and washcloth out of her provender bag. After she cleaned herself, she combed her hair and braided it, defiantly using the bag to provide a rubber band for the braid. She didn't have any idea how long she might be imprisoned, so she reached into the bag for a cup of hot, sugared tea, a roast beef sandwich, and a bowl of navy bean soup. After eating, she whisked everything back into the bag and stretched out on the pallet. She ached all over. She snuggled into the cloak and drifted off to sleep almost as soon as she pulled the cloak over her. Her last thought was that the duchess had given her the nicest present she had ever had.

Myst materialized briefly and flew around the cell, checking it thoroughly. It seemed safe enough. She returned her physical form to Lealor's wrist, and resumed invisibility, but her spirit arrowed through the ether, searching for her father. She needed Wyrd's advice.

Back at the cottage, Pook had almost worn a path in the floor pacing back and forth. Something told him Lealor was in danger, but he wasn't sure what to do about it. His keen hearing told him someone had entered the clearing. He padded to the door of the cottage and waited for the visitor. An old woman came up the path. When she saw him, she smiled. Her bright eyes looked at him and then she nodded and entered the cottage, passing him without any show of fear.

"Changer's greeting," she said.

Pook woofed companionably and settled beside the fire.

"I have news for Fafleen. Will you convince her to come here so we can plan what to do?"

Pook nodded and made a whining sound that Fialla correctly interpreted as a request for more information.

"The priests arrested Lealor for witchcraft and took her to the temple prison in Mancy."

Pook growled.

"I don't like it, either. The local priest waited until the duke was away, then brought in a witch finder. He locked Lealor in the witch wagon and whisked her out of the dukedom so quickly I'm sure the priest feared the duke's intervention. Lealor told me about Fafleen. I'll stay here and wait while you go into the mountains and find her. She must fly to rescue Lealor, if she can get to Mancy before it's too late."

With no sign he understood, Pook rose and left the room. Fialla watched as he headed west. She put the kettle on the fire, noting that Lealor used a fire sprite to keep it lit. The cottage was well-warded, for no sign of magic showed outside. It must have been Aldon's cure that alerted Lorsham. Then she sat to wait.

Pook crossed the river and headed into the mountains. He followed an almost invisible path that led west. He flinched when Berdu appeared before him, but he did not stop traveling.

"Wait, you fool bear," Berdu gasped. He trotted just behind Pook whose distance-eating lope never slackened. "I need to give you something."

Pook stopped and turned back toward a red-faced Berdu. He tipped his head to the side in inquiry.

In between puffs, the little man carried on a monologue. "How's an animal like you going to convince Fafleen to return?" He shook his head. "No sense. Nonsense. No sense," Berdu muttered to himself while searching in his pockets for something. At last he drew out a piece of birch bark. He took a moment to smooth the bark. Then he used his long second fingernail to inscribe a symbol on the bark.

"There. That should fetch her." He handed the message to Pook. "Just give her that. See you remember, now!" With these words, he disappeared. Pook wasted no time in returning to his original course with the bark clutched in his teeth.

Three days later through the gray mist that precedes dawn, Fafleen flew into the clearing before the cottage, dropping the disgruntled bear she had carried in her talons.

"I'm here," she announced unnecessarily, since she filled the clearing and only a blind man could have missed seeing her.

Fialla stood in the cottage door. "I am glad to make your acquaintance, Fafleen. I am Fialla," the old herbwoman introduced herself.

Fafleen wasted no time on courtesy. "I got your message. How did you learn the symbol for danger in dragon script? Few humans have the patience or intelligence to learn our language." Fafleen didn't wait for an answer, but continued talking rapidly. "How did this happen?" Fafleen fumed. "I leave Lealor alone for a few weeks, and the next thing I know, she's in trouble."

"Lealor went to heal the duke's son. She was successful, but the priest accused her of witchcraft and sent for a witch hunter. She originally met the witch hunter here at the fair. They didn't get along. He posed as a fortune teller."

Fafleen interjected a snort. "That explains it."

"Nelda, a village girl who works for the duke, sent Lealor's things to the village. I've taken charge of them."

"If witch hunters are active, I'd suggest you hide anything you have that might incriminate you," Fafleen advised, as if Fialla lacked the sense to know how dangerous any connection to Lealor might prove.

"I did." Fialla gave her a wintery smile. She could see exactly what Lealor meant about the dragon's attitude toward humans. Somehow the old parchments never mentioned how snobbish dragons could be.

"What do you suggest we do now?" Fafleen saw nothing incongruous in her asking a mere human for instructions.

"It will be necessary for you to rescue your friend."

Fafleen's nostrils expanded, the equivalent of a martyred look for a dragon. "I knew that," she hissed softly. "Have you any suggestions as to how?"

"I can draw you a map of the way to Mancy. I have already prepared an amulet to allow you to fly safe from the priests' traps."

"What traps?" Fafleen banged her tail in irritation. It took too long for humans to share information.

"When the priests banished the dragons, they set magical spells to guard the kingdom from them. If the dragons had not left, they would be no threat to the kingdom now, for the spells the priests set so long ago still exist."

"You know a great deal of magic for a simple herbalist."

"I am old. My family is dead. I study the old books that remain for me to guard. It is safe to share what pitiful magics remain to me. One who comes from the gate must be trustworthy. Your powers seem to augment my own." She smiled. "Also I have been careful so that the priests know nothing of me and my—abilities."

The dragon paid scant attention to Fialla's explanation. Saving Lealor held most of Fafleen's interest. "What should I do in Mancy?"

"Before I can tell you that, I must see what is happening to Lealor." Fialla took a bowl from within her cape and entered the cottage where she filled it with water.

Pook, who had watched the exchange, entered the cottage, too. Fafleen was too large to join them, so she laid her huge head outside the door with her eye positioned to watch what happened within.

The old woman poured hot water over a pinch of herbs and added a vial of some oily substance. The mixture reminded the dragon of an egg-coloring kit Seren had given her brother, except that the swirls of color arranged themselves to form a picture. Fialla put her finger to her lips and looked both Pook and Fafleen in the eye to make sure they understood before she muttered words in some outlandish tongue neither the bear nor the dragon had heard before. With the completion of the spell, the picture came to life and the three could also hear as if they were present in the room where Lealor was being tried.

Sleepy as she was from her early rising, Lealor sensed a different magic in the courtroom. She glanced around, but could see no source. The priests were all listening to a long roster of so-called charges that Lorsham read aloud.

"She did, willfully and with full knowledge, heal within the city of Mancy from the very witch wagon itself," Lorsham concluded, fiercely rolling, up the scroll from which he had read.

Several of the priests looked at Lealor as if doubting that she could heal from within the guarded witch wagon. Lealor smiled at them quietly, waiting her turn to speak.

"What say you?" the high priest of Sardoom asked, not of the accused, but of the assembled priests. They looked at one another and each nodded. "Guilty." The first priest in line began, "Therefore we pronounce—"

The high priest raised his hand and the voice fell silent. "Mardal, you may have a few minutes to speak to the witch."

From the shifting bodies and odd looks on the faces of the other priests, Lealor could tell how unusual a proceeding this was. Originally, she had expected a chance to speak in her own behalf. She did not want any of her friends or acquaintances to try to speak for her. In their priest-ridden society, who knew what might happen to them? She found out about the rules as her case continued. Now she knew that in the temple court, the accused was always guilty and so, granted no chance to speak.

Mardal, an old greybeard, tottered over to her and beckoned for her to follow. He moved slowly, tapping with his staff. Lealor followed, glad she had used a spell to lighten the chains they had loaded her with. Except for being awkward, the fetters intended to force her to the humiliation of asking the guards to support her or to make her fall to her knees, were of no importance. Once in the small antechamber, Mardal sat on a bench along the wall. Lealor got her first close look at her advocate.

The guards positioned her before the priest. He nodded his dismissal and they left.

Mardal's silvery eyes gazed unseeingly at her.

"Why, you're blind," Lealor burst out.

"Yes. Sardoom took my sight."

"How horrible!"

"Ah. No, child. The god in his mercy took it gradually, allowing me to get used to the darkness."

Lealor realized she was in the presence of one of the god's real followers. The lines in Mardal's face spoke of resignation and peace, not the hellishness and avarice ingrained in the faces of the other priests. "I'm sorry," she said, seeing nothing unusual in her compassion for suffering.

Mardal inclined his head. "I grieve also. That you should be a witch with so fair a voice is sad. Had you chosen to train that voice in Sardoom's service you would sing for him."

Lealor made a face, happy momentarily for Mardal's affliction. At least he couldn't see how disgusted the idea made her. "Did they make no attempt to save your sight?"

"I prayed to the god, but my superiors told me if it was the will of Sardoom I would see. If not, I would serve in darkness."

Lealor snorted. "Would you like your vision restored?"

"I am ill. The healers tell me I shall not see another harvest season. Which is true, in any case." Mardal chuckled at his little joke. He fell silent for a moment. "I should like to see the flowers in my garden and the birds that have sung so sweetly for me since the god took my sight."

Here sat a truly good priest. Lealor thought that Sardoom must be a poor god—if he existed. Her guards had taken her to the altar of Sardoom, so Lealor could be awed by the might of their god, but all she had seen was an outsize gilded statue. She felt none of the presence she felt on Achaea when she had seen the gods there during her childhood. Mardal believed in this sham! In a spontaneous excess of pity, she reached out and lightly touched Mardal's eyes.

Green light flared. Lealor's own eyes closed against the brightness. When she opened them, Mardal looked at her from eyes that saw again.

"Child," he gasped.

"Now you can see your garden," Lealor told him with a smile.

"You are a witch!"

"No. I am a healer. There is a difference. My powers were given to me when I was a child." She could tell Mardal felt very disturbed about his cure. "Sardoom," she called, feeling like a hypocrite, "if it was not your will that your faithful servant Mardal see, revoke the healing." She paused, waiting. Since she didn't believe Sardoom existed, she didn't expect anything to happen and it didn't.

"Sardoom, I thank you for your gift." Mardal's hand shook as he wiped a tear from his cheek.

Again, nothing occurred. Lealor relaxed. It was always risky betting against the gods on a strange world. If Sardoom had existed, he might have chosen to blast her to smithereens. A shaft of light came through the small window set high in the outer wall. It illumined Mardal.

"My child, my superior commanded me to tell you something."

Lealor lifted her eyebrows.

"If you claim to be a simple healer, your sentence will be death by the flames, for your powers go far beyond healing."

Lealor swallowed. Even with Myst to save her, the prospect didn't appeal.

Mardal raised an admonitory finger. "If you should choose, you might volunteer to be of service and so escape burning."

"What kind of service?" Lealor's experiences with the priesthood had left her suspicious of anything they planned.

"Many years ago we fought a war against ungodly magic wielders."

Lealor nodded. She knew about that.

"There still remained among us truly magical beings, the weren and the dragons."

"So I've heard."

"In Sardoom's name, we priests banished the dragons—for a price."

"What price?"

"Every year a great dragon comes to the sacrificial rock on the coast and takes from us a maiden." Mardal's face showed his grief. He seemed incapable of continuing.

"Nobody wants to be the sacrifice, right?"

Mardal nodded.

"Go on." Lealor's words dropped, cold as ice crystals into the silence in the chamber.

"No death by fire, if you volunteer to go to the dragon willingly."

"So that's what that guard meant by priest's meat," Lealor muttered too softly for Mardal to hear. She took a deep breath before answering. "I have no choice but to agree." Privately, Lealor thought it would be easier for Myst to handle a dragon than a crowd of maniacal priests and deluded citizens. She had only one question to ask of the kindhearted priest. "When?"

Mardal looked at his hands, which he folded in his lap.

"Tomorrow morning at sunrise," he said.

CHAPTER SIXTEEN

Fafleen raised her head and snorted a gout of fire into the air. "Tomorrow!" she hissed.

"The sacrifice always occurs at dawn on the first day of spring. I did not plan on the priests' cunning. They gave her a choice of which death she prefers." Fialla spoke as she rummaged in her cloak pockets. "Now where did I put . . . ah . . . here it is." With these words she drew out a small silver box.

"What do you have there?" Fafleen put her eye to the doorway again like a gigantic peeping Tom.

Fialla took a parchment packet from another pocket in the cloak and went to the blocked opening. "If you'll move back a bit, I'll come out," she said calmly.

The dragon moved away, dropped her head, and waited. Pook followed Fialla from the cottage. Intent on the problem of rescuing Lealor, they didn't notice when Berdu materialized at the edge of the clearing. He moved himself to a good vantage point and slowly faded from sight without any of them realizing he was listening.

Fialla opened the parchment. The dragon and the bear saw it was a map as she spread it on the ground in front of Fafleen. "This is where we are now," Fialla told them, placing a small stone on the map. "This circle"—her finger touched it lightly—"is where you must go. You cannot reach her within her temple cell. To the east of Mancy lies Spellcape. The sacrificial rock is on this spur of land that juts out into the water. The great dragon will come out of the east."

Fafleen extended a claw and delicately, for a dragon, scratched a line on the map. "This is the distance I must fly?"

"Yes, but you will also have need of this." Fialla offered the silver box.

"What's in here?" Fafleen took the box in her talons. She cocked her head like an inquisitive robin and shook it gently.

"During the war between the magic users and the priests, the ordinary citizens were always afraid the dragons would side with those with the power. The priesthood placed bane wards over the countryside to protect the people."

"Fine thing. The priests using magic when they warred against those with the power. How—human." Fafleen couldn't resist a chance to draw attention to human hypocrisy.

"The priests have ever used magic. They only forbid its use to any who are not priests." Fialla's grim smile showed she understood the irony in the situation.

Pook growled softly at Fialla's words. His keen nose detected Berdu, but since the little creature had helped with the message to Fafleen, the bear saw no need to expose him.

Fialla continued speaking. "Within this box is a powerful charm against dragon bane wards. Carrying this, you can fly overland without harm or hindrance."

"I wish I had flown around more so I'd know the area. If I had, I could just pop over there." Fafleen's talon touched the location of Spellcape. "Now, I'll have to fly the whole way. It's going to be close, but I think I can make it by tomorrow morning." Fafleen's second claw retracted in the dragon sign for luck.

Fialla held out a pouch she took from her belt. "Do you want to carry the box in your talons, or shall I put it in the pouch and tie it to your leg?"

Fafleen clutched the box tightly. It almost fell from her talons when she stretched her wings in a brief warm-up. "All right. I guess I'd better have you truss me up like a carrier pigeon. I won't have any time to waste looking for the box if I should drop it. Why humans don't make things a reasonable size, I don't know."

Fialla hid a smile from the dragon as she placed the silver charm box in the pouch and tied it carefully to the dragon's leg. She refrained from telling Fafleen that anything a dragon considered reasonable in size would be so huge she couldn't have carried it to the cottage.

"If I start now and fly all night, with time out for a tiny snack to keep up my strength, I should just make it," Fafleen said.

Pook woofed. He had seen the dragon eat. Her tiny snack would be a whole cow or deer. He waddled over to Fafleen and reared to his full ten-foot height. The dragon towered over him by another ten feet. She paid no attention to him. He roared.

"Yes, Pook. What do you want?"

Fialla watched quietly. The bear's size was impressive, but standing before the dragon made him seem like a small boy asking his mother for something he wanted desperately and feared he would not get.

Pook waved his paws for attention and roared again.

Fafleen hissed her disdain. "How am I supposed to know what this berserk bear wants?"

"He wants you to take him with you."

Pook dropped down to all fours and nodded to Fialla.

Fafleen flexed her wings. "You weigh a ton, bear."

Pook growled.

"All right. I'll try. If I feel you're slowing me down, I'll drop you off somewhere in the woods though."

Pook nodded.

Fafleen grabbed him, rather ungently, Fialla thought, and spread her wings. With the first wingbeat they rose into the air. The takeoff wobbled badly, but the small clearing hindered the dragon. By the time her sixth wingbeat pulled them high above the forest, she had compensated for Pook's weight and size. She flew rapidly for a few minutes before she remembered the length of her flight and slowed. How should she confront the evil dragon that would accept Lealor for a sacrifice? She shifted ideas around in her head until she felt dizzy. Then she simply told herself she would wait and wing it, never realizing how funny her thoughts would seem if anyone heard them.

While Fafleen's takeoff appeared casual, she had used her photographic memory to imprint the map in her mind. She estimated time of arrival. Pook hung, most ungracefully, clutched in her talons. His thick pelt protected him from their sharpness, but hanging for hours above the ground was uncomfortable, Fafleen knew. She wondered what part he planned to play in Lealor's rescue. After several hours of flight, the dragon began to notice the not inconsiderable weight of the bear. She flew on, mentally gauging the distance she covered. An hour before sunset, she could see that carrying Pook slowed her. She watched until she saw a broad meadow surrounded by trees. No human habitation marred the landscape, so she decided to set Pook down.

Pook growled as Fafleen lost altitude, but the dragon ignored him. She settled to the ground and released her hold on the bear.

He immediately rose on his hind legs and roared.

"Forget it, bear. I'm sorry, but I'm starting to feel tired. Fialla's charm does work. I can fly through the warded areas, but it takes a lot more effort than I ever thought it would. The closer I get to Mancy the more wards I will meet. Carrying you is just too much. Both of us on the way won't equal one of us there tomorrow at dawn. It will be a close thing, now."

Pook dropped to the ground and growled.

"No sense arguing. This is where you get off," Fafleen said. "Bye, Pook. I'll tell Lealor you meant to come."

With these words, Fafleen stretched her mighty wings and ascended, leaving an angry bear behind her on the ground.

Pook wasted no time roaring after she disappeared in the distance. He started walking after her although he knew it was futile. Darkness fell as he labored onward. His fastest pace put him so far behind the dragon that he growled to himself. He stopped at several streams to drink, but he took no time for food. He would be too late to take part in Lealor's rescue, but he would be near and perhaps he could still be of some assistance. He waddled down a steep slope, the shortest distance across the area being a straight line. One of the rocks to which he trusted his weight slipped, wrenching the paw that Lealor had helped heal. From that time on, Pook limped. After a while his paw swelled. It became harder and harder to put weight on it. Finally, Pook sat down under the bright moon and complained as bears do with a woo-oh sound. His part in Lealor's rescue was over.

Then he felt a strange ruffling in his mind. He thought he heard a voice say, "Poor bear. I help." For a moment, everything went black. His nose felt the cold, but his fur kept his body warm. When the blackness ceased and he could see again, he was on the point of land next to the pole that was outfitted with the manacles to hold the sacrifice. His paw no longer ached. He looked up at the moon and bowed his head. The strange feeling in his mind retreated, but he felt his thanks appreciated.

He began to look for a good place to wait for dawn.

Lealor, too, awaited the dawn. She had a rough idea of time from the meals the priests served her. After the last one, she found herself pacing the floor. A movement in the far corner caught her eye. It did not surprise her. She had placed the meals the priests brought her on the floor for the mice. They didn't find the food inedible. She used the provender bag to provide her meals. Something about the movement in the corner was different. She went over to see and for a moment, she froze in horror. She couldn't help it. She hated snakes. The horrid thing had probably eaten those nice little mice. Worst of all, there wasn't a stick in the room to keep it away!

She sat on her bunk and drew her feet off the floor. She watched as a three-foot snake drew itself out of the hole. When the entire creature was within the room, it drew itself up and inflated before Lealor's fascinated gaze. In a matter of seconds Berdu stood before her.

"Berdu!" Lealor cried, her happy face ample reward for any visitor.

"Shhh!" Berdu placed a finger to his lips. "I can't stay. Powerful magic . . . powerful magic . . . " He muttered to himself as if he had forgotten Lealor entirely. "So weak, so weak . . . "

"Berdu—-"

Berdu's eyes lit up. He raised a finger. "That's it!"

"What is?" Lealor asked, relieved he had come to the point at last.

"Steakfruit!" he announced triumphantly.

"Steakfruit?" Lealor hoped Berdu wasn't part of any rescue operation. He'd probably get everybody concerned killed.

"Do you have any steakfruit?"

"Well, I still have the provender bag . . . "

"Excellent. Let me have it."

Lealor untied it from her belt and passed it to him.

"Good," he said, and tipped the bag into his mouth which, snakelike, seemed to be able to hold a bushel at a time.

Lealor watched as he gobbled the fruit straight from the bag. He didn't even seem to chew. He ate just like Fafleen, she thought.

"What did you come to tell me?" Lealor asked as he finally lowered the bag and passed it back to her.

"Not to worry," Berdu said with a reassuring smile, but all Lealor could think of was his pointed teeth—not human.

"Not to worry!" Lealor's words almost exploded. "That's a ridiculous message! Here I am waiting for dawn so I can be fed to some overgrown Saurian—

"Tsk, Tsk, mortal."

Berdu reminded her of Rory. How Lealor wished he were here. He wouldn't stand there eating as if that were the most important thing in the whole world.

Berdu interrupted her thoughts as if he knew what she was thinking. "That old herbwoman friend of yours has sent Fafleen and that tame bear to rescue you." He paused to think. "If, that is, the dragon can fly fast enough and she doesn't forget and drop the bear."

"How did Fialla manage to find out what happened to me?"

"Water witching. Saw it in a bowl, she did. Uses bits and pieces of the old powers . . . magic . . . evil magic . . . dangerous . . . No magic," he warned, looking around fearfully. "Be ready tomorrow at dawn." With these words, he became thinner and thinner, and vanished like quicksilver into the mouse hole he had used as an entrance.

"Berdu! Wait! I want to know more!" The snake's tail vanished even as she spoke. "Myst! Did you hear that?" Lealor asked. The bracelet lay like dead metal on her wrist, refusing to tighten or move. When would Myst get over the sulking fit? "Be ready? What in the world can he mean by that?" she muttered to herself as she paced up and down her cell. She had no way of knowing Myst had sent her essence to visit her father to ask for guidance.

Lealor couldn't convince herself to try sleeping. Sleep seemed too close to death for her to want anything to do with it. To Lealor, dawn seemed far away and all too close at the same time.

Fafleen stopped only long enough to bolt a farmer's sheep whole. She had no time for a decent meal, but if she did not eat, she might lack the strength to fight the dragon at dawn.

Well, she thought to herself, at least that's settled. First I fight the dragon and then I free Lealor and fly away with her. One part of her mind thought, "A piece of cake." At the same time, she remembered her mother's words, "If your eyes are bigger than your stomach, you may end up with a tummyache, daughter." Fafleen hissed. Those human sayings her family had a tendency to use could be quite disconcerting!

She would have sold her scales for a chance to rest. Air freighting that bear had been a mistake. What business did a dragon have carting around a friend of a friend, anyway? Her wings ached with the effort. She had never before flown so far and so fast. Her breath became a series of short hisses. She felt the tremor in her wings as she forced them up and down. Finally, she began looking for a place to land. She had to rest or she would arrive at the rock too weak to do anything except hiss—if she had that much breath left. The road below had widened. A good sign. She must be approaching the capital. She saw a flat field a distance away from the road. Excellent, she told herself. She cold take time for twenty winks and still arrive at dawn. She settled wearily to the ground, trying to ignore the hunger pangs. A growing dragon needed a great deal of food. She felt like a hero for snacking on that sheep instead of decimating the farmer's flock. He didn't know how fortunate he was, she decided, carefully tucking her tail under her body so the tip stayed warm. Cold tail, bad cold, the dragon saying went. At least she could report to her mother that she had followed good hygienic practices while on this adventure. She sat, meaning to rest only a few moments, but shortly, her eyes closed and a gently snore seared the grasses before her as her head sank to the ground. She slept.

Fialla, always a light sleeper, awoke. She had returned home after the dragon and bear left for Mancy. Someone was in the room with her!

She nodded at the fire, which flared up, lighting the room. A little man stood beside her table, looking into her magic bowl.

"And who are you?" she asked as she rose from her bed.

"Blood and bones, woman! Ask something important! Can't you feel that the young dragon is in trouble?"

"Are you sure?"

"If I was sure, don't you think I'd be doing something about it? Use this to see where she is!"

Fialla filled the bowl with the correct ingredients and snapped her fingers. All the candles in the room bloomed with light. She looked into the bowl and saw Fafleen sound asleep.

"Let me see where she is, mortal woman," Berdu said.

"Can you do anything to help?" Fialla asked.

"How am I to know? Me, against that dragon. Oh, dear. No good ever comes of meddling . . . no good . . . those wards are so painful . . . meddle, meddle."

Fialla watched as the little man faded to a misty outline and then disappeared!

CHAPTER SEVENTEEN

Berdu materialized behind Fafleen. "You're getting ancient, Berdu," he murmured to himself. "At one time you made pinpoint landings half the world away. To be young and magical—that's real treasure." As he spoke, Berdu walked around to stand before the dragon. "Oh, my scales and talons," he whispered. "She doesn't know me. If I yell to wake her up, she may singe me like a roast rainbird." He paused, deep in thought. Then he took three steps forward so he was directly in front of Fafleen's nose. He drew back his foot as if he intended to make the point after a touchdown. At the same time he brought his foot forward he screamed, "Wake up, youngling." He dematerialized just as his toe connected with the dragon's nose. Fafleen didn't even take time to consider the little man in her strange dream. The gray mist hung over the field, waiting for the sun to burn it away. In the east, a lighter band of sky half hidden by clouds indicated where the sun would rise shortly. She propelled herself into the air and flew as she had never flown before.

Pook hid on a ledge facing the sea, away from the crowd of people and priests that accompanied the sacrifice to the appointed place. He took a chance and reared up enough to see over the lip of rock that hid him from the people. He scanned the sky. Where was Fafleen? He knew his eyesight was bad, but surely he should be able to see a dragon coming!

He dropped down from the awkward position and looked eastward. The edge of the sun's disc rose above the sea. In the brightening day he could just make out a speck that grew larger even as he watched. He heard a priest say, "The dragon comes."

The great red dragon was as big as a pad on his paws when Pook decided he could wait no longer for Fafleen. The sea was deep at the bottom of the cliff. If he could free Lealor and push her into the sea, they might still escape. The dolphins served the weren. They would help Lealor get to the sailboat they were to bring him. As prince, he had proved his were ability by staying in bear shape for a full year. He was eager to return home and to help Lealor. He hoped she knew how to swim. It would certainly simplify matters if she could. If not, he would have to manage. On land, they had no chance of surviving.

Back at Fialla's, Berdu hopped in anguish, holding one foot. "Well, woman," he said between hops, "Can you see what's happening?"

"The dragon rose in the air and flew like an arrow. I don't know if she reached Lealor in time." Berdu's bravery surprised Fialla, so she only smiled a little at the weird figure he cut jumping up and down on one foot.

"Well, look!" Berdu commanded with a screech of exasperation.

"Someone spilled all my herbs while trying to use my bowl," Fialla said gently.

A shamefaced Berdu replied, "Don't you have any spare herbs that will do?"

"No. The spilled herbs will not work for farseeing. It takes hours to set the spell without the special ingredient," Fialla explained. "I have no more of it, either."

"Special ingredient? What is it?"

"Powered dragon's scale. I doubt I can ever get any more."

"Have you a file?" Berdu peered at her from under his bushy eyebrows.

"Yes, but—"

"Then get it, woman! The dawn is breaking!"

The puzzled old lady gave him her file. He rubbed it over his long second fingernail. "Try this," he told her, tapping the fine power from his nail out of the palm of his hand into hers.

"But—" Fialla believed it would never work, but she decided to humor her guest.

"Button your lip, and just do it!" Berdu hobbled next to Fialla to watch her set the spell on a fresh bowl of water with the powder from his nail filing in it. "Got to stop meddling in human affairs," he murmured to himself.

For one brief instant, they saw Lealor at the stake and a red dragon in the distance, flying over the waves. They did not see Fafleen. Then the colors ran together and everything disappeared.

"Bring it back, woman! I wish to see!"

"I can do no more. It is in the hands of the Lady," Fialla said. She rubbed her tired eyes.

The animation Berdu had displayed dwindled. "Gone . . . all gone . . . all my power . . . all gone . . . gone . . . " As he spoke, he became paler and paler and finally with a pop he disappeared, leaving a puzzled Fialla to rock and worry all alone.

Pook climbed over the ledge, stood on his hind legs, and roared the terrible challenge of an angry bear. The priests and their guards, who had backed away to a respectful distance, turned and hurried farther down the hill.

Once the priests stood at the bottom of the hill with the people, the high priest turned to the captain of the honor guard. "Command your men to shoot the bear!"

"What if an arrow should hit the girl?"

"Fool! Can't you see that the bear is between the sacrifice and us? Have your men fire, I tell you!"

The archers were awaiting the command, having nocked their arrows when they heard the high priest. The captain said, "Fire, but don't hit the girl."

The high priest had shrieked his command, so Pook and Lealor heard him over the growing murmurs of the incredulous crowd. The wood on the stake that held the chains was old. Pook's great strength allowed him to paw the chains free as the first flight of arrows flew around them.

"What now?" Lealor did not see how she and Pook could escape. The crowd and the guards cut off any chance of getting down from the promontory. The red dragon flamed the air as he prepared to dive.

Pook looked over his shoulder at the dragon. He saw the archers ready to shoot again. He wasted no time in pushing Lealor to the edge of the cliff and over. He humped, glad to be out of the hail of arrows. He ignored the two wounds he had gained shielding Lealor.

Below, a pod of dolphins had taken charge of Lealor, chains and all. They gathered around her in the water, buoying her up until she understood they would give her a ride if she would grab hold of one of them.

Pook commanded them to take the girl to the boat that awaited him.

Not daring to change into his human form where the priests might see, he paddled after them. Already the dolphins and Lealor were far enough from shore that the bowmen posed no threat. It would take some time for the priests to organize ships to search for Lealor. He looked up in time to see the red dragon diving directly at Lealor and her escorts. Pook stopped trying to paddle after them and sank beneath the waves.

Fafleen was easily a mile from the scene when Lealor and Pook hit the water. She had the excellent vision of a bird of prey and could see the red dragon diving. "Oh, my scales and talons. I hope I can do this." She used her dragonly ability to travel and popped into view right under the nose of the red dragon, uttering a von Fafnir war cry that would have pleased her granddragon Fafnir, if he had heard it.

The look on the red dragon's face was ludicrous. A pale blue female with silver eyes, half his size, threatened him. In his surprise, he vanished.

Fafleen gritted her teeth. She felt as a human might if someone hung up a telephone in her ear. How dare that red devil disappear from before her eyes! Two could play that game. Her brother delighted in teasing her, then disappearing with some item she wanted. He had never been able to escape her wrath. This big bully should know what it meant to tamper with one of her friends! She wanted to find dragons to help her translate the old books she had found, too. With no more thought than that, she disappeared as well.

The confrontation between the dragons caused consternation in the priests and populace. The question on everyone's mind was whether the dragon thought that the treaty had been broken. He might reappear and flame everyone on the headland! As that thought occurred to people, they started to leave. The high priest wanted to be well away from the place in case the dragon felt cheated of his prey. How had the blue dragon been able to fly over the land? Considering the problems posed by the dragons, one redheaded witch seemed very unimportant. Now that the dragons were gone, it was too late to retrieve the witch. The high priest dispersed the remaining crowd and returned with the other priests to the temple, making plans to renew the dragon bane wards and offer sacrifices to Sardoom.

The cold sea water revived Lealor's wits. The farther the dolphins took her, the stronger her powers became. She wondered exactly what the priests did to turn the sacrifices into mental flyweights. It had to be a spell over the headland, for she had deliberately refrained from eating anything the priests sent her for food, fearing some mind-altering herb.

She murmured a spell of unbinding and her chains fell from her. She released her hold on the dolphin she rode long enough to kick off her shoes, which the seawater had ruined anyway. A second dolphin waited until she was ready, then nudged her. She understood this dolphin would give her a ride next. By the time the sun set she felt exhausted. She also felt like a prune, as if the water had wrinkled her into her eighties long before her time. The dolphins, like steeds, took turns bearing her onward all day. She had no idea where they were taking her, but anywhere was better than where she had come from, she decided.

The waters gradually grew warmer as they made their way southward. A bleeding dolphin joined the pod. Lealor gestured until the others let her use a healing spell. The dolphins surrounded the newcomer, leaving Lealor to tread water, tired as she was. Finally two of the pod helped the dolphin. They swam faster than the group that returned to continue giving Lealor a ride. Soon they were so far ahead she lost track of them.

At moonrise she looked over the silvered sea and saw a sailboat coming toward her. Lealor's dolphins brought her to the side, the young skipper leaned over and smiled. "Your sailboat awaits, milady."

Lealor thanked the dolphins and turned to climb into the boat. Her tiredness made her awkward. To her horror she found she could not pull herself up. The man took her hands and one of the dolphins flustered her greatly by giving her a needed boost from the rear.

"Upsadaisy," he said as she landed ungracefully over the side.

The young man turned to adjust the sails, giving her a moment to catch her breath and regain her composure. Although there was almost no breeze, the sailboat whizzed through the water. Lealor recognized that they traveled by the power of magic. The more she thought about her rescue, the more questions she had. By the time the skipper of the boat turned to her, she had a half dozen of the most important ones ready for him.

"Why do I think I recognize you from somewhere?" she asked, feeling foolish, for surely she wouldn't forget so attractive a man.

"Question time already?"

It annoyed Lealor that her question amused him. While grateful for her rescue, she felt tired and hungry and hardly able to cope. Her patience had evaporated along with most of the water that was in her clothes. Even her thoughts were cross. *It wouldn't be in good form to demand he feed me, but how I'd like to eat!* Could she ask him to return so she could look for Pook? A hollow feeling inside her told her the bear might well be dead, but she wanted to know for sure. Never before had she become so attached to an animal.

As if he heard her mental conversation with herself, he passed her a flagon of some sweet drink. After she swallowed a few mouthfuls, she felt amazingly restored. When he turned to get some food, Lealor saw two fresh wounds along his back.

"Strange," she thought. "How does a man get marks like that? I'd swear they were made by arrows . . . "

He returned to her with a basket of fruit. She looked into his eyes. The moonlight changed the colors of everything, but she was ready to swear his eyes were brown, like his dark hair. "Pook?" she whispered softly.

He made the same sound the bear had when not pleased. It was Pook! No matter what he said, she recognized him now, moon glamoured or not. "Pook!"

The happiness in her voice would have made a stone sing. He nodded. "No, not Pook," he told her. "My name's Rand."

"Let me put some salve on your back," she said, reaching into her provender bag. Her fingers groped, but the bag remained empty. "Oh, what a time for the charm to give out!"

"Don't worry. The salt water stung, but it cleansed the wounds. I do have some healing ointment here somewhere," he said, rummaging under one of the boxlike seats. "Here it is!"

Lealor took the ointment from him. "Turn around," she commanded. "This may hurt," she warned.

"Like old times," he joked.

"Shapeshifter?"

"Weren," he corrected. "I'm glad you don't mind. Many women would have a fit, here alone on the sea with a weren. Then, I guess a girl who has dragons for friends is pretty shockproof."

"All the members of my family have dragons for friends. Besides, Fafleen is really quite nice when you get used to her."

"She didn't improve much on closer acquaintance with me," he said, remembering his trip while clutched in her talons.

"If you're flying Air Fafleen, it's better to ride on her back. Her talons are sharp."

"My fur protected me."

Fed, and somewhat revitalized by the sweet drink, Lealor wanted some answers. "Might I ask where you're taking me?"

"Home," he answered.

"Where might that be?" Lealor hoped her remark didn't sound sarcastic, but she felt too tired to be polite.

"Fire Mountain Island," Rand looked at her and continued. "The place where the weren live since we left Magilan. We trade to the east and south of the island, but most of us long for news of our old home. I spent a year in wereshape to learn what is happening there. I couldn't turn back into a man until I had completed my time. It's a rite of passage with the members of my clan."

Only one piece of information registered with Lealor. "An island with an active volcano on it?" The weren could certainly pick winners, she thought. First they were forced out of Magilan by the priests and their people, and now they lived on an island that could blow its top at any minute.

"We monitor the volcano closely. Our wisewomen can often predict the future. We'd have plenty of warning before an eruption," he told her as if he knew what she was thinking.

"How will I return to my cottage?"

"You should stay away from there for a time. It might not be safe to return too soon. You must have come through that old gate with the dragon. Perhaps our wisewomen can help you return through the gate if that is your wish."

The food and drink on Lealor's empty stomach were making her sleepy. She smiled at Rand, blinking her eyes like a child who want to stay up even though it's past her bedtime. "I'd like that."

"Then sleep now. Tomorrow at dawn we'll be home!"

"Home," Lealor thought. "What a lovely word. I promise I'll try to appreciate it more—if I ever return." Her eyes closed. She never felt the brief kiss Rand gave her before he covered her lightly so she wouldn't get chilled.

Through the night he watched so no harm could come to her. The dolphins returned and rejoiced with the prince who was coming home at last.

CHAPTER EIGHTEEN

Lealor awoke as Rand lowered the sails. A city sprawled at the foot of a high peak. Halfway up the side a fairy-tale castle glistened in the clear morning air. The harbor curved along the crescent of a bay. No wonder Rand loved his home. She couldn't believe she had slept through the bustle of the busy docks. "Why didn't you wake me?" she asked as he tossed the mooring line to an old man.

"There was nothing you could do until we landed," he said, waving his thanks to the man who tied up the sailboat.

"Isn't it kind of dangerous to have a small craft like this moored in such a busy place with all these bigger vessels?"

"Don't worry. This is the royal mooring. No one will so much as chip the paint on the rail," he said, helping her onto the dock.

"Won't you get in trouble—" she began.

"So many questions for such an early hour in the day." He waved at the man who brought a horse to the end of the dock. "Come on," he urged, pulling Lealor along with him.

"Here's Talisman, Your Hi—" the man said with a bob of the head.

Rand interrupted him in mid-word. "Rand, Jonn." Then he turned to Lealor. "This is Jonn, the best friend and servant one could have."

Lealor smiled shyly. Everything was moving so fast! She watched Rand clap Jonn on the shoulder as a token of his thanks.

"Can you ride?" Rand asked.

"Of course!" Lealor was most indignant. She had already made friends with the horse. Her father had proudly said that if a beast had four legs,

CAROL L. DENNIS

Lealor could ride it. She had ridden wild unicorns as a child. She had no qualms about this beauty.

"May I?" Rand gestured to Jonn's mount, waiting behind him.

"Of course, Your—"

Rand's finger silenced him. "Let's go," he told Lealor.

As they rode through the city, the early morning sun gilded the pastel houses that lined the streets. Rand led the way higher and higher. Finally they climbed so high that Lealor knew their destination was the castle. The road widened, so they rode side by side. Lealor, filled with questions, hardly knew what to ask first.

"Do you live in the castle?"

"Yes. It's a nice old place. Hundreds of retainers live there to serve the royal family."

"Who are the king and queen?"

"The king is Erik and his queen's name is Alian. They have three children."

"What do you do?" Lealor eyed the brilliant flowers that seemed to spring naturally from every patch of ground beside the road. Some, she was sure, were species she had never seen on Earth or Realm.

"Me? Mostly errands and things for King Erik and Queen Alian."

"Things like checking up on Magilan?"

"Sometimes. The kingdom of Magilan is northwest of here. I've traveled on merchant ships to the southwest where the wildings are and to the southeast to trade with the desert dwellers. The dragons live far to the northeast of our island. I've even visited the Witch's Wood on Aerie Island several weeks' journey south of here."

"Widdershins is a lot bigger than I thought. I've never heard of any of the places you mentioned."

"No reason why you should. No Widdershins kingdom has people with your fiery hair."

Lealor blushed. She hoped her hair wouldn't make her seem alien. For a moment, Lealor debated telling Rand about the mistake that brought her to Widdershins, but then she decided to wait. As nice as Fire Mountain Island was, she was not sure she should trust Rand's people with the gate secret. After she had stayed a few days, she would make up her mind about what to do. "Surely some people here must have red hair!"

"Oh, yes, we have some folks we call redheads, but their hair isn't half as beautiful as yours."

The compliment drove Lealor's next question from her mind. Which was just as well, for Rand started talking about his family.

'I haven't been home for a year, but I'm sure my mother and father will be glad to have you stay with us. My little sister Silanna will probably drive you mad with questions. My father says he would have named her Curiosity if he had known what she would be like as she grew. My married older sister won't be home for a visit until next year."

Lealor felt a little pang of homesickness as she listened to Rand talk about his family. For the first time she wished Seren and Argen, her brothers, were on this adventure with her. In a pinch, Argen and she could have trained Seren to help with the gate although he hated to use his powers. Then they would have needed only one more person to stabilize the group and they could have fixed the gate. She thought that Baloo had done something to the Realm gate as she left. Why had the young Bright One wanted her on Widdershins? No wonder her mother sang him back to sleep when he awoke if he caused such trouble!

The guard on the battlements of the castle saluted them as they clattered into the courtyard. Servants hurried to take their horses. Everyone was very glad to see Rand, she could tell. He kept shushing them for some reason or other.

"The king and queen will be here directly," a man dressed in silver silks told Rand.

"We won't wait. We'll go right in," Rand said as if he owned the palace.

Lealor tried to hide her astonishment. He must be one of the favored nobles, she decided. She watched as the doors of the castle opened. A tall, silver-haired woman dressed in purple came down the stairs and opened her arms to Rand. Lealor saw them embrace. The queen certainly was young, she thought. Her silver hair marked her as a user of moon magic. Just then a little woman in a stained gown bustled down the steps. She stuck a pair of garden gloves in her pocket as she came.

"It's been so long, my son," she said as Rand enveloped her in a bearhug.

A huge man lumbered out of the castle. "Where is that ne'er-do-well traveler?" His voice boomed so loudly in the courtyard that it echoed.

The servants bowed their heads briefly in respect. Lealor decided this must be King Erik.

Rand received a hug that would have crushed a smaller man. Their coming together reminded Lealor of films she had seen of two mountain sheep butting heads. Then King Erik swung Rand to the side as if he were a small child. "Who is this?" he said, in quieter tones.

Lealor, for one, was glad King Erik had spoken quietly. If he had boomed at her, she would have died of fright. He was certainly an imposing figure.

"For shame, Rand. You have forgotten to introduce your friend," the gardening woman remonstrated, even as Rand wiped a smudge of soil from her cheek.

"This is Lealor." The way he said her name made Lealor's heart bump against her ribs. It sounded so official and proprietary, somehow. He pulled her out of the crowd she had faded into and to the forefront of the group. "These are my parents, King Erik and Queen Alian." The woman in purple raised her eyebrows. "And my little sister, Silanna, of course."

Lealor curtsied and hid her surprise as well as she could. She hoped her mother never found out what she looked like when she met Rand's parents. Mirza didn't stand on ceremony often, but she had inflexible standards about a few things. "Your Majesties," Lealor said with a smile. "Silanna," she added with a nod. Little sister, indeed, she thought. She didn't fit Rand's description of her at all.

The look on Silanna's face would have soured milk. Lealor sighed inwardly. At least one person here on Fire Mountain Island didn't like her much. She wondered what she had done to make an enemy of Rand's sister at first meeting. She didn't have much time for wondering, because Rand's mother gave her a hug like those Lealor received from her own family.

"I'm so glad to meet you," the queen said, making Lealor feel truly welcome.

Lealor smiled at Queen Alian. She loved her already. The queen wiped her hands on her skirt, leaving stains. Lealor often forgot that she was wearing a skirt when she was gardening and did the same thing. It made a bond between them.

"Mother," Silanna spoke for the first time, "it's only a few hours until the noon meal. Don't you think we should allow Rand's guest time to—clean up?" Silanna's look at Lealor's sea-soaked outfit, dried by the wind far from the touch of an iron, said clearly she didn't care much for the wearer.

"I suppose I can plant those bulbs this afternoon," Alian announced with a smile. "Are you interested in plants, my dear?"

"Mother—" Silanna began.

Rand, who had been watching, broke in. "The answer to that is definitely. She's an herbalist, mother."

Alian looked at Lealor with delight. "Really?"

Lealor's eyes danced as she answered the queen. "Really and definitely."

"All that dirt—" Silanna began.

King Erik said, "Silanna, why don't you hurry lunch along a bit? All this greeting has made me hungry and I know Rand can always eat. After the sea air, I'll bet even Lealor has a great appetite. This afternoon I've a council meeting. Rand can give his official report then." A frown marred the king's face momentarily. Then he forced a smile. "I'm glad to have you home, son. Especially since you brought proof of your good taste." He winked at Lealor. "She can blush!" he announced with a chuckle.

"Father, give her time to get used to you before you tease her to death," Rand said, obviously pleased with his father's opinion of Lealor.

"You two!" Alian said. "Behave yourselves or Lealor will be wishing she had never come." She turned to her daughter. "Please see to the meal, dear. Cook's so ingenious. Tell her in about an hour. I'm sure with your help she'll think of something. I'll take care of our guest."

Silanna nodded quietly and walked away.

Lealor wondered how Alian and her gruff but genial husband became the parents of such a regal daughter. Rand was very like his father in looks and his temperament matched his mother's. Silanna, however, seemed like a changeling. She certainly didn't resemble her parents.

"Be sure to give Lealor a chance to clean up before you drag her out to the gardens, mother," Rand said, "We'll probably have to take on extra help to keep the mud from the marble," he teased, sounding exactly like a harried housewife.

"Come along, my dainty cleaning maiden," his father said, clapping Rand on the back with a blow that would have felled half the men Lealor knew.

The queen led Lealor inside. No pictures adorned the walls of the wide corridors, but large windows allowed generous amounts of sunshine and flower-scented air to enter. Alian noticed Lealor looking out of the windows. "The bare walls seem to fit best on Fire Mountain Island. Although we haven't had an eruption in years, it's always so much easier to clean up with a fresh coat of whitewash, rather than worry about all those dusty wall hangings and ancestral portraits. I was never much good at sewing, although I can cook when I get the chance. As a girl, it always seemed so dreary to sit around sewing. Grace knows there are chests full of linens in reserve. When Erik found out how I felt, he allowed me to put the tapestries and portraits in the audience chamber to awe visiting dignitaries. At least there, they do some good." She ushered Lealor into a bedroom where a huge tub of water invited a guest to bathe. "Give your clothes to one of the maids, and we'll soon find something to fit you."

"Thank you, Your Majesty." Lealor turned to find Queen Alian gone. "Is she always so—precipitate?" Lealor hoped the maids wouldn't be angry at her choice of words.

Both of the maids giggled. "Oh, no, mistress. She's just so happy Rand is home," the taller maid answered.

"We all are," her companion added.

Lealor could see from the maid's demeanor that Rand was a universal favorite among the ladies.

"Lady Berith will be especially glad he's home. She's Silanna's best friend, you see."

"Mitalla, don't gossip!" the larger girl said, turning to Lealor in the same breath. "If you'll give Mitalla your clothes, she can set about getting you some new ones."

"Unless you'd like me to stay and help you with your bath," Mitalla said.

The little maid's brown eyes reminded Lealor of a cocker spaniel she had once owned. She felt almost guilty at refusing help, but she didn't want to be waited on, and this wasn't the time to start a bad habit. "Sorry," she said to both girls. "I'll take my own bath, thank you."

The maids placed a screen around the tub and Lealor stepped out of her clothes, tossing them over.

"The green flask is for your hair," Mitalla called softly just before the door closed.

Lealor swathed herself in the oversize towel after her bath and stretched out on the bed. *Time for a nappy, Myst,* she told her bracelet, which gave no sign of life. "I do hope you get over your sulks soon," Lealor said, enjoying the feel of the soft pillow at her head. She turned to look out of her window at the birds that glided past. She thought briefly of Fafleen, but realized there was nothing she could do for her friend. Then she dozed as she waited for Mitalla to bring her clothes.

She felt so comfortable, she didn't answer the knock on the door. It opened quietly. Mitalla and the other maid entered.

"Oh, isn't she pretty!" Mitalla whispered. "Much prettier than Lady Berith."

"Shhh! What if Lady Berith found out what you said?"

"Oh, Fia, the princess can't spend all her time spying on the servants."

"I'd curb my tongue if I were you. Lady Berith can be difficult to get along with as it is."

"Because she's the special friend of the princess . . . "

"Your gossipy ways will get you in trouble yet," Fia warned as she straightened the room.

"Isn't it funny that Lady Berith has red hair and green eyes? Only Lealor's eyes are the soft green of moss and Berith's are harsh, almost a yellow green. Lealor's hair is such a rich color. Wait until they come face to face. Berith's hair will look like feather root compared to hers. The prince will never marry Berith now in spite of Silanna's plan."

"Put the clothes at the foot of the bed. I'm afraid we'll have to waken her, or she'll miss lunch."

Lealor had been waiting for a chance to speak at some juncture that would not embarrass either maid. This innocuous speech seemed her best opportunity. She didn't care much for eavesdropping, but now she understood why Silanna disliked her. She yawned and turned over, giving her best imitation of someone waking from a nap. "Oh, are you back already? I must have dozed off. Are these the clothes you brought me?" She hitched her towel under her arms and swung her feet to the floor. "How did you ever find so many?"

Fia answered. "All of the ladies of the court sent you something to choose from."

Lealor picked up a bright pink dress with a neckline that plunged almost to the waist. She shook her head no and set it aside.

"Lady Berith sent that one," Mitalla said. "She wore it only once. Someone said she looked like a lady from a joy house in it. Nobody ever saw her wear it again."

"Mitalla," Fia warned.

"I won't tell," Lealor said, earning Mitalla's loyalty forever. "Mitalla, you'd best be careful. I bet some folks can hold a grudge over almost nothing."

Fia's smile showed her gratitude for Lealor's cautionary attempt.

"You've met Lady Berith?" Mitalla asked, unaware of the silent communication between Lealor and Fia.

"Hold your tongue!" Fia said, plumping pillows as if she had her companion under her hands.

A knock on the door interrupted them.

"Come in," Lealor said, pulling a soft yellow dress over her hair.

"Are you ready, child?" Queen Alian asked.

"Almost, Your Majesty," Fia said, running a brush through Lealor's mane and preparing to pull it to the top of her head.

"Nothing fancy, Fia. A couple of combs to pull it back so I can see where I'm going. I wouldn't want anyone to have to wait for me." She smiled at the maid. "Besides, I'm starving!" she added for Queen Alian's benefit.

"We'll soon fix that," the queen said, opening the door.

"Thank you both for everything," Lealor called over her shoulder as she followed the queen from the room.

Queen Alian began talking as they walked down the corridor. "I hope you'll have time to see the gardens after the council meeting."

'I've been looking forward to that," Lealor told her. "I enjoyed the flowers coming up the mountain to the castle. Some of the ones growing here I've never seen before."

"Everyone is so kind. They bring me starts of plants from all over. Almost every ambassador and trader brings me something or other. I hope the council meeting won't keep you too long."

"Am I supposed to attend the meeting?"

"Ordinarily, no, but you were a prisoner of the priests of Sardoom, our old enemies, and they'll want to question you."

"As a prisoner, you don't learn much, but I'll be glad to tell them anything I can. Those priests are no friends of mine."

"I suppose they're still squeezing every copper they can from everyone."

Lealor nodded. "That's them, all right." They passed a window wreathed in a yellow-flowered vine. "That scent is wonderful! What plant is this?"

"It's called maiden's glory. I've been especially lucky with it. Most places it's only a tiny shrubby vine, but here, at this window, it climbs two stories. It's magical, you know. If a maiden casts it into boiling water and wishes, it gives her a true vision of her beloved."

"Then it's a kind of farseeing herb?"

"I've never thought of using it for farseeing, but it should work. Most seers use a combination of other herbs."

"Clear sight, honesty, and evilbane?"

Alian's delighted look told Lealor she was correct. "I've taken you the back way," Alian said. "Once we get down these stairs, it's only a few steps to the main hall. The dining hall is likely to be full of hungry courtiers, eager to see Rand, of course, and to get first word of Rand's decision."

Lealor looked at the queen inquiringly.

"Yes. It must be his decision whether to sail north to find the cause of the sudden sea rise. Our captains say it must be caused by ice melt, but why would the ice melt now? Here on the island we're losing valuable feet of shoreline. It threatens Fire Mountain if it rises much more." They turned a corner and entered a busy hallway. "Oh, dear, it's all so complicated. You'll hear all about it at the meeting."

In spite of Lealor's curiosity, she hoped the meeting would be short. She wanted to try to use the maiden's glory to see what had happened to Fafleen. She had a feeling that Fafleen might get into difficulty. Fafleen was a very brilliant dragon, but she was young. No matter how intelligent someone was, a certain amount of experience made one wise. Although Lealor felt relatively safe, considering she was on a volcanic-island that might explode, her magical senses were on the alert, warning her of possible danger.

CHAPTER NINETEEN

"Mind trap!" Fafleen's ejaculation sounded like a curse. The red dragon turned his head to find the smaller blue dragon right behind him. She could not see the amused twinkle in his eyes as he flew directly at the tall cliffs that rose before them. He flew so low that the spray from the immense waves attacking the cliffs wet them both. At the last possible minute, he turned his immense power from speed into a thrust to provide altitude. He flew straight up the side of the cliff nearest him and settled with a swish of his wings on the flat top of the escarpment. He felt, rather than saw, the breeze created by the blue dragon's landing behind him.

"Well done, little blue lady," he hissed in the ancient tongue of the dragons.

My name is Fafleen von Fafnoddle, daughter of Ebony von Drak Fafnir and granddaughter to Fafnir von Fafnir, she answered in the mindspeech that dragons had used since the Beginning.

Beautiful flying, Fafleen von Fafnoddle.

Fafleen ruffled her scales as she caught his mental comment that her title was longer than she was. *Thank you.* Her nod of acknowledgment was curt, showing him that she had not yet forgiven him for his transgressions.

Why do you consider yourself the protectress of the young human with the fiery hair? I can sense no magical spell which binds you to her.

The bonds between us are of our own choosing.

Since when has a dragon made compact with mere Widdershins humanity? The sun struck scarlet fire from the male dragon's scales when he stretched his neck upward to look down his nose at Fafleen.

I wouldn't know. We are not from Widdershins.

I am Flare von Berdularion, last of my line. Do not tell me anything that is not true.

Not lie, truth. Lealor—

She of the fiery hair?

Do you want me to tell you this, or not? Fafleen did not wait for his answer. *We came through a gate long abandoned.*

An existing gate in Magilan?

Yes. Activated by a young Bright One called Baloo. We were pulled from our world to this one. Baloo has meddled once too often. Something must be done about him. Lealor's mother will be most unhappy with him. Did you not sense the mind net set to trap me as we journeyed here?

Flare shook his head. *No. Escaping a blue fury who threatened to harm me took all my concentration.*

I'm sorry I lost my temper. Fafleen gritted her teeth. She hated to apologize, but she knew she owed the red dragon the courtesy. At least when she told her mother of her foolishness, she could say she followed the proper dragon rituals. It would go far in mollifying her parent. She muttered the ritual words of dragonly abasement required by the Dragon Code.

Accepted, Flare told her.

Fafleen considered his terse acceptance a gracious response. In a few words, she told the red dragon all she knew of Lealor's stay in Magilan and about the books in the cave system.

Flare nodded his understanding. *Now, it is my turn. You feared for the life of your friend. Those fears were not necessary. For many years my people have sent me to collect the priests' sacrifice.* He backed up a pace as Fafleen bared her teeth and hissed.

Human sacrifice is barbaric! Her silver-blue tail slithered from side to side, indicating her readiness to attack if necessary.

You do not understand. When we dragons fled Magilan, we brought with us—at their request—a number of humans who formed a colony in the valley below. At first, the sacrifices were very important because so many men chose to come with us. They needed mates, you see. Now their numbers have swelled. In a few short years, they will form a force to return to their homeland and free the populace from the priests' injustices.

Now I truly mean my apology, Fafleen said.

Let's forget past misunderstandings.

Again Fafleen was favorably impressed with Flare's graciousness.

Agreed, Fafleen said, watching as a group of dragons flew across the valley toward them. *Is this the welcoming party?*

You might say it is. They are probably wondering why I did not land in the town square below. Usually the sacrifices are quite upset when I fly them here.

Humans are emotional. You get used to it in time.

Flare didn't think he would ever get used to the screaming maidens he delivered to the townspeople. He had no intention of admitting his weakness to this attractive female, who probably wanted a fierce mate to help rear her young.

Is there any dragonmage who might help me see what has happened to Lealor? She needs to know about the mind net.

Our Ancient One knows many things. In her cave she has stored the books we dragons brought with us. She can answer most of our questions. Perhaps she can aid you.

That'll solve all my problems! Fafleen's enthusiasm shone in her silver eyes.

I said perhaps, pretty one. Flare returned her inquisitive look quietly. *The Ancient One is going blind. She can no longer use her books. If what you seek to know is not in her mind already, it's lost to you.*

Not ssso! For I can read! Fafleen hissed proudly.

One so youthful can read?

Of course. In several dragon tongues and also in some human languages.

Why would a dragon have need of human scratchings?

Fafleen stretched her neck to look Flare in the eye. *Some humans are wise. The lore in human books is no mere scratching.*

Flare decided to avoid argument. Instead, he said, *Here comes the welcoming party.* Fafleen and he watched as four dragons landed on the cliff top near them.

All four lowered their heads in dragon obeisance. *SSire, have you news we sshould carry?*

Indeed, yes, heralds, Flare said. *This year's ssacrifice*—he paused, carefully selecting his words—*was diverted elsewhere. I shall inform the humans in the valley below in good time.*

The heralds bowed again and flew back across the valley to the dragons' home caves high in the surrounding mountains.

Flare turned to the astonished Fafleen. *Have you nothing to say?* He waited, but Fafleen remained quiet. *A rarity, I'll wager. Well, now we go to the Ancient One.* With no further word, he rose into the air and angled toward the northern peak in the valley.

Fafleen tried to gather her scattered wits as they flew. Royalty, for scales' sake. No civilized planet had seen a royal red dragon for thousands of years. The dragons believed the royal line had died out. If she didn't manage to translate the old books, she'd still have news of great value to redeem her foolishness in winging into that gate so blindly!

As they neared the mountain, Fafleen saw a dragon-sized opening about one-fourth of the way down. Now that they were closer, she could see an almost invisible plume of steam rising from the top of the peak. She flinched as Flare trumpeted out a call before they landed.

Who comes to the Ancient One? The thin hiss made Fafleen's blood run colder than usual.

I, Flare von Berdularion, her companion answered in High Dragon.

Welcome. You may enter.

Flare disappeared through the opening. Fafleen gave herself a mental shake, and followed him. The inside was nothing she could have imagined. A thin beam of light entered from a crack high in the ceiling of the vast cave. A million slivers of light answered the single ray, turning the huge cavern into a fairyland of delicate colors as it reflected from the surface of the interior walls. A vast geode formed the entire cave.

Fafleen's first thought was, *and she can't see this? A tragedy.* As her eyes adjusted to the light, she saw the Ancient One. A giant of dragonkind, age had turned her scales to purest white. Where Fafleen's scales were hand sized, the old dragon's were small, no larger than teardrops, a mark of royal lineage.

The Ancient One turned her raised head in Fafleen's direction. *Who is this you bring to visit me? She is not of our world.*

You are well-deserving of your reputation for wisdom, Ancient One, Flare said respectfully.

Fafleen shifted into her best High Dragon, hoping she wouldn't mispronounce any of the words. No dragon on Realm ever spoke it except for ceremonial occasions. Her mother would scale her if she didn't show proper respect. She carefully crossed two claws, hoping the good-luck gesture worked for dragons as well as humans. *Greetings, Ancient One, Mother of Knowledge, Keeper of the Laws and Lore.*

Ahhh. The old dragon's answer was a hiss of pure pleasure. *Come, daughter, and speak to me of your quest.*

You—you know her? Flame said, as astonished as Fafleen had been earlier.

Yesss. She has come to me in dreams. The silver Seeker has a task to perform here on Widdershins.

She's blue, Ancient One.

Then her youth hides her true color which will come at her maturity. She shall stand, a silver dragon, a blessing on Widdershins dragonhood. Since you bring no sacrifice for the human colony below, you have done well in choosing her as a substitute guest.

I shall need to inform them, Ancient One. Flare's tone showed his respect as did his lowered head. His gesture reflected itself in the million facets of the cave's crystalline walls.

Being discussed as if she were not actually present felt distinctly odd to Fafleen. She certainly didn't feel as if she were a seeker. The idea had never slithered through her mind—-a Silver Seeker! Well, they were legendary. The last one had died centuries before she was born.

We have things to discuss. You may go, the Ancient One told Flare.

Flare went.

Now, daughter, you wish to see those who are absent?

Yes, Mother of Knowledge. Nothing had awed Fafleen as did this ancient dragonmage. Her form of address showed it. For once, she was glad her mother had been such a martinet about forms and protocol.

Well-reared, a credit to your parents, the Ancient One hissed, pleased with the ceremony Fafleen knew that young Widdershins dragons hadn't learned since leaving Magilan. *Through there, you will find my scrying place.* She gestured to a narrow fissure in the rock at the back of the cave.

Fafleen stifled a squeamish twinge. How she hated narrow openings! Especially those that led deeper into a volcanic mountain. She crossed the cave slowly, positioning her wings as tightly to her body as possible. The diamond shards were capable of ripping scales from flesh, she was sure. Just before she entered the crack, the Ancient One spoke.

Ask to see those you know who are on the world of Widdershins.

Mercifully, the fissure was short. Fafleen gasped as she came to an immense pool of liquid fire, clearly fueled by the volcano itself. Fafleen paused on the edge, hesitant about disturbing such a magical place.

Ask, daughter. The old dragoness had entered silently and stood behind the younger dragon.

I would see those I know from Realm who are here with me.

For a second, the pool bubbled fiercely, then smoothed into a red mirror, showing the crystal form of Myst trapped within the silver strands of pure force that created the mind net.

Myst, can you hear me? Fafleen had experience with the mind net, but her brush with it had given her no idea that Lealor's talisman was trapped in it.

Behind Fafleen the Ancient One moved her head in a series of magical passes.

Myst opened her mouth to speak, then remembered her father's command. The twitch of her tail showed her anger. She nodded.

Where is Lealor?

A shrug of crystal shoulders answered Fafleen.

Not trapped with you? Fafleen continued without waiting for Myst's negative gesture. *Baloo put you in there, yes?* Fafleen answered her own question. Her talons clenched. *Then Lealor is unprotected!* Myst's head drooped. Fafleen's slow breath of realization fogged the pool. When the mist cleared the scene had changed.

The dragon saw Lealor standing in a garden admiring the flowers with an older woman. *Lealor!* Fafleen called, but she got no response. She quickly described the scene to the white dragonmage.

It is no use, daughter. Queen Alian has bespelled Fire Mountain Island. All mind communications must come through the seers.

But—

Daughter, your friend is safe on the island. I shall cast a spell to tell us if she leaves. Now I would hear your story. She led the way back to the other cave.

Behind them in the empty cavern, the red magma formed yet another image. In it, Mirza and Jarl stood in the gate.

CHAPTER TWENTY

Berdu watched the gate, wide-eyed, as an older version of Lealor material-ized with a tall, blond man.

"Well, I hope this is Widdershins," Mirza said with a sigh.

"It had better be. It was hard enough to force entry here. Now to find Lealor." Jarl stepped out of the gate, pulling Mirza with him. He stamped on the ground. "Nothing like a solid world under you," he muttered.

"You seek the flame-haired one?" Berdu asked, peering from behind a tree.

"Yes," Jarl said, hiding his surprise.

Berdu paled around the edges. The man sounded very fierce.

"Let me handle this, dear," Mirza whispered, giving her husband's hand an admonitory squeeze. "My name is Mirza and I am Lealor's mother. This is Jarl Koenig, her father. She and her friend disappeared some time ago from Realm, where we live. It has taken us all this time to find where she went. Her absence even now worries us. Can you help us, please?"

Berdu slowly solidified and pointed. "Follow this path, cross the river, and wait at the cottage in the clearing," he said before disappearing.

"Well, milady," Jarl said, offering his arm to his wife. "The cottage awaits."

"What a strange little man. How can a wizened creature like that remind me of Old Fafnir from home?"

"I haven't the slightest notion, but he did give us some advice, although it sounded like an order. If a building awaits us at the end of this path, it's worth checking out." He dropped Mirza's arm. "The path is too narrow to walk abreast. I'll lead the way."

Mirza followed, watching the woods around them with bright eyes. She saw some familiar plants and many that were not. After they found Lealor, she wanted to speak to a person who knew about local herbs. Some interesting remedies might turn up.

"All right. I could use a hand here," Jarl said.

Mirza smiled to herself. Jarl acted so helpless about magic. He had learned much since he first wore the dragon bracelet and arrived in Realm. Yet, with all their adventures, when it came to something magical, he always deferred to his wife. Mirza wondered if he understood how powerful a mage he actually was.

"The fact I don't want wet feet requires a little magic here," he said, looking down at the swiftly flowing current of the river.

Mirza muttered a spell and the river obligingly hardened. "Come on," she said, starting to cross the water. "I don't want to expend much magical energy. We might need it later."

Jarl raced across like a long distance runner making a sprint for the finish line. He puffed ostentatiously. "I'm across," he told her.

"Not any too soon." Mirza laughed at the look on his face as he turned to find the river behind him.

"You weren't going to hold it for me until I was safe on this side!"

"You're wearing hiking boots. They'd dry," she said over her shoulder. She took the lead in finding the cottage.

"Well, at least your strange little man didn't lie about this," Jarl said, pushing open the door.

"Feel the protection spell?" Mirza said. "I'd recognize it anywhere. It's one of Lealor's."

Jarl prowled around the room. "Yes, and these are her belongings. She's been here!"

Mirza noticed the thin layer of dust on the table. "Not for a while. Now what do we do?"

"We have no choice but to give your little friend a chance. I wonder where he disappeared to? I hope he went to get someone who knows what's going on."

Mirza sat at the table. "Sit, Jarl. There's nothing to do but wait."

Jarl sat and drummed his fingers on the table top. Mirza's thoughts whirled. Rescuing their daughter was not going to be as easy as they had supposed.

Fialla jumped when Berdu materialized beside her with a little *pop*. "Blessed be. You frightened me, Berdu."

"You didn't turn a scale—er, hair." Berdu told her. "Steady as a rock, you were."

"Do you have any news of Lealor?" Fialla finished pouring a distilled herbal remedy into a small jar. She covered it and wiped her hands on her apron.

"Not news of her, but news." Berdu helped himself to six cookies from a plate.

Fialla drew a short breath, sensing that Berdu would tell her when he was ready. Her foot tapped impatiently on the floor.

"Humans. No patience . . . " Berdu mused absently before popping all the rest of the cookies into his mouth at once.

Fialla bit her tongue. Berdu was starting one of his rambling intervals. "Berdu!" she said sharply, hoping he wouldn't disappear, taking his news with him.

"Magic is dangerous," he said, looking around the room carefully, "but this is an emergency!" With these words he took her hand, and closed his eyes.

Fialla had no time to blink before she was at the door to Lealor's cottage. "Widdershins' sake, Berdu!" she said, making no effort to hide her exasperation. "You could give a body warning before rushing her hither and yon so rudely."

"Only hither." Berdu chuckled at his own joke. "Humans are so persnickety," he murmured to himself as he faded out.

"Berdu! You come right back here! I've got to walk all the way home without a wrap and this breeze is chilly!" Her words were wasted on the air. Berdu had vanished. "Maybe Lealor has something I might borrow," Fialla said, pushing open the door.

When she entered the cottage, Fialla, Mirza, and Jarl stared at one another.

Fialla recovered first. "That Berdu!" she said before she smiled at Mirza and Jarl. "You must be Lealor's mother." She sketched a blessing sign in the air and looked at Jarl.

"Like two peas in a pod," Jarl referred to his look-alike daughter and wife.

Mirza gave her husband a look, then said to Fialla, "Yes, of course. I'm Mirza. And this is Jarl Koenig, her father."

"My pleasure, I'm sure." Fialla offered the old courtesy with a smile. "I can guess that you are here to find your daughter." She didn't wait for confirmation. "I wish I could give you her exact whereabouts, but I do not know. The last time I saw her. Sardoom's priests had chained her to a post on Sacrifice Rock, and a red dragon flew towards her."

"What!" Jarl banged his fist on the table. 'See if she ever gets a chance to use another gate"—he looked at Mirza's shocked face—"once we get her home safe," he concluded in a voice whose loudness compensated for his uncertainty.

"Where is this rock?" Mirza asked, leaning forward as if she were prepared to leave for it at once.

At the same time Mirza spoke, Jarl was asking, "Who's this Sardoom? How did those scurvy priests get her? Why hasn't anyone done anything? Someone's going to be sorry they chained my daughter to a rock!"

Fialla decided to answer Mirza's question first. "East of the city of Mancy." Fialla took pity on the distraught parents and added, "I do believe she is safe—-somewhere—because neither Pook nor Fafleen returned."

"Pook?" Jarl's gruff voice rumbled. 'What's a pooka got to do with Lealor?"

Fialla looked puzzled by Jarl's use of the word *pooka*, but explained, "Pook is a bear she rescued and nursed back to health."

"I should have known," Jarl said. "Lealor's better than an Animal Welfare Division. So you sent a bear and a dragon to rescue her?"

"Not exactly. They insisted on going," Fialla said, sitting on the cot, since Mirza and Jarl were using both chairs. She rummaged on the shelf above it for the map she left the day Fafleen needed directions. "Here is where we are," she said, placing it on the table and using a spoon to mark the spot. "Here is Mancy." She pointed to it before she sat down again.

"How far away is that?" Jarl asked.

"Several days travel on a fast horse."

"If you will excuse us," Mirza said. "We must go now."

By the time Fialla followed them to the door, she was in time to see Mirza's form shift to that of a horse with wings.

"Oh, my," she gasped.

Jarl mounted the winged beast. "Just like old times, isn't it? Notice I didn't even argue about this." He said to Fialla, "Thank you for the help."

The winged horse bowed to Fialla, snorted once, and sprang into the air with one beat of its henna-hued wings.

"Oh, dear me! I hope the wards will give them no trouble."

"Use your head, human! Of course they won't." Berdu materialized before the awed Fialla.

"How can you know that?" Fialla bent over to look Berdu in the eye.

"Because they're not dragons! She's not even human!"

Understanding dawned. "Ohhh. I see!"

"Weren mage!" With this pronouncement giving him the last word, Berdu vanished once again, leaving Fialla to borrow a cloak and walk home alone. She wondered what Mirza and Jarl could do against the priesthood of Sardoom. Everything happened so fast she had not had time to warn them.

Mirza flew at top speed for hours before she allowed herself to sink to the ground.

"About time, Love," Jarl said. "As late as we are finding Lealor, a few hours one way or the other won't make much difference."

Yes, but we don't know where she is. Perhaps seconds count, Mirza communicated mentally. Her wings vanished, but she remained a horse.

"Well, if I had known why you were hoarding magical energy for days, I might have tried to argue you out of it. You were using some kind of augmentation spell the whole time, weren't you?"

What if I was? Mirza trotted down the road, intent on reaching Mancy before nightfall if possible.

"I don't like to take advantage of you. You seem to be doing all the work." Mirza slowed to ford a stream, Jarl resettled himself, blessing her for materializing a saddle. He had never been much of a rider, and without a saddle, he would have fallen off most horses. Of course, his wife could always keep him astride by magic, but it always irked him that he couldn't do it alone.

Don't fret, Jarl. Soon we'll come to Mancy. You can get yourself a pleasant room in the inn and put me in the stables. Mind you pick a nice one!

"Now wait just a minute! If you think I'm going to spend the night in a cold, lonely bed while you're standing all night in the stables . . . "

Don't be silly! You'll spend time listening in the inn and I'll be listening to the stableboys as they groomed me.

"That's another thing—"

All right. You groom me yourself, then.

"Better." Jarl whistled happily, having made his point, not realizing that he had conceded all of the important points to Mirza.

She whickered and settled to a walk. She was feeling pleased with herself.

Within the next hour, traffic picked up on the road. Jarl talked to several farmers and merchants. He already disliked the priests, and what he heard from his informants did little to foster respect or affection for the priesthood.

Mirza's thought startled him. *No one has ever figured out why people set up governments and priesthoods and let evil men take over. It is a weakness of the human race.*

Jarl nodded and reined her into the line that was passing inside the city gates under the watchful eyes of the guards. He felt her shiver. "What is it?"

Can't you sense it? Mirza paused, but did not wait for Jarl's answer. *Nasty magic. Evil. The priesthood of this city has a great deal to answer for.*

"Lealor, for one." Jarl's voice sounded as if he intended to ask for some of those answers very soon.

The next morning, Jarl and Mirza pooled the information they had gathered. The yearly festival of Sardoom would be celebrated in three days' time. All of the priests were required to be present at the temple ceremonies that began on the next day. As Jarl's informant said, "The place is crawlin' with priests like buzzy bugs around a honey pot."

Mirza's contribution was the fear of the stable boys. Children "disappeared" more frequently than usual at the time of the ceremonies. They stayed inside the barn as much as possible. Their master was a kind one and did not send them on errands out of the inn yard. She concluded, *For ceremonies, read sacrifices.*

"What do you propose we do now?" Jarl asked, an admission that her plans so far had been good.

Let's find a secluded spot where I can change into a rich courtier. You had better be an emissary from the kingdom of Realm, on the other side of the great desert.

"What desert?"

How am I to know? I've never been here before. There must be one someplace.

"Right," Jarl said, guiding her down a street lined with imposing houses.

Mirza caught the bit in her teeth and turned into an alley that led to the rear of one of the houses. When they reached a door in the side wall, she stopped and Jarl dismounted.

Thanks, she told him. *I do believe you've been putting on some weight, dear.* The air around her shimmered with magic.

"You certainly look as fetching as ever," he replied. Swept into an imposing style and decorated with diamonds and emeralds, her long red hair glistened. Her dress was gold which matched her opulent jewels. Jarl noted that every finger wore a ring, and a series of huge emeralds formed a necklace that almost covered the skin revealed by the low neck of her gown.

"Don't you think you're—um—" Jarl paused for thoughts. Even though he had been married to Mirza for years, he hesitated to be undiplomatic about articles of dress. After all, she was a powerful magic wielder in her own right and he didn't fancy spending the rest of his days croaking and hopping. "—Perhaps overgilding the lily as it were?" he said after suitable thought.

"Not at all, my dear," she said with a giggle and a gesture.

Jarl glanced down to see himself resplendent in rubies and silver. "Mirza—" he began.

"No, this is not a whim on my part. We must look very rich indeed. We are seeking an audience with the king, after all."

"We are?"

"We are," she echoed him positively. "I do hope you're saving your magic. It will take me hours to recharge after this little display." Before them on the ground a flying carpet appeared.

"Ye gods and little fishes!" Jarl said.

"Necessary disguise," Mirza replied, seating herself on the carpet. "Are you coming or not?"

It was well that Jarl wasted no time in joining his wife, for in seconds the carpet was airborne, heading for the palace.

Is this really going to work? Jarl asked himself as Mirza landed the carpet in front of the castle.

Evidently it was, because an awed functionary duly escorted him and Mirza into the throne room of King Yve.

"See? Wealth impresses royalty."

Jarl nodded, thinking royalty were not the only ones susceptible to the clink of gold. He turned his attention to the much-bedecked functionary, who introduced them word-for-word as Mirza had told him. At least he had a good memory. Jarl himself couldn't remember half of what Mirza had told him about their titles.

King Yve motioned them forward.

Mirza took Jarl's arm and advanced. Which turned out to be a good thing because the high priest in attendance on His Royal Majesty captured Jarl's whole attention. Jarl had learned enough about Sardoom and his priests to know that any priest left in the kingdom was Sardoom's. The unhealthy pallor and general demeanor of the priest shouted self-righteousness and cruelty to Jarl. In Jarl's eyes, the priest might as well have worn a sign saying: *Evil.*

Mirza and King Yve made diplomatic overtures to one another while the priest and Jarl glowered at one another in mutual animosity. The king's next words caught Jarl's full attention.

"Your daughter Lealor?" King Yve repeated Mirza's words as a question. "Er—I—"

The high priest hurried into speech to assist his floundering monarch. "An unfortunate incident occurred, milady. Lealor herself volunteered to be the spring sacrifice, but before the red dragon king could carry her away, a huge bear pushed her into the sea." He neglected to mention the fact that Lealor had been chained to the post on Sacrifice Rock.

"Into the sea?" A muscle twitched in Jarl's cheek. No one but Mirza knew it masked his anger.

The priest looked sad. "She would have made a very acceptable sacrifice," he said with a sniff. "However, we were unable to recover her. A smaller blue dragon chased away the red one. We are searching the texts of Sardoom to see what such events mean."

"Then she is dead?" Jarl's tone showed clearly how he felt.

Mirza said nothing, but she placed her hand on her throat and tears glittered in her eyes.

"Quite likely," the priest said. His unfeeling attitude chilled the room as much as Jarl's anger heated it.

"You can tell us no more?"

"No." The high priest was unaccustomed to being questioned by anyone. "We are planning a number of sacrifices to Sardoom so he will protect us from the dragons. This is the first time anything broke the pact between us."

"You have an agreement to sacrifice people yearly to the dragons?" Mirza's voice tinkled like ice.

"Just maidens, milady," the high priest told her, attempting to propitiate her.

"Oh, Jarl!" she said, turning to her husband for the first time.

Her stricken look released something in him. His anger, which had grown greater by the minute, was almost palpable. Jarl willed energy to him. Those who watched saw him acquire a green aura. "Begone!" he commanded as he pointed to the high priest, who promptly vanished from the hall, black robes and all.

King Yve, white as the ermine fur on his robe, sat speechless.

Jarl turned to him. "Where is the temple? Can you see it from this room?"

Wordlessly, the king rose and pointed to a window.

Jarl crossed the floor in a dozen steps. He looked at the vast marble edifice rising above the rooftops across the town. Jarl raised both hands, paused a moment as green fire flared, and clapped them once.

Mirza turned as pale as the king. She knew what Jarl had done. That flash of fire destroyed the temple and its grounds, including all its devil priests. The truly powerful wielders of magic had not joined with the amoral priesthood so they had only the defense of their god, Sardoom. Mirza would have hesitated before attacking the temple of a god. If he existed, even Sardoom must have felt disgusted with his worshippers, for he did nothing to protect them. Mirza never could have unleashed such power, and if she could have, she would not have dared.

Jarl, acting instantaneously, was an outraged father, and he desired to punish by obliteration. She worried about how he would feel when the extent of his power actually registered on him. He was angry still.

"Do you have farseers here?" Jarl asked as if nothing had happened. His voice swept through the room, cold as a winter that kills every living thing exposed to it.

"That is magic," King Yve explained, trying to sound unafraid, although his hands gripped the arms of his throne tightly so they would not shake. "No one but Sardoom's priests may work magic. I shall send for one."

"That's not necessary, Your Majesty," Mirza said, attempting to break the news gently. "Sardoom's priests are no more."

"You mean, they're all gone? Vanished like their temple?" The king's eyes goggled at the news.

Mirza nodded.

"Very well," he said, quite courageously, Mirza thought. "Am I to retain my life and my throne?"

Jarl gazed at him. He seemed dazed at the devastation he had unleashed. Surely he was not so powerful a mage! His anger had shielded him from full realization.

"You may," Mirza spoke for them both. "So long, of course, as you rule justly and redress the woes the priesthood has inflicted on your subjects."

"They're really gone?" The king allowed a relieved look to form on his face when Mirza said he was correct.

"Now what?" Jarl asked Mirza. He grew paler by the minute as he realized what he had done without thinking.

"To Fialla. She can help us best now." Mirza felt weak, but she knew she had to get Jarl and herself away before full realization of what he had accomplished with his wrath registered on Jarl. After such a use, it might well be that he could never summon power again. Some of Sardoom's followers might take revenge on a powerless pair of magic users.

Mirza summoned the carpet, hoping the magic that remained to her would be adequate for the demands she was making. She and Jarl sat upon it, unhindered by anyone in the court. The destruction of the temple had occurred in a moment. It took time for human minds to comprehend what had happened. The carpet sailed out the window towards the west. If it wobbled a bit, no one noticed.

CHAPTER TWENTY-ONE

The Ancient One sat quietly after Fafleen finished her tale.

The young dragon repeated herself, hoping the old, white dragonmage could help her. *So that's why I need someone to work with me to decipher the books in the old dragon tongue.*

I would gladly teach you, but I cannot see the symbols. So what will you do now?

Lealor is unprotected. I must go to her. Perhaps she will be able to help you see again. She knows both Earthly science and Realmish healing. Surely she can do something. Then you can help me translate the books I will bring here.

The Ancient One indicated an old chest sitting against the back wall of the cave. *Open it for me,* she commanded.

Fafleen crossed the cavern and did as the old dragon told her. Within the chest, ropes of pearls lay over layers of gold, rubies, emeralds, sapphires, and gems of every imaginable color. The whole cavern scintillated with the shades of the rainbow, reflected thousands of times by the faceted diamondlike gems that lined the cave. Fafleen expelled her breath in a long hiss.

Beautiful, are they not? The Ancient One arched her neck. *Over the centuries I gathered them, not by force of claw, but through the gifts my magic won for me. Dig down to the bottom front right-hand corner and bring me the stone you find there.*

Fafleen followed directions and discovered an ordinary piece of obsidian. Perhaps the Ancient One was growing senile. Fafleen had been around her grandfather, Old Fafnir, enough to know that elderly dragons developed quirks of personality. *"This is just volcanic glass!* she said, voicing her disappointment.

Do you not find it strange that in a vast chest of jewels, each more beautiful than the last, I hoard such a keepsake?

Fafleen tried to be as tactful as she could. *I'm sure you have a reason,* she lied politely.

What you hold in your talons is an Odyssey stone.

An Odyssey stone? Fafleen had read the Greek Homer's story of the sailor's attempts to return home. It was exciting, but she couldn't see how the Ancient One knew of the book.

When the gates still functioned on Widdershins, stories traveled between worlds as well as goods. The Odyssey stone is a fitting name for what you now hold. It is the greatest of my treasures.

How so? Fafleen looked at what she held, searching for enlightenment.

Two times only in the life of the owner it may transport anyone or anything to any location specified.

Then what happens?

It renews its energy by being given to its next owner.

Have you used it yet? Fafleen peered at the stone, trying to see if it looked used.

Only once, therefore I may use it to speed you to Fire Mountain Island. The Ancient One held out her talon for the obsidian.

Fafleen placed it in her talons. *Can you send me now?*

Such haste! The young are always in a hurry. One tends to forget, you know. The ancient mage hissed her amusement. *One thing before you go. To return here, you fly east from the island, then north along the coast. Eventually you will reach these mountains.*

Yes, Fafleen said, stretching her wings. *I already know where the landing spot is.* She didn't try to explain her method of instantaneous travel, since the Ancient One could not see.

Very well.

Fafleen blinked. She stood atop a flat rock overlooking a large garden area. Lealor and the woman with her had identical looks of surprise on their faces.

Lealor broke the stillness. "Fafleen!" she cried, running to her and rubbing the nose the dragon obligingly lowered to the ground.

"I take it you know this dragon?" Queen Alian said, adding soil to the pot she was holding.

"Oh, yes! Queen Alian, this is my friend Fafleen from Realm—-you remember I told you about her. Faffie, this is Queen Alian, Pook's mother!"

Fafleen decided to overlook her friend's use of the childish nickname. The dragon stared rudely for a moment before saying, "Doesn't look a bit like him."

Lealor and the queen burst into laughter

Fafleen hissed her distress. She thought they were laughing at her.

The queen saw the problem before Lealor did. "Oh, Lealor, why didn't you tell me how clever your friend was?" Then she turned to the dragon. "She told me how learned and intelligent you were, knowing so many languages and all. She never mentioned your sense of humor. I'm sure we shall be great friends."

"No doubt," Fafleen replied as she reached out a talon and rescued the partially transplanted herb that was ready to fall out of the pot.

"You like flowers, too," The queen beamed while making a mental note to strengthen the wards of the island.

Lealor rushed in with her questions, wanting to spare them both a botany lecture on the habits of herbs. "Are you all right? What happened to the red dragon? Where have you been all these days?"

Fafleen answered the questions, explaining about the need for the Ancient One to see.

Lealor promised to try to help.

Then Fafleen wanted to know all about what happened to Lealor and Pook. Lealor and the dragon had forgotten all about the queen, who sat down on a convenient rock and prepared to listen to Lealor's version of events.

" . . . So after we got here, the council held a meeting."

"It must have been pretty boring," Fafleen said, knowing something of the human propensity to talk a problem to death instead of acting.

"Not really," Lealor said, ignoring the queen's nod of approval. "It's been an interesting two weeks, although I've been concerned about Rand. The seers of Fire Mountain Island have visions of the mage who is causing the ice to melt far to the north on Misty Island."

"Why is it important to the seers here?" Fafleen fluffed her scales and settled her head on a different spot of ground. "Sharp rock," she explained. She closed her eyes to double-check the feel of the ground, then opened them, indicating she was ready to continue listening.

"The ice melting from all those glaciers has caused a rise in the sea level. If it rises another couple of feet, it will pour over into part of the volcano through a crack on the other side of the island."

"Ohhh," Fafleen's eyes grew round. "All that steam wouldn't be very good for humans."

"Not only that," Lealor said. "The volcano might explode from the cold water. Then there would be no more island at all!"

"What are you doing about it?" Fafleen asked the queen.

"The council has sent my son Rand—you know him as Pook—to visit the island. He left two weeks ago."

"Didn't you want to go with him?" Fafleen asked Lealor.

"Of course, but Rand's sister said she didn't see me in her vision about the trip, so I stayed here. When Rand returns he will take me back to my cottage."

"By then, we believe some of our magicians will have studied enough to be able to renew the gate," the queen said.

"Then we can go home?" Fafleen didn't sound very happy at the news.

"We have to let our parents know what happened to us, Fafleen." Lealor smiled to take the sting from her remark.

"Oh, sure. It's just that I want to stay a while and work with the Ancient One on those translations."

"Once the gate is open, your mother will probably come here to see those old books you found."

"If I know father, he'll come too. Then my brother will show up. He can't stand missing anything." Fafleen sighed. "Probably grandfather will come as well." She rolled her eyes and covered her snout with her talons.

Lealor hid her smile with her hand. Widdershins would never be the same once the Realmish dragons arrived. "Well," she said, "now you know all my news and I know yours."

"Not all of it, you don't." Fafleen shot a triumphant smoke ring into the air. For once, she knew something Lealor needed to know. She was aware of how often Lealor prevented her from telling everything she knew about some subject. What sense was it to know tons of facts and not be able to share the information with someone?

"What else can there be?"

"Have you tried to communicate with Myst lately?"

"Yes, but you know how stubborn she is. She's been sulking ever since I was in the priests' power."

"She's not sulking," Fafleen told her. "She's caught in Baloo's mind net."

"Poor Myst." Lealor frowned. "Baloo's made a mind net? I've read of them, but never actually seen one."

The queen said, "Once they were used here on Widdershins. Whenever someone with power wanted to remove an enemy for a while, he would create a mind net. It isn't too difficult to do if you can manipulate the power. A mind net is a portion of another plane, bounded by magical force. No one but the creator can release anything placed within it."

"That settles it. We must do something about Baloo. Bright One or not, he's still a child. He can't whisk beings into mind nets willy-nilly." Lealor's clenched fists showed her determination. "Baloo!" she called.

"Don't waste your time trying to get his attention. After he does something naughty, he always hides for a while. He's dreadfully afraid your mother will find out what he's done." Fafleen chuckled at her mental picture of Mirza castigating the immensely powerful Bright One.

"It's not funny."

"You're right. It's not." Fafleen looked suitably grave. "You now have no talisman to protect you."

"Oh, I'll be all right. I have you and Fialla—"

"And us," the queen added.

"Hasn't it dawned on you yet?" Fafleen gave the two humans an exasperated look. "Add things up: powerful mage, dramatic changes with no thought of what those changes may do to people, secrecy, a shadowy figure, removed from humanity—"

Lealor's eyes registered her horror. "The Shadowlord!" she gasped.

"The one who caused so much trouble on Realm and Achaea?" the queen asked.

Fafleen gave her an approving look. "The same,"

"We must go help Rand. Will you carry me to his ship?" Lealor asked the dragon.

"Wait." Queen Alian's expression was grim. "If the mage we detected is your Shadowlord, the visions of my daughter should have seen Rand and Lealor facing him together. I must talk to my daughter before you go. Lealor, will you take our guest to the kitchen for some refreshments before you leave? Ask someone to prepare you a satchel of food to take with you. Please don't leave until I speak with you again." The queen looked at each of them. "Promise?"

Lealor and Fafleen agreed. When the queen left them, she heard Fafleen say, "I am a bit hungry." Alian hoped there would be enough in the kitchen to feed a dragon. It had been years since one visited.

Queen Alian wasted no time in finding her daughter, Silanna. She found her within the seer's vision room. She thought her daughter looked disturbed by her presence, which confirmed her idea that Silanna had not been honestly reporting her visions.

"Silanna." The single word dropped into the silence like a stone into a pool. The spreading ripples were Silanna's hurried explanations.

"I'm sorry, mother. The mist distorted the visions so that I wasn't certain who Rand's companion was. He is only going to reconnoiter. He won't actually face the mist mage until he confers with the council and father."

"Have you searched the mists for your brother today?"

"Yes. Some spell keeps him from going farther north. He will try to return here and take our magicians with him when he returns."

"You are fortunate nothing worse has happened. Look once more into the scrying bowl. Seek to see Rand's companion on his quest."

Alian and Silanna positioned themselves around the magic container. Since the question was Alian's, she poured the herbal liquid into the bowl. Silanna spoke the words of summoning. The liquid turned gray. It roiled within the sides of the container, resisting Silanna's summoning.

"The mage thwarts our clear vision with his magic."

Silanna placed her hand on the silvery stone she wore on a chain around her neck. She repeated the summons. Then for an instant, the roiling ceased, showing them Lealor and Rand in a room made of ice. They saw a shadowy figure in a robe. For one second the image clearly revealed the mage. The watchers blanched. He had no face. The magical liquid turned to icy vapor that rose into the room until it dispersed in the air.

Alian and Silanna looked at one another. Alian spoke first, "Your father and Lealor must know of this."

Lealor had fed Fafleen and introduced her to King Erik, who came to see what the commotion was. The servants were fascinated to see a real dragon. They had heard old tales of the days in Magilan, but no one on Fire Mountain Island had ever seen a live dragon until Fafleen arrived. Fafleen was on her best behavior, carefully answering any questions that were her put to her. No one would be able to say she had been anything but a perfect dragon lady—if her mother should ever inquire.

Alian heard Lealor's last words as she entered the huge area behind the kitchen garden where a table, covered with empty dishes, proved Fafleen had eaten.

"That's all there is to tell, I guess," Lealor said to King Erik She turned to Fafleen. "Unless I've left something out."

"Not a thing," Fafleen managed to say, licking the last of the icing from the top layer of the four-tiered cake she had politely divided with her tongue. Unable to resist, she gulped it down in two bites. She caught Lealor's look. "I'm ssorry."

"You won't be able to get off the ground if you eat much more," Lealor warned, pretending she did not see the look on the cook's face as the dragon finished off the last cake in the castle.

"Don't worry. I know exactly where we're going. We'll fly Air Fafleen."

Lealor hid a shudder. The business of climbing on a dragon, closing your eyes, and being there always unnerved her.

Queen Alian waved the servants and gawkers away to their places. "Erik, I have news. Silanna and I managed to get one clear vision of the mage. Lealor and Rand were facing him together."

"This slip of a girl?" Erik's loud rumbling remark showed his astonishment. He modulated his voice and added, "When?"

Silanna appreciated her mother's tact. She understood her dereliction of duty would not become public knowledge. So she answered rather humbly for her. "Soon, father."

"Well, what should we be doing to help?"

"Lealor and I need to consult with the Ancient One. Perhaps her magic will aid us," Fafleen said.

"Fafleen and I will find Rand," Lealor promised. "He won't have to face the Shadowlord alone."

"Ready?" Fafleen asked.

Lealor nodded, knowing dragons were notorious for abrupt departures.

Fafleen unfurled her wings to get the kinks out. She took Lealor firmly in her talons and warned, "Careful!" as she gave a tremendous wingbeat to move Lealor and all the food she had ingested into the air. Once afloat, Lealor had time to cry out, "Goodbye!" before Fafleen used her magical power to travel instantaneously to the cave of the Ancient One.

So you have returned, daughter. The ancient dragonmage hissed her pleasure.

Yes, Lore Mistress, this is my friend, Lealor. May we speak aloud?

The rapidity of the trip, the vast cavern with its crystalline walls, and the old dragon who stood before them stunned Lealor. "Greetings to you, Lore Mother," she said, remembering that Fafleen told her the Ancient One liked ceremonial address.

"A most interesting human," she murmured to Fafleen as if Lealor had no feelings. The Ancient One turned toward Fafleen. "You believe this one knows enough to restore my sight?"

Impressed as Lealor was, she knew better than to allow a potential patient to expect too much from her. For the millionth—or was it the billionth—time she wished she dare turn herself into another form. If she wore dragonshape she would not be so dwarfed by her surroundings. "I can but try if you wish it," she said, hoping it sounded acceptable in dragonish.

"Bend down your head, Ancient One, so Lealor can see."

A jet of warm air blew over Lealor, who was thankful that this dragon was so old her fires would not light.

"For the first and only time, I bow before a human," she hissed.

Lealor walked up to the dragon and looked at her eye. Then she walked around the dragon's snout to view the other one. "Yes, it is as I thought from Fafleen's description. You have growths over your eyes called cataracts," she told her patient, for she now believed she could cure her.

"Do I need to return to the cottage and find your medical supplies?" Fafleen asked.

"I don't think so. Since dragons are mystical creatures, I can use my knowledge of surgery to help in the magical removal of the cataracts."

"What will you need?" Fafleen asked.

"Although I will remove the cataracts magically, you will feel some pain. It will take several days for your eyes to heal completely," Lealor told the Ancient One.

"I agree," the old dragoness hissed.

"Have you some painease?" Lealor asked the dragon.

"Yes. The people in the valley keep me supplied with herbs. Sometimes I can bespell illness for them." The dragon held her head still, afraid she might hurt the human who could restore her vision. "Daughter, beside the chest is a rack holding my herbs. Bring the ground leaves in the small bag made of rabbit fur."

Fafleen found the bag and handed it to Lealor. "Do you need boiling water to make a tea?"

"Yes." Lealor waved her hands to make glowing patterns over the eyes of the Ancient One.

By the time she had finished, Fafleen had filled a bowl with hot water. The Ancient One drank it to the lees. That the dragon drank the steeped leaves as well surprised Lealor, but she said nothing.

"Please don't move," Lealor said.

The old dragon's eyelids closed while Lealor and Fafleen watched.

"Fafleen," Lealor said softly, "I'll need your help."

"What should I do?"

"Lift me onto her nose."

When Lealor was safely on her patient's snout, she said, "Now raise her eyelids for me—gently!" Lealor reached in the pouch she had tied around her waist to replace her magic bag. She took out a container filled with a creamy substance. A green glow formed around Lealor's hands as she chanted. Lealor rubbed the substance over the old dragon's eyes. Fafleen watched, fascinated, as the cataracts became first translucent, then transparent. In the next few seconds, they disappeared!

"I never heard of that spell before. What did you use?" Fafleen asked.

Lealor, seeing her patient cured, giggled. "Vanishing cream!"

"I hope you can come up with as good an idea when you face the Shadowlord."

"I wish I knew what was happening to Rand," Lealor said.

"While the Ancient One finishes her nap, let's go see," Fafleen said, leading the way to the lava pool.

CHAPTER TWENTY-TWO

The sight of the pool awed Lealor.

Fafleen formed her question carefully, hoping she would be able to bend the magic to her desire. "We would see Rand, the prince of Fire Mountain Island." To the young dragon's relief, an image formed instantly.

The ship lay becalmed in the middle of an icy sea filled with bergs. Lealor saw Rand's frosty breath as he looked to the north.

"You did well, daughter." The Ancient One's hissed words at their backs startled both Fafleen and Lealor.

"Thank you," Lealor said, noting that the old dragon had called her daughter. "Can you see the image?" she asked.

The old dragon nodded. Lealor could feel her pleasure.

"Look," Fafleen said, "someone's talking to Rand. Can you fix it so we can hear?"

The old dragoness hissed a word and the figures in the image began to speak aloud.

"Prince, how long must we wait here? The bergs grow more numerous daily."

"Captain, this is no ordinary calm. Some magic keeps us from sailing northward."

"We didn't take the time to get provisioned for a long wait. If we do not leave in two days we will not have food or water enough to return home."

"Let your wizard study possible ways to get through for one more day and then we shall return," Rand said.

"Very well, sire," the captain replied.

Rand nodded his dismissal, turning his back on the captain to look north again. He pulled his cape about him, for the air stung with cold, although no wind blew.

Lealor watched, wishing she could speak to Rand. She turned to the Ancient One. "Can we speak with him?"

"It is long since I wove that spell. Let me see . . . " Strange noises came from the throat of the Ancient One. Lealor supposed the sounds to be words, but they formed no language she could recognize.

"Speak now," the Ancient One said.

"Rand! It's me, Lealor!"

"Lealor? Where are you?" Rand's face lit with joy.

"Safe with dragons. I'm using a magical mirror."

"The two who swooped down at Sacrifice Rock?"

"Waste no time. The spell weakens," the Ancient One hissed.

Lealor hurried. She was sure Fafleen, at least, would help. "We'll come, if a dragon can fly through the magic shield."

"The ship's wizard says that whoever designed this spell did it to stop all human magic and shape changing. That's why I can't change into a whale and swim to the island."

"We'll be flying dragonback and that's perfectly natural," Lealor said. "Get ready. We're coming."

Rand nodded as the image disappeared into the bubbles formed by the slowly boiling lava.

"You will take me, won't you, Fafleen?"

"Of course, but I can't carry double in that cold. I can probably fly you to the island, but I'll have to come back here and warm up before I can return and get Rand."

"Come, daughters." The answer to your problem lies in my cavern."

Fafleen and Lealor exchanged puzzled looks, but they followed the old dragoness back into the main cave.

"Ancient One, have you seen—Fafleen!" the red dragon said.

The Ancient One chuckled. "Did I not say the answer to your problems awaited?"

Fafleen and the red dragon were busy talking. Lealor watched the three saurians. The Ancient One waited quietly, certainly an unnatural behavior for so powerful a being. Lealor smiled. Why, the Old One was match-making! Fafleen and the red dragon made an imposing pair. Now, however, was not the time for romance. Lealor drew a deep breath and said, "Fafleen, will you introduce me to your friend?"

Fafleen jerked her head around and looked at Lealor as if she had never seen her before. Then she said, "Oh, I forgot. This is Flare."

A heavy fur coat and a pack materialized on the cavern floor. The Ancient One said, "This is for you, Lealor." Then she turned to the younger dragons and spoke some words. A pale golden shimmer surrounded each of them. "You will be warm. This spell will last for three days, no more. By then, you must be on your way home."

"How—" Fafleen began as Lealor put on the coat.

"I am in contact with the magic users in the human colony below. They prepared the pack with the things humans find necessary." The old dragon had a smug look on her face. She could still show the young ones a trick or two.

"I know a rock four days' flight from here. It's in the middle of the sea. If you can follow me, we can save some time."

"I followed you here, didn't I?" Fafleen answered Flare with fire in her eyes. "Lead the way."

"Let's leave from the ledge outside. Are you ready, human?"

Lealor winced at the word. Flare was clearly willing to participate, but only because the Ancient One and Fafleen were taking an interest. She felt very small and powerless as she crawled to her place on Fafleen's back.

"Farewell—" blackness cut off the Ancient One's hiss. The transition had been almost instantaneous. Far below, Lealor could see a single spur of rock sticking out of the roaring sea. If Rand's ship was becalmed, it must be magic, she thought to herself. Look at those waves!

"Do you need to rest?" Flare roared over the noise below.

"Let's go!" Fafleen answered, shooting past him toward the north, watching for Rand's ship.

After the first three or four wingbeats, Lealor's stomach caught up with her, and she started to feel the cold. She pulled part of her cloak over her face and, forsaking the view of the wild sea, rested her face against Fafleen. How like a dragon, she thought. The warmth spell covered Fafleen, but not her.

After a day of flight, Flare swooped down to the sea and returned with a large fish, which he fed to Fafleen. Fafleen's hiss of pleasure reminded Lealor of her mother's reaction when her father presented her with a box of candy. She wondered what Mirza would say if Jarl gave her a big fish on

Valentine's Day. Lealor felt the stiffness in her face when she tried to smile. She changed position enough to rub her mittens on her face. She had no desire for frostbite now. The moon shed cool beams on the three.

She felt Fafleen lurch slightly. *Faffie! What is it?* she asked in mindspeech.

The calm place is this way, the dragon replied. *I can feel the magic.*

Several hours later, Lealor could see the moonlit ship. The deck was too small to hold both dragons and their tails, so Fafleen draped hers over the mast.

Everyone who could find a dragon-free inch or two of deck crowded around to watch as Rand heaved a pack containing supplies on the deck. Lealor introduced Fafleen and Flare. Rand wasted no time climbing aboard the red dragon.

"Hold on," Lealor warned.

"We go," Flare announced as he and Fafleen winged their way aloft.

The captain, the ship's wizard, and the crew watched as the dragons flew northward. They reached the magical barrier that shimmered and disappeared as they passed. With the barrier gone, a cold wind tore down from the north. The captain gave the order and the crew hurried to set sail for Fire Mountain Island. The wind filled the sails and the ship fairly flew southward to warmth and safety.

The moon sank and the sky lightened. Noon passed and Lealor and Rand could feel the dragons tiring. Rand had never carried on a mental conversation with a dragon, but when he yelled to ask Flare if he could do anything to help, he felt the dragon's chuckle in his mind.

Human eyes are not as keen as a dragon's. I can already see the patch of fog that surrounds Misty Island. This wind has vapor streaming for miles.

Rand squinted, wishing he could change to hawk form for long enough to see, but in a few minutes the foggy air passed them in ragged wisps, then formed a solid cloud around them. "How are we going to see it when we get there?" he asked.

Dragons know what kind of terrain is below whether they can see it or not. We are superior hunters because of our magical senses.

Rand wisely kept silence. He was only a passenger, after all.

Ready? Flare asked.

"Yes," Rand answered, knowing they were going to land when and where it suited the scarlet dragon.

Even with the prior warning, Rand's stomach lurched as the dragons plummeted to earth. They landed on a sandy beach, wind-scoured and snow-free. Rand and Lealor dismounted hastily—Lealor, because she knew the dragons needed to return home before the heat spell expired and Rand because he was following her lead.

'Thank you, Faffie," Lealor said. "Take care going home."

Rand thanked Flare, who merely nodded before turning to Fafleen. *Can you follow me, Seeker?* Seeing Fafleen's nod, he rose into the air so rapidly that he almost blew Rand over.

Fafleen was beside him. *Be careful*, she warned mentally as both dragons winked out of sight.

"Was that normal?" an awed Rand asked Lealor.

"'Fraid so," she answered, fitting her pack to her back. "Let's go. We have to find shelter before night falls."

"Lealor, if dragons can travel like that, why didn't they just zip us here?" Rand settled his pack and kept pace with her.

"They have to visit a place at least once before they can travel there instantaneously. Sometimes dragons can whisk themselves to places they've never visited, but they have to study or read the mind of their riders if they know the place. It's a pretty risky way to travel. Only great need would cause a dragon to do it. Misty Isle is somewhat off the beaten track, in case you haven't noticed." Her words came in short bursts.

Rand saw how hard it was for Lealor to move in the knee-high snow they encountered as soon as they left the shore, so he took the lead. "Let me break a path," he said. "Do you have any idea which way we should go?"

"Your mother told me a mountain ridge forms the northern half of the island. If the Shadowlord is here, he would create his castle on the south side of the mountains, out of the northern gales."

"If we are going to find a safe place to stay for the night, we should look for shelter somewhere off this flat plain," Rand said.

An hour or so later, Lealor spoke. "It's not as windy here as it was when we landed on the beach. Perhaps we're already approaching the mountains."

The light faded until they were slogging through a gray landscape. Both Lealor and Rand felt the cold beneath the layers of clothes they wore. Rand had tried to get Lealor to agree to stop several times. Thick snow fell from the night sky. It was impossible to see more than a few feet ahead. Lealor staggered on through sheer willpower. When Rand stopped without warning, she ran into him.

"Look!" he whispered to her.

The bulky form of a huge white beast rose up before them in the snow. Rand reached for his sword, ready to protect Lealor.

"No," she told him. "Wait."

"For what?" He expected the beast to charge any moment.

The mouth of the gigantic form opened, showing sharp fangs.

Carnivore, Rand thought, placing his gloved hand on his sword.

A plant eater would starve to death here. Lealor's gentle mental answer surprised him.

We're talking mind to mind, he thought to her.

I never really tried before. When you were a bear, I didn't think of it, and later, it was habit to talk to you out loud.

Their mental voices were joined by the voice of the beast. *I, Sleet of the Snow People, am glad you know our tongue.*

Rand looked at Lealor in puzzlement. *How does he speak our language?*

Mind speech uses raw ideas, not words, for communication, Lealor told him. *I am Lealor of Realm and he*—she gestured to her companion—*is Rand of Fire Mountain Island. It is an honor to speak with Sleet of the Snow People.*

A great storm comes, Sleet said. *Would you guest with my people until it is over?"*

Yes, Lealor and Rand thought in unison.

Follow me, the beast said and lumbered off into the snow, leaving a path for the humans who trailed after him.

The walking was much easier with someone else breaking a pathway through the snow. Lealor and Rand could sense how much the speed of their travel picked up as they followed Sleet. The hope of being sheltered refreshed them enough so they could keep going.

Without any warning, a cliff rose up from the plain. Sleet turned to make sure his guests were still with him and gestured. After a few minutes of walking, he paused for Rand and Lealor to come close to him. *Come*, he thought to them, and disappeared into the cliff.

"Illusion," Lealor murmured to herself as she advanced with her hands held before her.

When she disappeared, Rand followed blindly. He blinked in the soft light that illuminated a great cave. The walls seemed cut from solid ice that glowed.

Sleet led them forward into the center of the cave. From the openings in the wall a number of huge snow beasts emerged and gathered around Sleet, Rand, and Lealor.

The small ones are my guests, Sleet said.

They are like the Evil one, a smaller snow beast said, growling.

No. Sense their thoughts and know their hearts, another beast said.

Lealor and Rand stood very still, trying to project friendly thoughts. It didn't seem to be making much of an impression until a tiny snow beast toddled through the circle and held up his arms to Lealor.

Hello, small one, she said, unable to resist picking him up.

A chorus of mental chuckles broke the silence. They were accepted.

Sleet took the baby from Lealor. *My son*, he said.

Within a few minutes they were settled in a small alcove within the cavern. Sleet offered them food, but Rand and Lealor opened their packs and retrieved their own. Sleet's nose quivered when he scented the fruit in Lealor's pack.

It is long since I tasted fruit. When I was a cub, sometimes ships would come to trade with my people, but none come now. When the Evil One took the castle for his own, things changed. Now we are the hunted. Sleet's eyes gleamed red with his rage. *The Evil One poisons my people to remove their will. Only our power over illusions and magic has saved some of us from bondage.*

We are here to see this Evil One. I believe he is a mage I have met before. My people call him Shadowlord.

Sleet looked at them. *What can such small ones do to the Evil One? His magic is great.*

My people drove him from Realm, our home. Later we helped drive him from Achaea. Perhaps we can defeat him again. Lealor spoke quietly, hoping her fear did not show.

Sleep. Tomorrow I will take you to his castle, Sleet told them.

The caverns were somewhat warmer than the outside, but not warm enough for Lealor and Rand to take off their coats or sleep comfortably. Lealor woke the next morning with her head pillowed on Rand's chest. Rand smiled at her. She sat up quickly. She hoped he didn't notice the flush on her cheeks. She rummaged to find something in her pack for their breakfast. She set aside the rest of their fruit for the little snow beast.

Just as they finished, Sleet came. He took them through a series of underground passageways. When he led them to an opening, they could see the gray walls of a forbidding castle. Someone had cut it from solid rock.

Sleet pointed across the valley where moving white figures were barely visible. *My people captured to be slaves to the Evil One.*

Lealor nodded her understanding. She remembered tales of the Shadowlord's behavior on Realm. Fafleen's mother, Ebony, had been enslaved by a magical chain.

Sleet said, *If you have need of our illusions, we will aid you. Think of me and I will speak in your mind.* He raised a paw in farewell and disappeared into the mountain.

Rand looked at the wide expanse of snow before them and said, "Well, how do you propose we cross that unseen?"

"If you can turn yourself into a bear again—a white one, preferably—you can move unnoticed in the snow."

"What about you?"

Lealor thought how simple it would be to change herself into a white bear. Silanna had enjoyed telling Lealor that Rand could only marry a shapeshifter. Lealor felt the familiar pang as she remembered she could never marry Rand. Then she thought what it would be like to stay in bear form forever. While she was thinking, she searched through her pack. Inside was a square of white cloth. She thought it was a sheet, but it didn't matter to her why she had it. She opened it and draped it over her head, covering her flame-colored hair. "How will this do?" she asked.

Rand answered with a woof. He had already changed into a great polar bear. She felt his grin. *I forgot I'd have to mindspeak when I was in bear form. Now you get on my back and I'll give you a ride to the castle.*

I can walk.

I suppose you can. How will it look if the Shadowlord's servants see human boot tracks in the snow? A bear is easy to explain. In fact, my paw prints look a little like Sleet's.

Lealor stifled her wish to be independent and mounted. Rand set out across the snow at a lope in spite of his rider. In a little over an hour they reached the castle. Lealor felt uneasy. Everything was working out too well! The snow beasts wore silver collars and seemed intent on nothing but their tasks, although Lealor and Rand couldn't figure out the purpose of their leaden comings and goings.

The guards were visible on the main gate to the castle, so Rand and Lealor started walking around the castle's perimeter. Finally, they came to a small door in the side. They expected to find the door locked, but it opened easily. Once inside, Rand changed back to human form before he and Lealor looked for a place to hide.

Rand drew his sword and led the way. A short distance down the passageway he found stairs cut into the rock. He started upward. When they came to the first landing they saw a door. "Up or in?" Rand asked.

"Let's take a minute to rest. We need to talk. In," Lealor whispered.

They entered a windowless room. Lealor risked a small sphere of mage light. Rows of barrels filled the floor space. Rand peered into an uncovered barrel near the door. He wrinkled his nose. "Fish—and none too fresh. It must be what the slaves eat."

Lealor made a face. Rand helped her climb on top of a barrel and sat on one himself. He unlaced the neck of his shirt and pulled out a stone on a chain. Lealor watched silently. Within seconds, the stone began to glow. Queen Alian's worried face peered at them. *Children*, she said, *are you all right?*

Fine, so far. We're in the castle. We don't know yet what the Shadowlord is doing to melt the ice, or why, but when we find out, I'll try the earth stone.

Be careful, Alian said as her face faded from the pendant.

"What's an earth stone? All stones come from the earth," Lealor said.

"It's a magical artifact that uses the forces of nature to restore the balance when someone disturbs the proper order of things. This is probably the only one left in existence. We have lost the knowledge the power wielders used to make this."

"How does it work?"

"If we knew that, we could probably make another."

"That's not what I should have asked. I meant what do you have to do with it to stop the Shadowlord?"

"I'll know when the time comes. You can just take that look off your face. I know it's crazy, but that's what our wisewomen told me. Speaking of wisewomen," Rand said, "what is it you're going to do to drive the Shadowlord away?"

Lealor hid her worry with a smile. "Oh, I'll know when the time comes," she told him.

The walls of the room began to shimmer. Lealor felt a moment of vertigo, then she and Rand were in a huge chamber. She saw the Shadowlord standing before them on a raised platform. "Welcome," he said. "My trap worked very well, didn't it?"

Lealor bit her lip in chagrin. "I should have known things were too good to be true."

"I remember you, although you were a good deal younger when last I saw you. And more destructive," he added as an afterthought.

"I remember, too." Lealor said, keeping her voice steady with an effort. She had too much pride to let him know how frightened she was.

The Shadowlord motioned her aside. She looked behind her and saw Rand, frozen in time, his sword drawn, one foot ready to take his first step to battle the Shadowlord.

"Who is your warlike young companion?" he asked.

Lealor hesitated. Should she tell him, or would it put Rand in more danger?

"You might as well. I can take it from your mind if you don't."

"This is Prince Rand from Fire Mountain Island."

"Oh, you've found yourself a weren all of your own. How clever. You shapeshifters will probably be very happy together—if you cooperate with me."

Lealor's instinctive reply quivered in her throat. *Never,* she wanted to shout, but she wisely decided to wait and see what she could learn before she had to act, although what she could do against so powerful a magic worker, she didn't know.

Lealor took a deep breath. "Do you know you are melting the ice and raising the level of the sea?" she asked.

"My castle is high," the Shadowlord replied.

"The volcano on Fire Mountain Island has one very low place. The cold sea water is almost ready to run into it!"

"That explains why the prince is here. What is their island to me?"

"You really don't care what happens to others, do you? Yet, when I look at you I see a golden sparkling rod-shape hiding under some kind of—gray covering." Lealor bit her lip. She didn't know the right words to discuss what she saw within the Shadowlord. If there was ever a time when she needed to be eloquent, this was it!

"Womanly foolishness!"

Lealor felt a familiar ruffling through her mind. She recognized the touch of Baloo, the Bright One. She allowed her thoughts to expand until she touched him. *Baloo, can you help me?*

It's such fun to watch you have adventures, Lealor.

This is serious! I need you to tell my mother and father where I am. Can you bring them here? Release Myst from the mind net, too.

Okay.

For the first time in weeks, Lealor felt Myst tighten on her wrist. It was surprising how much better she felt.

"Who are you communicating with now? Another companion?" The Shadowlord's words cut into Baloo's and Lealor's thoughts like a sharp shard of glass. He waved a hand and muttered a word, but nothing happened to Lealor. He stopped to look at her and tried again. This time Myst flared into incandescence. His eyes peered at the dragon talisman. "You have gained a dragon guardian. This proves that I am right. Your abilities are the key. Now, if you will not aid me to save yourself, perhaps you have an interest in this young man. He has no dragon talisman!"

Bad man! Baloo said before disappearing from Lealor's mind, leaving Lealor alone, remembering that Fafleen said the Bright One always ran and hid when he was afraid.

Lealor watched in horror as the Shadowlord raised a bony finger and pointed it at Rand. Blue fire outlined Rand's body and encased him in ice that continued to thicken.

"Now answer me! Who aided you?"

"It was the small Bright One from Achaea. The one you almost destroyed when you meddled with the sun there."

"Not very brave, is he? I give you credit, Lealor. You have courage," the Shadowlord admitted grudgingly. "I hope you are not as stubborn as your mother was. I want you to lend me your magical power so I can complete my plans here. It you want Rand to survive, you will join me. The ice spell kills if it encases someone too long. I give you five minutes to decide. I shall return for your answer." With these words, the Shadowlord disappeared.

Lealor's thoughts scurried like mice. What could she do to stop the Shadowlord?

CHAPTER TWENTY-THREE

As Baloo fled through the planes of existence, he worried. It was his fault that Lealor faced the Shadowlord alone. He slowed, then stopped. He would return to Mirza and confess.

He scintillated brilliantly for a moment, the Bright Ones' equivalent of a sigh, then raced for Mirza on Widdershins. Before he could reach the plane where Widdershins was, he saw a great golden light materialize before him.

Stop, foolish child!

Who are you? Baloo asked, filled with wonder at so powerful a being.

I am Oron, an adult Bright One.

Please let me get by. I have to tell Mirza what's happening and take my punishment. I did a bad thing. Baloo's golden form drooped in a shame.

Oron's form grew larger and larger, becoming white-hot. *Who dares punish a Bright One?*

Mirza never actually punished me, but I know I deserve to be. Lealor wanted an adventure and it was so easy to have the gate take her to Widdershins. The Shadowlord was there and she could have an exciting time and convince her mother and father that she was really a grown-up being and—

Stop! Oron winced. *Child, you are very young to be out of the nest alone.*

That's why I hide from Auntie Mirza. She catches me and sings me back to sleep. She thinks I'm too little to be out, too. Please let me go. The Shadowlord is a very evil being. He hurt me once and Auntie Mirza saved me.

Auntie Mirza indeed! Oron roared.

Baloo extruded hands and covered his mental ears. He sobbed and two drops of molten gold dripped down his column.

Oron saw and relented. *The humans must do without your help, child. I despise them because the Shadowlord is one of their race. Why they have not destroyed him long before this, I cannot understand. Years ago, I made a vow. If the Shadowlord wins, all the worlds with humans on them are forfeit to the Black Universe. I shall see to it myself as I promised.*

But—Baloo began.

If you are quiet, I will allow you to watch with me. Baloo fell silent.

Lealor rushed over to Rand. She tried to rouse him, but quickly saw it was no use. Then she remembered the earth stone. She could pretend to join the Shadowlord to get a chance to use it herself. She tried to undo the shirt pocket where Rand kept the stone, but the ice was already too thick.

"I'm back," the Shadowlord announced.

Lealor kissed Rand through the ice, hoping the Shadowlord would not find out about the stone.

"What is it you work so hard not to think of? Hmmm?"

"A pendant he wears," Lealor admitted, trying to look subservient.

The Shadowlord held out his hand and the pendant materialized within it. "Simple device of no real value," he murmured, glancing at it before dropping it to the floor. "I take it this means you do intend to assist me," he told Lealor. "I chose this place because it is the heart of all the most powerful magic on Widdershins. In this world, the dragons control most of the old magic, so I need to wear a dragon's shape. All is ready to forge a universal gate that will take me and my armies to any gate world at any time I wish. Holding this power in control is melting the ice, so when you aid me, you stop the sea from rising."

"What do you want of me?"

"First, I wish to change shape. You gave me the answer when your dragon bracelet flared. On this world only a dragon may wield the powers I need. You will change shape first to teach me how."

"If I change, I'll have to remain in that form forever. You told me so yourself."

"Yes, that's right. I did. So you've remembered all these years."

"How could I forget?" Lealor's simple question let the Shadowlord know how grieved she had been.

"Well, then, I'll be magnanimous. I'll let you choose the form you change into. If I learn to change into one beast, I can become another, can I not?"

"Yes. The process is the same."

"Do you choose to be a bear like your weren friend? Or perhaps a bird to sail the skies or a fish to swim the waters of Realm forever." His eyes sparkled maliciously as he watched Lealor's face.

"If I may never be human again, I choose to be a dragon," she told him.

"Fortuitous. You'll be the very queen of dragons, I'm sure. Let's begin."

"We must hold hands so you're in contact with me. It's been a long time since I shapeshifted. You'll have to follow my thoughts as I change." Lealor didn't try to hide her grimace of disgust

She sent a mental call to the snow beast for help. "Sleet! Create an illusion. We must both seem to be dragons!" She broke mental contact before the Shadowlord touched her. He would have to be sharing her mind to change, she knew.

The Shadowlord advanced and took her hands. His bony fingers were gnarled with arthritis and icy cold. Except for his forcing her to give up her human shape, Lealor might have found it in her heart to pity him as she noticed the brown age spots on his hands. How old was he, anyway?

"One more thing. You promise not to harm the people here and you will free the snow beasts after I have aided you?"

"The sun will be cooler, for I must steal some of its energy. I will not harm the people, and I will free my slaves if I am successful."

"How much cooler?"

"Eventually they will have an ice age here. The water from the seas will turn to ice and snow. This will free large portions of the sea beds for human habitation."

Lealor shrank from the Shadowlord in horror. "But—"

"Begin!"

As Lealor watched, she saw the Shadowlord take on dragonshape. She looked down at her hands and saw dragon's talons. Sleet had heard. The illusion was perfect.

The Shadowlord-dragon rose to the ceiling, intending to break through and be outside, but as his head hit the stone, he dropped back down beside her.

He was so angry he could hardly speak. "You agreed to help me. None of these tricks, or Rand will suffer for them." The dragon illusion vanished. The Shadowlord pointed toward Rand and this time the blue fire doubled the thickness of the ice block that encased him. "You have cut his survival time in half with your foolishness. If you wish him to live, begin the transformation now. Dragon Queen!"

Lealor cast one despairing look at the ice that held Rand captive and began.

While years had passed since Lealor had changed her shape, she remembered the sensation as she initiated the process. She took great care to think of what she was doing.. First, her neck must lengthen, her skull must reform with sharp teeth along the lengthy jawline. Next, a long tail to balance, a larger body, strong hind legs, and front legs with long talons to hold her prey. Now, scales to cover her body from snout to tail tip. Last of all, she formed the strong wings that would carry her aloft. Her eyes watched as the Shadowlord followed her gradual transformation, shifting himself slowly, then more rapidly as he understood the process. While Lealor waited for him to complete his scales; she used all her magic senses to make certain he was truly shifting and not merely creating the illusion of a dragon.

Lealor, look! He's just like me! Baloo's voice broke the stillness.

Quiet, young one! You were supposed to watch and northing more. The tall golden plume that was Oron joined the slighter form of Baloo.

As the gray veil disappeared from the Shadowlord, Lealor could see him more clearly with her magical senses. She gasped as she realized what she was seeing. Baloo was right! A gout of hot flame burst from her nostrils.

"Why have these two meddlesome entities arrived here?" the grey dragon, who was the Shadowlord, asked.

Excited by her discovery, Lealor failed to notice his question. "You're like Baloo, only dimmer. You're a Bright One yourself!"

"A being of such power? Of course I'm not. I'd know if I had the powers of an energy being."

"You are! You're a Bright One! You must be the Bright One who disappeared so many years ago when the great dragonmage Wyrd was experimenting with a sun!" Lealor became so excited that she forgot she was in dragonshape and almost knocked a hole in the wall of the castle, solid as it was.

You lie, human! Oron's golden column shook with outrage. *I am Oron of the Bright Ones! This creature cannot be one of us!*

Yes, he is. Baloo's tiny voice protested, unheard by any of the others. Oron's mental voice was so loud, Lealor held her talons over the place where her ears would have been if she was in human form.

"Use your powers to look at his essence," Lealor told Oron, so excited by her discovery that she gave orders to the Bright One as if he were a child. "Can't you sense he is one of you?"

Oron's golden column expanded until it encompassed the grey dragon.

Baloo's childish mindthought broke the stillness. *Oh,* he said, *look at the dragon! Just like I said! He's one of us, too!*

Under the tutelage of Oron, the former Shadowlord was gradually assuming the pure energy form of a Bright One, except he was silver, rather than gold.

Are you going to destroy the human worlds of the gate, Oron? Baloo asked, with no conception of what his question did to Lealor.

No, Baloo, Oron's mental voice was as gentle as it had been harsh before. *It has been millennia since I was in error, but this time I was wrong. The Shadowlord was not a human problem. I should have looked into this more deeply.*

Why is he silver? Baloo asked as he watched the grey dragon turn into shimmering energy. *You and I are golden.*

Because his development has been repressed by being in a material form so long.

Is he going to be good now? Baloo asked.

Lealor sensed that Oron was fast nearing the end of his patience, so she answered. "Of course. He didn't mean to be evil. Whenever we try to be something we're not, it makes us miserable and selfish. Now that the Shadowlord knows who he is, he'll be happier."

More to the point, I shall be watching him, Oron added.

He isn't Lord of Shadows anymore, Baloo said to Lealor. *He's all silvery light.*

Perhaps I should choose another name, the silvery column said. Turning to Lealor he continued, *May I call myself Lor after you, Lealor? You saw me for what I really was, even when you were a child.*

"Of course," Lealor said. "Would you free Rand now?"

As she spoke the words, the ice surrounding Rand shattered into a thousand pieces, and he stepped over to her side.

"You have my word that I shall teach these young Bright Ones. They will not meddle with you humans again," Oron promised. "Baloo, Lor, follow me." The golden column that was Oron dispersed rapidly until it was an incandescent light, which winked out abruptly.

Two tears rolled down Lealor's snout. The defeated Shadowlord was a Bright One, and she was prisoner in a dragon's form forever!

"What are you crying for?" the silver column asked as it stopped dwindling.

"While we are both happy that you have found your true form at last, Shadow—er, Lor." Rand answered for the dragon, "Lealor, here, is condemned to be a dragon forever! I heard you talking about it while I was under your spell."

I really fooled her, didn't I? Lor's form quivered with his mirth.

"Fooled?" Lealor fluffed her scales. "What do you mean?"

You remember when I told you about changing? You had taken baby dragon form and destroyed my laboratory, upsetting my plans. I was very angry at you, so I told you if you changed, you'd stay that way. I didn't actually form a spell. I had no time, and I didn't know how to effect such a spell. I'm not sure anyone can keep a shapeshifter from changing if he wishes. You can be in human form any time you choose! Lor winked out abruptly.

Wait for me! On second thought, don't. He's still going to get into trouble. Baloo sighed, starting to dwindle erratically. Then he stopped. *Oh, I forgot. I'd better send you to your parents. They're really worried!* He grew and solidified.

Lealor asked, "Rand, what about the earth stone?"

In answer, Rand walked to the window and tossed the stone to the ground far below. "That should do it," he said.

Before Lealor could look to see what happened, she found herself changed and with Rand at the door to her cottage.

"Mother! Father!" Lealor cried as they rushed out to greet her.

Rand stood quietly to the side. Finally, Lealor remembered him. She introduced Rand to her parents.

They smiled at him politely, but he could tell they needed to hear about Lealor's adventures before they seriously considered anything else—like a wedding.

Berdu and Fialla materialized in the clearing. "See! I told you she was back!" he said. "I was able to transport us both here in spite of your doubts."

The cottage did not have enough seats for everyone, so Mirza waved a hand and created some chairs and refreshments. They were all listening to Lealor and Rand tell their adventures, when Fafleen arrived.

"Now where can he be?" she said.

Seeing the dragon, Berdu jumped from his chair, but Jarl took hold of his arm. "Don't wink out now," he told the little man.

With a gout of flame, carefully, aimed upward, Flare arrived. He took one look at Berdu and said, "The Ancient One was right! Father, don't you remember me?" Then, without waiting for an answer, he shook power from a bag he brought with him over Berdu. As the silvery motes settled on the tiny man, he began to change until a mighty dragon joined the other two.

Jarl backed away from the dragon. The clearing remained crowded although the three dragons had snaked their tails through the trees.

"That's Berdularion, the dragon king," Fialla whispered to the other humans in the clearing.

"Look out below!" called a familiar voice, as Young Fafnir, Fafleen's brother, materialized over the clearing.

The humans hurriedly vacated their seats as the young dragon made an awkward landing, crushing the chairs into kindling. "Humph," he said. "They don't make chairs very well here."

Fafleen forgot a good bit of her new-found dignity as she spoke to her brother. "I've found some important volumes of dragon lore, and I'm staying here to translate them. You can go home and tell mother and father. Besides, there's no gold for you here."

Flare and Berdularion watched the spirited exchange between brother and sister, while the humans were busy sharing information that was important to them.

Rand turned to Jarl and Mirza. "How long will it be before you can repair the gate?"

"Now that Berdularion has returned to his proper form, he has released the old magic that was fettered so long ago," Fialla said. "Probably all those transformed so long ago have returned to their original forms."

Rand looked a little puzzled by the information.

Mirza explained to him. "You see, now that things are being set right, the gate will return to its old form as well, but I don't understand what magic is working to fix everything."

Lealor said, "Rand fixed it."

"How?" Jarl asked, taking another look at Lealor's friend.

"He threw the earth stone," Lealor said, too happy to realize her answer was not clear to anyone but Rand and her. "I don't understand why you want to know about the gate, Rand."

"Our parents should meet before our wedding."

"What makes you think—" Lealor began.

"Oh, I remember a certain indication I had when we were in the Shadowlord's power—"

Lealor blushed and didn't say another word when Rand took her hand in his.

Jarl put his arm around Mirza and they smiled, misty-eyed.

The dragons turned their attention to the humans. Young Fafnir took one look, and said, "Oh, yuck!" He reared his head as high as it would go and looked Flare in the eye. "I suppose you're going to tell me you and my sister—"

Berdularion sent a jet of fire at Fafnir's tail as Fafleen ruffled her scales in a dragon's blush.

Fafnir waved his warmed tail to cool it before he gave the couples a disgusted look. "I hate mush!" he said, and disappeared.

EPILOGUE

Lealor looked down at her bracelet as Myst continued explaining. "So, Wyrd finally admits he was in error when he commanded me to silence."

"I've always been rather envious of my brothers. They had Soladon and Nyct to talk to, and we couldn't share our thoughts," Lealor said. "Now, all that's changed."

"The Shadowlord is no longer a danger to you or the gate. Wyrd created me to protect you. You no longer need me as a talisman."

Myst's musical voice was so pleasant, Lealor almost missed her message. "You mean you won't be staying with me?"

"No. I have other things I wish to do. It isn't as if you actually need me as a companion. You will be busy preparing for your wedding to Rand. Then he will come first with you, as is only right."

"But—"

"However," Myst's voice added. "I will leave my material form with you. If you ever have need of me, you have but to call and I will come." The dragon's form began to coalesce in the air before Lealor.

Myst's shape dwarfed the size of the other dragons Lealor had met. She realized how great a being she had worn as if Myst were a simple piece of jewelry. "Thank you for your care all these years," she said, removing the bracelet from her wrist.

"May you be happy," Myst said, fading from view as Lealor watched.

Cibby, Mirza, and Jarl watched from a window.

"Well, that's a relief. Our problems are over, witch," Jarl said to his wife.

"Lealor will always be my baby." Mirza sighed. "I hope she isn't too badly hurt by Myst's leaving."

"She couldn't have had much of a bond. They didn't talk to one another," Jarl said, thinking like all fathers, that he understood his daughter perfectly.

Cibby shook her head. "The pain will fade. Rand will see to it." She watched Jarl and Mirza stroll away like lovers without a care in the world.

"No problems?" Cibby repeated Jarl's words, remembering all the worrying she had done since Mirza and Jarl met. "They still have a lot to learn about parenting." She chuckled as she went to tell Andronan.

Are you content to leave, Baloo? Oron said from the far spaces where he and Lor, the former Shadowlord, watched with the youngest Bright One.

Perhaps we should stay to keep an eye on them, Baloo said. *I have this funny feeling—*

He's right, Oron. I sense the faintest of shadows gathering . . . Lor shimmered silver between the stars.

Enough! Oron's words flared through the ether. *The first lesson you both have to learn is that Bright Ones have no interest in the doings of material beings! Now come!* he commanded, streaking away.

Lor and Baloo streamed after him, but Baloo looked behind him as he followed, leaving a trail of golden teardrops to mark his passage.